THE CROSSOVER WARS

THE CROSSOVER WARS

Goodbye Angeline, unabridged

S. Warren Winslow

To order additional copies of this book, contact:
Xlibris
1-888-795-4274
www.Xlibris.com
Orders@Xlibris.com
795214

Thanks to my family and friends for doing without me while I was struggling to pull this story from the realm of fantastic imagination and put it in writing.

I should also thank the fine folks at the Lake Skaneateles Chamber of Commerce for patiently answering my questions about their charming village.

Thank goodness for Google Earth!

S. Warren Winslow

CONTENTS

Interlude II

Interlude III

Interlude IV

Prelude II

Interlude V

Interlude VI

PRE-STORY

The woman was dying. He held her in his arms, knowing that it was so. She was becoming weaker—he could feel it. "Fight!" he told her. "Fight it! Please. I-I love you. I don't want to let you go . . ."

Her eyes fluttered open, and upon catching sight of him, recognition flashed in them. She tried to smile. "HE did this to you, didn't he?" This being more of a statement of fact than a question from the man. She raised her arm to touch his cheek with her hand, and the effort it took was a tremendous one for her. He covered her hand with his own, holding it there, trying his best to keep her alive, hoping to do so by sheer power of love or force of will. As his tears fell gently on her breast, he whispered a few lines from a poem he once knew well: "I loved you before I saw you . . . I was yours before we met . . . never a question of want . . . just a fact of what life is . . ." A sob was wrenched from the depths of his heart at the memory of what those words meant for the two of them. "Please stay with me. Please."

But she was in pain and fading. Still, she found the strength of will to focus her eyes on his, manage a small smile, and tell him a secret that she'd cherished for so long: "I loved you too. All along it was you that I . . . I . . . wan—" Then she was gone.

He felt his heart laboring, and the dam of his soul seemed to break as the tears and great heaving sobs poured out of him like liquid life flowing from a broken vase. A part of him wanted to surrender, to let his world go dark, for if he couldn't keep her here, he was tempted to go with her there, wherever there might be. He was still holding her when the other woman got there, her cheeks flushed from having run up the stairs to the pool deck of this beautiful beachside home. She stood still, regarding the tableau in front of her eyes for a moment, a mosaic of different emotions crossing her face. Taking a deep breath, she composed herself with deliberation. Speaking flatly, she said, "He did it, didn't he? We couldn't stop him. You couldn't stop him."

Not raising his head, the man quietly responded, "Yes. He did it and I couldn't stop him." The recently arrived woman looked at her feet for a second then once again spoke. "We need to leave. I called the police before I came onto the pool deck. This place is sort of remote, but I'm sure they'll be here soon."

"I'm not leaving her here like this."

"You have to. If they find you or any clues that you were here, you know what they'll do. You can't let things end for you that way. You have too much more to do. This was never your home, anyway. You already know that." They locked eyes for just a moment.

"You're right," the man said, and gently laying the victim down, he whispered two words that seemed to always be the end of every encounter with the person lying dead. Wincing as if the sound of those words burned her, the other woman looked away. She was right, he thought. It was time to go. He could already hear the sirens a long way off.

The police, ambulance, and rescue vehicles passed them as they were driving in the opposite direction. Breaking the silence, she asked, "How?"

"How what?" he replied.

"How did I get here this quickly, or how did he do it?"

"Both." Resentment at the memory of his inability to stop the tragedy of the pool deck touched his face as he answered, "The railing on the master bedroom's balcony. She must have been pushed from behind, but there didn't seem to be anyone else in the house."

"So how can you know?" the driver asked.

Angry tears seemed to well up in his voice as he answered, "I arrived in the bedroom, went to the balcony, and when I saw the railing screws, it was obvious that they were previously cut almost all the way through with a grinder or linemen's pliers. That railing was lying on the deck below, beside her.

"She must've been in the shower when it all began because her towel was lying near where she fell." He continued.

"Yeah, I saw that, and I'm sure you never peeked," she replied with a touch of her old sarcasm. A quick glance passed between the couple.

"Well, anyway, there was a little bit of an alcoholic smell on her, but she never *drinks in the morning*."

"Sounds like a real angel," the woman said.

He looked at her again. "Yeah, okay. To answer your other question, I got here through a temporal shortcut. A portal. That's also how I sent you the message."

Now she looked genuinely surprised. "You can do that?"

"Yeah. Can make them too. Just learned. You know, I think this is a good time to try out that backpulse tech that you got from him." A sudden smile flirted with the corners of her mouth then. "What?" he asked defensively.

"The way your voice sounds when you say 'him' like that. Are you jealous?"

The man turned his face to look out of the window at the passing scenery. "No. I don't have time for the luxury of feeling that way. I'm just surprised that he would help me out."

With an air of frustration, the woman answered, "I don't think you're the one he's trying to help out. He's already lost her once." He turned to look at the driver again. "Don't sell yourself short. It might be all about helping you."

After another silence, the woman seemed to think of something else. "You might have left prints or evidence. The CSI teams will find it, you know."

"No, they won't," came the reply.

"How can you be sure?" she asked.

"They trained me for this sort of thing, remember? Reconnaissance, evasion, observation, acquisition, aggression, escape. How to be their secret weapon and do it all without detection. I didn't even disturb the pooling blood." For just a moment, she saw his inner pain show on his face. For just a moment.

"By the way," he continued, "will they be able to trace the cell phone you called them with?"

"Not this one," she assured him. "What if he gets away with it again?" she continued.

He answered in a very quiet, menacing way, "If that happens, then may God have mercy on his soul 'cause I definitely won't."

After a short silence, the woman said, "You can be a scary person sometimes."

Turning to look at her, the man replied, "I'm a very scary person. All the time."

INTRODUCTION TO A MYSTERY

The man walked with an air of competence. He could hear the resounding echoes of his own footsteps bouncing off the walls he walked past. *These places remind me of deceptive caves. I always wondered why they paint the walls white in these insane asylums*, he thought. *Oh well, here we go again. Another nutcase. Another façade to rip away. This is for you, Laura.* Bitterness welled up within him at the thought of Laura, gone these long years past. It always depressed him when he had to take on "deluded criminal" cases, for this had been *her* field of expertise. Still, the other messages he'd received seemed to suggest that this particular patient had a background that called for someone with a skill set more like the sort he himself had been gifted with.

Eventually, he arrived at the location specified by the front office, where a sour-faced excuse for a guard stood at a nondescript white door. *Of course*, the competent man thought. *Why would it be any other color?* "Okay, bring the creep out to the visitation area," he said to the guard.

"Our guests ain't creeps, sir," sourpuss replied defensively. "They're just troubled people who needs help."

"Yeah right, friend," the man replied. "Just tell my troubled creep of a patient that his doctor is here and bring him on out so we can talk. Maybe we can get some help for him *and* his victim."

The whitewashed visitation room they met in smelled of Lysol that long ago failed in its attempt to cover the odor of desperation and human waste. *How fitting*, the competent man thought. *Let's try to cover the filth in sanitizers and call it cleaned. Can't wait to meet this one.* Just then, the patient was brought in by a different fellow, an orderly who seemed, to the doctor, to be a little *too* concerned with the man's safety, behaving more like a bodyguard for the patient than a disgruntled and underpaid health service worker who was supposed to double as a prison guard. The employee, a huge dark-skinned fellow, seemed to be taking whispered orders from the man in his charge more than pushing the guy around the way that many orderlies do.

What's going on here? the visitor wondered. *Has he got everyone here convinced that he's that great a guy or what? These types can be very charming and convincing when they want something—or when they want to get away with something. Wouldn't be surprised at all to find out that she wasn't his first victim. I just need to make sure that she's his last.*

"I don't know how to tell this story," said the patient, as he settled into the chair across from his visitor.

"Why don't you just, as they say, start from the beginning?" the doctor urged in that calming way that doctors for mental maladies have.

"You won't believe me—no one else does. How do you think I wound up in here?" the patient asked. Sounding as reasonable and compassionate as any man could, the doctor replied with, "Well, why don't you just tell me the story the way you told it to the judge at the hearing?"

The patient leaned forwarded a little, and his eyes seemed to light up with a glow of fanaticism. "It's about *realities*, Doc, and more specifically, the multiplicity of *alternate* realities." After looking around the room as if he were the kingpin in some lunatic's conspiracy, the patient added, "They *do* exist, you know."

"And is that the only thing involved?" the doctor asked in that serenely understanding manner of the consummate mental health professional.

"No," the patient replied with a self-depreciating smile. "It's about a woman too. I mean, after all, isn't that what almost *every* man's story is about?"

The doctor stared, unmoved, at his patient for a moment before answering, "Yes, normally, but in your case, wasn't there more than one woman involved?"

The patient looked at his feet. "Yes," he replied in a whispered admission that the doctor almost had to strain to hear.

"So let's start from the beginning of those relationships," his therapist replied.

"You make it all sound so simple," the patient responded. "'The *beginning* of *those* relationships.' Doc, 'those *relationships*,' as you so succinctly put it, were well in place long before this business began, but just so as not to waste your precious time, maybe I'll record my story so that you can listen to it without going too far back into the unimportant past."

"If that would make it easier for you," the doctor conceded, not mentioning that he was already in the process of making a recording.

"Tell you what, I'll just see how far I can go today. It's not easy to tell this tale, you know."

***

Where did these relationships begin? About three years ago, when my godfather—I've known him for a long time now, but we only see each other off and on whenever he and his wife are in town. I just call him the colonel. I can't remember why, you know. Well, anyway, he introduced Dana Lacy and me. Her father was also a military man and had worked with my godfather, no doubt on some supersecret government project—you know, the kind that conspiracy theorists love to talk about. (As he said this, the patient wiggled his eyebrows as if he were talking to an old friend. The doctor's only response, however, was a stone-faced stare.) Okay, okay, you're not amused, Doc. I get it.

Anyway, I'd only been here for about three months when I had to go to a doctor's office for a checkup after a traffic accident, and she was working the front desk there. Because he spends a lot of his time doing god only knows *what* important work with some classified section of the military, we don't see as much of each other as we did when I was younger, so it was understandably surprising that The Colonel came to see me after the accident. Actually, in retrospect, I think he was the one who'd suggested that particular office and insisted on the checkup because he *wanted* Dana and I to meet, and when I feel like lying to myself, I almost believe that he was only trying to help me find someone to alleviate the loneliness that comes along when a person first leaves home for good to find their own place.

Pardon me, you want to know what I mean by that part about 'when I feel like lying to myself'? Well, you must understand, Doc, as much as I love The Colonel, I'm just not sure that he does *anything* for *anyone* without some top secret agenda being involved.

Well, anyway, if he did have any agenda of his own, it worked out pretty well for Dana and me—at first. When I left the doctor's office, she was the only person here that I was acquainted with other than my godfather, and it seemed as if we'd known each other for years. She was so likeable to me back then, and that made it easy. I decided to stay here in Florida after finding work in the field I knew best. Dana and I got closer, and the days went on.

Eventually, we moved into the same house, but no matter how warm and fuzzy our life together seemed to be, there was always, deep inside, a sort of space—like a failure to connect between us. We never could seem to become as close as people with those types of relationships do. Our passion started to fade, you know, sorta like a memory of yesterday's sunset or something, and that chasm was becoming more obvious every week. Without a doubt, our *thing*, my life with this woman, was moving into the history books, sooo . . . on to the next woman, and oh god, *what* a woman!

***

"Excuse me for interrupting again," the doctor politely began, "but did you get involved with this other person before or after Ms. Lacy disappeared?" The patient's whimsical look faded away, and for just a second, an iron-like hardness seemed to glint in his eye then disappear within the space of a single heartbeat. *Yeaaah*, the doctor thought. *Let's see the real you. Show me that inner beast. What did you* do *to her?*

Almost as if he could hear these thoughts, the man shrugged then smiled again. "I guess you got me all figgered out then, Doc, so why are you wasting your time here? Why aren't you kicking down the door of my very nicely padded cell with some interrogation team goons?" He leaned forward again. "Oh, I forgot. You're a *head* mechanic, right? So you need to know *why* I committed whatever heinous crime you have already decided that I'm guilty of, then you'll piece together all the rest, and off to the needle with another bad guy, isn't that it?"

The doctor just stared at his subject with a slight smile that to the patient seemed to hide a secret menace; then he mildly said, "Oh, I'm sorry. Please continue." The patient sat back, cocked his head ever so slightly to the right, nodded as if some new understanding had just occurred to him, then continued with his tale.

***

As you probably know, I've been a waiter in some of the best restaurants in the Southeast. It's a strange life, that of a waiter. Oh, I know that most people think that's a "dead-end" job, but for many of us who do the work, it's an honored profession that requires fast thinking and intense mental focus to succeed. Waiters are real prima donnas when it comes to their ability to do their job right. It's like being in showbiz with all the same types of egomania involved. Come to think of it, like all other waiters, I always had a lot of pride, too, and in retrospect, I think that particular quality of conceit has caused most of the of problems in my life.

Anyway, we who work in the restaurant service industry live in a sort of reverse existence from that of the normal human being. Your daytime is our nighttime, and the beginning of your workweek is the beginning of our weekend. So living in this sort of inverted world, it's not always easy to maintain any personal relationships with those who don't, and it always seems a lot easier to make anything like that last longer with people who live the same day-equals-night lifestyle.

Well, of course, as time went on, Dana and I began to drift apart emotionally, and neither of us seemed to notice how that gap was widening. During that time, I knew that she may also have had and pursued other interests, as far as men go, and she probably would have been long gone with some replacement loser a lot sooner, but her father approved of me greatly, which, apparently, was a rare thing for him, so she stuck it out just to avoid a lot of aggravation, I think.

Because I was a career waiter, almost everyone in my life lived and worked in the same world. That's how Angeline and I met. Oh, Angeline, Angeline. She was a waiter too and good at the job in a different sort of way than me. She's like sunrise over the Atlantic, the full moon over a serene lake in the spring, the soft smell of sweet perfume, and long nights of dancing to warm love songs. Angeline has the biggest, most lovable personality that I've ever known, it seems. And all wrapped up in the prettiest package, to boot.

***

"Excuse me, please," the doctor interrupted, "but would that be"—looking at his notes, he finished—"Angeline Arlander?"

The patient looked down, as if the sound of that name hurt him, and answered, almost in a whisper: "Yes, that's her." The two men stared at each other for a moment before the doctor, with that same quiet understanding tone that he'd so effectively exhibited earlier, said, "I'm sorry for interrupting, please continue."

The patient looked down, took a deep breath, and began.

***

Knowing what I now know, I can honestly say that there simply was *no possible way* for the two of us to *not* be drawn to each other. We were *meant* to be together, and that was all. But in this reality, I was in a dying relationship with a woman who seemed to have had enough of it all, and Angeline is in an excellent marriage with a man who adores her. Knowing these facts of life didn't change the strength of the attraction we felt toward each other. Still, she kept encouraging me to do all I could to fix things up with Dana, and I kept a respectful distance from interference in her relationship with George, her husband. After all, he was a sort of likeable fellow too.

Angeline and I worked together for a year and a half, and I can't begin to explain how we got as close as we did, but very often, after the night was ended, we would talk for hours, just the two of us, and anytime one felt down, the other's presence would make everything better. We seemed to be two sides of the same coin. Our ways of thinking are surprisingly identical, and our opinions are practically the same on all sorts of everything. We could talk to each other about *any* subject with complete trust.

Something grew between the two of us, and though we were both extremely cautious about how we dealt with each other, our affinity for each other just would not go away. Sometimes it would show—just a glance between us, a snatch of understanding, with a suggestion of a smile in her eyes, and an answering trace of merriment in mine, I suppose. The odd thing about this rapport, though, is how we both just understood that for as much as we loved each other, we would never allow this to disrupt those other bonds in our lives. Oh, we were *so* honorable!

Eventually, Angeline left the place where we worked together. She was forced out, actually, by a manager who became enamored of her, tried to get close, was rejected, and became frustrated at his failure. She left, and if not for the experience I have, my job in that place might have ended too. I wanted to walk out with her, to follow her into the night, come what may.

But I *needed* the work, she didn't. She just needed something to do. George makes a *great* living installing and maintaining security systems, and by this time, Dana and I were suffering under the effects of some bad financial decisions. Still, I intended to try and fix this thing we had, for I'd promised Angeline as much. So I didn't call and didn't go to see Angel either, even though she would have welcomed me to her home. Pardon me? You want to know how I could be so sure of that? I know this because I'd been there before, and even George seemed to have no problem with it. Now that I think of it, he was never there when I was because he was a day worker.

Anyway, Dana and I tried. We went to the movies. We went to dinner when we could. I went with her on those silly shopping excursions that were driving us deeper into debt, but through it all, my heart wasn't in it the same as before, and in retrospect, I guess hers wasn't either. Between us, there was just nothing authentic to say. We seemed more like roommates than a couple."

***

"Wait a minute, please," the doctor politely requested. "Can you tell me a little bit more about Dana Lacy? The authorities are still trying to locate her. Do you know where she might be now?"

"What you mean, sir," replied the patient, with a touch of ire, "is that the authorities think that I may have caused her some harm. Rest assured, though, that isn't the case. Dana Lacy is in a very safe, happy place and is just fine, but if you really want to learn anything about it, you'd at least listen to my story."

"I apologize for the interruption," the doctor answered in his most empathetic tone. "Please, continue."

***

Three months passed, and one day, Angeline returned to visit us at the restaurant, and when I saw her again, my emotions just skyrocketed. She *knew* when business would be slow enough for me to talk, and that's why she came at that time. My god, that woman is *smooth*. She knew that I *had* to be the one to walk her out to her car and I did. We hugged and held each other all the way to her vehicle, we talked a lot, just as we always did. We couldn't let go, it seemed. I kissed her hands and said, "You're *so* precious to me. Goodbye, Angeline. I'll try to come visit you . . . and George."

But enough about this stuff, Doc. I suppose you want to hear about the alternate realities, don't you? *Please*, don't act surprised. I expected that the court would send someone like you once I told the judge about the alternate realities . . .

Well, okay. During all those times when Angeline and I would talk, I'd always tell her that in some alternate reality, we are together. In some other world, we live and breathe each other. Most people would've said "in some past or future life," but I've never thought that was the truth of it. Not for us. Angeline and I had to be together *now*. Subsequent events have shown me just how right I was in believing that.

I was driving home one night when the whole chain of events that has brought us to this moment began. The evening had been a very busy one, and I'd worked for most of the previous day with Angeline's husband George. What? No, I'm not a regular employee of his, but when things get really busy, he sometimes takes on part-time help to meet his deadlines, and he almost always brings me on board then. The extra money helped Dana and me out a lot too.

As I was driving home, though, something really bizarre happened. I wish that it was a flash or a bang, a storm, or a beam of light, but it wasn't that way at all. A slight temporary temperature drop, sort of like those sudden chills that a person gets for no apparent reason, a gentle bend to the left in the road where there wasn't one before, and maybe, my mind told me, at the time, it was the tiredness from working so much that caused it, but everything seemed *strange*—different somehow. You know, any other person might have been unaware of the change, but I've always had a high sensitivity to the mysterious and weird. Some odd feeling of being in a different *where* or *when* crept up my back and made the hairs on my neck sort of rise, you know.

It seemed like it was only a momentary thing, so I just drove on home. But when I got to the house that Dana and I shared, I found it abandoned and, apparently, a long time ago. Appropriately, the street was deserted, the hour was late, and those dark evil-looking clouds that one sees in Halloween pictures were occasionally floating lazily across the full moon. I thought that I must be going crazy—it was *so* completely *different* from my own place back home, but it *was* the same place, and this *was* the same night.

Somehow, I knew that this was an *elsewhere*. My body tingled all over, and my bones felt as if they wanted to jump out of my body for sheer excitement or confusion. *Something* was right, but everything was *wrong*. I walked around and around, holding my hands to my head and looking like a hen who had lost her chicks, I suppose. This went on and on until a police cruiser passed by for the second time and the officer who was driving just had to stop and ask me for identification.

Oh wonderful! thought I, but what was there to do? Still dazed, I fished out my wallet and handed the man my driver's license, fully expecting to be hauled off to the jailhouse when his background check exposed me as a cipher who did not belong in this place at all.

Of course, it was quite a surprise when, after completing the verification check, my pal the police officer came over and politely informed me that everything was fine, and yes, he'd heard of that robbery attempt at the restaurant that was foiled by my "heroic" actions, and how the suspect whacked my head pretty hard with his gun before all the other waiters ganged up on him, and by the way, did I know that the man was wanted in Iowa in connection with a cop killing?

Needless to say, there had been no robbery attempt at *any* restaurant that *I* remembered, and the possibility of my having drifted into a different *somewhere* in reality seemed more concrete. Apparently, this was *not* the place I'd left when going to work earlier that evening. We were not in Kansas anymore, if you know what I mean, Toto.

Stunned, but not wanting to show it, actually, on second thought, I made *sure* to show it—after all, who wouldn't want to help a hometown hero suffering from a pretty bad noggin thump? Anyway, I just sort of mumbled, "I used to live here" in a spaced-out sort of way. The helpful officer informed me then that this was probably so, but it had been a long time ago since anyone lived in *this* house. Yet he seemed to remember that somebody once told him I'd lived in this part of town before.

Playing the head trauma card to the reasonable limit seemed like a good idea at the time, so I told him how it was sort of embarrassing the way these memory lapses kept plaguing me, causing me to forget my own address and all, so would he kindly tell me what that was? He was only too happy to help, considering the circumstances. He told me that he'd found my correct (a little too much emphasis on that "correct," it seemed) address when checking my driver's license, and was I able to drive? Yes? Well, would I like to follow him there? Yes, I'd appreciate the help.

When he mentioned where it was, the location seemed vaguely familiar, and as we got closer, it became increasingly clear that this was that first apartment I'd rented a long time ago—the one over on the beachside, right there on A1A. When the owner decided to "renovate" the place and triple the rent, my residence there came to an unhappy end. I really liked that place, you know . . .

Anyway, once we'd arrived, Officer Friendly pulled over, said good night, and after making sure that I'd be okay and could make it in all right, he shook my hand once more then went off to do more protecting and serving. The lights in the apartment were on, and not wanting to risk any more public scenes or embarrassments, I chose to drive around the back, where I always used to park.

The first thing I noticed was the car. It was the same one I was driving, right down to the tag number—a black '96 Chevy Impala with black tinted windows, and I *knew* that vehicle well. But *his* looked like it was a little cleaner and in better shape than mine. Maybe he has a better self-image than I do. Well, anyway, I parked right behind it then got out to take a look around.

The apartment's windows were open, just the way I always used to leave them on warmer nights, when you could hear the crashing waves and feel that ocean breeze. Something was going on inside too, for the voices of a man and a woman could be easily heard if one stood close enough. Already, I knew who the man *had* to be; thus, there was no surprise in hearing my own voice asking the woman how her night had gone at work. No, that was really no shock. But when I heard *Angeline* answering—*Angeline*, mind you! And the *way* she spoke to him, with that tone in her voice that always told me when I'd said the right thing—

Oh, Angeline! Angeline! I will always love you . . .

In my mind was no longer any doubt. This was that reality I'd always suspected could exist, and we were *together* here, in *this* place, a place where all I amounted to was just a doppelganger of a happier man . . .

There was no resisting the urge to creep closer and peek through that window on the side, the one I always forgot to cover at night, and as expected, he'd forgotten to cover his too. I looked in, Doc, and you no doubt know what I had to see. There he was, another me/him, sitting in what used to be my favorite chair, and Angeline was on his/my lap, kissing him, the way a woman does with a man whom she loves and will forever be content to live with. In the background, my favorite female singer, Sade Adu, sang the touching words of the song "Somebody Already Broke My Heart."

She moved back a little, looking at him with all the affection that I ever hoped to see in her eyes, and asked, "How's my hero tonight?" He rubbed his head and answered that the guy had gotten him pretty good, but he was lucky to have been born tough as he was dumb for acting like he wanted to be Batman or somebody. That was just the type of thing I would have answered with, and Angeline laughed just the way she always did whenever she found anything amusing. She said that she would rather not have *her* dumb and tough man taking risks like that, so watch it, pal, because the real Batman was still single last she heard.

She put her head on his/my shoulder, like that of a woman who'd found all she ever wanted. I could tell that he felt the same way too, just by the way he was holding her.

Something inside of me felt like it was shredding, and . . . and I couldn't stop the sobbing that was banging at the doors of my heart. Blackness was flirting with the edges of my vision, and there wasn't enough air in all the world for me to breathe.

He must have heard something, it seemed. Maybe I'd made some small sound or whatever—it was obvious in the sudden way he lifted his head as his eyes narrowed. He tried to get up, but between being gentle with Angeline, *his* Angeline, and that head injury, this "me" wasn't as fast as he normally would have been, or as I was, and that meant plenty of time for me to duck around the back and try to hide between the two cars before he'd made it to the door. I hid behind his vehicle, hoping that he wouldn't come out far enough to see two cars instead of one, all the while knowing he would, when I heard *his* Angeline telling him to come back in and let her just call the police to look around because after all, he wasn't in any shape to be tangling with bad guys tonight, and who did he think he was anyway, Superman or a waiter?

He laughed the way I did whenever she would say something that cut through my serious demeanor and touched my sense of humor. "Forget it—there's lots of other things we can do tonight." Hearing that laughter gave me a feeling like being stabbed in the chest because he *had* her, *his* Angeline, and *I* would never have *mine*.

There's a certain perfume that I'd bought once as a gift for the Angeline of my world, and this one was wearing the same scent that *he'd* no doubt bought for her. When the smell of that perfume touched my senses, an emotional earthquake of epic proportions struck me inside, and it seemed that again, my heart was shattering like some old forgotten and worthless plate. Sade sang "It's Only Love that Gets You Through" as they turned off the lights in what was in another location my old apartment, my favorite place, and went for a walk on the beach—together.

I, for my part, went down to the sand, watched them go, then sat down, and cried like a lost soul, shedding tears for a woman that I wished for and never would have, sobbing for every moment of my life that went past without *her* in it.

I finally cursed myself out enough to pull it together and walk back the other way. In an emotional daze, I found myself getting into my car, wondering what to do next—should I go to that other adaptation of me and tell him about everything? Or just relocate and start my life over within this reality? There was another place that I'd once called home, so maybe just going back there and leaving this version of me to his happiness was the best thing to do.

Besides, it seemed that "he" was probably a pretty good person and all, something which *I* am definitely *not*. So why mess his life up? What was that, Doc? Why didn't I think of finding Dana? Well, truthfully, it seemed we wouldn't be too happy together in this alternate place either since that was decidedly the case back where I'd come from. Besides, I was pretty sure that she was just as sorry to have met me as I sometimes was to have met her.

There was so much to consider, but it seemed that the best thing to do, at the moment, was just to drive around and try to clear my head. Even if I wanted to confront that other "me," he probably wouldn't have taken too well to having this dumped into his life right now anyway, so I found myself saying just what it seemed I *always* wound up saying when it came to *her*: "Goodbye, Angeline . . ." while driving away into the night.

The restaurant seemed as good a place as any to start in finding a place in this world, and it was as if the car, on its own, headed in that direction; but along the way, *it* happened again. that same sort of temperature drop, a bend in the road where it wasn't there before, and once more, something was changed. By the time I'd arrived at the workplace, it was obvious that this was the same location where the journey started, the world I came from, where Angeline was living happily ever after with someone else while Dana and I were stuck in a relationship that had all the intensity of a frozen waffle.

When I got back to the house we shared, I sat down on the nicely mown lawn, staring at the stars—those uninvolved twinkling eyes above

———

xxvi

that had no feeling for the pathetic out-of-place man that I now saw myself as, and realization of the fact that I could alter *nothing* made me want to scream in desperation. Instead, I just went on inside. She was there, doing whatever she could to ignore me and I went, as usual, to the bedroom in the back of the house. With that arrangement, we wouldn't have to bear the pain of arguing with each other.

I used to wonder, on nights like these, would it *really* have been different if *Angeline* were the person living with me? But now I no longer had the luxury of guessing. Do you know, Doc, what's worse than finding out you were wrong? Finding out that you were right about being in the wrong life. Then finding yourself unable to change any of it. Maybe that's why it seemed that a sort of numbness became set inside of me. Saying "Goodbye, Angeline" instead of "I'm happy to be home with you" was becoming too much to bear.

***

"Did that 'event' cause any sort of escalation in the tension between yourself and Ms. Lacy?" the doctor interrupted, with the extremely concerned manner that is common to those who care for the mentally challenged and emotionally broken.

"Wait a minute," replied the patient. "You've got to understand there wasn't any 'tension' between us. It's just that we both knew that being together wasn't really what either one of us wanted anymore."

"Then why did you stay with her there in the same home and so forth?"

"I stayed because we were in debt, and the idea of just dumping it all on her and running was repulsive to me—I couldn't really leave the woman in a bind like that. As for Dana, well, I can't really say why she didn't just take off any sooner than she did. It's not as if she were in love with me or anything."

"So you still maintain that she's alive and well?"

"*Of course* she is, man! I would hurt never hurt her or any other person—and causing harm to a woman just to end a lousy relationship is a very stupid thing to do. Walking off would be a lot easier."

"Maybe for someone else, but not necessarily for you, isn't that so?"

The patient's eyes narrowed, and for a moment, it seemed that he was trying to stare right through the doctor. "What are you trying to say, Doc?"

"I've seen your military record. Men like you don't normally accept defeat very easily—in anything." *Don't back down*, the doctor thought. *They told you he'd deny having any involvement with the armed forces.*

"I was *never* in any branch of the military," the patient replied, as if on cue. "And I'm tired of talking to you, so forget about it, Doc. Just call the white coats and have 'em escort me back to my padded cell, okay? You're not interested in the real story, and that makes this all a waste of time."

Ace in the Hole

When the doctor got home, he replayed the recording he'd made during the interview. To any other person, it would no doubt have been quite apparent that the patient was delusional. That was why the prosecutor had called him in. He, for his part, was pretty good at seeming to be someone he really wasn't, such as a psych doctor. At one time, he'd thought he *wanted* to be a behavioral psychologist, even spending four precious years attending the university in pursuit of his goal. But vicissitudes of life and scarcity of funds had driven him into law enforcement a long time ago. He'd found that he treasured the work in that field more than he ever thought he would, though, and love of his occupation spurred him on enough to make detective and eventually become one of the best there was.

Whenever he found himself reflecting on those years spent in the realm of elite education, it always seemed as if he'd just been wandering in a wilderness until he found his true calling. The only valuable thing he'd found in the esteemed halls of higher learning was Laura. Laura, with her dark, dark lovely skin, easy sense of humor, and that dazzling smile.

She was a little heavier than what was considered the acceptable norm in the world of plastic self-engrossed people that surrounded her, but she was by no means unattractive, sloppy, or self-despising because of it. When he really thought about it, he realized that Laura had never really been physically heavy at all. It was just that the majority of the people they had known in those years, for all their claims of being mentally enlightened, were prone to judge as "too fat" any adult female who didn't look like one of the top fashion models of the day: tall, pretty, self-absorbed, and close to anorexic—a physical template into which his girlfriend would never fit. She'd always said of herself, "I may never be able to knock 'em dead with my looks, but I will *always* beat 'em out with my brains." She never saw herself as a really good-looking woman, his Laura.

But in fact, she was altogether beautiful, and being a person who could not fit into the plastic doll mold had taken a woman who had physical beauty coupled with an attractive persona and made her into an irresistible point of light for him. When they met, he liked her instantly; and with the time they spent together talking, discussing, even occasionally arguing over their common subjects of interest, he fell in love. And every time he thought of those wonderful days of their lives, he'd recall a line remembered from a poem he'd read somewhere, and it seemed to fit: "When I met you, I fell, like a boulder into the sea—I loved you before I knew you, I was yours before we met."

He and Laura both loved that poem, written as it was by some amateur poet whose name they never remembered, as they'd loved so many other poems. Just one of a million shared interests between the two of them. Shared interests led to shared time, shared time led to shared feelings, and they were married the year after he left school.

He fell into life with Laura in very much the same manner as any huge boulder would have fallen into the depths of the unending sea. Buoyed by the power of their relationship, he became a star in his field, working on some of the city's most memorable cases, not a few of which would have gone into the cryogenic wasteland of cold-case status had it not been for his perceptions and actions.

Eventually, their daughter Giselle was born, and little Marjorie came along two years later. For a long time, his heart was as bound to his home as to his work. Later, when the darkest days of his existence rolled around, he'd always look back and feel that these were the moments when life had handed him the best that it ever would.

In retrospect, he could honestly say that his family life was responsible for his ability to keep hold of his tendency to look for any little bit of good in even the worst of people, although having such a disposition often earned sarcasm from his coworkers, who, never sharing his optimism regarding the better nature of people, tagged him with the not-entirely unwelcome moniker "Detective Bright Eyes," something the detective never saw any reason to change.

Still, his dogged determination, coupled with the inspired brilliance with which he solved some of the most difficult cases, earned him a prominent spot in the Major Crimes Unit, along with a healthy dose of press coverage for each time he solved a seemingly unsolvable crime; and gradually, "Detective Bright Eyes" became a celebrity within the gritty world of law enforcement.

Gradually, though, his work would begin to alter his perspective toward the darker end of the spectrum; and although it in no way changed the quality of their marriage, Laura, a behavioral psychologist, never failed to see the changes in her husband and apportioned a good quantity of her time and energy to the task of helping him retain his humanity. Again, and again, she'd save him, always bringing him back from the edge of indifferent anger to an emotional state that would allow him to remain true to himself.

Throughout all of his following years, he'd believe that her insights were what helped him get through the hardest times—times when he saw the worst of the human race. It was her love and patience that helped him retain a (relatively) positive view of the entirety of humanity during those days.

Living with his profession was never idyllic, but he felt that a fine line of peace had been established between his love of home and love of work. He could pour all of his efforts into his occupation while doing the job and still summon up the needed energy to help Laura produce a warm family atmosphere when he got home. His future should have held joy and warmth. He should have retired to a happy life in the beachside bungalow he and his wife bought down in Florida. Marjorie and Giselle should have grown to beautiful womanhood, started their own families, and had children that he and Laura could spoil on weekends and holiday visits. That should have been how his crime-fighting career ended. That should have been the reward for his mighty efforts in helping to keep one of the greatest cities in America safe from the chaos of lawless men and women. It should have ended that way.

But it didn't. That possible future disappeared with the coming of a psycho whose favorite hunting grounds were anywhere within the most hopelessly insolvent portions of the city. All of his victims were found posed (postmortem) in near-abandoned tenements, thus earning him a nickname: the Tenement Slasher. Like many serial killers, his victims of choice were those broken butterflies of the night—the prostitutes. But as time after time, in city after city, he evaded the long arm of the law enforcement, he got bolder and, somewhere along the way, developed a taste for the torment and torture of children, preferably orphaned or abandoned little girls.

He even had the temerity to be proud of the fact that he never raped, only murdered. He made that quite clear every time that he'd use a prepaid phone to call his favorite television reporter, letting her know where they could find his last work of "slum art," as he called it. That maniac would have gone on killing for years had he not mistaken an undercover agent for a cheap prostitute and committed a crime that brought the wrath of the law enforcement community as well as the ire of the public down on his head—hard.

But the Tenement Slasher was a wily one. He was a sociopath who had planned years in advance, preparing subterfuge after subterfuge designed to mislead and misdirect the long arm of the law. No serial killer had ever been so smart, so *prepared* to evade capture. Investigation after investigation kept winding up right back at square one, causing John Q. Public to doubt the ability of the police to protect them; and still, the man's identity remained hidden.

It was "Detective Bright Eyes" who eventually stalked and caged this animal. He acquired a suspect, going so far as to set up an entire "clinic for psychological counseling for the impoverished" as a facade, just to be sure he got both the suspect and enough evidence to put the person in any position that would keep him from ever walking a public street again. It was during Operation Tenement Slasher that what would become his favorite and most effective cover, "the Doctor," was born.

To lend credence to the whole charade, Laura took time off from her own job to help and coach him. The mayor went so far as to grant her a special commission authorizing her to work with the police on the case. Just to ensure legality, he said. As things turned out, the Tenement Slasher was hiding within the very structure designed to help the investigation, just as the detective thought. The man had been employed as a sort of traveling records checker for the US Justice Department's various field offices all along. Unquestionably, the Slasher had been entirely brilliant. Everything he did was carefully orchestrated, right down to his choice of victims. Still, he was exposed and caught. He may have been good, but "Detective Bright Eyes" was better.

When they finally arrested the man, wrung a confession out of him, and got him in front of a judge, the detective thought it was over. It wasn't, though, for the Tenement Slasher was also resourceful. He managed to convince all the "head doctors" that he lived in a delusional world as the representative of an alien race, he didn't know right from wrong, yada yada. Everyone bought it. Even Laura, and she was one of the shrewdest. But the detective *knew*. He couldn't explain how; he just *knew*. There had never been any other target of his who attained to this level of evil. The Slasher had been planning his course of life since elementary school, when other boys his age were still playing with matchbox cars and bug collections. He'd created a whole structure of falsehood, preparing for his inevitable capture, from sometime in those early years. Just so that he could escape punishment. The ultimate cowardice.

Yet his subterfuge worked. The Tenement Slasher was sent to what turned out to be a low-security mental asylum, and a year later, he escaped. But he didn't run. He worked his way to the home of the one man who saw through his act. At that time, the detective was involved in a deep-cover assignment, in conjunction with the FBI, so no one was there to protect Laura and their two girls because, of course, why would "Detective Bright Eyes" ever need a partner to watch out for his loved ones while he was gone? What hubris!

The Slasher was tracked and found, but not until after he took his own brand of vengeance on the detective's family. Making things worse, the department didn't even let him know of the danger to his own until the last minute, after his home had been invaded and his loved ones spirited away. The undercover operation was just too important to the district attorney's office to pull their best man off it, they said. They thought they could handle it without him. But he abandoned his assignment when he found out, as he felt any man would have. Still, it wasn't soon enough to stop the Slasher. The man murdered every beloved member of the detective's family, ending with little Marjorie, whom he slaughtered right in front of her father's eyes, all while gibbering with laughter and talking on and on about how he'd get away with it again. That was a bridge too far, and in a flash of anger and grief, his sight gone red, the detective did the only thing that seemed sane to him at the time. He drew his service weapon and ended the threat of the Tenement Slasher once and for all.

Of course, there were inevitable repercussions, for he truly had taken the law into his own hands and felt not a bit of remorse over that. His actions had also set a federal undercover investigation back by at least five years. Yet to John Q. Public, he was a hero, and the police were admired among the people once again. The powers that be couldn't get rid of their most popular civil servant, but none of his bosses were very happy with his actions so he would not be "on the streets" anymore. They felt he couldn't be trusted, that maybe he was prone now to vigilantism, or perhaps in danger of losing it altogether out there. Maybe they were right, he sometimes thought.

For many years thereafter, it seemed to him that his passion for the work died with his family. The formerly great "Detective Bright Eyes" became a desk jockey, a "house mouse" who was making it to work day by day only because he could think of nothing else to do with his time. When a chance for early retirement came around, he blandly accepted it because the heartbreak of living with one-half of a dead love was becoming too much for him. He moved into the Floridian beachside bungalow that he couldn't bear to let go of and prepared to rot the rest of his life away, never expecting the day would come when he'd make friends among his community's police, but it did. As time went by, he found himself becoming an informal tutor for many of the local officers and academy grads. Sometimes, these days, he'd say that maybe the law enforcement gods just weren't through with him yet. Under his tutelage, his students' achievements received recognition among their contemporaries and teachers, and so did he.

After a while, he was invited to do part-time teaching at the regional police academy. He still felt too burned out to be a full-time instructor and, without a doubt, he would never be asked to teach any classes on respecting the rights of the suspected perpetrators, but his detection methods were considered priceless knowledge. And he found, to his consummate surprise, that he was actually a very good teacher.

He was never given a large paycheck for his work with the youngsters, but that never really bothered him. Besides, he felt, the informal reward of helping to create some of the best detectives in the country as well as the chance to continue doing his preferred work without personal involvement helped keep him going day by day. His new world grew, gradually, to encompass the friendship and families of some of the brightest young detectives in his new neighborhood. His love for the thrill of solving crimes and catching bad guys had even found new life here.

Because sitting on the sidelines never was good enough for him, though, he became a private investigator, choosing this path because he felt it was less encumbered than that of a formal police officer's and, unfortunately, he'd also developed a propensity for bending, almost to the breaking point, certain rules that bound the public's law enforcement officers.

Still, as time progressed, some of his students became police chiefs, and a couple of them even wound up going back to law school, emerging as prosecuting attorneys. He, for his part, always found himself especially drawn to those cases involving people who seemed criminally insane to the rest of the world. The detective's observations became outstandingly useful in several of these, even to the point of assisting the DA in exposing as cold, calculating pretenders several criminals who had opted for an insanity plea.

Eventually he'd become known in the prosecutor's office as a man who could see through any charade, especially those put up by really clever suspects. His favorite "cover" as the doctor, a behavioral psychologist, remained, persisted, and became ever more believable to the criminals he stalked. His friends on the right side of the law never forgot him, and his enemies on the wrong side of the law found that there were plenty of reasons to be seriously afraid of him. Before long, he was the preferred consultant for many of the major cases that came along. His reputation grew and with it his client list, as well as his paychecks.

Nowadays, that reputation always brought many of the cases involving suspects who may have been subject to lighter sentences due to mental disabilities to his door. He loved getting the so-called "deluded" ones. He'd always felt that if an observant person listened to the whole story as told by the suspect, the idea of using "delusional" as some sort of doorstep into an insanity plea could be shattered by the very words of the n'er-do-well who was trying to put forward that false front. So he was totally in character now.

Considering the patient, he was thinking, *This one is clever, there's no doubt about that. But he's just another scumbag. He does have a service record, but it seems to have been altered in some way. It might be a good idea to put the squeeze on a few sources and find out what they really used this guy for. I'll keep on being "the Doctor" at least long enough to find out the truth. I owe Dana Lacy that much.*

Before calling him in, the prosecutor had met with someone from the military (what branch, he never said), and that meeting was fruitful in that a certain personnel file came into the possession of the DA's office. The liaison explained that Dana Lacy's father was an officer who had been involved in quite a few classified missions, and none of the military brass wanted anything to happen that could expose his record to public scrutiny.

It was beginning to appear that someone would have liked to have had the patient quietly cared for while kept hidden, but someone else seemed to have been diametrically opposed to that idea and was providing just enough material to give a few good leads into a way to rip this "delusion" thing up. A tug-of-war seemed to be going on within the shadow realms of national intelligence agencies, being fought by extension between mystery people with different intentions. Apparently, however, this anonymous person or persons really didn't want to get their own hands dirty or have their collective or individual faces exposed. Thus, the secret maneuvering and investigation by proxy. Thus, the call to *his* office.

In review, the patient's record suggested that he'd played some small part in certain high-risk classified "events." Yet it also seemed that he had only been a sort of personal errand boy for a few top-ranking officers, though never gaining much rank himself. His boss may have been the go-to guy for those risky missions, but this man only got credit for excessive persistence in being the butler. A classic case of an unhappy underachiever.

The problem with underachievers was that you never knew just what they might have been had all circumstances been right for them. Such a person may have had the makings of a mad bomber, a world-class physicist, slippery serial killer, a "Teflon Don," some sort of musical genius, or even the president. Whatever they *might* have been, these people almost always knew just enough about higher fields of learning to make them dangerous if their inner frustration could be combined with their natural intelligence and put to a criminal use.

The detective was determined, though, to remain focused on one thing: whatever his story, the fact remained that Dana Lacy was missing, and this man was a prime suspect in the case. Why he was in a mental health facility for observation instead of a cell, the DA hadn't explained. He just made it clear that he wasn't happy with it. "The doctor," however, knew what he was expected to do—find a way to justice for another victim, and he was going to do it.

It took a week to get the patient to see him once more, but eventually, the man did agree to another session. It seemed that he believed he was running out of time for something, and he wanted his story known, maybe even published. When the patient finally sat across from him again, "the doctor" thought that the man seemed more calm and self-composed than he did before.

"Are you ready to hear more of my sad and sorry tale, Doc?" he began.

"I'll listen, but first, I'd like you to know that I'm aware of where you've been and what you used to do," the doctor/detective replied.

___

"I told you, sir, I'm just a career waiter. That's all I do, and all I've done."

"So it would seem," the doctor ceded. *Don't push him off the subject. Let him prattle. He may wind up giving me more information about what happened to Dana. Time to set his tongue free.* He leaned forward, looked around with the same conspiratorial air that this patient had effected with him on their first visit, then continued. "I'd like to have you complete your story, please. It is important that I hear it. Tell me what you did after that first 'Elsewhere' episode." The patient looked at "the doctor" for a while and gave a half smile. "Thank you, Doc. I need to tell somebody about this."

***

On several occasions, during the two weeks after that first event, I drove up and down Benson Bay Road at least once and sometimes four or more times every day and night, hoping to find a way back to that alternate reality, to see myself living happily ever after with *her*, but it never happened—the change didn't occur again. Eventually, I quit looking for it, finally convincing myself that it must've been just a dream based on my personal infatuation with a false hope.

The next time I saw Angeline was at Roper's sandwich shop. Dana had been gone for a week out to the Carolinas on a camping trip with several of her "friends," but I'd found out by various means that she'd actually gone with one certain "friend," some dirtbag bartender from that tavern over on Landry Street. They'd be away together for the next two weeks too. Whatever.

What? Did that bother me? No, Doc, it didn't. Ours was a dead affair anyway. May I continue? Okay, so I'd just wandered in during Roper's breakfast that day, and there *she* was, Angeline, at a table with a couple of the other waiters who used to work with us. When she saw me, she jumped up and screamed my name, as if it had been years instead of weeks since we'd seen each other. Angel was always that way about me. We hugged each other, as usual, and I felt tears coming, but held them back. One of the others brought over a chair, and we all sat together, Angeline and I somehow managing holding hands off and on while having lunch.

What was that, Doc? Was she worried about what the others would think? No, you have to understand something: this is one of the most up-front people I've ever met. There are times when she's a little more outgoing and blunter about things than I'd ever be, but that is one of the many refreshing things about this woman. She is who she is. No facades, no false fronts. Angeline is with George and would never get involved with anyone outside of her marriage, let alone leave her husband for any selfish reason, so that's that. I, for my part, would never try to push my way between them either. I love her too much to bring trouble into her life. As far as seeing the two of us holding hands while talking, that wasn't unusual to people who knew us.

Well, we both wound up sitting there together long after the others had gone, anyway. We could talk and talk forever, you know. I still remember how that late afternoon seasonal fog was rising when I walked Angeline to her car. She told me that George was taking tomorrow, which was a Friday, off, and they were having a few friends over, so did I think that maybe Dana and I could come over and get together with them for a cookout or something? I told her Dana was out of town for a couple of days and would probably not be interested even if she were here. I, for my part, would be working the closing shift tonight and tomorrow.

Angeline looked at me with those eyes of hers, and I think she understood how I was trying so hard to say, without words, that *she* was the person I was in love with. She put her hand on the side of my face and said, "Don't give up on her." I remember that I sort of laughed and told her that without a doubt, she, Angeline, and I were together in some other reality.

"If you keep saying that, I'm gonna start believing it too," she answered me in that lighthearted way that she has.

"Believe it, Angeline," I told her, "I *know* it's true!" She kissed me the way friends do and said, "You are *so* romantic—fix your relationship because you need it." I kissed her hands and replied, "Thank you for caring about me."

She got in and drove away. As the taillights of her car disappeared into the fog, I once more found those same old words on my lips: "Goodbye, Angeline." My litany of defeat. I went home and got ready for work.

***

Seeing the deep sadness on the patient's face almost made the detective feel hurt for the man. *I have to remember that this is most likely a murderer and an innocent woman is unaccounted for because of something he did.* Trying to convey as much understanding and reasonability as he could, he said,

"I know that having one person who cares can make a major difference in anybody's life. We go through our whole existence alone in our thoughts, and finding anyone who seems to understand us on such a deep level could change our view of those who are already a part of our lives." Then he added, "Tell me how things went after that."

The patient raised his eyes, and to the detective, it seemed that the man was again trying to stare right through him. But his gaze softened after a moment, and he said, in that quiet whispering way, "Of course, you need to hear it all, don't you? Someone here needs to remember."

DOUBLE, DOUBLE

It was a week later, two months, to the day after the first time that it happened once more. It. That *change*. The restaurant was going through one of its rare slow-volume periods and we needed to catch up on the bills, so I'd gotten with an associate who owned a janitorial business for some extra overnight work stripping floors, and that after finishing a long shift. Dana wasn't home, having taken a trip the night before—off to stay with a friend of hers for a few days, she'd said. I didn't even ask who he was. Angeline called to see how I was doing, though. She'd just had a feeling that I needed to talk to someone who cared. It's always been like that with us. We always just . . . *knew* when we needed each other. Well, we'd talked for a very long time before my heading off to floor-cleaning land.

My mind was on her that morning, after that floor-stripping job, as was my heart. Again, as before, I was on my way home, traveling Benson Bay road, when there was a temperature drop, a slight bending to the right in the road where there hadn't been one before; and I somehow *knew* that I was back *there*. There, in that alternate world. Immediately, I pulled over, got out, and looked behind me to see if there were any discernible effects, some lingering afterglow, or maybe some sort of static electricity sizzling and zigzagging in the air behind me; but there was nothing.

As you can guess, I immediately headed over to the apartment on the beachside, thinking of how, just one more time, it would've been nice to see the two of us living happily together, Angeline and someone who seemed very much like me. In this variation of existence, it was again about the same time of day as in the place of my origin, so it seemed that time was running at about the same rate in both dimensions, realities, alternates, whatever.

Upon arriving at the old beachside apartment, however, I found it empty, with a For Rent sign on it. No one was living there anymore. I was standing there wondering where they'd moved off to, when I heard a familiar voice hailing me. The source of that friendly greeting proved to be a fellow who, in my world, had died a little while before. His name was Walter, and I remembered him well.

"Coming back to see how I've kept the place up?" he asked.

Of course, he wouldn't be dead here. Why expect anything to be the same? Hasn't been the case so far. "Well, um, yes, I guess so," was my reply. "How's everything been, Walt?"

"Pretty good, and I want to thank that wife of yours for inviting me to your anniversary party."

??? thought I. "Yeah, Walt, she's always been the best, but you're probably getting so old till you can't even remember what anniversary it was, man." That was how I'd get what I needed to know out of the old geezer, I decided.

Old Walt rose to the bait. "How could I forget? It was about five years ago, right after you moved out, and I always felt bad because I couldn't make the wedding—I was in the hospital, my heart surgery—you remember, and this was your fifth."

WHAT? thought I.

Walt prattled on. He always did that after his long nights with the vodka bottle. "You know, I'm happy that Angeline convinced you to buy the place after that. I always thought you got one hell of a deal, but then, considering that heart problem, if I were going to go, I'd rather have sold the building to you before anybody else."

I thought I would fall down.

Yeah, it would be Angeline. Who else? But five years? Five years*!* was going through my mind like an incredulous pedal tone, a repetitious mental statement of surprise and disbelief. It didn't seem that it could have been possible that so much time had passed here, *if* this "me" moved out after I'd last seen the two of them together in this place.

Walter sounded far, far away, but when my flagging attention returned, I could hear him asking if maybe Angeline and I had been working too hard to get that new place of ours open, and did I need a glass of water, or something stronger, maybe? I began to notice now that he was going on and on about this new "place" that we were working on, apparently with the idea of having it open up before winter and the snowbirds got here.

What place? Snowbirds? Where do I—no, where do they live, this other "me" and his Angeline?

Hoping to cover my befuddled state of mind, though, I asked him, "Hey, Walter, how long has it been since you were by the house?" He suddenly became serious. "Sorry, I only made it that one time. I meant to get back by there to see you kids, but I guess I kinda felt more and more guilty because of how long it took me to. You gotta know that you mean a lot to me. After all, if it hadn't been for your CPR, I'd have been gone."

"Wait a minute," I interrupted him. "You know you'll always be welcome there, and by the way, you *do* know where our house is, I mean, I gave you directions, and you remember, don't you?"

"Sure, I do! I'm not that old yet."

So saying, he gave me directions to another location over on the beachside. It was in one of those new developments, he thought; and although he couldn't remember the exact address, he could tell me what street "my" house was on, what it looked like, and so forth. As I saw it, getting to the right street would be a good first step since the odds were high that upon arriving, I'd easily find any house that another version of myself would choose. It was pretty much a sure thing that I would also know what type of place Angeline would like too. We've always had a rapport that way—we love so many of the same things, Doc, until we just *have* to be meant for each other.

Well, anyway, off I went, headed toward my counterpart's home, expecting to see this version of me happily living a life that was, in my reality, nothing more than an empty shadow of an impossible dream.

Somewhere along the way, I decided that this time, it may be good to actually talk to him. *Her,* if I could. Why, Doc? Because I had to know what *their* story was. How they managed to get together, and what it was really like to be her husband. Was he happy with her, now that they were married? Yes, I may have been more interested in speaking to Angeline than to myself—there had to be some reason other than coincidence for her choosing *me* over whatever version of George was here.

Well, after a couple of wrong turns for which the absent Walter got covered in verbally abusive terms, the right location began to show on my GPS. It wasn't really a subdivision, as Walter had thought, being more of an outskirts-of-town sort of location where several new homes had been recently built, tastefully separated by generous sizing of the individual lots. As expected, it didn't take much effort for me to pick out the one that seemed to be my/his most likely domicile. I even drove around a couple of times just to be sure. Seeing my last name on the mailbox helped out a lot too. I parked a little farther away, this time, opting to walk the rest of the way.

On closer observation, I was better able to size up the place, and one thing was pretty obvious—this person was not struggling like I was. They had a *really* nice home. It was everything I hoped my own would one day be. There were some differences, no doubt attributable to Angeline's influence, but that only made it look better. The yard still had plenty of trees because, of course, no version of myself would ever cut down all the trees on the lot since the summer heat would torture anyone living on such a bare desert.

Their grass was nicely trimmed, and there was that wraparound screened-in porch that was just great for sitting with your mint julep and enjoying the end of the day. And oh yes, there was water—I love homes near the water, Doc. You don't feel so closed in with that type of place. Can you believe he actually owned two lots? All in all, the house wasn't bad. Not small and cramped like the place I had here, and not too large and ostentatious either. Looking at it once again verified my feeling that this version of me was doing a lot better than I ever had.

Things were clearly changed for him, now, as compared to my last visit here. Five years and one woman had made a real big difference. For the first time that I can recall, Doc, I truly, deeply *coveted*. Oh, *how* I coveted! I wanted *this* house, *this* life, and the pain of not having it could have driven me to desperation; but I realized that for all that I saw, the possibility existed that their marriage, and this whole scene, could really be a pretty package with nothing in it. Not much of a consolation prize, I know, but the thought kept me grounded.

How did he manage to live this well? Maybe this guy was a lot smarter than I was. Or at the very least, luckier. After all, *he* was the one who had his Angeline, wasn't he? How was I going to handle this, anyway? I asked myself. Walk right up to the door and say, "Hello, I'm your evil twin from another dimension. May I have your dear sweet wife? I've wanted her for a long time, you see." If someone appeared at *my* door with that statement, especially after my having achieved such a wonderful life as this guy had, well, I'd want to shoot first, ask who what and why later, or at least, call the law and have him committed.

But then this fellow *was* me, wasn't he? Surely, I would *listen* to my own double before shooting him down. Still, there was no way to tell how it would play out. What would we say to each other? The thought of not saying anything crossed my mind too. Turning around and trying to find my way back to that drab reality that spawned me seemed less daunting than possibly meeting this all-too-happy-with-everything-I've-ever-wanted version of myself. I stood in front of his house and considered.

This was the home that he shared with *his* Angeline. What if she was the one who answered the door? Would she be able to tell the difference? Maybe she'd put her arms around me and embrace me like a wife and a friend instead of *just* another friend. Maybe we wouldn't have to try so hard to hold back, just for a moment, before our kiss revealed to her that I was a different man than the one she married. Maybe . . .

I stood on the sidewalk in front of their address, muddling about in a personal quandary for a few moments and, emboldened by such thoughts as "fortune favors the bold," "nothing ventured, nothing gained," et cetera, et cetera, finally climbed the stairs, stepped onto that nicely screened porch, and knocked (really loudly) on their front door.

No one answered. While that was a relief, it was also frustrating. So what now? I wondered, as I went over to sit in a very inviting chair that just seemed to offer itself. There was nowhere else to go in this reality, and since the differences between this visit and my last were piling up, what guarantees could there be that one lost stranger could find his way anywhere? What else might have changed? What if my money was no good here? Back in New Orleans (if that's where they lived in this reality), how were the rest of my family members faring? Could I get back "home"? Did I really want to? Was the beer in this place any good? How did he get to this point in his life? What lucky break allowed this version of me to own such a residence as this? Didn't that Walter say something about Angeline and me "opening up a new place"? *What* new place? What work did I do in this reality? On and on the unfathomable questions kept coming, wearing me out with their cumbersome inscrutability. The spring sea breeze was coming in about that time, seeming to caress me like a loving mother, and I was so tired.

I have no idea how long I was asleep, but *he* was there when I awakened. He sat in the chair that had been next to mine, apparently after pulling it around to face me. There was a wicked-looking Glock G17 in the right hand that rested on his leg. The heel of his left hand, fingers curled under, was on his chin as he leaned forward in an all-too-familiar position. People have told me that I have a way of staring at them as if trying to see through their souls. I've been told that it makes folks feel uncomfortable when I do that. Now I could understand why. I wanted to speak, but some instinct for self-preservation must've stopped me.

In a calm voice saturated with quiet menace, he asked, "Who are *you* and why are you sitting on *my* front porch, in *my* favorite chair?" I wanted to come back with a smart-aleck's reply, something demeaning and clever like "What are you, blind or dumb? Who do you *think* I am, genius? I'm sitting here 'cause I didn't want to sleep in the car." But in my mind was an intimate understanding of the imminent danger when *this* man spoke in *that* particular tone of voice. He meant business when he got that gun out, and why not? It *was* his house after all, so he would defend it. Knowing these things, I simply looked him straight in the eye and answered, "I'm you."

FAMILY TIME

Coming face-to-face with "myself" was the eeriest moment of my life. "You're sitting in my favorite chair, and who are you supposed to be?" he demanded again, slowly and quietly stressing every word. He was also raising his pistol.

"You know, a certain woman once told me that I can be very scary when I 'quiet-talk' like that," I replied, without thinking. Angeline once told me that my "quiet-talking voice," as she called it, could really sound threatening; and deny it as I would, it seemed that she was right. I could tell by the look in his eyes that he'd heard the same thing, probably from his Angeline no less. I could also tell that he wasn't too far from pulling the trigger anyway. "Wait a minute before you shoot me, will ya? I'm YOU, dumbass! I know it doesn't seem possible, but it's me . . . uh . . . *you. I swear, I'm not lying!* What do your own eyes tell you?"

He was softening up, but still wasn't too keen on believing me. "A lot of things are possible in this day and age, pal, but as far as I've ever known, I have no twin and there's only ever been one of me. So you can see why this seems sort of fake . . ."

"Look, I could tell you how old you were when you first ever got kissed by a girl if that'll convince you." With suspicion in his eyes, he answered, "Talk."

"It was Candice Honicutt who first kissed *me*. We were in the back of her dad's car, and our families were moving because both our fathers were being reassigned to Fort McClellan. I was seven, and so was she. She kissed me three times that night. I'd never told *anyone* about that because of thinking I'd done something wrong." He lowered the weapon, his eyes seeing yesteryear, as he took up the telling. "Mom *snatched* me out of their car when she saw it. I actually got a little mad because she did that, although I had no idea of where it could possibly have gone. I was just too young . . ."

Now I was taking up the story. "But later on, I figured it was the best and only way she could handle it at the moment." He added my next thought, "And I had a notion that there would without a doubt be a good ol' momma-style whipping coming, but she never did it. I still wonder why not."

"So do I, and you know, I don't think she ever told my poppa either. Did yours?"

"No, but I think that mine was just too much of a romantic."

"Yeah, maybe so. And maybe that was part of what made her go all berserk in the end. She did a lot of damage to all of us, you know."

He lowered that gun and bowed his head, covering his eyes with his free hand for a moment. When he looked up again, I could see a lot of very familiar old rue in his gaze. He stared at me for a minute and simply said, "I know."

His eyes again became sort of unfocused and confused for a moment. "What is going on here?" he asked no one in particular. "What in the world is going on?" Looking at me then, he said, "You know that when a man sees his doppelganger, supposedly, he's about to die soon and be replaced. So what's on your mind, dop? You intend to be taking my place soon?"

I gulped. "No, that wasn't why I wound up here or anything. . ."

"Well that's a relief because if you were intending to dispatch me and take my life over, the least you could have done was come over here looking decent—I mean, why does *my* dop have to show up looking like someone who slept under a bridge and got doused with floor stripper?"

I suddenly found myself laughing, which seemed to get my double a little riled at first. "What's so funny?" he demanded.

"I was just thinking about how that sounded like something I'd say under the same sort of circumstances, and then it occurred to me that I *am* the one saying it."

He looked at me for a minute then began to laugh also. "Okay, good point. You just might be me." Then he put the weapon down. (I did notice that it was safely out of my reach.) "You don't intend to blast me, then?" asked I, feeling more than a little relief.

"Not yet. I'm not good about doing something as unnatural as shooting somebody who looks like my double. Besides, I really don't want to have to clean up the mess this thing would make of you. This *is* my own home, you know. Not to mention that I can gun sling pretty quickly if it comes to it. So tell me, dop, where did you come from? Are you a product of one of those new clone labs that the government authorized?"

Clone labs? thought I. *What clone labs?* "They don't have anything like that where I come from," I told him.

"Well, that's good. Beside the fact that I'm not so important until they would clone *me*, it's mostly still experimental and limited to the *very* wealthy or *very* important, last I heard. So where are you from, then?"

"This same place, this same town, only in a different reality—a different world, really, and with a very different set of circumstances," I answered. He just looked at me in silence for a moment then went on. "That brings up more questions, and we'll get to them later. But right now, tell me, why are you here?"

"I don't know why I'm in this place where you exist. I was just driving along—hey, quit looking at me like that. Honest, there was this temperature drop, a quick fog from nowhere, and here I was. But if you're asking why I'm on your front porch, it's because I had nowhere else to go."

"That almost makes sense . . . Well, not really, but moving on, how did all this come about? What do you want here?"

"I have no idea."

"You have the answer to at least one of those. I can tell when you're lying, you know."

"Yes, I know."

"Why are you so *dirty*?"

"Because I spent last night stripping a floor to make extra money. I was headed home when I wound up here. I did not, however, sleep under a bridge."

"Okay, yeah, that's funny, but *how?* I mean, assuming you're telling the truth—and by the way, the jury's still out on that one—assuming, that is, how did you wind up in *my* neighborhood, at *my* house?"

"I conned the location out of Walter—or at least, most of the location. The rest of it was more a case of 'know thyself.' Oh, hey, Walter thought he was talking to you and says he's sorry he hasn't been able to make it over. That's been bothering him."

He looked at me like he couldn't believe it was that easy. "I always thought Walter talked too much." *Funny how he ignored that part about knowing thyself.* "Great guy, and I really like him, but good gosh, he can be *simple* sometimes. And you're trying to distract me. I can see through that trick, dop. Why don't you just tell me the truth about what you want here? Remember, I've still got the gun."

The interrogation could've gone on for hours because each answer only raised more questions for both of us. The possibilities seemed to be endless. But something occurred to him, all of a sudden, and I could tell what was on his mind. He was asking himself how he would explain me to Angeline, and she was probably due to return at any moment. "I'm supposed to be somewhere, so this fun's gonna have to end," said he. "Go back to wherever you came from."

"You've got to meet Angeline, don't you? Are you two opening a restaurant or something?" I blurted. Again, he seemed to be trying to stare right through me as he answered, "Yes, and almost yes. Did you just guess that or what?" I told him what Walter had said, and we both agreed that, yes, the old fellow was sort of a chatterbox at times. More laughter. It was beginning to feel like we were just a couple of family members visiting one another, when he asked the one question whose answer he *had* to have.

"I can accept that you're at least a very close facsimile of me. What this is all about and who you are really are, though, is still a mystery. This sort of thing just doesn't happen, but here you are right in front of my eyes, there's no denying that. You said you're from another world, which would be scary enough if I were a person who scared easily, but I don't. I also don't believe everything I see. But I noticed that look in your eye when you mentioned Angie. So what's it like between you and your Angeline? Does she exist in your world?"

There came an old familiar pain in my heart as I told him that where I came from, she wasn't *my* Angeline—about how she was living happily ever after, married to another man, and though I loved her dearly and we are close friends, it doesn't seem that she felt the same way toward me. She was married to George, and I would not do anything to ruin her life or risk our friendship, so then, as far as I could see, we would never ever be together—not in my world. I wouldn't even try. What I did have of her was just too precious to me.

He jumped up, eyes hardening, and that gun seemed to snap back into his hand with the swiftness of a snake. "You covetous, secretive *bastard*! That's what you're after, isn't it! You want to off me and take my *wife*!"

"No no, *wait a minute, man! I couldn't get away with that!* There's too much that I don't know! If I were to pretend to be you, the Angeline *I* know would see through me in a New York second! There're too many blanks that won't fill in! No need to kill me, man! I have a life too, you know!" He didn't budge. That weapon was still pointed at me. I must have sounded even more desperate now. "Look at me, dude. Do I *look* like I came here ready to pull an ambush and do a murder? I was *sleeping* on your front *porch*, for chrissake!"

"Good point," he conceded, lowering the Glock a little. "But I still don't trust you."

I exhaled, for truly, this man would have shot the life out of me to protect his with Angeline. "I don't blame you," I told him. "But I'll give you my promise that I won't do anything that'll bring hurt or harm to Angeline, so any idea of murdering you and taking your place are outta bounds." We both knew that prospect had already crossed my mind, anyway, and there was no sense in trying to fool myself— literally.

Angeline *was* what I wanted. He stared into my eyes for a long while. "Okay, if you're saying that you have no intention of trying to take over my life, I'll take that promise," he replied, finally stashing the gun somewhere on his person and returning to the chair. But I did notice that he made no such promise to me. Apparently, he knew he had the life I wanted, but mine wasn't one *he* wanted. No promise needed. Leaning forward, he asked, "How do you *live* without her?"

Again, there was that familiar twinge in my heart. I wanted to talk about only being able to see her every now and then, the hapless and hopeless relationship with Dana, and how Angeline kept trying to encourage me not to give up on it because she only wanted what seemed best for me, so she must have known that despite any attraction there may have been between us, we would not have each other. Ever. In my thoughts I answered, *It . . . it's the hardest part of living for me. I know the woman that I was born to love but cannot have her. I know that she and I were meant for each other but have no right to desire her. I have found my mate, but she needs me to stay away from her.*

The only thing I could say, though, was, "I manage to live." I had to put my head down and rub my eyes with my fingertips because they were burning with unshed tears. *Ahh, my tears—unshed, unbid, never heeded. Oh, my words—unsaid, deeply hid, always needed.* He turned his face away and simply said, "I see."

"You know," I said to him, "I was just thinking that another advantage of talking to yourself is—"

He finished the statement, "That you don't have to waste words trying to explain everything you're feeling and hope it's understood." We both nodded at the same time. Still, I *had* to ask, "Tell me this much, at least, about her. Is it any easier with Angeline as your wife?"

"I don't want to give you any more hurt than you already have, man. You're carrying a lot as it is." *No*, I thought. *I have to know.* So I begged. "Please?" Again, he stared at me in silence for a moment that seemed to stretch on. In the end, though, he must have known what it took for me to use that word, *please*, because he answered.

"Okay. You know that part about not having to waste words because the person you're with just *understands*? Well, living with Angeline is like that. Most of the time, anyway. You're right on at least one point. She and I *were* meant to be. Oh, we . . . we have had our differences and fusses, even some quarrels, but there has never been any other woman in my life that was so easy to agree with, so easy to work through problems with." His eyes seemed to stare into yesterday as he spoke further. "I have been close with a lot of them in my time, and it always ends with bruises and heartaches. Even the amiable breakups hurt too much. But when it comes to Angeline, it's just all around, a lot more painless, like being home at last, you know. Oh, pardon me—you *don't* know, do you?"

Ooo, nasty too, thought I. *He really must not like me.*

My reply was, in turn, a little sarcastic. "Thanks. That does make the pain worse." Raising his eyes, he said, "You did ask. But I will also tell you this. The way you live, that would be more than I could do—going through life without Angeline. I can't imagine living with that empty space in my heart. And it bothers me to see someone who's so similar to myself defeated and content with it. It's like you're some sort of professional loser."

I'll tell you, Doc. That almost set off a storm, but then, he was armed and I wasn't. I wanted to yell at him, something like "I am *not* a loser—you just *think* I am because you're afraid of being one *yourself*!" But that would have sounded seriously juvenile, and there was no sense in making this thing harder to deal with.

His cell rang, and I knew it had to be her. He stepped aside and talked quietly for a while. I took a look around me. *Sure, I'd choose to sit in his favorite chair. What did I expect? What could he expect?* He apparently had gotten Angeline's chair, and then I noticed something else—there were children's toys lying around, here and there. *Oh my god, they have kids!* Another shocking realization. The type of toys I saw said at least two and would've put the children between four to six years old. More than anything else now, I knew that I wanted this life with Angeline, but I also knew that there could be no taking his. No child of mine, or any child that might've been mine, deserved to lose Daddy. This "me" was safe from any homicidal intent I may have harbored toward him. When his phoneversation was over, I told him, "I see the children's toys . . ."

"And?" he demanded, with the old suspicion creeping back into his voice. "They deserve to have their father." *Truce declared.*

He nodded slowly. "One's ours, one's Devvie's."

I couldn't believe it. *"Devvie has a kid?"* DeVries. I have two brothers, and though I love them both, everyone seems to think that he's my favorite brother. But then, he's everybody's favorite anything. We used to call him Devvie for short. Criminal to the bone, that guy, but I've never met a person who didn't like him immediately. He was a bit of a bon vivant, lots of "lady friends" and no kids—in my world. Somebody else I loved and had to say "goodbye" to.

"Yeah, Devvie," my double reassured me. *Oh, the questions, the questions! So many differences—and how many more were there?*

"Come on inside," he said, unlocking the door. "Let's get you cleaned up. That was Angel. You were right, I was supposed to meet her, but goofing around here with you caused me to miss our appointment. The girl gets worried. She's doing some shopping, and she'll be a little late. You were only half right about the restaurant. What we're actually working on is a cafe where we'll feature jazz musicians, some lyric poets, as well as any tasteful local talent on the weekends, and it's kept us busy as ever. But now that Dev's pitching in, things have loosened up a bit." I was about to ask to meet her when he turned to me and said, "The answer is no. Not today, definitely, and maybe not *any* day, in my world. Ever."

The inside of the house was even nicer than the outside—Angeline's touch, no doubt. As we entered, something that seemed a little odd struck my thinking. "You don't seem to be too freaked out about this whole affair," I mentioned, knowing what his answer had to be.

"I don't 'freak out' too easily—I've seen too much."

Something occurred to me then. "Say, Dub, I want to ask you a personal question."

He stared at me, and there was more suspicion in his eyes. "Well? *I'm waiting . . .*"

"Has it helped your self-image any, having Angeline as part of your life? Do you care any more about yourself than you used to?" It got through, I could tell. For just a moment, a bit of shock showed in his eyes.

"Oookay . . . that was freaky. Yeah. Maybe you really are me. But there's no doubt now you've gotta go. Get yourself cleaned up. You can grab a bite here and I'll give you something for the ride, but you really ought to leave."

We both agreed that it wouldn't be a good idea for me to stick around and get some sleep though I could've used it. He still wasn't very trusting of his "dop" from nowhere, and I wasn't sure how long I could take being tantalized by the life of my desire, which would never come to be. Then there was the reality bending thing that neither of us understood, and as far as we knew, there was no way to tell when something would change and land me back in my world, but he definitely did not want to be around or with me when that happened. Proof positive that he didn't have the hots for my alternate existence.

***

"Wait just a minute, please," the detective once again politely interrupted. "I know that explaining your entire story is important to you." *Telling his own story was important to Ted Bundy too.* "And in many ways, it's quite meaningful to me. But surely, you must understand this—a woman is missing, and it seems that you are the only key we have to finding her. Think of her family and how it must be for them."

"Have you had the chance to talk to her family, Doc?" the patient replied. "Because if you did, you may have noticed that they didn't seem too emotional about her supposed 'disappearance.' Her mommy dearest cut out on her a long time ago, poppa's too busy being the big dog on some military base somewhere, with little or no time to talk to his child. And here you're talking like I'm a serial killer or something. I can promise you that that no harm has come to Dana, and she truly is where she ought to be. It's probably the safest place for her right now. It'll all be very clear to you, if you just let me finish telling everything that happened."

The detective looked the patient in the eye for a moment. *So he's wanting to drag it out, but in his mind seems to think he's telling the truth. He acts as if she may still be alive, and if she is, there's a little hope and probably less time left for the poor girl. This guy's also made it very clear that he wants to tell the story his way. What type of game is he playing? A few moments alone, and maybe I'd get more out of him.* "Just tell me this one thing, and I'll let you get on with your side of it. If she's alive, as you say, is Dana Lacy's life in any sort of grave danger?"

The patient leaned forward, and the detective thought that for the first time since this began, he may have seen something besides mockery in the man's eyes. "You've got to hear me out . . . please. It's all intertwined, and after I've finished, whoever you're really working for can do whatever they want with me, *Detective.*"

THE COULD'VE-BEEN LIFE

For a long time, they stared at each other, formerly "doctor" and "patient," now detective and suspect. "Okay, so you know that I'm not a doctor," the detective eventually said. "When did you figure it out?"

"After our first session, Doc," the patient replied. "It was the tenor of your questions that caused me to wonder. A brain mechanic would have tried to find out why I'm mentally messed up then use that to prove what they thought I did. A detective would have already thought he knew what I'd done and would try to use questions to find a 'victim' or, at least, force some sort of confession out of me. I'll admit, there was also a little help from the outside."

"Who?"

"It doesn't really matter, Doc. Do you want to know about Dana or not? Do you want to break this case or not? Yes? Okay then, let me take up the story from where I left off."

"How do I know you're telling the truth? And how are you able to recall all the details so as to be able to talk with such accuracy?" The patient heaved a long sigh. "First, Doc, you have already decided that I'm lying, and secondly, I have total recall, or something like that. Remembering details, facts, events, and conversations with acute clarity is easy for me. Especially when I focus really well. May I, please?"

"If this is the only way to find Ms. Lacy, I'll go ahead and listen to your tale. But if she dies or has died while I'm here screwing around with you, I'll do everything in my power to see to it that you get to the hell you deserve, by the needle or any *other* means," the detective answered. The patient stared for a moment, approval in his eyes. After a noncommittal shrug, he began. "I'm counting on your personal integrity in such things, Doc. Now do you mind if I continue?"

"Go on, but don't think that listening to your garbage is going to stop me from cracking you open sooner or later." They looked each other in the eye for a few moments, willpower against willpower; but eventually, the patient seemed to accept and concede. "Thank you for listening, anyway."

***

When my "dub" suggested I leave as soon as possible, there really was nothing else to be done, considering the circumstances. He gave me some of his old clothing, and I must say, his old clothing were a great deal nicer than any new clothing that I currently own. Well, anyway, after I'd cleaned up and changed, he showed me into a room that was stacked top to bottom with neatly shelved books, almost all of which I'd read and owned at one time or another or wanted to own. There was a sort of coffee/reading table in the center of the room, and it was obvious that he must have also been used to eating here sometime. We had a quick lunch—roast beef, ham and cheese po-boys with everything on 'em, washed down with a coupla Grolsch beers, my favorite quick-fixin' meal.

After finishing lunch, we took a little time to talk then, and I had to ask him, "How did you get to this point? You have everything I've ever wanted but could never attain. I'm a waiter who has to find side jobs so that ends meet, but you . . . you're about to open a business, I'd guess, and it seems that while I'm in debt, you have a fat bank account, not to mention a house the likes of which I'll never own. What did you do, rob an armored car and get away with it?"

He looked down for a moment. "No, dop, it wasn't anything like that. My financial advantages came from some of the problems caused by Katrina." *Katrina? Katrina who?* thought I. "After she passed through, our family home was wiped out. Dad lost our house on the river and the one in Gentilly because of that storm. He wanted to rebuild, but before he could, the state seized his land with some hoked-up crap about taxes from twenty years earlier—in fact, that was being done to a lot of Katrina victims, from New Orleans straight through the Mississippi Gulf Coast. They were especially bad over there.

"Joanna and Lisa had evacuated to Houston before the storm, and Poppa joined them there after everyone in the family called and yelled at him consecutively. The three of them were crossing an intersection when some oil exec's kid who was driving drunk, in a company car and on company time, sped through the light and ran them down. The situation got a lot of coverage in the news and all, and it wasn't like his lousy reputation hadn't preceded him. So it seemed as if this was it for the guy, and maybe he'd be spending a lot of time in prison. But his dear old rich daddy could afford to pay the tab for a few public officials' diverse pleasures and hire the best law firm in the business. Consequently and unbelievably, the murderer got off."

I'd never faced the thought of losing any of my sisters to death, Doc, and I don't like that idea even today. I love my sisters—and the three of us boys were, of course, close. My dad has been there every day of my life, and though there were times when it seemed like we just had something between us that prohibited our getting as close a relationship as he had with my two brothers, we still loved each other. Well, I guess my double had a different sort of relationship with his father because I could see how deeply the thought of recalling all of those deaths hurt him. Just the thought of someone killing my family members got my blood boiling. Still, it was his turn to talk, so he continued on with his recollection.

"After the killer got off, DeVries and Marvin came down, and we started to make plans to go out to Houston and make that guy disappear, but Angeline held us off with the phrase 'file a civil suit.' We were newlyweds then, and at that time I was a waiter too. Devvie, of course, knew plenty of lawyers—one of the necessities of his chosen way of life at that time, and Marvin was willing to wait when he thought of the money, so we sued.

"It seemed that the case was going to be dragged out from now 'til forever, but a few things worked out in our favor. First, there were traffic cams all over that city, and several of them caught the whole incident on tape. How that fact was ignored, nobody knew, or at least nobody who knew would admit what they knew. It also helped that a lot of DeVries's pals and, shall I say, 'associates' had also evacuated to Houston, and those folks know how to get people to tell the truth in a courtroom. They'd do anything for my brother, you know.

"Even all of that may not have made much of a difference had not another event occurred. Execu dad's kid decided to hire some local lowlifes to shake us up, not knowing what kind of people *we* were. Devvie's shady contacts and pals told him what was in the wind, so after making sure they could find us, we went home to New Orleans to wait for 'em. We were thoroughly prepared for them knuckleheads when they got there. The police questioned what was left of 'em in the hospital and, from that, determined who the money came from.

"I personally made sure that the press found out. You would not *believe* how pissed off people get when they hear of that kind of behavior. In addition to that, oil prices were going through the roof, gasoline costs shot out of sight, and while the average person was going broke from all the effects of that situation, oil companies' profits exceeded all previous records, allowing their executives tremendous bonuses. People were angry, and any chance to stick it to the fat cats who were screwing the little guy would have easily been jumped on by John Q. Public, and it was. We won, and boy, did we ever win *big*.

"We went to the bank, and even though he'd gotten away with a triple murder the first time, Richie Rich eventually went to prison. It seems that he and some of his friends bought a truckload of cocaine from some unidentified person who sent incontestable evidence of his crime to the authorities. Another person even sent a film catching him in the act of committing a murder—he whacked some poor idiot who had been accused of stealing from him, I believe."

I looked him in the eye for a long while, searching . . . searching, and after a while, yes—it was there: a slight smile on the corners of his lips, a glint in his eyes.

"And," I said, "I suppose that our family had nothing to do with all of those fortuitous exposures."

"Of course not." he answered, sounding almost honest. "That poor little rich boy wound up in a cell with the worst rapist in prison and eventually hung himself. Very sad, you know. We'd never back anything like that."

"Riiight," I said. We both started laughing then. Another almost warm moment, but he continued.

"A short time later, Angeline and I convinced DeVries to move out here because we figured that the longer he stayed in New Orleans, the shorter his potential lifespan would be. It was her idea, you see. She told me later that she just knew how I would feel if anything happened to him. It's that middle brother syndrome, as she calls it." *Middle brother. Yeah. Marvin, Joanna, me, Lisa, and DeVries.*

"Life was a lot easier after that, but about two years ago, we lost Marvin. To him, being well-off meant all the liquor, beer, and whatever that he could have for the rest of his life, and that wasn't very long. He was out doing his thing one night when a coupla guys jacked him for his vehicle. He was too drunk or high to even dial 911 on his cell. He dialed 411. In that condition, he tried, but couldn't put up much of a fight. The goons left him dead on the side of the road. Dev and I inherited his portion of the 'loot from the suit' as we called it."

I was stunned. *Poppa, Joanna, Lisa, and Marvin? And who or what the* HELL *is this "Katrina"? So much loss . . .* He wasn't done, though, so I waited. "DeVries was never the same person after that. He doesn't have the contacts here that he had in New Orleans, so the cops got those two guys before he did. He didn't have anybody like Angeline, and it was hard on him. The night they found Marv I thought was one of the darkest in my life too. I wanted to go out and do some sort of violence to ease the pain, but when Angeline put her arms around me, I must have cried like a baby—I've never been able to let go like that. Dude, I don't know how you can *live* without her, if you really *are* me."

"Who or what is this *Katrina*?" I demanded. When he raised his head, he had that I-can't-believe -it look on his face again as he answered, "You mean, you don't know about *Katrina*? You really must be from a different world if you've never heard of *Hurricane Katrina? S*he was the BIG one, a cat 5 monster storm that nearly made New Orleans a part of Lake Pontchartrain! That city will never be the same, man!"

"I already told you, I *am* from a different world! Mostly different, anyway. But there hasn't been any Hurricane Katrina there, and New Orleans is still the same old Big Easy. Poppa, Joanna, Lisa, and Marvin are all alive and well, but we never talk much. DeVries, well, we lost him about three years ago. Took a bullet when he was doing whatever he does, or used to do, out in the Desire Projects one night."

He fought back tears for a moment, put his head down, and rubbed his eyes. Looking up, he said to me, "You need to spend more time with whoever's left then. I would give every bit of this *stuff*, with the exception of Angeline, up if I could have all of them back, if I could just go to one of those family dinners Poppa was so sentimental about, just one more time, and I wouldn't trade DeVries for any amount of money I have. He was always my favorite sibling, you know."

"Yes," I answered. "I know." For a quiet space of minutes, we understood each other, that other man who wore my form and I.

"How is your Devvie doing now?" I asked him.

"He's got a very decent woman who can stand him and put up with his wild-child side. Met her last year." There seemed to be a bit of a lump in my throat, but I managed to say, "I hope she has a great sense of humor. My brother Dev was always a bit of a joker."

"Mine *is* a bit of a joker, and yes, his girl does have a great sense of humor." I had to turn my face away. *I don't know if . . . if I can abide being here too much longer.* He evidently couldn't stand my presence for too much more time either. This was taking an emotional toll on both of us.

Eventually, things had to wind down. It was getting late, and he had a million tasks that needed to be done, considering what was going on in his life. Also, he was not going to let me meet his Angeline, and that was that. She was on an acquisition trip, getting her hands on those fancy blue glasses for the business and would be bringing them back to the house later. So I had to go. Thus we agreed that if I could not find any way back to my own reality, we would work together to find a place for me here in this world (just as long as it wasn't anywhere close to his wife and him).

We both wanted to talk more but decided to hold off our inevitable long conversation and meet at his old apartment tomorrow, if I was still around. And yes, I could spend the night there, if necessary. Yes, the spare key was still hidden under the loose brick on the front windowsill. Oh yeah . . . Walter. Well, he would probably see me there and just know without a doubt that there was some marital strife between Angeline and my double and would want to help fix it, but at the very least, it would get him off his duff and over to visit, thereby easing his conscience. Especially if I refused to talk to him while I was at the other place. There was just one more thing to tell him before heading out. "You know, this isn't the first visit to this realty," I started, and his eyes lit up as he again focused that stare on me.

"Go on, tell me about it," he said, with that dangerous edge of suspicion creeping back into his voice.

"It was about, I don't know how long ago in your world, but you were still living in the beachside apartment and had stopped some robbery attempt where the goon clocked you on the head before you kicked his butt, it seemed, because that's the only reason you didn't catch me that night. I'd crept up to that side window—you know, the one we always forgot to cover—and saw you sitting in that big blue chair I used to have, with Angeline on your lap." His eyes sort of narrowed; he was looking at me as if I were a madman, no doubt with anger at my past act of near voyeurism, maybe, but I continued on.

"I thought, at first, that you must've heard something because you got up and headed toward that side door. I had my black Impala—that's it down the street there—and parked it right behind the one you had then, your black Impala, and it was exactly the same, wasn't it?

"Anyway, now that I think about it, you must have felt my presence there. It had to be something like that because I *know* I didn't make any sound, and you got up then came outside to catch me. Maybe that head injury sort of slowed you down because by the time you got out the door, I was hidden behind the two cars. Even then, you would've caught me, but Angeline told you to just let her call the cops and asked you who you thought you were, Superman or a waiter, so you went back inside and later took a walk on the beach. The idea of hanging around to meet you or just lurking outside and peeking in to make sure I was seeing what I thought I was seeing did cross my mind then, but instead, I just left."

He looked down for a minute and then sort of laughed. "Superman or a waiter, huh? That sounds like something she would say, but it couldn't have happened because I've never stopped any robbery attempt at any restaurant, and even though I met Angeline when we were both working in the same place, she *never* came to visit me there. She was a little worried about getting in too deep too soon, despite the way we just seemed to be drawn to each other, and I'd pretty much decided to give up on the love-'em-and-leave-'em game forever, so we were understandably afraid of getting too close and ruining our relationship.

"I was about to move away from here," he continued, as my head began to reel. "Maybe try out living in New York, when we realized that we couldn't do without each other and would do very well together, so we got engaged and, later on, married. And by the way, I sold my black Chevy two weeks after I started working in that restaurant where I met Angeline." Once again, I was shocked. How could that night have *never happened*? It must have shown on my face because he said, "You know, you look like Marvin used to look whenever he got caught doing something dumb. Your mouth is open."

"How old are you?" I asked him.

"Thirty."

What! "I'm twenty-five."

———

33

It hit us both at the same time, the realization that there must have been yet another reality that I'd visited. "What year is it in your world?" he asked.

"Two thousand four."

"It's two thousand nine here," he told me quietly. "You're five years younger than I am, dop. Shame you don't look five years better."

Petty, petty. Twist the knife that got stuck in, thought I. "What about that guy, the other one of us?"

"How would I know? It's *your* party, pal. *I* never needed any other realities or alternate endings or whatever you got going here."

"Yeah, but you've got *your* Angeline too. So does *he*! What wrong did *I* do to be the only left-out Lamont in this whole thing?"

"I can't answer that for you, dop, but whatever is going on, I'd just feel better if you left my house right now. If you need to grab a nap before you go, you can use the old apartment. I'll just come around to meet with you there later, and we'll see if we can find some way to work you into life in this place or something—that's if you can't get back to wherever. While you were in the shower, I put together a duffel bag full of decent clothing for you to take along in case this world-changing thing does happen again. You can go take a look at the store if you want. It's located on Benson Bay road and Main. You'll *know* which place ours is, and if you don't disappear, you might even have a few useful ideas so swing by and take a look, but you gotta get there by yourself 'cause there's no *way* I'm going to ride along with you to show you where."

Suddenly, his eyes sort of *snapped* into a sort of clarity. He looked at me with an intensity that even I can't match today. Grabbing my arms, he asked, "Hey, I just thought of something! Do you know what this time difference means, dop?"

"That I'm younger than you are?" I said, no doubt sounding like one of those students who sit at the back of the classroom.

"No, you idiot!" he replied. *"It means that you can save them!"*

"Save *who*?" was my illustrious reply.

"Poppa, Joanna, Lisa, and maybe even Marvin, not to mention all of those unsuspecting people who died as a result of Katrina! That hurricane struck in 2005—for you, that's *next year!*"

"But how do I know that this 'Hurricane Katrina' will ever happen in my world? And even if I did know for sure, who in the world would believe *me?* I'm a waiter, not a weatherman! I mean, I'd have no *proof*!"

"Look, dop, I can print out tracking maps of all the hurricanes that went that way. You're right about never being able to convince the whole world, but all you really need is to convince the whole family. It's 2004 where you came from, what month is it?"

"It's late April, almost May." He looked at me in surprise. "It didn't occur to me that the months would be the same. I just assumed that hurricane season had already passed by where you came from. But it hasn't. You have no idea what your world is about to go through—it'll be bad. Real bad."

FRESH CONCERNS

"What are you ranting about now?" I asked him. "Didn't you already say that this big hurricane would happen next year, not this year?"

"Dop, there were *four* hurricanes that crossed the state of Florida in 2004, starting in the month of August—"

"Wait!" I stopped him. "I've never heard of anything like that! It could be that this sort of thing only happens in this reality."

"No *no!* Believe me, *we* never visualized anything like that happening here either, but it did!

"Their names were Charley, Francis, Ivan, and Jeanne, and they kept the state of Florida in plywood for months! Ivan was the worst—he made landfall as a cat 5 in the Panhandle and wreaked havoc from Pensacola to Mobile, Alabama. A lot of people were hurt and lost a lot, up to and including their lives, but even all that turned out to be lightweight damage compared to what happened after Katrina!"

I reminded him that even if *anyone* believed me, the people whose lives would be saved were not *his* people—they were just like the two of us: different, though being the same. They would be *my* people, and none of us were that close these days.

In return, he said something that in my mind proved without a doubt that he was the better man. "It doesn't matter, dop. Your life is hard enough without Angeline in it. Don't you think it would be worse if you lost everyone else who really mattered?" *What a difference one woman can make in a man.* He went over to his computer and began making a printout—hurricane facts and figures, I presumed. When the printing stopped, he handed some of the information to me, saying that I should head over to the other place, and he would be there tomorrow morning to see how things were and if I was still around. It was getting on toward evening, and he just knew that soon, Angeline would be back. And again, the answer was no. Emphatically *no.*

In taking one last look around at this house, this life that I would never have, my eye landed on a twenty-four-by-eighteen-inch picture of Angeline. "This is your room, isn't it? Your study."

"Yes," he answered.

"She's beautiful," I told him while we both looked at that lovely portrait.

"She'll always be that way to me, I mean, to us, anyway."

"Are you going to tell her about me?"

"Maybe, but there's no way she would ever believe it was real, and I'd rather not have my wife seriously questioning my sanity."

I pulled my wallet out and handed him one of my treasured possessions—a picture of Angeline, George, and I, taken during New Year's Eve function last year at the restaurant. Her left hand and his right held glasses of champagne raised for a toast, her head was on my shoulder, and her right arm was around my waist. George had his left arm around my shoulder in the classic "here's my buddy" pose while I held two glasses of champagne aloft.

I, the clown. What great fun. Never found out who it was that made the picture, but Angeline wound up in possession of it and gave it to me, just before she left that place. Their wedding rings were rather obviously displayed and were clearly nothing like the one she had on in his picture of her or the one he wore. *At least he was able to get a more expensive ring for her. It's so like her too—precious, without being gaudy.*

"Here's proof. You can keep it for yourself if you want to. This picture meant a lot to me, but my heart really wasn't in it anyway." Accepting it, he watched the way I looked at the big beautiful image of *her* that hung on his wall and said, "No way, guy. You're *not* gonna meet her, and you aren't getting that picture or any copy of it."

"Okay," I replied. His house, his world, his rules. And once again, that same old refrain came to my lips. "Goodbye, Angeline," I said to the portrait and was out, headed for my car, carrying my charity package along.

Surprisingly, I did make it back to the old apartment, even stopping along the way at what was in another place, my favorite package store. The owner always had Absenthe from New Orleans in stock, so I always went there. It was, in this place, the same store, with the same owner, who generously asked if this purchase should be put on my tab. Just to see, I asked, "By the way, that tab does get settled every month, doesn't it?"

"Absolutely, sir," replied the same English gentleman who probably runs the place in every reality there is.

"Well, add it on," I cheerfully replied, thinking that of getting that three-thousand-dollar bottle of Louis the Thirteenth while I had the chance, since my double here could probably afford it. He had told me how much they'd won, and lord, was it ever a lotta *money*! But that would have been too selfish and irresponsible, even for me. Two bottles of Absenthe would be enough, though. One to drink, one to go. At 138 proof, this stuff was no joke.

So I went to my old place that was also my favorite apartment at one time and got plastered, Doc. I shamelessly gave in to self-pity. The sky was gray with a promise of evening rain; the waves broke against the shore again and again, just as they always have, just as they always will. Angeline lived with another version of me that wasn't me here, and in this place it was a happy union, the type of thing people write songs and poems about.

In the meantime, I was once again just a spectator in the stands on the side of my own hopes. My heart was breaking for love of a cherished mist that would never be a solid and real woman held in my arms, and I didn't want to take the pain anymore. Besides, I was afraid of the dreams that might have tortured my mind during the wee hours of the night in this world. The best solution seemed to be to get too inebriated to dream, so I tried.

Morning came. Somebody was opening the curtain, and the sun was far too bright. "Hey, dop!" my own voice was shouting at me "Get up, man! You gotta move on."

"Whuzzit?" I managed to mutter. "Quit the yellin', would ya . . . my hea's a-hurtin'."

"I haven't been yelling, dop, you're just hung over. But man, you have got to focus your mind on what I'm about to say."

"I'll get outta your worl', okay, dub? Jus' gimme anudda hour an' I'm outta here."

"Focus, man—jeez, you really get a thick New Orleans accent when you've been drinking."

"Ahh hell, you prob'ly do too, dub . . ."

"Hey, enough already! Look, if you don't get back to that place you came from, the Angeline you know might be a widow soon! Or dead!"

That got my attention, all right. The pain in my head seemed to lessen, and the mental clouds parted. "What're you saying?" I asked. He said, "I took a good look at that picture you gave me last night. That guy with your Angeline, is his name George Arlander? Yes? Well, there was an alarm tech by that name here. He owned a small company and things looked pretty bright for him, but he died when his truck went off of a bridge in Pensacola. It was during Hurricane Ivan. I remember him because he was always in the restaurant flirting with Angie. He was a nice enough guy, but he was already outclassed 'cause by that time, Angel and I were seriously interested in each other. Later on, some really suspicious things about him came out. There were rumors of some sort of double life, and his first wife did have a very unhappy ending."

"Yes, his name is Arlander. He is an alarm tech, he does have contacts and family in Pensacola, but I don't think he'd be stupid enough to try to drive through a hurricane or stupid enough to endanger his marriage with some secret life that way. This first wife of his, was her name Irene in this world?" He raised his right eyebrow, a sure indication that I was right. "Yes? Well, I only know because Angeline told me their story. She said that his first wife died in some sort of accident—driving drunk, I believe."

The eyebrow rose again. "Yeah, dop, that's how this guy's first wife went out, sure enough."

"After losing one wife, I don't think George would risk losing Angeline too. And I really don't see him as a guy who would leave her to herself in order to drive off into the middle of some hurricane," I told him. His eyes got sharper as he concentrated on me. "Well, normally, this guy wouldn't have either, but I think he had someone there. He hadn't been able to contact them, his business was set to lose a lot of money. He didn't trust his friends to do the right thing about it. Whatever the reason, he decided to go there himself, and his wife, who normally went along for the ride, tried to stop him. Maybe he had some other agenda. But it seems that nothing she said could influence his decision.

"This one time, though, he never made it home. She went with him, but had already called one of her kinfolks to say goodbye—can you believe that?" My head felt as if some vicious gnome was using it as a drum, but I could still answer, "After all o' this, I c'n believe anything, dub. Normally, though, Angeline does stay home when George is out. I know this because now that I think about it, those are the times when she calls me the most. I've even been invited by when George is gone."

A sort of smile was playing around the corners of his eyes as he asked, "Are you two . . ."

"No way, man!" I answered his unformed question. "Don't you know Angeline better than that? She wouldn't do anything like that, and I wouldn't try!" He looked at me the same way that a person would regard some roach that had crawled across his dinner plate then said, "So maybe that's why she wouldn't do anything like that, dop. Because you wouldn't try. Don't forget, I'm *married* to Angie in this world, so I can say that I, without a doubt, know her better than you do—provided the two Angelines are as much the same as we seem to be.

"So," he continued, as his voice took a softer, more sympathetic tone, "I can honestly tell you this much. If she let you into her house when her man was gone, it wasn't because she had no feelings at all for you. Quite the opposite, I'd think. If I were this George guy, I'd shoot you if I ever saw you again. Proof or not. Just the threat you represent, when it comes to Angie's affection, would be enough for me." Feeling like a defeated battle veteran, I whined, "What would you have me do? Push her into destroying her life? I have nothing to offer her, except debt, struggle, and a guilty conscience. I do have to consider someone else's feelings too."

The hardness returned to his eyes as he replied, "If you're referring to that poor unfortunate girl you live with, I'd say that you stopped considering her feelings the day you met your Angeline."

This was becoming a little annoying now, so I looked him straight in the eye and started to say something my mother always repeated, but he joined in and said the exact same thing at the exact same time. "Remember, boy, the way you get a woman is the way you gonna lose that woman." *Touché.*

"Oookay . . . that was freaky. Yeah," said I.

"Well, dop," said he, "it seems that you're at an impasse here. If your Angeline becomes a widow, you may finally have her. If you save her current husband, well, at least you'll have a clearer picture of what sort of man you are and how to work with that. But you still won't have Angie. Maybe you should really have a long talk with your current excuse for a girlfriend—the one you live with. What's her name, anyway?"

Right then, however, his phone rang. Angeline again. "Yes, Ange, everything's okay. Yeah . . . it's just some crazy kid—got drunk and found his way into the place last night. I'm dealing with it. Nah. No need to call the cops. Kid's harmless, just a little lost. Yeah. I know his parents, and I'm sending him home right now. Walter? Well, that's good—it's nice to see that he is trying to keep an eye on it, anyway. I'll go over and tell Mr. Due Diligence to calm down, get out from under the bed, and put his shotgun away." He laughed. "All right, babe, see ya inna few. Bye."

Then his attention was back on me. "Dop, I've printed up some old headlines and other material to help you prove your point to whomever it may concern when you get back there. I've also given you far more than plenty of cash to take care of some of those problems you have. There's a whole suitcase of money, as well as a small amount of gold and diamonds here. You will be well loaded when you get back home. Maybe having enough in *that* place will stop you from ever wanting to come to *this* place again.

"There's even instructions that I've written to help you figure out how to put this away without attracting too much of the wrong type of attention. I saw enough of the few bucks in your wallet to know that our money looks the same. And even if this reality-twisting thing doesn't happen again, you ought to at least be able to set yourself up somewhere else in this world. Key phrase, *somewhere else*. Don't forget it."

My eyes were misting. "Thanks. That's more than anyone ever did for me."

Once again, his eyes hardened. "Everybody needs a break, man. Whether you get Angeline or not, just make sure you don't let Poppa dem (New Orleanian for Poppa and the others) die like they did here. *Promise* me."

"You got my word," I told him.

"Good enough, dop. Go on, get outta here now, *mon ami*." He turned as if to leave; then a thought came to his mind. Looking at me with that familiar hardness in his eyes, he said, "Oh yeah, one other thing. Talk to that girl you live with. She deserves something better from you than what she's gotten so far. Now *go*, please. This ain't been easy for me, man. I'm gonna go talk to Walt. Maybe he won't look too closely at you when you get in your car. Put that hat over there on. Oh, and en passant, dop, the answer to that question about my self-image is *yes*. She made *all* that much of a difference. Now leave. Please."

"Where do I go?" I asked. "I don't know how to make this thing happen. It just *does*. There's no telling for me when or where I'll wind up."

"Listen, dop, I don't *know*. Maybe if you head down Benson Bay Road . . . I mean, isn't that the way you say you were going when you wound up here? If nothing else, go back to New Orleans or head out for New York. If you're half the waiter I was, you ought to be able to do pretty good there, and the money you have will get you a decent apartment—even there. But you have to go, man—I'm getting more and more irritated every time I see you, and it's getting pretty bad. I mean, you seem like such a loser until you just *can't* be me."

You know what, Doc? That was something I'd noticed too. The more we hung around each other, the greater the feeling of irritation that just sort of tugged at the fringes of my emotions got. I'd just chalked it up to jealousy over his situation as compared to mine, but his words confirmed the mutuality of the feeling. Maybe it had a lot to do with the normal human tendency to pick ourselves apart. Since I was what he never wanted to be, though, it made sense that he would be more aggravated at seeing me in my sorry state than I would be at seeing him in his happy one.

I couldn't leave without one last dig, though. "Maybe you ought to exercise, more, dub—your bottom is getting awful fat there." He looked at me for a moment, nodded sort of to himself, I guess, then said, "Better a fat butt and a happy life with a happy wife than a permanently broken heart." *Home run, bull's eye. The last touché, whatever.* "Now go, before we really hurt each other, *s'il vous plait.*" That was the second time he asked politely. The second time he said "please." There wouldn't be a third. So I left.

BUSTED

"Okay, look," the detective began. "Going by your own words, you're a person with some serious criminal tendencies, even if you never committed a crime before now. I mean, this 'other' you immediately threatened your life with a loaded weapon, obviously has violent behavior in *his* past, and comes from a violent family. Since you're both the same guy, is it possible that *he* could have been the one who caused Dana's disappearance?"

Give him an "out." Let him have a chance to blame someone else for his actions—sometimes that's all it takes to get a criminal to start telling everything.

There was a moment of silence between the two men. The patient looked around in exasperation, his gaze finally falling on the orderly who brought him in. The man just shrugged as if within this very room there may have been the presence of a white elephant that no one could see but the two of them. "You're still not seeing it, Doc," the patient responded. "I'm not looking to get away with or run from anything I've done. Dana is gone because she *had* to go. My actions just opened a way for this to come about. And that other fellow, well, he wasn't a murderer or anything. He was just a man trying to protect his family and his home. Very different from myself. It seems that we walked the same life path up until we each left Poppa's house for good. As near as I can pinpoint it, that's when things diverged in our worlds. Probably in the first alternate guy's world too."

"So you do admit that even if he wasn't a dangerous or violent person, *you* could be? That you could have a potential for violence, maybe even being able to take another person's life?"

The patient sat back in his chair with a frustrated sigh.

Seems like that rattled him. What's he thinking of now?

"Let me just tell you how things went with Dana." *It's about time,* thought the detective. "Go ahead, I'm listening."

"I hope you are because if you just hear me out, you'll know what you have to do."

***

Of course, it happened again along the way, just as expected. A drop in the temperature, a slight bend to the left, and I was pretty sure that it was my own world that I returned to. This notion was confirmed as soon as I got to the house. Same house, same place as before, the hour of the day being just the same as in the location I'd just left. Almost as if it never happened, except for his seabag and suitcase left lying on the backseat. Once inside the house, I took a look at the maps and printouts that he gave me. Here and there were handwritten notes on the papers, drawing my attention to something or another that he considered important or essential to proving any case that could be made concerning the authenticity of the facts.

God, there seemed to be no end to the list of things to do now. Since I hadn't yet counted the money that my double generously gave me, there was no way to tell, at that time, that I'd never have to worry about having to work in that place again, so I thought that it would be a good idea to call the job and explain last night's absence. I remember thinking that maybe it would probably be better to claim that the schedule wasn't up when I last worked, so I had no idea, yada, yada, yada. That done, I had to figure out how in the world *I* was going to be able to convince George not to make that trip up to Pensacola or if he did, at least stay there until this "Ivan" blew over. Yeah I know, Doc, it seemed that would be the last thing I'd want to do, considering how I felt for Angeline. But if I at least tried and the guy didn't listen, my conscience would feel a little clearer should Angie and I get together afterward.

The morning passed, noon rolled around. I'd started looking over some of his printouts and trying to put the events they reported in context with my world. These great and mighty thoughts were still running through my mind when there occurred the sound of tires screeching in the driveway. A look out the window confirmed that it was indeed the return of Ms. Dana Lacy but, I'd never seen her driving like that. *Something must be really bugging her,* I thought, as she got out and slammed the door.

Her keys were in the front entrance now, and when it flung open, there she stood: tall, beautiful, and angry. She stormed over and slapped me—hard. *"Why didn't you tell me!"* she demanded. After that, she stormed into her room. I could hear her in there, sobbing over whatever it was that got me smacked. The words of my double came back to me then. I realized how right he was when he said that I hadn't considered her feelings since meeting Angeline. You know, Doc, there was a time when it seemed that Dana and I were really working out well, but I don't know what happened. Sometimes I think that our thing was just superficial, anyway. Truthfully, I really wanted to talk, maybe find out what was hurting her so, but we hadn't *talked* in such a long time.

Eventually I did knock. She didn't answer, so I just went in. She lay on the bed now, not saying anything, not talking, not really crying. I remember looking around, thinking of how long it had been since we'd shared our passion in this room, on that bed.

Not knowing how else to do it, I just decided to just start speaking. "Tell *what?*" was the only thing I could say, when what I really felt was a need to tell her how I wished it had not been so difficult, that I wished we had real love between us, not just jealousy over possession; but the words just wouldn't come out that way. Hell, they wouldn't come out at all.

She shifted, as if to make room for me; and just for a moment, I became that guy who had once found her so irresistible, so satisfying. I wanted to touch her again, to make the pain I had caused go away, so I sat on her bed and reached out to stroke her face. "Please don't touch me," she said flatly.

Defeated again. "What was it that you needed to know?" I mildly asked. *Now is not the time to let my emotions out of the box. This relationship ended a long time ago, and there's been enough pain dealt out since all these things started. Just because you're heartbroken doesn't mean that she has to suffer more for it,* I remember thinking.

But her answer shocked me at the time. "That you had another life, you *liar!* That you go down that weird foggy road and live in some mansion with Ms. *Angelie,* or whatever that so-called 'friend' of yours is named."

"Wait a minute, Dana . . . What are you talking about? *What* weird foggy road?"

Two of a Kind

She wasn't really calming down, but at least her yelling was decreasing by a few decibels, and it seemed that we could discuss things a bit more. Dana sat upright on the bed, facing me now. "That road you take . . . It comes from nowhere, and this is the second time that I followed you down it, only this time, you *left* me!" My mouth was hanging to the floor, it seemed, but some half words still stammered out of it. "Wha, whas . . ."

"Don't tell me that other place of yours doesn't exist either because I went right up to that house, knocked on the door, and you and her both were there—*together!* You acted all surprised to see me, so I knew you two were up to something, and that really got me pissed when you acted like I wasn't supposed to be there or like anything I had to say wasn't as important as she was, and when I started yelling at you, calling you a cheat and all, then you said that I was your dead brother's girlfriend! I called you a liar and was going to slap you right there, but that *Angelie* said to call the police because I was sampling drugs again, but I've *never tried any drugs*, and I've never been in trouble, and couldn't find my way back, and there you were bellowing something about my not having any nose piercing, so I left. I ran away, and . . ."

She was getting a bit hysterical now, and I was still trying to wrap my mind around the implications of her words while the whole world seemed to be spinning out of kilter because some memory was coming back—something about how to avoid being followed. Other images started circling around within my mind with ghostlike memoirs of Dana's face from somewhere and sometime before, when she was a teenager, and all I could think of was the question of why I hadn't been able evade the someone who was behind me. There were more voices, like boot camp instructors yelling in my head.

Pushing those phantoms aside for the moment took an effort, but Dana needed me now and I owed it to her to be here right now. "It was an *Elsewhere . . .*" I whispered it, I guess, because it seemed that Dana couldn't hear me; for there she was, still going on about how she'd been left behind. "DANA! *STOP! Listen to me! IT WAS A DIFFERENT WORLD!*"

Well, that got her attention, all right. She just sat there looking totally astonished, her eyes as wide as those of a deer caught in the headlights of a truck, and I don't know if the realization of the truth that there were *elseworlds* out there or my shouting elicited such a reaction. "Dana, I can't tell you about any road or fog or anything. Whenever I've crossed into the other places, I've never seen any road, just felt a temperature drop and a sensation like going around a slight bend."

"Well, they are bends," she said, leaving me totally astonished, "and you always go down one or the other of them. The first time I followed you was some months ago, at night. I was going to the restaurant to talk to you when I saw you leaving. I followed you because . . . well, anyway, I followed you. That fog came up then, and you drove right into it, which I thought was strange since it came up so suddenly, out of nowhere, and anyone with any sense probably would've avoided it or something, but there you went, driving along like it was all normal to you. I saw you head down the first bend to the left, and then you sped up and were gone. I turned around and got out of that crap. It was too weird for me.

"When you got back home that night, you just sat there on the lawn, looking like you lost something, then you came in and went to your cave at the back of the house."

"Dana, I . . .," I started to say something but realized that I had no idea what to say. "I wanted to talk to you, to tell you what it was like, but . . ."

She was recovering, but her confusion was becoming anger now. "Since *when* did you want to talk to *me*? About *anything*! Besides, you don't have to tell me what it's like! I know what it's like because I followed you that second time too! What do you *mean* how did I know it was going to happen again? I can't explain that, but I did. It was something in the air around you, like a ripple. Whenever you get into one of those *moods* of yours, like you're wishing for something but can't find it, that's when it happens, but I wasn't sure if it was really there or my eyes were just going bad, until recently because the ripples really have become more obvious.

"I followed you twice after that first time, but you just passed right through that fog and nothing would change, but this last time, you went somewhere else and I followed, but you stayed there for two days and I had to sleep in my car because my house wasn't where it was supposed to be, and you went to that old apartment, the one you used to live in, and I didn't want you to know I was there, and—" Dana was rambling again, so I grabbed her shoulders and held her eyes until they clarified.

"Dana, those places were *elsewheres*. That's the only name I can give them. I didn't know you or anyone else could see a fog, a road, or whatever it is. I only know when things change because of the temperature drop and the bend in the road, but why did you follow me? Why didn't you just catch up with me and let me know you were there? How did you find your way back here if I left you? Can you see that road all the time?" She seemed to be getting it together now.

"After that first time, when I turned around and came home, I called Daddy. He'd told me that he had a bad feeling about you lately, that maybe you were into drugs or something. If you ever started doing strange things, he said to call him and he would help me. I went out to the base and spent a couple of days with him. We were out to eat with that old colonel guy you know and some lab rat friend of his . . . By the way, is he related to you somehow? I know he's just your godfather, but he looks a lot like . . ."

"I know, he looks a lot like an older version of my father, but we're not related. Poppa saved his butt in the War, or Conflict, whatever, but will you get back to the *point*, please, Dana?" She looked at me for a moment, and it seemed that another argument was shaping up. But she took a deep breath, exhaled, and went on. "Anyway, so Daddy and his pals had a few drinks and pressured me into telling them about everything. They didn't seem to believe me but said that I should follow you if it happened again. They even gave me some 'special GPS' that would help me get back to the base if I were lost, but really, it was all a big joke to them—they were even sort of laughing a little bit, but not so bad as to embarrass me. Still, they laughed, so that's why I came here instead of going there."

"A 'special GPS'? What was so special about it?"

"I was supposed to put it on the roof above the driver's side, like one of those police sirens on TV. But every one that I ever heard of goes inside the car. They said this one had to be on the outside to work. The screen inside the car told me how to find the foggy road and what direction to go in. What do you mean, where is it? I left it all out there because something's wrong with it. I could smell wiring burning up."

I was once again astounded. A "special GPS"? While, to Dana, it looked as if no one believed her, to me, it all appeared quite different. Dana was without a doubt telling the truth. She knew too many details about the other place to be lying. That, coupled with the way she started falling apart was enough to establish the truthfulness of her words, and Dana was never the drama-queen-actress type. I knew the colonel could be trusted, but as for Captain Robin Lacy, there was no way to know for sure. Still, I wondered, why would the colonel stick with a man who seemed to be out spying on me? Concerning Captain Lacy, I asked myself, would any decent father intentionally cause harm to his only daughter?

I didn't think so, and as far as he'd shown, Captain Lacy was a decent father although he was a bit of a stiff-collared sort of guy. I'd once told Dana how I believed that if her dad ever dared to fart, it would probably come out as a long high-pitched squeal. The man was just wrapped far too tightly, in my opinion. Stringent. I'd also thought that this world-walking thing was something that only happened to me and wasn't too sure of my own sanity. But Dana could do it too, albeit her way of moving from here to *Elsewhere* wasn't the same as mine, and something seemed to be missing in her ability.

The colonel had introduced us, and I *knew* he sometimes did pretty classified spy sort of things. There were times when it seemed he had an agenda, but I always knew that the old man had affection for me. Or at least I *thought* I knew. He treated me like a son or, in his case, a grandson. And without a doubt, we weren't relatives, but now, even that fact seemed suspect. Captain Lacy worked for him from time to time, so their being together, with Dana pouring out her heart about elseworlds and foggy roads definitely implied that they were working together now. And what was a "lab rat" doing there? The colonel didn't think very highly of lab guys, I knew.

Still . . . could have just been one of the old guy's drinking buddies, but that didn't seem likely. It sounded like they were "running an operation" (a term I vaguely remembered hearing before, but wasn't sure where at the time). I was pretty sure of that too. Too many coincidences to make any other conclusion possible. What was more, for some reason, it also was something I'd somehow expected to happen. Actually, something I felt that I was *waiting* on.

———

But there was still so much to be done. Save George Arlander's butt. Go over the paperwork that "dub" had given me (it was hard to think of that man as being me sometimes), hopefully to find some way to convince the people who could make a difference. Had to talk to Poppa about this upcoming "Katrina" (of course, he would probably think nothing of anything I had to say—we weren't very close) or maybe just forget all about it and go to work. Going back to my double's world and try to fix any damage that Dana or I had caused seemed like a good idea too, but how? I wanted to count the money *he* gave me and figure out if it could be used to pay bills here. So much that needed to be done, and soon. Now I was beginning to remember a training session that was aimed at teaching how to handle crises of unexpected developments. Step one, mentally prioritize. It was a bit like working a crowded restaurant on Mother's Day. Handle the most important item first. Don't forget your timing, but don't obsess over the clock. Delegate that task to the back part of your mind and proceed.

Taking a close look at the "special GPS" had become priority number one. So I went outside to Dana's car, but a careful search turned up no trace of any GPS, car siren-looking item, or anything else. Hers is a white Ford Focus Coupe, and although it's always kept tidy, she doesn't always wash it well, so the roof was a little dusty. There was no sign of any gadget, gidget, or anything else on top of the vehicle, but anyone could see by the way the road dust was disturbed that something that was there had been moved.

I had the driver's side door opened and was looking around for any sign of a GPS monitor screen when, suddenly, there was a furtive movement to my left, a strike aimed at my temple. My left forearm flew up, deflecting the coming blow from its target to the back left side of my head. I fell back into the front seat, lashed out with a kick aimed into his groin, heard him grunt in pain, pulled myself up and charged him—uppercut from him to my jaw, felt it coming, got me, but just barely, hit the car and fell forward. On my hands and knees now, a swift kick to my rib cage. Don't pass out; that's what he wants. Look hurt worse than you are. He approaches, put all my strength into a power jump, my head catches the point of his chin, his head hits the outside wall of the house, he's out.

All that happened in less than three minutes without a lot of sound, except when his head thunked the wall. I dragged my assailant into the house to see if Dana knew the guy—he looked very familiar to me, but I couldn't place him. Besides, getting knocked around like that left me a little woozy. When she saw who the man was, Dana's eyes widened.

She said, "That's one of Daddy's men! I think he's some kind of aide or something. His name is Gibson . . . Sergeant Gibson. He's always around the Captain. That's where I've seen him before." Whenever she was angry with her father, she called him "the Captain." We decided to tie Sarge Gibson up, let him sleep it off and, in the meantime, go outside to see if there were any sign of the special equipment that Dana had been given. We looked around all over the place, but nothing turned up. When we got back to the scene of the fight, I noticed something odd about the tracks in the grass around the garage—*there were two sets!* So there were at least two people out here while all that was happening! "Why didn't the other person join in on the fun?" I wondered aloud. Dana answered that one for me.

"Maybe they weren't here to fight," she said. "If they were Daddy's men, and he sent them here for something specific, they wouldn't want to stray too far from their mission. He doesn't like it when people let their minds wander from the primary objective." The voice of experience, I knew.

We stood looking at each other for a few minutes, and it seemed that I was seeing Dana for the first time in a long time. "The sarge isn't going to be there when we go back in," I told her.

"I know," was the answer.

"He and whoever else were here for the equipment they gave you."

"Yes."

"Did you know they would be out here?"

"No." Her face tightened up, and tears started to form at the corners of her eyes.

"Why are you crying?"

"Because you want to leave again. I can see the air is rippling around you. Because you don't love me, and I don't love you. Because we've wasted so much time, and I wish things were different, but they aren't, and I can't trust anybody if I can't trust Daddy and I can't trust you."

The spring breeze was gently blowing her hair. Dana raised her hand to push it back into place, and in that moment of time, she was so beautiful. I had hurt her, I knew, as much as she had hurt me with the occasional other men; but this day, it was just the two of us—that's all we had right then. She was scared and crying because her world was being rocked by the reality of mistrust and the pain of being different. I was the only person who was there with her, and I hurt for her, for both of us. I wanted to kiss her and hold her, to allay the fear and give her comfort, for just that moment, at least. So I did. Apparently, she wanted to kiss me too. So she did. Something happened to both of us during that touch. *Something* passed between us, and we each traded off a part of our ability to the other.

It didn't hurt, it didn't burn, and there was no bolt or jolt of electricity. We held the kiss for a while, our passions almost aroused, and then it was over. When we separated, I looked at her and saw *ripples* in the air around her—faint, like the waves of heat that you see floating over the roads when they put tarmac down in the summer, and it was apparent that some new perception was now added to the individual sum totals of whatever we were. We both knew it although neither of us could explain it all.

I don't know the whys, where, or what of it; and right now, it really doesn't matter, Doc. "We have some things to straighten out, Dana," I told her. She started to tell me that it was too late for us, but I put my finger to her lips as gently as I could. "No, Dana, it's not our situation that I had in mind. We blew it a long time ago, and I don't know how to fix things. Since you don't know either, that's an indication that we probably aren't in too much of a hurry to patch this up at all. I was thinking of those people in that other world where we interacted with them. We affected their lives, and I don't think it's been for the best."

I could see her anger welling up, and she answered, "You're just trying to find an excuse to go back to that house you have with that b—"

"Dana, don't you *understand?*" I interrupted her before it became another tirade. "That guy wasn't *me!* He's another person, who has had a different life than mine, with different circumstances. He's about five years older than I am even."

"Well, apparently, he's also got the woman you wish you had too," she added. *Okay, let's be nasty now.*

Before we could get into a major argument, though, I forced myself to calm down, just enough to say, "Someone like you exists there too, and apparently, *that* Dana also has the man *she* preferred."

That deflated her sarcasm. "How do you know all this?" she asked icily.

"You told me that he said you were my dead brother's girlfriend, right? Yes? Well, in their world, the only member of my family that's left alive *is* my brother DeVries. But here, he's the only one who's gone. And whoever Dana is in that place, she's finally found a man she can be content with. It was my double who told me about it, and he knew nothing about your existence. It was just sort of in passing that he mentioned it at all. "

"How do you know she's content?"

"Let's go see."

Interlude I

A Brave New Life

She was walking along the beach in her new residence when she saw him again. He was sitting on the boardwalk, painting. Even with his back to her that way, she still could tell who he was. She could have picked him out of any crowd. Why was he here? she wondered. Did he think she'd needed to be watched or something? Hadn't they ended everything almost a month ago? Selling that house was all they had left to do, and it wasn't likely to have sold so soon, the way the economy was going back home, what with the recession and all. Maybe it had sold, anyway, and that's why he'd come back here again, to give her share and say goodbye for good. If so, then her connection with him would be severed forever. She'd be free. Yet somehow, the thought of her upcoming "freedom" didn't thrill her as she expected it would. Well, she thought, as she neared the artist, he did just lose the love of his life. In one place, that woman belonged to another man with whom she was happy; and in the other, she was with a man who was wealthy, so he could never have had her, anyway. Still, even then, that *one had been the one he'd seen as the love of his life. The woman for him. A small jealous part of her feelings reminded her that* she *wasn't the one. It hadn't been her. Maybe it never could have been so.*

Suppressing that sentiment, she asked him, "Why are you here? Didn't you have other things you needed to get done?" As she spoke, she thought of how much she hated it when her voice came out flatly like that. She could still hear her daddy saying, "That's okay, baby, it's just the way you sound when you're trying to hold your feelings in." Tears came to her eyes as she thought of Daddy. The man who had his soldiers attack her a month ago seemed *to have been Daddy. But the artist whom she'd just addressed had assured her that it wasn't really* him, *just an impostor who was very much* like *him. She had known it was true too because of that man's reaction to her screams for his help during the attack. Or rather, his lack of reaction. Even his eyes seemed emotionless as he watched his men try to capture and bind her. But then the man who she'd once thought she loved burst upon the scene and was enraged at seeing her hurt, even more so over the way that she was being endangered. At that moment, if no other, he had been hers and acted like he was. Just as she felt herself passing out from one of her attackers' blows, she also felt his arms around her, protecting her, because she mattered to him. He brought her here, stayed until she recovered, and then left when the old frostiness of their past began to reassert itself. He'd told her how he needed to save that other woman, whom he loved, and promised to find her daddy. He reminded her that the man she'd caught a momentary glimpse of wasn't the one who lovingly raised her. No matter. She really would like to have seen Daddy before she left that other place for good. Maybe he'd move here with her.*

Finally, she heard the artist's voice. She hadn't realized that tears were rolling from her eyes and he'd been speaking. "Pardon me, dear," he was saying. "I'm not sure I've had the privilege of meeting you." When her eyes focused again, she realized with a shock just how wrong and right she'd been. It was him, but he was older, with gray at his temples and a kinder demeanor, as if he'd accepted something he couldn't have changed. He also had a patch over his left eye and was alone in this place. She knew him well enough to discern that much. He lived alone, existed alone, and that was the way it had been for him. He didn't even realize how the loneliness of his life had marked him, but to her eyes, it was as plain as a handwritten tale.

"You're crying," he said gently. "I'm sorry if I hurt your feelings, ma'am, although I have no idea how I could have done that."

She felt his concern. "Is this the way you speak to every woman you've just met?" she asked, happy to hear the flat emotionlessness of her words disappearing. With an almost shy smile, he looked at his feet and replied, "No, honestly, I don't speak to any women much these days. I'm just not that . . . sociable . . . a fella anymore. But I can tell that you're just as attractive on the inside as you are on the outside, and any human being like that is a person whose feelings I'd never want to hurt. Your eyes tell me that somehow, you're walking around with a lot of inner distress. I don't like it. Whether we know each other or not, I don't think you deserve that."

This was something that was different about him, his being so concerned for her feelings. He smiled, and she remembered what originally made him so attractive all those years ago. "It's okay, it wasn't you," she answered. She then added, "Or maybe it was. Never mind. Thank you for your concern. Why don't you let me take you to lunch?" He hesitated, as if not believing what he'd heard, and she could almost tell what he was thinking. "No, you're not too old to charm a lady, and you're not as burned out as you think," she said and felt satisfaction at his look of surprise. "Why don't we go over there?" she asked, gesturing toward a nearby beachside restaurant, which happened to have been one of his and her favorites in that other place.

"The jazz is great there," he told her.

"They make good rum runners too," she said.

"Hey, that's my favorite beachside drink!" he told her, and she could almost see the old boyish excitement he used to exhibit whenever something new came into his life.

"Somehow, I knew that," she told him, adding, "and I'll bet you used to sit there when the moon was full and drink cognac too." He stopped walking, looked at her for a minute. "Wait a minute," he said suspiciously, "how did you know that? I mean, I just met you, and—"

"Don't be an idiot," she said. "Do you think you're the only person in existence who likes to drink cognac, gaze at the full moon, and listen to music?"

"Uh no, but I mean—"

"So are you coming or not?" she asked, walking on.

His smile returned. "Well, I guess I oughta. It's not every day that a beautiful woman walks up and invites me to lunch."

She turned her head to hide her smile. He called me a beautiful woman, *she thought.* I haven't heard that from him in a long time. *"You* left *your painting," she told him, pointing.*

"That's okay," he answered. "I'm well known around these parts. Nobody's going to mess with it. It isn't finished yet, anyway. Not worth as much as it will be." She looked at it. The painting was becoming his rendition of a dark powerful thunderstorm coming ashore. Yet the weather out here today was sunny, bright, and beautiful.

"No," she said. "I guess it isn't finished yet." She put her arm in his, and they went to lunch.

After another month, they were living together (again, for her). She knew his story now and had to remind herself, Don't think of it as "again" *because even though he was very much the same as the other man, he was also an entirely different one too. The only other woman whom he'd once loved died years before, when war and battle had enveloped this world. He'd gone to fight, lost his eye, then wandered hopelessly until the rebirth of his talent, not as a warrior, but as a telecom and biometrics inventor. The man he worked for then with was also someone who existed in that other place, someone who had known the other version of this man from his childhood and was about twenty years older, but here they were within months of being the same age. Yes, things were going to be different this time, she often thought, as she spent her mornings drinking coffee out on their front porch. The two of them were happy together, as it could have been in that other place. That he was six or seven years older than her and had lost the other woman a long time ago undoubtedly helped things along too. Still, she would love to have seen Daddy again. Just once more.*

That's when it happened. The one from her former life just appeared in *front of her, a transparent outline, speaking to her. He was here, he said, and needed help. Against her inclination, she chose to respond. But she wouldn't do it alone. She trusted the version of him that she currently had and told him everything. He wasn't surprised in the least and even put his arms around her to comfort her fears that he might be displeased over the information she'd held back. He would be there for her till the end, no matter what, he told her, and she knew both versions of him well enough to know he meant it. So together, they went to the other one's aid.*

NEW DIRECTIONS

The detective was feeling more and more annoyed with the patient. *All this talking, and he's still not saying anything that points me in the right direction. This guy is getting on my nerves. I'll have to find another way to crack him.* "Let's talk about something else for a while. Most Americans go throughout their whole lives never being able to pay their bills, but over the past year, *all* of yours have been paid and you haven't accrued any more. So how did you do it? Were you planning to leave the country before you wound up locked in the loony bin here? Maybe somebody paid you to make Dana disappear, promised protection from the law and more money, then snatched the rug out from under you after paying the first installment on the job."

Seeing no immediate reaction in his suspect, the detective continued on. "I've seen it before, you know. If that's the case, you're on your own, and you can't expect a bailout. So you hokey up this detailed story that's almost believable and really self-contained. That means that there's no substantiation anywhere that anything you say is true, but it sounds so *real*, and the head shrinkers come up with what seems to them to be the only possible conclusion under the circumstances—you're suffering from some sort of delusion and need to be cured before we can bring you to trail, blah, blah, blish.

"But in the meantime, Dana is still missing, and no one's been able to link you to her disappearance or find a body. Yet. Even with no proof that there was any foul play involved, it seems that you're still the last person to have seen her, and her blood was found in your house."

The patient was visibly irritated now. "Her house, Doc. *Her* house. I was able to pay off all of her debts and mine, as well as buy the place and put it in her name before my intended departure. My double just *gave* me enough money to do all of that, and more. I used the cash in what seemed the best way to allay suspicion and avoid drawing too much attention, but I was the one who was going to go, not Dana." As he listened, the detective felt that he was seeing more of the picture. "You saying you set up some type of offshore account? What banking system did you use? Swiss bank? Cayman Islands?"

The patient became a bit more irritated at hearing this. "That's beside the point, Doc. What you want to do, accordant to your bosses, is find Dana, or failing that, verify beyond any doubt that I, big bad ogre that I am, have taken her life and hidden the body. That is nowhere near the truth, but I'll never get to proving anything else if you keep interrupting my narrative here."

"Forensics found her blood in your house," the detective reiterated, "and that alone should have been enough to convict you, but it didn't happen. Maybe your employer didn't snatch the rug out from under you after all. Maybe you made some sort of stupid mistake, threatened to give up someone, and your cash cow pulled a few strings to help you wind up here instead of on death row. You'll screw up again, if that's the case, because criminals always do. Just so you know, I'm going to find whoever's been helping you out, and when I'm done with you, I'll go after that person's head too."

The patient sat back, looking appraisingly at the detective. "I'm glad that you're the guy doing this. You really are dedicated, and you have the anger you need to see it through. When I found out they'd hired you, I was worried about whether you'd become just another washed-out ex-detective who was just trying to while away the years till the Grim Reaper came for him. But you haven't given up, have you? And you never will."

The detective glared. *What is this scumbag thinking? Maybe he's developing some type of attachment to me because he knows that I am going to take him down. Very hard and very painfully. He's got a Joker-Batman complex. Maybe he thinks that we'll be "best frenemies" or something. This guy doesn't realize that I don't have a good side for people like him to get on.*

He leaned in, beckoning the patient forward. Pitching his voice low enough so as not to be heard by the attendant standing at the door of the room, he said, "Why don't you just tell me where she is? That's all I care about. Don't think for a minute that you and I have any friendship connection or anything else. I'm not going to spend years of my life going after you while you joyfully lead me on some merry chase. Should I find proof that you are a monster and Dana was your victim, you are *not* going to get away with it, no matter what the *court system* decides.

"Remember that I am *not* a cop anymore," he continued, as all the anger he'd been holding in bubbled to the surface of his words. "Remember that I have no moral duty to the taxpayer to worry about. I just hate dirtbags who victimize innocent women. Remember that I have all the connections I need to simply make *you* disappear. I can put people next to you and get it done that way or pull a few strings, maybe have you moved to some place where you would be just a sitting duck and I would be the hunter. Whatever you think you are or want to be, *don't try to be my pal.*"

The two men sat back, staring each other in the eye again, and this time, no one gave in. Finally, the patient looked around for a minute, rubbed his head, and leaning forward again, asked, "Have you spoken to Angeline or George Arlander since we started these little chats of ours?"

Intrigued, the detective responded, "No, I did not."

"Why not? Was my 'guilt' such a foregone conclusion until you felt you didn't need to do any footwork? That's not competence, *Detective Bright Eyes.*"

That this man would know of that old moniker wasn't at all surprising to the detective. Apparently, *someone* was feeding him some pretty good information, which was an issue that would have to be dealt with later. For now, though, he had made a pretty good point. "Why should I? Give me one good reason why I should do that," the detective asked.

The patient sat back once more. After a minute, he answered, "How about five? Because there's something you need to see among Angeline's possessions. Because no matter what you think, there's nothing false about what I've told you. Because if you go to the Arlanders, you will find out more than anyone else has so far, and because something serious happened at their beach house recently, and it was something that *Dana* saw."

The patient then turned to the man standing at the door and raised his voice. "Hey, guard dog! Take me back to my padded cell, wouldya? This doc is giving me the creepies, and I'm about ta have a whack attack here!" Even louder, he yelled, "You wouldn't want me to have a whack attack. Hey, Lucius!" Lucius came over. A big dark-skinned man with a handsome smiling face, he seemed to view his charge more as an errant little brother than a dangerous mental case, further convincing the detective that something suspicious was going on with this particular "patient" and his whole situation. Orderlies at facilities for the criminally insane may usually be large guys, but they were not normally as relaxed and congenial as this "Lucius" was when dealing with their wards.

Maybe this was the person who was doing the footwork for this animal. Serial killers often accrued fan clubs, so it makes sense that someone like this would wind up with at least one fan, thought the detective. "Armchair murderers," he'd always called such people because in his opinion, that's what they were. Cowardly lowlifes who didn't have the ability to actually go out and do what their idols did, although they did have the same twisted desire. *They're usually big guys like this "Lucius" too*, he thought as he considered the man. *I'll have to look into his background, find out what his story is and how these two are managing to operate together. I know that this dirtbag wound up with a lot of money, somehow, so I'll have to see what big Lucius's bank accounts look like—maybe that crooked banking accountant whose behind I saved last year will come in handy now.*

***

Tempted as he was to ignore his suspect's suggestion, the detective could not deny the reasonability of the thought; he really did need to talk to the Arlanders. Even a rookie could tell that this picture wasn't coming together as expected. The patient was responsible for or knew more than he was telling about Dana Lacy's disappearance, of that he was sure. Yet there was something missing, and for lack of that thing or fact, nothing was adding up. That any investigation could go in a totally wrong direction due to deficient information, the detective knew from bitter personal experience.

He'd also found that for some reason, his not having thought to speak to that couple until the patient mentioned it bothered him way more than he thought it should have. So although believing that it would prove to be just another dead end in his suspect's sociopathic game, he resolved to go ahead and talk to the Arlanders. Before going, however, he did do a little research on one George Arlander. He was the sole titleholder and proprietor of AA Protection, specializing in fire alarm and home protection systems. His slogan was "Don't delay, call double A, do it today!" Cheesy and unimaginative, the detective thought.

George Arlander had married Angeline Duplessis four years before. *So they were just newlyweds when that slug wormed his way into their life,* the detective thought bitterly. George's business began to pick up speed about three years back, and yes, he did have a few clients in the Florida Panhandle, his highest-paying one being a prominent pharmaceutical supply company. AA Protection was not a large-enough operation to sustain a regular workforce of more than twenty people, but they were on the way up. More and more frequently, George Arlander began to have an occasional busy season that required the use of temporary labor. He also noticed that AA Protection was on the verge of facing a lawsuit over some installation work that seemed to be substandard, the customer wound up getting burglarized, the alarm system didn't do what it was supposed to do, hundreds of thousands of dollars in merchandise had been stolen, a security guard who tried to activate the alarm during the robbery got shocked with just enough juice to send him into cardiac arrest because of his weak heart, his widow was joining in on the lawsuit, so on and so forth. The firm they'd hired for representation was Woosner and Wilcox, a group he'd done some investigative work for in the past. That would be his "in." The folks over at W & W would allow him to question Arlander and the missus under their banner, trusting him to uncover the truth or falsehood of the accusations upon which the suit was based.

After making the necessary arrangements to represent the law firm in the discovery phase of the case, the detective sought a meeting with Mr. Arlander. The man seemed willing to, at first, but suddenly didn't look to be in much of a hurry to convene with the person who was supposedly the point man in W & W's efforts to clear AA Protection's good name, and this gave the detective cause for concern. In considering the quick alteration in the man's behavior, the detective realized that Arlander had become evasive after he was told that the law firm's representative wanted to meet with both him and his wife. That was when his attitude seemed to change. Whenever the detective tried to make arrangements to meet with George himself, the man's personal secretary, "Wes," seemed to have already scheduled Mr. Arlander for an important meeting or a trip out to some potential job that "needs to be bid on real soon." This evasion continued for weeks. Reasoning that such behavior seemed peculiarly suspicious in the context of the Dana Lacy case, the detective that decided the best way to force an interview was the old unexpected Sunday afternoon visit out to the Arlander domicile on the beachside. *Not really a big place, just a really nice one*, he thought when he arrived there. At least someone was home today for certain. He could smell the grill going and could hear music. Classic rock, of course. George Arlander was at what the detective considered as that classic rock age, being between forty-one and forty-five.

Reaching for his badge (oh yes, he had a badge; several, really, but this one was authentic, a bounty hunter badge), which he considered as one of his universal door openers, he unlatched the front gate and walked into the yard. The sounds of music and smells of grilling were, of course, emanating from the backyard pool area. Preferring not to violate the man's privacy too much more than he already had, the detective decided to call out in his best "come out with your hands up" voice. "ARLANDER! GEORGE ARLANDER! WE'VE GOTTA TALK!" Satisfyingly, the music suddenly stopped. A man in his early forties appeared, walking around the side of the house from the direction of the swimming pool area, a puzzled and concerned look on his face. "Who are you?" he rightfully demanded.

"I'm the guy from Woosner & Wilcox who's going to save your butt," the detective responded. "Now, I've been trying to get in touch with you for about two and a half weeks. You were gonna meet with me to discuss the details of the Cline Group's lawsuit. Everything seemed on track until I told your guy Wes that Mrs. Arlander had to be involved in the meeting. You turned into the invisible man after that. Do you mind if I ask why?"

"Wesley said that you sounded like some pissed-off cop," George replied.

"I *was* a cop," came the answer. "That's why I'm working for the law firm now. The money's way better. Get back on point, Mr. Arlander. Is Mrs. Arlander here today? We need to get this done."

George seemed a little uncomfortable now. "Why?" he asked, sounding almost petulant.

"Why what? Why do we need to discuss how you handled that job, or why do both of you have to meet with me?"

"Why does Angeline have to be there?" George replied. "I mean, I know that you need to have more details in order to poke holes in their complaint, but what help could she be?"

"The Cline Group has suggested that the break-in may have been an inside job, with some of your people involved, considering how easily the bad guys circumvented the alarm system. They're going to be trying every imaginable angle, possibly up to and including accusations leveled against your wife." The more he mentioned Angeline, the more uncomfortable George Arlander seemed to become, the detective noticed. *I wonder what's going on here,* he was thinking, when a smiling blond man in his late twenties came around the side of the house from the direction of the pool deck.

"Hey, sugar daddy boss man!" he yelled. "You gonna come back and finish playing the—" Seeing the detective's gun, the smile disappeared, and the young man's expression changed. "Oh, I'm sorry . . . I didn't know that there was . . ."

A little annoyed now, George turned and said, "It's okay, Wesley. I'll be back in a minute. He was just leaving."

To the detective, he said, "I'll meet with you Monday. We have company today, and this is not a good time. Give me your card, and I'll call you. Definitely."

"Fair enough," the detective replied, handing over the Woosner & Wilcox card that he'd created. "Remember, Mr. Arlander, it has to be you and your wife. Woosner & Wilcox will not take the case if I don't think they can win."

Determination
and Duplicity

Monday. *Everybody hates Monday*, the detective thought as he headed for his meeting at the Arlander home. George Arlander's secretary "Wesley" had called and hinted at postponing off the meeting again, but the detective's phone call to Woosner & Wilcox ended that procrastination. Arlander agreed to meet that afternoon. But Angeline would not be there. The husband said she had not been there in some time. He'd have an explanation when the two of them spoke today, he'd assured his guest. Upon arriving at the beachfront home, the detective did notice, however, that the same vehicles were there as had been last Sunday. *Company stayed over, I guess. This guy had better not try to use that as an excuse to cut it short.* George Arlander himself, dressed in a robe, his hair still wet from the shower he'd just abandoned, opened the door. "Company still in town, Mr. Arlander?" the detective asked.

"Uh no . . .," came a nervous reply. He just stared at Arlander for a minute. "Those are Angeline's and Wesley's cars," George answered in a tone that sounded more like a defensive retort than anything else. "They, uh, they park them there and, uh . . ."

"Then who was here this past weekend, Mr. Arlander?" the detective asked in an even tone. "Somebody was here having a grill out with you."

"That would be me," said Wesley, coming from the direction of the bathroom with wet hair and a towel around his waist. "Sometimes George lets me stay here. We normally do a little grilling when that happens."

The detective turned his attention back to George Arlander, staring at him until the man turned beet red. *This foolish embarrassment is something I*

---

don't have time for, he was thinking. *Dana Lacy, or her remains, haven't got the time either.* "Mr. Arlander," he began, no doubt sounding like an irritated old barber, "how you live your life is your business, and I couldn't care less about your preferences. But I really need to talk to both you and your wife together. She is still your wife, isn't she?"

"Of course!" George answered, seemingly offended. "Why would anybody think otherwise?"

"I've noticed that you're not wearing your wedding ring while you and your buddy 'Wesley' here are each showering at the same time. What a coincidence. Now I don't know what that's supposed to mean in your world, but I do know what it means in mine. But as I said, that part of your life is not my business. I'm working another case in addition to doing the preliminary investigation on this one for Woosner & Wilcox. You and your wife, if she can still be called that, have both been mentioned by the suspect in that case."

George and Wesley looked at each other in astonishment. "What is this person suspected of?" George asked.

"Murder, maybe. At the very least, possibly kidnapping and false imprisonment," the detective answered.

"It's that waiter guy, isn't it?" Wesley demanded. "I always thought he was creepy, and everyone said that he might be locked up somewhere."

Perceptive, the detective thought. *Not just another boy toy. He's slimier than the dirtbag at the kook house, though. I can see it in his eyes. This guy could take a life, and his conscience would never bother him. I'll pinprick him a little. See how he reacts.* "Listen, *Wessie*," the detective began, putting as much sarcasm as possible in his voice, "I don't think you have anything to say here. Why don't you go bake raisin bread or ducky cookies or something? Just let the *men* talk." Wesley's eyes widened and for a moment, and for just a second, the detective saw a terrible hatred in them. But this Wesley wasn't a totally empty-headed person. He realized how he had exposed himself, and in an instant, the hatred was gone, replaced by sarcasm.

"Yeah okay, ex-cop burnout. I'd better get out of here before you shoot me like you did to that guy back where you came from. So why don't I just go and let you 'men' talk. Call me if you need me, *Georgie*," Wesley replied, flashing a handsome smile.

So they researched me. Why? Why does it mean so much to him? Or . . . maybe he's trying to remind dear old George of something, like why he shouldn't talk too much with me. There's something more than the obvious between these two, the detective thought. *Suspiciouser and suspiciouser. This reminds me of the Two Tower Killers, the way that they interacted.*

Turning to George, he asked, "Where?" The man gestured to the living room.

After they were seated, he started. "I really wish you hadn't talked to him like that. He's been good to me."

"Yeah, I'll bet." The detective replied. George Arlander began to say something else, but the detective interrupted. "So where *is* Mrs. Arlander?" Avoiding the detective's glare, George stammered, "She, uh, she isn't here now."

"She went missing and turned up dead," Wesley came in and interjected. "About two months ago."

The detective couldn't hide the look that came across his face at that announcement, made in such a matter-of-fact way. His shock must've shown on his face, he thought, for Wes now had a smug, satisfied look about him; he'd hit the ol' ex-cop with a shocking fact and was reveling in the reaction. *So this guy knows how to play the psych game too. Something serious is going on here. I need to separate these two.*

Turning to look at George, the detective said, "Get him out of here. I have many close friends, both in the local police department and in a couple of federal agencies. If boy toy here interrupts one more time, not only will you lose this current case, but there will seldom ever be another peaceful night's sleep for you in this town. There is also every possibility that with a few well-placed phone calls, I can see to it that the IRS *will* audit your books, perhaps going back for the last ten years. Now, get this *excuse* for a human out of here. Do you *understand* me, Mr. Arlander?"

The way his eyes widened told the detective that Mr. George Arlander did indeed understand; this was no bluff. "Wes, please leave," he said calmly.

"Ahh Georgie, this guy's full of sh—"

"Wesley, LEAVE NOW!" George cut him off.

That's the most authoritative I've seen this fella act since I met him, the detective was thinking. *I wonder if boy toy knows that he's not really the ringmaster of the circus here.* Wesley slinked out, sulking.

Turning to George Arlander, the detective fairly spat out his next words. "Now, *Mr.* Arlander, you will *tell me what happened to her.*" George was stammering again. "Uh, well, she, uh, she had an accident, and uh . . ." The detective leaned back a little and said, "Look, George, I know you're not the helpless stumblebum that you're pretending to be. You built a company that is almost a two-million-dollar-a-year enterprise and still growing. I mean, just counting the profit, it's still growing. Guys like you don't cower or stutter. Drop the act and talk to me. What *happened*?"

"Okay," George replied. "But first, tell me something. Wes is right, isn't he? That waiter of hers is the guy you're looking at, isn't he? I don't need to know what for, but he is the suspect you mentioned, right?"

"Maybe. But if you want information, you need to give information."

George nodded. "Okay, go ahead. Question away," George replied.

"Okay, for starters, what happened to your wife?" the detective started. "She fell off of a second-floor balcony onto the pool deck." George said. "The fall hurt her pretty badly. She was staying in our house in Mexico, and by the time I got there, she was gone, wandering around somewhere in the town, lost. They found her about a week later. She'd gotten a head injury, and that's why she wandered away, because of that head injury, which eventually killed her."

"How did all that happen, Mr. Arlander?"

George got up and paced. Then he poured himself a drink. "I believe that she was having an affair. That wouldn't have really bothered me, I suppose. I mean, it's not like she didn't know that I had . . . other preferences. And her other guy was a friend to both of us, really. He'd even done some work with me on a couple of my jobs. He was really bright, for a waiter. Weird how most people think they're all dumb guys who do that work. There was something between him and Angeline, though. I'd have to have been blind not to see it. She knew what I . . . what I was sometimes doing, and although she acted like she had no idea, never made any scene or fought about it, she started going for long walks on the beach at night, supposedly alone, and we'd stopped sleeping in the same bed a long time ago."

George Arlander was standing at a window now, holding his drink in his hand. The detective concentrated on the man's body language, his facial expressions. For a man who had lost his wife in a foreign country, his reaction was just *wrong*. No anger at the unfairness of it all. No tears of remorse for how he had denied her needs. Even the most estranged of husbands would show *some* regret after the death of the woman he'd married. But George Arlander seemed angrier over something else, and by his experience, the detective *knew* that his anger had nothing to do with the man in the asylum. *He's trying to mislead me for some reason. This man has a secret hidden inside, and it's not his relationship with his pal.*

Oblivious to the turn of his visitor's thinking, George continued speaking. "But I still had love for her. It's just that, well, I am what I am, she wasn't very accepting of it, and that's probably what made everything go wrong. There were times when I still wanted her, but she just couldn't deal with things being the way they were. You'd think that she'd at least be grateful. I mean, I could have just cut her off—she did sign a prenup, you know. But no, my generosity and kindness wasn't *good* enough for her." George's tone was becoming slightly angrier now. "She developed some type of relationship with that 'friend' of hers, but she always maintained that it was never carnal in nature. Still, about three months ago, they took off together for a few days. We own a place down in Beach City, on the coast, and I believe they went there."

George Arlander took a deep breath, composed himself, and began again. "When the hospital in Mexico released her and the authorities cleared me after investigating, something had changed with her. Angeline started drinking almost all the time and became even more distant. I believe that maybe her conscience was beating her, as it ought to have been. She had never been much of a cheat—she was just generally too honest. We had a good marriage at first, you know. I mean, I guess it wasn't her, really. It was *him*. I just had to try other things and some of those things I sort of liked, that's all. I mean, I work hard, you know, I'm entitled to a little enjoyment."

Anger was beginning to work its way back into Mr. Arlander's voice as he continued. "She *should* have been okay with it. I was still a pretty good husband, and she . . . I gave her *everything* and *anything* she would ask for. Do you have any *idea* how many women would have been okay with a man who would get them any and everything they *wanted?* But oh no, not *her.* From the moment they met, it was like a part of her was always absent, always thinking about *him.*"

Realizing how he'd let his emotions take over, George stopped, took another deep breath, and carried on his narrative. "She didn't talk about it, but I *knew* where her mind was. She must've done something she shouldn't have with him, and maybe her conscience was bugging her pretty badly. Maybe she *remembered* whose wife she was *supposed* to be or who pays the bills, at least. She wouldn't lay off of the liquor, and one day, under the influence of alcohol, she fell off of the balcony at the other place. The railing broke while she was leaning on it."

As much as he tried to contain himself, George was still becoming visibly angry. The detective noticed how his complexion was reddening as the veins in the man's neck bulged. *He's not grieving a bit for his wife*, the detective thought. *Actually, it sounds like he's angry at her, but wants to blame her for his own choices. How could anybody expect a woman to be happy when her husband does what this guy did? That's not realistic. Besides, there are a few things in his story that aren't adding up.*

The detective stared at George for a minute. *Human jealousy is an amazing thing. He lives this double life and then gets so pissed off when it seems that his wife, whom he's been lying to all this time, has found another interest. Too bad that the other guy is probably more of a scum than he is.* The man seemed to wither a little under his scrutiny. "Did the local authorities suspect any foul play, Mr. Arlander?" he asked as dispassionately as he could.

"No." George's reply was quick and affirmative.

He's hiding something, thought the detective *Considering the circumstances, he may have paid my perp to take out his wife.* "I have a picture of my suspect in the other case. Tell me if he looks familiar to you." Opening his portfolio, the detective drew out the patient's picture, handing it to George. "Here. Take a look." After one glance, George answered, "Yeah. That's the waiter that Angeline was involved with. What did he do?"

"He's been implicated in a situation regarding another woman. Her name was Dana Lacy. Did you or Mrs. Arlander know her?" George looked openly shocked. *"He's* been implicated in a murder? Are you sure? I mean, I know him, and it never seemed that . . ."

I never mentioned murder. He knows something that I *need to know.* "You seem surprised, Mr. Arlander. How well do you know this man?"

George regained his composure, and the detective was sure that he saw a calculating look in the man's eyes before he looked at his feet again, saying, "I mean, you never know what goes on in people's minds, you know? The guy was strange, but I never really thought he was capable of . . . but you know, in retrospect, I really believe he was closer to Angeline than I thought at the time. I mean, I missed a very important meeting in the Panhandle once because of whatever was between them, and that cost me a lot of money."

"So how long ago was it that you said he and Mrs. Arlander went away together? About six months?" the detective asked.

"Yes," George Arlander replied. "It was about six months ago."

"Thank you, Mr. Arlander. You've helped me out a great deal. So now I'll help you out. You fired one of your installation techs last year. Remember a fellow named Phil Redland? Yes?"

George Arlander's demeanor suddenly changed. He became the successful businessman again—sharp eyed, alert. *In an instant*, the detective thought. *This guy should have been an actor. He's almost good at it.*

"Yeah, I remember Phil. He'd been with me since I started, but he was a broke-down drunk before we got that Cline job. He screwed up so much until I had let him go by that time."

Nodding, the detective replied, "Well, he went to work for the Cline Group, but not as an alarm tech. He went in as a temporary laborer. His cousin Scott was into the burglary thing. He and his crew had Phil sabotage your system and gave him a cut. Your former client never did any background check on him, so they had no idea of what he was capable of. Just out of sheer mean-spiritedness, Phil rewired the primary power supply so that it would give a nasty shock to anyone trying to open the master panel. No one expected that jury rig to kill another person. It's amazing how fast his cousin spilled his guts when he thought he'd be the one saddled with a murder charge. They will, of course, both be charged.

"Furthermore, I've turned the information and proof over to a couple of my friends in the department. Phil's not going anywhere because he still thinks he's under the radar. They'll pick him up on the breaking and entering after Wednesday. By that time, the detectives on the case will have the hard-copied financial proof that they need, and AA protection and the Cline Group will have already started their litigation. That'll put Woosner & Wilcox in a stronger position." George Arlander understood the implications of these facts almost immediately, as was evident by the enthusiasm with which he began shaking the detective's hand.

"Thanks, Detective! Thank you! Thank you!" He was exuberant. "If there's ever anything I can do . . ." The detective turned as if to leave, stopped, and began. "In fact, Mr. Arlander, there might be something that you *can* do for me. I'd like your consent to enter the premises of the place you own on the Mexican coast. Or at least the one down in Beach City." *His reaction will tell me a lot.*

George Arlander's enthusiasm disappeared. His face set like stone, he replied, "That's where Angeline died. I won't let you disturb her memory that way. Besides, the house is up for sale, and whatever you might be looking for would probably be gone by now."

The detective gave a half smile. "Well, Mr. Arlander, maybe you're right. Oh, by the way, did you hear anything else from the authorities there?"

"What?" George asked, looking like a man who had just been reminded of something unimportant. "About who? Oh . . . *Angeline.*" The embarrassment showed in his face for a moment before his expression changed to one more suitable for a grieving husband. "They suspect that someone else may have been involved, maybe another man, but they really didn't have anything concrete, and even though they're supposedly investigating, nothing's turned up."

He looks even more pathetic and sad. How sweet of him. "Was there an autopsy? A death certificate? Was there an insurance policy on her?" George Arlander raised his eyes to meet the detective's, saying, "There is a death certificate, and I didn't need any autopsy. She died in Mexico. I think we're done here, *Detective.*" There was no more hesitation, no looking down at his feet, just a straight stare with a quiet smugness on George's face.

They held each other's eyes for a moment, and the words of an old children's story kept going through the detective's mind: *Run, run as fast as you can; you can't catch me, I'm the gingerbread man! Something is very, very wrong here. First, he says Beach City, but now it was in Mexico.* Mr. George Arlander could be as self-satisfied as he liked, the detective thought. There was no way he could have realized the depth of determination in the man he was taunting with that attitude. *One psychopath at a time*, the detective was thinking. *The gingerbread man got eaten by a wolf at the end, I believe.* With a gray cold smile, the detective said, "Thanks for your time, and good luck in court. I'll let myself out."

As he was leaving, he could see George and Wesley engaged in an animated discussion on the front porch, George appearing angry, Wesley looking as if he was trying to explain something. The detective watched for a few moments, just long enough to gauge their body language. It looked as if George was pretty hot about Wesley's "letting the cat out of the bag." His eyes narrowed as the wheels within his mind spun.

Love to be able to hear what that's about. Arlander's lying. There's a big difference between three months ago and six months ago. He couldn't even say which month it supposedly was. But why would he lie? It's as if he's trying to implicate the other guy in something, which would make sense only if his wife's death wasn't an accident, and he knew it. Anger welled up within as he thought further.

Even in a screwed-up marriage like this one, a man as possessive as he is would not *be mistaken about when his wife went on a sabbatical with someone he thought she had the hots for. If it happened at all. More puzzles. But I love puzzles. George Arlander will be hearing from me again. But first, it's time for a return to the nuthouse to crack the kook who sent me here. I am going to find out what this was about. Maybe he's jealous of this Wesley guy taking his place or something.*

A Night of Waves
and Shadows

Later that night, the detective sat in his living room, staring through his opened french double doors at the restless ocean outside his craftsman-cottage-styled bungalow on the beach. He'd been contacted by some of his students before making it back to the facility where his suspect was being held. The kids needed his help on a different, but equally puzzling case; and as much as he loved catching bad guys, he'd learned to love both teaching as well as the people he taught even more. There would never be a time when someone he taught would be unable to reach him. By the time he'd finished up with the pupil who had the problem, it was far too late to talk to the patient again before the place where his own suspect was being held had closed up for the night. So the day had ended as so many law enforcement officer's days did. A lot of good done, but still not enough. There were still too many evils in this system of things. Evils that would take a man's family but leave him with the home he'd prepared for them. The *empty* home he'd prepared for them. Three bedrooms and an office, not to mention living room, den, etc., etc. He had never thought to ask himself why he felt the need to hold on to what seemed like far too much house for a single man. *Laura would have loved the place*, he thought. *That's why.*

It always seemed, to him, that the sound of the surf, coupled with the warm night breeze, helped in the furtherance of deep thought needed to work out the abstract questions that popped up with every investigation. He'd sit in his favorite chair, sip a little bourbon, face the never-ending waves, and let his mind wander through the maze of case-related information stored therein. But this one was becoming more and more perplexing. Something wasn't quite right about George Arlander—even a rookie cop could've seen that. For an experienced detective, the red lights and buzzers would go off at top volume. He couldn't put a finger on the problem yet, but he knew that there was one.

A thunderstorm was trying to work its way onshore, and he could see the tendrils of lightning far off over the ocean. The direction of the breeze told him that the storm would most likely succeed in its efforts to step onto the land. Probably by tomorrow. *The direction of the breeze . . .*, he thought. *That's what's bugging me. I don't like the direction of the flow in this case. Things seemed so clear when I first reviewed it, but now, something else is on the horizon—I can feel it.* He got up, went to the liquor cabinet to refill. He'd been given one of the finest bourbon whiskeys once. A gift from the innocent parties in another case he'd solved. Thanks for all your hard work, etc., etc., and tonight, in some mood of melancholy or despondency, that was the stuff he was drinking.

Miles Davis was working "Kind of Blue" in the CD player, and this case was pricking at the detective like some overly insistent memory that refused to coalesce out of the edges of his awareness. The Suspect would have him think that it was all about love, this mystery, but the detective had seen some horrible things perpetrated upon innocents in the name of that elusive emotion. People used to burn their children alive for false gods in the name of love too. Something else was involved. Jealousy, money—*something*.

He knew there was a villain here. There had to be. There always was. Someone who had done something terribly wrong and thought that they could find asylum by hiding in anonymity, hoping that what they did and who their victims were would be lost and forgotten within the shadows of time. Innocent victims didn't deserve to be forgotten. Not for the first time, he once again wished that Laura were here with him now. She'd be sitting in that chair over there—it had always been her favorite one, that's why he'd kept it—and he could say, "Hey, babe, I've got this really weird, convoluted case I'm working. Your input on these guys sure would help."

Laura would reply with something like, "I'm not the detective, dear, you are." Then she'd put down whatever she was reading or doing at that time and come over with that look of interest that she always had when it came to such things. Hell, she'd probably have been a better detective than he had she chosen this type of work. *I can imagine what she'd say about the money I've made as a private detective. Probably wouldn't like me hiring myself out like that, but the pay would tell her that I finally knew my worth. She always said I needed to.* "Oh lord. Laura, I miss you so much," he found himself saying to the empty place in his heart that would always be hers. "I wish I could believe you were in some happy heaven tonight, baby. You and the girls. But people don't go to heaven when they die. They don't go to hell either. They just go. Wish you girls were here. Love you. Love you all."

He drained the last of the bottle into his glass and, raising it as if calling for a toast to futility, spoke to the otherwise empty room. "Here's to the last of the best." *Guess I've had too much. I'm talking to the walls. Kind of early in the evening for this, barely even 9:00 p.m. and I'm already close to being sloshed. I'm having pointless conversations with memories of the dead now.* He felt tears rolling down his face. Aloud, he spoke to the majestically rolling, but deaf sea waves. "God, I miss my *wife.*" The sea gave no answers as Miles played on. The detective returned to his chair, watched the thunderstorm approaching like the end of some ominous prophecy, and fell asleep, hoping that sweet oblivion would claim him, if only for tonight.

He awoke with a start. *Someone else* was in his house—he knew it. Even in his state of near inebriation, he could *feel* it. There was an intruder. Snatching the Sig Sauer that he kept within reach right under his favorite chair, the detective immediately adopted that "stop or I'll shoot" stance that law enforcement officers everywhere find useful. Moving quietly, he went to each room, clearing. Nobody. Empty house. He knew what he'd felt, though. In more than one situation, that feeling had saved his life or someone else's, so he trusted it. There *had* been an intruder, he knew. Who, what, and why, he'd find out. Taking a flashlight and the Sig, he did as close an inspection as he could, under the circumstances, looking over every possible entry and exit point inside and outside of the bungalow. Nothing. No sign of any other person than himself having been here. *Maybe I should have Arlander install a system for me.* That seemed like a comical or sarcastic thought.

Wondering why, he suddenly realized something: another theory of the crime was beginning to shape up inside his head, and Mr. George Arlander was stepping out into the limelight as a major player in the show. Co-conspirator? Financial backer? The man had something to do with this (whatever this was), and the detective now had a potential second suspect. How did Dana fit into the picture? The patient had mentioned something about Dana witnessing some sort of event that happened at the Arlanders' place. Which place? Did these guys kill Angeline Arlander? He strongly felt that her untimely demise was an orchestrated event, but was there any way to prove it? Not sure. Still, she too would be remembered when he brought the hammer down. Thus thinking, the detective decided to hit the shower for the night. Staying awake until almost 12:00 a.m., drinking up more bourbon wouldn't help him come up with any possible answers or new avenues of probability.

What about the feeling that someone has been in my house? Probably nothing to worry about. Maybe it was a false alarm set off by the total creepiness of this case. After all, it might have been an effect of the drinking. Still, no one was going to invade his home ever again. *Maybe I did have a little too much bourbon tonight,* he thought, casting an accusatory glance at the liquor cabinet as he passed by it. *This investigation is working my nerves. There's something huge under the surface of this thing. I know it, I feel it. Just have to expose it.*

He was in the shower when a sudden realization hit his mind with the chill of a winter blast. *Go look again at the liquor cabinet!* Almost losing the towel he'd hastily wrapped in, the detective raced to the living room, stopping to stare incredulously at what he saw. There was a full bottle of the very bourbon he had just finished not too long before! Yes, that was it. He read the label: *Pappy Van Winkle.* Yes, again, that *was* it. But there was only one bottle here, and he'd finished and tossed that one. A quick look into his garbage can prove that the other empty bottle was still there. *So someone with serious skills came into my house while I was asleep, just to drop off a bottle of the world's finest bourbon, and I never even knew they were doing it? Yeah right. Probably had it in there all along. Ye gods! I've been drinking too much tonight.*

Still uncomfortable, he pulled on a pair of latex gloves and, using a magnifying glass, went over every inch of the bottle as best as he could. Nothing. No indication of tampering, tomfoolery, or anything else. It seemed to be just what it was. A bottle of the world's finest bourbon, left in his liquor cabinet, presumably as a gift. He'd take it to the county crime lab tomorrow; Billy would be on duty. He was the top lab rat there, and he was another one of the detective's many reliable friends in the department. Tonight, though, he'd get his rest. If the "intruder" wanted to hurt him, he definitely had the skills to have already done so. If there were any intruder at all, that is.

The Sig would be with him when he went to bed tonight, though, so he wasn't too incredibly uneasy.

A set of eyes regarded the detective from their place of concealment. There was no way that the man could be seen or located in this space where he was. He approved of this detective. Actually, he thought very well of the guy. *He deserves something better than what he got. I'll see what I can do to help him when this is over. Detective, you need not worry. Just wanted to see if I could get away with setting something down out there. Had to test you. Sleep well. You've got a big load to work out; this whole thing is really taking a lot out of you. It'll take more as we go, and you'll need every ounce of that mental acuity you're so famous for.* The man turned away and disappeared into the background of his observation post.

VISITORS INVITED AND
VISITORS UNEXPECTED

The detective wasn't able to see the patient throughout the next week. For some reason, his chief suspect, who at one time seemed so eager to blather on and on about the fantasy life that led him to the loony bin, no longer wished to see him. He'd tried to use every lead and favor that anyone owed him in order to force his way into the place, but nothing worked out. That alone was enough to ensure his continued interest and involvement. His connections were many and powerful. For any of them to be stonewalled so effectively pointed to the possibility that someone in a very high governmental position was exerting a lot of muscle to keep the patient isolated all of a sudden. Maybe the man had talked too much. With nothing else to do, he split the next week between walking in the surf and hanging around at his favorite beachside restaurant while waiting to hear from Billy. He'd decided to get his friend's opinion on this case before going any further.

Jazz Tuesday at the Bistro and a renowned saxophonist was the featured entertainment. That was where the young forensics lab tech found him. There was nothing wrong with the bourbon, Billy assured him. No prints on the bottle other than the detective's, which may have been normal, except for one thing. "Did you wipe the surface of the bottle before you touched or brought it to me?"

"No, I didn't," he answered.

Billy's brow furrowed in confusion. "Well, that's weird. I mean, a normal bottle of anything should have *some* sort of prints on it. Especially a brand new one like that. Somebody packaged it, somebody bought it, somebody bagged it, and who knows how many people may have picked it up to look at it before it was sold?"

"So there should have been something there, right?" his mentor asked.

"Right," Billy replied.

"Well, someone left it as a gift for me. Would've been no big deal, but it seemed that they left it at my place while I was away. Would've been nice to know who it was," the detective said. *No need to tell him that some unknown person slipped it into my house while I was on a binge. The kid will be worried to death about me.*

"Well, it's definitely good bourbon, I'll tell ya that," Billy replied.

"Billy! Did you take a nip of my bourbon?" the detective asked chidingly.

Billy blushed. "Well, you did ask me to test it thoroughly, remember?"

"It's okay, kid. By the way, how's Meredith doing?" he continued. "I heard about that Willie Potts thing."

Billy dropped his eyes for a moment. "Yeah, that was pretty bad. But she did what she had to do, you know."

Willie Potts had been, by any officer's definition, a real dirtbag. The man had built a crack cocaine ring with forced labor dredged out of the several low-rent properties that he owned in the poorest part of the city. When single mothers fell behind in the rent, he would hold their children under threat, forcing Mom into work at one of his "factories" until the "debt" was paid. After the first batch was produced, the children would (supposedly) no longer be in any danger, but the woman would then be blackmailed into staying where she was, working for Willie Potts's crack cocaine ring. What made the man so detestable was his façade as a prominent preacher in the low-income community. He had his own church as well as the trust of many a family in that area, but at the same time, he used their sons as gunsels for his muscle and personal protection while his product fueled gang warfare within the same neighborhoods.

There was one woman, however, who refused to go along with Mr. Potts's extortion. By coincidence, Meredith Compton, Billy's wife, had been the detective she first talked to when LaTonya "Pinky" Wilson came to the precinct to report a threat on her three-year-old son's life. An undercover investigation was launched, with Meredith working point. By the time it was over, gutsy little Pinky was dead, shot down by no less than the great Mr. Potts himself. He'd also tried to gun Meredith down, but had underestimated her. The Reverend Willie Potts did not survive that encounter.

There was, of course, an uproar produced over the man's death. Most of the people in his community had no idea what kind of person he really had been, acquainted as they were with only with the façade they'd been shown. Some people suggested that he may have been "framed" or "set up." City councilmen with their own agendas pushed for the termination of Officer Compton with such intensity that the department felt that an internal investigation was warranted, if only to put an end to the speculation that was now beginning to stir up such unrest.

Meredith Compton was put on paid leave until the matter could be resolved. Eventually, though, Pinky's mother, Ruth, got several of Willie Potts's victims to come forward with their stories, and a clear picture of the monster behind the man's civilized veneer was exposed. Ruth Wilson wasn't satisfied with that, though, so together with some of the former victims, she bought Meredith a plaque with their lost children's names engraved on it. Also engraved on it was their expression of appreciation for Detective Compton's actions in their behalf.

The situation thus resolved, Meredith was pronounced innocent of any misbehavior and reinstated. She agreed, but before returning to duty, she and her husband decided to take advantage of their accumulated vacation time. It was Billy's idea. He saw what a toll Pinky's death and the ensuing turmoil had taken on his wife and, convinced that she needed this break, pushed until she'd agreed. The couple had an open invitation to stay at the detective's place whenever they needed it, and that was what they were going to do. Red-haired affable Billy always reminded his mentor of a cheerful college freshman. He liked the kid. The guy could keep his mouth shut when he had to and could also remember details and facts from any one of the infinite number of cold cases that he loved to delve into. "You can never assume that the information you have is all the information there is," the young man always repeated that phrase. Something else the detective had taught him along the way.

He himself had introduced Billy to the girl that later became his wife, another one of his promising students, Meredith Yates. She was a real hotshot of a detective herself, and after working with Meredith, the detective just knew that this woman and Billy were made for each other. It was a strange way to look at things, but in their mentor's mind were happy visions of how many crooks this dynamic duo could put away together.

When they finally did meet, at a cookout on the detective's backyard deck, Meredith didn't seem to be too impressed with Billy, though, and why should she have been? She was a hot blond bombshell of a woman, a visibly rising star in the law enforcement community, while he was the typical red-haired computer lab nerd: underweight, shy, clumsy, and seemingly too frightened to speak to any woman on any subject other than forensics and cold cases. Although his star in the department was rising, it wasn't rising as visibly as hers. The two people just didn't seem attracted to each other at first (actually, Meredith didn't seem attracted to Billy; he and every other guy at the gathering was attracted to *her*).

Maneuvering matters so that the three of them were sitting together at the same table, the detective casually brought up a subject that they both would be interested in: a current case that Detective Yates was working on and William "Billy" Compton was doing lab work for. The two young people warmed to the subject immediately and were still deep in conversation when their mentor quietly took his leave. Meredith was a classic beauty of a woman, but she was by no means shallow, arrogant, or self-centered. She was also sharp enough to know a good man when she met one, and yeah, Billy was a good student as well as a good man. Always had been. They did make a great couple. Still. That was eight years ago. He still called them his Dynamic Duo.

Later on that night, the three of them once again sat together on the detective's front porch, tossing back shots of bourbon and discussing his current case. "The Dynamic Duo" were going to start their vacation the next day, and tonight, they had time to spend with "the Old Man" as they affectionately referred to him. ("I'm not that much older than you two," he would always say. They would always laugh.) All three felt that the patient had a lot to hide, but it was George and Wesley who got their attention. Particularly George Arlander. It seemed that there was some past case with Arlander's name included, in which another woman had died under strange circumstances—Mr. Arlander's first wife, the kids thought. A big insurance settlement had been involved, and though foul play was considered, nothing of that nature had ever been proven. And yes, a younger man was mentioned as George's possible accomplice then too, though it was not Wesley. Something went awry in the investigation, and George was never charged with anything. He was cleared of suspicion, in fact. Billy, for his part, was intrigued when Arlander's name came up, linked to another dead wife. Meredith was the only thing that would get him more interested and excited than an old unsolved case. She, for her part, was just as interested in seeing justice done for the victim as the detective himself was, and the thought of some villain going free made her blood boil. Many a criminal who had gotten off on technicalities or with the help of clever defense lawyers had only Billy's mellowing effect on Meredith to thank for their continued existence in the land of the living. *Yes, they are a perfect match*, the detective was thinking. *If necessary, they'll get on the George Arlander situation, I'll continue with the other one.*

Bill and Meredith wound up staying over at the detective's house, just as they always did whenever they'd had a drink-a-thon the previous night. No problem. The bungalow originally had four bedrooms. One was his, one had been changed into his office, and the other two doubled as guest rooms or temporary storage areas, depending on what was going on at the time. When morning arrived, Meredith, as usual, would be up before anyone else because she had to have her coffee and quiet time to think about her cases. The detective would wake up next, start breakfast, and chat with her as he cooked. Billy was always the last one up, arising just in time to make sure that he didn't miss the meal. This morning, though, something broke the normal pattern.

Their host awoke to the sound of Meredith banging on his bedroom door. There was a huge guy out on the front porch "requesting an audience" with him—that's how the visitor put it anyway. It was important and had something to do with the suspect in the case. Meredith had awakened Billy first, and they both concluded that the caller was unarmed and harmless. The man was in the living room. All this she told the detective through the door as he was throwing on a pair of jeans and a shirt. He wasn't really concerned about his safety, for without a doubt, Meredith and Billy would not have let a dangerous person into the house; and if they had, that person was in way more trouble than he even realized, with those two on the premises. Besides, he did, at times, use his living room as a reception area.

Still, he was surprised when he saw who the visitor was. There was Billy, leaning casually against the front door, doing a pretty good job of looking harmless and unarmed himself. *Never knew a lab rat who could hide and handle a firearm as well as that kid. Meredith's taught him a few things. Toughened him up*, he thought.

"Okay, here he is, mister," Meredith was saying in her most intimidating-to-suspects voice. "Now let's hear what was so important that you had to tell him face-to-face." There, sitting on the couch, totally unintimidated, was the hulking form of Lucius, the guard from the facility for the criminally insane. A broad, warm smile on his face, he stood and extended his hand. Billy stood alert, and Meredith moved to interpose herself between Lucius and her mentor.

"Hold on, guys," the detective told them. "It's okay. He's Lucius, one of the guards at Sand Ridge. In a way, he's one of us." The Dynamic Duo relaxed visibly. "So what's up, Lucius? Is our guy still under wraps?"

"Yes, sir!" Lucius replied with a military crispness, looking torn between standing at attention or shaking his host's hand.

"Relax, man," the detective told him. "What brings you here? Is there something you need to tell me?"

"He told me to tell you that he's leaving, sir," Lucius replied with military crispness. "He wants to be gone before the end of the week and said that it's time to tell you everything. You're the only one he'll talk to."

"And what if I say no?" the detective asked suspiciously.

"He told me to tell you to check out the box that is in your office at the back of the house, sir. Says that if you look in it, you will without a doubt want to see him."

The detective glanced at Meredith. She gave a slight nod and turned to go verify. Having spent some time training with the bomb squad, she was the most likely person to do so. After a few moments, she returned to the living room with a plain white packing box. It had been checked for tripwires, he knew. There must not have been any. Still, she looked as if something was wrong. "What's wrong, Meredith?"

Looking at Lucius, Meredith answered, "This wasn't here when we sacked out last night. I checked that room beforehand. Just had a gut feeling."

"You sure? We *were* drinking."

"I didn't drink that much. I'm telling you, it wasn't here."

Looking suspiciously at Lucius, he asked, "Did you have anything to do with this?"

"No, *sir*!" Lucius replied, and this time, he did stand to attention.

"How did it get here, then?" the detective demanded. He was starting to feel that old anger again as he went on. "Did that *psycho* break into my house while we were out last night?"

"I don't know how he did it, but I can without a doubt assure you that he did not break into your home, sir. He has ways of doing things that no one can explain."

"Where were you last night, Lucius?" he asked suspiciously.

"My wife and I were on the road, sir, returning from Miami. We spent the weekend there for our anniversary. It was around oh one hundred when we finally pulled in, and he had left me a message. I went to see him as soon as I could, *sir*. He expected you to ask that question, so he insisted that I do a lot of selfies with my wife while we were there. I don't usually allow strangers to see my pictures, sir, but I will produce them if you'd like."

The detective sighed. "I guess he thought of everything, huh? Forget about it."

"Yes, *sir!*" the big man replied, looking for all the world as if a salute was imminent.

"Lucius, will you please stop with the 'sir'? Neither of us are in the military, okay?" Lucius visibly relaxed again, and his smile returned. "Why do you run these errands for him, anyway? Does he have something on you?" the detective asked.

"No . . .," Lucius replied, struggling not to say "sir" again. For just a moment, his eyes took on the slightly out-of-focus look of a man returning to some point of memories past. "He gave me back my life, . . . sir."

Detective didn't want to alienate a potential witness, so he asked in a calming (and friendly, he hoped) voice, "Do you have any idea how this box got here then, Lucius?"

The big man answered, "He told me to tell you that the answers are in it. That he ran out of time, so he'd decided to come in and leave it for you just before I got here this morning. He also told me to tell you that he went to make sure that Dana Lacy was out of danger. Said to let you know that the man she's living with is more than capable of protecting her."

MORE MYSTERIES

The trio stood stunned, staring at Lucius, who apparently had less answers than they did. Every possible scenario only created more questions. Dana Lacy, missing or not? Alive or dead? Was the man locked up in the mental facility because he belonged there, or was there something else going on? What kind of agent could infiltrate a house with the likes of these three people in it? Drinking or not, that was still not likely to happen without *someone* noticing *something*. The detective asked, "If he was already here this morning, why didn't he stay to talk?"

Lucius bowed his head as a slight smile crossed his face. "Because he would likely have been shot on sight, sir. He said that since you think he's done something to Ms. Lacy, that would make him a suspect, and if you had caught him in your house when you didn't know he was here, you'd have assumed the worst. Anybody would."

Meredith interrupted with a question then. "Where is he now?"

"He's back in the facility, ma'am. Says it's probably the safest place for him at the moment."

Meredith sneered. "So this guy left Sand Ridge, came here to put this box in a back room within a house filled with armed investigators, then just went back to the loony bin? And all without being heard or caught, no less. Now why doesn't that make a whole lotta sense to me?"

Lucius looked at her like a teacher who was trying to explain a problem to a particularly annoying student. "Ma'am, I don't always know how or even why he does the things that he does. We've trusted each other with a lot over the years, and he's never let me down or caused any harm. He told me it would be here by the time I got here and where he would place it. If he did want to hurt any of you, believe me, he could. But he didn't.

Apparently, he's asking for your help in the only way he can," Lucius continued.

Meredith was ready to begin another round of interrogation when the detective said, "Well, I guess we ought to look in the little box. By the way, Lucius, I think you need to stay in town. There may be people who want to talk to you. Is that a problem?"

"Not at all, sir," Lucius replied. "I'll be at home later."

"I guess telling you to stay away from him won't work?" Lucius smiled again as he turned and headed for the door. Stopping for a moment, he turned to the detective and said, as if to put an end to all suspicion, "He's a good man, sir. I trust him."

After Lucius had taken his leave, Bill, Meredith, and their mentor took the box to the kitchen table. Inside were two or three eight-by-eleven-inch envelopes. Meredith insisted on being the person who opened them. She took the first one out and, after checking it, handed it to the detective. The foremost thing in it was a picture of Angeline and the patient. She was sitting, he was standing behind her, his arms around her shoulders, and her left hand was on his left wrist, making their wedding rings obvious. *Precious without being gaudy* . . . Written across the front in what was obviously a woman's handwriting were the words "Jazz festival '02! First anniversary, New Orleans—loved it!"

He looks different in that picture, the detective thought. *Something's not the same.* "Meredith, something about this picture . . ."

She looked at it and called Billy over. When he saw it, Bill's eyes lit up. "Wow! This quality of digital reproduction isn't even available yet! How was he able to get his hands on a copier that could do *this?* I read about it, and it may be available soon, but right now, you'd have to—"

"Okay, billy!" both detectives said in unison.

"We get the point, lab rat," Meredith continued, smiling at her husband's enthusiasm.

The second item in the envelope was a letter. The handwriting was more masculine than that on the picture. *Probably his writing*, the detective thought. He had begun reading it when Billy politely cleared his throat. The detective got the point. He began reading aloud.

My dear Angeline

As you can see, it was all real. I wish that you and I were happily together, as they are. I am, however, also hoping that George will listen to me about the upcoming hurricanes. I know that you thought something was wrong with me the last time the three of us got together - the tears in your eyes told me how you felt. The proof in this photo will assure you that I am not insane, as he suggested. I didn't even know that other "me" had packed it until after I got back to this world.

I did ask him for proof that you would believe, and I thought he'd denied me that, but your life is on the line, and in any world, any reality, he could not have stopped himself from caring about and loving you. I will not try to see you anymore, as a friend or anything else. You deserve the happy life you have with George, and I will not cause you problems.

As much as I may wish it were so, the simple fact is that we are not married in this reality, and so I must show my love for you by leaving you alone. Still, I want you to know something;

When I was fifteen, I drew the face of a woman. A face I fell in love with. You wear that face. When I was eighteen, I wrote a poem for that woman, though I didn't know who she could possibly be. I sent that poem to a popular magazine anonymously, because I wanted the whole world to see it.

I thought that if they published it, maybe it would bring you into my life. They did, but it never seemed to have found its way to the person it was meant for. Now I have sent it to you. Wherever you go, whatever you do, please, always know that I have loved you even before I met you.

"Where's this poem?" Meredith asked. The detective just looked at her. "Hey, I'm a girl who likes a little romance in my psychopaths every now and then," she said in mock defense.

He smiled. *Marjorie probably would've been a lot like her one day.* "I guess it's in the other envelope, Meredith. Hey, take a look at this. Do you see how there are spots where the ink is smudged? What do you think caused that?"

"Tears," Billy replied. "She was crying when she read it. Or maybe he was crying when he wrote it. Waitaminit, no, the smudges would look different if the reader were crying."

"How do you know?" the detective asked. "You've seen this in your lab before?"

"Well, uh, . . . actually, I may have cried over a letter once. Or twice." Meredith and the detective both looked surprised. Billy shrugged. "Guess you gotta be there to know it. So I've gotten a few Dear Johns. Who hasn't?" The detective busied himself with opening the other envelope while Meredith stared at Billy, who looked like a man about to step on a live bomb. "Um, yes, dear?" he queried.

"I was just wondering what idiot of a woman would write you a Dear John?" she replied.

The detective rolled his eyes. Billy grinned. "Okay," the detective said, "let's look at the rest of this stuff before all this sweetness makes me diabetic. Here's the poem."

When I met you, I fell
Like a boulder into the sea
I loved you before I saw you
I was yours before we met
it was never a matter of thought
never a question of want;
just a fact of what life is,
a simple truth of what must be;
You would come, and I would fall
like a boulder into the sea
So here is the statement of what my life is
a simple truth throughout all my years
loving you has been for me,
the substance of my destiny
and in every way of my walk
through the emotions of my life
you are now, and always have been
as perennial as the sun,
the love of my life from those days
when I was very young.
I hadn't seen you, but I loved you
had never touched you, but I felt you
and now
you have come into my heart

and you flow through my body
with the blood of my life . . .
in the light of my eyes
and the thoughts of my mind
there's a simple truth I find
that all the treasures of men and time
will never equal you
When I met you, I fell
Like a boulder into the sea
I loved you before I saw you
I was yours before we met
it was never a matter of thought
never a question of want;
but just a fact of what life is,
a simple truth of what must be;
You would come, and I would fall
like a boulder into the sea
You are, and always will be
The finer part of me
That woman who I adored
Long before
I knew what girls were for
All for love, none for war
Listen, my dear
you have come into my heart
and you flow through my body
with the blood of my life
all the treasures of men and time
will never equal you
I don't know what I would not give
just to be with you, but
I do know that I could not live
could not abide
just being alive without you . . .

The detective's eyes widened. *Now I know where I read that, I guess.*
Meredith was staring intently when he looked up. "What's wrong?"

"This . . . this poem. It meant a lot to me at one time. I read it in some magazine I was looking at, then took it to Laura. I told her that it . . . it . . . Excuse me a moment." He got up and walked to the front porch. *Laura! I miss you so . . . I thought this pain was healed or at least temporarily stopped. This bastard is playing me. Maybe not. How could he know? But then, how did he get this crap into our house in the first place?* He felt Meredith walk up. She stood next to him for a while before he spoke: "See those clouds? They've been there for a couple of days now, just staying in one place, like some sort of lurker. It's one hell of a thunderstorm brewing. I thought it would be here by Tuesday, but here it is Wednesday, and that storm is still out there. Like it's waiting for something. The wind's died down too."

"Do you think he's playing you?" she asked.

"I thought of that, Merry," he answered, unaware of the tears in his eyes and voice. "But how could he possibly know what those words meant to Laura and me?" She took a deep breath then added, "I don't like this guy, Roan. How could he get a box into this house without any of us knowing he was here? How could he get into your head if that's what he's done? This is too weird. Way too weird. He must have some outside help. Maybe we should look a little deeper into this 'Lucius' character."

The detective stared at the black thunderhead that still hadn't made it ashore yet. Billy appeared, somehow managing to carry three glasses of bourbon. He started handing them out. Accepting the offering, the detective began. "Know what's really bothering me, kids? I found a guy that I like for the disappearance of one woman. He directed me to another guy who may have been involved in the death of a different woman, maybe the first man's lover and the second man's wife, and I can't put the two together, even though I know there's a connection. It's like having the right word on the tip of your tongue and being unable to remember what that word is.

"The guy who's locked up in the nuthouse wants me to believe that he's some kind of interdimensional superhero fighting for love and justice, yet all the signs say he's a psychodelusional crackpot, but I don't think he's insane at all, and it seems, more and more, that he may be the only player in the game who's trying to do the right thing. The guy who may have killed his own wife wants me to think that Dimension Boy did it, but Dimension Boy's the one who sent me to Mr. Probable Wife Killer. If I believe anything, it's that at least one woman has died when she should have lived, and maybe the other one is no better off."

Meredith and Billy exchanged a look. Billy, still holding on to his drink, put his long arms around both the detective and her, saying, "Come on, guys. We're on vacation. Take a break."

"You and Meredith are on vacation, Billy. I'm working a case that is becoming more and more complicated."

"You need help, Roan," Billy said. "Merry and I live for this sort of thing. Yes, we are on leave, but this is the most interesting affair we've come across in a long time. We're in it with you, old man. That's that. Let's take a break."

He's right. I might as well let them in on the rest of this story. "Okay, guys. You're in. I have some recordings I want you to hear." As they went into the house, the wind picked up outside, and the thunderstorm resumed its slow march toward the shore.

DEPTH OF THE CONUNDRUM

It was late afternoon and a few pizzas later by the time they'd listened to the last of the detective's recordings and began to work on the puzzles facing them. A white expo board that was in the living room had been adorned with pictures of all known parties involved. The patient, George and Angeline Arlander, Dana Lacy, and Wesley's likenesses were all present. Nobody asked Roan where these had been acquired. He wouldn't have told them, anyway. Besides, his guests seemed too astonished after hearing the patient's narrative to concern themselves with Roan's sources. A long silence set in while each person took time to allow themselves time to consider the known facts.

Finally, Billy spoke into the silence. "This guy's really gone if he thinks anybody's buying this load of crap."

"Somebody is," Meredith said. "That's probably why he's neither doing life in some hellhole nor sitting on death row right now because somebody with a lotta clout bought into this. The world would be so much better off without psychologists or lawyers."

"He definitely has someone looking out for him," the detective told them.

"What, like an angel or something?" Billy asked.

"No, Bill. I mean like a person or persons who provide him information and continue to look after his interests. Somebody gave him intel about me. He brought it up in one of the recordings you heard, remember? Okay, you two, let's brainstorm here. What do you think, is he really insane or just devilishly clever?"

"He's obviously trying to go somewhere with this long and convoluted tale he's spinning," Meredith answered. Continuing, she said, "All along, he's been trying to get your attention turned onto the Arlanders while hoping that this rambling about 'other worlds' will convince you that he's just a helpless loonie."

"So are you saying that this fella's trying to distract me, Merry?"

"Well yes, I guess so, Roan."

"Okay, say he is trying to outfox the wolf. Why?" Roan asked.

Meredith sort of frowned. "Let me think about that a minute," she replied.

"Did you notice how he refers to Angeline as if she's still alive?" Billy asked then continued. "Is it possible that he doesn't know she's dead?"

The detective nodded sagely. "That's definitely possible, but then why the runaround? Why try to point me toward the Arlanders if she's still alive?"

"Maybe he was hoping that you would heroically swoop in and prevent her demise since he couldn't get there himself," Billy replied hopefully. Meredith, however, just snorted derisively.

"Okay, okay," Billy conceded, "probably not. He may have wanted to seem innocent in the case of Angeline Arlander, but at the same time wanted George's name on her dead body."

"So do you both think that George and he worked together in killing Mrs. Arlander?"

"Yes," said Meredith at the same time that Billy said no.

"Oh, . . . so there's a difference of opinion among the young Turks. Okay, so let's set Angeline Arlander's case on a back burner for a minute while we look at Dana Lacy's disappearance.

"Okay, kids, here's what we've got on that case," Roan began, standing in front of the expo board that had the pictures of his suspect, Dana, Angeline and George Arlander, as well as Wesley Whatever-His-Last-Name-Was.

"This man and Ms. Lacy lived together for almost two years. They shared a home. They shared a bank account. They were both listed as co-owners of their house. It also looks like either this mysterious colonel or Dana Lacy's father had cosigned for the original loan since it was endorsed by a representative of the State Department, a fact that I could only have verified through the use of one of my sources who works in a certain federal crime-fighting agency. Then there was a second mortgage debt in both of their names, said mortgage having been taken out as a means to take care of accrued credit card debts, and even though that mortgage was slowly being paid off, it still kept them both stuck in the same house as well as the stale relationship despite the fact that the thrill was already gone. All of a sudden, in steps Angeline Arlander, who seems to be the woman of his dreams, only she's married to a guy who, as it turns out, likes an occasional boy toy on the side—"

"Boy toy sounds like something you ought to have to go to McDonald's for," Meredith interjected.

The detective stopped, confused for a moment "'Something you have to go to MacDonald's for'? What are you . . ."

Billy started laughing. Meredith stifled a chuckle. The detective shook his head. "Okay, children, let's get back to the lesson. Mr. George Arlander, as it turns out, is also loaded and on his way to greater wealth. His company is doing fine, and sometimes he even hires our guy to work with him. Our suspect occasionally parties together with the Arlanders, and he definitely has been to their home. Ms. Lacy apparently is no part of the merry crew, though. We only have our suspect's word for what went on between Dana and himself so I'm not inclined to believe much of it, but it seems that she had her own life while he had his. They were going to go their separate ways, he said, but according to George Arlander, this guy was getting pretty cozy with Mrs. Arlander, if we're to take the errant husband's word for it."

"Doesn't seem like that would have been much of a problem to Arlander," Billy observed. "Especially if he was busy doing his thing with this Wesley person." Meredith agreed.

"It *would* seem that way," the detective said. "But George Arlander is a very possessive man. I know this because we've all had to deal with his type. How many murders were committed by men who couldn't or wouldn't let go?"

"He's right, Meredith," Billy said. "Remember the Lawton case? That guy had no reason to do what he did."

"No reason except jealousy and perverted possessiveness," his wife added.

"Okay, now that we all agree, may I finish my lecture?" the detective asked.

"By all means, sir, please continue," Meredith said with a wave of the hand.

"Moving forward," the detective picked up the narrative. "The sequence of events seems to have gone this way: Angeline Arlander died by falling off of a balcony at a second home the Arlanders owned in some remote location in Mexico. Her husband said it was a result of overdrinking, had the body cremated, likely has a death certificate on file somewhere, and may even have gotten some insurance settlement out of it that has yet to be determined. Before all this happened, though, Mr. Loonie suddenly paid off all the debt that kept him stuck with Dana Lacy and had given her sole ownership of their house. But after Angeline Arlander died, Dana disappeared under circumstances suspicious enough to rouse the curiosity of the department. That would be you guys, in case you didn't notice.

"After he was questioned, the DA wanted to charge him, but couldn't for lack of evidence. They found her blood in the house, as well as signs of a struggle that looked like it originated in the kitchen and ended in the living room, but no other sign of my suspect having been there after he moved out. The rest of the evidence suggested that the door was kicked off of its hinges from the inside, but there wasn't a footprint or even a shoe indentation on it. When Detective Wilkes interrogated the suspect, he told him this tall tale about alternate realities and secret military plots. He also insists that Dana Lacy is alive and well, and the way the story is going, it looks as if he's going to say that she's found her own little alternate reality and is living happily ever after there. Psychological eval indicated that the guy was delusional, but the prosecutor was ready to charge him anyway. That's when things got screwy.

"Some shadowy military person or persons got with Paulson and convinced him that taking this fellow to trial may endanger Dana Lacy's father, as the man is involved in some sort of top secret classified military work, and our nutcase may have had a small part in past ops under Captain Robin Lacy's command."

"That doesn't sound like Paulson, pulling off of a case because of some government geek's shadowy threat," Billy said.

"I know the man," Meredith agreed. "His son and I dated a little back in high school. He's not a candy-ass when it comes to letting a crook go, so something pretty serious must have been involved. Did this mental patient have a military record?"

Roan picked up a sheet of paper, looked it over, ad replied, "He denies it, but yes, he did. He spent a little time in the Marine Corps. Even made it through boot camp, but it seems that he turned out to be a cross between Beetle Bailey and Gomer Pyle—willing, but unable. Some rare lung disease that only strikes one out of every five hundred thousand persons rendered him unfit for duty a little while after he got out of basic training. He got a medical discharge and disappeared out of the military world. He later resurfaced as a guy who can barely eke out a living as a waiter, and it seems that he's pretty proud of it."

Billy and Meredith both laughed. "What a loser!" Billy finally said. The detective glared. The laughter stopped.

"I was a waiter for a little while, guys, when I was in college. It's not an easy job."

Meredith stifled another chortle. "Sorry, boss. Go ahead."

"Thank you, Ms. Merry. Well, anyway, our loser, he—" Billy started snickering and stopped. "He was locked up in Sand Ridge until the head shrinkers decide that he's fit for trial. That was Paulson's decision, locking him up there. It keeps this guy within our reach. Now it gets weirder. Someone *else* provided Paulson with confidential information that gave him the impression that this whole 'don't prosecute because you may endanger a few good men' story may have been a fabrication invented by some friend of the suspect who's got connections in the armed forces. I was called in because the DA's office wasn't sure if it wanted to proceed in an official manner. That's where we stand right now, guys. Give me some feedback, folks. You don't agree as to whether our boy and Arlander worked together against Angeline. What do you think about Dana Lacy? Dead or alive? Meredith?"

"I think she's dead and buried in some shallow grave," Meredith bluntly replied.

"Okay. Billy, what's your thinking? Dana Lacy, dead or alive?" Roan asked.

"I think she's dead and buried in some shallow grave," Billy answered. Roan nodded. "Ah yes. The sweet sound of agreement. So now, everyone who thinks that these two cases are connected raise your hand." Both of his companions did so. "All right then, let's go with theories. Billy, you don't think the hapless loonie and the cheating husband are in it together. So what do you think happened?"

"Which case?" Billy asked.

"In general. Let's just hear what you've got," his mentor said.

"The loonie had some knowledge of Mrs. Arlander's death. Either before or after. He somehow figured that George was going to do it or had already done it. He tried to point you in that direction, hoping that it would get more of your attention than he did with his own misdeed. He was having an affair with Mrs. Arlander, and the possessive hubby found out about it. She might have given the Sand Ridge guy the money he needed to bail himself out of the relationship with the other girl, and her husband found out. Maybe she knew that George had murder in his eye and called the other fellow. Maybe not." Roan nodded, so Billy proceeded with his hypothesis.

"George killed his wife, either for the insurance or because she was going to divorce him. I would think it more likely that a potential loss of assets by divorce was involved. The guy really didn't need insurance capital that badly. You said that his company was pretty solidly making money, right? Yes? Okay, no problem there. But a divorce could have cost him his business, as well as stuck him in a position where he'd have to watch his ex-wife live happily ever after with half of everything he had and another man. What was that, Merry? Yes, I know that there weren't any divorce proceedings started, but you don't get to be a CEO of a successful up-and-coming security company without having a little insight. This George guy may be nasty, but I don't think he's dumb. Besides, he *is* the type who wants to keep it all and collect everything else at the same time."

"So you're suggesting that Loonie Boy acted in the best interests of Angeline Arlander?" Roan asked.

Billy's face reddened. "Well, he *was* in love with her."

His wife rolled her eyes. "My man thinks that all guys are as romantic as he is. Unfortunately, I know better."

The detective nodded. "Well, what about Dana Lacy, Billy? What do you think happened there?"

"I believe the mental patient killed her. She somehow found out about what was going on between Angeline and him. Mrs. Arlander gave him the money he needed to pay off the debt that kept him stuck to Dana, thinking that after he dumped the girl and she divorced George, they would move in together. Probably in the house way down South. Didn't he tell you that something happened at the Arlanders' that Dana saw? Yes? Well, I think she followed him. I mean, in the recording, didn't he also claim that she followed him to never-never land one time? That was how she caught them together. She followed him to his girlfriend's place, seeing them there while hubby was at work or off with his pretty boy, whatever. Later on, Dana confronted him, raised holy hell, maybe threatened to go to Mr. Arlander or her own daddy, and the guy saw all his hopes of being with Angeline disappearing, so he killed her then hid the body, after which he convinced himself that something else happened. That's why he seemed so truthfully whacked out when the psychological evaluation came around."

The detective looked out of his window, considering Billy's hypothesis. *Three people, sitting in a living room, theorizing about things that will have a deep impact on someone else's existence. These bad guys have no idea what's about to happen to them if they're guilty. We're gonna wreck some lives here, I know, but the perpetrators do worse. They don't stop at wrecking lives, they take lives. That storm is getting closer. It looks like it's gonna be a really big one.* "Meredith, what's your thinking on this?"

"I believe that your nutcase was trying to get next to Angeline Arlander, but somewhere along the way, he saw another opportunity and got pretty close with George instead. He was trying to worm his way into an easy life because nobody gets rich by waiting tables no matter how classy the place is, and after a while, your feet start aching and giving out. So he got chummy with dear old hubby, who paid him to take out Mrs. Arlander, promising that the two of them could settle down together, or whatever it is that these people do."

"Do I detect a little bit of prejudice here?" Billy interjected.

"You know how I feel about those things, dear," Meredith replied with her sweetest be-quiet-or-else voice.

"Go ahead, Merry," Roan encouraged, giving Billy his best shut-up-or-else look.

"Well, this guy, he thinks that he and George are going to cohabitate, but dear ole George, he gets tired of your suspect, maybe the guy's too old for him anymore, so when he meets this Wesley, the other guy is dumped. Well, here he is now, with no money and no hope for an easy life with sugar daddy, so he tries to go back to his old girlfriend. But he's paid off the debt they had, put the house in her name because he wanted to get rid of her without a fight, and she's as done with him as he is with her. He started off trying to take the rich guy's wife because he was tired of the dead-end job and the girlfriend who had stuck with him all this time, then he hooked up with the rich guy, killed the ex-lover after getting the money, and now he's right back where he started, but the welcome home mat is gone, meaning that door is closed to him too. So he kills the ex-girlfriend, thinking about how *his* dirty-deeds money was what paid everything off, and he should be entitled to live in the house for free, but this chick is saying 'no way' because she's had enough of his crap and she's not going away, so he makes her disappear."

She was warming up to her theory now, Roan noticed, as Meredith went on. "He doesn't expect it, but the law catches up with him, so he puts on this 'I'm a whack job' act, hoping to escape the consequences. When you go to talk to him, he spins this yarn that's designed to turn your attention onto George Arlander because as you said, he has already been given information about you, so he probably knows a lot about your reputation. You'll can Arlander for his wife's death, and even if this fellow gets another body put on him, he's already safe in the loony bin, so he does no prison time, and gets back at sugar daddy for bumping him out of the picture." Meredith had sat back after finishing her narrative, and Billy gave a low whistle.

"That's brutal, babe." Now she regarded Billy for a moment. Arms folded, she told him, "That's the difference between where we work, darling. I'm out in the streets hunting the scumbags down while you're in the lab, making sure they stay put away. I see more of the dirt than you do. People who do these types of crimes aren't committing forgivable transgressions out of love or romance. They're doing evil things out of selfishness, viciousness, and malice."

The detective stood, turning to look at his students as he told them, "The primary difference between your two theories is motive. That's what determines what kind of perp this guy is. But there's one thing I didn't hear from either of you." Billy and Meredith looked a little confused.

Holding up the poem and the photograph, the detective asked them, "How do you explain these? And didn't Arlander say that there was a prenup?" Billy's mouth opened then shut. Meredith raised an eyebrow. "You know, we never did look at the other envelope in that box either." Roan continued. The other two looked at each other as if they couldn't believe it.

"No, we didn't, Billy," Meredith said, drawing the other envelope out. It contained a compact disc and a handwritten note.

Here are answers to the questions that you must have by now, Doc. Don't even try to find out how I came by it - I made use of a technology that doesn't even exist here. Not yet, anyway. By the time I clearly understood the danger she was in, it was too late. I couldn't get there fast enough to stop this from happening. Please, do for her what I could not do. Give her justice. I have other lives to save. Please.

After you start the cd, put your remote on aux. If you have two, that's even better. You can use the second one on aux. In that mode, you use the channel controls to change the angle, and use the numbers to zoom in or out.

The three looked at one another, obvious questions on their faces. "A DVD? How is that supposed to . . .," Meredith began. Billy put it into the DVD player. "Popcorn, anybody?" His friends just stared. "Okay, okay, let's just see what the interdimensional superhero has for us."

***

It was filmed inside a home. Brief views of the scenery outside of the windows indicated a beachside residence. It also showed them enough for the viewer to realize that the scene was being played out in a second-story master bedroom. The camera was recording from a high angle, as if it had been set in one of the corners where the wall and ceiling met. A woman came into the picture, wrapped in a towel, and headed for the bathroom. In her hand was a glass of what looked like ice water. As she passed her dresser, she stopped, picked up one of the pictures on it, stared at it for a few moments. Her body language said that whatever thought was going through her mind at the sight of the picture she held was painful enough to make her cry. She put the picture back in its place and headed for the shower, leaving the glass on the dresser.

As soon as she had closed the bathroom door, another person with the slight build of a younger man entered the room from the direction of the door. He was wearing a green jogger's suit with a hooded jacket. His hood was pulled up, covering just enough of his face to hide its features. He went to the thermostat, turned it off, then headed slowly toward the dresser, constantly casting fearful glances at the bathroom door. It seemed that he was trying to get to her glass before she finished her shower. Once he was at the bureau, he withdrew a small vial from his jacket pocket and swiftly dumped its contents into her glass. Hurriedly, he stepped to the sliding glass door leading to the balcony, opened it, stepped out, and spoke to someone who was most likely standing below. Leaving that door slightly open, the man then seemed to leave.

About fifteen minutes after she entered the shower, the woman came out, dry and wearing her towel, her hair wrapped in an additional one.

She went to the dresser and had started selecting some things from one of its drawers when she seemed to notice that the room was too warm. She took a long drink out of her glass, went over to the thermostat, turned it on. For a minute, it appeared that she was wondering if it had been on at all. She was also starting to stumble when she walked. Confusion was showing on her face.

Suddenly, she turned her head, looking toward the balcony door. Someone was calling her. Her mouth formed a name: *George.* She tried to make it to the balcony, stumbling as if having had too much to drink. Her lips were saying, *I'm coming.* By the time she reached the balcony, she seemed truly drunk. Her hands clasped its railing as she tried to hold herself up. The railing broke. Still she held on to it, for it was partially connected yet, looking as if one of its screws may have still been holding. She began to back away from the traitorous railing in horror, when the hooded man dashed back onto the scene, brutally pushing her from behind. Her body went over the edge, the towel flying off. The man stood for a moment, looking at what he had wrought. He appeared to be yelling in agitation at someone who was standing below. Then he turned around and walked toward the room's door. As he passed the dresser, he snatched up the glass and hurled it into a corner of the room, close to the bed. Pulling the hood off his head, he walked out.

Roan, Meredith, and Billy just stared at the television screen in astonishment. Roan looked at his companions. "Lady and gentleman, I believe that we have just witnessed the murder of Angeline Arlander." Meredith started to speak, saying, "How did—" when Billy interrupted with, "The show's not over yet. Look at *this* guy." She turned to the television. "Where did *he* come from, Billy?" she asked, for there in the picture was a new person on the scene.

"I don't know, baby, but it looks like he's in a big hurry to do something," Billy answered as he leaned closer to the screen. The man was wearing what appeared to be a USMC flight suit minus the flight gear. The suit was belted with what looked like some sort of futuristic web belt, segmented with pockets of some type. His face was covered entirely by a pullover mask with glowing covered eyeholes. He was looking around in a desperate manner when he saw the balcony. He ran over to where the railing had been, looking down. After that, he turned into the room as if to sprint for the door. Instead, he just took a step and disappeared.

Meredith gasped. Billy's mouth dropped, and Roan's right eyebrow disappeared somewhere under his hairline. "What did we just see? Billy, *what was that*?" Meredith demanded.

"It must have been some kind of camera glitch, Merry," Billy was saying, when Roan asked, "Did you try the aux thingy that he told us about?"

"Roan, this is one of those universal remotes that you buy separately, right?" Billy asked.

"Yeah."

"If you'll get the remote that came with this cool plasma screen TV for me, we'll do that. I think the instant appearance of the big scary guy in the Spiderman mask was a camera glitch. Who or whatever recorded this missed his entrance. Maybe they stopped the recording and restarted when he showed up."

"Then your camera glitch just reappeared out of nowhere again," Meredith cut in.

"Rewind that if you can, kid. I want to see this," Roan added. Billy turned the remote toward the detective's home theater and pressed the reverse function. The picture on the screen was once again showing an empty room. Suddenly, the man in the flight suit was there again. Once more, Billy reversed then proceeded ahead in extra-slow speed. The manner of the man's entrance could be more clearly discerned now. First a leg then the left side of his body entered, followed by the rest.

"Looks like he stepped through a door that no one else could see," Meredith observed. "What's that he's doing now?"

"Looks like some kind of invisible wall thing," Billy said. "Maybe he's practicing his mime routine." Nobody laughed.

The masked man was holding his hands up, palms outward, and his audience could now see that he was wearing gauntlet-styled gloves. Sewn into each glove were evenly placed oval bulges, each being about the size of a thin cigarette lighter. They were located on the upper side of the gauntlets, along the length. There were three on each glove. He rotated in a slow 360-degree turn, carefully keeping his hands in the same position. After completing his slow circle, the man pulled his hood off and stared at the corner where the assailant had thrown the glass. He replaced the mask, stared for another few seconds, and going over to the corner, began rubbing his fingertips on the wall and the carpet.

After that, he picked up one of the fractions of glass, stowing it in a pocket sewn into the leg of his outfit. That done, he looked directly at the camera then turned his gaze to the other four corners of the ceiling and wall junction. Working his way around the room, he held his left hand up again, palms up, as before, aimed at each of those junctions. When he got to the one where the camera angle was filming from, he did the same. The palm of his hand emitted a small swift flash.

"What is he doing?" Meredith asked again. The detective thought for a few moments. "Billy," he said.

"Yes?"

"Don't you and Meredith have those fancy cell phones with the camcorders or cameras or something like that inside?"

"Yeah, Roan, but what . . ." He could see the realization dawning on Billy. It hit Meredith at the same time. "He was recording the crime scene!" she exclaimed. Punching Billy's arm, she repeated, "He was recording the crime scene! And that last thing he did was him taking a picture of the cameras! Who is this guy, some hotshot cop with a prototype investigation suit?" Billy mouthed a silent "Owww."

"Actually, boys and girls, I think that was our mental patient slash murder suspect. Or someone he knows very well," Roan told them. "Remember the box that was left in the back room? We know that he had something to do with our little surprise package getting here, but none of us knew how that happened. We may have just seen the explanation. I think it's time for me to visit our friend in Sand Ridge again."

"I'll go with you," Meredith said.

"No," Roan answered. "I don't know how he would react to your presence. I'm beginning to think that this man is quite lucid, but if he really is a criminally insane serial killer, I don't want you in contact with him."

She walked over to Roan and gave him a hug. "You're so much like my daddy, Roan. That's why I love you. But believe me, you don't have to protect me from this guy. I'm a long way from being that scared little rookie fresh out of the academy."

Roan smiled, a rare thing for him. "I wasn't trying to protect you, dear. I was thinking of protecting *him*." Billy laughed. Roan turned to him and said, "And you, Mr. Lab Whiz, see what you can do with the remotes. We need to get everything we can out of this video thingy or whatever it is. If it is what we think it is, it'll answer a lot of questions. See if you can find some way to put sound in it."

"Got it, boss," Billy replied. "While you're there, don't forget to ask the koo-koo where he found the suit guy, will ya?"

Roan looked worried. "That suit is what really concerns me, Bill. If he or anyone he knows can do what we saw that fellow do, the question remains, where can he *not* go? No one could be safe anywhere if there's some way that a dangerous man can just *appear* in their bedrooms. And people deserve to at least feel safe in their own homes. Another thing is that I don't see that sort of technology being in existence without somebody in *some* official position being aware of it. This is bigger than we thought. It's time to get the truth out of this guy." He went out the front door.

Meredith followed and, standing on the porch, watched him drive off. Something about this was making her feel apprehensive. Like most good detectives, Meredith could tell when something was not quite right. A hunch, a gut feeling, sixth sense. Whatever name anyone chose, such feelings should never be casually dismissed. But sometimes they are. She looked up at the sky, turning grayer as it was with the approach of the storm, shrugged off what she took as her own overprotectiveness, and went inside to help Billy.

After the front door was closed, a white Crown Victoria with dark-tinted windows that had been parked down the street pulled onto the road and headed in the direction that Roan had. Lightning flashed across the sky, and a clap of thunder seemed to bellow a loud warning.

Enter, Stage Left

Sand Ridge Asylum for the Criminally Insane had been a home built in the grandiose style of the old Greek temples. Plenty of stairs and pillars. It was once a mansion owned by a con artist who escaped imprisonment in some Central American country. After his successful escape, he'd made his way to Brazil, where he'd gotten lucky (for someone like him) and had become the "kept man" of a wealthy coffee exporter's lonely widow. As time went by, the man somehow got his hands on most of her money, killed her, then fled, resurfacing as "Cesare del Toro," charismatic leader of the Del Toro cult, only to later be found drowned in his own bathtub after having had too much tequila and, for some undecipherable reason, having chosen to wear a diaper following Sunday services. With his ignominious fall from grace, the "outraged" in-laws donated the palace to the State (after divvying up the remainder of their relative's assets, of course), and it later became Sand Ridge Asylum for the Criminally Insane. The sad history of this building was going through Roan's mind when he arrived and pulled into the parking lot.

There was no way he could have known about the encrypted message that had been sent ahead, alerting certain parties to his imminent arrival and providing instructions. He climbed the stairs and was headed for the front entrance when four men seemed to materialize from thin air. Actually, two came from in front of the doorway, and two others stepped out from behind the huge Corinthian-style pillars he'd just passed, immediately surrounding him. Roan noticed that the man coming from the left side wasn't wearing his jacket; instead, it was slung over his right arm, effectively concealing any weapon he may have had in his hand.

"Excuse me, sir," began the obvious leader of the party, a kid who had to be twenty-five years younger than he and seemed to be twenty times larger.

"Yes, son, what is it?"

"We cannot allow you to see him, sir," the baby-faced leader of the group told him.

"Why not?" Roan demanded.

"Need to know, Detective Caldwell. Please wait here," the young man replied with that military politeness that tells you things could get ugly if you don't comply.

"Who are you boys with?" Roan asked, trying his best to sound fatherly. The leader of the crew just gave him a frosty smile. *Probably didn't get along well with his father*, Roan thought, sizing his delayers up. *All four of them have military cuts. They're also wearing tailored suits and probably are well armed. Their mannerisms just shout out "Federal agents! Covert military!"*

"You do realize that you are obstructing an investigation authorized by the district attorney, don't you, son?" he asked, hoping for a reaction. There was none. "If you are working with a federal agency, you also need to know that *someone* will have to answer for this later. The DA just loves having the feds step all over his jurisdiction. Tell you what, I'm going to go on in there and talk to my suspect. What are you going to do about it, shoot me?" He moved to push past the group leader, but the younger man also moved to interpose himself between the detective and the entrance of the building again.

"This is a matter of national security, Detective Caldwell, so to be quite frank, sir, yes, I *am* prepared to shoot you if need be." As he spoke, the man to his right stepped forward, pulling the jacket that was slung over his arm just far enough back so that the barrel of the gun he was holding could be seen. The pistol had a silencer.

Roan began to reach for his own weapon, carried in a hip holster on his right side, and the third man grabbed his right hand from behind. As his head instinctively started to turn in that direction, he felt something wet slap the back left side of his neck. It felt like a moist nicotine patch, and its effect was instantaneous. Suddenly, Roan's knees were buckling while strong hands and arms supported him as though he were drunk. *It was that easy for them. That easy. I can't believe it*, he thought. Even as he fell, he also heard a voice saying, "Target secured, sir. You may collect." *That sounds like the team leader.* Roan fought to focus his concentration on *seeing*, forcing his eyesight away from the comfort of blurring or fading to black, but the fight wasn't going his way.

The white Crown Victoria appeared at the edges of his awareness, its door opened, and he was deposited within, not ungently. Someone whose voice sounded strangely familiar, although a little fuzzy, was speaking. "You didn't have to handle him that roughly. How high was the dosage?"

"One slappy, sir," Team Leader replied.

"Let's get him back to base," said Familiar Voice, "and I hope, for your sake, that he doesn't go into cardiac arrest." Roan's vision lost the battle. Everything faded to black. Outside of the vehicle, lightning flashed, thunderclaps seemed to roar in anger, and rain began to fall. The long-approaching storm had finally reached its destination.

***

Meanwhile, Billy and Meredith had indeed worked on the recording with quite a bit of success. They'd moved the camera angle again and again, eventually finding that there were four perspectives from which the dastardly deed had been captured. Following the directions on the note, they had been able to magnify the scene several times. Doing so enabled them to recognize the face of the primary murderer. It was Wesley.

They saw who he was when he snatched his hood off on the way out of the room door. They had also seen enough to know the identity of the mysterious disappearing man in the flight suit. He was the same man who was suspect in the Dana Lacy matter. No longer was there any question concerning who had murdered Angeline Arlander. The recording resolved that for them. They didn't think that any court of law would accept this evidence, though, what with it coming from such questionable sources as it had. But something needed to be done about it, that much was clear. They tried to call Roan, but his cell phone was turned off. Maybe he just didn't want to be distracted, they thought.

What really worried them, though, was the ease with which the suspect could move about. If he *were* responsible for the death of Dana Lacy, he'd be able to confound any normal investigation that may not have the information needed to consider what he could do in that outfit he was wearing. "I think Roan was right," Billy told Meredith. "This has to be bigger than we thought. I wonder what his guy in Sand Ridge will say about this suit. It seems that he trusts Roan, if no one else."

Hearing no reply from his wife, Billy turned his attention from the television to see Meredith going through a stack of paper. *She looks angry,* he thought. "What are you looking at, Merry?"

"There was more stuff in this box," she answered. "Look at this." Billy came over, taking the proffered paperwork and looking it over. It was a printout of several newspaper articles concerning an investigation into the murder of one Evelyn Arlander.

Her husband had, of course, been George Arlander. In this article, however, he was referred to as "the *late* George Arlander. "Late" because apparently, *this* man had died in the Florida Panhandle during Hurricane Ivan. At least, that was what was being reported by the newspaper that the article had originally been printed in. The George in this story had become the main suspect in his estranged wife's demise, and the authorities were closing in on him when his fatal accident occurred. The case was being handled by one Roan Caldwell, a determined detective with a reputation for being a relentless investigator who normally won. He was the person who positively identified George Arlander's body. *This* Detective Caldwell, however, was being assisted in the investigation by his wife, Laura, whose ability as a profiler was well respected in the entire Southeastern United States. The George Arlander that they were investigating had also been a suspect in the murder of his first wife, Irene Arlander, but the State's district attorney's office had stepped in and ended that pursuit despite the well-vocalized objection of Police Sergeant Laura Caldwell, the lead officer in that effort. The problem was that all the evidence unmistakably pointed to Robert "Bobby" Landis, who, as things turned out, had been George Arlander's lover at the time.

Roan and Laura Caldwell, however, were pretty sure that Mr. Arlander had been the person behind the act, although Bobby was the one who was convicted, largely as a result of George Arlander's testimony against him. After the trial's results were placed into public record, George Arlander received a very hefty insurance settlement. He used that money to start his security system installation business. When Evelyn Arlander also died under suspicious circumstances, the Caldwells were once again assigned to investigate. This was an unexpected development for Arlander, considering the fact that he had moved more than one thousand miles south of the city wherein his first wife died. He'd never expected Roan and Laura Caldwell to once again be assigned to scrutinize him as a suspect. Unbeknownst to *that* George Arlander, the Caldwells had moved away from their former location in the same city after the death of their two daughters at the hands of the Tenement Slasher. They were still involved in law enforcement, though, having been hired to head up a newly formed profiling division of the local police department. It was largely their work that built that particular house into one that was well respected among its contemporaries, and their involvement in this case was just happenstance. Now, though, George Arlander was once more in their crosshairs, much to their pleasure and his discomfort.

The Caldwell team managed to get a full confession out of one Wesley Keller, a confession that implicated George Arlander as complicit in the homicide of his second wife, Evelyn. There was an insurance settlement involved in this affair also, and yes, Wesley *was* George's latest paramour. This time, however, it looked as if Mr. Arlander wouldn't get away with masterminding this crime as he had the other one. Roan and Laura Caldwell, having dealt with this type of situation before, inclusive of the same man as a suspect, weren't going to let their quarry escape justice again. They were closing in on their suspect when Hurricane Ivan came along. Even though George had no idea how fast the hammer was going to fall, he had to have known something, the newspapers speculated. Some of the comments he'd made to his acquaintances and employees seemed, in retrospect, seemed oddly fatalistic, as though he knew he'd be imprisoned soon. Conversations with his friends and employees had been overheard, conversations that involved placing his affairs in order in case he lost in court, so on and so forth.

The Wesley Keller of the newspaper articles had confessed to having committed the murder in the exact same way that Roan, Meredith, and Billy had seen Angeline Arlander assaulted. He told the authorities that George had set the whole thing up, promising that they could be together afterward. He'd supplied Wesley with a drug that simulated drunkenness when ingested. Wesley was to slip into the Arlander's beachside home where Evelyn would be staying. He would wait in concealment in the master bedroom upstairs because Mrs. Arlander normally stood on the bedroom balcony to smoke. Wesley was to slip some of the drug into her drink, whether that drink was water or anything else. George would stand outside on the pool deck below and call to his wife, screaming that he'd been hurt. Wesley would make sure that she fell when the balcony's railing, having already had its fastenings weakened, broke. If things did not go according to plan, then Wesley was to push her over. Unlike Angeline

Arlander, Evelyn Arlander was a serious drinker, though not remembered as an alcoholic. No one would find it overly suspicious, however, if she fell to her death after having had one too many.

Things did not, however, go according to plan. Wesley put too much of the drug into Evelyn's vodka tonic, and the woman passed out before she could even reach the balcony. She was already near death when he picked her up, leaned her on the railing, and pushed. "Sound familiar, Bill?" Meredith asked after they had both read the news reports.

"Almost, babe," Billy answered. "The location was different, though. In these articles, the murder scene was reported as being a home located in Beach City, a remote, unincorporated location not far from Roan and Laura's bungalow, but our crime supposedly occurred in Mexico." Meredith, in the meantime, had begun to look through the other things in the box, and her brow was furrowed. "Oh boy. I know that look," Billy said. "What are you thinking, Merry?"

After a short pause, Meredith replied, "Let's suppose this were all true and that these events happened in some other world. Their Roan seems to be as determined as ours. In some of these interviews, this guy says the same sort of things that the old man would say, and he even uses the same words and types of phrasing.

"He found this place by looking into Arlander's expense accounts and figuring out that the worm had another residence they frequently used," she continued. "It was a house listed as the property of AA, his company. *That* was the crime scene, not their home in Mexico. But our Roan wasn't looking into Mrs. Arlander's death until after the mental guy mentioned her, so that's why he wouldn't have tried to find any other residence slash murder scene, and look at this, Bill. Their Roan was quoted a few times in the newspaper, and again, the way this guy chooses his words and expresses himself sounds so much like *our* guy that it makes me wonder if we should go down the road to Beach City and see if there's a house that looks like the one in these newspaper pictures."

Billy shrugged. "Well, Merry, why not? Roan's out of reach right now, and we can't ask his opinion, so let's go see. Looks like that storm's finally made it here, though. We ought to try to get back before it gets really bad." As if to underscore his words, fat raindrops began splattering against the windows while thunder and lightning danced together in the sky above.

Beach City was a relatively remote neighborhood located thirty miles south of Roan's bungalow, with several large homes, most of them owned by well-to-do six-figure-or-more-a-year CEOs who normally stayed only during the winter. With few exceptions, the houses tended toward being large beautiful places with two, maybe even three, floors, and every one of them had pools. Because it was unincorporated, there was no permanent law enforcement presence, the area being within the purview of state or county law enforcement. Not that anything requiring the attention of the authorities ever seemed to happen in that location. There weren't even any sidewalks, and most of the homes had been built on the only rise in the area, a line of dune-like hills that followed the coastline. The access road was a frontage street that ran alongside A1A, and just climbing up the long flights of stairs that connected most of the homes to the road must have seemed a daunting task to anyone with criminal intent or lack of good physical condition. Any attempt at burglarizing these places had to involve a lot of walking up and down to make off with the goods, unless the burglars had access to the dugout garages attached to the homes, most of which could only be opened by fingerprint-activated garage door openers, a technology that, although still in its infancy, was quite effective here.

The house they were looking for had once been owned by the main publisher of a popular "men's magazine," the type concerning which some say things like, "I only got it because I wanted to read the articles." It was a three-story affair with a large balcony on its second floor and a lavish pool deck attached. The George Arlander of the otherworldly newspaper articles had acquired the home as the major part of a settlement in a dispute about payment for a security job done for the same company in another part of the country. Just as suspected, the two of them did locate the house that was depicted in the newspaper pictures found in the mystery box. A laptop search of the ownership listings brought out the fact that this place, like its counterpart, was listed as a holding of AA security systems; but unlike its counterpart had been deeded to one Angeline Arlander (instead of an Evelyn Arlander) as a part of an adjustment to their prenuptial agreement, designed with the intent of allowing her soon-to-be- ex-husband to retain the controlling interest in his security company since that company did not exist before their marriage, thus leaving it unenclosed in the original prenuptial documentation.

The first property owner normally had out of towners put in security systems for any of his properties anywhere. It was his way of lessening the odds of any locals having access to "free viewings of the commodities" as the man used to say. So while George Arlander now owned the home, he may not necessarily have been acquainted with its security system, a fact for which Meredith and Billy Compton would later be grateful. The rain had already begun by the time the two found the address they were looking for, but Meredith still wanted to go up the stairs to look around. The house was beautifully built in all modernist architectural style, but it stood darkened and silent, like a mute witness against the coming storm. The climb from the road was long, but the slope was an easy one. The stairs, they found, landed right on the pool deck, which had to be crossed to gain entry to the house.

Something bad happened in this place. I can feel it. It's like some kind of living grief is just floating in the air here, Billy thought. *What was I thinking, letting Merry drag us out here like this? That storm's almost on us, and it's a big one.*

They were headed for the front door when Meredith stopped, pointing to something lying beside the pool. They went over to look and found two roses, one red and one black, along with a paper that at first glance appeared to be encased in a thin plastic sheeting. Four naturally blue conch shells had been put at each corner of the paper to serve as weights. The spot where the items had been placed was cleaner than its surroundings in a way that indicated the use of a powerful cleansing agent. Its shape indicated what may once have been the location of a blood pool.

"Billy, do you have your kit?" Meredith asked, settling down beside the shrine.

"Yes. It's right here in my backpack."

Meredith looked up at him and smiled. "And here I thought you were just being your nerdy self when you brought that thing."

"Be prepared," Billy answered, taking out his camera as well as a pair of latex gloves. After handing them to Meredith, he looked around again. "Whatever we're going to do, we'd better get it done fast. If this is a crime scene, it's about to be washed out even more by the rain. Besides, I don't feel comfortable being here."

"Yes, dear." Meredith answered in a way that he'd come to understand meant "I'll finish when I'm done."

The raindrops were coming more frequently now. Billy took back the camera Merry offered to him while she picked up and scrutinized the roses and the paper. "Hey, this black rose, it's *real*!" she exclaimed.

Billy was more interested now. "What do you mean 'it's real'? There are no true black roses, are there? I mean, what's called a black rose is normally a deep purple or a dark red or something, isn't it?"

"That's what I'm telling you, Bill. This rose is a *true* black rose, not deep red or anything like that. And this paper, I thought it was wrapped in plastic sheeting, but it *is* plastic. It's another one of his poems, I guess. The writing is the same." Billy was getting livelier now. As Meredith handed him the paper, he went on. "It's probably written on a sheet of a weatherproof polymer paper. I read in one of *Popular Mechanics'* latest articles that something like that was being developed for the military. The pen point makes a sort of a split in the coating while writing, but then, the polymer surface recovers and encapsulates the writing, making it effectively waterproof." He stopped short as Meredith's gun suddenly seemed to *appear* in her hand, pointed right at him. "Wait a minute, babe. I know I bore you when I prattle, but—"

"Billy, move to your right. Slowly," Meredith whispered in her all-business "cop" voice. "Thought I spotted someone with a rifle on that balcony just now. Saw him when I looked up at you. He moved a little, but I think he's still there." Billy slowly began to step to his right, reaching into his pack, which he'd been holding in front of himself, for his own gun. "Dammit, he's gone!" Meredith said.

"You sure you saw him?" Billy asked. Her look answered the question. "Nobody's supposed to be here," he said.

"But, hon, this place belongs to a deceased person, and it's not closed off or anything," Meredith answered. "Maybe it was just some beach bum hiding out, looking for a place to sleep, but I could've sworn it was that stealth-suit guy," she continued.

Billy felt a chill. "Why would he be here?" he asked no one in particular. "It seemed that he got everything he needed the last time." Meredith held up the roses and the poem. Billy said, "Oh yeah." Thunder sounded off in the heavens, and the breeze picked up considerably. Pushing his fingers through his wind-tousled hair, Billy told Meredith, "We probably need to leave. That storm's coming in off of the Atlantic, and it doesn't look like it's gonna get any better out here." Turning to Meredith, he saw that she was reading the poem, still holding the roses. "We should probably bag 'n' tag that stuff, babe. It is evidence, after all."

"I would rather you didn't do that," came a voice from behind him. Meredith's eyes hardened as she drew her Glock. *My god, she is fast!* Billy was thinking, even as he pulled his weapon out of the backpack, spun around, and fired two shots in addition to Meredith's one. His went wide because hers had already hit the man in the stealth suit and he was spinning around, falling from the impact. Before what should have been a dead man could hit the ground, however, he just *disappeared*.

The sky darkened, and lightning flashed again. The two detectives were standing back to back now, weapons drawn, when they both felt something wet slap the backside of their necks. Immediately, their weapons dropped as their knees buckled. Billy hit the ground first, and Meredith fell on top of him, both landing faceup. The man in the stealth suit stepped out of nowhere and stood over them. He picked up the roses and the paper, looked up at the sky, then down at them.

"You're right, Detective Compton. This weather isn't going to get any better, and I had better get you two out of it," he said. Their vision darkened as a drug-induced sleep claimed them.

Faces Unmasked

Drums. He was trying to get some rest, but they wouldn't stop with the drums. Another boom, and Billy began to realize that he was hearing thunder. The rain was falling in full force, and there was another flash. He was lying down, and Meredith . . . *Oh god, where's Meredith?* He didn't know if he was speaking, but it felt like it. Someone was saying, "She's okay. She hasn't been hurt, and she's right here beside you." He tried to rise, and gentle hands came to his aid.

Suddenly remembering the circumstances that led to this state of affairs, he tried to fight against his unseen helper, but the man's strength was incredible. "Calm down, Mr. Compton. She'll be okay," said a voice that sounded like Lucius's baritone. As his vision cleared further, he could make out the man's form; and yes, it was indeed Lucius, holding him up, one huge hand supporting Billy's back while the other held his hands. They were zip-tied. So were his feet. He had been lying on a king-sized bed with Meredith next to him, still seemingly asleep. "If you struggle after coming out of a slappy sleep, you could go right back under or get sick."

"What—" For a moment, he felt as if he'd forgotten how to speak. "What is a 'slappy sleep'?"

"A 'slappy' is what I hit you and the other Detective Compton with," said the man in the stealth suit, walking into the bedroom. His hood was pulled off, exposing the features of the patient as he pulled up a chair and sat down beside the sliding glass door. "I had no intentions of doing you or your wife any harm. My name is Nigel Boyd Renoir, and I believed that you were looking for me."

"Not really," Billy replied, taking a perverse joy in being able to say that. Meredith groaned, came to, and tried to rise too fast. Dizziness would have caused her to fall back, but Lucius moved with superhuman speed to get over to her side of the bed and support her as he had Billy. She, for her part, let loose with a powerful stream of expletives.

"Easy, Detective," Nigel cautioned. "You're in no danger whatsoever."

"Then why are my hands and feet zip tied?" she demanded.

"Because I know that you're an expert hand-to-hand combatant, you're hotheaded, and you would raise hell first and listen later. I didn't want you to wake up and come out attacking anyone. Without a doubt, you'd shoot first and ask questions afterward. The little tableau out on the pool deck proved that. You'd have gotten yourself hurt here."

Meredith reddened. "Wanna try that theory out, dirtbag?" she asked.

Nigel's smile disappeared. "Believe me, it wouldn't have been good for you," he answered quietly. "Just to be sure that no one got hurt, I also zip-tied your husband here and took your weapons. All of them." He gestured toward a side table that held four guns and a knife. "You really do go strapped, Ms. Detective. Three guns and a knife. Wow."

"What do you want, mister?" Billy asked icily.

"Get your hands off of me!" Meredith spat at Lucius, who complied with a complete lack of animosity.

"The first thing I want is for you to be kinder to Luke there. I was pretty pissed off after you shot me. He's the guy who talked me out of the temptation to take you to a far less comfortable location for our 'let's get acquainted' party."

Billy spoke up calmly. "You attacked two law enforcement personnel, Nigel, and now you're holding us captive. That's assault on police officers, kidnapping and unlawful imprisonment charges, just for starters, not to mention whatever else you might have done. Put an end to this now. We walk out, and maybe you get a head start before we finally catch up with you."

Nigel blinked. Lucius smiled. Meredith glared. After a tense moment, Nigel exhaled, shook his head, and looked down for a minute. He ran his fingers through his hair and, looking up, said to the captive couple, "Look, this is all going way wrong, and it's gotta stop. You're good people, I know it. And while neither of you are the detective I was looking for, it seems that maybe you are trying to find a way to bring her killer to justice, or you wouldn't have been here in the first place."

"Who were you hoping for?" Billy asked.

Nigel took his chair over to the sliding glass door, seated himself, and looked out over a rain-swept world. The thunderstorm was in full force now. "Did you notice that this was her master bedroom?" he asked. "They never cut the power, never turned off the water. Never put any For Sale signs up. George has plans for the place, I suspect. That shouldn't be happening. People who do the things that he did should be penalized. They should pay for their actions."

Awareness dawned on both of the detectives. This *was* the bedroom they'd seen in the recording. The balcony outside still had a missing railing. "I was hoping Doc would be here," Nigel continued.

"You mean Roan?" Meredith asked.

"Yes," Nigel replied. He got up, went to the table where the weapons were, and picked them up, one by one, stashing them in the pockets of his suit. "I'll be right back," he said as he stepped forward and disappeared again. Meredith and Billy couldn't believe what they'd seen. "Where did he go?" Meredith asked Lucius.

"Why don't you ask him? He'll be back," Lucius replied.

"I was pretty sure I hit him at least once," Meredith said to Billy. "How the hell did he survive that?"

"Lucius," Billy started, "listen. Whatever is going on here, there still may be a chance for you. I *know* that you're not a bad man. Didn't you tell us that you have a wife and maybe even a family? If you break with this guy now, we may be able to do something for you with the DA."

"Thank you, sir," Lucius politely answered. "But there won't be any need for that. You aren't going to be hurt in any way. He intends to let you go. He really was just trying to avoid being shot again."

"How did he survive the first time?" Meredith demanded again. "He isn't even scratched, and I know I lit him up. I saw him spin from the impact. He should be hurt pretty badly, if not dead."

"Were you trying to kill him, ma'am?" Lucius asked.

"He's a murder suspect," Meredith answered. "People like that don't get second chances when they sneak up on cops. I was reacting to a potentially dangerous situation."

"So was he," Lucius said, as Nigel stepped out of nowhere and back into the room without their weapons.

"How does that suit work?" Billy asked.

"Where did you go?" Meredith demanded. Nigel looked at them for a moment as if trying to decide whether or not to answer then replied, "I took your gear to Doc's house. It's all on the kitchen table. Luke, cut them loose please. Please don't try attacking us or whatever, you two. That sort of thing could be potentially fatal. You're free to go. By the way, don't waste your time trying to track us down or anything. We won't be anywhere you can get to."

"I wouldn't bet the house on that if I were you, you son of a—" Meredith began as Lucius produced a commando's blade and cut their bonds. A hardness welled up in his eyes as he looked at Meredith and simply said, "Don't. He really could hurt you. Badly." The intensity in his eyes and voice was enough to stop her threat before it went too far. The two police officers abandoned the bed and rubbed their wrists and ankles. "The ties weren't too tight, were they?" Lucius asked, the very embodiment of concern. Nigel and Meredith simultaneously rolled their eyes at that.

"Let's go, Luke," Nigel said. "I guess they weren't really here to help us. It seems that Doc's bailed out of the whole thing, and these guys may have been after me."

He had turned to walk off when Billy said, "I thought you wanted justice for Angeline. That's what you said in your note. Are you gonna bail on *her*?" Nigel stopped, turned. He stared at Billy for a moment.

"Nige," Lucius began, "I think you ought to give them a chance. They must have been doing some work on the case we gave them if they found their way here on their own. Something made them want to do that. I think maybe they *were* trying to help Angeline." Nigel put his head down and rubbed his eyes with his fingers. *Trying to stop tears*, Billy thought.

He raised his head, and the wetness of his eyes told the truth of his internal pain. "You know, I never did ask why you were here, did I?" he asked.

"Why were *you* here?" Meredith shot back.

He made an expansive gesture that took in all of their surroundings. "Because this was *her* house, and I never even realized the type of danger she was in until it was too late." Tears seemed to well up in Nigel's voice as he continued. "She told me once that if I needed to escape, they'd . . ." Nigel stopped, took a moment to control his emotion, then corrected himself. "No, not *they*—*she*, Angeline. She told that she'd let me stay here for a little while if I ever needed a quiet escape. I loved her and failed her when she really needed me. I *owe* her, so I came back to . . . to look for something else." He stopped speaking for a moment, looked around as if searching for anything that might have brought Angeline back, took a deep breath, then resumed speaking.

"Also, I was hoping that Doc would show up here. How much of what's happened do you already know?"

"We've been staying with Roan for a few days now," Billy answered him. "We've listened to his recordings up until your last conversation. We watched your recording of her murder. By the way, how did you make that footage? I didn't see any cameras in the—"

"Bill, stay on point," Meredith interrupted.

"Oh. Yeah. Sorry," Billy said, embarrassment showing on his face. "Well, anyway, we know just about everything that you told Roan."

"Then I guess I can tell you the rest of it. It doesn't look like that storm is going away anytime soon. Can we have a temporary truce, Madam Detective? Just long enough for me to tell you some other things you may need to know?" Nigel was waiting on Meredith's reply now.

"Okay," she responded. "But don't think that I'm going to let you off easy afterward. We're not old chums here or anything. Remember that."

Nigel looked surprised for a moment, as if a memory of someone else had come to him. "Good god, you could really *so* be *his* daughter," he said. Everyone seemed to know who he was referring to. It had to be Roan. Lucius and Billy both laughed. While neither Nigel nor Meredith joined in, it did seem to lessen the tension between the two. Thunders sounded off in the atmosphere, and rain belted the windows.

***

Laura was calling him. She needed him to get home as soon as possible, but he couldn't leave the scene right now. They had to do mop-up work. The victims needed to get to the hospital, or for some, the morgue. The suspects needed to get to prison. She didn't like that answer much, so she called louder. He tried to tell her again, but the words got carried away with the water. Laura really was getting louder now. Her voice sounded more and more like . . .

Thunder. That was what he kept hearing. It was thunder. He tried to concentrate, but with the lightning, he seemed to remember a Stevie Ray Vaughan tune, "The Sky Is Crying."

"He's coming out of it," someone said, and their words were framed by flashes. He couldn't see it, but he knew it was there. *The sky is crying, and tears are rolling down the street. This guy is crying, and tears are rolling down his face—Laura, Giselle, Marjorie . . .*

"He's crying, honey," a woman was saying. *There's smile in her words. She loves this guy.* "What did your gorillas do to him?"

"It was a new tool, my dear," the man with the familiar-sounding voice was replying, and Roan could hear the fondness in his tone. *They miss each other. Did I sound like that whenever I talked to you, Laura?* "They weren't sure of the dosage. That's why I asked you here. The only doctor I trust is my wife. How is he? Does it look like he's going to have any cardio problems?"

"No," she answered. "His heart is just fine. He's waking up and probably hears us right now. I should stay around, but I already know you won't have that."

"Come on," the man's familiar voice was saying. "I'll walk out with you, babe. Sergeant Little and his squad will be here to look out for the detective." Lightning flashed again somewhere outside, and thunder sounded.

That storm finally made it in, Roan was thinking. Figures were coming into focus. Four men sitting and standing in different locations around the room, and one really large figure was close to Roan. *The kid from Sand Ridge. "Sergeant Little," I guess. Why are there so many huge people with tiny names?* He tried to rise, but a sudden dizziness caught him. So did Sergeant Little.

"Please be careful, sir. The old man says that if anything happens to you, he'll have my hide, and I really don't want that."

"Thanks for the concern," Roan muttered. "What did you hit me with, anyway?"

"Sir, the general told us that you are to be treated as a friendly, but I'm still not sure how much I can tell you." *What a very crisp, very military answer*, thought Roan. The dizziness disappeared as quickly as it had come on, and Roan felt better. *The colonel, the general, whatever. So he was telling that much of the truth.* The man with the familiar voice reentered the room through a side door, and once again, Roan was struck with a sense of acquaintance when he saw. *He looks like somebody I've seen before. Older, but the same person. Who could . . .*

"You're his godfather? The Colonel?" he blurted. The Colonel smiled. "If the 'his' to whom you are referring is Nigel, yes, I am his godfather." The two men regarded each other for a moment. *He's old, older than I am, but in great shape*, Roan thought. *Tailor-made suit. His is different from the others because it's more expensive. No medals, no emblems of rank anywhere on him. Intelligence agency. Senior field agent or team leader. Which agency, I can't tell yet. Where am I?*

The man's eyes smiled as if he'd heard Roan's question. "You are currently in a secure location used for our VIPs," he answered before the words could even be said.

"It does look like a hotel room at the Ritz-Carlton. I'm not a furniture guy, but it doesn't take a genius to see that this is a seriously expensive secure location," Roan said after a look around. He had been lying on a couch within a room that truly had all the amenities one would expect in the penthouse suite of a five-diamond hotel. "The windows are lousy, though. They look more like *muertieres*. Can't possibly give much light or ventilation," he observed.

The Colonel smiled again. "They're seriously important VIPs. Besides, we have skylights," he answered. "*Muertieres*, eh? Slotted windows built into medieval castles that allowed the defenders to rain crossbow bolts down upon the heads of their attackers. Not too many people are aware of that term's existence, let alone its meaning. You continue to impress me in all of your incarnations, Detective Caldwell."

All of . . . my . . . "incarnations"? Whatever, Roan thought. "What did your people hit me with, Colonel?" he demanded.

"We call them 'slappies.' The preferred mode of application is to slap them onto a target, the neck being the favored location, especially close to or on top of the jugular or the carotid. They're patches, about the size of nicotine patch, and they deliver a drug that incapacitates the target almost immediately then breaks down inside the bloodstream, later being completely metabolized by the human body. All in a matter of minutes or seconds, depending on circumstance and dosage size," The Colonel answered in a businesslike manner.

"Untraceable," Roan muttered.

His host smiled. "Always thinking like a cop, aye, Detective?"

"Well, that is what I do," Roan said. "Now, tell me, please, why you saw fit to do a snatch 'n' grab on me."

At that, The Colonel stopped smiling. "Because *he* trusts you, Caldwell, and we need to make use of that trust. We've lost contact with Nigel and Dana. We know where he is and can go get him at any moment despite his thinking otherwise. It's just that things would go so much better for everyone if he came on board voluntarily. We also have an idea of where Dana is but are unable to reacquire her. Nigel's doing. And believe me, we *really* want to reacquire Dana Lacy."

Roan's interest sharpened. *So she's not dead? I wonder if he's holding her captive or hiding her. Where would he hide her? Why?*

"I need to know who you people are, Colonel. In my experience, anybody who shows up with a bunch of ex-military goons in tailored suits is either some top secret fed or the guy who needs to be sent up on a RICO or arms-smuggling charge. If you're a fed, then this Nigel guy is probably a problem *you* created. If you're organized crime or an arms dealer, then we already have issues between us."

His host regarded him for a moment. Without breaking eye contact, he called out, "Sergeant Little!"

"Sir!" The sergeant and his men snapped to attention.

"Set up a conference call. We are going to verify our identity for Detective Caldwell." A flurry of activity followed as Sergeant Little and his men began working. They moved the chairs and pushed the dining table aside. "We will also identify the source of my authority for the detective here." The action stopped for a minute as Sergeant Little and his squad exchanged glances.

"Sir . . .," the sergeant began, but The Colonel cut him off. "That's an order, Sergeant," he said in a quiet voice. The men resumed their preparations. Telecom wiring was produced from who knew where; then they removed the flat screen off the wall and connected the wiring to a port that had been built in, obviously for that purpose. After a while, with the exception of Sergeant Little, they all stepped out of the room.

He went over to a wall on the left, opened a panel that only one with prior knowledge of its existence would have known of, and punched in a code. The wall beside the port where the wiring had been inserted slid into the ceiling, revealing a huge flat screen. A panel on the side wall did likewise while a console with a chair and telecommunications equipment slowly issued forth from that location. A different section on the opposite wall also proceeded to glide away into the ceiling, revealing another bank of monitors.

Roan couldn't believe his eyes. *What have I stumbled on? Some secret government agency? How secret? How far will they go to ensure my silence after this is over? What about Billy and Meredith? What have I gotten them into?* That seemed to be a moot point at the moment since there was nothing he could do about any of it right now. *Guess I have to just go along for the ride and see where it takes me.* Meanwhile, his host had stood and turned to face the extra-large flat screen.

"Detective Caldwell, please come here," he said, sounding like a parent whose patience had been sorely tried or a disappointed schoolteacher. Roan resented that tone of voice, but he complied, anyway. He felt that there was too much at stake to make a big deal out of it, and he was, as he later found out, completely right.

"Contact in five, four, three, two, one," Sergeant Little was saying, and when the screen that they were facing spoke to The Colonel in some strange code language, he, in turn, answered and replied in the same tongue. The exchange ended, Sergeant Little left the room; and after a few short seconds, the screen lit up, providing Roan Caldwell with a view of the inner office of the Vice President of the United States.

"Good day, sir. Thank you for taking the time for this. I have a good man here who needs to be convinced. Yes, sir, I have *thoroughly* checked him out, and we do need his cooperation that badly," his host began.

The agency was called IDEA Control, the acronym having been based on the initials for the title given to one Nigel Boyd Renoir, once his unique talent could be labeled. He was Inter Dimensional Asset One, and Dana Emily Lacy was Inter Dimensional Asset Two. The Colonel had explained all these things after a brief meeting with his immediate superior, the Vice Commander-In-Chief of the United States of America. Roan would never forget the things he learned that day or the way his host sounded as he told an amazing tale of people with abilities that no one thought possible outside of science fiction stories. But these were real people, and there were only two of them: Nigel Boyd Renoir and Dana Emily Lacy.

In the Beginning . . .

"Detective Caldwell," The Colonel had begun, "you are about to become privy to classified information. You will be required to swear a vow of secrecy. Should you choose to compromise that vow, you will be sought out and dispatched with all possible alacrity. Do you understand this?"

"What if I don't agree? Or if I were to, say, refuse to cooperate and decide to walk out on whatever is happening here? Am I free to go?" Roan asked. *Ever the wise ass*, he could still hear his father saying. "Even the *title* of your outfit is frightening, Colonel," he continued, feeling a momentary anger take hold. "*Idea* Control? Did the name-picking gurus really consider what it sounded like before they stuck you with that label?"

"You will be allowed to leave, if you like," his host answered in a quiet tone that although being polite, still carried a nuance of threat. Then his eyes took on an intensity that made it seem as if he could stare right through the detective. He leaned in and spoke quietly. "But you will not arrive at your intended destination, and no one will ever know where you went. Make no mistake about that, Detective."

Roan felt a chill. *Long time since that happened.* He stared right back at the man. "It may not be that easy to make me disappear," he said. A smile flashed in The Colonel's eyes then, "Okay, you won't go out without a fight, yada yada yada. If you'd reacted any other way, I would have had serious doubts. But one thing I can say about Nigel, I do trust his judgment when it comes to people. Just to show you how little danger you're in here, I'll see to it that you get your weapons back. Three guns and a knife. My, oh my, you *do* go strapped, Detective."

You are also trying to let me see just how little you're worried about what I may be able to do. "By the way," Roan said aloud, "I'm not officially a detective. I haven't been one for a long time now."

The general looked at him for a long moment. "By the way, I'm not a colonel anymore. Haven't been for a very long time now, either. You, however, have always been what you are, Detective Caldwell. That's what made you honest. At any rate, you will soon be an acting federal agent as much as I am. Have a seat, make yourself at home. It's time to brief you on what we're dealing with."

***

The first thing you need to understand is who I am and where I came from. These facts will help you understand who and what both Nigel and Dana are. I wasn't born here, in this world, although I was born in a world that *is* this one, just in a different location and a different time frame. I'm originally from New Orleans, as is my wife and both of our families. My mother was a genuine New Orleans Creole girl, all a mix of Black 'n' French. Poppa was an African American. Middle kid in a large family of exceptional people, that was me. All during my years in high school considered a gifted student. After high school, I chose to go to Annapolis, eventually graduating as a Marine Corps second lieutenant at the top of my class.

During the week of my graduation, some of the senior officers I'd met along the way got together with me for a little powwow. They wanted to persuade me to go into the administrative fields of the corps, to preserve myself for a special project that they had in mind. One even went so far as to say that I was too intelligent to waste as a "bullet stopper." Sometimes I wish that I'd listened, but only sometimes. Back in those days, I wanted to fight, though, and fight I did. Got pretty good at it too. I was a first lieutenant when the call that sped up my career came. One of those officers had the ear of the Commandant of the Marine Corps, and a new program was in the works. They were going to start an elite Special Forces program exclusive to the Corps. There were no Navy SEALs where I come from, and the need for that type of outfit was becoming more and more evident. A call went out, and as ever, the corps was going to answer it. I went when they sent for me and became a member of the first graduating class of the Marine Intensive Specific Training unit. They called us the MIST, and we struck fear in the hearts of enemies everywhere. "Death from the Shadows" was our calling card.

I was promoted to the rank of captain upon completion, and my whole life after that was spent fighting proxy wars, secret wars, and some that weren't so secret. Our cold war ended, and wars against terrorist organizations began. China was a problem, the possibility of a return of the old communist block was a threat, so we were all very busy MISTmen. Eventually, after I was awarded the Congressional Medal of Honor, the brass decided to install me as commanding officer of an intel ops unit. I was a lieutenant colonel in the Marine Corps by that time, one of the youngest men to ever have held such rank and was now a classified ops man, working within The Division. That's what our intelligence apparatus was called back where I come from.

That was also when Nigel happened to step into my life. One day when I got home, there he was, sitting on the front porch with my wife, a five-year-old boy, small for his age, who seemed to wander in out of who knew where. They were eating snow cones, and he was as happy as if he were home with his own mother. I asked where he'd come from, and she really had no idea. I asked him, and he told me that this was his house, only people were living in it again. We told him to go home. He didn't want to, but after I threatened to take him to Child Services, he left. I thought no more of it until a week later, when, upon arrival, I found him there again, only this time he'd been beaten, and badly. He was afraid to even go knock on the door. He said he didn't want her to see him like that. At five, that's how he thought. I picked him up, took him inside, and when she saw the condition he was in, my wife was outraged. She'd never used our relationship for any favors before, but this time, those stops were pulled. She wanted me to do something for him, anything that would punish the person responsible and ensure that this didn't happen to him again. I found out that day that this kid was a regular visitor at my home, but she always sent him back to wherever he'd been staying before dark, normally giving him some little thing to take with him—a toy, sweets, whatever.

She's a doctor, my wife, and it wasn't always easy for her being married to me. We'd been sweethearts since my senior year of high school, and even though our career choices didn't allow us to spend as much time as we wanted with each other, we still managed to get married right after I finished up at Annapolis. Even after that, it seemed that we spent more time apart than together. We loved each other, though, and that never changed. It seems now that she'd always wanted a son, but we never had any and perhaps that's how it came about that she so welcomed little Nigel. She couldn't help but see some resemblance to me in him, I suppose.

Well, I did some inquiries, and the more we looked, the less we found. There was just no trace of him or anyone related to him *anywhere*. I even began to wonder if this kid was an enemy agent. So I decided to do a DNA test, hoping to at least find a country of origin. That was when the chain of events that landed us here, in this place, this world, began. The results of the test told me that this child couldn't possibly have existed in *our* world. The implications of that were sobering. I had every intent of revealing him to my superiors right away, but another crisis arose, and my unit had to be fast-tracked to Somalia. Another deeply secret operation requiring the involvement of my MISTmen, they said. Before our deployment, though, I told Nigel that he could stay there with her until I got back. He was thrilled and asked if he could go back to pick up some toy that his favorite brother gave him. He went, but still hadn't returned by the time we deployed.

It took us a month to wrap that crisis up, and I was back home. My unit had to stay there at the center for another week, though, because we all had to be debriefed. This one turned out to be a tougher mission than expected because some photography intel lab rat had fouled up one tiny detail. We lost a couple of guys on that assignment, and the director wanted a complete report and The Division had to concoct some cover story involving equipment malfunctions due to human error and take that false information to the loved ones left behind. (We had to say *human* error, for in that place, a private citizen could take the DOD to court over wrongful deaths, but not over human error.) That was . . . difficult. When we finished, I put in for leave because she was about to start her residency, and we really wanted to spend some time together. We were going to go to Cancun. Nigel, for his part, was, of course, at the house when I returned from the Somalia debriefing, and he smugly showed me the tooth he'd lost. Said it was already loose and came out when one of the bigger boys punched him, but he still won the fight. My wife insisted I listen to his story since he'd been eager to tell me, as little boys can be. He'd been looking out of the window for me from the time he heard of our return, so I did what she asked. I listened. He told us how some bullying kid tried to take the toy he'd gone back for, and they fought. It was a Batman action figure, and later on, I learned why it meant so much to him. Nigel had gotten in trouble for that fight, and "they" grounded him, even barring as well as locking his door to block any possible escape.

Although whoever had custody of him had tried to take away his toy, Nigel managed to keep it concealed until he could escape and return to us with it. He was pretty proud of that, and not too oddly, so was I. That kid always had a lotta moxie. Additionally, he proudly informed us that he was six now. I knew then why she'd had me listen to his story; she wanted to take Nigel with us, but there was no way, I told her. After all, what did we know about this kid other than the fact that he kept showing up on our doorstep? Even though she wasn't privy to the results of his DNA test, she still had some idea as who the boy really was, I believe, and that didn't help my case any. She went along though, and together we told him that we were about to leave the country for a while and, yes, he could stick around and say goodbye.

All that night, Nigel cried like he was losing his family. We let him sleep on the couch, but the next morning, I had to talk to him again, for he'd come up with a clever, though childlike, plan to stow away in our suitcases. I assured him we'd be back and then I would go with him to see where he lived. That cheered him up, the idea of my going to visit his home. Apparently he'd been bragging about us to the other kids (whoever they were), and none of them believed him. He wanted to go that day, immediately, but we got him to settle for our just walking a little way toward his home with him if he remembered how to find the place. Yes, he assured us, he did. I remember the details of that day as if it were yesterday, Detective, and for good reason. Since the weather was turning cold, she'd bought him a little black trench coat. He was proud of that and was pretty sure that it would keep the others quiet for a while. He asked her to keep his Batman for him so it would be safe. We walked, and for the first time, I actually *listened* to his chatter. He went on and on about his parents and how they were lost, but the "Ghost Card" had saved him. He was still excited about the ride in the helicopter. He said he had brothers and sisters, but they too got lost in the storm. His favorite brother had thrown his action figure to him when he was falling off the roof into the water—he wanted Batman saved, Nigel told us. It all sounded like something out of a kid's imagination, and while that may have made the veracity of his story suspect, one thing remained noticeably true—this child was an orphan.

Finally, his talking stopped, and he fell silent. We both looked at him, seeing that he was crying again. "Do I have to go? Can't you take me with you?" he asked. My wife could hardly bear it, but she knew not to ask again about bringing him along. Truthfully, we'd already been over it again and again, but this was to be *our* time together. Even so, had she pushed the issue, I would still have given in because it was *she* who asked; but neither of us knew anything about the kid's legal status, having only now found out that he was truly alone, and even that needed to be verified. Kneeling to put herself at his eye level, she embraced him, gave him a motherly kiss on his little forehead, and asked, "Nigel, do you know how long a month is?" He told her he was pretty sure it was thirty days. He was six, and he knew that. She told him to count thirty-one days and come back.

"Okay," he said. But then he asked again, "Do I have to go back *there*?" She promised him that when we arrived home, we would bring a surprise for him and maybe even allow him to spend more time with us—if he went home now. That cheered him up somewhat, but we both could still see that for some reason, he dreaded the excuse for a home he'd be returning to. He promised to be good, count thirty-one days, and come back. The boy put on the bravest war face he could muster up in order to fight back his tears, hugged both of us in turn, and walked off. He went a few feet, blurred, and disappeared.

I thought she would have a heart attack. I could not believe what we'd just seen either, but for me, it confirmed what that DNA test had already shown. This boy had to have come from somewhere *else*. I just had no idea until now, how he moved between here and there. Fortunately, I had two concealed cameras, one in my belt and one in my sunglasses, because of my suspicions regarding his origin, and it seemed best to see and record where he would go. Thus my suggestion that we walk a little way with him. On the way home, we didn't talk much of what we had seen, but it was clear that something other than the obvious was bothering her. Finally, I coerced her into saying what was on her mind. "You're going to find a way to *use* him, aren't you?" she demanded. I explained to her that it was the nature of my oath. That my first loyalties were to her and my country. If Nigel had something that we could use against the forces that threatened our way of life, or if he somehow represented a threat, I was honor-bound to inform myself and, by extension, our government of the possibility. I wanted to tell her of the DNA results, but at the time, it didn't seem to be the best idea.

She hated the possibility that the boy might become a top secret weapon or top ten most wanted enemy, but she also knew that it was something else she had to live with. Still, she told me, on that day that if

I ever allowed Nigel to come to any harm, ever abandoned him to enemy hands, or if he lost his life and no one would tell her the truth of how it happened, if I did less than my very best to keep him safe, she would leave me and never look back. I would give up a lot for God and country, but not my wife. So I made her a promise, on my honor as her husband, a man and a marine officer, to do what she asked as far as that.

That's one of the reasons why you are here now, Detective Caldwell. Things have happened that not only represent a danger to Nigel, but to this world also and other ones. We'll get back to that, but for now, I'd like to completely brief you concerning the history of my relationship with him.

We went to Cancun, Mexico, my wife and I, but before we took off, Nigel's existence and ability had to be revealed to the division. They, in turn, dispatched a report to our bosses in the Pentagon. I also forwarded them the footage I had of his strange way of moving between here and there, wherever *there* was. Before we were allowed to go, however, I had to have a talk with my director. He needed to understand that despite their stated preference that we get on "this thing with the kid" immediately, my wife *desperately* needed time alone with me, as I'd had a close call on the last deployment, and vacationing with her for a little while would really help us both out. Despite our losses, The Division was happy with the overall way the Somalia mission went, not to mention being thrilled over the aftereffects, so Director Rocklin promised that at least for the next month, my wife and I would have our time together, with no urgent messages from headquarters, no sudden assignments taking me away in the middle of the night, to be gone for weeks before I saw her again.

He almost kept that promise. Twenty-eight days went by before they contacted me. After the lab rats had finished doing whatever they did with the pictures and film, The Division set a constant watch on our place, looking for Nigel. They'd caught up with him because apparently, he couldn't wait the whole thirty days. He'd come back the morning before and sat on the bench swing on the front porch, staying there all day and spending the night, eating some popcorn that he had brought along in his pockets for his meals and drinking out of the water hose. One of our agents, posing as a policeman, had talked to him, and Nigel told the man that he was watching the place till we returned, even saying that we were paying him to do so. He'd been beaten again, and they considered the possibility that either a real policeman would observe the bruised-up kid and get curious, or some nosy neighbor would notice the child on the porch of a home whose owner was most likely out of town, and the local authorities would still get involved. They therefore chose to take him into custody and now he was in Washington, being poked and prodded by the lab rats while asking for us. He'd tried to escape a couple of times and almost got away, but after the last time, they sedated him.

The first time he attempted to disappear, they managed to keep him there by revealing the fact that I worked for them, but the boy was perceptive, and after not seeing myself or my spouse in evidence anywhere, once again made a break for freedom. The only reason his getaway attempt had failed was because one of the field agents made a diving grab and caught his foot just as he was disappearing. Even then, Nigel nearly got away, dragging the man neck deep into nowhere. But he was outweighed and couldn't move fast enough before two or three of the others grasped the agent's body and tugged, thus pulling the both of them back into the center. They'd gotten the kid back and prevented him from attempting any more escapes, but at a price. The agent who grabbed Nigel seemed to be suffering from some sort of mental break. Something about the *in-between* space had that effect on the man. He'd become catatonic. It was a miracle that he'd even been able to hold on to Nigel during that, but the head shrinkers were suggesting that fear might have been the motivator behind it. After all, they did have to pry his fingers loose. In their opinion, that poor unfortunate's condition didn't matter much when compared to what the group learned about the boy and the zone he disappeared into. The agent got an honorary promotion, was awarded a medal, and immediately honorably discharged into the care of a VA hospital near his hometown.

I still remember how disappointed she was when I told her that our vacation was going to be cut short. Actually she was pretty nearly enraged. But when I also told her that they had Nigel and he needed us, she calmed down. After hearing the rest of the story, she was livid again. Packing never went so quickly before. They even sent a Concorde to bring us home. Once we got back to New Orleans, they told me that Washington was my next destination. I was expected to talk to Nigel alone, but after some discussion with my superiors, convinced them that she should be there too. He saw her as a mother, I explained, and with her there, he'd be more prone to trust us all. After looking over my report about the boy's behavior with her, the division agreed. Going forward, they also felt that it would be better if Nigel was brought back to our house as the newest member of the family.

"Congrats, son, you just became a father, and your wife didn't even have to deal with labor pains!" Director Rocklin roared. The old man even shared a drink with me and demanded that we bring some of those illegal Cuban cigars home the next time I was out that way (that being a big hint as to where my next planned mission might have taken me). To make him feel even more like trusting us, we were to come into the military hospital where he was, make a scene, and take Nigel home. She had no idea this was expected of her, but it couldn't have gone better. She really loves that kid.

As soon as we landed in New Orleans, and before we got to where Nigel was being held in Washington, the director took me aside and presented my new orders. I was to go with Nigel to his place of origin, scout around, and make a report. As far as the possible effects of the *in-between* space, well, they couldn't predict anything, not even my odds of survival, but they felt that no one else was more qualified and likely to endure. Also, I did have MIST training, and there wasn't anything tougher in our world. There was one other mission parameter; if any of his ability was attainable for me, I was under orders to acquire it—by whatever means necessary. Should that prove unfeasible, I was to bring back both Nigel and enough information to help the division produce a good threat assessment, just in case there was any possibility of menace emanating from his home, wherever that was. In the meantime, while the mission was undergoing congressional review, they wanted us to keep the child in our house for a little while, or forever, whichever was needed to keep the mission on a positive track.

A think tank was also being put together, and for now, Nigel's conversations while he lived with us were to be taped, replayed, and analyzed enough to give them a pretty good idea of some facts regarding wherever he came from. I talked to her about this, and although she wasn't crazy about the idea of my undertaking a journey that could possibly leave me mentally incapacitated, she could also understand the need. She also needed to know the results of his DNA testing and, to my disbelief, didn't seem to exhibit any surprise whatsoever. It was as if this was what she'd expected. Her biggest concern was more about what type of life Nigel was suffering through back in his home because that was the second time he'd shown up in such terrible physical condition. The brass had decided, therefore, to allow her to talk to him, with the intent of solving that little mystery. The boy had refused to tell anyone why he was in such bad shape when he was brought to The Division, and even the most empathetically skilled interrogators kept coming up empty-handed on that one. But of course, when my wife asked him about it, his clam impression ended abruptly.

He never wanted to cry in front of anyone, but she wasn't just *anyone*, so through quite a few tears, he informed her that the nuns took his trench coat after someone named Robby Dubois had told them it was stolen. (Apparently this was the same kid who knocked his tooth out earlier.) He further told her that they were trying to, as he put it, "beat the debbils" out of him because he kept escaping every time they tried to lock him in, and to these superstitious whack jobs, it seemed that he must be "possessed." In their Torquemadan minds, that little black trench coat was a manifestation of his possession by whatever Trinitarian Satan they believed in, so they took it and burned the thing. She wanted this abuse stopped, whether we kept the boy with us or not.

When the time for the next phase of the mission came, I made sure that I was the control officer for the project of installing a boatload of bugs and minicams in my own house. I didn't tell her about that part of it, though truthfully, she probably had an idea. We went ahead and fixed up a room for Nigel, with plenty of eyes and ears in it. I made sure, though, that I knew where every camera and microphone were located. Absolutely *none* would be allowed in our bedroom or the bathrooms, though, and that was nonnegotiable. After we finished, the kid and my wife were brought from the hotel in Washington. Nigel went home with us, and he was absolutely thrilled to see that he had his own room. His little world was complete. She was happy about it too, but knowing why it had been done dampened her joy. She hadn't forgotten his surprise either. There was a huge gift-wrapped box waiting in his room when he first stepped into it. The thing contained every accessory a kid with a Batman toy could want. Bat car, other action figures, a bat cave, all that stuff. She'd even bought another little black trench coat. How it was all put together so fast, I don't know, but she kept her word to him.

We went back, and while she started her residency, I commenced the easiest part of the mission. Staying home and talking to Nigel. I even played with him. During the short time we spent in The Division's headquarters, the director had told my wife that I would likely be promoted to colonel, and that was what she began to call me. Nigel heard that and took up the practice. All these years, that has never changed. It's even become my code name among the men with me today. That would be a demotion, actually, but misleading enough to enemy ears. Throughout the following months, he and I got to know each other much better while a new section of The Division, known as the Think Tank learned a lot more about him and his world. Apparently, their money looked exactly like ours. He also knew that the diamond in her ring was very expensive, so these existed and held value in his home world too. I'd shown him a gold coin, and he talked on about all the toys he could buy with it, so gold was likely the same precious metal there as here. I gave him the coin. Later on, I'd wished I hadn't. Eventually, The Division and its Think Tank got back with us to present their assessment.

Nigel had been through a traumatic experience, they said (as if that were news to me). But his world obviously held the same type of people and comparable values. This they could tell by the games he played with his toys. After assessing all the video and audio of the boy's day-to-day behavior, the general conclusion was that there weren't too many differences between our societies, the lab rats assured us. He lived in a New Orleans that was in a Louisiana that was part of a United States, they had a president and probably congressional and judiciary governmental branches just as we did, and although their president was not the same man as ours, his office was the same. Whatever harrowing event had happened in Nigel's New Orleans, though, did not sound like anything we had seen, though it must have been big, the Think Tank said. In the course of our conversations, the boy mentioned things that led the analysts to believe that his city must've recently suffered some serious natural disaster, the event having occurred within a month or so before Nigel's first trip into our New Orleans. He'd lost his family and had been looking for them when he wound up at my doorstep. Or maybe he was just trying to find his house, thinking that they would be there, which seemed the more likely scenario.

Eventually, the word came down from Rocklin, the mission was to commence in two weeks. Meanwhile, our science geeks had come up with a few things, and I was to be outfitted and geared up in preparation. Nigel, from what he told us, seemed to always step out of the *in-between* space into the orphanage where he stayed, so I was to be disguised as a priest for our journey. For some reason, the child hated that costume. I couldn't blame him, though. I'd seen my share of movies with creepy priests in them. Didn't matter, they said. My holy man outfit was hooked up with more cameras, recording devices, and transmitters than anyone in recent history ever carried before. I was armed with a silencer-equipped Sig Sauer, a dozen extra small dart tranquilizers, a mini-computer (new technology in my world), a backpack with changes of clothing for Nigel and myself, $300 in small bills (not too many, as we couldn't be sure of the serial numbers); about $80,000 in diamonds and thirty gold coins that would have fetched around $13,800 where I came from. The diamonds and the gold were sewn into an inner pocket within my Holy Man getup, and in a sinister gesture intended to make a point, a cyanide capsule was integrated onto one of my molars.

Nigel didn't want to go, but knowing that I would be going with him was what got his cooperation, and my promise to give Robby Dubois a belt lashing for getting his coat taken gave the whole affair an added impetus for him. I took the little guy to see my dear wife; she spent some time cooing over and babying him; then we did what we always would before my deployments. She and I spent the long night before my deployment loving each other and, the next day, danced to a quiet Sade tune; then we said goodbye. She was worried but would not allow herself to break down with it. This was just a thing that had to be done, she knew. I can still remember looking back, seeing her standing there in her whites, a stethoscope around her neck, and her hands clasped in front of her heart. *Please come home safely*, she mouthed to me. There were tears in her eyes. Nigel and I climbed into the SUV and left.

Into the Rabbit Hole

The Division wanted us to commence our trip from its headquarters in Washington, but after considering Nigel's age and place of origin, decided it was best that we leave from our New Orleans location. They wanted us to take off from the building we had there, but I took exception to that idea. After all, we had no idea what was on the other side of the passage. Helpfully, all of the brass did agree on one point: if I were to suffer a mental break, no one in the other government's service should be allowed to find me first. A catatonic wouldn't even be able to break that cyanide capsule tooth. The fact that we had a headquarters in that location led them to consider the possibility that there was some sort of official building on the other side too.

So we decided to try it from our house, and I told Nigel what to do if I fell. He was worried, but they told him I was a specially trained superhero, and that convinced him enough. He still hated the priest suit, he told me. We were all set to go, when someone at the top changed their minds again. We were flown back to Washington "because of the immediacy of resources," they said. Some other "advisor" had also convinced my boss's bosses that driving from Washington to New Orleans would afford a better opportunity for learning about Nigel's America. Later, the fact was exposed that this noncommittal hesitating stop-go behavior resulted from infighting over command of The Division, a situation aggravated by lack of strong leadership that would later have terrible repercussions.

They had us all set up to commence the passage from some secret sub-basement, but Nigel said that he didn't think he could find the way from inside, so they took us to an abandoned lot and we started off. I held his little hand and told him that it was time. I'll always remember how he gave me the biggest smile and, with all the confidence in the world, said, "Okay, Colonel, let's go." The next thing I remember was a feeling of *wrongness*—as if the laws of physics were in open rebellion. Air currents with solidity, pushing at me with what seemed like malevolent intent, colors screaming out sounds that were as dangerous as jagged glass shards, moods that you could taste and feelings with their own different smells, merciless rays of light that howled like wind and bore down on me, my head hitting the ground repeatedly and Nigel screaming for help. The taste of cyanide in my mouth and I knew that I'd bitten the capsule and would be dead soon. Hands grabbed my feet, and Nigel was yelling, telling someone to leave me alone. We went back into *there*, came out again, and I curled into a ball and slept.

When I awakened, my head was on Nigel's lap, and he was asleep. I tried to stand, succeeded with just a little bit of dizziness. That passed, and I gently woke Nigel. He was overjoyed to see that I was better. I asked him what happened, and from what he told me, I gathered that we came out in the main walkway of a shopping mall. I was having convulsions when he smelled almonds, and I went limp. People were trying to drag me away or hold me, he didn't know which, but he'd gotten me back into the *in-between* space, where they couldn't follow. The rays of blue light cured me while we were in there, he said. He told me that he normally ran from them, but one had hit me and made me better, so he waited for a long time until another one came. After the second ray had done whatever it did, he got me back out of the *passageway* into an abandoned store whose entrance was shut to the rest of the mall and covered with plywood, then tried to keep watch while I slept; but he was very tired and fell asleep himself, he said. I told him that the exertions had been pretty hard for him, and that was probably why that happened. Nigel felt better after hearing that he hadn't let me down by failing to keep watch.

I gathered that we'd arrived early in the evening, at about 1700 on a Tuesday, this day and time having been selected by The Division for its lack of evening traffic. They hadn't expected us to turn up in the main walkway of a Washington DC shopping mall, though. Apparently, I was convulsing when we got out of wherever or whatever that middle passage was. So now I had a better idea of what its effects could be. A couple of people had come over, maybe with the intent of helping, it seemed, but they tried to reach into my pockets even while I was still convulsing. Nigel said that he thought they were "crackheads" (a term I was unfamiliar with), so he had to get us away from them. A six-year-old couldn't have dragged a man of my size away very easily, though, if at all. So I guessed that Nigel had to have been under the influence of a fear-inspired adrenaline rush. Scared. I asked him about that, and he told me that he didn't drag me, he just pulled the *otherspace* around us and pushed it away when he felt safe. That was something new for him, and he was afraid to try it at first. But he said that it just *seemed* like the right thing at the time, so fear and all, he tried and was still able to do it or else God only knows where we both would have been by now. The kid even managed to hang on to the backpack.

Of course, I'd lost the mini-computer immediately when we first entered that hell zone, but the Sig was still fastened to my chest holster. I didn't know how long it took for these "rays" to pop up and do whatever they did, but my internal clocking said that about three or four hours had passed. (No, Detective Caldwell, I do not have an actual clock within my body; the internal clocking was part of MIST deep mental training.) It should be around 2100 out there, I felt. This place would be closing soon, and we had to get out and on our way.

I tested my teeth and found that the fake molar had somehow been replaced with a real tooth—*my* tooth. This was to be only the first of several shocking discoveries along this journey, though. I wanted to question the boy about the healing light beams, but here and now was not the time. Filed it away under "To be exploited later" and moved on. We got out through a door located in the back of the space that led us into an exit hallway and out a different side door. Once we got outside, I stole a car, an act that just thrilled Nigel. It was a 1984 Monte Carlo and the only one in the vicinity. We later learned that it once belonged to a crooked jewelry store manager who'd made it available for certain criminals to use in robbing his store, a robbery he himself set up. As a result of my interference, the thieves ran out and found their transportation gone, tried to foot it to a safe place, but were caught and arrested by the local LEOs. That too would later come back to haunt me.

We dumped the car when we got back to the more populated areas of the city and went ahead by public transportation and on foot. I wondered why it seemed that we were getting so many stares, though. Most people in big cities tend to keep their eyes cast away from seeing anything out of the ordinary, but the stares just kept coming, every now and then being accompanied by a few muttered insults aimed at the two of us—more specifically at me. Eventually, we found that shady pawnshop owner who lurks in the shadowy areas of every city in America—you know the one, that guy who would give anybody cash for anything, no questions asked, and with his crooked assistance, managed to get more than enough money to set us up in a decent motel. I wondered why the girl at the front desk kept giving me such dirty looks, though. After attaining our room, Nigel changed, watched a lot of cartoons, then sacked out. I was surprised to find so many channels on television that were operating so late, but apparently there had been some sort of cable TV revolution here, which meant plenty of twenty-four-hour broadcasting, including news channels. I'd also gotten a newspaper and knew now that this place was the same or extremely similar to my own home, but here, it was a different era. Nigel's world was twenty years ahead of mine in time, but only about five years ahead in technology. Still, five years, when it comes to technology, is a lot of time.

In this place, the year was 2005; and the month was, just as in my world, early October. The paper was the *Washington Post*, and it contained an article about how reports of pandemonium in the Superdome may have slowed aid to the victims of Katrina. So that was it, I remember thinking. That was the traumatic event that had stripped Nigel of his family and driven him to walk the deadly corridor between worlds. A killer storm. The sheer magnitude of human suffering involved seemed unrealistic and unbelievable. *How could this have happened on American soil?* I wondered. What corruption within this government could have enabled such lack of concern about the sheer devastation that was visited upon American citizens? I had a really hard time with that, finding myself sitting for a while, simply stunned.

Soon enough, there came an official-sounding knock on my door. I thought, for a moment, that maybe they were on to me already. Sig in hand, I looked through the peephole. There, on the stoop, holding his badge up, stood a lone police detective with one of those short little Clint Eastwood mini-cigars in his mouth. I put the gun down, out of sight. Cracking the door just a bit, I did my best irritated-dad act. "Can I help you, Officer?"

Yes, he said I could. Front-desk gal had called, telling him that a priest, traveling alone with a little boy, was occupying this room, and the detective wanted to see if everything was all right. He had no warrant and no disturbance had been reported, but the owner was a friend of his and had reservations about this situation. Understandable, the detective said, what with the way things had been going with priests and boys lately. I had no idea at the time what he was implying, but it didn't sound too good.

"He's my son, Officer," I told him.

"Yeah, pal, I'm sure," he answered, looking as if I'd just tried to sell him a fried chicken franchise in the Everglades. "That's Detective, pal. Detective O'Malley. An' I wasn't born yesterday, fella. Everybody knows youse guys don't have nuthin' to do with women."

"Not all priests belong to the same church," I told him. "The priests of my faith are permitted to marry. We're from New Orleans, and my son and I are headed back there, hoping to find anything we can of his mother, my wife. She was visiting her parents down there, but we've heard nothing since Katrina, and we fear that she has been lost in the storm."

Detective O'Malley was looking less incredulous now. Doing my best to look as much like a man under duress as possible, I even sniffled a bit as I told him, with tears in my voice, "We've had eight good years together, Detective. I had a really bad feeling about her taking that trip, you know."

O'Malley was looking a bit embarrassed now. "Yeah, guess I don't know everything, do I? I mean, I ain't no religious guy myself or nothing, an' I had a wife once too, Father, Brother, or cuz, whatever *youse* guys are called."

Trying to sound priestly, I asked, "And did you lose her in death, my son?"

"Nah," Detective O'Malley answered with a lecherous grin. "I lost her to Jane Levostky, and boy, you shoulda seen that gal's—" Cutting him short with a disapproving glare, I said, "Please, don't speak that way. The Lord is listening, and my boy need not . . ."

Right then, Nigel walked up, rubbing his eyes as if he had been sleeping. Putting his hand in mine, he said, "I couldn't sleep, Dad. I'm worried about Mom." Looking suspiciously at the detective, he asked, "Who's he?"

"He's a detective, son," I answered.

Immediately, Nigel appeared overjoyed. "Is he gonna help us find Mom?" he asked hopefully. "I know she survived, Mom's tough!"

Hearing this seemed to be softening our visitor up somewhat. He looked at his feet, shuffled them in embarrassment for just a few seconds, then said, "Look, mister, I'm sorry to have bothered you. But if you're gonna travel with your kid, maybe you oughta wear somethin' different. I mean, you guys can do that, can't you? Wear normal clothes? 'Cause if you don't, this is gonna happen a lot more before you get back home."

"I'll keep that in mind, Detective O'Malley," I replied, acting just a little insulted. He looked down at Nigel, and I thought I saw real concern in his eyes. He would probably have asked more questions, but I said the one priestly thing that makes people leave every time. "Would you like to take a moment to pray with us, my son?"

"Er . . . uh, no thanks, pal, I got real work to do, and you got a wife to locate, so yeah, well, uh, good luck," he said and disappeared into the darkness. *Not an extremely brilliant cop*, thought I, *but definitely a compassionate one. This kid is almost too smart, though.* The first thing I did in the morning was go buy some normal-looking clothing.

I thought that we should journey around the city by bus for a little while because that means of travel would allow more opportunity to learn how to use the new laptop I'd bought to assist in my catching up as much as possible with the computer tech that was current in this place. Such tourist-type wandering would also give me time to observe more details about their governmental departments and workers. My home world was, indeed, behind this one in technological knowledge, but a fast learner can learn a lot in a little time if he's willing to ask questions and pay close attention to the answers. The only question was, who do you ask about current computer technology without attracting too much attention to yourself? When we went back to the shopping mall, I'd noticed a lot of computer gaming stores with geeky people working in them. It seemed logical that those guys would be the ones with the savvy needed to answer my questions while providing free updates and refresher courses. They also were the type that most needed others' approval and would talk for long hours if given that much time to show off their techno acuity. This turned out to be the correct assumption. So we spent a lot of time in computer stores, as well as electronics departments at "Super Targets" and "Super Walmarts" (something else I'd never heard of). Nigel, for his part, didn't mind it one bit. He loved computers and computer games. He would go play with the "demos" while I pumped information out of the Poindexters' brains. With the boy thus occupied, I could take as much time as I needed with my nerdy teachers.

We stayed around the DC area for about three weeks, and then I decided that it was time to leave. This place was the center of their government, after all; and no matter how far under the radar we were, sooner or later, someone was bound to get too curious. We'd also seen Detective O'Malley at least one more time, and although he was too far away to positively identify me, he did a double take and seemed about to approach us when some emergency call came in. He jumped into a car with his partner, and they zoomed away. He did peer pretty closely at us as they passed, though. We'd already changed our lodging location, so it wasn't as if he'd catch up with us at the motel or anything. But it was still time to leave. I paid cash for a used car from a private owner, and we took off. Two hundred and fifty miles away down the road, that car was sold off, and we caught the bus. Doing it that way wouldn't allow O'Malley to be able to track us too easily if he decided that was something he had the desire to do. Taking his advice, I'd long ago ditched the Dirty Priest outfit (what a relief *that* was!) and found other ways to conceal my valuables and weapons. Cargo pants are the best invention ever for that sort of thing.

Because it was the same time of year there as it was at home, around late October, wearing a trench coat wouldn't be considered too unusual, so we bought some. Two for each of us. One for use, and one for backup. Nigel needed a new one anyway because he'd left his at our house, not wanting to lose it again. Finding that little lady who has the alteration shop in a strip mall and would sew pockets inside my coat was no problem either. I paid her in cash. We'd gotten two new backpacks too. It's amazing that people don't realize how easily having the same backpack can help a pair of observant eyes to easily identify you. I bought all sorts of books on computers as well as digital technology and read them as we traveled. Nigel mostly slept.

We stopped riding the bus in Birmingham, Alabama. I hustled off a couple more diamonds and some gold then found a "Hummer." (I was surprised to find they'd been adapted to civilian use) for sale by a private owner in an affluent suburb. My plan was to drive the rest of the way to New Orleans and set up shop there. I knew there had been a disaster of epic proportions in the city, but nothing could have prepared me for what it looked like when we arrived. I've seen many, many war zones, destroyed many cities and towns, but none of them were ever on the soil of my own country. What I saw was heartbreaking. It really looked as if an enemy army had invaded this part of the United States and driven away after demolishing the land. The media had even been referring to our fellow American citizens as "refugees" at one point.

Nevertheless, it did seem that the resultant chaos might afford me an opportunity to work as a mole without detection in this world. Anyone could pretend to be anybody in this ambiance and get away with it—for a little while, at least. The Ninth Ward was my first preferred shop site, especially since it had been utterly trashed and abandoned. The place was a desert. It would have been perfect, but upon reconsidering, I'd decided that we needed to be nearer to the living center of things since my mission required access to plenty of persons with weaknesses. Such people could be bought easily. So of course, I chose to set up shop in the French Quarter. There was a building on Rue Burgundy that would work perfectly, and it was a typical New Orleans French Quarter dwelling, divided into apartments with an inner courtyard. I bought the whole affair. After all, it wasn't like the price of real estate was high or anything, and no one was questioning cold, hard cash. Nigel, for his part, was just happy that he didn't have to go back to the orphanage. He was starting to miss our home in the other world, though, as was I. We talked now and then about what she might be doing, but there was work to be done and mooning over home would not help. I put an end to those conversations by finding books that kept the boy interested while I worked.

The cameras and transmitters had not survived the passage, so the next best option was to take pictures and make hard copies. I'd purchased a computer, a printer, and a camera-video recorder in one of the stores that had struggled back into business. I'd also bought a what he referred to as a "camcorder" for Nigel, which also helped to keep him busy. All this equipment came in handy for storing and copying information. I, for my part, wanted to know the state-of-world affairs and spent most of my time in the history portions of their internet, recording, documenting, preserving whatever facts seemed to be the type that could prove invaluable information for The Division to use in making the world a safer place—my world, of course. There wasn't much I could do to help here.

I remember the day I found out about 9/11. The scope of that one destructive act of terrorism utterly stunned me on so many levels. It wasn't just the terrorist act that shocked me so; it was the identity of the man behind it and the way the perpetrators had been so easily enabled to pull it off. I had personally worked with the mastermind of that affair in chasing the Russians out of Afghanistan, and this was the repayment that was going to be given us. I made it a point to take this guy out as soon as we got back.

So far, we were still making nice with the Taliban back home. Good. Keep your friends close and your enemies closer. It was also quite surprising to find that both Iraq and Afghanistan had been invaded, but thank God, that was not my war. All of our best brains in the Think Tank back home felt that there was just no way to achieve anything worthwhile or implement a clean break from something like that. The current mission had to remain my top priority, though, so eventually, I went looking for people who could be twisted into moles and agents. There were plenty of them around. So many who needed help and assistance that was just not coming soon enough. With these conditions being so prevalent, I built a network in less than a month. The value of gold was higher there than expected, but then, it was a time of war. That made it easier to convert a great quantity of my bullion and diamond stash into money and set up accounts in places that were out of the legal reach of this country's government, although admittedly, such places had become fewer since 9/11.

In order to ensure payment without too much personal interaction with them, each of my workers were issued a card that would authorize them a monetary allowance for every time they worked in my behalf. It operated as a debit card paycheck, and the funds for each card were allotted for one preassigned amount per mission upon completion. My people were given a special activation code after their assignments were concluded and checked. The best approach seemed to be to set up a business front and convince some of more nearly honest bankers and potential temporary employees that I was a historical researcher, trying to preserve what I could of the city, and it worked. My "group" was even given a name that went along with its stated purpose. It was known as the Preservation Hall Society. No one was ever hired on a permanent basis; instead, they were all "paid by the job," as it were. For security purposes, very few of the employees were allowed to meet me in person.

Using the mafia model, every one of their assignments were communicated by buffers and other people who were paid to relay an accurate message to still other people. For every success, they were well rewarded, even receiving bonuses for work over and above what was asked or expected. Those who were known to be more (relatively) scrupulous people were given things to do that wouldn't violate their moral code. Of necessity, there were also less-worthwhile citizens in our employ, folks who didn't care what the assignment was, as long as they got paid. These were the ones who were sent to attain information in ways that bordered on being illegal. Still, with all this in place, I needed someone to hold the fort, as they say, while we returned home and made our report.

Of all the individuals with moral frailties in the employ of the PHS, all the people that had been twisted, coerced, or coaxed into serving this arm of the division, my crowning achievement was Bernard "Big Bernie" Syminsky—an optimistic overweight employee of a store that was called "GameStop," a person who'd long hoped for a better life on an alien planet. I knew of these stores because they had existed in my world although the idea was new in that location. It seemed like a logical environment within which to find someone like this. Still, I checked everything there was to check out regarding Bernie: his hopes, dreams, likes and dislikes, past and present behaviors, both of his "friends," as well as his mother's garage where he was living when I found him. Once I had a pretty good handle on what his psychological needs were, I had Nigel do his *otherspace* thing for him a few times, and that pretty much convinced him that we were the "real deal"—aliens who needed his help in saving planet Earth. Cheesy, I know, but it was the only way in this case, and Bernie bought into it with genuine zeal and dedication. He did more to expand our reach than I ever could have.

Facebook was new and limited to college campuses, but of course, Bernie told me he had friends in such locations whose accounts he could make use of. In reality, these were people he'd gone to high school with; they'd gone on to attend local colleges, but he hadn't been able to. Still, he wanted to show his worth, so I allowed him what leeway he needed to get things done. Many talented people slip through the cracks, as it were, because of some social or economic disadvantages; and Bernie happened to be one of them. In a short time, he had set up AOL and instant messenger, with countless names and accounts, and he was generously rewarded. I can honestly say that Bernie's contributions became so totally dependable that I put him in charge of caring for the network when I was away. He was also given leeway to use whatever impersonation, personification, person, or persons he needed to further his assignment of gathering as much historical and political fact as possible without committing any overt acts of espionage. He was truly creative, but between his past choices and current circumstances, this was the only chance he'd ever be likely to get toward being all that he could be, and he knew it, so this was just the right fit for the man. Under his oversight, my mission sped ahead far faster than it ever would have without him.

Every now and then, he would receive a diamond, gold, or cash bonus as an appreciation gift, then buy himself time with an expensive out-of-town call girl who didn't mind having her skin temporarily dyed blue or whatever. The man's quality of life having become much better, he was totally sold. He was also totally reliable. Bernie quit his other job to become my first and only full-time employee.

We also took the time to go see Nigel's old home. It was a disaster still. And, yes, it was the same house as my own, there in Gentilly. The devastation was more mind-numbing in this spot because it really could have been our own home back in my world. I insisted that Nigel take me to the orphanage, a location he hated going back to, and I could see why. The place was a nightmare. A Nightmare that was was pathetically understaffed, and most of the church people who worked there were real psychos. Additionally, there were just too many lost children there for their care to be anything but substandard. When we got to the location, we lay in wait for the villainous Robby Dubois; and when that kid passed by, I grabbed him, dragged him off to the side, and let Nigel watch while he got that belt whipping that I promised. A few serious-sounding threats convinced the hapless youngster to keep his mouth shut and never ever so much as *touch* another little kid. Yeah, I know that seems heartless, but at that moment, Nigel was one of the most important resources that my America had, and keeping his trust was a priority. That action helped out a lot. Besides, the Dubois kid was a really serious bully. I was impressed that Nigel had even been able to hold his own against a boy who was two years older and that much bigger, but he had.

We wanted to get home before late December, but even with Bernie's help, it took longer than I expected to set my mole network up. Since the only thing required from our assets would be information that seemed to be harmless common knowledge, the outfit needed to be structured as some innocuous, unimportant, pacifistic organization that wouldn't attract too much attention from the authorities; and things needed to stay that way. We needed to remain under the radar indefinitely, if possible. Still, there always seemed to be one delay after another. Again and again, different individuals would do things that came close to bringing far too much official consideration to my presence and surreptitious activities. Eventually, Bernie and I came up with what we called a "disclaimer program" for the cards. If anyone was caught, they should be unable to implicate the PHS in any concrete manner, so the cards' magnetic strips would "blank out" under certain preprogrammed conditions. I further made it clear to Bernie that *no* crime against anyone was to be perpetrated by *any* agent acting in our service, unless I personally approved such. No classified or illegal item or information would be accepted although a note would be made if such were offered. It could make us look good to the authorities if those type of people were turned in, but we would also want to know who the seller was and what organization, if any, they represented before taking such action. That type of information could be handy to have later on.

If any of our information-gathering agents deviated, the person's card would be automatically disavowed, and no connection with our network should be evident. Everything was set up so that if the powers that be did uncover us, Bernie would be the ultimate fall guy. I never told him this, but I think he had a pretty good idea of how it would go. My clandestine education on computer technology in this world had enabled me in setting up a system of checks and balances in my financial structure here. It was making money, though not enough to be red flagged by any governmental agency, and Bernie couldn't embezzle any amount that would cripple it. I figured he'd embezzle some, anyway, so I set up a limit that he couldn't get past.

Late January came, and it was finally time to go home. Nigel and I were both chafing to get back. I'd given the passage a lot of thought and decided to purchase welder's goggles and an insulated jumpsuit. It seemed logical to assume that my convulsions after the first passage may have either been the result of some sort of stray unidentifiable current that had hit me or of electrical harmonics in *otherspace*. After all, harmonics could cause seizures for epileptics who stare at computer screens too long. So it just made sense to try whatever I could think of for protection. Something else learned in the trip here.

Additionally, I was going to try to take the camcorder through with me, though having no real hopes of its survival. The micro circuitry within could really be a lot of help in developing materials and weapons back home, even if it burned out on the way. I stuffed three seabags with as much relevant information as I could carry and put more in Nigel's backpack. After that, we went to the wreck that had been Nigel's home and was now owned and being renovated by my "company." It was time to go at last. I knew that the boy was worried about me, but he had also shown his ability to adapt and overcome if the circumstances warranted it. Besides, we would come out of the *passageway* right in my yard, he assured me. He liked my outfit too and wanted one for himself. I told him he'd get one after we got home, and he was ready. He grabbed my hand, and once again, we stepped into *otherspace*.

The Troubled Horizon

There's no way to describe that *in-between* zone to you, Detective Caldwell. Suffice it to say that it was as if the abstract and solid were engaged in pitched battle. A combination war of Dalis, Corberts, and Picassos. I was more than halfway right about wearing the welder's goggles, though. They even allowed my eyes to *see* while within that accursed place, though that may have been more of a disadvantage than not. I didn't lose consciousness this time, but my body was having convulsions when we exited the nether realm between the worlds, though these weren't as violent as before.

Time wobbled; reality drained away then spun back in. We emerged exactly where we'd hoped, and suddenly, I was on my knees, unable to quit shaking. Little Nigel was holding both of my hands and calling out, "Colonel! Colonel!" It was daylight; we'd left the other world at 0900 on a day when she was normally off, and as before, it was the same time of day here. We were in my backyard, and I just barely managed to say to Nigel, "Go . . . get . . . her!" He ran for the door, yelling, while I curled into a ball on the grass, shaking. Hearing her voice calling my name was, at that moment, the sweetest sound of my life. My metabolism was beginning to get that shaking under control, allowing me to rise to my knees, and now her arms were around me. She was crying. I wanted to, but wouldn't, not in front of the boy. I held my head up, caught his eyes, and managed to say, "I'm . . . p-proud . . . of . . . you, . . . N-Nigel." He beamed.

The Division sent my unit over as soon as possible. For them, that meant arriving about fifteen minutes after I got home. Originally, an agent had been posted to watch the house when Nigel and I left, but after three months with no communication, the division had very nearly been ready to give me up as lost so the agent was pulled just one week prior to our return. That's why it took so long for them to arrive. They took Nigel and me to headquarters, and yes, my wife insisted on accompanying us. It was my turn to be poked and prodded, and she wanted to make sure that we would be well. They took our seabags and immediately sent them over to the Think Tank. The poking and prodding gave them a wealth of information concerning the effects of *otherspace* travel on a man who did not have Nigel's natural ability. For some reason, he himself had proven immune to any adverse reactions from making that trip, but for me, it was different. They estimated that I had survived only because of my particular DNA. To the best of their understanding, the nil zone seemed to destroy electrical conductors (biological as well as metallic) by rapidly draining their internal energy, pouring in more electrical energy, then draining it out again; and apparently, this occurred with a wavelength-type frequency. The reaction somehow caused the victim's nervous system to misfire or burn out, depending on the person's metabolic makeup. Still, some people's bodies could store more electricity than others. I made a good capacitor, I guess. Someone else may not have.

My camcorder had, of course, not made it, but everyone was surprised to find that Nigel's had. He'd instinctively known to find some rubbery substance that was used in the other place for insulating industrial pipes and wrap his camcorder in it. The Think Tank therefore surmised that if my jumpsuit had been insulated with rubber or some nonconductive polymer instead of that cottony rayon crap, I might have been able to make the passage without any ill effects at all. A duly insulated and specially designed outfit might allow me to move electronics between the worlds, they further postulated. My next journey to Nigel's home was going to be different, I could see. The Division also wanted to assemble a MIST - trained team, equip them, and send them with me on the next trip across the zone. Because those men would be stationed there for an indefinite period, they were all to be single, with no tendency toward forming attachments, and unshakably, unquestionably, even fanatically loyal to the duty they choose. The psych doctors were already starting work on the guys.

In the meantime, that power struggle in the top ranks had also gotten worse, and as a result, there was talk of taking Nigel away from us, thereby cutting down on my importance to the mission. Someone was trying to edge me out. They even had an agent try to initiate a friendly relationship with him in an attempt to gain his trust, but the boy hated him so much that he disappeared into *otherspace* and came out in our backyard, leaving the agent standing slack-jawed in the hallway at our New Orleans headquarters. One thing I will always be able to say about Nigel, he is a good judge of character.

I'd also brought back the most comprehensive almanac available from the other world. Admittedly, Detective, the information inside did come in handy with regard to some of Angeline and my personal monetary investments, and I chose to use it accordingly, having no illusions as to the eventual poverty that most loyal federal agents come to. Should I not survive to the golden years, I was determined that my wife wouldn't have to deal with economic problems; for I'd seen what was happening in Nigel's world, a future version of the one we lived in. I'd seen tomorrow, and there was, in my view, no sound basis for any ill-founded hope that this world's political element would make life any better for its veterans than that one's had. Thus, I'd brought two of everything informational back, one for using to our advantage and the other to turn over to the Think Tank, who used the almanac to start their analysis with the weather patterns (and other things), in order to see if they matched. They did. Certain historical events matched the ones here also, and even though some of the minor participants in those events were different, the major players were the same with the same results. So the big brains saw this as a pretty good sign that our worlds were on parallel paths.

The Division therefore decided that I should go back and return with more historical data, especially where terrorist organizations, domestic and abroad, were involved. Not a problem for me, I assured them, but Nigel would not at all be likely to want to return. He liked being here, where he had a safe, secure home and semblance of family. They told me to find a way to make him want to help, so I did. I convinced the kid that we needed him as a "junior adjutant to the commanding colonel." They even made a miniature dress uniform for him to wear whenever he came to the building. The thought of going on adventurous missions to different realities totally caught his imagination. He was convinced that we were also going to explore "all the *other* worlds," as he called them, not just his. But we had to start somewhere, I told him. (*All the worlds?* I thought.) He bought it. My wife wasn't too happy about the whole affair, but the simple fact was, if we didn't make the most use of his talent, someone else would. They would have found a way to take the boy and place him with foster parents who would have no problem with doing whatever the government asked, as long as they got their pay and perks. I reminded her of this, and while she chose not to openly go along with it, she also chose not to fight me about it either. At the same time, however, she reminded me of her original promise when it came to Nigel.

All matters in my home having been settled, The Division set about the business of assembling two teams. One would be assigned to deal with threats foreign and domestic, dangers extant and menaces to come, while the other was assigned to make excursions into *otherspace* and beyond. Each team had a redundant, so altogether, there were four teams involved in activities springing from information gathered out of Nigel's world. The only one who couldn't be replaced was Nigel himself.

It really was a good thing for them that the boy was too young to understand his value to national security. He could've demanded just about anything and gotten it. But Nigel has never been that kind of person. Not then, not now. He always was too much the hero type. Very much the same as I was at his age. But by the time he wandered into my life, all those missions and years as a shadow warrior had taught me that there are moments when you can't be a hero. There were times when I had to be a villain, a liar, even pretend to be a coward. Whatever served the best interests of my country was what I would be. It's strange, sometimes, how a little twist to the proverbial left or right in someone's life can make two people who have every reason to be exactly the same into totally different individuals. He still has that "hero" mentality, Nigel does. I fear, sometimes, that it'll be the death of that boy.

I was home for six months while the great and mighty plans of the Think Tank were being put into action. During that time, I discovered the source of the disunity in The Division. It had begun within the Think Tank itself. When The Division originally put that group together, they'd searched high and low for the most mentally talented, unquestionably bright people in the United States and eventually created a collection of the greatest American minds of that time. The problem, though, was this: with great minds often come great egos. So while they were wonderfully effective, the Think Tankers could also be excessively petty and capable of astonishing guile. Sometimes their egos would not just allow but would also seem to *force* them to go to shocking lengths in their pointless games of one-upmanship.

The worst two were Blacen Muldowney and Devin Craine, probably because they were also the smartest pigs in the pen. The Tank had been divided into two departments, and each of these fellows were in command of one of the two wings. Muldowney was a microphysicist and a miniaturization engineer (whatever that was), and the man had all the moral fortitude of a wild hog. He was a licentious, narcissistic, pretentious fellow who'd had the good fortune of having been born the only child of a very wealthy family. Blacen was a handsome man of average height, about six feet or so, with a carefully combed head of wavy dark hair. He wore the most expensive clothes and colognes that money could buy, as well as one of those skinny mustaches that men who are overly proud of their personal prowess with the ladies tend toward wearing. I believe, though, that most of the time the women encountered by guys like him wind up wishing these fellows would get emasculated.

His family's prosperity and influence may have been the only reason why Muldowney wasn't doing time in some grubby prison as a convicted sexual predator. He had an almost uncanny knack for detecting and exploiting weaknesses in women and loved the idea of defaming, deflowering, and/or demoralizing those who were most respected among their peers. Most of his off-duty time seemed to be spent in the many cathouses and other establishments for indulgence in carnal deviancies that thrived within New Orleans. He often bragged to fellow coworkers (usually the males since it seemed that he also wanted all of them to admire him as the "alpha dog" as some say) about how he could corrupt even the best of women. Of course, this piece of breathing slime had even decided, while I was in Nigel's world, to try his hand at adulterating *my* marriage. Honestly, he couldn't have resisted that temptation had he wanted to. Muldowney was *impelled* to try to put himself in the position of "top dog," even if the results of his efforts caused him many personal pains. When it came to his ego, he just couldn't always think that far ahead. The man showed up at my home unexpectedly one day, claiming to have brought flowers for my wife only as a thoughtful gesture, to see how she was holding up, he said.

She'd met Blacen Muldowney the first time we took Nigel to the division and immediately knew what he was. She found him despicable. When she politely declined the flowers and asked him to leave, he actually tried to step into the house instead, but having her point her Mauser M2 at his face backed him down. I know, because I saw the taped interchange between them. Blacen always was too wrapped up in himself to discern when his own stupidity was endangering his life. Even then with my girl pointing a pistol at his face, the man's anger at being rebuffed seemed to make him want to force his way into our home, regardless. Just at that time, Sergeant Puccini, one of my MISTmen who was assigned to the house that day, appeared behind Muldowney and snatched him, with a noticeable lack of gentleness, out of my doorway, tossing him onto the sidewalk. With plenty of intimidation and no friendliness whatsoever involved, he ordered that piece of dirt off the property. Blacen was stupid, not dumb, so he left with no further resistance. After that story got around the Think Tank, though, he wore his bruised ego like a black eye for the next month.

Devin Craine, for his part, was very different, in physical appearance at least, from his rival. As unto all men with that last name it seems, Devin Craine was tall and thin, with a neck exhibiting a prominent Adam's apple. According to his psych evals, he had an inexplicable hatred of any type of sexuality, viewing intimacy as a tool that could and without a doubt be used against him and occasionally by him against others. The kid had a nice head of brown curly hair that irritated bald guys whenever they saw him and was a bit more of a handsome fellow than most tall and skinny lab geeks, but none of that meant as much to him as being a DNA whiz of some sort did. Biowarfare theory had been his specialty before the Tank, but because most of his proposals were only hypotheses and conjecture, very few people paid any serious attention to his ideas. Resultantly, he constantly felt marginalized and ignored. That only made him more miserable. Being hired by the federal government, however, put more resources at his fingertips than he'd ever dreamed of having access to, which allowed him to develop many of his ideas. The majority of them worked out well, too. Things changed for him afterward.

Unlike Muldowney, he'd had no advantages beyond a hardworking mother whose husband had abandoned the family when his only son took sick, seemingly to the point of death. Craine was nine when that happened. For the rest of his youth, the young man was bullied and teased. Even otherwise kindhearted girls beat him up. Still, his mother was there for him. She worked job after job, sometimes two or three at a time, paying for his college education for as long as she could afford it; and when it seemed that she was about to run out of money, Craine was noticed by a forward-thinking Division recruiter who could see the genius in him. Our agency took care of his educational fees in return for Craine's involvement in developing certain projects. He was one of a very few persons who went straight to work after earning his first college degree. Still, Craine was talented beyond even his own realization. His IQ for the development and use of biological weaponry as well as the incorporation of that science into military application was stratospheric. He was also mean beyond belief. In his opinion, it was the magnitude of his genius that propelled him into his position, and anyone who could do what he could with the power of natural science deserved the adulation of the masses. The man had no gratitude whatsoever for the effort and sacrifice his mother had put forth in his behalf. Actually, he seemed to hate both of his parents, as well as the rest of the human race. In his estimation, the entirety of humanity was one rung above bathtub scum; and in his own words, he alone, through his personal brilliance, had earned the authority to correct their evolutionary path. The boy was a megalomaniac with something missing in the middle.

Despite this, Devin Craine was a decent enough administrator to be put in charge of one of the two research branches of the division. He despised his people though, treated them badly, and would have treated them even worse; but his fear of official reprisal kept him in check during that time, as much as Muldowney's dread of my reaction to his attempt on my doorstep kept *him* in check. When we got back, *that* one tried his best to disappear into the backdrop of everyday life in the division, I'll tell you. No matter. I cornered Blacen while he was sneaking back in from a two-hour lunch break one Friday and had a deeply significant heart-to-heart talk with the man. He had to go home, change his pants, and take two weeks' vacation after that.

During that time, I cut orders for Sergeant Puccini to perform a clandestine investigation with the goal of uncovering whatever mischief may have been afoot within the tank. Something strange was going on between Muldowney and Craine, you see. It didn't seem like much more than petty foolishness at first, though. They'd hated each other immediately when they met, and their teams were constantly in bitter competition with each other. Not that that's such a bad thing. Even in military training, we try to instill a sense of competition in our men. It produces good results in most scenarios. But those two lab rats had sown dissension the way a farmer sows corn. They couldn't stand each other, but they couldn't do without each other either. No matter how wonderful their individual accomplishments, it would be worthless in one's eyes if it didn't upstage the other. Anything that one would do, the other would have to outdo. In the beginning, some very amazing advances resulted and upper-level management in The Division was thrilled; but for the geeks who worked in the tank, the results were not as positive.

Our agency had an employee assistance program, and one or another of those poor people were constantly talking to the motivational department about how their bosses' antipathy were causing them so much undue stress. Again and again, the human resources people sent advisories to the two heads of the tank, but for the employees, nothing ever changed. Then again, that may have been because the division's leadership was so unconcerned and incompetent in understanding the people who worked under them. Craine and Muldowney were also essentially unconcerned with the effect their shenanigans had on everyone else. There were times when the psych people in our human resource department had to jump through hoops, as the saying goes, to keep their best and most brilliant minds on board. Nobody up top wanted any of the talent to walk out of the Think Tank. Not as if they would have survived had they chosen that route, anyway.

Hindsight is twenty-twenty vision, Detective Caldwell; and in hindsight, I think a couple of my men should have been secretly ordered to make both of those self-aggrandizing troublemakers disappear. Would have prevented a lot of grief and literally saved a world of human lives. We thought we needed them, though. National security. Keeping ahead of the bad guys and all that guff. We didn't realize the seriousness or the nature of the real threat coming from inside the Tank. We'd learn a lot more later.

Director Rocklin, for his part, thoroughly believed that Muldowney was his man in the Think Tank. The assistant director, on the other hand, was close with Craine. Unbeknownst to me at the time, those two, Muldowney and Craine, were really the ones running the show. They'd reversed the status quo of command and rank, somehow managing to pitch their bosses against each other in the process. This was a masterpiece of manipulation by two men who were far more brilliant than their victims. The divisive trend had all along become more and more obvious, but it seemed that Rocklin had it under control so there was no need for me to stick my fingers into that particular pot, and this was too far along for me to correct it alone in the short time that I wound up having there. My observations on the schisms forming within the lab rat cage, as well as some recommendations as to the best way of managing the problem before things got too far out of control, were, nevertheless, included within my report to the man at the top; and Rocklin assured me that he'd follow those suggestions since they were the best he'd gotten so far. Thus comforted, I settled on my own work, leaving the Think Tank up to the boss. He would, of course, handle it with efficiency and capability, just as he always had.

I was wrong, but there were other things that had to be done. My unit was ready to go, and it was time for the next mission. For this expedition, the troops were outfitted with jumpsuits made of a thin nonconductive polymer fabric. Each outfit had an attached full-head cowl that the men would pull over their faces before we entered the nil zone. All were armed with M-14 assault weapons as well as their personal handguns, then bugged with transmitters and cameras covered in the protective rubbery goop. The division wanted us to enter our side in my backyard and exit the other side in the backyard of Nigel's family home in Gentilly. The PHS owned that place now in the other world, and that meant more privacy. We were to commence at 0300 because the late hour would likely mean less eyes observing. The team consisted of six guys, all of them tough and ready. Nigel and I would make eight.

When we got to my house, I went in to dance with my wife and say goodbye. She was so beautiful that morning. Sade's "Your Love Is King" was playing on the system, and her perfume was so sweet. She held her tears as she sang softly along and held me as tightly as I was holding her. We did that before every mission. There was no way to know if the last time we saw each other would be the last time we'd ever see each other, and it was important that before the mission commenced, she'd know how much I truly loved her. The song ended, another one began, and we held on just a few moments longer before duty called and I had to answer. Time to wake Nigel. Time to go. The boy was a little grumpy and didn't want to do anything at that moment, but the promise of a McDonald's happy meal was thrown in, and he was ready. Nigel was very sleepy though, and it would be hard to keep him awake throughout the passage, I thought, so I wanted to move fast. He did too and asked if we could drive there. I didn't think that was possible, though, because we had moved through on foot before. But then, I wasn't the reality walker either. It was worth a try, I told him.

So all of us piled into a specially made van, pulled our hoods (Nigel being the only exception), and I took off, driving way slower than normal. The boy asked me to go faster, and I did. Suddenly, we were in *otherspace* again—and out. Just like that. Amazing. The implications were astounding. *We could bring vehicles!* This mode of movement between the worlds could be faster as well as safer, and amazingly, the vehicle suffered no damage. Why, I can't say. That's still a mystery.

———

When we came out of the *in between*, we were down the street a little ways from the house, still headed in the direction that we'd been going when the boy opened the *passageway* from our world, so I did a U-turn and headed back. Once we made it into the backyard, the van from our reality was put in the garage. It would be better to use the Hummer I'd bought while we were there, as it was a civilian vehicle, with tags and registration that made it legal. My team had arrived in Nigel's world in the same month, on the same day, and the same hour, twenty years ahead of our own world. I had the men go to their racks immediately and wanted to put Nigel in his own room. He didn't want to stay in the house, though. It had, after all, been where he lived with his family and was the place where he thought they died. I hadn't realized how much it tortured him being there. Out of consideration for his feelings, I decided to take him to the building on Burgundy. He could sleep better there. I'd wait till the next day to meet with my XO. We had a lot of work to do.

TRAGEDY IN SILHOUETTE

"Wait a minute, there, Colonel," Roan interrupted the older man's narrative. "You're telling me that our government knew about this kid all these years, and it's been kept secret?"

"Yes and no, Detective Caldwell," the colonel replied wearily. "Your government has only known about Nigel since we brought him here. Neither he nor I are originally from this place."

Roan stared. "Then how did—"

"How did we wind up here?" the colonel completed his question. "Once again, Detective Caldwell, I can tell you that it was blind coincidence, coupled with the evil that men do for lusting after the power of Nigel's abilities that landed us two worlds away from what used to be my home."

Roan thought for a moment. "You know, old man, when all this started, I was only supposed to be helping the DA get to the bottom of a question regarding your boy Nigel's involvement in the death or disappearance of Dana Lacy. He's told me a completely different story of his origin, though. He said nothing about his family being lost in some hurricane or himself being some superkid associated with the military. So how am I to believe either of you? You could both be lying, and as far as the conference call with 'Mr. Vice President,' well, I've seen all kinds of fraud."

The colonel stood, walked over to the wall, and pushed a button. All the screens and monitors disappeared as the plush furnishings returned from whatever nook or cranny they'd rotated to, leaving the one large plasma screen on the wall and restoring the expensive penthouse look to the room. After doing so, he went to the bar, poured himself a drink, and stood in silence for a little while longer. Thunder boomed again above the room's skylights. Occasional flashes of light through the windows cast more luminosity on his face. Viewing the man in those circumstances evoked a weird sense of familiarity within the detective, as if he'd met this person somewhere before. Suppressing that sensation, Roan thought, *He's asking himself how much of the truth he can tell me. If this is all as important as he claims, he's got to give me something more to go on.*

"Dana Lacy is not dead," The Colonel said after a while. "There was an attempt on her life, and Nigel saved her. They fled into *otherspace,* and we have not seen her since."

"What happened to her?" Roan asked. His captor turned to look at him, and there was a hint of dangerous anger in the man's eyes as he spoke. "She was assaulted in her own home. As near as we could tell, the assailants were waiting for her when she entered. They expected her to go in through the front door, but for some reason, she entered the back door instead. They jumped her when she went to put her things away in the front room. She fought back. Young Ms. Lacy was bleeding from a blow to her face when Nigel appeared on the scene. His arrival spelled the end of the fight as well as, quite possibly, the end of the attackers. All the evidence seems to indicate that Nigel seized Dana out of their clutches, dealt with them, then kicked the back door off to facilitate his escape with Dana. We believe that the reason he exited in that fashion was because there was someone waiting out front. Someone that Nigel did not wish to confront."

"Maybe your knight in tainted armor was just outnumbered, Colonel. Why else do you explain his kicking out the back door to run away?"

The Colonel stared at Roan for a moment, and it seemed that there was a hint of laughter—or maybe pride?—in his eyes as he answered, "You have no idea what the number of enemies would have to be in order for Nigel to have to flee a battle in such a hurried fashion. I do. I *know* what mettle he is made of, and I have never fought beside a more capable and combat-qualified marine."

Roan had to mentally "take a knee" as they say in boxing lingo for a moment after that answer. *Wait a minute, all the military records that I saw indicated that this kid never saw battle. He was too sick or too much of a screwup. But this colonel guy acts as if the boy was the next James Bond combined with Sergeant York. So far, nothing he's said has added up. But that's beside the point for what I need to know. I need him to get to whatever he was trying to say to keep me on board. He hasn't explained how a door could be kicked out with no shoe imprint being left in it, nor has he mentioned anything about that stealth suit. He'll expect me to ask about the lack of evidence on the door's wreckage, but maybe he isn't aware of how much I already know and he wants to get me to start blathering out revealing questions.*

"Well then, who tried to kill Dana, and where did he take her?" Roan asked. *I won't ask the obvious questions—he's waiting for that. I'll just keep him waiting. Maybe it'll throw him off balance, just for a second. Of course, this guy probably hasn't been off balance since he wore diapers.*

The Colonel smiled, very slightly. "They were not trying to kill her, it seems. We believe that the objective was her capture, nothing else. Things probably got out of hand when she put up resistance. She knew who sent the men that ambushed her. She knew that there would be someone else waiting out front, and what's more, she knew the person's identity. Very, very well."

The detective sat upright. "What are you saying?" he asked.

The Colonel looked at him for a silent moment. "I'm saying that the person behind the attack was Major Robin Lacy. Not the man who fathered Dana, though she was unaware of that fact. This man came from Nigel's home world, although neither of the younger people knew it on that occasion. He took our major's place and has been operating as a mole for an undetermined length of time. He was also the person who first reported Dana as having gone missing, and his comments to the investigators were meant to cast all possible suspicion on Nigel. He'd hoped to have a potentially valuable asset turned over to his personal custody as a prisoner. That's why he posed as an NCIS agent when talking to your district attorney. The man never knew that he was discussing case information with a double of Dana's own father."

Roan asked, "Didn't you tell me that only Nigel and Dana could do this 'crossover' thing?"

"That is true, Detective," The Colonel answered. "But not too long ago, we made a major breakthrough on a technology that will allow travel between the worlds for people without that natural ability. All we need is a bit of Nigel's DNA to make it work. Our major, uncharacteristically, crossed over without backup while testing it, and recent events have shown that he may have been captured or killed and replaced."

"And you think this man may represent a danger to your top secret plans, right? So why do you need me involved?" Roan asked. *This rabbit hole is getting deeper. Sounds to me like they lost control of it all. Maybe he thinks he can use Nigel to sweep in and put it all back together.* Once again answering as if he could hear thoughts, the colonel said, "It's not that we expect Nigel to sweep in and fix it all or anything like that, Detective. But he trusts you, which means that you represent our best chance of bringing him onboard voluntarily, and his abilities can be formidable when he's motivated to use them. But in order for us to access the gamut of his power, his use of it in our behalf must be willing."

"So you think I can talk him into helping you handle this multidimensional threat, huh? So why me and not you yourself? It seems at the moment that you have a more fatherly relationship with him than I ever will."

The Colonel looked at his feet for a moment. "Because he doesn't trust me anymore. There were some . . . things . . . that were done with Nigel, and as far as he is aware, I *had* to be the one who authorized them. He has recently discovered part of the truth, and heaven only knows what he believes was my role in all of it. He wouldn't so much as speak to me right now, no matter what was at stake." *He doesn't want to tell me everything,* Roan thought. *But I'm not going into this business without knowing. Secret agent crap is dangerous enough as it is, and this "colonel" has already indicated that he's willing to use people and pitch them.* "Let's get some things straight here, Colonel. You need me, but you also tend to use people like soap and pop them like bubbles when you're done.

"Before my getting involved with anything, I want to know *everything*, or I can't help out. You may be able to buffalo me into jumping on this bandwagon you've got going, but you can't *make* me do the job well. If you want my best work, you've got to hand over everything that I need to work with. And I'd rather not disappear after all this is over. Provide an assurance of my future safety. Something tangible, faxed, delivered, or e-mailed to an address that I give you. I won't be a person that you can rely on if after we save the whole wide world, there's a distinct possibility of my disappearance, and the way it looks right now, you're not that guy who can be relied on to value *my* life."

In response, The Colonel sat down in a very comfortable-looking chair right across from Roan. For a moment, he appeared lost in thought, sitting there in the universal armchair thinker's pose, occasionally staring at the detective as if seeing him and at the same time seeing someone or something from a time past. After a moment, he came to a decision.

"I'm the person who arranged for Nigel to be briefed on you while you were interviewing him in that nuthouse. Some of my agents even smuggled your file in to him there, Detective Caldwell." He started, "I requested your involvement in this case, and my sources persuaded the DA to put you on it. Do you care to know why? Yes, I thought you would. To be quite frank, Roan Caldwell and Nigel *already* have history. He learned to trust you or someone very, very much like you a long time ago, during one of the many episodes in his life. Don't look so surprised, Detective. Didn't it occur to you that you too might have a counterpart or counterparts in at least one or more of the many, many different alternate realities that Nigel has access to? Although he isn't entirely sure why he trusts you, I am. Your personality in every place is the same, so it goes without saying that you'll keep your word according to your sworn oath. That's why I have no intentions of making you 'disappear' if we succeed in what must now be done. You . . . meant a lot to the boy in another place, and your face was the only one he trusted there. Besides, if we fail, it won't matter, anyway. The quality of life for any survivors in this reality would become much, much worse." Roan felt a chill at that.

The Colonel spoke on. "My answer is no. I won't give you anything that could be held over the head of this government just so you can be assured of your life. You'll do your best work, regardless, because you never could stop yourself from caring; and because if you don't, many lives may be lost when such an outcome could have been avoided. It's who you are."

The Colonel downed his drink in one shot, sat quietly for a moment, then resumed. "But I will give you my word as a man, as a marine officer, and as a representative of the President of the United States of America— that you will be allowed to return to your life after you have done all you can to serve in this crisis. That's all you'll get. And as I have previously told you, Detective, you're not being offered the option of refusing."

Roan was, once again, stunned. *I'm there, in these other places or worlds? ME? What about Laura? My little girls? They could be* alive *out there somewhere, in some other place, but if they are, then so would I be, so there would still be no way that . . .* His eyes glazed over with the ramifications of what he heard. *He knew me? But it seemed . . . how could he hide that so well? Wait a minute, Roan! When did you start believing all of this garbage? Nothing's been proven. Laura's gone. Giselle and Marjorie are gone. Even if this stuff were real and they were alive in some alternate dimension, they still wouldn't be mine. They'd belong to a different me, someone like me, but not me—I can't let myself think this way. My mind has to be in the here and now. Focus, Roan, focus. Put the possibilities out of your mind and move on with the realities. The here and now. The here and now.* Internal crisis settled, Roan came out of his mental reverie. The Colonel was still sitting across from him, staring with an owlish look that seemed to border on concern. *He knew what that thought would do to me*, Roan realized. *I really hate mind games.*

"Why?" Roan demanded, his voice and eyes as hard as flint. "If you know me as well as you claim to, why are you trying to play games with my head?"

The Colonel leaned forward. "Because the ultimate moral challenge is to be able to *take* what you want by force, but to refuse to do it that way because it wouldn't be *right*. You would love to go, find your lost beloved, and take them back, even if it means the death of another man who wears your form. But Roan Caldwell is a moral man, and both of us needed to know that about you."

"Thanks for the synopsis, Master Splinter, but that wasn't what I was asking about."

"What were you inquiring about, then, Detective?"

"Why isn't Nigel aware of the fact that he has encountered another version of me before?" The Colonel's eyes widened slightly. "Anger's showing in those eyes, Colonel sir," Roan said. "You said that *some things had to be done with Nigel*. What did you do? Burn the kid's brain out?"

Once again adopting his thinker's pose, The Colonel answered calmly, "No. I didn't 'burn the kid's brain out.' The Division had his memories altered. Some of them were erased later, but that was not my doing."

"Why did you allow it, then?" Roan asked, "Why would a man who blathers on about 'moral right and wrong' do that to an *innocent child*?"

"Because Nigel was not like other innocent children," The Colonel answered with a steely firmness. "The things he could do meant life or death for thousands, maybe millions. We knew that. Any of our enemies, foreign or domestic, might have known that. His existence was one of our most important classified secrets, and we needed to have a handle on his whereabouts at all times. The Division worried that the constant deployments to the world of his birth may one day have caused the boy to want to return to remain there. So Rocklin had the Think Tank work on a process that could target and eliminate certain pathways of memory, in preparation for future application on Nigel. They didn't want him to remember anything that may have made him want to choose his own reality over ours.

"However, The Division had also made a grave error in their estimation of the extent of my loyalty to king and country in areas where that duty might conflict with my love of family. And make no mistake, sir, the boy was family, both to my dear wife and me. Nigel had been legally transferred into our custody, which meant that authorization from both of us would be needed for any medical procedures. That arrangement was precipitated as a precaution in case any of the common accidents or illnesses of childhood should have befallen the boy, and civilians in the medical field have to be the ones to treat him. In such a situation, we were expected to only allow whatever would have been necessary at the moment and refuse permission for any deeper involvement of civilian doctors. What this meant for the division, however, was that they too would have to have our legal consent before they could initiate any medical treatments on Nigel either. They spoke to us of the memory alteration they'd hoped to inflict upon our boy and even gave us permission forms to sign. We refused to give *any* permission. Not even for *one* treatment. We reasoned that if the wrong people got their hands on him, he'd never have any chance at even an excuse for a normal life, anyway. But that didn't stop them. Things that need to be done for the good of the state trump all other concerns. We're wasting time with this part of it, though. You asked for everything, Caldwell. There are still other things I need to tell you about."

"What 'wrong people' are you talking about, man?" Roan's voice was rising; he could hear it himself, but honest anger was fueling this, so he didn't feel like stopping. "I mean, it seems to me that there couldn't have been too many other people more wrong than the ones that had him! What were you people doing that some foreign power *wouldn't* have done?"

The Colonel bowed his head for a moment, rubbed his eyes with his fingers, then looking at Roan, quietly answered, "I wasn't worried about any *foreign* power. It was *our* power. The things that may have been done with this boy had he been taken and placed in any other person's custody were too much for even me to consider allowing. He is, after all, a member of what is considered, here as much as there, a minority ethnicity. Sadly enough, such people were not always as highly valued as others, no matter what their capabilities." A leaden silence dropped between the two men at the implications of that statement.

"Okay, so it's not too much better where you come from than here. Racism lives. I get that. Still, you've got a story to finish. Finish it. I'm getting the impression that we need to get this situation under control before it escalates. I have to know what happened between you and him, what made you come here, and what the hell is the big threat you're so afraid of, because even a rookie could see that the big bad Colonel is afraid of *something*," Roan replied.

The Colonel studied Roan for a moment. He held his glass up to the light and stared into the amber liquid as if searching for a softer time or a sweeter memory. Speaking introspectively, he began. "You know, Detective Caldwell, I used to think that scotch was an old man's liquor. Swore I would never take up drinking the stuff. I guess I'm an old man, now. It happens to everyone. We are subject to time throughout all of our years, and time changes us. Nigel too. It happened with him. He grew bored with his young-boy games, as he inevitably would. In retrospect, it's obvious that I should have been more vigilant. When we took the first infiltration team in, Nigel and I stayed in the French Quarter. Bernie was overjoyed to see us again but wasn't entirely happy about my decision to retire him. The Division had given me everything needed to set our organization up very well financially, so Bernie received a twenty-million-dollar severance package that included a new identity, a very nice villa located in the Italian countryside with surrounding acreage and an all-female service staff, something he'd always wanted. Feeling no further unhappiness about leaving us, he packed his bags and hit the road."

***

In retrospect, I can see that he could and should have been retained to keep an eye on Nigel, as everyone else quickly became very busy. My squad had to be trained in their respective duties, the whole PHS network needed to be restructured and updated, investments had to be checked, duty rosters had to be created and applied, our troops needed day-to-day regimens outlined, and on and on. Meanwhile, the boy was left to his own devices for much of the time. He began spending a lot of time out of doors, wandering off somewhere. That was a security lapse that should not have been allowed. We'd had tracers sown into all of his garments, so his general location was never a mystery, but since we were positive that his existence as a natural phenomenon was yet unknown to the powers that be in his own reality, he was still not under complete surveillance during those absences.

When I finally noticed how long he was staying away and began wondering where he was going, my XO assigned a man to find out. He followed the boy and returned to report that Nigel had, seemingly, found a sweetheart back in the neighborhood where the orphanage was. Or at least a little female playmate. My MISTmen found it quite amusing, that the boy would have a "sweetie" at his age. They called him "Baby Marine," and that eventually became his nickname among them. Meanwhile, the kid was soaking all the extra attention in and thinking that was the greatest thing ever. It all encouraged him to keep on visiting her. I was, however, not amused. Nigel wasn't an ordinary kid. He was a national resource, and the secret of his ability needed to be protected. Since he should have been in school, anyway, I assigned Sgt. Lucius Carver, one of my most intelligent MISTmen, to be his tutor/bodyguard/teacher and keep the boy out of sight, under the radar of school officials.

So Nigel was, in effect, homeschooled. For all his ability as a fighter, though, Lucius was still a romantic at heart and was a very young man, being only twenty-one at the time. So of course, he developed the habit of occasionally taking Nigel to see the little girl after school hours were over. Oh, he "chaperoned" all the while, but I still wasn't too keen on the situation until my XO explained how that little ditty was improving spirits in the unit.

Our men were hardcore fighters who needed more than just data research and errand-running assignments to hold off the type of mental stagnation that leads to low morale among such people. They were a long way from home and hadn't found a decent fight yet, so the situation was wearing on them, and inventing clever ways of helping their "Baby Marine" see his playmate without being caught by the commanding officer (myself) or the old birds who ran that orphanage had become a game that kept their minds occupied. Okay. I let the thing alone, but still made a mental note to bring less high-spirited guys along on our next excursion into this place. These men had been selected because of their mental acuity just as much as their physical toughness, but now that vehicles could cross the barrier faster and with less risk to their occupants, though, I also knew that the makeup of the next incursion unit could be different. Maybe we could use a coma-inducing drug on some supply clerks and bring them through *otherspace* without their falling apart. Eventually, after a six-month tour, we returned to our own world, leaving my XO in command of the newly overhauled PHS network.

Nigel wasn't in as much of a hurry to get back this time and even began pouting a bit, so I figured it had something to do with his mystery playmate and the way the troops had made such a big deal of it. He kept mentioning too that when he let her know he was going, the little girl told him she'd seen his younger brother, still alive and well—an impossibility since that lad had been lost a long time ago. I made a mental note to ask my wife if she'd have a discussion with the boy on the subject of little girls after we'd arrived at home. Nigel was way too young for that kind of thing, in my opinion. His morose attitude vanished, though, when we arrived back home into our reality. He was happy to see my wife again, and of course, she had taken the time to fix his favorite dinner, following that up with her homemade banana pudding, his favorite dessert. Not a problem for me, as it was my favorite dinner and dessert too.

Later that night, after Nigel had been tucked in and fallen asleep, we sat on our balcony, enjoying a couple of snifters of Louis XIII, a gift from the DOD, congratulations on another successful mission and your promotion to brigadier general, blah, blah, and so on. She'd gotten Sade Adu's latest release, knowing that was my favorite female vocalist, and as we enjoyed the sound of her beautiful voice asking, "Is it a Crime?" I told her how the mission had gone. She was, of course, most interested in how Nigel had done. I reluctantly told her that I'd let things get a little out of control, what with taking care of all the acquisitions that were required by the division, assessing the functionality of the PHS as it was, tracking our agents' actions and movements from the time Bernie (whom she considered a totally detestable person) had been left in charge, setting up bank accounts with our government's financial assets, and on and on. I told her how Nigel had found himself a playmate while I was doing all this. Yes, it was a little girl, I answered, as Sade sang "War of the Hearts" in the background. I told her more about that business and how I'd assigned Lucius to keep track of the little man, and would she, please, discuss this issue with Nigel? After I'd stopped talking, she sat with a contemplative look on her face. A moment passed while Sade finished one song, started another. Then she asked me, "What's the little girl's name?"

I was surprised by that question. Of course, I'd never bothered to find that detail out. Why, the other child may have been planted by *their* government in an effort to find out more about *us* or maybe even gain control of the boy's amazing abilities! I could have kicked myself for not thinking of it sooner. I expressed these thoughts to her, and surprisingly, it really made her somewhat angry. She told me to stop thinking like a soldier (she called me a "soldier" whenever I irritated her) and try to think like a man who still knew what love was. What was her point? I asked, and she glared at me the way a teacher glares at that smart student who keeps on doing dumb things. "I'll talk to him tomorrow," she finally answered and went to bed. Sade was now singing "You're Not the Man." I was feeling stupid. What was I missing?

After reporting for our debriefing the day after, we were informed of several key changes made within The Division during our absence. Devin Craine had gotten himself fired, and apparently, it hadn't been pretty. After receiving anonymous tips, NIS began to suspect him of handing top secret information over to some racially intolerant militia group that he'd somehow gotten close with. Nobody could prove anything, though, because Craine was pretty much smarter than most of the NIS people who were looking into him, and he'd covered his tracks well. The final blow fell upon his federal career only after Muldowney finally went in, broke his pass codes, hacked his computer, and turned the information over to Director Rocklin.

When the powers that be met to assess the damage and pass judgment, Assistant Director McGillian intervened in Craine's behalf, pointing out that the man had not actually passed any real secrets on to this scum. He was just guilty of faulty reasoning in choosing his associates, McGillian argued. So instead of being prosecuted, Craine had just been fired with no disciplinary action to be taken (in other words, no "scrub team" was to be sent to neutralize the man). That dissent, in its turn, began a sort of political melee. Seeing an opportunity in the pursuant chaotic and doubt-ridden environment within the division, Assistant Director McGillian's camp then attempted a blatant in-house coup. This didn't occur until after a long bout of infighting among the top Division officials.

When it was over, and all the dust had settled, Rocklin was still The Division's director while as collateral damage of the Craine affair, McGillian was promoted and put in charge of a military recycling facility in the Antarctic. Craine was given his "get out of the Think Tank free card" as a tradeoff, and shockingly, Rocklin was perfectly willing to let him disappear into civilian life. He was to be allowed to live on, free of any surveillance, provided he never again became involved in any DNA research or laboratory work for the rest of his existence. That to me was the most shocking news of the whole affair. How in the *world* could that decision be justified? I asked the director. Did he realize what a *threat* this man could become? I demanded. What's more, did he really comprehend how much *damage* could be wrought if Craine found the right backing? Still, all this fell upon deaf ears. The director seemed quite confident in his own actions, so I reluctantly let the matter go. Perhaps the boss had some classified ace up his sleeve. Besides, if he found some rich bigot to back his research, Craine *would* turn up again—that would have been a move he couldn't have resisted no matter what. If that resurfacing ever occurred, well, who knows what horrible coincidence could befall him? My MISTmen were on constant lookout.

Blacen Muldowney was posted in Devin Craine's old position, and now, the two main research arms of the Think Tank were consolidated under his command. He had effectively become the sole head of that department and was, surprisingly, very successful at it once he concentrated his thinking above waist level. In combining each department's research projects, they'd come up with what was called "smart micro-weaponry," such as bullets that could home in on a person's DNA signature, bombs that would only detonate if a certain target was in the blast range of where it had been dropped or would totally, completely self-destruct, protecting its precious internal secrets.

Oh, what wonderful ways to kill people, I remember thinking, as the lab rats gleefully explained the capabilities of their newest inventions. *These people never have seen real death.* All this wonderful weaponry, however, had the same weakness: a bit of Nigel's DNA would be needed to activate it.

As things went, it seemed that his DNA carried a specific energy that couldn't be duplicated by any means we had at the time. Therefore, The Division had to satisfy this need by reaping a bit of DNA from the source or in some instances, from bits of blood that the lab had taken for testing. Since there was no way in hell that we'd allow them to take his, the geeks had to satisfy themselves with using the few samples of Nigel's blood that were already in their custody. I was becoming far less popular within the walls of the Pentagon during those days.

Muldowney had also acquired a couple of wonder kids who had begun work on a "cloaking outfit" as he called it. This was to be a uniform that could bend and refract light to whatever extent the wearer needed in order to stay camouflaged. Its effectiveness would be increased by the fact that it too was interwoven with "smart" micro-circuitry, making it responsive to its wearer on a genetic level. The microchips in the camcorders that Nigel and I brought back from our earlier trip had been reverse engineered, and that was one of the reasons why our own advances could be implemented so swiftly. The other world may have been twenty years ahead in its timeline, but it had only been five years ahead in its technological development.

Our own advancements would begin outpacing theirs, eventually, but we weren't there yet.

For that reason, when Crossover Team Alpha returned from its mission, our vehicle was expected to be loaded with gidgets and gadgets that had *any* type of microchip and/or digital technology involved in its makeup. N-Prime, as we called it, was laden with digital toys, recorders, home entertainment systems, all kinds of things and devices. Since we were not even going to think of trying to steal anything that could possibly have drawn the least amount of official attention, especially from the military, these would have to do.

We were interested in advancing our technology, and since our world wasn't that far behind his, it wasn't as if there were some technological chasm that we had to overcome. None of us ever viewed our activities as espionage or theft either, preferring to see it more as a little brother borrowing from an older brother. We recorded the nightly news, Discovery Channel shows, Science channel shows, and collected *Popular Mechanics* magazines by the dozen. All of it went straight to the think tank, and a lot of experimentation time was saved because we could see what planned advancements of our own would work and what wouldn't. We would love to have gotten some eyes on the inside of their military, but taking that type of risk wasn't necessary for what we needed . . . yet. Additionally, Blacen tasked a team of big brains with finding the key to Nigel's "door-opening ability" as he referred to it. Echoing Craine's work, the think tank concluded that whatever this key was, it must've been concealed in the boy's DNA. So Nigel had to be poked and prodded a bit more. He really hated that, as did my wife. She offered to do it for them so that things wouldn't be so hard on Nigel, but Muldowney stonewalled her, rudely and immediately. As I think back, I realize that his reaction to her offer was what first raised some suspicion in my mind regarding his motives. So I *ordered* him to allow her to take the lead in any procedures, and cry as he would, no one in The Division would ever *dare* trying to countermand *my* orders—not even Director Rocklin. From then on, I assigned one of my MISTmen whom he'd never met to follow and observe Blacen Muldowney. Constantly.

Darkness Stirring

A few months passed, and the FBI informed the division that Craine had formally become a member of the "Sons of Freedom," his pet hate group. These seemed to be the only type of people that he could commiserate with. The only people who could revere him in the way that he wanted. I should quit referring to them as a hate group, I suppose, because actually, the Sons of Freedom formed more of an antigovernmental organization that treasured and cherished all the evils that people, American or foreign, hated within this country. They were more like homegrown terrorists by the time Devin hooked up with them.

All along, Craine had been keeping them in the loop on what Nigel could do, and that along with his former position as an employee in a stealth governmental agency was how he kept these types of people interested in himself. But knowing about the boy eventually became too much for them to bear. The "Sons of Freedom" at first tried to make known Nigel's existence to other like-minded groups, but The Division had already seen to it that Craine could provide no concrete proof of Nigel's existence and abilities because anything that he had appeared to be a dead end when researched. After all, Nigel didn't even exist in our world as a child anyway, so there was no means of proving anything Craine said. Actually, if anyone seriously looked into it, they'd mistake Devin Craine for a brilliant nutcase. Resultantly, these other groups laughed the SOF right out of their proverbial front doors. Craine's future activity was now limited to the confines of this one group and its backers. With their credibility among their peers in tatters and now seen as a bunch of crazies by the rest of the intolerance community, the "Sons" were totally on their own. Just like we wanted.

So before his becoming an official member, Craine's pals hatched a plot to kill Nigel, for they felt it was morally wrong that a kid of his particular ethnicity should have this world-walking ability. Why? My best guess— guess, Detective?—is that people like that have so much self-abhorrence until they have to find any possible excuse for believing that some other type of person has to be worth a lot less than they themselves are. They live in constant fear that someone of another race or ethnicity might come along and wipe them off the surface of the earth because they know that they are so little and mean until that's what they would do to themselves, if they could.

Well, anyway, their first, last, and only attempt on Nigel's life was a phenomenal failure. Lucius went to the home of their hit squad's leader, when all six of them were there together, preparing for their mission. The man disappeared out of his own home, and that was the last his cohorts ever saw of him. They claimed that a huge unarmed black man had attacked them and taken their friend. Not a likely story, the detectives decided, since they were, all six, heavily armed at the time of the alleged attack; and in addition, no person could be found who fit their given description and had the ability to do what they claimed this mystery man did. Their own background didn't help any either. While investigating their claims, however, the FBI's agents were able to uncover conclusive evidence against the others in their own team leader's kidnapping and murder. The aforementioned evidence also contained other damning facts: that these men had been involved in some failed domestic terrorist activity involving the kidnapping of a postal employee, whose identification badge they wanted to use in an attempt at firebombing a federal building. Additionally, since they'd crossed State lines after kidnapping their former leader, who had now been murdered, these particular "Sons of Freedom" were headed to a federal prison. Unfortunately, a traffic accident along the journey killed all of them. Only the transport guards survived. Tragic. Don't look at me like that, Detective Caldwell. As I have already explained to you, I have no mercy for enemies of the flag. Not a whit.

After Craine officially joined the SOF, it wasn't long before he became the top man. He was a sneaky and manipulative person in any group dynamic and always had a perverse need to be the alpha dog in every situation (except when it came to Muldowney). So of course, as things went, he wound up in bed with the former leader's wife. The man's personal frailties and vulnerabilities were exposed to Craine during postcoital pillow talk, and he used that information to destroy his target and usurp the lead position. Exposed as a fraud and a thief who had used almost all the money in the SOF mutual bank account for himself, the man was deposed and, of course, Devin Craine replaced him. The man's soon-to-be ex-wife also disappeared somehow. That had to be Craine's doing. For some reason, that man always hated any woman with whom he'd had the slightest intimacy. Like a pack of wild dogs then, the Sons of Freedom turned on their former leader and beat him to the bottom of the bunch. It was too much for the man. I had a NIS agent pick him up as he was on his way to commit suicide. By the time the Think Tank's psych department finished manipulating his head, that guy was totally ours. We planted him right back into the SOF, and Terry Tilden became our eyes and ears within.

Summer vacation rolled around, and with Craine now at the helm, the SOF tried something different. This time, though, they altered their aim. One day, while Nigel and my wife were sitting on the porch, having their usual snow cone, some little kid, who seemed to be aimlessly walking past, decided to spit out some really nasty racist remarks at Nigel. Of course, he was ready to fight over the matter, but she stopped him. She was worried because the kid was a couple of years older and so much bigger than ours. The little troublemaker went down the street and, after a moment, returned with more garbage to spout. This time, though, it was directed at her. That was it. Nigel could take no more. Before she could stop him again, he had jumped on the other boy and was fighting like a professional. She had to pull him off. The larger youngster got a few blows in, but apparently, during his time at the orphanage, Nigel had watched lots of recordings of boxing matches and read plenty of books about various fighting styles whenever he was allowed library time.

He forgot nothing, and it showed. Everything about Nigel was constantly being taped and recorded, so later on, when I watched the footage of that fight, it was obvious how this kid could hold his own against someone like Robby Dubois. He was good. Very good. Born a fighter, I'd say. That recording became the number one hit among the MISTmen, after Lucius asked my permission to show it to the unit. I guess I allowed it because of being pretty proud of the boy, myself. Besides, there were other affairs to oversee, and what entertained the guys was the last thing any of the officers wanted to be worried about, as long as it kept their morale up.

Meanwhile, the intel from Nigel's home world actually began producing mixed results; our Foreign Threat Neutralization MIST team was on the ground in the Middle East, using whatever means necessary to tag individuals who would represent future threats. The Domestic Threat MIST team was doing the same thing at home. The Division had eyes on Timothy McVeigh and Terry Nichols. The FBI was gathering evidence on the Green River Killer, and the Unabomber was already in custody. The Justice Department had several future serial killers under the gun, and a lot of heinous crimes had been prevented before they began. Yet these advances seemed to open the way for different threats that the other reality had never faced. Even though FBI behavioral analysis units were working on ways to readjust the thinking of future serial killers who had not even started yet, new ones were arising from unexpected directions. Our digital technology, however, began blasting ahead at an incredible rate. The information gathered from Nigel's world was paying off. In good ways, mostly, but unfortunately, there were always one or two new problems that popped up. For example, there was the time when one of the members of the Think Tank came up with the idea of capitalizing on future stock market information to earn operating funds for our work.

That move, though illegal, would have taken us out from under the thumb of Congress, he said. We could operate as an ultrasecret self-contained protective unit for our country and, maybe even for the rest of the world, an international police force, he preached. Truthfully, he was really trying to enrich himself with the information that others had risked themselves to attain. Many of his fellow lab rats, as well as a few of our agents, were beginning to think he had a good idea; and as he gained support among his peers, it looked as if another power struggle might be shaping up within the think tank. But the man disappeared before things got too far out of hand. That ended his movement, and it put the rest of the lab rats on the straight and narrow, including (seemingly), Blacen Muldowney.

I still had to work with that scum Blacen, though, regardless of the fact that he was detestable to me. And one day, after we'd reviewed the tank's progress reports, Director Rocklin called me to meet with him. Some disturbing information had come to his attention.

The division had cameras planted on every block within a two-mile radius of my home, and four days after Nigel's fight with the racist kid, they were finally reviewing the input. The cameras followed that boy's progress down the street after his ignominious defeat. He walked two blocks down the road, crying all the way and was approaching a white pickup truck.

Suddenly, the driver's side door swung open, and a very angry man wearing a dirty flannel shirt and a baseball cap, got out and stood, hands on hips, glaring. He yelled something at the kid and seemed about to slap him when the passenger side door opened, and Devin Craine got out. The man, apparently the kid's dad, froze with his hand still held high. Fear crossed his face, and he lowered his arm, backing away. Craine looked at the father for a few moments, his face showing even less emotion than he normally did. Something in his eyes, something that the camera hadn't been able to pick up, had caused a lot of fear in that other man. I know because I've seen that reaction before. Craine then approached the boy, tousled his hair, and drew DNA swabs out of his bag.

He swabbed the boy's hands and bruises with gauze pads, swabbed his knuckles with the giant Q-tip, then put these items into a plastic evidence bag. Giving the child's father a withering look, which caused the man to shift uneasily from foot to foot, Craine returned to his side of the vehicle and got in; the other two did the same. The trio then left. My blood boiled. All along, I had the feeling that the fight had been a setup. Now the person behind it was exposed, as well as the reason for the ruse. Devin Craine wanted some of Nigel's DNA and intended to use any means he could contrive to achieve his aims. As far as I knew, he didn't have access to any lab as advanced as ours, but there had been some intel suggesting that he definitely had the support of at least one very wealthy backer, maybe more. He could build or buy a completely equipped laboratory with the money these people could afford to throw at him. I asked Rocklin why it had taken so long for us to get this footage. A lot of villainous deeds could be done in four days.

After my asking that, the man couldn't look me in the eyes, a first for Rocklin. Then he mumbled that Blacen Muldowney had been given the footage initially. For some as-yet-undisclosed reason, the Think Tank held it for three days before giving it back to the director. I placed Craine on an "open" short list and considered putting Blacen on a secret one. However it could be done, we needed, at the moment, to find Craine before any other federal agency did. He wasn't going to make it to trial, regardless, but The Division needed to clean its own house before things got too much worse.

***

"You mean, your people carried out 'hits'?" Roan interrupted.

The Colonel looked at him without blinking. "I've already told you, Detective Caldwell. I have no mercy, no regrets, no sympathy when it comes to our enemies. I will do whatever is needed to preserve my country and carry out my commission."

"That sounds like a lot of self-righteous drivel," Roan answered, feeling anger well up inside himself. "If you claim to be doing your patriotic duty while you stomp on people's constitutional right to a fair trial, you're no better than the racist mobsters who lynched innocent men on the basis of their own prejudice and then claimed to be doing God's work."

The Colonel continued to stare at the detective. "We don't have the time to argue ideologies, Detective. Some of the evils that were set in motion in my home world are now threatening this one, and maybe others," he said.

"Why did you ever leave your own world, anyway? Why are you here?" the detective wanted to know.

The Colonel remained quiet for a moment, his head down, rubbing his eyes. When he raised it again, Roan could see that the man was close to shedding tears but wouldn't. The Colonel leaned forward again, and his voice became a little more than an angry whisper as he answered with a passion that fairly burned out of his stare. "Because my world *died*, Detective. Blacen Muldowney and Devin Craine set into motion events that *murdered* an entire *world*. Despite that, I too bear a measure of responsibility for those deaths. Six billion people *dead. And why?* Because I *didn't* act as judge, jury, and executioner on the one occasion when *someone* should have. And I am, by God, *not* going to let it happen again."

INTERLUDE II

RETROSPECT

It should have been an idyllic existence. By this time in their lives, they should have been living happily ever after, he having retired and she being semiretired. That had been their plan, or rather, their hope. But he was gone now, lost two years ago, during the last of those classified missions they'd so often used him for.

After he was deceased, life had gone on around her, but not for her. Still, she concentrated on her work: saving lives. To her, it seemed to be the best way that she could honor him and continue to move forward with her own life. He'd been a warrior, and not just any warrior—he was the perfect *warrior. Always had been. Such a man would never have wanted his wife to fade into despair, to quit because of being wounded. In retrospect, she never could understand how their marriage had worked for as long as it did. Maybe it was a love rooted in shared tenacity. Maybe it was just the yin and yang of a lifesaver being so in love with a lifetaker. Maybe their individual natures just created a combined force that was always meant to be.*

Fifty-one years, and it still hadn't been enough time. Many people hadn't even been alive that long. She was twenty-one when they got married, seventy-two when the "Blind Widowmaker" took him away. 'The Blind Widowmaker," she thought. His term. Oh, how she'd hated that idiom, never with a personal disdain, or anything, it's just that such speech seemed so martial and calloused toward those who were experiencing so traumatic a loss.

Then it happened to her. She was working an overnight at the hospital when two generals appeared, seemingly out of nowhere. They said that he was gone, and for a moment, she didn't know where. He was seventy-two! She'd thought that active military duty should have been over for him! She'd been told that the DOD summoned him to DC for a simple consultation! What did they ask him to do? The generals claimed that it was classified; they couldn't talk about it.

But he still had friends inside the shadow world within which he'd long operated. Friends who cared about whether or not his wife knew how his life had ended. Yes, it was one last mission, those friends informed her. One last time when he was the only man alive who could do what was needed. This time, the threat was domestic terrorism. Two mad scientists had arisen, and they were professing to have concocted a DNA-based doomsday disease, even claiming to have tested it on homeless elderly human subjects.

Intelligence reports verified the disappearances of several elderly homeless persons and further verified the fact that when their bodies were found and autopsied, there existed undeniable evidence of DNA degradation that bore all the earmarks of a man-made plague. Moreover, command believed the masterminds were operating out of some homeless community located in the western United States.

Further intelligence reports confirmed that the two terrorists preferred to kidnap elderly persons of African American descent for test subjects because they also believed no one would miss people of that ethnicity and age. That was how her husband had been chosen as the man for the mission. He was deployed because of his ethnicity, his age, and the fact that such egomaniacal villains as these two would never suspect that a seemingly doddering seventy-two-year-old man could be as dangerous as some steely-eyed twenty-five-year-old. The brass, on the other hand, knew better. They'd never measured an upper limit to what he could do in battle. He would go as far as giving up his life before he gave up in combat. They counted on that. He didn't disappoint either. Her husband had performed his final mission in the fashion of the truly gifted hero that he'd always been. No other military man ever ended his career with as many commendations, medals, awards, and promotions as he. Valiant to the end, he had, indeed, broken with deadly force the threat of the two psychotics whose treacherous activities almost plunged the entire earth into World War Three amid accusations and suspicions that their country was involved in development of biological weapons of mass destruction.

After eliminating the traitors and battling his way out of their lair, he found himself left alone without support among enemy henchmen, yet he'd still managed to send more than quite a few of his assailants along their way to the silent halls of nonexistence, as well as get away with a cure for the plague that the two mad geniuses had unleashed in the name of God and country. Almost, anyway.

Communication breakdowns, her contacts had told her. That was why he couldn't get extracted in a timely fashion and at the predetermined location. Still, he'd escaped the pursuers long enough to transmit the most vital information to headquarters. But he was still seventy-two and couldn't run forever. Before he could completely communicate the entire code and by the time his men got to him, he was dying. Too many mortal wounds coupled with too much time spent fighting against enemy empires finally took its toll, and a hero fell. Rest well in the hallowed halls of Elysium, his heartbroken troops declared while crying into their drinks.

The nightmare began shortly after he went. People were dying by the hundreds the world over because although the fighters in the medical field had more than half of the cure to the most frightening and unprecedented disease ever concocted by humanity, there were still pieces missing out of the formula. It seemed, at first, that his final self-sacrifice in the name of the Deity of War had been a pointless failure.

That failure continued until the day his closing transmission hit her subdermal COMM card. It was his last message, conveyed over a private mental frequency that only two people who had spent so many years together could share. Eventually, once she could make sense of the static within her mind, she found it: the rest of the formula that would render a cure for the plague, ending with his last loving expressions, and two other words that he'd never before had to say with such finality—his goodbye to her name. Because it was his dying transmittal, the code words containing the cure seemed to take forever to cut through her grief. But it had, and now humanity might survive.

The mob was moving closer now. Actually, they were more misled religious fanatics than anything else. She could hear their frenetic shouts for blood as they made their way through the hallways of the building, a former school transformed into a makeshift hospital. They'd just bombed the rest of the place out with their Molotov cocktails and were moving toward her little party of survivors with the inevitability of a rising tide. She could also hear the clerics egging them on with their megaphones. They'd even made sure that their mob was armed, with everything from AK-47 rifles to pitchforks, if necessary.

Always the religious leaders, she thought. They always were the ones who pushed governments and masses to murder their fellowmen in the names of their compassionless gods. Here and back home, in the United States, it was always the same story with those people. Same story, different hardhearted gods. After her intent to bring the cure to the Muslim world just as she'd done for the lands of Christendom became public knowledge, the American clergy had instigated a dangerous firestorm within the ranks of grassroots true believers, intensifying those efforts when they realized that she was still determined to move ahead with her mission. No difference between them and these clerics, she thought.

———

The Muslim clerics, on the other hand, were divided in their reception of her attempts. Some welcomed it, but those were the minority. Others chose to ignore her because of her gender. Still others chose to order her death. Why and on what basis she neither knew nor cared, overwhelmed as she was by the very idea that such men would use religion to deny their followers a lifesaving treatment. It was on the order of these that she and her party found themselves in the current situation.

Clergy and clerics be damned. She'd done what was right. *She made up her face for the last time then looked at her reflection in the mirror. If she had to face death, she would at least look her best while doing so. He would have approved. Of course.*

There was yelling in the outer lobby now. She could hear the medical professionals who'd chosen to accompany her—they were fighting as best as they could out there, trying to buy her time to get away somehow, though no one could figure out how to open the solid steel fire escape door that was rusted shut. Still, she did have a "trump card," as they say, that being the presence of some of his former troops Lucius, Archimus, Benjamin, Gabriel, Thomas, and Antoine as her attendants. No one else in the party knew who they were or what they could do. Her small troop of personal bodyguards were checking their knives and weapons now, every one of them having chosen to bring those small extremely powerful machine guns and pistols they favored. She hated the thought of them having to shoot anyone but had also accepted the possibility.

Now the fanatics were in the hallway that led to this large gym, and it appeared that her career, along with her life, would end here, in the heart of her temporary hospital. The double thick wooden doors at the other end of the room were shaking, and their barring wouldn't hold out much longer. There didn't seem to be any way out other than in the company of the Blind Widowmaker. It may be unavoidable, she thought, but she would not go down without a fight. She checked her MauserM2, made sure she had extra ammo, just as he'd taught her. Having agreed on a defensive strategy, her men (yes, they were her *men at this point) began moving into position, for the fanatics were throwing Molotovs and the doors were beginning to buckle. The clerics on their bullhorns could be heard over the angry cries of their followers now.*

The men formed a hexagon with her in its center and prepared for their final fight. How she wished it hadn't come to this. People would die today, and she could not stop thinking of the words of her oath, the Hippocratic oath:

I will apply, for the benefit of the sick, all measures [that] are required.

The door splintered, began to buckle.

I will remember that there is art to medicine as well as science.

The crowd started to surge forward like a wave of bloodthirsty fire ants.

And that warmth, sympathy, and understanding may outweigh the surgeon's knife or the chemist's drug.

Their frenzied eyes seemed to reflect white luminosity from the low-level lighting.

Most especially must I tread with care in matters of life and death. If it is given to me to save a life, all thanks.

She could sense her attendants' tension, could see it in the way their shoulders set.

But it may also be within my power to take a life.

This was going to be costly.

This awesome responsibility must be faced with great humbleness and awareness of my own frailty. Above all, I must not play at God.

Gunfire mixed with the screams of the religious fanatics.

If I do not violate this oath, may I enjoy life and art, be respected while I live and remembered with affection thereafter.

She felt so much regret right now. This was never supposed to go so badly...

May I always act so as to preserve the finest traditions of my calling and may I long experience the joy of healing those who seek my help.

She did not want anyone to die. She was a healer, not a killer. In a moment of epiphany, she realized and accepted the fact that she would have to let the fanatics take her life before allowing any more of them to be shot. The assailants' behavior wasn't entirely their fault. The DNA pathogen began its kill by breaking down its victims' ability to reason correctly, she knew. She put the Mauser down and stood up from behind her guard, Lucius. The mob stopped for a moment, shocked at her bravery or foolhardiness. That act alone could have put an end to the fiasco, but the clerics wouldn't have it. They began a new tirade, and the people once more became a bloodthirsty mob. They surged forward.

That was when the impossible happened. For just a second, the air in the room suddenly seemed electrically charged on some subliminal level, and HE was there with six other men, obviously his troops, standing beside her, shouting orders as if he'd been here all along. "They want to KILL her!" he yelled, and for a moment she couldn't tell who he spoke to. But then the boy, a lad of about thirteen years old, stepped forward.

Oh yes, she could tell that the youngster must have been his—they moved too much alike for anything else—but something seemed slightly wrong with the youth. She could see it in his movements but couldn't pinpoint what the problem may have been. It must be mental illness, she thought. Still, the boy knew who she was, that she had been endangered, and it enraged him. Instantly, she surmised that he must also have been hers. He seemed to spread his arms as if reaching for water to splash onto the assailants, and . . .

Something that looked like liquid fire came from wherever they stepped out of. He threw it against the crowd, and their bodies simply disintegrated. With blurring speed, the lad then moved his hands as if he were throwing baseballs; and something that her mind would only process as solid sound flew over the shocked remainders of the throng, soared along the waves of noise being emitted through the clerics' bullhorns, striking those devices, smashing them and driving their splinters into the faces of the users. They died, painfully, swiftly. The wonder child then reached out or into somewhere and dragged out more of the liquid fire, using that to disintegrate the cleric's lifeless bodies. Anger appeared to boil over within the lad as he prepared to hurl more of the conflagration in the direction from which the crowd had come.

"Stand down, son! She's not hurt! She's okay!" the man who so closely resembled her husband bellowed in a voice that she'd never before heard him use. But the men with her knew that voice and reacted to it as if it were all they'd ever waited to hear. They stood to attention, their eyes gleaming with pride at his return. Yes, indeed, they fairly worshipped him, she could see that, but he, for his part, only had eyes for her. The boy also stood stock-still, at ease, as if he too were military. The angry mob that had been after her party's blood were simply

gone. The troops who had come in with him then began using some type of laser weapon to remove the rusted doors that had obstructed her party's escape route. Still, he *only had eyes for her.*

She thought her heart would break. The air was thick and heavy with the weight of his presence. He reached out his hand and gently lifted her from the ground that she never even realized she'd been sitting down on. She didn't want to look at him anymore, younger and stronger as he was, but her eyes wouldn't look away either. "We need to leave here. Now," he told her with that gentleness *that she loved him so much for. She took his hand, and they all left.*

A Competition in
Malevolence

My man Puccini, who was tailing Muldowney, contacted me that very night. The target had actually *met* with Craine, exposing his own traitorous character. They'd had their little rendezvous at Jacque-Imo's, a very pleasant place over in the Garden District, on Oak Street. The recon agent had actually gotten close enough to make a recording of their conversation with one of the new multiwavelength mini-receivers and image recorders invented by the Think Tank. He then sent everything in dispatch to my house, where I reviewed it in a clean unwired room.

That night seemed darker after the recording had stopped. The implications of its contents were chilling. These two brilliant idiots were still playing *games* with each other! Games that would have horrible repercussions in other people's lives. They'd even gotten to the point where murder became a part of their plans.

As it began, Muldowney could be heard congratulating Craine on his skillfulness in masterminding the attempt to harvest some of Nigel's DNA, though chiding him for not having foreseen the possibility of "that useless brainless, jarheaded caveman commander" (referring to me) managing to get in the way and jam up the works. Craine, for his part, wanted to know how far along his buddy had gotten in *his* master plan to take over The Division, then chided Muldowney for the same reason he himself had been reproached. As the night wore on, the direction of their conversation revealed the fact that they were planning something extremely dangerous, and having Muldowney in control of The Division would help them implement it all.

The worst part of the whole affair was the way these two were playing at some competition between themselves that would be considered won by whoever could pull off the most stunning masterpieces of manipulation with the lesser beings among whom they worked and lived, those not blessed with such phenomenal genius. They did not realize the horrible outcome their games would lead to, and even had they known, it would not have mattered to them. Human lives meant nothing to these two. Admittedly, I've ended more than a few in my own time, but that's what marines are made for, yet never have I killed for sport. These men, on the other hand, never had any humanly understandable reason for doing what they planned to do. Their references and words implied a calloused belief that common people who didn't have *their* mental ability weren't even *real*. In the course of their little love chat, Blacen gave Terry Tilden up, and Craine said that he'd have some of his "stupid rednecks" take the man and lynch him.

That murder having been planned, the two of them even went so far as to sketch out their next "challenges." Muldowney was to try to find and destroy Craine's secret lab, thus establishing credibility for himself; and Craine, for his part, would kidnap Nigel, as his work with the DNA he had wasn't going very well and having the boy on hand could move his research into duplication of Nigel's world-walking ability ahead more rapidly. As the libations of the evening went to their heads, they became chattier. In the course of their blathering, they began to toy with the idea of attempting to discredit me by having the proposed kidnapping pulled off right under my very nose. Should that goal be achieved, then Muldowney might be in a position to move ahead with his takeover scheme. They knocked back a few more, got drunker and ruder with their waitstaff, demanded a couple of cigars, then smoked them while Craine talked more raucously and Muldowney sexually harassed their waitress until the manager threatened to have them escorted off the property. Even then, those two scum shook hands and parted ways as if nothing was wrong.

It was time to act without delay. A team was sent in to extract Tilden, and I demanded an immediate meeting with Rocklin. We got together at headquarters, and the recording was played for him. His face was ashen by the time it was finished. He confessed that as of yesterday, he'd promoted Muldowney to the position of assistant director, thereby making the man my boss. Silver-tongued Blacen had convinced him that this was necessary because I was too militant. Had that position been given to me, he'd contended, then the possibility existed that the MISTmen could and would take control of The Division, not a good thing, considering how Congress could easily view it as a clandestine military organization with the strength and capability to secretly overthrow the United States government if it happened.

Stunning. That posting had never even been listed as being open to active military. Nor would I have ever rebelled against my government. Not that it mattered, anyway. Something was excessively off base and just plain wrong with Rocklin's reasoning. The simple fact was that Blacen needed to be arrested. He'd deliberately put a confidential informant in a position that would cost the man his life. That alone made him guilty of attempted murder. The Director of The Division shouldn't ignore the fact that we had all the proof we needed. Rocklin just couldn't do it, though. At that time, I still didn't understand how Muldowney had inserted himself so deeply into the man's mind and told him so. We had that type of relationship, Rocklin and me. He'd once asked me to never, under any circumstances, hold my tongue when speaking with him. I didn't. Yes, he recalled this, he said, but he also reminded me that the open-communication agreement between us still didn't obligate his accepting my advice. Our meeting ended on that note. As we were leaving, the director ordered me not to touch either of the men. "Now that we have an idea of what they're planning," he explained, "we may be in a better position to take them to trial if we catch them in the act." That was the only reasonable conclusion he had drawn that night.

I went to my office and called off the strike team that had been sent out to neutralize both men. During the meeting, Rocklin had also ordered a confidential operation to take Nigel and return to his home world. His reason? A new type of radical threat seemed to be surfacing in the Chechen Republic, and the division needed more information on foreign terrorists from the eastern European region, the type of stuff that would be found deep within the other United States' Justice Department and DOD databases. They wanted those databases hacked, every bit of relevant and important information duplicated, then left intact and unharmed. It was imperative that after the mission was completed, the other reality remain unaware of our existence. To ensure that policy, every man in the insertion team was fitted with one false tooth loaded with suicide gas. Nigel was the only exception (not one person alive could have forced it on him either). They also chose not to implant one in my dental work either. I understood why. Should this mission fail and all be lost, a scapegoat would be needed. That would, of, course, be me. Baaa, baaa.

Clearly, this excursion into Nigel's world was shaping up to be a suicide mission, and no doubt Muldowney had quite a hand in cutting the orders. As usual, however, the man's ego sabotaged his own plans. Within the Think Tank, there happened to be an extremely gifted wonderkid who only wanted to be called by his last name, Kruger. The guy was the best hacker of his generation, but he could also do amazing feats in the laboratories and research pools. He'd earned renown among the lab in relation to some past event that involved his having called Muldowney out over some whacko experiment that threatened the security of those implementing it and could well have blown the entire Division to smithereens, literally. His boss hated him entirely, and Kruger had disrespectfully made it quite clear how he reciprocated that feeling.

Despite the fact that his questioning Muldowney's work had saved many of their lives, Kruger, for his part, still couldn't get along with all the other big brains in the tank. Unlike his coworkers, he just refused to be afraid of getting fired. He'd made one reliable friend therein, and that man wasn't going to be coming along with us. During the process of reading his file, I began to like the kid. Even a moron could tell, however, that his boss sent him along with hopes that the youngster wouldn't make it back any more than I would. Rumor had it that when he told Kruger how unlikely his survival was, the boy flipped him off and questioned Muldowney's mother's morality right in front of everyone. Yeah, I liked my computer geek nerd already and hadn't even met him yet.

That night, I called my entire unit together. Eighty-four men, seven squads of twelve each. We met on our urban infiltration course. The Muldowney-Craine digital recording was shown, and our man who was shadowing Muldowney was contacted for verification. I talked to my commanding officers and laid out a duty schedule for each team that would not interfere with their current assignments. In addition to carrying out whatever orders they'd be given as a regular part of their duty rotations, they were also to protect my home while I was away. Those with me were also to protect Nigel, whether here or in his own world. All of them were gung ho. The Baby Marine would be safe, they'd see to that. Thus assured and prepared for our next incursion, I went home and talked to my wife about the developments in The Division. She was frightened for Nigel and for me, never once thinking of the danger that she herself may have been in, but I guess that's why she's a doctor.

The next day, Kruger and I met. He was a twenty-year-old kid, about six two and maybe one hundred and sixty pounds after a heavy meal, who had once succeeded in hacking the Department of Defense computer on a dare. He was so good at it that he'd almost managed to evade detection and capture by any of the federal government's own cybersecurity guys. Almost. The FBI only found him because his mother caught him at his act of treason and called the police. She was tired of his living in her basement, and her boyfriend, who was only two years older than Kruger, couldn't stand him, anyway. Having been given only two options by the judge who handled his case, he worked in the Think Tank now. Federal employee, or not, he still refused to dress as anything other than a "punk rocker." Purple hair done up in a tall mohawk and all that. Ultimately, his all-around nonconformity was one of the reasons Muldowney selected him as the first non-MIST-trained lab rat to make the crossing. He was a guinea pig. Okay with me. Considering the fact that he was a civilian male, how he dressed didn't matter to me; I just wanted his loyalty.

Any commanding officer with a trained eye could also see that he was tougher than he looked. Not physically strong by any means, but tough. When he understood that we were going into a world that was twenty years ahead in time, but originally only five years ahead in technology (less now, thanks to Nigel's world-crossing ability and The Division's borrowing, coupled with the fact that we were already way ahead of them in microengineering), he could wrap his mind around the need to change a few things. In Nigel's world, the punk rocker look was "so yesterday" as the kids there would say. Yes, he said, he would be willing to cut his hair and change his look, especially if it meant the difference between whether he'd be able to go with us or not. He just wanted permission to download as much music as he could while we were there. Permission granted. I explained to him that he would be sedated for transport to the mission site, and he thought that the opportunity to "legally get loaded" was "way cool." Kruger even offered to supply his own drugs. Request denied. We talked for a long time that morning, and when he left, I believed we both felt as if we'd made another friend. Per my request, Kruger had been only too happy to plant a time-released bug into the surveillance software in my house. That whole system would be useless in less than a week and no one would be able to figure out why, he told me. Great job, kid. It was time to introduce him to the rest of the team.

We left five days later. Before our departure, I deployed my home protection detail without informing anyone else at The Division. No one there needed to know. We took the same crossover team that had gone the first time, adding an additional six men so that Crossover Team Alpha now became a marine squad. I personally handpicked these particular MISTmen and, before leaving, secretly rearranged things so that Puccini would remain in his current assignment although it would appear that he had gone with us. Along for the trip was an almost-normal-looking Kruger, who, by the way, was a big hit with Nigel.

This time, we used a Ford Econoline E350 twelve-passenger crew van and pulled a trailer along. Our driver went onto I-10 and five, four, three, two, one: Nigel opened the door to *otherspace*, and we were through it again. This time, the going was a lot quicker. The men patted his back and cheered him. Especially Lucius, who had been officially appointed as Nigel's personal bodyguard/babysitter. He hated Kruger, who was busily snoring in the back of the van. Likely because of some rivalry over Nigel's affections. We headed for Gentilly again, and when we pulled into the house, I could see that Captain Gary, my XO, had been busy. The place was renovated, telecom ports and extra outlets having been added everywhere, and a meeting room prepared. One of my men, First Lieutenant Archimus Marcelon, was also a medic who had psych training, and his first assignment was to see how my XO was holding up. Benjamin Gary was doing very well here. Back home, he'd lost his wife and children to a drunken driver who slammed his car into their house one night while then-lieutenant Gary was deployed on a mission; and after the incident, Benjamin never adjusted to living there without them, as he felt they were all he had. He was selected for the first crossover team because the head shrinks in the tank predicted that the psychological effect of actually being in another world could be a relief for him. His productivity was expected to increase incrementally with every month spent away from his formerly happy home, and it had. That's just the way he was wired.

The fact that he'd met another woman here helped out, although it worried me. Of course, these things were expected to happen, but now we had to deal with the possibility that he would have to go back to our world and be deployed God knew where without her. If the woman were a vindictive or angry sort of individual, that could lead to many unnecessary complications. Still, he'd learned a lot more about this place from his girlfriend than from all of our research. Well, marines weren't allowed to bring their wives along unless they paid out of their own pockets, anyway, let alone their girlfriends; so if it came to another deployment, he'd do just fine. He'd have to. I gave the man his promotion, anyway. He was now Major Benjamin Gary.

We spent another six months in that place, during which time, I saw a lot less of Nigel. He was off with Lucius, visiting his friend, I supposed. At that point, no one in N-Prime knew what he could do; so to them, he was just another little kid. He'd get no more official attention than any other child would. The memory of what my wife said when we talked about that situation with the little girl kept coming back to my mind, though. Maybe it *was* just a harmless case of two kids playing together. Still, I had Lucius take pictures of her, anyway. Kruger's first assignment was hacking into the excuse for a computer system that the orphanage had. He, of course performed brilliantly and reported that the little lady was due to be adopted by her uncle and aunt very soon. Scratch one problem, thought I. Back to business.

Kruger's ability to hack computer systems and remain unnoticed turned out to be nothing short of superhuman. Or in his case, supergeekly. We got what we needed from N-Prime America's DOD and Justice Department databases and didn't even have a close call, as far as being caught in the act. He was so far ahead of his time until even cyber safeguards that were nonexistent within our own world presented no challenges to his immeasurable talent. They had lots of advantages and lots of good people, but they didn't have anyone like Kruger. Within thirteen weeks, we'd accomplished our mission with brilliance, speed, and efficiency. Going above and beyond, however, we'd also taken two months more and planted what Kruger called a "foundation protocol" in their worldwide net. This contained advanced coding kernels that would integrate themselves into any and all new cyberdevelopments to such an extent that the composite program they'd formed would have to become a foundation for all future applications. Now their whole World Wide Web was bugged, and not a soul in that world knows about it to this day. After having filled The Division's acquisitions, I was more than ready for the trip back home. That ongoing situation with Muldowney and Craine had me worried, and I felt that my absence allowed Muldowney too much additional latitude for working mischief within The Division. Damn those two men!

You know, Detective Caldwell, during the wee dark hours of the night, when my mind wanders among memories of the dead, and it's impossible to sleep, I've pondered, again and again, the question of how two men with such vast mental gifts could have been so occupied with their own little competition until they couldn't see the ultimate endgame of their narcissism. Maybe their far-reaching mental vision occluded their ability to foresee the immediate. I think of the law of cause and effect. Maybe the persons whose actions are the cause can't see the truth of their own effect. Well, enough of that. Another issue was soon to arise. Now at this crucial time, we began to have a problem with Nigel, who had become more and more morose as his little girlfriend's adoption date neared. He wasn't ready to leave yet. Claimed he had forgotten how to open the pathway. So we were stuck here on the whim of a seven-year-old boy. I grounded him (as if I really could; still, he did obey). Next, a special muster with Crossover Team Alpha was called, just so I could give them an old-fashioned marine-style collective butt ripping for encouraging this foolishness.

Since we were going to be stuck here until the kid got his head together, the house in Gentilly, as well as the building on Burgundy, were both scrubbed inch by inch with toothbrushes. Hundreds of them. Benjamin Gary and Kruger, for their part, were assigned the task of totally securing the properties so that our presence there could remain a secret. If they both burned their brains out trying to foresee and prevent any future cyberthreats to our national interests, well, so what? They, too, had been involved in this stupidity. Another month passed, and finally, I allowed Lucius to take the boy to see his playmate one more time before her new family came to get her. He just *had* to be there to see her off. The whole situation made me livid, but I had to allow it. Never again, I promised.

At long last, after yet another three weeks, Nigel was ready to leave. He kept crying, but also tried really hard to suck it up and be tough. Of course, all the men felt really bad for him (and for themselves, as their knees and hands were beginning to ache). Kruger, for his part, had his waterworks going like Noah's flood over the thing, and that didn't do much to help the boy keep his game face on. Lucius wanted to slap Kruger for that, but was forbidden, mainly because I really felt hurt for Nigel myself. A kid that young should never have known the pain of seeing a girlfriend go. I finally took him aside to talk, and that was when he told me the little girl's name. I guess it should have been a surprise to me, but it wasn't. I hadn't even had time to look at Lucius's pictures, but still should have expected it

---

195

to be her. On a deeply personal level, I could now understand why it had to hurt him so. I also knew that there would never have been any possible way for that particular person, adult or child, to ever be any enemy of his. He was ready now, he said. So we left Nigel's home behind one more time. We couldn't know that when we saw this place again, we'd be returning as refugees escaping a dying world.

No one was prepared for what we encountered when we got to our own reality. The city was thick with tension, and people were carrying those dime-a-dozen filter masks while casting furtive, fearful glances around as they walked along the street. I wondered what the hell had happened. Were we in the right place? I asked Nigel. He said we had to be because he could always feel which place was which, and he'd never been to the other places. *What other places?* I wondered, but didn't pursue the thought. It wasn't the right time.

We went to my home first, but she wasn't there. Some of my MISTmen were, though, and their CO approached us with masks in hand, ready to make his report. There had been two attempts to attack my house while I was gone. Of course, both failed, with the assailants having been dispatched before even coming within two blocks of the place. Two men were in the custody of my unit and, under "intense scrutiny," had already confessed to being affiliated with the "Sons of Freedom." Since these two geniuses and those who accompanied them had a military background, Craine sent them in with orders to kidnap my wife, thinking to use her as leverage in forcing me to hand Nigel over. Needless to say, that didn't work out too well for those guys. Even Blacen Muldowney hadn't known that my MISTmen would be there, so there had been no information about the guard detail leaked to the SOF. That meant the assailants never had a chance. Our captives had also disclosed Craine's plan to release some sort of bio agent into the air within the city limits of New Orleans. The attack would be designed to target one particular ethnicity, African Americans, and that may have indicated the use of a DNA-specific bio agent. The lieutenant colonel in command of the MIST force had seen to it that The Division and NIS were warned of the danger; and as a result, all medical workers, first responders, and security forces were on standby.

At first, quite a bit of trouble had been caused when someone within the Think Tank leaked vital information about the matter to a journalist, but The Division's press department got a handle on things, and the general public had been warned through the news media of a possible flu outbreak. But for The Division, Craine's threat was not something to be dismissed lightly, for if anyone could manufacture a DNA-specific bio agent, *he* could. Yes, my men assured me, my wife was still under guard, and after The Division was made aware of the attempt, President Kennedy himself had the Secret Service assign agents to help out. She had, of course, gone into the hospital that she was assigned to in order to help out instead of staying home. Said that only a coward would shirk duty and hide behind a wall of security when they were needed to fight. That was why the MISTmen hadn't detained her and hadn't allowed anyone else to either. They admired her bravery and honor. She was a healer, and that was that. I couldn't hide my pride in her, which they shared. Lucius and the rest of Crossover Team Alpha were ordered to stay and guard Nigel while I went to headquarters.

The place was a mess, and no one was sure of what to do. When I arrived, Director Rocklin was just coming out of a meeting with the secretary of state and most of the heads of our national security agencies. One look at his ashen face, and I knew right then that the man was up a very smelly creek without the slightest possibility of anyone throwing him a paddle. He halted his panic long enough to sit with me in his office and explain what all the commotion was about.

DUPLICITY ESTABLISHED

Blacen Muldowney was missing. He'd gone AWOL. It seemed that all along, his relationship with Craine's outfit had been closer than anyone realized (closer than *you* realized, I reminded him), and the whole truth of his treachery was coming out. How? I asked. Right after my incursion team left, Muldowney once again met with Craine. As a result of an "anonymous" tip (mine, but Rocklin didn't need to know that) to the NIS, a whole surveillance team tailed the man, and he was so obtuse that he never knew it. The two of them met at Muriel's, a restaurant on the corner of Chartres and St. Anne. They sat outside on the second-floor balcony and discussed their next moves against each other as if they were just chatting over a chessboard. Craine had a secret lab that would be operational soon, and Muldowney was supposed to try to find it before the bio agent could be completed. Craine, on the other hand, was to complete its fabrication and seed my house with it before Blacen could catch up with him. If Nigel got sick, then Blacen would have to supply Craine with as much of the boy's DNA as that kook desired, even if it meant turning over the kid's entire body to Craine. If Blacen appeared to be a hero of some sort, as if he could protect my own home better than I could, then he'd be a step or two closer to attaining his goal of controlling The Division. He depended on the possibility that such an event would also weaken my position with the MIST teams since none of them could fully respect a commander who had to have some lab geek like Blacen's help in saving his own. Neither one gave the other any clear directions to the goals, but they both gave plenty of encrypted hints.

After finishing their meal and laying out the rules for their self-centered contest, they loudly and rudely ordered cognacs (speaking to their server like the lesser being they saw her as, of course), lit up cigars, and started going on and on about how good they were at what they were doing. Their conversation soon became maudlin over the sad fact that there were no other human beings on earth with the mental acuity that they had. No one else to understand their great and mighty minds. All they had was each other. Boo hoo. A month later, Blacen did find Craine's laboratory and warehouse. Or at least he *thought* he did. He never even realized how much clandestine assistance he'd gotten from NIS and the FBI because Craine's lab *needed* to be located, and Blacen Muldowney just wasn't smart enough to break his rival's encryption soon enough. Not without help. When its location was finally confirmed, an NIS-FBI joint task force raided the lab, and a firefight ensued.

Survivors were taken into custody, but would not give up any information. They committed suicide by biting into cyanide-filled molars. Craine's work again. Blacen attempted to stall the autopsies, failing only because he was under investigation at the time, although he'd had no idea up until that failure that anyone was onto him. He realized though that his subterfuge was blown on the day he walked into the coroner's lab and was forcibly removed by a marine guard detail. Once he realized how he had been locked out, he left the ME's office in a big hurry. It was at that time that Rocklin finally recognized this man as a serious problem, so he ordered Muldowney detained. It was too late, though. When they finally broke into his office, he was, of course, long gone, his computer's hard drive burned out and all of his files taken. What neither Muldowney nor Rocklin had known was that I'd had an "ace up the sleeve," as they say, in the person of Dr. Derron Leonard, my other whiz kid inside the think tank and Kruger's first and only friend therein. He was a quiet genius who could have been mistaken for any NFL linebacker. That young man received a doctorate at the tender age of twenty. He was another true genius.

While he was the youngster's boss, Muldowney couldn't resist the temptation to try bullying the kid. He constantly mistook the boy's quietness for weakness. Oh, no one could ever doubt Leonard's brilliance, not even Muldowney. The issue he had was jealousy. He couldn't stand the fact that this kid was far more brilliant than he himself would ever be, had no more respect for him than Kruger did, was far more popular among the other Think Tankers than either Muldowney or Kruger, was a better-looking fellow and all-around better man, and so of course, most of the women who worked in the tank really liked Leonard. Of course, Leonard couldn't stand Muldowney either, though he never made a big show of it. It was he who had overseen the planting of surveillance devices all over Muldowney's home. We even had "bugeyes" set above his desk. The information they transmitted wasn't always consistent because the effects of Muldowney's bad conscience had increased his paranoia to a point where he'd programmed his specialized home security system to randomly sweep for bugs, and they'd have to shut down during the sweep. Still, the system's parameters allowed plenty of snapshots of some of Muldowney's secret files as he read them, and now that information would come in handy.

Our sweep squad took Muldowney's computer to what was left of the Think Tank. Even though he'd tried his best to destroy all data and evidence of his dirty deeds, Leonard found everything. Plans within plans and wheels within wheels. They really *did* intend to release that DNA killer disease. It was designed to be both airborne and communicable by touch. The virus could live in warm food and be ingested too. Craine had rightly estimated that their best chance of spreading the bug would be by infecting workers in the food service industry in the Southeastern United States. Those people had no unions, which meant no health care, and they could hardly ever afford to take off work, let alone go to any doctors, which would be important, because the virus was extremely fragile for its first two weeks when the immune system would fight its hardest.

If any of those infected were treated for influenza or pneumonia, that treatment would kill the virus. If it could live past its first two weeks within a human body, it would seemingly become dormant, but would actually be attaching itself to its victim's DNA, begin duplicating, and proceed to destroy the DNA's amino acids. It would be at it most contagious during its "dormancy," and that would last for fifteen days. Still, something, some vital information or statistics were not there, Leonard had told the division leadership. He felt that there were gaps in the information on Muldowney's . computer, and some of the links that should have been in the disease's chain of mutation were missing, as if perhaps our two homegrown homicidal maniacs had deliberately left them out. The best biological geniuses the tank had were working on it, but that gap in the information was eluding them at every turn. Still, they had, of course, found more of the story regarding the game Muldowney and Craine were playing.

If none of Craine's attempts at acquiring Nigel succeeded, he was to give Muldowney the antidote after infecting a few people. Muldowney would then present the serum to the Think Tank, crediting himself with its discovery. He would get the credit for Craine's work (since Craine would have, at that point, been the loser in their little game) then move on to having the FBI attack all the hideouts and base camps belonging to the "Sons of Freedom," capture a few prisoners, and use one of his own newest inventions: a nanochip that could suppress its host's free will, to wring a "confession" out of these guys. He'd look like a hero, while the current director appeared to be a failure, and would then, hopefully be forced to retire and name Blacen as his successor, after which Muldowney, as the new director of The Division, would order my arrest on charges of treason then see to it that Craine would be pardoned and reinstated so that round two could begin.

This "will killer" chip idea was of great interest to the tank, so they dug deeper and found that Muldowney had, in one of his encrypted e-mails to his partner, made reference to one of his nanochips that was being tried out on a living person who never suspected that the thing was embedded in his mind. Blacen complained though that the chip could only be activated if he were within a fifty-yard radius of it, and its will suppression wasn't as powerful as he'd hoped. Its remote control was too just limited to do any better. He did, however, admit that one of the thing's advantages was its residual effect on the subject's behavior. His living guinea pig never realized that he was under someone else's control and would implement suggestions made during the time when the chip was active up to ten days after its deactivation. It was as if the subject had been exposed to a very efficient posthypnotic suggestion and would comply even if that compliance forced the subject to invent baseless rationalizations for the actions they took while under the influence of his device. Once he got that information, Rocklin ordered a complete search of everything Blacen had ever touched, from his house to the lab at headquarters, and all things in between. As a result of that search, NIS agents were able to locate some of Blacen's prototypes, which went straight to the Think Tank, of course.

In a week, they had a scanner that could home in on the nanochip's unique electrical pulses. They used that to check every living person in The Division, finally finding what they were looking for in Director Rocklin's head. How it got there and for how long it had been there, only Muldowney would have known, but he was gone, and no one knew where. Meanwhile, back at the farm, the Tank had stopped all its other projects in order to concentrate on ways to remove or destroy the will killer without harming Rocklin himself. Even without Muldowney and Craine, these people were still a formidable mental power, and it showed. In two weeks, they reported a success to the acting director. Someone among them (they never said who) had estimated that an ultrasonic sound spike would destroy the will killer chip's circuits, and they were right.

With the solution to the problem discovered, it was time to test it out on Rocklin. It worked. All this played out within the six-month period that Crossover Team Alpha spent in Nigel's world. The Director of The Division had only recently been freed of the thing, but now, his directorship was most likely over. No one knew how much classified information the man may have leaked to Muldowney, and that had been the subject of this meeting he'd just walked out of. Another priority discussed among them had been finding Blacen. They weren't even sure of where to start with that search. Rocklin had no one else to turn to, so he'd decided to ask me for my help. Of course, I'd gladly help, I said. Just give me a day or so and let me see what can be done.

I contacted my Muldowney shadow, and he gave me the man's location. Just like that. He was hiding out in Central Mississippi. There was a small town named Wiggins there, where absolutely nothing ever happened and the people lived pretty far apart mostly. Muldowney had a very nice house just outside the town, and that was where he could be found. I personally led the MIST team that crept through the shadows that night. We stormed into his bedroom and dragged him out of the sack. We took both of the call girls into custody too. I didn't even allow him the dignity of putting on any clothing. He stood there, his hands ziptied, yakking on and on about how he was The Assistant Director of The Division, one of the two most enlightened minds of our era; how none of these troglodyte imbeciles had any business touching him; and how he'd see to it that we paid for this, and . . .

I walked up to him and punched him in his mouth. Knocked him and one of his front teeth out. His hideout house was searched from top to bottom, then we tore it apart and searched more. There were false walls, false floors, and hidden compartments all over that place. There was so much stuff that we brought in dogs and scanners. Top secret papers, plots, money, jewels, cocaine, all kinds of contraband was found in his secret little stashes. Blacen Muldowney was going to go away forever, if I could help it. Because of this fool, The Division had been compromised beyond redemption, though, and we were all under scrutiny, as the Administration had no desire to take any chances with a problem this enormous in scope. That was the only reason why his fate was no longer in my hands.

All the evidence had to go to NIS (by the way, they'd just become NCIS) and they took over the investigation since they were still considered airtight. As expected, my unit and I were cleared almost immediately. The team that had Blacen in custody finally brought in a gifted FBI profiler who knew just the right formula for sending him into an egomaniacal rant. He spilled his guts without ever realizing how much he was telling. Everything the tank had dragged out of what was left of his computer was confirmed. Yes, they had created a DNA-based bio agent. Yes, they were going to release it into the air, and yes, they planned to infect all food service workers, and yes, they were going to rule the world, and on and on.

We knew now that we *had* to find his partner. The idiot was going to release that toxin into some hapless restaurant somewhere, and God only knew what would ultimately result from that. This was no simple organic bacteria; it was a genetic virus, so it wasn't likely that it would behave according to any established or predictable pattern. Kruger had rejoined the Tank by then, once more working with Leonard, the only coworker whom he'd ever gotten along with; and together with the rest of the Think Tankers, they all worked up a computer model of where this could go. The answer, when it came, was not at all hopeful. It seemed that the two most enlightened minds of our era had not taken into consideration the fact that viruses can mutate. What might start as an attempted genocide of one ethnicity could end as the death of all humanity. Even if the virus were programmed to attack a certain ethnicity's DNA, there was no telling how many people may have had trace amounts of that very same in their own gene code. It could then adapt itself to prey on other types of individual DNA in order to survive. This thing seriously could threaten the entire human race. If it were already released, lots of death would follow. Craine was counting on Muldowney to swoop in, get the antidote, and play his part, but he had no way of knowing that Blacen was not likely to make it. We needed to catch up with this man, and time wasn't on our side. My people, along with any available outside personnel, were working with NCIS and the FBI to locate Craine, but nothing was going our way. Finally, I hit upon a plan.

The Division had spent the last year and a half working on microtechnology, and it was time to make use of the fruitage of that labor. Blacen had his will killer chip, which was now ours, and we also had microtracers that could be implanted under the skin. They were thumbnail size, thin as a potato chip, flimsy as wet cloth, and the person who was tagged that way would, conceivably, not even know what had been done to them if it happened while they were in a deep sleep. The two men we captured were high-ranking members of the SOF, and they could be expected to make their way to their boss if we arranged their release, saying that it was because they couldn't be taken to trial or something like that. We did it. They were released and, within another month, headed toward North Alabama. Meanwhile, the CDC sent out e-mails, circulars, faxes, and inspectors to all the restaurants in the Crescent City, warning management to be on the lookout for flu-like symptoms among their waitstaff and to call in immediately if anything like this was noticed. Local health departments were contacted and apprised of what they were supposed to be watching out for: sudden flu-like symptoms that seemed to have no reason for occurring in the healthy but would. Blacen, meanwhile, was dead set on not assisting. In fact, he would supply false information designed to cause a wild-goose chase and stall us whenever he saw an opportunity. So NCIS finally decided it was time to try out the will killer on its inventor. Don't look at me like that, Detective. The mother of all plagues was about to be released into the general population of our country, and there truly was no other way to stop it.

Muldowney had to play his part, and if he refused to do so willingly, we would simply take his will away, forcing him to do what we needed him to. Our hope was to find Craine before he could put his portion of the plot into action and use his pal to convince him that the game was over. Within the week, we'd located target Devin Craine. He was holed up in the woods outside of Anniston, Alabama, with a number of his cronies. Through infrared imagery, we'd also found out that there were far more warm bodies present than anyone possibly could have expected. The figure had increased to a little over fifteen hundred. We later learned that these people had been invited by means of hand-delivered invitations. Because the SOF used their family members to distribute the invites, Rocklin completely missed that. In his summons, Craine put the word out that he was going to demonstrate his race-targeting bio agent for them. When like-minded groups had learned of the existence of the ethnic killer virus, most of them had also chosen to throw in their lot with him while others stood in opposition, believing that his wonder disease should be used on all people of Arabic and Jewish descent first. Surprisingly, some of the more sensible among them actually were fearful of releasing such a deadly bio agent on US soil. I guess all prejudiced people aren't stupid.

With the idea of resolving the conflict, the major players of their world of intolerance were gathering there with him, having brought along as many of their members as they could for backup and protection. It was becoming a hate convention. We, for our part, didn't care. We wanted Craine, and if Muldowney couldn't get him to divulge the antidote, there would, as a last resort, always be the Muldowney will killer. President Kennedy didn't want to use MISTmen on domestic soil, so we dropped four SWAT teams in those woods, along with NCIS and FBI agents, but just as our forces were converging on the location, a firefight broke out. Our people could hear gunfire, and they charged in, defending themselves along the way. The clearing in the woods was starting to become a minor battlefield. There were Klansmen with guns, skinheads with guns, neo-Nazis with guns, militiamen with guns, every one of them using their weapons to the full on one another. In the middle of all this, federal agents had to get to Craine. They kept their focus, though, and eventually fought their way to the inside of a huge sheet metal structure that resembled a hangar, for that was the place where Craine and his allies were meeting with their rivals. Meanwhile, the fighting outside got heavier, so federal forces scrambled choppers to scatter the ground targets and spirit Craine out of there once he was captured.

Because many of the people on the ground were ex-military, it wasn't long before they spotted our air support and began firing on it as much as on one another. That escalated the conflict. The choppers dropped lead rain on the combatants, and our National Guard backup that had been deployed to hold the perimeter began closing in on the scene, detaining everyone without federal credentials. The raid was becoming a genuine cluster copulation, but finally, it ended. Heroic deeds were done in that little battle, but there's no time to go into all of them. One day, I'll write my memoirs and tell the tales of all the valiant fallen that I have known. It'll probably be all classified, though.

Whatever. When it was over, we found Craine's dead body in the structure. Our crime scene units went through every bit of evidence that was there with a "fine-toothed comb" as they say, and their reconstruction told us that he'd gone down with a bullet right between the eyes. That was what initiated the gunfight. The evidence collected on the scene also exposed the underlying reason for the conflict itself. Apparently, someone had done some digging and turned up Craine's mixed ancestry. Needless to say, that was a problem for these types, and all the more so for the Sons of Freedom. Yes, Detective Caldwell, he was "mixed," as they say. His grandfather was French, his grandmother African American, but there was just no way that anyone could tell by looking at him. You see, Craine was never a racist. He was just using these hatemongers in his game. He knew how those sorts of people felt, had seen how deeply their hatreds ran, and counted on the power of such emotion to provide him with willing puppets. Oh, how he loved being a puppet master, that Devin Craine. In his mind, human emotion was considered a tool. The man was never known to express much of it himself, except when he was denigrating someone else or when Muldowney was involved. That was the only person Craine ever seemed to care anything about. Every other human was beneath him.

What? Were they . . . no, Detective, they were not, to my knowledge, homosexuals. Craine needed a father figure, and Blacen was just . . . Blacen. They were just two narcissistic egomaniacs bound by some shared vision that they held dear. Muldowney could play other people's feelings like a fiddle whenever he wanted them to do things for him, and he seemed to have a talent with certain types of men and women. His talent wasn't always sexual, it was just in his ability to exude false empathy that deeply moved people in need of acceptance or validation.

Craine saw Muldowney as his only friend, his only confidant, and the one person in the whole world who was his equal. His supporters, however, and every other person in existence rated as little more than idiotic subhumans on standby for the doing of his will. As far as his extremist supporters were concerned, he'd decided to manipulate their fears and develop a "solution" to what they saw as a threat, just so he could make these human beings do what he wanted and one-up Muldowney, but he paid the ultimate price for that arrogance.

After his death, NCIS searched and searched for his formula and serums. By whatever means necessary, Craine's kitchen would be located. Certain elements of what used to be the investigative arm of The Division were brought into the case, and suspects were interrogated, cajoled, threatened. Still, nothing new came out. Blacen Muldowney got several visits from different agencies during the weeks that followed. We used the will killer on him so often until it seemed he had no capacity for free will left. There was no mercy, no quarter. He was pumped for every bit of information he could give about his late partner. We pressed him harder and harder to reveal the location of Craine's lab notes and data records. Finally, he told us that Craine never wrote *anything* down. It wasn't necessary for him since he could remember everything.

Then people started falling sick. Thousands of them, all around the world, as far as we could tell. We knew, then, that one or more of Craine's cannon fodder had to have done it. They'd released the disease, perhaps having no idea of how evil a genie they'd let out of the bottle. It was decided that his chief ally should be told. Maybe knowing about this would coerce him. But when Blacen found out, he started laughing and crying. He almost became hysterical, he laughed so much. They didn't know what to do, so the agents just left the room, fearing that they would have been overwhelmed by the temptation to kill him right then. He kept saying, "We won, Devin, we won."

The Evil that Men Do

It was time to take a step back and formulate a new approach. I'd always been his chief antagonist, and for that reason, I was assigned the unenviable task of going in to Muldowney, appear utterly beaten, and make an effort to get the formula for the antidote from him. Beg, if necessary. They gave me a script to memorize, even. When it came down to it, though, I couldn't do it. Not that way. I just sat across from Blacen and glared at him. I knew him too well. He was a braggart and would have to talk, now that he was looking into the face of a man whom he felt he'd personally defeated. I was right. He started laughing again. "I beat you, I beat you . . .," he started singing, "you thought you knew, and I beat yooou." He seemed a little unhinged.

Possible effects of long-term use of the will killer? All he got from me was a wintry smile. "Maybe you did. Perhaps this round is yours." I started getting up to walk out, then turned, and as if just remembering something of only minimal importance, said, "By the way, Devin Craine is dead. I killed him myself."

The effect was more than could have been hoped for. His face whitened. In a near whisper, he said, "They told me that . . . that . . ."

"Riiight," I said softly. "They told you he died in the crossfire? Or that one of his racist buddies did it? Nah, Blacen, my boy. It was me. I took him from you. I'm the one who made your grand plan fail." Pointing two fingers at him, gun-style, I said, as if I'd enjoyed it, "*Pow . . . pow.* Looks like I beat both of you, and all it took was a bullet." That insult to his ego did what all our interrogation techniques and the brutal use of the will killer failed to do. It broke him open like artillery firing on a dam. He ranted and raged all about how there was no way that a rock-throwing Neanderthal like me could win against Blacen Muldowney and Devin Craine, going on and on about how we'd all lost and didn't even know it.

"Bulls——t," I said, walking out of the room. He became even more livid. He stood and demanded that I get back in there. I didn't.

Two days passed. More people died all over the globe. The populations of many third world countries were at risk of being decimated by the thousands. Blacen kept demanding my presence, but his guard had been instructed to tell him that I was out in the countryside, celebrating my big win over Craine and him. Finally, we were brought together again, Blacen and I. Before they brought me to the interrogation room, though, Blacen could hear over the intercom that his last questioner had "carelessly" left on my loud complaining over what a big waste of time this was, that this guy was just another loser with nothing else we needed and probably just wanted to make some last-ditch attempt at seeing me to beg for leniency, I had fish to catch, beer to drink, and on and on. Finally, I entered, wearing one of those stupid Hawaiian tourist shirts with a pair of mismatched overly colorful shorts and Margaritaville sandals. My three-day growth of facial hair and smug expression angered Muldowney even further. He'd never seen me out of uniform and demanded an explanation as if he were entitled to any such thing. I laughed.

"You think you have nothing to worry about?" he asked icily.

"So a few people have died," I answered. "Nobody here is sick (a lie, of course), and you still lost. Guess you two weren't so much smarter than the rest of us, after all, you and your precious Craine, because you still *lost!*"

It was too much for the man. I could see in his eyes that he had something really, really bad to tell me. He was dying to do it. A slow calmness seemed to work its way throughout his body, and his eyes were dancing with demoniacal laughter. I will never forget that day and the way that Blacen Muldowney calmly placed his fettered hands on the tabletop, leaned forward, and told how he and Craine had orchestrated the death of the human race on our earth. Oh yes, there were attempts to seed Craine's disease in a few people, but these had not produced the desired effect. Every waiter they'd infected had taken some type of cold medicine during the two weeks when the virus was in its infancy. They all killed the disease before it could reach its stage of dormancy, when it was at its most contagious. Why waitstaff? I asked.

"We hate them. They're creepy. They scrape, they bow, they're useless servants and nobody ever notices them, but they come in contact with dozens of people as well as their food and are generally uninsured." The evil laughter within his eyes began to bubble out as if he couldn't control it. He stopped his giggling, regained his composure, and continued. "They're good at being nice to you but secretly hate you, and they're all failures or they wouldn't be doing that job." *Okay, narcissistic and with a fetish hatred against waitstaff.* I thought. An intellectually superior human. Right. I said as much. He became angrier, but it didn't alter his deadly calmness. With insanity in his eyes, he told me everything we needed to know and could do nothing about.

After that first failure, Blacen stepped in to help Craine work out a stronger virus. They found a way to make the disease more virulent, more contagious, and less obvious. When they had what they wanted, they infected themselves. They also injected themselves with an antidote. Both the disease and its nemesis would attach to the DNA ladder, one on each side. The malevolent portion of the disease would reproduce and was highly contagious through touch, food, and airborne means. The infected would not know for two to four weeks that they were sick. In order to precipitate their mad plan, Muldowney and Craine both took trips abroad, touched people, hugged people. They also traveled throughout our own country, doing the same thing.

Wherever they went, Muldowney would hook up with as many call girls as he could find. Craine would hang around in airports or bus terminals striking up conversations and making "friends" with fellow travelers. That's what they did during the time they were acting as Typhoid Mary times two, spreading their death as far as possible. The antidote in their own bloodstream would release itself two weeks after their injections and, subsequent to that, once a month after reproducing. Three months later, it would break itself and its opposite down, leaving the host immune to Craine's virus forever. There was no cure for it now, as Muldowney's antidote was long gone and Craine was dead. Why? I asked. What were they going to do? Live happily ever after on an empty world? No. That was where Nigel came in. They were going to kidnap my wife and the boy, with the intent of using her to force him to do their bidding. With his ability, they would cross into his world, kidnap the most brilliant young women there, and bring them here. After infecting them with Craine's disease, they would force these to submit and have their children in order to be infused with the antidote. Since Nigel was to be rendered sterile, that would leave only Blacen Muldowney and Devin Craine to father a new human race in their images. They also thought they would pirate Nigel's gift and spread it among their own progeny, thereby creating a world of reality walkers who could hold all other worlds in thrall.

It was the most outlandish plot that I'd ever heard. What about my wife? I had to ask. She was to be given the disease and the antidote since as long as she was alive, Nigel could be manipulated (I knew that Muldowney also had other more carnal ideas in mind regarding her also). It had already been done. Blacen got close to one of the nurses who worked with her and had the woman put the virus in her meal when they went to lunch together. After that, his agent applied the antidote. They tried to raid our garbage in order to get some of her DNA and check it to see if everything worked out, but my guards ran their guy away, so Blacen's pet nurse had done the deed of checking for them. And yes, she was safe. Craine's tests had also shown that Nigel was immune for some reason. That nurse of theirs went missing after my day's conversation with Muldowney. Scratch one terrorists' accomplice. So why was he so happy to tell me that my family was safe? Because he'd personally seen to it that I'd been infected when I got back from my last mission. Maybe I should check the bar in my office, he said. How many people might I have infected? he asked. It was all too funny to him, yet I continued to act with nonchalance.

"Perhaps you failed. *Again*," I told him, stressing the last word. Those who died had shown flu-like symptoms and nosebleeds for weeks after the disease became obvious, and I had exhibited none. Nothing. That was impossible! He raged. He, the great Blacen Muldowney, had arranged my death. I *had* to be infected! What does this disease look like? I asked him, yawning. I'll check it out and see.

He wanted to clam up, but I reminded him that if he was right, well, he'd just been given a chance to watch me fade away. Here's some paper. Draw a picture. If I'm dying, you get to be there when they tell me. I also asked him, en passant, how he and Craine intended to manufacture the antidote. They wouldn't have had to, he smugly retorted. Craine's blood carried a version of it that would not break down and would reproduce itself indefinitely instead. He looked up at me then, with more than insanity in his eyes, and added, "Craine's *living* blood. Everything breaks down when the infected body dies. Oh, and by the way, everyone here is already infected. Here's your picture."

After that interview, I was quarantined while a sample of my bloodwork was sent to the NCIS lab. The Think Tank wasn't there anymore, and The

211

Division had been dissolved long ago, its most brilliant talent having been absorbed into other federal agencies. The price of failure. Yes, we had to have underestimated these two men. Nobody realized what a *faire la folie a deaux* they'd become. Blacen had conned the profiler because he wanted us to chase red herring while his antidote slid out of our reach. It had. Apparently, we failed to realize how capable he was when it came to sneakiness. We underestimated how tough he could be in resisting the will killer too. Maybe he was able to do that because it was his invention, after all, and perhaps he knew how to hold his own against it. I cursed him again.

The testing of my blood went on for three days. Three days of people dying while I waited. She had to have been busy, I thought. The hospitals were filling up. Lucius was probably Nigel's full-time babysitter right about now. I had not been home in such a long time and would have loved to have seen her face. I missed Nigel too and thought of how naive he was. The boy had no idea how much drama and mortality was centered on him. Nigel and his gift. We'd taken something that could have been good and turned it into a cause of death and strife. How human of us. Finally, two marines in biohazard gear dragged Blacen Muldowney in, chained and cuffed. We knew then that I was about to find out whether I was a living or dead man. Kruger and another lab rat entered, and despite his biohazard mask, anyone could have seen that Kruger had his waterworks going again. Blacen Muldowney became absolutely radiant. I prepared myself for the worst. Death is just a regular part of the risk when a man spends his life as I'd spent mine. Of course, like General Patton, I would have preferred to die by the last bullet fired in the last war and all that, but . . .

We almost didn't hear Kruger saying that I wasn't infected. Not only that, but everyone on Crossover Team Alpha seemed to have an immunity to Craine's disease. An antidote was being manufactured even now, and it looked like this was over. The marines saluted me. Muldowney whitened. I laughed at him. His guards dragged him back to whatever hole he was being held in, screaming, "Impossible! Impossible!" until his voice faded out of range.

After he left, Kruger dismissed his fellow tekkie and removed his bio hood. He was still crying when he ran over and hugged me. I don't do hugs with my men, but that didn't stop him. Then he pulled it together and got serious. It was true. I was safe and so were all the members of Crossover Team Alpha, but there really was no antidote in the works. He'd said that for the benefit of the marine guards and the other lab rat. I, for my part, was due to get together with some pretty important people, and since it was a top secret meeting, they'd only given him a few seconds without the camera to hand me an access card. I was to go to my house. That was all they told him.

When I got home, neither Nigel nor my wife was there. A Secret Service agent was. She motioned me to an SUV that was waiting nearby, which whisked me away to the airport, there to board a stealth transport to Washington. When we got there, my guards took me straight to the White House, where other Secret Service agents handed me off to marines who saluted then ushered me to an elevator that went down a very long way. Upon my arrival at the bottom, the troops ushered me into a large room somewhere underground, saluted again, and left after instructing me to use my access card to enter.

When the door opened, I came face-to-face with the fortieth president of the United Federation of American States, President Edward Moore "Teddy" Kennedy. I stood to attention, of course, and saluted.

THE DOGS OF WAR

"As you were, General," he started. "Well, it looks like we've got quite a mess here. All because a couple of nerds wanted to get some. Quite a mess. Let's have a scotch and talk a little bit, son. I'll have a Chivas and soda there. "

I, of course, poured for both of us (he was, after all, the President of the United States of America). We had a drink, sat for a moment, and then he began again. "You know, they tell me that you should have been the man running The Division, all along, that you had a gut feeling about these two nuts and might've stopped this from ever happening. How do you feel about that?"

"If I had been given that assignment sir, I would have carried it out to the best of my ability," I answered then added, "but The Division was a very powerful entity, and having something like that under the control of a military officer might have scared the pants off of more than a few members of Congress."

The President laughed, told me to relax, and that I had permission to speak freely. We talked for a while, and I knew that he was sizing me up for something. Then he told me to step out of the room. When I was summoned back, the place was filled with so much brass till the reflection could have lit up the moon. CMC, SECNAV, SOD, the Joint Chiefs, you name it, they were there. President Kennedy spoke then. He gave a pretty good speech and proceeded to explain to me that I was being sent on a mission that would have long-range effects for our country and maybe for the entire human race. I would be leaving this reality with Crossover Team Alpha. We were to go out and find a medical cure somewhere among the worlds that Nigel could access. It needed to be done, and in a hurry at that. The world was about to destroy itself, he explained.

The analysts all were predicting a war on the horizon, our enemies around the globe were becoming agitated, and though no other nation had the technological advantages we had, and were not likely to be able to stand against us, still, no one in our government wanted to risk the chance that some foreign hit squad might embark on a preemptive assassination attempt against Nigel, as he had become our number one asset in the military conflict that was bound to come. My wife had allowed a couple of the reputable staff members from Johns Hopkins to collect two vials of Nigel's blood and do some cheek swabs. The military now had more than enough of the Wonder Kid's DNA to power all of their superweapons several thousand times over. Additionally, trusted experts in the CDC had predicted that Craine's disease would most likely disappear before becoming a pandemic that could seriously endanger the existence of humanity. We later learned just how wrong they were.

If all went against us, then we were to return and evacuate the leaders of our fair nation to safety in some other preferably uninhabited location. Of course, certain key citizens (*no doubt the richest of the rich*, I remember thinking) were also to be evacuated to whatever safe haven we might find among the worlds. There they would (ideally) begin to reestablish our great civilization. What that meant, I guessed, was that the top people in government and business were probably going to be placed in some safe location with the idea of ensuring *their* preservation if this virus couldn't be stopped. Yes, The President assured me, that type of contingency plan did exist and, at the very worst, I'd have to return and fetch these folks off to some other realm untouched by the blight. He had me memorize the location and access protocols of their little hidey hole, just in case.

Furthermore, I was being given a double promotion, he said, a thing that was nonexistent to rare in any branch of the military, let alone The Corps. I would now be a major general of the United States Marine Corps. They wanted me to have enough rank to be taken seriously in any comparable reality that our new mission may lead us to infiltrate. That was it. There wasn't much more briefing to be done after that. Starting with the president, each brass in the room gave me a handshake and one of their coins then filed out, leaving General Alfred M. Gray Jr., commandant of the Marine Corps, alone with me. He told me to sit down. It was time to explain in more detail what was expected of my command on this mission. Before we started, though, I had to stop my in-depth briefing for a moment, for there was a something, a question, that needed to be addressed: why wasn't the reestablishment mission already under way? For a moment, the commandant looked as if he was too disgusted to answer, but he did.

"Some individuals thought that it should have been implemented immediately, but there was too much disagreement over one complication, Marine." He shifted a little uneasily then added, "The people that have the most influence also had doubts about undertaking a mission of such great magnitude with a 'dark green marine' in command." He continued then. "But no authority in the world could make that youngster of yours work with any other person, and you are also the highest-ranking officer we have whom we know to be both uninfected by and immune to Craine's virus. Even then, this almost didn't happen, but some of the most influential and powerful people in America have been struck down or have seen one or more of their relatives die. That has made this mission a top priority regardless of *who's* in command." So there it was. The ugly truth of limited human thinking once again.

General Gray continued. "Intelligence indicates that we will win the coming war, so that eased a lot of the tension. No other power on earth has our military muscle and capability. Not even the Russians or the Chinese. We *will* win, and after that, there won't be any need to reestablish in some foreign world. This is the second reason why you are not traveling with a host of the country's greatest citizens to care for. The first reason is because none of them want to be in a position where *you* are the person in control. Nevertheless, while we're cracking skulls here, you and your kid will still need to be out of reach of any enemy we have. I know you'd like to stay and fight—any good marine would, but these are your orders and you will follow them, General."

A C-130J was, at that very moment, getting loaded up with whatever might be needed to make our way among the worlds. We were being given the most advanced weaponry available, every workable thing developed from our phantom zone crossings, and all of Craine and Muldowney's research had been located and placed aboard. Kruger was going to go, along with Leonard, because command had finally come to realize that these were the two most brilliant minds from The Division's Think Tank, and we'd need them. My MISTmen had gotten their rubber suits on and ready while the lab geeks had gotten whatever lab geek stuff they needed.

Benjamin Gary was to be promoted to lieutenant colonel, placed as my second in command when we arrived in Nigel's world, and Lucius had also been promoted. He was Master Gunnery Sergeant Lucius Carver now.

I was, however, concerned about the size of the aircraft, as well as how it might react to changes within *otherspace*, and whether Nigel could move anything that big, but the CMC told me that it had been completely sprayed with a very thin layer of our polymer-rubber goop, and after drying out, the plane had been taken through to Nigel's world once already. The kid had been told that I'd ordered the flight; that's how they obtained his cooperation. The boy thought it was great fun, but Captain Martin Braggs, the air force pilot who had flown the aircraft, reported that they were picked up on radar as soon as he exited *otherspace* into Nigel's home world. In planning the test, our air force had deliberately picked an exit location that would give the pilot enough time to turn around and get back before their jets got to him, though. As things worked out, he didn't need to turn around. Nigel just took them right back into the nil zone when he understood that they could be shot down. I wasn't too happy about their risking the boy's life that way, but we now knew that he could open the pathway for something as large as a C-130J Super Hercules. Additionally, the CMC mentioned that he'd also seen Nigel's fight recording, saying how much he really liked the boy's moxie, and if I'd been anything like that when as a kid, well, no wonder my military career had been so stellar.

We were going over the essentials of the mission, double-checking everything to ensure success, when I thought of one more thing I *had* to have. This was likely to be a long-term mission. We would need a competent doctor, and I was *not* leaving my wife here this time. I respectfully informed the CMC that if they expected to me to go without her, I would rather relinquish command to the next man in line. He stared at me for a moment then laughed. The President had already ordered her along. He felt that Nigel would do better with her there than if she were left here, and no one wanted any possibility of the mission's success being threatened by having any of my family exposed. They were both at Keesler Air Force Base in Biloxi, waiting for me, along with the rest of my command. After a few more hours of planning, there was nothing more to say.

Finally, the old man looked me right in the eye and said, "General, there is every possibility that when you return, the world will be changed. There are countries who think that this bio attack was instigated by American citizens with the tacit approval of our government. We have been accused before the United Nations Security Council of attempting genocide on the Arabic people, as well as other ethnicities." The Commandant paused and took a drink, then continued. "There has been saber rattling and shield banging by some of our accusers. Despite all that, Great Britain has come out in our defense, and a few are listening. But for the most part, the others want war. In truth, however, they just want the genetic bug. We're not agitating them, but if they come against us, we will by *God* come out swinging, and swinging hard. Nukes are armed, and we are at def con 3. If you find this world dead and gone when you return, raise a memorial for us, then go to every one of these worlds, realities, or whatever they are, and kill every single Blacen Muldowney and Devin Craine in existence. Those are your orders from me, as of this moment."

I saluted him, holding the stance for a little longer, then turned and left. We both had work to do.

***

The General fell silent for a few moments while the sound of thunder and the almost inaudible crack of lightning invaded the empty air where his words once filled the room. His face held a look of deep sadness and melancholy. As he sat, head almost down, holding his scotch with both hands, Roan was once again struck with a strong sense of déjà vu, as if he knew this man. The answer was lying just out of the reach of recall, as if it were a puzzle only sensed with peripheral vision. *I know him. I've met him before, but . . .*

Roan's reverie was interrupted by The General's words: "I should never have separated him from her, you know."

"From *who*?" the detective demanded, feeling irritated at the interruption of his train of thought.

"From the little girl," The General answered. "I saw her as a security risk, a random factor that might have caused our expeditions into that reality to be exposed. But nothing is random. Everything has purpose. I knew that when I found out what her name was."

Roan leaned forward. *Puzzle, puzzle, piece of pie . . . . why do you try to dodge my eye?*

"It was Angeline Duplessis. She was later adopted by her uncle, Rene Emilien Duplessis, a mechanical engineer specializing in power plant development, and aunt Severine Cosette Fouche-Duplessis, and that was

218

the first time Nigel had to say goodbye to his Angeline." The General rubbed his eyes with his fingers after speaking.

Fighting back tears, Roan thought. *Click*. The puzzle in his mind's eye began to come together. *A few more pieces . . .*

ON FOREIGN GROUND

I did not want to leave any of my MISTmen behind in what could well have become a dying world, Detective, but I had to. I wanted to take *all* the teams under my command, but in the end, it was just Crossover Team Alpha that would go. The way things were shaping up back home, our America would need every bit of force it was capable of, anyway. Those two fools, Muldowney and Craine, had put us in the unenviable position of appearing to have made use of bioweaponry in an attempt to destroy our enemies, and the leaders of those governments were refusing to see that our country was suffering too. There was no way we were going to expose our weakness to them ourselves and no way in hell would we allow our America to be forced to give out any "reparations" to anyone, especially not those states that desired our downfall; so all of our enemies, foreign and domestic, seemed to be preparing to attack at once. For those reasons, World War III was already beginning when we flew out of that reality. The thirty-eighth parallel had been crossed, enemy naval units were approaching ours with hostility, and the nuclear arsenals were being prepared for launch. Our super weapons were already being effectively deployed in various theaters around the globe, and still the enemies were coming. We found out, years later, what happened after we left; and even attaining that bit of information cost too many lives. When I recall these things, only one word comes to mind: "Enough." Crossover Team Alpha couldn't help with the fighting, and we couldn't stop it. The only course of action for us was completion of our mission.

Meanwhile, we'd found a place in Nigel's world to land that huge plane with little or no notice from their air force. You see, Captain Braggs didn't really have to get the thing that high above the ground for our boy to do what he does. All that was needed was for the beast to be in motion. I thought I knew some good pilots, but Braggs had to be the best. How do you keep something as large as a C-130J below radar? I don't know, but he'd done it in a couple of practice runs. When we got into Nigel's world, we'd be headed for an abandoned airfield in Franklinton, Louisiana, and that wasn't very far for an airplane leaving out of Keesler Air Force Base in Biloxi to go. Even one this big. Some millionaire had built the target airfield for his planes, but the guy died of a heart attack while having a good ol' time with the ladies, leaving no inheritors, and the last time we'd been there, Major Gary had quickly bought the estate (with a little help from Kruger). So we had a landing field, one that could be accessed by a huge C-130J flying low out of Biloxi. There were even a few small aircraft still there. Another gift of Benjamin Gary's foresight was the extra acreage that had been purchased for use in keeping the men in shape as well as preparing lodging for them all. He'd positioned our outfit as a ranching arm of the Preservation Hall Society and contracted a construction company to go out there and build fifteen really nice cabins for the men, put in gates, and wire up security cameras. I wouldn't have been surprised if he'd even gotten his hands on a couple of cows.

Meanwhile, our flight plan called for us to fly most of the way in our own world, and Nigel would move us through within the last thirty miles; we just prayed that there would be no news choppers or police chases involving helicopters going on at the time of our exit. Nigel was pretty sure that if we went really fast, we could get through quickly. He wanted to know how fast a plane could go, and when Captain Braggs translated airspeed to miles per hour, the kid was ecstatic. He wanted to be a pilot now. God, to be eight years old and eternally optimistic again!

Braggs would have to fly on instruments for a short while when we were in the nil zone (as if any instruments could work in that place), but if anyone could do it, he could. A man that good should have been flying F-22s, some might think; but Marty Braggs came with a lot of baggage, as most gifted people do. He'd been embittered by some series of events in his life and was such a risk taker that he would take chances even fighter pilots feared. He was not to be trusted with jets that could move at supersonic speeds, but flying a huge cargo plane was just boring enough to keep his need for risk taking under control. He was also constantly prone to getting himself into some trouble with other officer's girlfriends, and that was the real reason why he always wound up being frequently assigned to fly cargo planes and the like. Typical for a guy like him. He was that fellow whom most young girls dream of—a tall blond guy with what people who spend their lives living in nice suburbs call "all-American" looks. Nigel heard Lucius calling Marty "Captain America" and took up the practice, so that was Marty's name among our men now. He'd been selected for this mission because his father was very close with President Kennedy and had pled for him. Otherwise, he may have ended his career being in charge of some air force comet-tracking station in the coldest part of Alaska. Even then, he would probably still have managed to find somebody else's wife to get in trouble with. Braggs wasn't crazy about this assignment, but it saved his life.

My wife, along with Amadeus Kruger and his new assistants, Carla Ryan, a computer whiz, and Dr. Derron Leonard, a former think tank member who'd mapped out Nigel's brain, both at his age and at mine, were loaded aboard in air-conditioned armored boxes that looked to me like coffins with observation glass. I should have visually inspected every piece of material that came aboard, but we were so short on time that it would have been an impossible task. Hence, only one other person was aware, at that point, of another unmarked coffin box with no climate controls or observation window that had been loaded onto our aircraft along with everything else.

Finally, we were ready to commence Mission CureSearch. I sent Lucius and Nigel off to get ice cream and talked to my men. It was time to be honest with them. We were going to embark on a mission that could possibly take years, and there was no way to know how many. If no cure could be found or fabricated, the world we knew would die. I relayed Commandant Gray's orders regarding Muldowneys and Craines to Crossover Team Alpha and reminded them that they'd been selected for the first crossover because of their lack of solid connection with anyone or anything here. If any of that had changed, I told them, now would be the time to say so because once we left, there could very well be no coming back. I waited for anyone to step forward. No one did. There were only nine of them there. That was the entirety of Crossover Team Alpha. First Sergeant Lucius Carver and Major Benjamin Gary had been reassigned to their current postings with this unit, and two more had been selected to replace them within the other units they'd been assigned to. My MISTmen stood ready to fight through hell, face the fire, battle to the death, and I was proud of them all. Semper fi. We took off.

Captain Braggs flew that bird high up into the air then began a fast descent toward our ultimate destination. Leave it to Marty Braggs to deviate from the flight plan. I asked what the hell he was doing, and he calmly explained that he intended to go in much faster than we planned. If we flew low, under the radar, not too many people would miss something of such size flying low through the night sky, he said. The less exposure, the better. Good point. I sent for Nigel and ordered the men to suit up. We were descending at an amazing speed, and I wondered if the man could pull this beast up fast enough to keep us from crashing into the ground. About that time, Nigel and Lucius arrived, Nigel all aglow with excitement. It appeared to me that "Captain America" was fighting the controls, but he took the time to smile and wink at the child, anyway. *What a cocky bastard!* I remember thinking. Finally, he said, "Do it!" Nigel opened the gateway, and we all blacked out.

We awoke on the landing field and in broad daylight. A look at my watch told me that the time was around 0900. *This shouldn't be happening,* I thought. *It was 1200 when we left. It should still be dark here.* No one knew what happened, and Nigel wasn't in the plane with us. Braggs was slumped in the pilot's chair, nose bleeding, a shiner on his right eye. I thought he may have been dead, but a quick pulse check told me that he was just knocked senseless. *First things first,* my mind admonished, so I went to check on my love and get her out of that damn box. The locks were keyed to my fingerprints, and all I had to do was touch the indentations on the control panel of each box. With a barely audible hiss, the top slid back, and I pulled her out. She was a little confused, but that didn't last long. I held her in my arms and did not want to let go. Finally, I did. I explained our situation to her; and when she understood that someone had been injured, she went straightaway to check on Captain Braggs. I awakened Kruger, Leonard, then Carla Ryan, all of whom immediately went in search of their geek gear. Lucius was, of course, next. I kicked him into consciousness and sent him out to locate Nigel, if he could. Then the rest of the team needed to be awakened. Every one of them was, of course, embarrassed and confused. They'd made this crossing so many times before and never came out of it in this condition.

I led them out of the aircraft and into the sunlight. We were definitely in the right place. A huge private airfield in Franklinton, Louisiana. The gigantic house that went with the estate was obvious in the background. I was beginning to worry a great deal over Nigel's absence, when our sentry called out. A golf cart was making its way toward our location, but no one could be sure who was in it. One of the men stood in front of me, and while he and the rest drew sidearms, Kruger hid inside the plane. As the cart got closer, everyone relaxed. It was Major Gary with Nigel, who, when he saw me, looked for all the world as if he knew he deserved a spanking for being caught stealing candy. The cart skidded to a halt right in front of us, and the major was out and saluting before its motion had even stopped, it seemed. He reported that Nigel had called him this morning, and he got out here from New Orleans as quickly as possible. Then he fell silent. So did everyone else. We were all staring at Nigel, waiting. He stood to attention, as he'd seen Lucius do. Okay. "Report, Little *Marine*," I demanded.

"It was Treple Clep, sir," he answered, sounding a lot like his babysitter/bodyguard. Our confusion must have shown on our faces.

"Sir." Major Gary stepped forward, saluting. "I have a picture here. The lad drew it for me when he was trying to explain." He handed the paper over, and what I saw on it only added to my confusion. It was some type of musical note. I called for Lieutenant Archimus Marcelon, who stepped forth, saluting. He was a music guy and our medic, as well as one of my best men with a Ka-Bar.

"This thing, or one like it, attacked us in there. What is it?" I asked, thrusting the drawing into his hand.

He couldn't believe what he was seeing either. "It's a treble clef, sir."

? thought I. My confusion must have been showing.

"When you read music, sir, it's an indicator of a G clef," he said, his face reddening.

"So it's a musical note?" I asked.

"Yes, sir. That's the easiest way to put it, sir."

We all stared at Nigel for a minute again. He was still trying to stand to attention, but was starting to fidget. "At ease, Nigel. Why don't you tell us what happened?" I said.

"When we were in the La Land (that's what he called *otherspace*), Treple Clep came through the walls and hit Captain America because he flew real fast through some finger waters where it was playing. The plane started turning over sideways. Nobody knew it, though cuz when Treple Clep came in, it was feeling sad mad, so it flattened and knocked everyone else to sleep. Except me, cuz I don't get hurt of anything in the La Land. That's why I used to go there to hide from the nuns."

There was dead silence among my MISTmen. "Nigel," I began softly, "if the plane was going sideways, how did we wind up here?"

He was visibly uncomfortable now. "I made the finger waters grab it and put it down neatly. They don't normally listen, but I made them do it this time. I was really tired too, but I opened the door to here and wouldn't let them go until they put us down. Some of them even fell out of the La Land, but they turned into sunlight and went away. It was still dark when we got here."

"Why didn't you wake us up, Nigel?" I asked.

He started to cry then stopped. "I tried to, Colonel sir, but no one could wake up, and I thought you were all dead, and I fell out to sleep 'cause I couldn't keep my eyes opened anymore. In the morning, I went in that house over there and remembered that you said to call Major Gary if things went bad, and that's what I did."

The silence among the men continued. "Sir," Major Gary began, "I don't know how he got into the house. The doorknob, the windows, everything, it's all been biometrically tuned to your palm print only." I looked at the kid. *I* knew how he got in. I was about to ask another question, when Lucius came double-timing it up to us at the same time that my wife came out of the plane, noticed what was going on, and angrily stomped over to protect the boy.

"What are you doing to him?" she began but then answered her own question. "You were talking to him in that scary quiet-talking voice of yours, weren't you? Look at him . . . he's positively frightened!" She put her arms around him, and he visibly reddened. It was a funny enough scene to make even me laugh—a little. Nigel trying to stand at ease at the age of eight while she hugged him like the mother figure she had become for all of Crossover Team Alpha. Great tension breaker for my marines. I let Lucius know that he was off the hook while Major Gary, my wife, and I hopped into the cart to go to the house. Nigel wanted to stay with Lucius and the other troops, so I let him.

I looked back once as we rolled off, and that scene will ever be a frozen moment among my memories, Detective. Captain Braggs had regained consciousness and was standing with my MISTmen, his arm in a sling and a broad grin underneath his black eye. The computer nerds were sitting in the shade of the plane, doing geek things with their mini-computers, having stopped working long enough to watch Lucius, who had picked Nigel up, and the other MISTmen beginning a game of toss-the-boy to one another. Nigel was loving being a football, and they loved him. He'd saved all of our lives, and they knew it. I can still hear him laughing. I remember thinking, *That's it. Crossover Team Alpha. All that's left of our Marine Corps, our country, and our world. She and I, twelve marines, a boy genius, and his assistants. Sixteen souls. We're all alone here, and there is so much to do.*

They were a young bunch, my team. Most of them were only in their twenties. I prayed that they would have what it took to face the tough times ahead.

A Devil in the Darkness

Click. The final piece of the puzzle in Roan Caldwell's mind found its place. He *knew* now. The General stood and began pacing the room, his scotch held in his hand. Roan rose slowly, walked over, and studied the lines of the man's face. The colonel seemed to accept the scrutiny as inevitable. "You said your original DNA test told you that he *couldn't* have existed in your world. You mentioned something about how two people who had every reason to be the same person could be different in different worlds, and you were referring to Nigel and yourself when you made that statement. You said that this boy got into a house whose security system was designed to answer only to *your* biometrics.

"Colonel, what's your wife's name?" Detective Caldwell asked. The General nodded, as if accepting something that he'd been waiting for. He even smiled as he turned and faced Roan with his answer.

"My wife . . .," he began. "My wife's name is Angeline. Angeline Claudia Duplessis-Renoir, and my name is Major General Nigel Boyd Renoir, United States Marine Corps, Second Division. The Nigel you know, well, he and I are the same person, only we're from different worlds. That makes us *almost* the same person, anyway. I am almost forty or so years older than he, as is my wife. My Angeline calls him 'Petit Nigey-Deaux,' meaning 'Little Nigel the Second.'"

Roan looked contemplatively at the taller man, and for a moment, his mind went back to something that he'd heard Nigel say before. "And you too have your Angeline while he's the one only one of all the different Nigels who doesn't."

"That's right, Detective Caldwell. It's true. I am living proof that he wasn't lying to you. Thinking of that boy now, I realize something. He was

---

227

an orphan of Katrina when we found him, and even then, he was playing in the schoolyard with a little girl named Angeline. We took him with us, posing as foster parents, believing that it was the least we could do, considering how much we owed this lost little boy child, but my personal feeling, nowadays, is that what we really did was upset some natural balance that existed between the worlds, and we paid the price for that act of presumptuousness then, as we continue paying for it now. At any rate," the senior Nigel continued, "there's no going back now. We can only move forward. I know you must have questions."

You bet I do, Roan thought. "Why doesn't he remember all of this history you're telling me?" Roan challenged. "When I talked to him, he wasn't even able to say how he did whatever it is he does. That's one reason why he wound up in Sand Ridge. He seemed to believe all of what he was saying, but there was no proof or indication that this thing had ever happened before in his life or could happen at all. The guy even passed a polygraph, and that's what convinced the court that he had mental issues."

General Renoir half smiled. "Actually, Detective Caldwell, *I'm* the reason he wound up in Sand Ridge. I needed Nigel put into an environment that would allow us to protect him, and considerable resources were used in order to secure a rack in a holding tank for the criminally insane instead of having him undergo a trial that could have exposed too much classified information and land our boy in some state or federal penitentiary. He didn't deserve to end up in any place like that. He . . . he has . . . *served* my country, your country, his own America, through three worlds at great personal risk and with extraordinary valiance. I see that you wonder how that could be. Well, I will explain all of that later." The elder Nigel looked down for a moment, once again rubbing his eyes with his fingers, a sign that Roan now knew indicated some deep internal grief within the man.

Roan waited a moment. The General began speaking again. "You see, we had to strip him of some of his memories. That's why he had no idea, originally, of how he was once again able to pass between the worlds. Yes. I did say once again because for a while, he'd lost that ability."

Roan turned his face away. His anger at the thought of stripping another person's memories was showing, and he'd never been one for emotional displays. *Sometimes your memories are the only thing you have to hold on to life with*, he was thinking. "How old was he?" he asked.

General Renoir didn't bat an eye as he went on to explain. "His life was in grave danger, Detective. We thought that we'd never hear of Blacen

Muldowney again, but that turned out to be a fallacy. His chapter in our lives hadn't ended yet, and he is once again posing a threat to an entire world. Two. This one and Nigel's home."

"How. Old. Was. He, *General*?" Roan asked again, his anger becoming almost palpable in the air between the two of them.

The general stopped in midsentence. Looking at Roan as if wondering what he had in mind, General Renoir answered, "Ten. He was about ten years old by the time the process was showing results and close to sixteen by the time the process had been completed. We started when he was eight."

Roan was stunned again. "You must be a soulless bastard," was all he could say. "He's *you*, man! Didn't it even bother you a *little bit*?"

The general looked away for just a moment, and that was the only indication that Roan would ever see of General Nigel B. Renoir's inner conflict. "As I said, Detective, it was what needed to be done."

"That's probably what Hitler said too," Roan answered.

The general's eyes hardened. "I have already told you, Detective Caldwell. I am willing to do whatever it takes and to be whatever I need to be in order to uphold my oath. Nigel was in danger, and by extension, so were the fifteen people that remained of our world. What we didn't know at the time was this—our greatest evil, Blacen Muldowney, had managed to get himself put on that airplane. He escaped before we were even fully aware that it was truly he himself who rode in the unmarked box we found in our cargo bay. Nigel, in the meantime, was too young to know that some of the things he did helped Muldowney to almost gain the upper hand in that reality. If he could not remember how to get back to where the problems started, he could not unwittingly endanger the people that even he had come to love as a family."

***

We found the empty box about a week after our arrival. That's how long it took to unload the cargo, and even then, not everything had been taken out of our C-130J. All work stopped when they found evidence that a stowaway had slipped on board. We had to determine who that had been. I deployed Crossover Team Alpha to search the surrounding acreage, and they found his trail almost immediately. It took a little longer for Lucius and the brain geeks to activate our portable DNA scanners and apply them. Meanwhile, I worried that one of the infected may have made the crossing, but also wondered, if such had been the case, wouldn't the ride through *otherspace* have destroyed the disease?

Unfortunately, my anxiety caused me to hover over our pet lab rats a little too much, but so what? They worked faster. Angeline also pitched in to help them, saying that her presence may make me behave like less of an ogre. The kids were happy to have her help. I behaved like less of an ogre. They were civilians, after all. Eventually, Dr. Leonard and Kruger came to me with confirmation of the stowaway's identity. It was definitely Blacen Muldowney's DNA they'd found in the box. He was here, and most likely, traveling with Carla Ryan who, somewhere along the way, stepped out for a smoke break and never came back. I could have choked Kruger. *How did this happen?* I demanded of him. He told me that when word of the classified mission came to him, he and his team were given carte blanche to gather whatever they wanted to take from what was left of The Division's laboratories. They could only speculate, but it seemed that Carla had an infatuation with Muldowney, and he may have used his persuasive charm to get extremely close with her so that whenever she took samples of his blood work, or anything else, she'd demand complete privacy with the man.

Since he was under a death sentence, anyway, no one felt the least bit sorry when his heart suddenly stopped one day and he went into a coma afterward, but they did have to move him into sickbay and chain him to a bunk there. Let him lie among his victims, she'd said. Maybe it'll soften him if he ever wakes up again. His two marine guards had no problem with that idea. That was the last anyone had seen of Muldowney. No one knew that she'd bring in a box and load the creep into it. She then put that box on an acquisition list. Since there was very little time left, the acquisition was simply filled. So that's how he did it. Once again, Blacen had used a young naive person in his nasty game. No matter now. Carla Ryan was put on the "scrub" list for aiding and abetting a domestic terrorist and murderer who was guilty of crimes against humanity.

When the trackers returned, we gave them the bad news. They were worried at first. Considering the fact that this was not our world and we did not have the full resources of the US government to work with, they asked, how would we find these two people? That, I told them, was *my* concern. Benjamin Gary and I were "the brass" now, and the brass would handle it. We were MISTmen marines, and MISTmen neither failed nor quailed. Boo-rah. Now was the time to play a trump card, and I did. The

Preservation Hall Society had become a multistate information-gathering organization. We even had sources in other countries. Lieutenant Colonel Gary had been under orders to build it into a usable organization for attaining data, and with the last infusion of funding from our government of fifty million dollars in diamonds and gold, he'd done better than expected.

In accordance with the government's plan, the idea behind The Division's original thinking in funding all this was the goal of building a place to hide federal witnesses or "priority personnel" (that would be anyone wealthy or politically influential enough to be of importance to our country's interests) if these had to flee and needed a place of concealment. Such preparation required our being in tune with whatever currents and ripples ran through the substance of this world, as well as being willing and able to use these to move anything or anyone into any location. That, in turn, meant having funds available for transplanting anyone from our home who may have had to be stashed here. There were overseas bank accounts that had grown nicely, as well as people who worked in every walk of life on our "payroll," such as it was. We'd paid attention to the disenfranchised. We'd run raffles that helped middle-class families get through those financially scarce months that had become all too frequent in this place. Everyone was a potential source. Lots of people needed things in this place. Lots of people were unhappy and victimized by the corrupt government here. They needed money, and the material they gave us got it for them. All we ever asked for in return had been simple, harmless, verifiable information.

That was how we built our bank accounts as well as our network by helping people who needed helping, attention-starved celebrities, mobsters, politicians, or clergymen who ran large churches being exceptions. Even though we'd give these ones information or leads, where it suited our purposes, we never sold to them or paid them for anything. Such people were not to be trusted with anything that could lead the press to the PHS. For when they got caught at their crooked dealings, as I was convinced they would, these type would throw any and everything to the sharks in the press in order to haul their own fat out of the fire. Our eyes and ears were those people who went about their everyday life ignored and normally under anyone's radar: the receptionist at the doctor's office; homeless guys who smelled bad, but were not too insane to notice and report things; the janitor of the local high school; the short-order cooks; and of course, waitstaff and bartenders in restaurants. Muldowney and Craine may have hated waiters, but they both loved restaurants, especially high-end ones.

If we'd bribed a few hospitality workers to eavesdrop on those two while back in our own world, they might have been canned before they got too far. I wasn't going to make the same mistake here. Major Gary put all of our associates on the lookout for Carla Ryan or Blacen Muldowney so that we had eyes in every nook and cranny that someone such as Muldowney would ignore. That was how we would find Carla and Blacen. It wasn't long before we got a lead from one of those restaurants. A busboy who worked at the Redfish Grill positively identified Carla Ryan as having come in to make reservations. Lieutenant Colonel Gary thanked the kid for helping us locate two potential investors in the city's rebuilding effort and gave him quite a nice finder's fee. That youngster was going to be able to pay the rent this month, for sure. Meanwhile, Lieutenant Marcelon was sent to hang out at the restaurant on the night of the reservations.

Sure enough, Muldowney arrived, but without Ms. Ryan. Right away, he began sizing up the wealthy-looking women who happened to be there that night. After having dinner and snapping at the waiter with his usual arrogance, he took off and wandered over to a bar on Decatur. He went in and spent a few hours there, looking for an easy mark. Most of the women ignored him that night (it might have been because of his missing front tooth) so he keyed in on the bartender. Maybe she'd been sampling too much of the business's wares or something because when he left, that's who he went home with. Understandably, we began to wonder now where his accomplice was. We needed to find Ms. Ryan for a couple of reasons. First, she'd emptied her bank account of a very large amount of money before we left home and was putting into circulation bills that may have been traceable since they didn't originate here, and the serial numbers wouldn't stand up to close examination in this world. Secondly, their version of Carla Ryan was thirteen years older and a federal department of transportation worker who ran a large office out of Atlanta. If anything were to happen that might bring our Carla's fingerprints and DNA information to their attention, a serious investigation may result. We were not prepared for that. Having eyes and ears everywhere is not the same as having fingers in the system.

Our best tracker and surveillance man was Gunnery Sergeant Gabriel Puccini, so he was sent to relieve Lieutenant Marcelon in watching Muldowney. We wanted Carla Ryan; and Marcelon, although being another one of our best trackers, was also a psychology major with an uncanny talent as a profiler. His ability would play a key role in finding Ms. Ryan, so we needed him back at base. Before dealing with Blacen, we needed to know where she was. I didn't want the man to be aware, just yet, of our knowledge of his whereabouts, and if Carla were still in contact with him, she'd need to be isolated first. She'd be easiest to break and use against him. There were also other things that needed to be done before we made any moves that could have exposed us to the authorities there. I had to know which people could be used in what circumstances, so Kruger was assigned to hack their system and find out what each of our doubles in this world were doing and where they were now. Knowing that would eventually tell us what direction to go in if we needed to stay here. He and Dr. Leonard were also to begin tutoring Nigel because he was a kid, after all, and kids have to go to school. They needed to be on hand to keep up the memory suppression work on the boy, anyway.

Because natural charm and his ability to think outside of the box made him a good motivator and judge of character, Captain Braggs, for his part, was assigned to quietly recruit people that we could put to work for us directly. There was an economic downturn occurring in that world, as well as wars on two fronts, and a lot of ex-marines needed secure jobs. Those were the ideal employees for the direction we intended to take. Braggs had a list of what sort of talent we needed as well as what types of ex-military personnel would be best suited for the jobs offered. We were set to begin building an organization that would serve our needs there when everything was thrown off track by an unexpected series of events.

SELF-RECRIMINATION

Nigel disappeared one day, and no one could find him. Sgt. Lucius Carver had taken him on a sort of field trip to the Audubon Zoo over in the Garden District and was enjoying having a pretty good day with him when suddenly the child seemed to recall something that made his mood turn sour. Nigel became morose and suddenly walked into the nil zone. Not being properly equipped for *otherspace*, Sergeant Carver was divided for just a second, as all the men were under strict orders to *never* enter there without being properly geared up. He hesitated just long enough for Nigel to close him out; otherwise, he would have followed the boy even into that place. He loves that kid just as much as I do, our "Master Guns" Carver.

Needless to say, the event caused quite an uproar among us. The boy was an asset, Detective, possibly the only worthwhile one we had, so Crossover Team Alpha was, by God, *not* going to lose him. We immediately started monitoring all law enforcement wavelengths. If he'd remained in his home world, someone would soon *see* something, we knew, and it would be reported. If he'd left, well, God bless our souls, for we too would be stuck here and the main source of our power probably lost to us. My MISTmen, with the necessary exceptions of Lieutenant Colonel Gary and Gunnery Sergeant Puccini, were mustered and garbed in camouflage fatigues, prepared for a forcible incursion and extraction, in case someone had captured Nigel. I would also be involved in such action (against the advice of my XO) should it become necessary. We were checking our weapons and preparing for movement in case Kruger turned anything up, when Angeline came in and pulled me aside.

She asked one simple question: "Where is his little girlfriend right now, dear?" My mouth stayed open for a few minutes before I thought to close it. Of course, he would recall *her*. That memory should have been deleted already, but who could possibly know for sure if *that* particular erasure would continue to work? Memories we had the technology to suppress, but not feelings. On my orders, Kruger redirected his search. He found little Angeline's home address and what elementary school the girl went to, and I was ready to take off with Lucius Carver, when my wife asked that we just let *her* go—alone.

"Okay," said I. "If you can bring him back, then do it." And she did it. By the Gods, Detective, that woman did it! What? No, she didn't have to use a bit of violence cajolery, coercion, or anything like that. It was far simpler for her. Captain Braggs flew her and Lucius into New Orleans with one of our Cessnas. They arrived at 0900; and she left the two of them at the airport, rented a car, and returned a little after 1830 with Nigel. He was back to himself again and felt a little better. She, on the other hand, didn't at all speak to Braggs or Carver during the return flight. As soon as I saw her face, I knew that there would be trouble for me. She gestured to the briefing room, and as we headed in that direction, I was pretty sure that Braggs, Carver, and Gary looked as if they were going to burst out in laughter. One look from me put an end to that merriment. For the moment. Then I had to face the fury.

"Why didn't you tell me who the little girl was?" she asked in a very nice voice, which really worried me. It was true. I'd forgotten to tell her, what with the crisis at home and everything that was going on. I myself had only learned her name on our last incursion before the Great Disaster. When we arrived back home, everything began happening far too fast, and it never stopped until after we got back here. I explained as much. Fine. Then she wanted to know why Nigel knew he had to see her but could not remember why she was of such importance to him. I told her that we'd used some of our microtech, applied it to Muldowney's will killer invention, coupled Dr. Leonard's research and some of Craine's to induce a process of gradual memory suppression within his brain cells. She was smoldering by the time I finished explaining.

"Why?" she asked, and there was a firestorm behind her words.

"Because Nigel has a great power that could be used against us," I began with the "party line," no doubt sounding a little self-righteous. "If his abilities became known to the government of this world, our activities within it could be seen as a hostile invasion. That would have very bad repercussions for all of us." Angeline folded her arms, and I could see the fires inside her gaze dampening—a little.

"I can see that most of that crap you just spouted had to come from your line of work, and maybe from the people that you worked for," she said then continued, "but I also think you know that Nigel would never allow himself to be used to hurt *us*. *You* wouldn't."

Truthfully, the possibility of Nigel's oncoming maturity bringing about a change in his choices regarding our use of his ability had been the express reason stated by the division for Operation Clean Slate, as this was called. Its main priority being this one thing; Nigel *must not* be allowed to fall into any other power's hands, be it friend or foe, but if he could continue to open the gates between the worlds with no reason to desire a return to his own world, this too would have been an acceptable solution. Of course, these same powers that be had originally preferred a more sure and *permanent* course of action to avoid such a catastrophe, but Kruger and I had gone to a lot of trouble in convincing Director Rocklin to allow the development of the memory-erasing process instead. What? You want to know what I mean when I say "a more sure and permanent course of action"? How about a bullet to his brain? Yes, that's right. Human government at work. For our part, the intent of the treatment was to only target certain memories that could expose classified information, but after the fall of the division, the DOD ordered a more aggressive development and application of the procedure in the case of Nigel; and despite how I felt about it, that was the only way to keep the boy alive.

It would have been so easy to say that they didn't give me any viable option, but I would never tell my beloved wife how I was only "following orders" when I did something she hated. Angeline deserved better than such self-serving platitudes from me. What? Okay, I'll put it simply, then; if my wife was going to be angry with me, I wasn't going to blame somebody else for whatever the problem was. "Good point," I answered her. "But he could be used in a way that would bring harm to us and never even know it. He is a child, Angel."

"I know that, Nigel *Senior*," she started, "and you're probably not going to tell me that you were under orders to do this to him. You'd do it as a good marine officer should, but you *can't* like it. So why won't you put an end to this? The government that ordered that monstrosity is probably long gone by now."

"It's a matter of protecting the boy as well as our own small group," I began in my best "let's be reasonable now" tone of voice. "Should an enemy capture Nigel, the possibility exists that because he would not allow himself to be cast against us, at worst, he could be killed after torture or, at the very best, spend the rest of his life being used as nothing more than a weapon," I explained, no doubt sounding, once again, like a military parrot to her.

"Why does his being used that way make a difference to you?" she asked me in a very sweet voice. I should have known how this was going to go, but forging ahead seemed to be the only sound strategy.

"A child is a human being, dear," I sanctimoniously began, "and that human being is ours, just as if he were our child. If the government of this country were to catch up with Nigel, he would have no other life than that of a convenience tool. He would be denied any normal life, ever. They'd exploit him as nothing more than a walking weapon of mass destruction, and no human being deserves a life so devoid of living. Nigel shouldn't be used as any government's secret utility weapon."

She raised her chin after my saying that, and I knew that a javelin was about to be hurled into my heart. "What do you think *you've* been used as?" she asked.

Stepping around me, she left the room. I just stood there, thinking. Angeline was right. While it was true that I had been used as a weapon for most of my life, it was also true that I'd grown up wanting nothing more than to be the best possible weapon I could be. My mind, my body, my pattern of thought, were trained to fighting and winning. Sun Tzu's *Art of War* was the first book I'd ever read through and through. I was five years old then. My father had been a master gunnery sergeant in the Marine Corps, but he tried his best to talk all of us, his children, into pursuing more peaceable careers. I was the only one who wouldn't listen, choosing, instead, to join MJROTC in high school, read as much military history as I could get my hands on, cultivate as many hand-to-hand fighting skills as possible, all the while studying and becoming more adept at the work of handling knives, guns, bombs, and any other transmitter of death, further disappointing the old man. He had once encouraged me to try out for sports, hoping that my attention would be distracted by these, and that maybe some college scholarship would come along and get me on what he felt was a better track in life. But for me, any involvement in school sports programs was motivated by the fact that leadership skills learned therein could be put to use later in a military career. I was as bored as one kid could be with school, but Father refused to allow any of his children to skip any grades. He was trying to delay the inevitable, I believe. That never quite worked out in my case, though.

Angeline and I met at the end of my junior year in high school. I was the captain of the defense for our football team, and we'd handed our rival school a royal trouncing. We all played well, and after the game, some of us went to their high school dance, hoping, no doubt, to provoke the inevitable brawl. That's when I first saw her. She was alone; their second-rate excuse for a quarterback was trying his best to talk to her, and I just *had* to walk over and sit right down on her left side, ignoring the fellow on her right side. She ignored him too. We immediately *knew* each other, but we'd never seen each other until that night. It was as if we'd been married for years, the way we just understood each other. Mr. Reject on her right eventually left in a huff while she and I continued talking. I'd almost forgotten my purpose in going there when the fight began. Mr. Reject had started in on our kicker because no one in their right mind would've started with *me*. I kissed her, we traded numbers, and I went to my calling. I was a weapon. That was that. Later, much later, she told me that I was the first boy who ever kissed her, and she'd hoped that we could have talked more that night. When it didn't happen, she'd just gone home.

She went to Tulane, I to Annapolis, and we kept in touch, seeing each other whenever we could. We were secretly married before we finished, but for her mother's sake, we had a public wedding again right after my graduation. My Angel never left me, yet we spent more time apart than together, it seemed. I was taking lives; she was learning to save them. I was a weapon. She was a curative. It was just the way it was. We got older and seemed to always be missing one another. I needed her, as she was the finer side of myself; but my government needed me, as I was the finest example of what a marine officer should be. I won a Purple Heart, two Silver Stars, three Bronze Stars, and finally, the Congressional Medal of Honor, an extremely rare double promotion, and still wasn't finished. She wasn't finished with me either, though I can think of no explanation for why she never left our marriage. She was the one woman in the whole world of mankind who could love me through whatever storms we faced, and I couldn't have done anything without her support, but most of our life together had been spent in separate locations. Why? Because I was the weapon I'd always wanted to be, and weapons do what they are intended to do; however, she still chose to live with what that meant. Yes, it was true. For my part, I'd *striven* to be this way. Little Nigel never did, and he deserved his own chance.

Okay, I silently promised, I'd do all that could be done to help him get the best he could out of living, without forcing the boy to actually *be* another me. He deserved to make his own choice. Sometimes I wonder, if we'd met sooner, maybe Angeline's presence would have influenced me into choosing a different path. One that would have allowed us to have more of that most precious thing two people could ever have with each other—time. This Nigel and this Angeline, however, *had* met sooner. They deserved a chance to be better together. That's what my dear wife wanted me to understand, to see. The memory wipe continued still since it was a necessity for our safety, but from that point on, the geeks were also ordered to leave his memories of little Angeline intact, if they could. Admittedly, this could mean that Nigel would never become a living weapon; but if so, then perhaps his life with his Angeline, *their* years, would also turn out to be much more superior for it. Believe me, Detective, I wanted them to have a life together, no matter how it looks to you or anyone else now.

Unexpected Developments

Meanwhile, Kruger's background check revealed that most of my people had no doubles in this universe. Of the few who did, Captain Braggs once had one, but that man died in their Korean Conflict. Lucius Carver's double had been twenty years older than he and was KIA in Iraq. He'd had a son who was a first lieutenant in the Marine Raiders and frequently used for classified missions. In fact, the young man was away on one of these at that very time. Three of the men who were with my current group also had younger doubles who were, not unexpectedly, members of the young Lieutenant Carver's squad. They were Roy Robert "Roy-Bob" Joseph from Lucedale, Mississippi, the best machinist in the military and inarguably *the* top MISTmen's expert with the "bull pup" shotgun as well as any pistol he'd get his hands on. He could build new weapons out of anything, as long as we gave him an adequate shop and working space. There was also one Antoine Rochon, whom the men referred to as "the Creole Assassin" because of his ability to move with amazing stealth. He was one of my best snipers and the man to go to for silent elimination of any enemy. The last one of these was "Wisconsin Wally," Walter Ralph Arthur McGrath, whom the men also referred to as "American Pie." He was one of our more angry MISTmen and hated the corporate world, no doubt because his father's fortune had been stolen by corrupt businessmen back home, resulting in the suicide of both of his parents. The McGrath of this reality had had his father's fortune handed down to him and then stolen by a corrupt Wall Street banking group whom he'd known and trusted from childhood on. This McGrath hated the whole corporate world as much as my Walter R. A. McGrath did.

These were some of the miscreants and borderline individuals who made up the junior Lucius Carver's Special Marine Ops unit, and they were constantly placed in perilous situations to handle the dirty deeds of that government, normally at the behest of a military branch called the MPIS. Their government never told them that if any of their top secret missions went bad, they'd be renounced and left on their own, but they knew that was the way it would go. Later on, this proved to be the best piece of intelligence that we ever could have gained. Lieutenant Marcelon's double was also older than he and was the director of the United States Marine Band. The Kruger here was three years old. Dr. Derron Leonard did not yet exist, but his parents were about to celebrate their first-year anniversary. *He'll probably be born in about nine months*, I remember thinking.

Muldowney's double was eight years older and incarcerated, having been convicted on a plea bargain of multiple serial rapes and murders. He was facing numerous counts and, because of his deal with the DA, had escaped the death by torture penalty that exists in that America, being sentenced instead to three thousand years in a federal "supermax" prison (another thing we didn't have back home) without the slightest possibility of parole. All in all, that monster had raped, tortured, and killed fifty women, maybe more, but that was all he would own up to doing. It seemed that Muldowney was detestable no matter what world he was in. Nevertheless, with Kruger's exceptional hacking skills and our DNA tracking equipment, we still managed to implement his execution before we left there. How? Oh well, it was simpler for us, at our level of scientific advancement with DNA, to locate at least two other victims who hadn't been found nor had he confessed to. We then inserted that information into a digital packet regarding an unrelated case that was headed for one of their police labs. On the basis of such damning new evidence, there was no further way for that Blacen Muldowney to evade their death by torture penalty. He was immediately relocated to death row.

It was Devin Craine's double that worried me, though. The man was twenty years older than ours had been, and he lived and worked (whenever he had a job) right in New Orleans. He'd mostly worked as a DNA researcher, but kept getting fired because of his behavior toward his fellow employees. He currently had an application in at a local hospital, which, if he got hired into, would give him access to a laboratory wherein he may have been able to pursue the same destructive course that the Craine of our world had. If our Muldowney met this unhappy man, there could be hell to pay. It wasn't going to happen again, I decided. Both Benjamin Gary and I wanted to order this Craine neutralized right away, but the idea occurred to us that he may be put to use in finding a cure for the other Craine's bioweapon. Of course, Muldowney had contributed to creating that nightmare, but Kruger and Dr. Leonard had shown themselves more than capable of duplicating anything Muldowney did since both of them were far more brilliant than he would ever be. No reason to spare that scumbag's life. As far as we were concerned, he was an enemy combatant and would be dealt with as such. Before our men could get to him, though, the inevitable meeting of Muldowney and Craine II occurred.

This Craine, like the one we'd previously known, was a loner, with no friends; but unlike our Craine, he often spent his time in one of the many bars of the city, trying to drink himself into happiness. As he was leaving one of those places, he bumped into Muldowney, practically knocking him over, and kept walking. It took a minute for Blacen to recognize the man, but when he realized who that person was, he abandoned his lady friend and ran down the street, calling "DEVIN! DEVIN *CRAINE*!" Alert to the danger, Gunnery Sergeant Puccini stopped long enough to put a 911 microchip comm call in to Kruger, gave a short synopsis, and was moving to follow when two sailors came staggering out of the Friends Bar and, seeing Puccini in his fatigues, one of them immediately jumped to the alcohol-assisted conclusion that my agent was an MPIS agent and he and his buddy had been "busted," so they attacked the gunnery sergeant, figuring their military careers were over, anyway. Why? Because that America had something that this one and my original one didn't have. Their country has had some harrowing encounters with lone wolf terrorists who arose out of their military. For that reason, there was a wing of the armed forces identified as the Military Policing and Investigating Services branch (MPIS) that existed solely for the investigation and elimination of illegal activities within the armed services. They also were tasked with clandestine elimination of terrorist threats, foreign or domestic; and that section of the services wore uniforms of a slate gray color.

On that day, Sergeant Puccini was wearing our camouflage fatigues, and ours are unlike anyone else's. You see, when in active mode, ours change to suit the background coloration no matter where the wearer may be. They're so effective that the marines wearing them can be invisible to most eyes. But when not in active mode, they're slate gray. Because it didn't seem necessary for that mission, Puccini's camos were not activated, thus they appeared as slate gray as the MPIS normal uniforms were. Moreover, the two men who attacked Sergeant Puccini were personally involved with each other in a capacity that was not approved by that country's military and would have resulted in court-martial as well as imprisonment without exception. What do I mean? They were secretly homosexuals, and during their incarceration, they would, in addition to being psychologically tortured, be issued a suicide kit. Needless to say, having only such a bleak existence to look forward to did not make them less capable or willing to fight.

When they caught sight of my tracker, they'd assumed themselves to be under some type of investigation by the MPIS section, which is, by the way, also the most ruthless division of their military. So they chose to assault Puccini. Over in that reality, all of their sailors are required to undergo intensive hand-to-hand combat training, which produces excellent fighters; additionally, these two had logged hours and hours of extra martial arts training, and they were angry. Two of them against one of my MISTmen. They were able to survive against him long enough to be a distraction, but ultimately, they didn't stand a chance. By the time he'd finished putting those men down, the gunnery sergeant was just receiving my orders to neutralize both of his previous targets at the earliest opportunity, but he'd lost track of his quarry, and the second Muldowney/Craine team up was in the making, somewhere. I was in the building on Burgundy at the time with Angeline, Marcelon, Lucius, and Nigel. Kruger was also with us, as he'd asked to come into town so as to hack the main NOPD computer and scan for any trace of Carla Ryan having turned up as a dead body in an alley somewhere. He couldn't do it in the other location because Dr. Leonard was installing the truckload of computers and programming that was brought from home over there, and that would take more than a day to get done.

Meanwhile, Kruger's search found no trace of Ms. Ryan, but did turn up more news. This Craine was already under investigation by their federal government, having been suspected of stealing and reselling materials from the New Orleans naval air station in Belle Chase, Louisiana, as well as possibly supplying a synthetic drug called meth to sailors who'd been stationed at Pascagoula naval station at the time. So this MPIS branch, as well as NCIS, would probably be involved. Great. Our only advantage with that was the fact that the various law enforcement agencies over there seem to hate to work together. Each one would rather hog the credit and get more of the financial backing of their Congress that way.

Still, Craine may also have had a tail placed on him by any one of these agencies, who, if he or she were any good, would have noticed Puccini sticking out like a sore thumb in our marine camos. He needed to get out of the field for a little while, so Gary and I decided that it was time to call my gunny in to the Rue Burgundy field base and debrief him. Muldowney was less important for the moment. In having his double placed on the death by torture list, we had severely limited his ability to freely move about in this reality's United States. I'll explain how that worked later in your briefing. We also knew that we would, without a doubt, find him again. As part of his psychosis, he *needed* to have *something*, one little thing, that the he did in the same fashion, at the same time, every day. It was just the way he was. There must have been a means to find this guy. He had to be sleeping somewhere. We'd found no trace of anything being bought or rented in his name or Carla's, so where could he be staying? Where would a rogue Division scientist have found a safe haven in this post-Katrina world? That was the question. If not Muldowney, then what of Devin Craine? He never stuck to any routine as his buddy had, but there were some consistencies that he too clung to.

I ordered Kruger back to the Franklinton property to access everything we had on our Craine. A day after he returned, he called back with the key. Devin Craine of our world had a base of operations across the state line, either in Pearl River or Waveland, Mississippi. He'd had some relative living there, and as it turned out, so did this Craine. The difference was that on this earth, he, not his relative, owned the land. Carla Ryan's name also turned up, sort of. Someone bought a trailer on a rental lot in Waveland, Mississippi, listing the name of Renetta Ryan, which was her middle name, as the owner. This had been done the week after Muldowney and Carla disappeared from our landing site. Blacen had known of Craine's association with the owner of that land back in our reality, so we surmised he must have had the trailer placed there in hopes of coming across Devin Craine's double sooner. It had to have been the location we were looking for.

That night, Lucius, Puccini, Marcelon, Eller, and I drove our Hummer across the state line into Waveland, Mississippi. We parked the vehicle about a half mile out and headed through the woods for the trailer park. We didn't need to get too close before we could see that there was a lot of activity going on there. The place was loaded with government vehicles, as well as an ambulance and a coroner's van. An NCIS crime scene unit was there too, and although we didn't see any of the MPIS people there, we had no doubt that they either knew already or would soon know what had happened to draw all the attention to this place. A short recon told us what the big event was.

They'd tracked their Craine to this location after he hooked up with Muldowney, and the agent who was following them decided to take them both in. A struggle ensued, and somehow, Muldowney managed to shoot the man in the back and escape with his pal. As we watched, we heard one of the agents call out to his boss. In another moment, we found out what happened to Carla Ryan. It hadn't been very pretty, and she'd been dead for a while. We saw the coroner pick up her purse and heard him announce that he'd found a DOD identification within. Our lives had just become more complex.

BATTLE SHOCK

Tantrum. I guess that's what they call it when a person comes into his house, kicks things around, and punches holes in the walls. That's what I felt like doing when we got back to the Rue Burgundy Field Base. I felt like throwing a tantrum, as the old folks used to say. Carla Ryan's body had just been found, and her DOD identification was now headed for some NCIS lab, probably in Washington DC. I wanted to curse her through all the seven hells or whatever for being such a damn fool as to trust an animal like Blacen Muldowney. Instead, I cursed the fact that I'd lost one of the last survivors of the human race on our earth. With that in mind, Ben Gary called Kruger and had him drop passive spyware on as many of their computer systems as we could. Captain Braggs was also ordered to have the C-130J ready for takeoff at all times. Having cut those orders, Lieutenant Colonel Gary and I cloistered ourselves and began to plan. If we had to leave in a hurry, he'd stay, and his identity had to be firm. We began to construct a believable history for him and the men he'd keep command of. I had nine MISTmen, and if it came to it, four would stay here with him and five would go with me. Dr. Leonard had to stay here and work on a way to duplicate Nigel's ability. Kruger would be doing the same thing from wherever we wound up should we have to retreat.

I thought, for just a moment, to leave Angeline, but Benjamin convinced me that would be the worst possible thing I could do to her and myself. We would take as much of our microtech as we could with us since it had been the thing that gave us the advantage in this world. We did all we could to arrange for tomorrow then did a little more. After that, there was nothing left to do but sit still and wait to see if their government would discover our existence. We were as prepared as we could be for that. At this crucial juncture, an unexpected opportunity to increase our strength came our way. Our spyware rendered some very useful information regarding the young USMC First Lieutenant Lucius Carver Junior's location and situation. He and his squad were soon to be inserted deep into Russia in order to perform some clandestine operation. Their Cold War had ended, but there was a new authority in the old USSR. Some political strongman who had formerly been head of that country's KGB had come to power as the "democratically" elected president of Russia.

The CIA had decided that this man had to be a predatory bear in sheepskin, and they weren't all wrong. Lieutenant Carver and his Raider squad were one of two squads that were deployed on a special Black Ops mission to handle the situation. They HALO jumped right into the Black Sea, one to the northwest of the man's billion-dollar palace on Cape Idokopas and the other to the southeast with orders to kidnap or kill Russia's top political strongman. All evidence of affiliation with the United States' military had been removed from both squads and they would be, in the case of capture, decried as a splinter group who had gone rogue and become mercenaries employed by religious terrorists from the Middle East. For that reason, none of them were to allow themselves to be captured alive, if it came to that. Both squads made it ashore and were working their way toward the target's domicile when things began to go very badly. The terrain they were traversing was rugged, densely wooded, and unfamiliar to them. Worse still, after the mission had been green lit and initiated, someone at the top on the American side got cold feet and concocted the idea of alerting the Russians that two teams of mercenaries were going to be out there that night, so the area was loaded with Spetsnaz. Those marines were going to be decimated.

Squad One was caught two miles inland from the beach they came out of the ocean onto. They'd fought hard, but in the end, the Blind Widowmaker claimed them. Fortunately, when the fighting was over, there was no possible way that the Russians could attain any evidence that pointed toward the identities and mission of the dead marines. Implanted under the skin of each Raider's chest was some type of enhanced incendiary device programmed to self-destruct and incinerate the entire human body before they could be captured (compliments of their CIA). Even the dead would self-destruct as soon as their vital signs ended. All that the enemy would ever find of them or their equipment would be piles of ash. Meanwhile, Squad Two, Lieutenant Carver's troops, was washed farther south than they expected, and that alone saved their lives. That particular group of men made it farther inland from the beach, but they were also aware of the fate of their fellow Raiders. They had encrypted electronic devices, providing instant communication between the two squads, you see. Though they knew that this was the end of their lives, though they knew that they'd been betrayed by their superiors, they were still going to try to complete the mission. Those were the type of men that made the Marine Corps great. But by that time, we were already on the scene. We, for our part, had dug a little deeper and found out that this was the original plan of the MPIS, to put the Raiders out there and then abandon them. They wanted to see if the mission were possible at all and, while they were at it, make the Russian president feel indebted to the American government somehow. Additionally, it was the MPIS that had influenced someone within the CIA to contact the target. Those men never stood a chance.

It was time to act, but before that, Lucius Carver needed to know about his double's son. I felt that it was the right thing to do. You see, Detective Caldwell, in our world, that youngster had been the victim of a late-term abortion forced upon his mother by her disapproving parents. They were members of one of the wealthiest families of an affluent African nation and felt that an Black American man was too far below their status for their daughter to have his child. That illegal operation, however, killed not only their grandson, but also their daughter. Lucius was about to meet his son that would have been, and I wanted the man to be mentally and emotionally prepared. Additionally, we would also have to use Nigel's ability in a way that may have been new to him, and if he knew how much this meant to Lucius, we believed that his commitment would be more . . . sure. I knew from my past with the lad that Nigel could move in and out of the *between* zone and stay within the same world. We had seen him disappear from Lucius's side and resurface in another location in the same reality back when my Angeline had gone to find him at little Angeline's home. We would now need him to tap into that ability for what we had planned, but he had to have a reason to want to do so.

For the sake of his dignity, I will not go into the depth of emotion that Master Gunnery Sergeant Carver felt when he learned of the Junior Lucius's existence as well as the situation that his double's son would soon be placed in. Although this version was a man not too much younger than he himself, it was still his boy. I understood. Nigel was my son, no matter that we were the same person. When I explained to him—Nigel, that is—what was going to be needed, as well as how much it meant to Master Sergeant Carver, he was, for his part, all too willing to try to get us to that location. He just had to be shown where Cape Idokopas was on the globe. He did, however, request a set of our special camouflage fatigues for himself. Request granted. By God, Detective, my boy also requested a rifle! That I refused. He would stay safely inside our transport with Captain Braggs while the MISTmen went out to retrieve Lieutenant Carver's Raiders, hopefully, without too much loss of life.

In order to complete the mission, our entire squad of MISTmen, including Lt. Col. Benjamin Gary and I had to be involved. Everyone except Nigel would have to equip themselves with their Otherspace Travel Outfits (which, by the way, in typical marine fashion, my men now referred to as OTTO gear). In addition, we needed a CH-53E Super Stallion, a helicopter that can transport up to forty people. To attain it, we'd paid some people who paid other people who eventually found and paid off a few corrupt officers within their transportation corps, and that got it done. The PHS definitely had deep enough pockets for it. One Super Stallion was ordered to a certain location for a refit, and while en route, that original order was belayed. But the chopper never made it back to its point of origin because all the paperwork showed it as having been scrapped due to irreparable electrical wiring faults. We were, however, apprised of the fact that unfortunately, the machine was located in a naval storage base's VTOL vertiport area that we would not likely be able to access from outside. We were also informed that for a few hundred thousand dollars more, the thing could be moved to any location we wished. Our answer was an unequivocal *no*. So how we got to it would be our problem. That was fine by us.

It was time to test Nigel's ability to move in and out of the nil zone while remaining in the same world. We showed the lad a picture of the location where we needed to go and got started. All of our men geared up; then we ran a mountain climber's rope from Lt. Col. Benjamin Gary at the back of our single-file line to me at the front. I held Nigel's hand, and the boy once again walked us into that horror that we called *otherspace*. We exited right in front of our newly acquired CH-53E Super Stallion, and it took less than three seconds. Even with the memory wipes, Nigel was getting better at crossing the nil zone. Captain Braggs, though, had never walked through *otherspace*, and we thought that he would heave right there on the deck in front of our chopper, but Lieutenant Eller held the man's mouth shut until we could get a catch bag under his chin. You see, Detective, we'd learned that somehow, their NCIS agency had gotten word that there would be an attempted theft of a CH-53E Super Stallion, and since that particular vertiport would be under surveillance that night, we dare not leave anything that could contain traceable DNA at the scene. Military police were stationed at the entrances, and there were also agents stationed on the roof, guarding the chopper's open-topped hangar. None of them ever knew we were there. Additionally, Dr. Leonard had even planted some sort of loop feed into all the cameras that had eyes on the place. We mounted up into our transport; Captain Braggs lifted off then sped out of the NCIS officers' line of sight, and my boy took us to Cape Idokopas.

There is a road that runs roughly alongside the Cape Idokopas Palace—it's in a valley and, from that one, ran another road in a southeasterly direction, the second one being more empty and abandoned than the first. Lieutenant Carver and his squad had fortified in a position under cover of the trees at the very end of that road and prepared for their final battle. They'd been able to fight off and evade their enemy along the way. Even though none of them had lost their lives, they still had wounded Raiders whom they were not going to abandon. They had no way of knowing that my squad was already there, waiting. Based on the psych profiles we'd fished out of their military software, Kruger and Leonard had come up with what they called a probability equation that should have been able to predict the location where these men would be found. They were dead right. At the very end of that unnamed road alongside the Black Sea in Russia, we'd waited almost throughout the night, listening to the sounds of the battle as it came closer and closer. As soon as we arrived, the auto-silence feature that had been added to our chopper was activated, keeping Captain Braggs and Nigel safe while we'd gone on to our locations. I'd deployed the MISTmen alongside Lieutenant Carver's most probable route, six to each side, so that when the Raiders came in, they would be between our two positions.

They made it there too, Detective Caldwell. Despite the odds against their survival, they came, carrying along their wounded and being harangued by the Spetsnaz squads that were tracking them. The enemy was having a very hard time keeping up, partly because they'd hoped to catch as many of Lieutenant Carver's men alive as they could and partly because these marines were just fighting too hard to be captured easily. Their enemy wanted to call in air support, but the forest was way too dense. The FSB wanted this fight to be conducted as quietly as possible, and burning up a dense woodland with ordnance would definitely draw too much attention. That's why they were driving the Raiders toward that road. It was out in the open, and any air strikes could have been carried out with more accuracy and efficiency. That's also why the Raiders were fighting to stay under cover of the trees.

It was almost over by the time they reached our position, though. Lieutenant Carver's Walking Dead Raiders (that's what they called themselves, for some reason) were out of options. They weren't going out in the open onto that road; they couldn't escape to the sea, and even if that had been possible, there would have been no one waiting to extract them. Having no expectation of living to see daylight, they prepared for the end. Just as the enemy troops got there, though, MISTmen broke cover and wiped them out. With our advanced camouflage, neither side could have seen us until it was too late. That act gave us a break in the action that lasted long enough for me to identify myself to the Walking Dead Squad as Maj. Gen. Nigel Boyd Renoir, United States Marine Corps, Second Division, and order them into the CH-53E Super Stallion that was just now deactivating its camo cover right past the tree line on that road. Landing it there had been challenging and risky, yet we needed to have it close enough for our escape, but far enough away to clear the trees when it took off.

Some of my MISTmen helped the Raiders to carry their wounded, and the rest provided covering fire. That run from the trees to the chopper was less than half a klick—about 400 meters or so, but it felt like a thousand. Meanwhile, more Spetsnaz began to arrive every minute, it seemed. We were now in a full-on firefight, but our small company kept moving. We were using DNA-specific ammunition that had been programmed to hone in on Russian DNA (our guys called them bigot bullets, and the name stuck), and what that meant was that every one of our shots took a man down, so that was helping. First Lieutenant Carver and I were going to be the last to arrive at the chopper, but about twenty meters out, a round hit him, and he fell. Seeing this, Master Gunnery Sergeant Lucius Carver charged out of the safety of the helicopter, past our troops who were laying down covering fire, and rushed to the man who would have been his son. I kept ordering him back, but he didn't seem to hear. As we pulled the Junior Carver to safety, we could hear the rotors of their air cover heading in our direction. More Spetsnaz were also charging us from under the tree line, and it seemed that we were doomed.

Lieutenant Colonel Gary's orders were clear in this situation. He was to take off and leave us there, but he wasn't doing that for some reason. I felt anger that he'd disobeyed orders when I saw the reason for the delay: Nigel had escaped the Super Stallion and was running toward us! *OH NO, oh no! Go back! GO BACK!* I thought. I must have been yelling it also because the boy hesitated. Seeing what was happening, the men tried to catch up with him, but Nigel ran into *otherspace* and disappeared. The Raiders who were healthy enough to fight stopped in their tracks for just a moment. But a moment is forever when men are in combat. A moment can make all the difference between life and death. The Spetsnaz hadn't seen the boy yet—his camouflage made it hard for them to, so they kept coming on, firing as they approached. These marines were going to die, I thought.

In that same moment, my boy, my Nigel, reappeared right next to the three of us: Lucius Sr., Lucius Jr., and me. His face was contorted in anger, and yellow light was spilling like tears of flame from his eyes. He reached into that *other* place, spreading his arms like a crucified man, and pulled destruction in the form of red-and-orange liquid-like illumination out of the *between* zone. It became a living fire in his hands, and he *whipped* it at our enemies. The conflagration burned through them at the speed of light then turned about and did it again, consuming men, armaments, ordnance, and equipment as well as their air support; and nothing of theirs caught within that inferno remained. When he let it go, it rolled like a wave in all directions away from him, skipping over our people and equipment as it went. Then it dissolved and was gone. All the enemy troops and their air support had been reduced to cinders. The trees, grass, and wildlife, however, were unharmed and silent. Everything was still. As crickets regained the courage to chirrup, Nigel almost fainted into my arms. I carried my son to the chopper, and Master Sergeant Lucius Carver carried his.

One of the men with the Raiders was a corpsman, and he helped me revive our boy. "Nigel," I asked, "what was that?"

"It was the finger waters, sir," the boy answered weakly. "They get mad when I do, and they wanted to help me too."

"Sir!" Captain Braggs interrupted, looking askance at Nigel.

"Yes, Captain?" I replied. He went on. "The skies are clear, and we can fly under the radar for some time while he revives, but we need your son to get us home."

"Can you do it, petit Nigey Deaux?" I asked my boy as I held him in my arms.

"Yes, Colonel sir," he replied. "I'm tired, but I can do it." At that moment, I felt so much pride in him, so much relief for him, Detective, that there is no way to adequately describe it.

I ordered Braggs to fly low out over the Black sea, ordered the Raiders to apply "slappies" and go under sedation, had the MISTmen gear up while we were flying. It was time to depart that place of death, for we'd attained the thing we needed most—potential reinforcements. Nigel needed to sleep for about thirty minutes or so before he tried it. Captain Braggs could fly that Super Stallion under the radar over the Black Sea for that long, we thought, but Nigel wanted to get home as soon as possible. He opened the way into the nil zone, and three seconds later, we were flying over our property in Franklinton, Louisiana. Again the men cheered for him, but he had fallen asleep and couldn't have heard them, anyway.

INTEGRATION AND
RECOVERY

I have always thought that Angeline has the most beautiful hands, and I knew what she did—she was a physician, but watching her work on the wounds our new men had, well, that experience moved me to an even higher respect for her and how she performed within her chosen profession. I realized something that day: to the extent that I was gifted and successful in my chosen field, she was even more so in hers. She was tender, caring, and soft enough to cure the wounded, but she could also be hard as diamond and unrelenting as steel when that was what her patients needed. We worked together so well in caring for our people, and without a doubt, we truly completed each other. The Walking Dead's navy corpsman, HMCM, Master Chief Hospital Corpsman Daniel Legget, was awestruck by her ability to work with such clarity of mind and purpose under duress; and she, for her part, was happy to have his assistance as another medical professional. She removed the incendiary devices from each of the men's chests, following which Leonard programmed them so that their GPS readouts placed them in Cape Idokopas and initiated all of their self-destruct sequences. That was that. The Walking Dead Raider squad had officially been killed in action, as far as their masters were concerned.

Lt. Lucius Carver Jr. was the least badly injured, mainly because his IOTV (that's shorthand for "improved outer tactical vest") had saved his life when the round hit him. All he suffered was a bruise to his upper back. For every day that the men were in the infirmary, either Lt. Col. Benjamin Gary or I would be there. Until he knew for a certainty that his men were all going to be fine, First Lieutenant Lucius Carver Jr., for his part, also refused to leave no matter what. I approved greatly. The young Carver was an excellent commanding officer. Eventually, our medical staff, such as it was, reassured us that all the troops recovered from Cape Idokopas would survive. Additionally, every one of them wanted to see "the Boy Wonder" as they called Nigel. They sincerely loved him, for he, at such a young age, had put his own life on the line for them. They were always asking how he was doing; and when they finally did meet our MISTmen and hear more about the boy, including his moniker of "the Baby Marine," they were even more moved.

Strained. That is the best way to describe both Nigel's physical and mental condition after the Cape Idokopas mission, as well as my relationship with Angeline when she treated him. Seeing Lucius Carver with his son did soften her attitude up eventually, but the atmosphere at our dinner table was still not at all pleasant for a time. As a couple, we had never been in such a sorry state before when it came to our boy or anything else. I had no desire to justify any of my choices in that matter, and she had no desire to fight with me over it. But Nigel's body and mind had undergone an excessive and hurtful exertion, and he was having a tough time healing. When Angel wasn't sitting beside his bed, I was, for we both feared that we might lose our boy, either to exhaustion or to some mental disconnect from which he could not recover.

During the days when we both had to be gone, Maureen Sampson, who was Lt. Col. Benjamin Gary's lady friend from N-Prime, would sit beside his bed and care for him. The child just slept on for days. When he was awake, he seemed unable to speak any words or feed himself. The longer that continued, the more distant my Angeline seemed to become. I watched her go to the infirmary every morning and loved her all the more for how compassionate she was. She didn't want to hurt me, but seeing little Nigel in that condition was hurting her. She was divided when she came home every day, and I, for one, would not fault her for that. I was sitting beside his bed one day when he reached his little hand out and grabbed mine. The boy looked at me and spoke for the first time since Cape Idokopas.

"It was right to do, Colonel," he said and then went back to sleep. He woke up a little while later, and I could see confusion in his eyes. But now, as I sat beside his bed, hearing Sam Cook singing "Bring It on Home to Me," a tune that Angeline and I know well, a thought crystallized within my mind, and I also *knew* what to do for him. I just *knew*. Holding his face between my hands, gently forcing him to look at me, this is what I told him: "Nigel, think about your Angeline and go into the La Land, get inside the blue lights, go visit your little Angeline, then come right back home. Angeline will always make the pain go away." Without another word, he got up, took an unsteady step, and disappeared.

When she came home, he was sitting at the dinner table, chattering on as kids do, and eating strawberry-vanilla bean ice cream. She stood unbelieving, but overjoyed for a moment, then ran over to the table, picked him up, and hugged him as if she were a mother grizzly. She looked at me and *knew*. *What did you do?* she mouthed silently through her tears. Nigel hugged her and told her with all childish innocence, "The Colonel told me to go into the La Land and then go find my Angie. He told me that she would always be able to make my hurt go away." The implications were not lost on my Angeline. She knew where that assured understanding had come from inside of me so that I could pass it on to Nigel the Second. She knew what I was saying about her effect on my life, my heart, my well-being, then, now, and forever, no matter what incarnation the worlds would cast me in. She would always hold the key, even as her double in this place held the same key for the double in our family, and that was beyond questioning for her. She didn't even get upset because I'd let him eat ice cream before dinner.

Life got a bit easier after that, but a certain amount of tension persisted for a while until one day when Nigel told her, in all honesty, that he would have found a way to follow me into that battle no matter what I may have tried to do to stop him. He wanted to be there for Lucius's sake and would have allowed nothing to prevent him. In one of those moments of profound wisdom that children sometimes have, the boy told her that because he was so kind, Lucius needed to know his son, so what if they were from different places? He even went as far as saying, in his own way, that wherever our long-term mission would take us, at least Master Gunnery Sergeant Lucius Carver's son would get to know his dad.

That moment of wisdom ended, and the boy became a child again; but the point had been made, and Angeline accepted that. She knew how he could move through space, and by extension, she also knew that what he'd told her was the indisputable truth. *No one* could have made him stay home that night. As a result of Nigel's actions, Lucius Carver and his double's son had become the friends that fathers and grown sons should be. They both deserved that second chance. Both then and now, Nigel would always be willing to put his life in danger for Master Sergeant Carver's sake. Lucius's wife of that world, however, had chosen *not* to meet with him. She'd told Lucius Carver Jr. that she couldn't have borne the pain of separating from her husband again if our group had to leave while she and her son stayed there. Besides, she wasn't sure that he would have been able to be *her* Lucius, whom she'd lost, and neither one of them wanted to be disappointed if that were so. The decision to avoid contact, therefore, had become mutual. Still, she wanted to live close to her son, who was now officially listed as KIA, so we had to make that happen. A few months after she got the official DOD notification of his death while carrying out a classified mission, it seemed that she perished in a fire that consumed their home, and that was that, as far as their authorities were concerned. In reality, however, Lucius Jr. had secretly presented himself to his mother long before that official notification came, and afterward, she moved into a new home that had been built for her and her son on our Franklinton ranch.

After seeing incontestable proof of how they had been betrayed, all the members of the Walking Dead Raider Squad chose to join our military, such as it was, and submitted to being thoroughly vetted by Lieutenant Colonel Benjamin Gary. It helped that he and I also held briefings and showed them evidence of who we were, where we'd come from, and what country we fought for. We enlightened them concerning what Nigel could do and where he was from, how he had crossed over into our world, and briefed them regarding the aftermath of events that led Crossover Team Alpha to be in this place at this point in time. It was important that we keep nothing at all from these men, for they were marines and subscribed wholeheartedly to the Code of Honor that the corps held dear. They had however, been betrayed by a dishonest and corrupt government, and we could not have them feeling that we were no better. To that end, they were told everything. Their decision as a squad or as individuals would be left up to them afterward.

First Lieutenant Archimus Marcelon was assigned to work along with Kruger and Leonard in building a profile of each man, then applying their probability equation to that profile to test their potential for loyalty to the PHS as opposed to the system that had abandoned them. This was also how we would build new identities for them if they chose to stay with us. So far, it was looking as every one of them were going to work out. They were all without family or any other ties, with Lt. Lucius Carver Jr. being the only exception, as he had his mother. We altered their identities right down to their fingerprints, and using Kruger/Leonard modifications that their cyber spyware had planted within the system on N-Prime, combined with applications from our Devin Craine's DNA science, we fixed things so that even if these men underwent testing for DNA results, such tests would render different data from what was on file with the military databases here.

Lucius and Lucius Jr. had, of course, grown close, as that young man saw only his father in our Master Sergeant Lucius Carver; and everything that Lucius said, did, or thought seemed to be exactly what the one who had existed here would have said, done, or thought. Master Sergeant Lucius Carver, on his side of things, was entirely grateful to have a part in the life of the man who would have been his son. Roy-Bob Joseph and his double got along as if they had been older and younger brothers who just learned about each other. They were always together, concocting some practical joke, working in the machine shop, or doing weapons training. It seemed that both men had grown up wishing for a brother, and that need was finally being filled.

Second Lt. Walter R. A. McGrath and his younger double were cordial to each other, and although they never exactly sought out each other's company, they would often drink together, but since their conversation on those occasions would often just embitter both of them more than they already were, Colonel Gary assigned Sgt. Richie Garfield to keep an eye on the two of them during those drinking sessions. It was a necessity. One highly trained MISTman and a Marine Raider could do unimaginable amounts of damage together if they decided to go off and destroy the banking and economic system of any country. Oddly enough, Gunny Antoine Rochon and his double seemed to prefer to avoid each other. They went out of their way to not be around or near each other, and that caused Benjamin and me quite a bit of concern. We never did figure that out, but on the occasions when they had to train together, it was like watching a martial arts performance of unforgettable grace. Together, they both moved with the smoothness of two panthers stalking in concert, and nothing was more inspiring for a commanding officer to see. It just seemed that outside of training exercises or field missions, they simply did not *want* to like each other, and that was their internal battle.

The new men entered MIST training, and it was, of course, twenty-one weeks of the toughest conditioning and battle preparation they'd ever endured. You have to understand, Detective Caldwell, that MIST training affects the candidates right down to the basic genes and proteins of their individual bodies. Lieutenant Colonel Gary placed Lieutenant Logan Eller in command of the project as their primary instructor, with Master Sergeant Lucius Carver, Gunnery Sergeant Gabriel Puccini, and Sergeant Richard "Richie" Garfield overseeing a team of four Raiders each. I didn't want any of the men who had living doubles involved in that training, and Colonel Gary made sure that Lieutenant Lucius Carver Jr. was not in his father's team of candidates. We weren't worried about anyone being too easy on their doubles; it was more of a concern over their being too hard on them. These men were already Special Forces, and they would never settle for being failures or quitters. So life went on. Angeline, for her part, saw how Lucius and Lucius Jr. were getting along and, as a medical professional, spent a lot of time with the late Lucius Sr.'s widow, who had a bachelor of science in nursing degree, never forgetting, all the while, what the little Nigel had told her, so she eventually forgave me for having to use him as I did, though I'd never have asked for such absolution.

A Provocation
of Outrage

Things continued on for a while. Nigel grew one year older while the Walking Dead Raider Squad completed MIST training and became everything that MISTmen should be. Eventually, it began to feel to us as if this world would be a good home base for Operation CureSearch until one day when matters outside of our compound suddenly took an unexpected turn. Like an omen of things to come, Kruger was monitoring his spyware one day when he picked up a reference to Blacen Muldowney. Zooming in on it, he found that once Carla Ryan's remains had been identified, and with Blacen's DNA having been found on the body, NCIS paid a visit to his supermax home and interviewed him.

Of course, there was no way he could have done it, based on the TOD, as well as Muldowney's current location on death row, so they thought more and more of the possibility of a copycat killer being involved. The problem with that theory, though, was this: no one had any access to the man, nor had any mail been allowed to come to him. He had one sister, and the woman hated him for the despicable things he'd done to her. She couldn't have children and their parents were dead, so no relatives had been in to see him. The guards at his facility were scrutinized, then, to see if anyone had imparted any information to the outside world that may have inspired a copycat killer.

They all came up clean, of course. E-mails that Kruger and Leonard captured from NCIS servers indicated that the field agent now in charge of the investigation was pretty bright, though, and he'd decided to go back and look over everything they'd gotten from their operative murdered at the Waveland scene, whose job was to shadow Devin Craine. This new agent was the man who had taken command over there that night, after NCIS found their previous agent's body as well as the gruesome remains of our Carla Ryan. We'd also learned that they had film of our Muldowney meeting their Craine and even a portion of Puccini's fight, though the preceding agent had only paid attention for a moment before having turned his attention back to his primary target, Devin Craine. This new guy chose to focus in on Puccini, though. He surmised that Muldowney might have a double who had been put into play by MPIS, maybe in an effort to find Craine's location, but was surprised that the tail would wear his camos while carrying out such a sensitive assignment. The agent also wondered why a Muldowney double would even be involved, and that was just another piece of the puzzle to him. MPIS was, as expected, not going to cooperate in any fashion and were stonewalling NCIS' every attempt to open up a dialogue. Because of that, NCIS wouldn't share anything with them either. A few weeks later, we got verification of all of these matters from a bartender who was having an affair with the wife of one of this hotshot agent's discontented underlings. We were pretty thankful for human jealousy keeping us in the loop when it came to that.

The miserable agent would always go home and gripe to his wife about his job, as he felt that he should have been promoted from the research section to field agent, and his immediate superiors had denied him promotion in favor of someone else whom this fellow truly hated. It seemed that the disgruntled man's ability to maintain confidentiality was suspect (rightfully so, apparently). Meanwhile, his unhappiness over his status within the NCIS agency was destroying their marriage and driving his wife into the barman's bed, and as long as that went on, we would always have access. Lieutenant Colonel Gary paid the man to continue the affair for a few more months, as well as for whatever information he gave us. Eventually, I decided, I'd tip Agent Hotshot off about that guy.

We thought we'd find him, but as it turned out, Muldowney found us first. Or at least the ones of us whom he desired most. While all the new developments were keeping Crossover Team Alpha and the Walking Dead Raider Squad busy, my Angeline had gotten into the habit of taking Nigel to see little Angeline every now and then. She wasn't aware that the Blacen Muldowney from our world was at large somewhere around New Orleans, and I wasn't aware that she'd been taking Nigel out that far without any sort of security. Lucius couldn't be present all the time, what with training the new men; and as far as we could see, there were no immediate threats to the boy, so we'd relaxed his guard somewhat. Basically, our vigilance flagged, and we were about to pay for it. Additionally, we'd been looking to the east, toward Mississippi, as the most probable place where we'd find Blacen. It was where we'd caught up with him in our reality, and the imprisoned version of him did own the same property in the same location here in N-Prime. Meanwhile, because it wasn't an everyday thing and because of who she was to me, to both teams and to Nigel, no one would ever try to prevent Angeline from taking our boy off to do fun things without a bodyguard.

That's how it came to pass. The two of them would sometimes be out and about in the city of New Orleans with no protection. Muldowney spotted them in traffic on one of those excursions, I later found out. He then followed them to a park near little Angeline's home where she would meet Nigel and they'd play together. Fortunately, for as observant a man as he was, Blacen Muldowney never figured out who that little girl was. I guess that his myopic focus on Nigel clouded his thinking ability. It's also probable that using himself as a mule for Craine's DNA virus could have adversely affected his psychological stability as well as his abstract reasoning ability. The virus does do that to the infected, and although his passage through the nil zone and into this place had destroyed the virus, it wasn't likely to have repaired any mental side effects associated with it.

Well anyway, he followed them, and Angel never noticed. One of our troops or I would have caught on if someone had been tailing us so, but not Angeline. The woman is a fighter but not a killer to suspect others as we soldiers do. She didn't know to be on the lookout for anyone who may have been paying too much attention to her for surveillance purposes. The two of them weren't out like that every day, but when they did go, they always went to the same park in the same neighborhood. That's how Blacen knew to wait for his chance to attack in that location. Additionally, the people who were raising this Angeline happened to be the doubles of the couple who was my Angeline's most beloved aunt Cosette and uncle Rene, and that had to have been an additional distraction for her. In our world, that dear woman had died too soon after losing her husband. My wife must have had a profound longing to go to their home and talk to her favorite aunt, who was always watching from her front porch, but she never did. To her credit, she'd stay on one side of the park and let Nigel go then wait for him to come back. Keeping that distance helped her resist her own inclination to reunite with her beloved kin.

Because of all this, she was unaware of Nigel's behavior in regards to his little Angeline. At the age of eleven, the boy had decided to marry the girl he loved. I believe that what he'd seen in Cape Idokopas had more than a little to do with that. It's a fact of life that when men see war and believe that they may be going back into it, they want to marry their sweethearts. Nigel always had maturity beyond his years, and it seems that he'd made a choice similar to what I had about what he wanted to do in his future. The boy believed he'd be going back to war. Little Angeline was his girl, so he wanted to do what seemed right in his young mind. Since there was this one drunk of an ex-preacher who was always on hand in that park, and that loser had convinced the kids that he could marry them if they had money, he was the person the boy decided to use. Nigel paid to the man that gold coin I'd given him, as it was the only currency he had. After biting the gold to make sure it was real, the debased clergyman immediately broke out a Bible he'd stolen from some poor depressed rehabilitated junkie at the halfway house and commenced. All the passersby and onlookers just thought that was the cutest thing, so a small crowd of onlookers gathered to coo and "aww" as they witnessed the spectacle.

Angeline noticed the "ceremony" from the bench where she was reading and got up to go see what was going on. Unfortunately, because she was trying to hurry to break up that scene before someone recorded it, she didn't notice the two thugs who were stalking her as she headed in the children's direction. Just as she got to Nigel, the men charged toward her. Nigel saw what was happening, ran past her, and sent them into *otherspace*. He opened a door under their feet, and they simply *fell* in, just like that. Though he has never been able to duplicate that act, still, the implications were astounding! *He could force others into the nil zone without going in himself!* Sometimes though, the memory of their screams still keep Angeline awake at night. Seeing his goons disposed of that way, Muldowney now knew that this was *the* Nigel, the one he'd been after. That maniac suddenly drove through the playground in his rental car, taking out one of the swing sets and killing one child, critically wounding two others. He screeched to a halt behind my wife, jumped out, and held a gun to her head while Craine got out of the passenger side with a pistol in his hand and shot two of the fathers in the park who attempted to rush them. The excuse for a minister tried to flee the scene, but Devin aimed carefully at the drunken old ex-preacher then shot him. Two rounds, center mass. An excellent double tap.

Apparently, this version of Devin Craine had lived long enough to become an excellent marksman with a pistol. Muldowney yelled to Nigel that he'd do the same to Angeline if the boy didn't go with him right *now*. Apparently, neither Blacen nor Devin noticed little Angeline running to get help. They forced my Angeline and Nigel into the car and took off through the playground. No one knew at the time that one of the members of a family that was there on an outing actually had brought a digital recorder and filmed the whole thing, starting with Nigel and his Angeline's mock wedding and ending with Muldowney's mad charge through the park along with Devin Craine's blatant triple murder. Because of the angle from which that recording was made, though, Blacen's face couldn't be seen, which was a bit of a break for our side.

I was looking over our contingency plans with Lieutenant Colonel Gary when Lucius and Marcelon slammed the door open and demanded that I come to see the "breaking news" report. We went to the living room, and there were my wife and "son" (for truthfully, that was what Nigel had become to me), being kidnapped by Craine and Muldowney. A red haze came over my vision. Those two were going to die for sure now. Meanwhile, Kruger called. He was hysterical. He wanted to come and help out, but I heard Lucius ask what he thought he was going to do, come out here and throw a computer at them? I ordered all of Crossover Team Alpha to the Rue Burgundy base. The Walking Dead Raiders were also demanding the right to get "in the mix" with this. They were put on standby while we put together an action plan. Kruger was to stay in the computer room on the Franklinton property because we had some of the most powerful systems money could buy installed therein, and we would need him working at that location.

Leonard was to come to Rue Burgundy with the rest of the MISTmen, as he could coordinate our efforts with Kruger when it came to computerspeak. We still had our CH-53E Super Stallion, carefully concealed because it was "too hot." No matter. We would need it now. The first thing on Kruger's to-do list was run a systemwide check to see what type of security force our targets may have enlisted and provide that information to Captain Braggs, who was, at the moment, flying the rest of the team down while Lieutenant Colonel Gary would muster the Walking Dead Raiders, who were preparing themselves to act as reinforcements in case it came to that. We were going to get our own *back*, and God help anyone who got in the way. I took three men and headed to the crime scene.

When we got there, we just blended in with the crowd. I wanted to see if that hotshot NCIS field agent would be on hand, and he was. The local police were arguing over jurisdiction with one of his people, but he wasn't wasting time with it himself. He picked up the gold coin that the preacher had dropped and bagged it. His body bus arrived before the city coroner's did, and whoever was officiating the jurisdiction dispute awarded it to the NCIS people. No doubt MPIS likely had some slinkers on the scene too, but they weren't sure whether they should move in and forcefully take over, watch from the sidelines, or buy ice cream and watch the show. We'd snatched their comm frequency and could hear all the conflicting orders they were being given. It seemed that the only acceptable action the MPIS agents knew for sure to take was that of trying their best to escape detection and blend in with the crowd so that none of the other agencies' representatives would notice their presence. To us, though, they stuck out like a handful of sore fingers. From personal experience, we of Crossover Team Alpha knew that such a lack of decisive action had to indicate some division within their leaders' ranks. Scratch one problem. The MPIS could never be as fully effective against our group as the other agencies could, with an upper-level bureaucratic power struggle dividing their ranks and hindering their efforts. I told the men not to concentrate on those agents. Just let 'em slink. They were powerless to act.

On our side of things, I also knew that we needed that hotshot NCIS guy's help. My own people were stretched thin; we had no one on the inside of any of their law enforcement agencies to do our bidding, so somebody needed to legally check all of Craine's hidey holes while we worked out our battle plans. Thinking thus, I worked my way to the front of the crowd, signaling Gunnery Sergeant Puccini, Master Gunnery Sergeant Carver, and Lieutenant Marcelon to do the same. I signaled "box formation" to them, and we positioned ourselves so. Once in position, I *willed* Agent Hotshot to look in my direction, and eventually, he did. We locked eyes. I put all the intensity of my emotion into that stare and, when I saw him rising to the bait, nodded in Lieutenant Marcelon's direction to my right. He looked and saw. Eyes back to me now, I indicated Sergeant Carver to my left. He looked in that direction, noticed Master Gunnery Sergeant Carver, who then nodded toward Puccini, whom he recognized. We'd all worn black overcoats as it was a little cool still, and I wanted us to look threatening enough to keep his attention. He saw that we had boxed in all the first responders from our locations and started slowly moving his hand toward his gun. We didn't move. He eased over to one of his agents, and I saw him alert the man. But when that one looked up, no one was evident, save myself. The crowd got jostled, people moved, and I disappeared from their view. The effect was exactly what we'd hoped for. He and his man tried to force their way through the crowd, and the jostling got a little worse.

By the time it eased down, we were in our vehicle, watching through a pair of extra powerful digital field binoculars. Agent Hotshot was turning his from head side to side, searching as far as he could, and speaking into a cell phone. Meanwhile, the MPIS slinkers had no idea what was going on. Good, we neither wanted nor needed them involved. Based on all we'd learned of them, it had become our opinion that as an agency, they amounted to untrustworthy, honorless cavemen who would beat down an entire forest to find one pine cone, with no desire or ability to consider cooperation with any other agency. It was just the culture of that particular institution. They didn't need to have any contact or involvement with us. Our purpose having been achieved, we left before Agent Hotshot's reinforcements arrived. It was time to put Kruger and Leonard to work.

FEINTS, COUNTERMOVES, AND CONSEQUENCES

We needed to find out where they would take Angeline and Nigel. When Agent Hotshot made his cell phone call, Leonard had swiped his number out of the airwaves, back traced its transmission, and now had an access point for intrusion into their cybernet. Next, Kruger sent an encrypted e-mail to Agent Hotshot, identifying himself as a member of the team he'd seen in the playground and exposing the properties Craine owned in Mississippi. Some had been listed under other names, and these were the ones their people needed to know about. We knew about them because our Craine had been owner of the same properties back home. (We also tipped him off about the blabbing underling of his whose words had originally pointed us in his direction.) When their people tried to trace the e-mail, Kruger and Leonard lost them somewhere in cyberspace.

While NCIS agents were notifying local cops across the state line of the need to kick in the doors at those properties we'd exposed, Leonard sent Agent Hotshot some of the information that we'd gotten on Craine before and after his death, including his psych profile. Actually, we thought they'd have this information already, but our sharing it would, hopefully, demonstrate that we were on the same side.

Even as they were downloading that, a Kruger cyberworm zipped into their system and recorded whatever they had from the crime scene, then retreated, leaving behind a window for passive observation. We hoped they would not notice its presence for a long while, if ever. Lieutenant Colonel Gary, for his part, had put all of our people out on the streets to work immediately after the incident in the park. "Hey, you saw that news report?

Yeah? Well. That lady who got kidnapped was your boss's wife and the kid was his son! Remember how well you get paid for information? Right. Just think of how much he'll pay for information on those two guys that worked for the kidnappers! Even more for anything leading to their top guys!" That was the word going throughout our whole network.

My team arrived, and we began to plan. Kruger sent Leonard the results of the worm's grab, and we found that they'd lifted Nigel's prints off the gold coin, ran it through AFIS, and scored a hit. The very same fingerprints had been lifted from a car located in Washington DC five years ago. It was a 1984 Monte Carlo, stolen by a couple of petty criminals who claimed that it, in turn, was stolen from *them*. What had confused the authorities, at the time, was the fact that the same fingerprints were on both the driver's side door and the steering wheel, as well as both doors and inside the car. One set of prints seemed larger than the other, but they were the same prints. Could one person drive the car and ride on the passenger side at the same time? No way. The two losers whose prints were also found had been sent to prison, anyway, so the whole mystery was forgotten. Until now.

The previously unidentified prints were now known to be those of Nigel Boyd Renoir, who had been in an orphanage in New Orleans after perhaps having lost the rest of his family to Katrina. Many of the Katrina orphans had been fingerprinted, in case an opportunity to reunite them with their families or other relatives ever came up. So how could this kid have possibly been in Washington DC and New Orleans at the same time? Their NCIS investigation into Gunnery Sergeant Puccini's identity, on the other hand, had turned up nothing; and they'd found that no Muldowney double had been introduced into any investigation of their Devin Craine that may have been conducted by MPIS or any of their other law enforcement services. They considered that information unreliable though, since none of these agencies cooperated with each other and not one of them *ever* trusted the veracity of *anything* that MPIS told them.

Agent Hotshot's people, therefore, decided that we must have represented some deep-cover government agency involved for reasons unknown since Puccini was positively identified now as having been on the scene when Blacen and Devin re-met and on the scene of the kidnapping murders. They sent us an inquiry on the matter, but in fact were trying to back hack us and find our location. For a few moments, the Burgundy base sounded like a machine-gun firing range, with Leonard typing so fast. I could just imagine how fast Kruger was typing in the control room there at the ranch. Our boys won whatever contest they had going because Leonard told me they'd dumped the attacker into the files of one Dr. Carlson Chubbs, and whoever that guy was, he would be getting a visit from the IRS after the NCIS and FBI people got done with him. Bye, Carlson. Have a good stay in federal prison. Embezzling millions of dollars from Uncle Sam as he had would come back to haunt anyone.

Finally, our network came through. Craine had recently come into an extremely large amount of money due to the death of one of his uncles in Mississippi and began using it to hire a boatload of goons for "protection." The hooligans that Nigel cast off into nowhere were cousins who reportedly lived together in one of the abandoned homes out in East New Orleans. Those men had been two of the hoods on Team Muldowney and Craine. Apparently, decent law-abiding citizens were not the only ones suffering through unemployment in post-Katrina New Orleans. Even good-for-nothing men were willing to work for food and board. They were reportedly based in a neighborhood near Read Boulevard East, the nearest intersection being Lake Forest Boulevard and South Eastover Drive. On South Eastover Drive itself, there were about eight gigantic homes, all of which had been gutted by flood, fire, rain, and looters.

The most prominent one was addressed as 5400, and it was strategically located at a point where the road intersected with a cul-de-sac that headed east while the main road continued to the south and curved. That home commanded the entire territory. Craine and Muldowney had been seen speeding in that general direction and were rumored to have taken over that whole vicinity of deserted homes. Of course, they'd set up in the most prominent one. We also found that some medical equipment was on its way to one of those places out there. A description of the minivan carrying it was even included in that tidbit of information. Since we had our chopper now, Captain Braggs was flying over that part of the city with Second Lieutenant Logan Eller and the two Antoine Rochons, searching for any signs of a vehicle fitting the description of Craine's, or a rat's nest of criminals that needed a visit from the MIST. After dropping both Rochons in to keep an eye on the objective, Braggs flew back to the ranch. The unfriendlies on the ground should have been able to hear them, but none of them considered the thought of shooting in the air at the sound or anything like that. I guess it was a classic example of "if I can't see it, it has nothing to do with me" thinking at its finest.

All in all, there were about thirty of them on hand. They evidently had a base camp of sorts, with five houses in the community that were under their control. We'd also learned that none of the equipment they were using had been purchased with Craine's money. They'd looted some sporting goods stores, I guess, because there were also tents, most of them located in the houses' front yards for the majority of their men, so that was most likely to have been where they slept. Additionally, all he'd paid was about three thousand dollars for the lot of them. That meant each man on the scene would net only about three hundred each if it were split fairly, which wasn't likely. Impressive. Gunsels were working cheap in this tough economy. We were readying weapons when Leonard contacted us via the 911 microchip comm that we all used for confidential communications. The MPIS had received an anonymous call and was on the way out to our target location, having been alerted that a team of ex-military domestic terrorists were going to be practicing maneuvers with stolen army weapons and ammunition on or near South Eastover Drive in East New Orleans. MPIS tactical units would have arrived around the same time or a little after our own ETA. Thank you, Blacen Muldowney. It seemed that his ability to apply abstract reasoning wasn't all gone. We knew it was him because Leonard had applied in-depth phrasing and syntax comparisons to our pirated recording of that very call, and the identity of the concerned citizen was confirmed; it was without a doubt our boy Blacen. Right about that time, the Rochons also confirmed what we knew of that location, and Braggs was dispatched to extract them. He would get there and be gone long before any MPIS agents arrived. At about the same time that MPIS was locating the target destination, our communications surveillance also revealed that Agent Hotshot had just found out where to begin looking.

When MPIS tac teams rolled onto South Eastover Drive, Craine's small army of hoodlums, seemingly well prepared for just such an encounter, commenced firing on the convoy, and the fight started. MPIS had only sent in three teams of six men each, but they were armored and loaded with weaponry. The gunsels, on their side of things, had no intention of going quietly or any other way. It was also common knowledge among nonmilitary law enforcement agencies that since weapons were easy enough to find on this post-hurricane-Katrina Gulf Coast, they'd *definitely* be well armed. It was just too bad that MPIS chose not to share intel because that meant none of these agencies shared intel with them. They had no idea what kind of desperation or armament they'd be facing in their enemy.

We learned later how these men had formed a relatively new gang with a reputation for excess brutality, whose actions contributed to the spike in homicides, robberies, and rape in New Orleans after Katrina; and every one of those big bad boys were scared of ghosts being in the houses, which was why most of them chose to stay outdoors. Only the hardest of the hard opted for the protection of the abandoned structures. Not at all convenient for the men in the gray fatigues. The bad guys saw them coming from a mile away, so to speak. Our geeks swiped some type of video and satellite feed, permitting us to review the whole encounter later. Someone within their ranks must have been former military, we surmised, because they positioned themselves in such excellent ambush locations as their adversaries neared. Intel we received after that event also revealed that their bosses had told these hoodlums to expect some type of lightly armed military medical convoy, and the degenerates thought that if they could eliminate the convoy, there'd be easy pickin's in pharmaceuticals and medicines that could be sold at a high profit. There was a lot of money to be made on the black market from that sort of haul.

Craine's Hoods-for-Hire also had no fear of MPIS since most of them had no idea who they were, anyhow. Once it started, though, the fighting became quite intense because many of those men had armor-piercing bullets loaded into fully automatic AK-47 rifles while others in the bunch of hooligans even had grenade launchers. All of them knew that area well, and the majority of them had warrants for various murders out on them. To tell things truthfully, every one of the gang members, if caught alive, would, at the very least, be facing life without the slightest possibility of parole while quite a number of them would also be eligible for either the death or death by torture penalties. This whole scenario had no choice but to become a bloodbath, and it did. We weren't there to see it though. Blacen had done exactly what we expected him to do. What? You want to know what I mean by that? You must remember, Detective Caldwell, that he had risen to the rank of Assistant Director of The Division, which was a position that carried a high-security clearance. He'd also mined all kinds of classified data from former Director Rocklin's brain, so he knew what the PHS really was and was aware of its information-gathering capabilities. He planted false leads as feints within feints because he *wanted* us to come into conflict with MPIS since the resultant backlash could only have worked in his favor. They would possibly have come to know about us and began taking some sort of countermeasures. We wouldn't have gone down easily, and they wouldn't have quit coming at us. Wars of that type can only end in oblivion for both sides.

Why didn't he go directly to the MPIS himself, you ask? Well, he wasn't about to expose himself to the authorities there because in that America, the law of the land was this: if a person who has been sentenced to death by torment were to escape, all citizens were expected to either call the police or kill them on sight, for which they would receive a hefty reward after being cleared by a Justice Department investigation while, conversely, anyone who carried on communication with or provided the least amount of aid or succor to such an escapee would receive the same death by torture punishment, without exception. No matter what their rank or political position in the country might have been and whether their actions ultimately benefited America or not, that was the penalty. Only their President himself was immune to such punishment or could issue any pardon for it. Their nationwide antiterrorist system facial-recognition software would have labeled Blacen an escapee as soon as any governmental or local law enforcement facility camera recorded his face. He knew that much about the system of N-Prime. Additionally, he would most likely have understood the need to know the legal status of his double in order to carry on with whatever plot he and this new version of Devin Craine were concocting. Such information wasn't hard to find in their internet. It was and still is a more ruthless world than yours or mine.

Oh yes, he knew all that, but *we* knew Blacen Muldowney. He had worked with us during the glory days of The Division, short-lived as those days turned out to be, and we knew not just what he was, but we also knew *who* he was. We also knew *who* Devin Craine was. Kruger and Leonard had applied the probability equation to all that we knew of both men's psyches; their mandatory evals from the old division days, their behavioral records, camera recordings of body language, and speech patterns, even the way they tied their shoes. We knew where Blacen Muldowney would be because we'd learned what properties their Devin Craine owned, and given the enormity of Blacen's failures and successes in our own reality, the probability equation told us where the two of them would most likely feel safe enough to try to rebuild the Craine virus. Another unexpected physical condition of Blacen's also assisted us. We'd never removed that will killer chip from his head, and although it wasn't originally intended for use as a tracking device, it did emit a small man-made electrical signal that couldn't have originated in this reality because it was on a wavelength that they had not yet discovered. That provided another means with which to find the man, one which had been theoretical up to that time.

You see, Detective Caldwell, as it turns out, human DNA does emit its own individual electrical waves. Normally, the wavelength seems random and inconsistent. But the will killer altered such waves just enough so that anyone checking that frequency could tell that the alteration had forced the wavelength into a consistent frequency, resulting in a coherent signal. We knew that particular one. It was emanating from Blacen Muldowney's DNA, and it led us straight to him. Antoine Rochon and his double had been dropped in East New Orleans only to confirm where Muldowney and Craine were *not* to be found.

They were located just to the northwest of Houma, Louisiana. In that place, there's a road called Savanne Road. It connects Martin Luther King Boulevard on the northern side to Little Bayou Black Drive on the southern side of town. Savanne Road is about three miles long, and dead center of its distance is another smaller unnamed road. In that reality, it was privately owned by the Craine family, although now, it belongs to Nigel. At the end of that unnamed road is a clearing with a home in the middle of it, a home that was big enough for any determined person to set up a medical clinic or lab within. Blacen and Devin were determined. Our two geniuses, Leonard and Kruger, had piggybacked into one of the American spy satellite feeds and confirmed that there was indeed activity caused by living human beings on that site, though none of them were likely to have been our targets at that time since Muldowney and Craine were still en route when we obtained the information. Okay, so someone or some ones other than those two were present. We needed to know who that would be. Our boys already had that part figured out, though.

Blacen believed in overkill when it came to his personal safety; and depending on how much money they had, as well as how much influence he wielded over this wealthier and more paranoid Devin Craine, we could be going in facing thirty to forty brigands, we thought. As things turned out though, there were more than that, and they weren't just brigands. Craine had plenty of money, and he'd hired Steele Bay Security to protect himself and his mentor. In this reality, you have a security company named Blackwater, and they are no joke. That's who Steele Bay parallels in that reality. All of their men were the best of the best when it came to ex-military, and they were well paid. Honestly, I believed they deserved every penny they earned, for their previous employers—a.k.a. their various governments—hadn't been able to pay them as much. What monetary value could any government place on a good man's life, anyway?

They had four men deployed on each end of Savanne Road, where it connected to Martin Luther King Boulevard on its northern end and to Little Bayou Black Drive on its southern end. These sentries were to be on alert for anyone who fit our description. All along the main road, there were lookout posts randomly interspersed. Their job would be to catch us in a crossfire if we headed down Savanne Road. Down the length of Craine's private road, there were also sentries posted, and additionally, they had about twelve men surrounding their headquarters. So without a doubt, the Walking Dead MISTmen (who still preferred to be called Raiders) would have to be involved in our operation along with Crossover Team Alpha. So it would be twenty-four MISTmen facing up to forty trained, armed, and disciplined professional soldiers, almost all of whom had been spec ops. We'd try to go easy on them and kill as few as possible. I really didn't want to slay any of those men, though, just because we all respected who they were and the services they'd rendered. We understood them, you see. So Kruger was ordered to send an untraceable message to their superiors, advising them of the danger facing their field operatives. Craine's public murders had undoubtedly put him in line for the death by torture penalty, and although we didn't reveal his cohort's identity, we did inform them that he was in league with an escapee who was under the same penalty. They had to know what that would mean for any of their field operatives who may be captured by law enforcement.

Additionally, we were bringing a vastly superior force to bear upon theirs; and if Steele Bay backed out and allowed us to attain our objective, none of them would die that night. Otherwise, all of them could. Hopefully, they would be influenced into pulling their people out. They weren't. They actually sent in ten more local men who were also Steele Bay operatives. Unable to resist being himself, Kruger sent them a picture of "the finger" in a communiqué that immediately fried all their transmission and computer systems as soon as they opened the digital packet and saw its image. Leonard, for his part, did nothing to stop Kruger. He was actually laughing harder than his associate collaborator was. Okay. Yuk it up, boys. Now we had fifty men to face.

As we got the news, Crossover Team Alpha geared up and drove to an abandoned area of the Ninth Ward. We left the Rue Burgundy office at the same time that Braggs took off from the ranch, refueled, and loaded up with the rest of our people, as well as more gear. There was one particular piece of technology that desperately needed to go in with us, and that was on the chopper with Braggs, headed in. He'd meet us there and take us to the drop zone, flying under the radar all the way. We all preferred a nighttime attack for the fear and confusion it could create. Things had to move fast because the Savanne Road in that world was a very quiet place with little or no traffic after the 1200 hour, and we intended to hit the pinpoint location as soon as our targets arrived, if not before. Few, if any, civilian casualties or spectators. Additionally, there was the fact that it had already been a little more than twenty-four hours since those guys grabbed my family, and they'd spent most of that time trying to throw us off their trail, what with making sure to be seen heading out to East New Orleans, then doubling back, driving along the surface roads toward Houma and all. That coupled with the fact that just like our Craine, this older, deadlier version of Devin Craine deeply despised any type of sexuality meant that Muldowney hadn't been able to stop moving long enough to assault Angeline, which was something he couldn't have resisted doing. I didn't want to wait anymore.

As I've mentioned to you, because we also sent him Craine's psych profile, our would-be nemesis from NCIS just figured out where to begin looking; and he was trying to convince his director that their efforts needed to be focused somewhere in Houma, Louisiana. He was having a hard time getting through, though. So while we were already in motion, Agent Hotshot, on the other hand, was put on hold until the next morning, when he could go in with limited local SWAT team support. He didn't feel the need for it, but there was that old jurisdiction fight again, tying his hands. Just as we'd hoped. See ya after the show, buddy.

We arrived at our rally point from two different directions. For this op, I chose to have Crossover Team Alpha use three high-security armored Toyota minivans. (Why? Because nothing looked more normal than a minivan.) After our troops disembarked, they activated the vehicles' internal remotes and had Dr. Derron Leonard guide them back to New Orleans, where we stashed them within a private parking facility. The PHS originally had settled on a long-term agreement to rent all the parking spots in that garage, supposedly for any conventions or guest speakers that may be featured in the city, but in reality, it was our motor pool. Eventually, we just bought the whole parking facility. While those vehicles were driving themselves back home, we checked gear and waited for our additional MISTmen. We did not have to wait long before Braggs arrived with the Walking Dead Raiders. In the interim, Gunnery Sergeant Puccini began playing the Eagles' "Heartache Tonight" as loudly as possible over his portable sound systems while we waited. It was his favorite fight song, and that sound, coupled with his own personalized cadence to the melody, always beefed up the team. We were feeling the adrenaline flow and loving it.

All twenty-four of us were going in, Lieutenant Colonel Gary, Master Guns Carver, and myself included. Muldowney had no idea that our ranks had doubled and, without a doubt, felt that he and Craine were quite safe behind that wall of hired security. Oh, they both had to know by now that we might be on the way, but they were also blissfully unaware of the capability of one MIST-trained marine, let alone twenty-four. That information was never included in the classified records that were open to The Division, so Blacen didn't have such knowledge to pass on to Devin Craine. Even Director Rocklin hadn't had that level of clearance. Fifty ex–Special Forces guys against twenty-four MISTmen and one elite pilot. That was how the deck was stacked. It was shaping up to be a nice fight, and we wanted it badly. Every one of Crossover Team Alpha had been ordered to wear their OTTO gear, our new MISTmen and Captain Braggs having been outfitted with OTTOs of their own. I had brought along a tranq for Angeline in case Nigel opened the gateway for some reason during the fight or should we have to escape in that direction. I was thinking of Agent Hotshot when that contingency was developed, for we couldn't be sure that he *would* wait until the next day before arriving with SWAT teams or even his own little NCIS team. I'd read his record and could see just how much this man hated leaving innocent lives at risk. He'd almost lost his family to some nut years ago, and had his partner not been there to help get them out and die doing it, Agent Hotshot would've been without his most beloved people now. I, for my part, wasn't ready to cast MISTmen against any law enforcement officers in this reality or any other, if retreat were a viable alternative option.

A CH-53E Super Stallion has a top speed of 196 miles per hour, and we had 74 klicks or 46 miles to go before we'd be above Savanne Road. As usual, Marty Braggs flew at top speed, under radar, with reckless abandon. In less than fourteen minutes, we'd be on site. Just before the ride started, though, Lieutenant Colonel Gary voiced his concern that either the enemy or someone else would hear our rotors, and without a doubt, we'd attract interest from anyone on the ground, flying as low as we were. Excellent point, and just the sort of thing that a good XO should bring to his commanding officer's attention. I gave Captain Braggs a signal; he flipped a switch, and the rotors' sound went silent. A little gift from the old think tank; a general wave refraction device that was designed to activate certain properties of the polymer goop that we'd sprayed onto our C-130J Super Hercules before flying it over from our own world. That same stuff had been applied to our chopper before the Cape Idokopas affair.

We simply called our device the Refractor, and it had been a classified development that only I had the clearance to know of. It could be mounted on any one of our military or civilian modes of transport, if needed. Anything coated with our polymer and subjected to the Refractor's effect would bend radar, sound, light, electrical, or magnetic waves around itself, becoming virtually undetectable by any modern means. My world's microengineering at work. Captain Braggs activated the Refractor, and basically, our CH-53E Super Stallion disappeared. It was now invisible and inaudible. The gleam of pride in my marines' eyes told me that the Old Man had once again proved himself fit to command in their estimation. They were confident in my leadership still, despite the setbacks we'd suffered.

We approached the target with Braggs flying treetop high, all dark. Our night-vision digital ocular enhancement eye covers (Night DOCS) told us all we needed to know as we circled the landing zone to look over the competition. Risky, should a small aircraft be flying overhead, but risk wasn't anything the MIST ever worried about. We needed to see how our enemy was deployed. These men were ready to go to the gates of hell to rescue my wife and boy, and I wouldn't have them go into a fight without being able to see what they were facing.

Yes, as our intel had informed us, there were eight soldiers located in the wetlands and woods beside the northeastern intersection, four on each side. There's a place called Dedeaux's Market there (in your world, it's called Rouse's Market), and behind it is a bayou. You'd call it a channel, I guess. A small bridge crosses that bayou, and there are wetlands on the other side. One unit of four sentries was hiding there, and another four-man unit was on the opposite side of the road, just in front of a small electrical transforming station, with the same number of men deployed in the same way at the Southwestern intersection. On that end of Savanne Road, there is a volunteer fire department building with a graveyard behind it on its northwestern side, and behind that is some sort of farm. The sentries were in the woods that followed that farm. On the opposite side, they were concealed behind saw grass that hid yet another farm. All the sentries were armed with SR-25 sniper rifles, night-vision scopes attached. At strategic points along the length of Savanne Road, there were three-man teams on opposite sides of the road, in a staggered formation, all armed with Colt 9-mm submachine guns, complete with sound-suppression attachments. They amounted to eighteen men, six sets of two each. That accounted for twenty-eight enemy combatants.

The private road that belonged to the Craine family was named Auberjon Road, after one of his grandfathers' side of the family tree. It was a very narrow road that had heavy undergrowth along both sides and stretched for five miles or so from Savanne Road to a large rectangular clearing. From the air, the whole thing appeared to be shaped like one of those old-school skeleton keys. All along that road were posted five two-man units each, staggered from one side of the road to the other, two men for every mile, each unit equipped with one M60E4 machine gun, made for cutting men down, and one M16A4 rifle. That accounted for ten enemy combatants.

The last twelve were, of course, located around or inside the rectangular clearing where Muldowney and Craine would be. On each corner of the rectangle was a man posted with a M60E4. On the shortest sides of the rectangle, a single soldier armed with a Colt 9-mm SMG was posted midway between the two corner gunners. On the long side of the clearing, there were two similarly armed men posted between the M60E4s that accounted for another ten. Within that clearing was the Steele Bay main encampment. There were temporary structures built, apparently, for the Security Force's men. In the middle of the clearing, there was a huge beautifully built two-story house, and it was well lit. That would be where Blacen Muldowney and Devin Craine were. The two guards, one stationed at the front and one stationed at the back doors, confirmed it for us. That was their headquarters.

We checked our M4s, making sure the sound suppression was attached; checked ammo; and synchronized ourselves. Each MISTman carried two Ka-Bars and one commando knife (Second Lieutenant Marcelon having added several throwing knives to his war belt). We needed to be able to move as fast as possible during this mission, so none of us were wearing armor or egg buckets. We knew the possibility existed that we'd be leaving many of them dead on the field in this place, so as forensic countermeasures, we equipped with biodegradable bullets. They're made to fall completely apart after impacting and traveling through a body. In our own world, they were only used for deep cover or Black Ops missions and were entirely illegal for any other use. Any person caught with them was eligible for a penalty of no less than twenty-five years to life in a federal penitentiary. Lieutenant Colonel Gary and I had the two Roy-Bobs tweak a few batches of them a little bit before using them for that operation, though, because there was no doubt that after it was over, every federal and state agency in the United States would be interested in finding us. A field full of dead mercenaries would have to draw their attention with urgency. That didn't need to happen. So we would use any and everything at our disposal to avoid it.

The Walking Dead Raiders would be deployed, six near the northwestern intersection, three on each side, and the other six would be deployed the same way near the southwestern intersection in the same formation. They dropped in one kilometer behind their targets and were expected to meet one another at the intersection of Auberjon Road in a maximum of twenty minutes after having neutralized every enemy combatant. They would then reinforce Crossover Team Alpha in whatever battle they'd be fighting. Yes, Detective Caldwell, a MISTman can do that. Unencumbered, one of us can move at thirty to thirty-five miles per hour for at least two klicks (that's about a mile and a half or so) in total silence without stopping. In full gear, that time is only decreased by about ten seconds or so. And that can be done in noncombat situations. During a fight, our speed increases. Our reaction time, strength, coordination, and all of our senses enhance themselves incrementally in direct proportion to our adrenaline output. How? I'll explain that in a few moments, but right now, I need to complete your briefing.

After deploying the Walking Dead Raiders, we divided our force into three teams: 1st Lt. Archimus Marcelon, Gunnery Sergeant Gabriel Puccini, Sgt. Roy Robert "Roy-Bob" Joseph, and Cpl. Thomas Bench, who was also equipped with an M40A5 sound-suppressed sniper's rifle. They were Team Charlie and were expected to clear the south side of Auberjon Road while moving along that side toward the rectangle.

Lieutenant Colonel Benjamin Gary, Second Lieutenant Walter Ralph Arthur McGrath, Sergeant Richard "Richie" Garfield (another M40A5-equipped sniper), and Corporal Demetrius Benson (our second-best hand-to-hand combatant) would make up Team Bravo and attack from the north side with the same orders and mission parameters. Second Lieutenant Logan Eller, Master Guns Lucius Carver, Gunnery Sergeant Antoine Rochon (with his M40A5), and I made up Team Alpha, and we would attack their headquarters, accessing from the back of the rectangle. We equipped with earwigs and dropped into our zones.

Crossover Team Alpha's objective was the head house. Alpha Team would neutralize Craine and Muldowney, snatch the hostages, exit out of the back, and proceed toward the extraction point, accompanied by teams Charlie and Bravo. Braggs would take Nigel, Angeline, Master Guns Lucius Carver, Naval Corpsman Vince Legget, and me to the ranch in Franklinton while the rest of Crossover Team Alpha, along with the Walking Dead Raiders, all under Lieutenant Colonel Benjamin Gary's command, would dispose of the bodies, their gear, and the temporary barracks, then wait on the rectangle for Captain Braggs to return and fly them from Houma back to Franklinton. Lieutenant Colonel Gary was assigned to hang around for a few days to see what, if anything, got out about the battle of Savanne Road then ride back in one of the minivans with Leonard or Kruger, who would have met him at Boudreau & Thibodeau's Cajun Cooking—a nice enough restaurant there in Houma.

No, I told them, they wouldn't be allowed to remotely drive the vehicle to Gary's location since N-Prime had no self-driving cars at that time. Also, the Refractor wouldn't be used for that ride—we needed intel from a living human eye, and if a Toyota minivan drove the distance from New Orleans to Houma without a visible driver, someone, most likely a policeman or a Louisiana state trooper, would notice it and possibly cause us more complications, exactly the sort of thing that we needed to avoid.

Let me shorten it for you, Detective; we neutralized every single one of them, and by the time they knew what was happening, teams Charlie and Bravo were on the front lawn of the main house. That was the only time that any one of them got off a shot, and he missed. It must've had something to do with the throwing knife that was suddenly piercing his neck. As the battle progressed, our side got a little surprise. Unbeknownst to us, there were fifteen more men in the house. While the firefight broke out in the front yard, Team Alpha was within the hideout, fighting from room to room, looking for our quarry. We found them at last, Devin Craine and Blacen Muldowney, in an upstairs gaming and theater room. I made it there first, as Eller and Lucius were doing mop-ups throughout the house.

When I kicked the door in, there was Nigel, lying on the bed, asleep. *Drugged, most likely.* Angeline was tied to a chair, her head down, and Muldowney was about to try to insert an IV into the boy's arm, hoping, no doubt, to take enough blood for a resumption of the same mad plan that caused the downfall of one world. Craine was at the window, aiming his pistol down into the front yard, and I knew he'd drawn a bead on one of my men. I called his name, he turned, and I shot him between the eyes, putting another one in his forehead before he went down. The effect on Muldowney was the same as if he'd been kicked in the chest by a mule. He screamed like a girl, dropped the IV, and ran over to Craine's body, crying his name. He held Devin's head in his arms and moaned.

Lucius and Eller joined me about that time, reporting that the fighting was over, but we were about to have company. A vehicle was zooming up Auberjon Road, and it looked like that NCIS agent's car. I walked over, kicked Muldowney in his face to stop his blubbering, and ordered my MISTmen to pull their hoods and blend into the shadows. They did. We needed to face this man. Meanwhile, I checked on my Angeline. One of those bastards (most likely Blacen) had hit her, and she was still out. Nigel was still unconscious. They'd cut his arm and swabbed some of the blood. I had no idea where that sample had been sent to, but that was not the time to worry about it. It was time to face a potential ally, who could also turn out to be a potent enemy. I was untying my wife when Agent Hotshot walked in with three other agents. *His team*, I thought. He was visibly angry too.

"I can't believe you killed all those men alone," he said.

"I can't believe you disobeyed orders, Agent Caldwell," I replied. "I didn't kill all of them, just a few in the house, the backyard, and Devin Craine here. I'm about to kill Blacen Muldowney," I told him. He raised his Sig and said, "You're not taking another life on my watch. Move away from the woman and the boy. Do not go *near* that man." He indicated Muldowney, who, having recovered somewhat, was blubbering once more and repeating himself again and again: "Don't go, Devin, don't go . . . We have to kill them all . . ."

I gave a signal. Lucius, Eller, and Rochon deactivated their battle fatigues' camouflage function and, with their rifles raised, seemingly stepped out from the walls that his team had passed by when they saw me in the middle of the room. Marcelon, Puccini, Bench, and Joseph came in the door behind the NCIS team again, seemingly from nowhere. His people's heads were turning right to left as if on swivels. They couldn't believe that they were so suddenly surrounded. "Maybe you should have waited for your SWAT teams," I said while Eller removed the agents' cell phones and firearms. I could see the anger in Hotshot's eyes as I walked over to Muldowney.

"Agent Roan Caldwell," I told him, "I am not from this world. None of us are. But we have been visiting here for more than two years. I'm telling you this because we've already ascertained that you have no recording devices, and you and your team arrived alone. I am the General Commanding Officer of MIST Unit One, Crossover Team Alpha, and all adjoining forces. This man, Blacen Muldowney, is under a death sentence back where we come from. You've wondered how it is that your Blacen Muldowney can be in a supermax federal penitentiary and still have managed to leave his DNA all over the woman you found across the state line. That's because this is the man who raped and murdered her. He's a double of your own. You've also wondered how that woman could have been twenty years younger than the Carla Ryan you have here and also have been in possession of a DOD identity card that identified her as an NCIS lab worker. That's because she too was a double of your own.

"In our world, this Blacen Muldowney and the double of Devin Craine, the gentleman lying there with the two extra eyes in his head, were responsible for fabricating a virus that may, even now, still be decimating the human race. It is entirely possible that their having deployed that virus from American soil has also caused a third world war. Blacen Muldowney escaped into this world, and I have chased him. Our intelligence reports indicated that he and the Devin Craine of your world were working on replicating the virus that may have already obliterated our home world, or perhaps they were creating something worse.

"Thus, Blacen Muldowney has demonstrated a virulence that knows neither remorse nor repentance. In addition to his previous crimes, he and his accessory, Devin Craine there, kidnapped my own family from a neighborhood park two days ago and have subsequently threatened both their lives and well-being. Now I will carry out the death warrant that our president signed off on him."

Hearing that, Muldowney tried to dive for Craine's pistol, but I caught him by his collar, pinned him with my boot, then reached down and twisted his neck as if he were an enemy sentry. He died with his head turned around backward. After executing the Presidential Death Sentence, I shot him through the ears with my Beretta. NCIS agent Roan Caldwell thought, at the time, that this was done out of malice. What he didn't know was that such action was simply the most effective way to immediately destroy the will killer chip as well as any evidence that it was ever there. Besides, I hated Blacen Muldowney so deeply that malice was indeed involved. The skinny guy on the NCIS team looked as if he was going to throw up. Your counterpart had rage in his eyes, but could not have stopped me from doing what I did. I looked into those eyes and told him that there was no way Muldowney could have ever had a so-called fair trial here, and that he would be receiving a copy of that presidentially issued death warrant.

I signaled again, my men stepped forward with slappies, and put every one of the NCIS Team members to sleep. Nigel was out for the count, which meant that any exit through otherspace was cut off, and we had to handle the NCIS team the best way we could without hurting any of them. They would wake up still in their car, in the parking lot of the Houma Police Department. I carried Angeline, Lucius carried Nigel, and we left that place of death and destruction. The authorities could do what they would when they found the bodies. They'd never find *any* of us.

PORT OF CALL

Roan's head was down. He didn't want to believe that if he'd only had a partner, the Tenement Slasher may never have killed his loved ones. *But I didn't think I needed one, did I? I was just too good at the job for some lesser cop to slow me down. Why is this man trying to break me down so? What does he really want?* Raising his head, he asked, "How do I fit into this game of yours, General?"

General Nigel Renoir looked at him for a moment. "I told you, Detective Caldwell, you and Nigel have history, and he trusts you more than he trusts me right now."

"If I'm supposed to believe anything you said, then you're a murderer, General Renoir," Roan began then continued. "By your own admission, you ordered the deaths of at least fifty men and are directly responsible for taking the lives of at least two more on what was for you, foreign ground. You weren't at war when you killed or ordered the death of those Security Forces. You were acting under the orders of a government in a different world, not those of that place."

Feeling even more anger well up within himself, Detective Caldwell spoke further. "The men who died weren't under the authority of your 'President Ted Kennedy' if such a person ever truly existed, and this 'Muldowney' person, if he's even real, was on the soil of a different country and still should have been extradited instead of murdered. You authorized illegal experimentation on a minor without that child's consent or his parents, and the list of felonies could go on and on. No wonder Nigel doesn't trust you! Look at what you've *done* to him!"

Even as he concluded his tirade, Roan knew within himself that General Renoir wasn't the person whom he was really angry with. This wasn't the person who'd made the wrong decision all those years ago, when Laura and their children had still been alive. General Renoir just stared at Roan for a moment then answered in an aggravatingly calm tone, "That being the case, Detective Caldwell, why don't you just arrest me, charge me with these crimes you speak of, or go to the press?"

"Because I wouldn't make it a mile down the road if I left here with that intent," Roan answered. "You've already made that perfectly clear, sir."

"So then, you do believe my story, yes?" the general asked again, with that aggravating calmness and owlish stare.

"What?" Roan replied, surprised at the turn of direction. "Yes, I mean, no, uh, well, I can't really say at the moment. I know what I see in comparing you to the man I met in Sand Ridge, so there's no denying the fact that you seem to be the same person or, at the very least, an extremely similar one, but . . ."

General Nigel Renoir stood up, and his whole demeanor seemed to change from confessor/storyteller to that of a hushed imminent threat. In a quiet voice laden with undertones of steel and nuances of danger, he began. "But what you're trying to say is that you don't want to believe that if you'd been less *conceited*, less willing to believe that *your* deductions had to be the *only* right ones, if you'd just *trusted* any of your fellow police officers, especially those gifted ones who *deserved* such trust, then your own life would have turned out differently so that you wouldn't have spent so many years beating yourself with feelings of bloodguilt and self-reproach over your beloved family. Even now you've begun to believe that they're dead because of your conceited, single-minded *arrogance*, and your thought is simply this, Roan Caldwell—you *failed to protect* your wife and children, and *you don't like that fact!*"

Roan sprang to his feet and swung at the general, but suddenly he felt movement of air, similar to a light breeze, while his intended target seemed to blur and shift, leaving nothing before Roan but empty space, and there was General Renoir sitting in a chair on the other side of the room, a sage smile on his face. "Now, you've seen just a touch of a MIST-trained marine's ability. If you would like to take the information you have to any of your authorities here or to the press, I wouldn't stop you, just so that you could see what would come of such a thoughtless decision." He began again in a quiet albeit less threatening tone and went on. "They wouldn't believe you, though. I also ask you to recall something else: I never said that *I'd* be the person to order your neutralization if you digressed from your sworn word of silence. Your own government would do that." Roan's eyes widened slightly at that thought while General Renoir added, "And one more thing." Now there seemed to be a quiet tone of amusement or laughter in his voice. "Only four men lost their lives in the skirmish on Savanne Road."

***

Do you remember that I mentioned how Sergeant Joseph tweaked the BD rounds? Yes? Well, we changed that whole batch into knockout slugs whose effects were similar to the slappy patch that we used on you, only those effects were far more powerful. The difference is that BDs modified in that fashion will put a person into a temporary coma that lasts two or three days and wipes their memories from up to ten days before the BD hit them. We had already attained a school bus to load the Steele Bay men into, and after the fight, that bus was left as a roadblock at the intersection of Lake Crescent Circle and Pelto Drive, located within the nearest residential neighborhood. Since that's the only direct access to Savanne Road from the Crescent Lake Subdivision there, a school bus loaded full of sixty comatose men and two deceased ones, all in military fatigues with ziptied hands, wouldn't long escape notice. Someone living in that community would *have* to call the police, if only to get the street cleared. When they recovered, Steele Bay's men would unable to remember anything from four to ten days before the action, so they'd no doubt spend a long time with the local authorities, who would chalk it up as just another mystery. No district attorney could even arraign them for anything since they were all victims, and none of their number had any pending warrants, charges, or indictments in their background reports. They also had no weapons that could be matched to the fatal wounds inflicted upon their deceased comrades. Actually, they had no weapons at all when they were found. Even their knives were gone.

For us, that left NCIS and, possibly, MPIS to be dealt with. Those agencies would attempt a more detailed investigation, so we created more confusion by planting drugs and other contraband in the main house then informing the DEA. What that wrought was this—three different governmental agencies involved in their own investigations, all trying to one-up each other and refusing to work together, each of them stonewalling the other. All the interagency fighting, combined with the resultant mud that it stirred up, further assured that any investigations would be obstructed for a long time. Only NCIS agent Roan Caldwell and his team would know what had really happened, and they couldn't share the entirety of that information with their agency without endangering their own careers. Still, with his customary brutal honesty, your duplicate probably did file a report somewhere.

My XO and I ultimately decided not to allow Craine's or Muldowney's remains to fall into the hands of anyone in that world, so we incinerated them. Their ashes were scattered over a huge garbage dump located in some third world country. That's how much we valued those men. The recording of Muldowney and the second Craine's meeting also disappeared. The digital archive where information regarding the DNA of our Carla Ryan had been stored somehow got corrupted right after they found the body, but when their cybertechs finally got everything sorted out, the match turned out to be wrong, and that DOD identification card turned out to be a fabrication. Though we hadn't mixed it up with them at that time, that unidentified woman with the fake identification had actually been exposed as an employee of Steele Bay who was deployed on some secret mission for an arms dealer who wanted to get his hands on a mutated bubonic plague sample for use in creating and selling bioweaponry.

Before any autopsy on her body could be performed, however, a directive ordering its cremation came from their CDC. As for Steele Bay, in the eyes of the law, all of this disjointed evidence, when put together with the bus full of comatose mercenaries wearing their uniforms, seemed to point toward that company's being involved with some profound and horribly underhanded villainy; but no substantiation of any offense could be found. To the paranoid Justice Department of theirs, that, in turn, seemed to indicate that Steele Bay was involved in covert activity on behalf of either organized crime or a rival government. Any attorney general or district attorney would take a dim view of such involvement on the part of a security corporation as large, well connected, and equipped as Steele Bay. The resultant investigations, combined with the total loss of their computer systems, contributed to keeping that company too busy with legal matters and unlikely to be able to interfere with our affairs for a very, very long time, if ever again.

Meanwhile, the recording of what happened in that park in Gentilly became a hit all over their World Wide Web, but the United States government thoroughly discredited it as a hoax. Still, at the highest levels, they *knew*. Later, the country elected their first, as they say, African American president; and after reviewing it, he tasked his attorney general with finding a way to compel their different agencies to work together and find out who Nigel was, how he'd been able to do those things he did, and so forth. The results of that effort had begun to show, meaning that we now had to find a way to remain out of their reach in order to continue Mission CureSearch. I suppose you could say that we had to "get out of Dodge" until the heat died down, so to speak. That meant drastic steps needed to be taken. That is why we left that reality after that. *All* of us. No one wanted to stay behind, especially since every possibility existed that they were on to us now. If we separated from each other, we would not be likely to ever see each other again, and for some reason, that thought had become too much for us to bear. We'd fought as a team again, and that event reminded all of us that we were all that was left of our world and our people. I promoted each of my men, including Captain Braggs, one rank, making sure that they had insignia and documentation.

When we were ready, I asked Nigel if he wanted to stay there in his home world. He could take us across then come back. He couldn't think of why he would want to stay, though, as he'd already begun to forget his little Angeline. My wife was hurt that the memory repression had that effect because neither of us expected him to be able to forget her. He boarded the plane with everyone else. Besides Nigel, there were sixteen of us making that second crossing, as Lieutenant Colonel Gary's girlfriend insisted on accompanying him, and I allowed it. As far as any of us knew, I was the highest-ranking military officer and marine left of our civilization, and the authority to change things was mine if I so desired. I so desired. When Nigel asked where we were going, I told him to just take us *across*, to anywhere that we hadn't already been and that wherever we came out, we wanted to be as close to the nation's capital as possible. He agreed, and Major Martin Braggs flew slower this time.

I ordered all of my marines into dress uniform, rank insignias, and medals openly displayed. We went high and headed for Washington DC. He brought us out almost right above the White House, here, in this world. Boy, did we ever have to scramble then. We signaled peaceful surrender over all bands as loudly as we could, and they had us land at Bolling AFB. I'd been given a packet marked *Classified* to present to any United States government that I chose and that was in my hand when they boarded. I was under orders from my former government not to open the packet myself, so it was still sealed. I also insisted that my men not be treated as prisoners, and they weren't. They found Angeline, Kruger, Leonard, and Ms. Maureen Sampson aboard in their boxes and were not sure what to do with them until I identified them. I further informed them that our story would not be told until their commander in chief and secretary of defense had seen what was in the packet. The year here was 1989, and Nigel was eleven years old, soon to become twelve.

INTERLUDE III

COLLATERAL AFTEREFFECTS

It had been four years since The Incident. Four years since the shadowy presence of a group that his government code-named "the Interlopers" touched the lives of The Agent and his team. Two years since the last time he'd been here, in Broussard Park, where his world had its first "we are not alone" moment, when a child from some other place made two men disappear into nowhere.

The event had simply become known all over the country then all around the world as "the Incident at Broussard Park," and oh, the theories and stories that had arisen from that day's activities! For months after the incident, all types of people from all over the world had crowded this place. There were religious fanatics, drug burnouts, sci-fi geeks, ghost hunters, vampire lovers, occultists, cultists, true believers, nonbelievers, unbelievers, scientists, pseudoscientists, and every other whacko or weirdo with the slightest ability to make his, her, or its way to Broussard Park on The Lakefront in New Orleans. Eventually though, the frenzy ran its course, and the parade ended. Even the shocking video of all that had gone on there was discredited. Forensic analysts proved that while the person who made the now-famous iPhone recording that day had, indeed, witnessed heinous acts of murder and malicious mayhem, the part of the film capture that documented a little kid making evil-looking thugs vanish into the ground had, in fact, been a hoax.

Later, the person who was responsible for the recording came forward to admit that she had, indeed, "photoshopped" the camera output to include ruffians disappearing at the hands of the little boy from the kid wedding video. She apologized profusely to the families of the victims, and although receiving public castigation by the media and the community, as well as being the subject of most late-night comedians' opening dialogue for a time, her injudicious deed eventually ceased to be the hot topic of the day. Ironically, as soon as she completed her senior year of undergraduate studies at Tulane University, the young lady was actually hired by a prominent contractor for the US military as an intern for their virtual reality development department. All was forgotten, forgiven, and the world kept turning. Things were different within the walls of top secret facilities and underground laboratories of the United States government, though. They knew that every event captured in that recording was authentic. The boy was real. What he did was real. Still, nowhere else could any other evidence of the child's existence be found.

Eventually, a different president came to power, a man who approached matters of state from an innovative perspective; and as one of his first (classified) official acts, he had his newly appointed Attorney General as well as his Joint Chiefs subject every report from every single law enforcement agency and branches of the military that had been filed during that time period to review. It was a daunting task, but they found certain reports of inexplicable actions taken by untraceable and unverifiable parties, all or most of these records having originated within duty reports submitted by one NCIS lead agent and his team. Closer scrutiny by the best analysts indicated that those events were without a doubt likely related to the incident in Broussard Park, and the very same child may have been involved. That was what they'd been looking for.

In the meantime, for NCIS Agent Roan Caldwell, as disturbing as The Incident in the park had been, it paled in comparison to another incident that kept haunting him, driving the sleep from his eyes. He thought of it as the Savanne Road Case. Over and over again, that horrendous scene within the top room of a big beautiful home at the end of a private unpaved road off Savanne Road in Houma, Louisiana, was replayed in his memory. That night, he'd looked right into the eyes of an individual who was either a highly trained killer or simply an emotionless sociopath. Without the slightest hint of regret or remorse, the man had blatantly admitted to the murder of one of the victims in the room, then with the same disregard, brutally slain the second victim right in front of Roan's eyes. Still he hadn't done it with the twisted joy of a killer who loved death. His behavior was more that of a soldier who was doing what his duty demanded, for without a doubt, he had chosen not to kill or have his troops kill the sixty or so other men who were fighting against his that night. He and his people had to have been the Interlopers because he had also been on the scene after the incident in Broussard Park.

Whenever his thoughts returned to the Savanne Road case, as they always did, Roan would also remember every word that the man who had to have been the Interlopers' leader said to him in a brightly lit upper room on that gloomy night: "I am not from this world. None of us are. But we have been visiting here for more than two years." He stood there, wearing the uniform and insignia of the United States Marine Corps, and identified himself as "... The General Commanding Officer of MIST Unit One, Crossover Team Alpha, and all adjoining forces." He said further that his two victims "...were working on replicating the virus that may have obliterated our home world, or perhaps creating something worse. Blacen Muldowney escaped into this world, and I have chased him." The dawning of Roan Caldwell's understanding of the facts, that the Interlopers were from some other possibly "obliterated" world, had "adjoining forces" and access to technology advanced enough to create a virus that could extinguish the entirety of the human race, were the most chilling details of that episode every time he replayed it in his mind.

He also remembered how their leader had told him that the two individuals whom he'd personally executed had "...kidnapped my own family from a neighborhood park two days ago and have subsequently threatened both their lives and well-being..." So the boy and the woman were his family, which meant that the Savanne Road affair and the incident in Broussard Park were linked. More than anything else, though, that statement told NCIS lead agent Roan Caldwell that no matter where they'd originated, the Interlopers were neither aliens nor unidentified life-forms; they were just other human beings—advanced in technology, but still human. No matter where they came from, only human beings could love and murder that way.

After the humiliation of he and his team's being found unconscious in the parking lot of the Houma Police Department, the then director of NCIS met with them to discuss the problem of what to place within their official reports. While the truth that the same police department had also found a stolen school bus loaded with unconscious unarmed mercenaries was a matter of public record and couldn't be denied, still, there remained no evidence anywhere of the on-site presence of either of the two men whom Roan's team identified as the victims of a double murder that allegedly happened there. One was supposedly the infamous serial killer, Blacen Muldowney, who had never even left ADX Florence, the federal supermax prison out in Colorado. Before being sent on his way to his final sentence, the man had been questioned under torture, and his answers revealed that there was no way he could possibly have been in Houma, Louisiana, on the night in question.

Further inquiry had indeed proved the existence of a Devin Crane, but Homeland Security's bridge surveillance cameras unmistakably identified that man as having been the person who jumped off the Huey P. Long Bridge early one Sunday morning, although his body was never recovered. Additionally, other items that warranted investigation were discovered within the house, so now more than one federal agency had become involved, making it harder to move any single investigation forward.

What was definite, what was real, The Director had stressed, was the matter of three separate federal agencies being involved in different although linked investigations at the scene where Roan's team had "allegedly" met the Interlopers. Every one of those agencies had to look good in the eyes of the Congress when the upcoming Annual Federal Funds Allotment hearings were completed. Each agency needed to have a certain budget for the upcoming fiscal year, so there was bound to be a lot of backstabbing and stonewalling going on with this, and the dirtiest players would get the rewards if they could make themselves look like the best.

Now, since NCIS didn't want to seem to be staffed with lunatic agents, The Director had further explained, Agent Caldwell and his team were asked in what was, for the most part, a reasonable way, to fabricate "less accurate" reports. Roan took The Director's urgings to heart, but had chosen to file the most accurate report that he could, anyway. There was just too much danger in the words of the Interlopers' General for him to exclude anything the man had said during those hours of darkness. Two of his team members, Billy and Meredith, chose to follow his example. Their third team member, Kevin McDinton, however, had taken the easiest way out. His report was a masterpiece of creative writing, for the way he omitted facts then substituted rationalizations and outright lies about what really occurred in Houma, Louisiana, that night. Resultantly, Roan, Billy, and Meredith were on the verge of being sacked when President Obama personally made the phone call that saved their jobs and changed their career paths. Kevin McDinton, on the other hand, was irrevocably transferred to a lifetime position with the Department of Housing and Urban Development as lead investigator of insect infestations, a one-man posting.

After a closed-session congressional review of the incident in Broussard Park along with Roan, Billy, and Meredith's reports regarding the Savanne Road case, the Obama Administration proposed the formation of a new federal agency for the interception of and defense against encroachment of alien threats, regardless of the point of origin of any such menace. The IDEA Threat Agency was commissioned with the approval of the majority of the divided Congress of the day; and because of his lack of political affiliation, as well as his direct contact with the Interlopers' leader, combined with the urgency of the need, Roan was appointed without partisan dissent as its first Director, to be code-named IDEA Control.

In order to prevent any public panic, the agency would have to remain classified at its inception, but all other state and federal agencies were to be subject to its orders when transdimensional, or any other types of unfamiliar threats were involved. Billy and Meredith Compton were the first of three federal agents to be placed in his agency, directly under his command. Against his wishes and better judgment, however, Roan would have to use MPIS people as tactical field operatives in situations where abundant or overwhelming force may be needed. Knowing that this compromise had to be made in order for IDEA Threat Agency to exist, however, still did nothing to alleviate IDEA Control's mistrust of MPIS.

Roan, as The Director of IDEA Threat Agency, decided that if the puzzle of the Interlopers were to be solved, it would have to be done by finding out more about the boy from the Broussard Park incident, as the child had come to be known. Again and again he reviewed the film record. He also sought out a report he'd read regarding the fingerprints found on the boy's gold coin, but that report was gone, and the coin had also come up missing. Apparently, some corrupt police officer had taken it for himself before it could be transferred into federal possession. Although the man's theft of that as well as other pieces of evidence was inarguably exposed by an anonymous source, the gold coin was never seen again, and he claimed he'd never taken it. That left the orphanage that the boy was supposed to be in.

IDEA Control visited that institution, and after leaving that place, he immediately put through an order to have DHS shut it down and take all the staff into custody. How could a child go missing for so long and not a soul in that place missed him? The nuns and priests that comprised its staff told him ridiculous tales about a youngster who may or may not have been The Boy. Some said that he'd been taken by adoptive parents, but their first explanation was that the child frequently disappeared into some place of perdition and iniquity, often returning with gifts given to him by the Evil One. They were actually serious when they said it. Certain members of the staff even had the audacity to show him the tools they'd used to try to exorcise the devil from the child he was searching for, as well as any other children of such evil inclination. Their basis for such brass self-exposure was the classified nature of his agency. These people had the wrong opinion of the reason for IDEA Control's visit. They thought Roan wanted to use their draconic methods to capture and force heretics into divulging their involvement with Lucifer or some such superstitious drivel. All four of the core members of IDEA Threat agency were simply disgusted with them. The orphanage turned out to be just another dead end. So Roan tried to find out the identity of the woman in the film. She looked familiar, but he couldn't place her. Further, he could barely make out her face because of the angle of the shot. He tried to find any way to put a finger on what was so familiar about her, but he simply couldn't place it. He regulated that little problem to his subconscious and moved on. Maybe discussing the puzzle with Laura tonight would help. There was another problem with this person, anyway. She didn't appear anywhere else. Not in the surveillance system that had been put into place since 9-11, not in ATMs or grocery stores' cameras. Nowhere. She had to be the wife of the Interlopers' General, but he could find no more trace of her than he could of the general himself. Another dead end.

That left only the little girl from the video record of The Incident in Broussard Park. He could see what direction she went in when she ran off the scene, and as a detective, he surmised that her home must have been near Broussard Park. Where else would a kid that young run off to in that type of situation? So for a moment, he considered the thought of going to the scene, look toward the direction she fled in to try identifying the group of homes most likely to contain the one she ran into, then work from there.

Roan felt that once he found the right domicile, to go alone and talk to the child's parents as a father, asking to be allowed to speak to their little girl, under their oversight, would be the best way of handling the matter. But he soon realized that no one viewing that iPhone capture could have positively identified the girl, including him. So he let it go for the moment. There was no sense in banging on all the doors in the neighborhood, hoping to stumble across the right one. That would alert the residents to the fact that the United States government was still investigating The Incident, which could, in turn, bring back the crowds of tourists and nuts. This little girl was only guilty of liking the wrong little boy and didn't need to be hunted like some criminal suspect.

IDEA Control rightfully surmised that soon enough, his agency would have to find her through investigative means, anyway, then her entire life would thereafter be subject to unending public scrutiny. Once MPIS got involved, things would get even worse for the kid's family. So Roan decided not to aggressively pursue that lead yet. Besides, there was a possibility that his agency would soon have a tool that could sense energy spiking in the immediate area of any other event. The lab had gone back over the atmospheric energy readings from that day in the location of Broussard Park, and their findings pointed toward a sudden extreme increase in the levels of ambient electromagnetic static in the area that occurred at the exact moment the event did. Such an energy flux never had been recorded anywhere else on earth. That made it an anomaly connected only to the exploit that the boy had performed. At the present, they would be able to know within a matter of moments if anything like that happened again.

Now that the IDEA Threat Agency could discern if, where, and when anything like The Broussard Park Incident happened again, IDEA Control could put off any intrusion into that unidentified little girl's life for the moment. The problem of finding the boy just got easier, he thought. That child would have to do what he did sooner or later, and the IDEA Threat Agency would have him then. Meanwhile, Roan decided to go and have another look at the location where it all began. Thinking thus, he returned to Broussard Park for the first time in two years. He had to look at the setting again, to remember as much as he could. That was how it came to occur that he was on hand to witness the next event.

He was walking alone in Broussard Park when he noticed a girl of about thirteen years of age standing by herself. She just stood there, alone, near the spot where the incident took place. Any rookie detective could have been able to see that the lass was expecting someone to meet her. There could be no mistaking the air of anticipation she exuded. Intuitively, Roan also recognized her as the one who had been in the kid wedding at the start of the now-classified iPhone capture. She'd emerged from one of the homes across the street, and he'd seen which one. So now he knew. He started to approach her when suddenly, The Boy *stepped out of nowhere. Without a doubt, that was the same kid from before, the very one who had been involved in the incident. Something was wrong with him, though. He seemed to be under the influence of some drug or another. Somehow the girl knew he'd be there, but seemed to have expected him to be in better shape. Her distress at his condition was too obvious for any other conclusion to be drawn. He seemed delirious, falling to his knees, shouting at times that they, whoever they were, were trying to kill "her" (whoever that "her" was, for he was clearly not referring to the girl in front of him) then, The Boy would commence yelling to someone who wasn't there while his body started shaking or shivering, Idea Control couldn't tell which.*

Thinking that the girl might have been in danger, Roan prepared to spring forward to her rescue, but something told him that he needed to wait. Wait just a moment to see how the scene would play out. He was glad that he did. The girl held both of the disappearing boy's hands in hers for a long moment. He fell to his knees, and she let his hands go then stepped back, pursing her lips while she thought. Having come to some conclusion, she knelt in front of the boy, put her arms around him, and held him. He responded by putting his arms around her, his shaking stopped, his shouts ended, and Director Caldwell could see that both of the teenaged children were crying. He eased toward them slowly, not wanting to spook The Boy from The Broussard Park Incident into fleeing.

Suddenly, three people in a MPIS government-issue Ford Fusion came speeding up the street and screeched to a halt, mounting the curb. Cursing mentally, Roan turned to see Billy, Meredith, and probationary agent Troy Quentin jump out of the vehicle. Not MPIS, then. His people in an MPIS vehicle. Billy and Meredith ran toward him, yelling about an energy spike while Quentin, in an act of inexperience, charged toward the two adolescents, gun drawn, ordering them to "Freeze! Halt!" The two kids stopped hugging each other and looked up like startled deer. They stood and when the boy saw Quentin's gun, his eyes seemed to exude yellow light as his expression twisted in anger. Then he started to reach for something that only he could see. The girl, however, jumped in front of him, held his face in her hands, and said something that changed his mind. He wrapped her in his arms and disappeared.

That was the end of that event. Because it occurred early in the morning after Black Friday, there hadn't been too many people in the park to witness it. Broussard Park had, for a short time, become the focus of tour groups and general weirdoes who hoped to be taken away by aliens (or whatever), but the city had discouraged such visits and it seemed that nothing like The Incident would ever again happen there, if it ever really had. So the crowds stopped coming, and the place became a quiet neighborhood park once more. John Q. Public had a short memory. One middle-aged businessman and his wife were the only ones there that day. The two people hadn't even seen what was happening with the children; they'd been so frightened by Agent Quentin's behavior that they immediately hit the ground. From such a prone position, there was no way they could have seen what happened. The adolescent girl was never reported missing because, of course, she wasn't missed. She'd been at home in her room the entire morning, her parents said. She'd even come down the stairs herself and said the same thing when Roan, having dropped by their home for a casual visit, asked about it.

That was two years ago, but the damage was done. Reports had to be made, and now The Administration expected IDEA Control to have Broussard Park under constant observation by MPIS agents at all times. Satellites were constantly watching the park, and all the adjoining corners now had covert surveillance cameras mounted on them. Somehow, though, the girl's involvement had been removed from every official account, so no one knew who she was. Roan just figured that maybe some of his superiors had more mercy than it seemed and kept her existence quiet that way. Still, here he was, another two years later, back in New Orleans, heading toward Broussard Park and perhaps another encounter.

If the same young lady were again implicated as complicit in further events, he didn't think anything could protect her future anymore.

Tonight he'd been informed that the energy signature accompanying every event had reoccurred in this same park, disappeared and come back, then disappeared again without The Boy. Being IDEA Control the Director meant that he had to get there with his original team and put more agents in that location regardless of whether The Boy showed up or not, so he did. Four years, and his agency was still using MPIS for the majority of their field work. Politics were involved. Top-level governmental representatives wanted them in this, and Roan wanted to keep them under his scrutiny because unlike his own agency, MPIS was a branch of the military, not a law enforcement agency, so Roan suspected them of possibly having numerous "off the books" operations and other activities of dubious legality that he himself would not be privy to. If this were true, only heaven and hell knew what they'd do if they were left to handle anyone connected to this event without the IDEA Threat Agency breathing down their necks, so to speak.

MPIS was primarily an apparatus designed to keep America's war machine clean and functional by whatever means necessary. Originally, their commission was to expose and eliminate any type of terrorist threat rising out of the ranks of the military. Suspicion was the code they lived by, and seeking out new wars was a function of theirs that had grown out of their original mission. Their power and reach had been broadened by the Patriot Act to include terrorist threats to the public as well as prevention of any actions attributable to "lone wolf" terrorists. It was very simple to them: a threat would be suspected, confirmed, identified, then destroyed with extreme prejudice no matter where it came from. IDEA Control felt that of all the military branches, that would most likely be the one that would find a way to impel the Interlopers into an all-out war against the United States. Roan's world couldn't have survived such a conflict, he knew. He'd seen what those people could do, what type of technology they had, and it frightened him.

He also knew that the Interlopers weren't out to conquer his world. His brief encounters with them indicated to his keen detective's mind that something else was involved. They'd taken out every man Steele Bay had on the scene, a platoon-sized force, with neither injuries nor exposure of their own forces. Not one shot had been heard, nor any spent cartridges located. Two men, both with GSR on their hands and clothing, died of knife wounds; yet no blades in existence matched those injuries. Further, not one person could be found who had seen a thing on Savanne Road that night. As for Roan and his NCIS team, they had been suddenly surrounded by men who came from nowhere in less than a second. The condition that his team as well as Steele Bay's mercenaries had been left in was unprecedented. No. The Interlopers couldn't have been out to conquer his world. If that were so, it could already have been done and over. Still, their nonaggression toward Roan's America wouldn't necessarily be reciprocated. Especially if MPIS were in the mix. That's why as the first director of IDEA threat agency, he continued to use the soldiers in gray as tactical units. It kept them under both his eye and his thumb.

Nevertheless, Roan was here again, staking out Broussard Park, accompanied by MPIS tactical units, lying in wait for an innocent fifteen-year-old boy who only wanted to see his girlfriend. They waited all night, though, and nothing changed. No one miraculously appeared in the park. Around daybreak, Roan ordered the men to prepare to leave, but looking across the park at the little girl's house, he saw when she stepped outside, caught sight of all the activity, then turned and walked down the block and around the corner.

She was cautious, but she was also only a fifteen-year-old kid and had no idea that Roan quietly slipped away to follow her alone. He saw when the boy appeared, but this time, there was another little girl with him. That child, well, unlike the one he'd followed, was scared to death since once more, something was wrong with him—his responses were slow and muddled, his gait wobbly, and the girls had to hold him up. Of course, there was a heated exchange between the two of them, but it ended when they caught sight of the director. They tried to run because apparently, the boy couldn't make them disappear suddenly as he had before, but Roan called the first girl by name, and the three children stopped.

Slowly, he approached, explaining to them that he wasn't totally alone and that all four of them needed to get out of sight so that they could have a discussion. He showed the children his badge and assured them that if he wanted to, he could have all three teenagers arrested and in custody right now, but he wouldn't do that if only they'd let him talk to them. They calmed down, and he began to ask questions. The conversation ended, and Roan had an even clearer understanding of what was going on. He knew the boy's name now and understood what the kid's present life was in that other world where he lived, but the boy could not remember anything past the last few days for some reason. It was as if he was born the moment he entered Roan's world. His young traveling companion, who was only thirteen, was far more informative, though.

After hearing as much as the youngsters could tell, he knew that these children would never be any threat to his country or his world. Their handlers, however, were a different matter. Still, he got the impression that they weren't about to launch an invasion or anything of that nature. *They wanted something else. For IDEA Control, it was just a matter of figuring out what that might be. Then maybe his world of humanity could be more prepared for anything that may come from the boy's world of origin. He decided, therefore, to allow the boy from The Incident and his traveling companion to go back home, warning them to never return to Broussard Park. The other teenaged girl even helped contrive a story that the little female visitor should tell the people who sent them there to begin with. Roan, meanwhile, had to admire the personal fortitude of the young lady whose charm kept drawing the boy from the Incident in Broussard Park to her. She clearly was in love with the fellow, but was also willing to give him up forever if it meant that he would be safe.*

She was a remarkable person, and Roan knew that nothing would keep the young man away from her as long as she was in this world. The boy would be back, and Roan had to be ready for it. During the course of the conversation between himself and the teenagers, the boy's reasoning had begun to clear up, and he made it quite clear that when he went back, he wanted to talk to the man who had put him in such poor condition whenever he arrived here this way. The teen was angry and only wanted to demand to be set free to return here forever. He said that he was tired of always having to say goodbye to her. Roan understood, but still, he sent the two visitors home and warned them again that they should never come back. He'd learned that the girl who lived beside Broussard Park had some instinctive ability to feel when the young Interloper was on the way. She would not only know when he was coming, but she'd also know where he'd be when entering their world.

The director also decided, as a father of two preteen girls himself, not to divulge that piece of information to his superiors when he made his official report. It wasn't necessary. Not at the moment, anyway. He didn't want MPIS tearing the young lady's life and family apart, which they surely would have done. If he chose to explain himself to his team, he knew they wouldn't go over his head to make a different report. He trusted them almost entirely. They'd trusted his leadership and went along with his decision two years ago, and he was reasonably sure they would do so again if he told them about this at all. He hoped he'd never have reason to regret his choice.

He never did.

TEENAGER TROUBLES

The President in this world was, of course, a different man than he had been in my world, as was the Secretary of Defense. Then-president Bush, after seeing the contents of the classified packet, sent for all of us. We'd brought over a lot of goodies and advancements that were going to be integrated into this country's military, as well as being curiosities ourselves, so he wanted to see if we were real and to tell all of us what had been in the package.

It contained a formal introduction on paper and DVD from our president, as well as an explanation of who we were and why we were there. Included was the same type of formal introduction from the secretary of defense, as well as the CMC. Our complete military records, in detail, up to the time we left home, were included. Nigel's role was also mentioned in further detail, and our former president suggested that the boy be kept close to me. Following that disclosure, each member of our party, with the exception of Ms. Sampson and Nigel, were identified by DNA and fingerprint analysis. A great deal of our technology was completely divulged to the DOD here, and considering our elite training, we were offered positions in the Marine Recon forces or the Navy SEALS, provided we could pass a battery of field tests, which, to their surprise, I insisted on going through along with my men. Actually, we performed better than their Special Forces did.

Eventually, Benjamin Gary and I were invited to the Oval Office for a confidential meeting with The President, his Chief of Staff, and the Joint Chiefs. They wanted to discuss the possibility of enemies of the United States crossing the dimensions as we had. We who had crossed the worlds knew that there was a very real possibility of some other person or persons being able to crack the DNA code that allowed Nigel to do what he did. Our people in The Think Tank were working on that very same thing when The Division fell. We explained all this, and they were alarmed at how close our people had come. Actually, that was the original reason for meeting with us. The majority of The Think Tank's work on duplicating Nigel's world-walking ability had been turned over, and the progress that had been made scared the people who were charged with protecting their country here.

President Bush decided, therefore, to form a new unit, specifically for preparation against dimension-crossing threats, also for the training of elite forces and running cross-dimension deep-cover missions, the unit that would be my command. They gave us the acronym IDEA Control and commissioned our activities. We were all once again in the United States Marine Corps. The DOD wanted to put us to work right away, but insisted that I not lead any more field missions, though Colonel Benjamin Gary could if he so chose, barring orders to the contrary.

Nigel was sent to a lab for testing, but he disappeared into the nil zone when they tried to get started, so they came to me. "How should we handle this?" they wanted to know. I let them know that such testing may not have been necessary and gave them the results of his past tests that paralleled the ones they wanted to try out on him here and, due to our level of advancement, happened to be even more complete. They wanted me to take Nigel and raise him as my son, but I sent a message to Kruger instead. He sent me an answer the next day. Yes, Nigel's family lived in this world too.

Their Nigel had been a musical virtuoso with the ability to play piano at the age of three. His aptitude for everything musical increased as he grew up. He could write composition, understand its theory, put together harmonies for songs. His parents held a hope that the boy would one day earn a scholarship to Julliard or some other prominent school, where his talents could be developed as fully as possible. They would never have been able to afford anything similar to the education they'd hoped he could have in such a place. His father was a first sergeant in the United States Marine Corps First Division. They lived in New Orleans, in Gentilly, and yes, it was the same house, in the same neighborhood. Yes, he did say their Nigel "had been." What happened? Well, the boy was missing. Since he'd been missing for three months now, the police had no expectation of finding him alive. The case was now under the purview of the FBI, and yes, he would have been the same age as our Nigel. Are you thinking what I think you're thinking? Is the DNA sweeper ready? Maybe. Yes, we can try it. We used our DNA tracer to find the other Nigel. He'd been molested, killed, and buried. It hurt me more than I'd thought, to see that what would have been a peaceful version of him and I had his life snuffed out so brutally. Our people positively identified the body then had it moved to headquarters and cremated, but we also went a step further on this. Because there were traces of his killer's DNA on the body, we could use our sweeper for the next step. We found that man, and Master Sergeant Antoine Rochon followed him for a few days.

When we found his home, First Lieutenant Logan Eller, Sargent Thomas Bench, and Sargent Demetrius Benson broke in and searched it. After locating what we needed to bring that animal under close FBI scrutiny, we called believable anonymous leads into their New Orleans field office, and they did what they do. They began investigating the man. In the course of their investigation, they found more evidence against the suspect. Additionally, their profilers were able to follow his development from random child pornography addict to full-blown perpetrator of heinous crimes against boys. With a little covert help from our computer geeks, they eventually found his dumpsite across the State line, in the woods near John C. Stennis Space Center, the same location where we found what was left of this reality's original Nigel. They were on the way out to pick him up when, with the wiliness and acuity common to predatory animals and serial murders in all realities, the man somehow discerned that he was about to be captured and fled. They were firmly on his trail, breathing down his neck, so to speak, but were having a devil of a time trying to catch up to him too. Honestly, in that case, the FBI were just too far behind to catch him. So Kruger and Leonard gave them a little more covert aid. They located the escape route that had been in his personal itinerary from his place of employment, and that was turned over to the FBI agency.

This worthless scum was on the way out of the country in the hold of a cargo ship, when one of our three-man MIST teams abducted the perpetrator, right under the FBI's collective nose, making it seem as if he escaped with the help of a partner in crime. We forced the truth out of him, then executed him, ensuring that the FBI would find their way to his torture chamber after locating the incriminating material he so carelessly had in his vehicle when he'd run it into Lake Pontchartrain. They're still searching for his supposed accomplice. We, for our part, handled it that way so that the DOD would be more prone to accept my next suggestion. Besides, having a hand in the elimination of that sort of human predator did not in any way cause me regret.

That done, I talked to the DOD about inserting Nigel back into his own family here. It was agreed that this was the best thing for him, as such a move would encourage normal development for the boy, as well as lessen the danger of any enemy using my wife or myself to bend him to their will since there would seem to be no connection between us. If the serial killer who had him did, in fact, have a partner, the FBI wanted to capture that man at all costs, and such enthusiasm could well expose IDEA Control's existence. His memory alterations were proceeding well, and many of his childhood recollections had been overlaid with my own in order to help him integrate, so it could reasonably be done. Consequently, they had an NCIS agent deliver Nigel to his family's home and explain that he'd fought against his abductor, managing to foil the man's attempts to molest him, but the ensuing scuffle resulted in Nigel's suffering a blow to his head that caused a temporary amnesia even though he'd managed to escape. He'd been living in a foster home until he was found by the agent. That was the story, and NCIS stuck by it.

As our next step, I sent for his father and explained that Nigel no longer had the musical ability he'd been born with, but instead had developed a code-breaking ability that made him a subject of special interest to the country's security and he would now be indispensable to the government. We thought that he'd reason out that his son had some ability in code breaking, anyway; and when he asked for details, the reply was simply, "That is definitely the situation, Marine, so your job is to raise your son as you would under any normal circumstances. No, you are not expected to coddle or baby the boy. He is your son, and you will raise him as you do your other two sons." I would be checking in on him from time to time, taking him with me on some of those occasions, and he was to be presented to the newly promoted Master Gunnery Sergeant's family as an old friend whose life Nigel's father had once saved. I would be considered Nigel's Godfather for that reason. After that, Nigel's father, my father, was transferred to my command, and I put him to work. His family would never again endure the hard times that ours sometimes had.

So things were proceeding along almost as before, Detective Caldwell. Nigel was used for exploratory missions into other realities, though we never went back into his own. This United States was, as mine had been before, profiting from his ability, though they limited their acquisitions to those of a technological nature. The administrations changed, and Nigel's special gift was used in different ways, with his memories being activated and suppressed before and after each mission. We stayed out of politics because we were considered immigrants, but still, we warned them about the attacks on the World Trade Center and even gave them proof. But neither my MISTmen nor any other Spec Ops were sent over to handle the mastermind of that fiendish plot before it got started. In fact, for political as well as financial reasons, we were all ordered to stand down on the matter. So it happened anyway. Our proclamations of faith in this new America began turning into dust in our mouths, and we hated that.

Kruger eventually asked to be relieved, as did Dr. Leonard. They were not military men, and neither one of them could abide the way that particular administration had chosen to allow such an atrocity, nor what was being done with Nigel. So they were allowed to leave. Both were offered very well-paying jobs in the research and development department of Apple electronics, which they accepted, of course. After a while, I couldn't stand seeing what was being done to Nigel either, but if I bailed out too, then my boy would be totally at the mercy of people who didn't know or love him. When he was thirteen, though, his ability to cross over without memory assistance resurfaced. Nigel saw *her* face in the crowd at Mardi Gras one year, and the next day, he passed through the nil zone on his own again without prompts or prodding.

IDEA Control labs went ballistic. As it was, one of our people was driving the lad back to his family in Gentilly when the vehicle just *disappeared*. It reappeared less than a second later with its driver unconscious, but safe and without Nigel. They were afraid to let me know, but in the end, there was no choice. They had no idea where to find him. Without even reviewing surveillance tapes, I knew. He'd be where I would have been. He'd go to that park where he'd always meet his Angeline. Our crossover tech was not as good then as it is now, but I knew where he had to have gone. Nigel had been implanted with a tracer that could (theoretically) lead a team across the zone, and we had large bulky handheld locators to find him with. Our ability to open the gate to *otherspace* was almost there, though untrustworthy. We were preparing to try an incursion when Nigel reappeared right outside of our headquarters. Again, the doctors applied his memory treatments. Nigel slept for two days.

He woke up unable to remember a thing. Back to what was normal for him nowadays. When Master Gunnery Sergeant Lucius Carver and I went to the Renoir home to check up on him, he cheerfully greeted me, the same as always: "Hello, Colonel sir. Yes, sir, I feel quite well. Nice to meet you, Master Guns Carver, sir." He didn't even remember Lucius. My heart felt so heavy. Also we'd found out there *was* an Angeline here too, I explained to Lucius. He thought that it shouldn't be mentioned, but I had to say what caused the problem in my report on the incident, and the DOD saw to it that her father in this reality, an Air Force Officer, was transferred to Patrick Air Force Base in Florida. He never knew why it happened, but was happy for the relocation. Master Sergeant Carver has barely spoken to me since.

Eventually, Nigel did it again. He was fifteen, and by that time, we'd discovered the one other person who could walk between the worlds that way. She was the daughter of Air Force Junior Grade Lieutenant Robin Lacy. Her mother was a "screamer," unhappily married, and one day, the teenaged girl just disappeared into thin air, right in front of Lieutenant and his wife. When she reappeared, full of fear and anxiety, having no idea what she had done, why, or how, the parents took her to the air force hospital. IDEA Control was on the lookout for people doing what Nigel did, and as soon as the report reached us and was confirmed, I was sent to the hospital to meet Robin Lacy so that we could get a better idea of the type of man he was. Over the next week or so, I observed his style of command and found it to be excellent. He handled his responsibilities with Marine Corps–level efficiency, but didn't forget how to earn an above-average level of genuine respect from his people. He treated them like valuable people and instilled self confidence in those who needed it. I liked him and had him transferred to my command. He was very underappreciated in his former posting, largely because his immediate superior succumbed to jealousy and had done all he could to discredit the man and his work, but I found him to be an outstanding officer. Junior Grade Lieutenant Robin Lacy handled the assignments he was given with above-average quality, so he received a well-deserved and long-delayed promotion. His daughter, Dana, was immediately subjected to a battery of tests, and the family's travel history was reviewed as well. Thus, we discovered that way back when she was about ten years old, her parents had visited New Orleans for the Jazz Fest, and she'd met our Nigel. They hung around each other for the duration of that visit, and then the family left. Her mother, on the other hand, wasn't happy with much of anything in her life, so she divorced and relinquished custody of the girl to her father. The woman ran off with some other person, who eventually wound up shooting her to death in a jealous rage.

The two kids had fallen out of touch eventually, but they'd met up again when her father brought her back to the Jazz Fest. She was thirteen, he was fifteen. That year, Nigel was under continual surveillance, his movements constantly traced. We'd seen when the two of them stumble across each other, watched while they crossed the river on the ferry a couple of times, holding hands and even doing the kissy thing a time or two. Typical teenagers, Nigel's surveillance team thought. But now, things seemed different. Dana too had the ability. It just seemed that she had to have been with or near Nigel for that to manifest itself.

We tested our theory this way: Nigel was sent through after having his memories manipulated again, and Dana was told to follow him for his own good. She did, but instead of just following him, she grabbed his hand and turned him around, bringing him home. She was unharmed, but her feelings were hurt. She now thought that Nigel was a "stoner" because of the condition she'd found him in and wanted nothing more to do with him. The psych lab rats took her and suppressed the memories with whatever arcane arts those people use. The boy, for his part, was angry, very angry, and demanding to see me. Knowing what he could do when in that state, I hesitated. No, Detective, my hesitation was not resultant from fear of death; it was because information regarding his ability to destroy had been withheld from the government here for Nigel's sake. Still, my boy was calling out to me, and for life or death, I was heading out to answer his cry when two of our marine guards subdued him and administered a tranquilizer.

Lieutenant Lacy refused to grant us permission to use his girl to open the way for excursions through the nil zone, and I did not override his wishes. Besides, she still couldn't do it without Nigel leading, and my boy was struggling so much against the memory suppression and deletion process that it was beginning to put him at risk for developing a bipolar disorder. IDEA Control could not chance losing him, I explained to my superiors. Nigel never deserved to become the head case he was, and I wouldn't let that happen to another kid. My official report stated the fact that Dana couldn't open the gateway unless she'd been in contact with Nigel, it seemed. So she'd not be likely to ever represent a threat. Her father was under my command, which meant that she wasn't going anywhere anytime soon. We'd check in on her, but would not force her into use.

***

"So what changed?" Roan asked. "Nigel told me that you were the one who introduced him to Dana Lacy. He even thought that you may have wanted them to become a couple."

"A lot of things happened to bring me to such a conclusion," General Renoir replied. "When we found that Dana too could walk between the worlds, we fully intended to keep her with the only other child that we knew of who could do this. Perhaps it was our hope that the two of them would stay together, maybe even produce a family of reality walkers, but the strength of his love for Angeline was too much for that plan to stand up against. We also underestimated the power of things that were simply meant to be.

"Dana was not Angeline, and that was the woman Nigel always wanted. He met and dated other young ladies as he grew, but none of those relationships could possibly have stood against who and what Angeline is to him. After that excursion into otherspace when he was fifteen, Nigel seemed to lose interest in everything. His grades began to suffer, but I'd started making more time for him, helping him with his schoolwork and his lessons, so he made it through high school with a very good grade point average."

"Did he ever recall any of the history that you two had?" Roan asked.

"No," the General answered, "and that was a hard thing to bear. Especially when I had to leave him on his own. Nigel graduated from high school a year early because he chose to attend summer school. He wanted to get schooling over with. I was at his graduation, but of his family members, only DeVries and Joanna attended. Right after the ceremony, I took the three of them to eat, and while we were enjoying a meal, I was called into action. I had to leave the two boys and their older sister there to finish without me."

"What happened, General?" Roan asked. He had begun to feel more and more anger at the way this man seemed to so casually dismiss the boy Nigel had been with the clinical detachment of a coroner. "What was so important that you bailed out on him *again*?" General Renoir considered Roan for a moment then replied, "We'd received intel that one of the lab rats who had worked with IDEA Control stole a great deal of information about Nigel, who he was and what he could do. That worker was going to try to defect to Russia and take as much information as he could, with the intent of bargaining with the Russians for political asylum and wealth. He'd been in contact with one of their top KGB operatives and was expected to meet him and show the veracity of what he had to offer. The Russians were even sending an extraction team in to evacuate the man, if their agent gave the word. I had to go handle the matter. The KGB agent is now in some black hole from which he'll never again be able to see daylight and he is giving up very valuable information even as we speak. That lab worker and the Russian extraction team are dead. So you see, Detective Caldwell, I hadn't 'bailed out' on Nigel. I was just called up in order to protect him from threats he never even knew were out there."

"Okay," Roan conceded, "you had to protect him. Did his family situation ever improve?"

"No, it did not," the general answered. Sounding as if he were speaking from his own memory, he continued. "His father did the best he could, but neither of Nigel's parents could endure the loss of his musical potential, and it showed through in the way they treated him over the years. We also believe that on some subliminal level, they *knew* that he wasn't their original boy. He has felt estranged from them and his siblings all the rest of his life. Only DeVries and he ever held some semblance of closeness. When he became seventeen, he was in full-out rebellion. His ears were pierced, he was wearing oddly trimmed facial hair, and was starting to hang around with a crew of losers who called themselves 'the Fight Club.' It seems that some popular movie inspired all this. All in all, Nigel was cheerfully becoming the worst possible role model for his younger siblings. Additionally, his father had chosen to retire from The Corps, which took him out from under my authority. The mother was a bipolar manic depressive and had left the family, but not before she'd done a sabotage job on all of her kids' emotions. That, at least, couldn't have been the fault of IDEA Control because my mother had taken the exact same course in the exact same way by the time I was seventeen. It was just the person the woman was. Besides, at that point, we had begun to leave him alone."

"Well, that sounds about right, General," Roan said. "You take a kid like that, make him into a weapon and a tool for the military, then leave him to try to find his own way when he needs you the most. Our government at work." The general looked down for a moment, rubbed his eyes with his fingers, then looked up again and began to reply, "I did not abandon Nigel, Detective Caldwell. Truthfully, I am the reason why he stopped his self-destructive behavior. It was at that point in his life that I began to make attempts at contriving some way to get him to move out to Florida, where he might have gotten close with either Angeline Duplessis or Dana Lacy. It seemed that either woman could have assuaged his loneliness. It just took a while for my suggestions to sink in.

"Meanwhile, Nigel beat his way to the leadership of his gang of fist fighters, commenced a training regimen for the gang, then began to pursue more dangerous brawls with similarly disposed groups of young men. They'd all agreed on a certain set of rules for their activities: they never fought with any weapons, the loser of any bout wasn't permitted to seek revenge anywhere other than in the ring, whichever fist-fighting crew won the overall match got to host the next fight, and the bouts were always fought by appointment. Other fight clubs sprang up, of all ethnicities and from all different parts of the southeastern states, with names like 'the Rolling Dragons,' 'the Celtic Crossmen,' 'Black Plague,' 'German Panzers,' and 'the Gulfport Brawlers.' That's one of the most memorable ones, mainly because of their leader, a short angry overmuscled Black kid with some Italian-sounding name. I think it was Genardo or Bennarro, something like that. The brawling events doubled as revelries, word spread among the young folks the way it always does, and kids as well as young adults from all over were invited to come witness the battles, make bets and party, while the Fight Club took ten percent of the loot since they hosted most of the time.

"Nigel had DeVries working as the DJ and talent scout for the musical entertainment, with his older brother and sister, Marvin and Joanne, in charge of acquiring liquor, which was sold at a makeshift bar within every venue. The young man was gracious enough, however, to have his crew sit out a few bouts so that the other fight clubs could host and earn more money. Overall," General Renoir added with what seemed to Roan to be a bit of misplaced fatherly pride, "that was an amazingly sound strategy, given the world these youngsters were building, as it helped cement the allegiance of the Fight Club's competitors to the system and, indirectly, to Nigel himself. Because I had to know how my boy was doing, I even attended some of his fighting bouts.

"One night, I was there when my understanding of what the DNA splicing of my childhood memories into his mind was doing to his physiology clarified for me. The kids were blaring songs from Green Day's *Insomniac*, from Nirvana, Tupac, Biggie, and one favorite, from a fellow named Dr. Dre, whom I do not believe to have been an actual doctor, rapping 'Keep Their Heads Ringin'. Illicit liquor was flowing, various couples were making out in the shadows of the warehouse, their sounds mixing with the expletives uttered from the mouths of the gamblers and the smoke of cigarettes and marijuana in the air while, in the center ring, Nigel was battling a particularly talented young fighter who was in the best condition I'd ever seen. Because he'd been drinking in excess before the match, Nigel was getting the worst of it at the beginning.

"Any person who has ever seen underground gambling would know. It seemed, to the crowd, that an upset was in the offing. Everyone could tell that he wasn't fighting at his best, and the money was changing hands swiftly. The other young man knocked Nigel down, stunning the crowd into silence for a moment, but something within Nigel suddenly seemed to go *click*, as if the pieces were just coming together. Only a MIST-trained eye would have recognized that sudden change; it would be indiscernible to any other type of person. Nigel's physiology had 'leveled up' into MIST mode. The change wasn't as drastic as it is with us, but it still happened. To the untrained eyes of the audience, however, he seemed to find strength or common sense enough to realize that he was on the verge of losing.

"Nigel sprung up before the five count and went on the offense. His hands moved so fast that they looked like nothing more than twin blurs. His drunkenness started to disappear as his body used the remaining ethanol in his system as fuel, the bruises on his torso as well as the nosebleed he had were fading. He danced around his man at unbelievable speed, but not so fast that the fight fans noticed that it was above normal. It occurred to me then, at that moment, that they probably didn't seem to notice because it *was* normal for him, and they expected it. What they didn't expect was the beating he'd been taking earlier. Still, his opponent was good as well as sober, and he didn't go down swiftly. That youngster was bigger than Nigel and quite tough. Actually, in retrospect, I believe that he looked a great deal like the Robby Dubois lad, all grown up. Maybe that was who he was. No matter. Nigel eventually landed an uppercut with his left then danced to the other fellow's left and came down with the right in an overhand that caught his opponent behind his left jawbone, ending the match.

As I watched the money changing hands again, I saw a pattern. From the few snatches of conversation I heard, these people never bet on Nigel's possibly losing because it seemed that he simply didn't lose. What they did was place bets on which round he'd knock the other man out in, if at all. I thought for a moment of calling Kruger or Leonard to see what may have been going on with our kid, but then it occurred to me that Nigel had already been experimented on enough. I chose not to mention it. The boy was doing this because he thought he'd never see his Angeline again. Let him make his money. Let him beat out his grief on others. The DA wasn't interested in the Fight Club's activities, so no one would be investigating anything . . . yet. Eventually, he and his crew began doing quite well for themselves financially and started to need the services of armed security, which meant hiring gun-toting hoods, and that drew the attention of Local Law Enforcement, as well as organized crime. Now, they wanted a piece of the action too.

"When the local Mafia sent men to 'talk to them' about it, no doubt with the idea of forcing the gang into their service, the Fight Club, with the brashness of youth, pounded the men into senselessness and robbed them. My boy was not in town at the time so as to prevent or facilitate anything associated with that act, though. Nigel's father had taken his children out to Arizona to see the Grand Canyon, so he wasn't with the Fight Club when they offended 'the Family,' but the Mob didn't exempt him from their immediate reprisal list. They killed his crew and were looking for him, supposedly to offer him a chance to work for them fighting for money, at least that was the word they'd put out among his peers, but in reality, their true intention involved torturing him to death in some dark abandoned building.

"IDEA Control's policy was to allow Nigel to pursue his own life, but although he seemed unable to ever cross the nil zone again, he was still considered an asset of the DOD and could not be allowed to fall under the Mafia's domination. When my sources told me about all this, it was quite clear that IDEA Control had to intervene. We were the driving force behind the Renoir family trip out west, thereby saving Nigel's life, but I knew my boy. He'd look for vengeance, if he could, and would likely go after it, dragging DeVries and Marvin along in such a fool's quest. Although we hadn't seen each other in quite a while, I got a message to Master Gunnery Sergeant Lucius Carver; and because Nigel was in danger, he, Rochon, Bench, Puccini, Benson, and I paid a visit to the head of the Family. We showed him a few things that changed his mind about ever having anything to do with Nigel again.

315

"Also, it was politely made crystal-clear to him that the particular men who murdered the Fight Club members were going to die no matter what; and when that happened, the New Orleans Mafia would have to move on to other things that were going to come up for them, such as a federal investigation into their activities, so they left Nigel and his family members alone. Furthermore, when the men who actually committed the murders of the Fight Club's members were found, it needed to look as if they'd been beaten to death. That way, Nigel's reputation would prevent any of the other violent youth from his rival clubs seeing him as a coward or a pushover. When the word hit the streets, Nigel's anger cooled off and his common sense returned. You know, those Mafia types probably have no idea that any torture they had in mind may have pushed the teen to call that instant destruction from out of the nil zone upon them, anyway.

"One night, after the loss of his friends, and the dissemination of the whole underground fight scene, my boy called me for help. He was feeling lonely and adrift, in need of direction. His father had grown more distant, and DeVries was out of state, visiting relatives up north. He felt very alone, and I was the only person he could think of calling. I wished my Angeline could have been there, but that would not have been good for either of them, it seemed, so I went alone. He met me at about 0100 in a park that he knew of on the Lakefront. We talked for a long time, about girls, angels, love, fighting, parents, school, and siblings. During the course of our conversation, he indicated that he was going to join the Marine Corps. He wanted to know what I thought of it. I convinced him that I would not have any objection if he chose The Corps. He also wanted to know that I would not try to use my position to attain any unfair advantages for him in his career. I gave him my word that would not happen. For those precious few hours, it was as if he were once again my adoptive son, the happy, naive child that had just walked into our lives from nowhere eleven years and two worlds ago."

For a long moment, General Renoir fell silent and sat still, head down, holding a clenched fist against his lips as if he were holding back a cough; but Roan could see that the man was putting a herculean effort into keeping control, holding back tears, and maybe even sobs of regret. *I guess Nigel and the Angelines aren't the only ones who have had to suffer from the decisions this man has made,* Roan thought. *He has a lot to answer for, and it looks as if it's already starting. The devil's begun demanding his due.* The only sound in the room was that of the thunderstorm outside, which now seemed to have become a torrential downpour. Thunder boomed, lightning flashed over again. The General finally regained what he'd lost of his composure and resumed his narrative.

"We talked until daybreak," he began once more in a quiet, worn voice, "but when the sun arose, I looked around and could not believe the mistake I'd made. We had met in the very same park where he was when Muldowney and Craine the Second captured him in the other world. I turned toward Nigel, to tell him that we should leave, and could see the confusion in his eyes. He too had taken a look around, now that daylight had arisen, and he was frowning, trying to figure something out, as if he were struggling between images present and memories past. He fell to his hands and knees, pounded the earth a few times, stood up, and looked at me with even more confusion in his eyes. He held out both hands to me, the way children do when asking to be picked up and held and for all the world. He seemed to be asking for help that I could not give. He put those hands that had just plead for my help against both sides of his head then blinked out. Disappeared. He went into *otherspace* again.

"But for some while by then, we'd kept miniature cameras in both Nigel's earrings as well as the buttons on his clothing, and when he went through this time, his actions were recorded. The things got nothing but static within the nil zone, but when he came out, it was in the park where he last saw little Angeline. The last time he went there, people were waiting for him in that location. That much we'd expected from what was learned during young Dana Lacy's last debriefing, and although she'd said she'd been unable to recall how they evaded those watchers, she had told us about them. We believed, however, that her memory was inaccurate since that had been the first time she'd made the crossing. Her memory had not at all been inaccurate, though. As soon as he stepped out of the zone, they were expecting him and were waiting with a couple of tac teams wearing the gray fatigues of MPIS, along with two of Agent Caldwell's former team members and a third man whom we'd not met. Included were a couple of corpsmen at the forefront. These approached Nigel gently then began to attempt drawing blood samples while he was disoriented from the passage. Things would have gone their way, but an MPIS lieutenant suddenly charged toward Nigel and grabbed his arm.

"He has always been an excellent fighter and had learned even more over the years. That's why it wasn't too hard for him to break free of the medical staff and run. When MPIS pursued, Nigel escaped into *otherspace*, reemerging a few miles away from them, and your counterpart, who somehow must also have known he'd be there, arrived and dragged him into his car, which put an end to the chase. Our analysts believe that someone else might have been in the vehicle speaking to Nigel, but if that were so, that person stayed out of the camera. He seemed to be able to calm and assure Nigel that Agent Caldwell would keep his word, not allowing him to fall into the hands of the pursuers. That's why he trusts you. We didn't have sound, but your double's outrage over Nigel's condition was evident as he spoke to the boy, who was in a mental daze. Finally, our lip readers were able to tell us what NCIS agent Roan Caldwell was saying."

Roan already knew. He could guess what *he'd* be saying in such a situation. Looking up at the General, he said, "He told you that you were risking the boy's life by doing this to him. He probably did not at all appreciate the state the kid was in when he arrived and hoped that you had him bugged enough to finally get the message. He may have told you that he'd find a way to keep the boy there the next time and may have even threatened your life, if he could have. Then he'd take Nigel someplace safe, tell him to go home, and watch to make sure he got away into that nowhere zone."

The General smiled. "A rose in any other world is still a rose," he said.

"I couldn't do it anymore after that," he continued. "I called Kruger and Dr. Leonard, both of whom were working in the civilian sector now. We had to put an end to this. We met in my Angeline's office and planned a deletion of all of Nigel's memory of the nil zone. I gave them a password enabling access to everything we had in our computer records and let them get to work. They called back later. One of them needed unrestricted access to our operation here. I decided on Kruger because we went back farther. He'd also been closer with Nigel. The man gave up his cushy civilian job and once more came on board."

***

By the time he was nineteen, Nigel was showing signs of inability to open the gateway anymore. And later that year, everything ended. That was also the year Colonel Benjamin Gary and his girlfriend, Maureen Sampson, died in an airplane crash. I told Nigel, and he looked at me blankly then awkwardly expressed sympathy for the loss of my friend. After a brief moment, he proudly showed me his acceptance notification and ASFAB results from the United States Marine Corps, which were stratospheric, better than mine had been. I sincerely congratulated the boy. He couldn't cross into otherspace anymore, though, and was unable to remember that he ever had. For the DOD, that meant no crossover ability, no gateway into the nil zone, no more new weapons and technology from other realities. So Nigel was placed under passive occasional surveillance and all but forgotten. IDEA Control was then reassigned to the task of developing the vast amount of information and technology that his previous excursions had yielded. Crossover Team Alpha was also reassigned to be used as a top secret Black Ops and preemptive strike team aimed at confirming and eradicating terrorist threats. I was to be in command of both IDEA Control and my team's missions. An excellent strategy should a scapegoat ever be needed.

Even as these developments were proceeding, Kruger continued working on his next creation: a durable, indestructible camouflage suit that would have all the characteristics of our original Refractor device. Only the original Crossover Team Alpha knew of its existence, as well as what it was expected to achieve. With this work of art, Amadeus Kruger had truly blossomed into his full potential. That suit was designed to be bullet proof, laser proof, and knife proof, as well as invisible. It is entirely built to ensure the survival of its user, but I wouldn't be surprised if it has some type of seriously destructive microarmament. He also nanocomputerized it or something like that, to cause it to react with one person's DNA. Of course, that person was Nigel. Kruger loved Nigel, as did every one of us who had gone through all that we had with him. This scheme was one that he'd been developing ever since we first commenced Mission CureSearch. The reason Kruger even came up with that idea, all those years before, had been Nigel's safety, and he'd continued working on it all this time for the same reason.

We'd long ago decided it would be best if we kept the existence of the cloaking suit under wraps. Kruger and Leonard had a little research and development lab of their own, assembled with proceeds from their civilian jobs, where they had been faithfully getting together to work on the Refraction suit, developing it more fully in a well-hidden off-the-grid location. We all knew that it had to be done that way because several reasons for distrust had arisen between the MISTmen and the government of our current United States. Additionally, IDEA Control had been forced to take on a new young gun, some teenaged prodigy whom none of us trusted and all of us wanted to kill. His name was Devin Craine, and he was a DNA research genius. For Crossover Team Alpha, keeping him as far away from Nigel as we could was a top priority at all times in those days.

We wouldn't be allowed to kill this Craine per our original orders, the Secretary of Defense told me, because the country needed his brainpower. The people in Nigel's home world may be developing a way to cross the zone, he said. If we could do it, they could, and Craine's talent with manipulation of DNA could be used for our advantage, provided we kept him away from Blacen Muldowney. Additionally, like injury to insult, he was to continue under my wing because the psych doctors, upon reviewing all of our previous intel on his two predecessors, seemed to think that Craine's problem was centered on his need for a father figure, and I was selected to be *it* this time. Hopefully, that would eliminate the vacuum in his persona that Muldowney had stepped in to fulfill. Nigel was lost to me, they'd assumed, and in their eyes, that indicated that I too had a vacuum that needed to be filled. So now Devin Craine was to be my child. They could not have selected a poorer replacement for Nigel.

A Purging and a Redemption

I knew, by the way that SECNAV spoke of the man, they'd probably located a Blacen here too. It worried me, so I talked to Kruger about hacking their NSA system and telling me what he found. Not a problem since he and Dr. Derron Leonard had originally designed it. He got back to me with the bad news pretty quickly. Yes, they had a Blacen Muldowney on their radar. He'd been working for Boeing, but his nefarious behaviors toward coworkers of the opposite sex kept becoming a problem for that company. Still, they tried to hold on to him as long as they could, and for good reason. You see, Detective Caldwell, this Muldowney was far more brilliant than his two doppelgangers had been. He was also far more cunning, secretive, evil, and wicked, with wealthier parents. One of his coworkers had even come up missing after turning his advances down, and although he'd been investigated and questioned, Blacen was never charged with anything. There was simply no proof of wrongdoing on his part, nor any real proof that the woman hadn't simply chosen to walk out of her current life and disappear. His parents hadn't escaped suspicion in the matter either. The detective investigating the case actually postulated a theory that they may have been complicit in the woman's disappearance. Still, they had an army of overpriced attorneys with questionable morals in their employment, though, and these people kept the Muldowney Family out of trouble. Yet for Blacen, there was more trouble to come out of the affair. An FBI investigation into one of their employees' association with a missing person who also happened to be one of their employees proved too much for the human resources department of Boeing, and they had to let

Blacen go. They bought out his contract, gave him a wonderful severance package, and off he went.

However, as I've mentioned, this Muldowney was a truly brilliant man, with capabilities way past those of his two counterparts; plus he was a deeper thinker, which pointed to his also being a very thorough planner. He'd developed microbots that could penetrate security systems by integrating with the electrical signals and actually becoming part of the system, so he began using them for infiltrating Boeing's computer systems and stealing their R & D plans. Next, he constructed a nonexistent persona, Tim Saeng, alias "Silent Saeng," who would sell these off to the highest bidder through dark net connections. Silent Saeng's activities were known to NSA, but they hadn't been able to catch up to him until he made a mistake. As things turned out, Blacen, true to form, had been using his Silent Saeng persona to get familiar with a pornographic actress who also dabbled in certain activities that could only be broadcast over the dark internet. He made a date with her, gaining her trust by showing proof that he himself was, indeed, the one and only "Silent Tim" Saeng. However, he had no idea that the woman recorded everything she did in her illicit activity, for use in future blackmail schemes against her unwitting and unwilling co-stars. When it was all said and done, though, she was dead, murdered at his hands, but her recordings were acquired by the NSA, who now had a lead toward the identity of Silent Tim Saeng and were going to send that information over to the FBI.

Unfortunately, the DOD, upon realizing that this was *the* Blacen Muldowney, the man who, in another reality, had spearheaded the development of the only known supervirus based in human DNA, complete with microscopic delivery systems, *had* to have him. Furthermore, they were determined to get him to come on board as a microweaponry *engineer.* This Blacen was ten years older than my Craine, and they sometimes used the same jogging route, though not having met up yet. They were going to send a team over to make contact and force him to join IDEA Control when I found out about it and brought my own people in. This Blacen's destiny wasn't going to be spending the rest of his life in IDEA Control. Oh yes, the DOD thought they'd gotten a pretty good handle on how to control the man, yet as I've told you, Detective, we *knew* Blacen. We knew the potential that both of his counterparts had, and it was always in the direction of progression toward greater vileness. The one here, well, he was our Blacen, only worse. The life course of the man they were looking at had been a steady movement from one act of evil to another, despite his brainpower. He was an amplified, augmented version of our own greatest villains of two other realities. Crossover Team Alpha considered the possibility of finding his victims and discrediting him publicly, but with the way the legal system in this world works in favor of the wealthy, there was a distinct possibility that he'd never see justice, let alone some death penalty, as a result of his murders. No, he needed to be exposed to the media then eliminated. That way, IDEA Control's higher management would forget about trying to find out what may really have happened to him. They wouldn't want the light of public attention upon their dark activities.

So we put our knowledge of Blacen Muldowney to work one more time. We knew that he'd owned a home and property in Wiggins, Mississippi, and he loved that place, so we started there. Yes, there was the same house on the same property, owned by one Blacen Theodore Muldowney, and considering how often he went there, this one also must have cherished that locale. Our two geniuses, Leonard and Kruger, outsmarted his security system installed therein, so McGrath, Garfield, and Benson could silently break in and capture him. They did. This house was different, though, in that it had additions that the one in our reality never had. There was a large basement in the place, and inside were torture rooms loaded with accoutrements used in his ever-spiraling pursuit of sexual sadism, some with leftover victims still tied or buckled in. He also had a makeshift prison out in the woods of that property. Within it we found sixteen women, all captives, all having been tortured and abused in a variety of most unspeakably perverse ways. Some of them died in the hospital, but most lived to tell the tales of what horrors had been visited upon them at the hands of that fiend. They would all need physical therapy and psychological assistance for the rest of their lives.

The media had a field day with it. He became the Most Hated Man in America pretty quickly, and there were countless BOLOs out for him. Yes, you *do* remember that, don't you, Detective Caldwell? Not surprising, considering all that you yourself have been through at the hands of such a man. Why couldn't law enforcement find him? Well, Blacen went "off the grid" as they say and vanished. Not a hard thing to do, considering his parents' wealth and connections. Strangely, every single bit and byte of Blacen's technology had disappeared along with him, and nowhere could he be found. The publicity was so bad that his parents took off in their private jet, ostensibly to find some nice quiet location where they could weather the storm. Coincidentally, though, as they were flying over the Gulf of Mexico, the plane's engines caught fire and blew up, tearing the whole thing apart in midair. Blacen Muldowney would never have any possibility of siblings in this world. Additionally, the Justice Department was hunting him now, and sooner or later, they'd get their man. Even with all this, the DOD still wanted the guy. As these episodes were proceeding, I was invited to meet with the Secretary of Defense again; there was an assignment that he wanted my MISTmen to plan and train for.

They wanted us prepared to break an unnamed person out of any prison, jail, or other type of penal institution should the need arise. The person's identity would be classified, and even I would not be informed of who he was. Before actually securing the package, the SOD's personal representative, who would accompany the MISTmen on the mission (although I wouldn't be allowed to), was to speak to the potential alone. If he bagged the man's head, they were to bring him to IDEA Control. If not, they were to kill him. That wasn't a very opaque mission objective, I tell you. Obviously, there could only have been one person that they had such plans for. We needed to find him first. Eventually, Blacen Muldowney surfaced, at least for Crossover Team Alpha, that is. We knew of a backwoods brothel club that he frequented, and we also knew this man's psyche. Blacen couldn't have stayed away from the place no matter what. It catered to his perverse desires far too much for him to let it go. True to form, he had always been extremely rude to the waitstaff and cocktail waitresses there. That's how they remembered him so easily when we'd gone in asking questions. That's also why we were able to set up an advance notice system that would make him easy to catch.

The place was named the Cottonmouth Gentleman's Club, located well off the beaten track, in the backwoods of Bush, Louisiana. Truthfully, nothing at all gentle ever went on there, and the place was far less than genteel for its female staff. Additionally, it was, so far, unknown to law enforcement as a location where he may have been captured. But as I said, *we* knew Blacen Muldowney. With the amount of stress that he had to be under, there was no possible way he could have *not* visited the Cottonmouth. The next time he went, we caught him outside before he ever got in. He spent the next sixty days in Master Gunnery Sergeant Lucius Carver, First Sergeant Antoine Rochon, Kruger, and Leonard's hands, and he talked about how his nanobots and microbots (all of which were in our possession) worked. Oh my, did he *ever* talk. He was in decent physical shape, but he was also unfamiliar with the will killer and so had no knowledge of how to resist it, as the Muldowney who invented it had. Besides, Kruger and Leonard had upgraded the thing. Along with that, everything he told them was tested, and if it turned out to be falsehood, Lucius and Rochon used extremely physical methods of persuasion to convince Blacen of the horrible consequences of lying, which helped to increase his chattiness. For all of his love of inflicting pain on women, Blacen couldn't take any. If only we had used that sort of thing on the original! Maybe none of this would have ever happened. But that was illegal in our society. I honestly believe that at one time or another during his visit with us, every single one of our remaining MISTmen took turns spending some quality time with him. Finally, when he'd given all that he had, we took him back to his secret backwoods play place.

Unfortunately, it appeared that some robber shot him to death in the forest behind the club. The killer was never found. The brothel itself was owned by the New Orleans crime family whom we'd dealt with earlier, and they didn't want the attention that would have come with several federal marshals searching for a fugitive in that area. Nor did they want the scrutiny that would have resulted from that same fugitive's body being found in the parking lot of their hidden cathouse. That would have been bad for business. Three days went by before the Justice Department finally identified the John Doe that the St. Tammany Parish Sheriff's Department found floating in a lake beside Evans Road in Bush, Louisiana, as Blacen Muldowney. The condition he was in when found was considered a result of the hardship he must've endured while out in the woods, trying to stay hidden from the law. Obviously. No, Detective. This Blacen Muldowney's destiny was not to spend his life forced into government service, after all. Additionally, more extensive details of his vicious deeds had been anonymously leaked to the media. That signaled the end of any DOD interest in him or his unhappy demise. Bye-bye, Blacen.

Meanwhile, it seemed that the head doctors were right about Craine. The kid took to me very well and would willingly work on whatever I asked of him. I did not like his attitude toward his fellow workers, though. He seemed to consider everyone else as beneath him, and yes, he despised restaurant waitstaff. He'd been put under my authority when he was about seventeen and had just graduated from MIT. I hated the kid and would have been hard put not to make him disappear, but once again, it was Angeline who intervened, saving his life. She'd been distraught over Nigel being removed from our family, and the thought of my mentoring a version of Devin Craine who had been made our Ward had at the first been extremely distasteful to her. That was the way she felt until she learned how young he was. I've told you, she is a healer; and as such, she needs to be able to see any trace of good within people and never lose hope in them. Angel insisted that she be allowed to meet the new Craine, and after that, she told me that he wasn't entirely good, but hadn't been ruined beyond redemption yet, either. She said that he was just a little broken. I thought of ways to break him even more, hopefully beyond repair.

Apparently, his father was quite the worthless sort and, for all of Devin's life, had been demeaning the boy's mother, blaming all or any of the family's problems on her. The man had convinced his son that his mother's withholding from marital intimacy was the reason for the father's drunkenness, his infidelity, the beatings he'd subjected the boy to, and all the unkind words and hateful speech that started curdling Devin's emotions. Additionally, Devin Craine was almost convinced that because he was special, his mother's every effort was intended to force him together with some woman who would use her sexuality to ruin everything that made him stand out. The boy's father actually thought that teaching his son such garbage was funny. As a result, Devin was also beginning to develop a deep aversion toward any type of human intimacy. He was beginning to see the desire for such as a weakness. In reality, his mother was only guilty of refusing to allow herself to see what type of monster her husband was trying to twist the boy into, but she did ask the man to leave after catching him in their bed with his fourth girlfriend in two months. Mrs. Craine hadn't withheld any part of herself from her husband. He was just greedy and a pig.

Devin was nine years old and sick with pneumonia when his father left him for good. The boy blamed his mother for that too. Still, when he was invited to MIT at the age of fourteen, she did all she could to pay for whatever his scholarship wouldn't cover. Of course, he never thanked her. As time went by, he also began to develop an aversion toward all the softer human emotions, for he felt that these were the root causes of all sorts of betrayal. Just like his two predecessors had thought. Furthermore, in his eyes, the social activities that his fellow freshmen involved themselves in were examples of people wasting their chances on foolishness. So he went through college as a lonely youngster who, in the late hours of the night, cried over losing his father. When he met Angel, the boy was inexcusably rude to her. I wanted to cuff him a few times, but she told me that, instead, I should just take him outside and talk to him, that he wasn't a person who needed to be subjected to physical punishment from *me* of all people. She told me to explain that *I* was the one he'd insulted, not her, because an approach of that type would have the most positive long-term effect. I listened to her and, over the course of time, held many such conversations with the young Devin Craine. To my complete surprise, he responded well. The boy began to respect me in a way that his first counterpart never did. That man feared me, and the second one hated me, but then, they both just hated all of their fellow humans.

Eventually, Angeline told me that it was time to break Devin free of his father's influence. I was ready to capture the man, force him to record a confession of his schemes and misdeeds against his own son, then eliminate him with extreme prejudice, and even told her as much. After I did, Angel gently placed her cup of Earl Grey down, and for a moment, we both listened to the soft early spring rain, enjoyed the smell of that tea and the early evening rainfall, while Alicia Keys sang "A Woman's Worth" in the other room (at that time the artist was only eight years old, but we'd brought over our own personal top secret music collection from Nigel's world, some of hers included). Then Angel answered me with the sweetest rebuke I'd ever heard. She began with, "Do it that way if you want to, Nige, but . . ." She continued, "If you do, then this boy will hate you because he's observant and smart enough to see through that sort of thing. He has a mental idea of the wonderful person he thinks his father is, and if you break that, then he'll feel betrayed again, this time by you. And because he's way smarter than the other two, he'd likely wind up creating a more efficient and deadlier version of the original Craine Virus. All because you'd have used a military solution when you should have used a humane one. You don't need to add that level of guilt to what you're already feeling over Petit Nigey Deaux." Okay. Point made. So how do we do this, then? I asked.

Devin's father, Ronald Craine, was located and arrested for an identity theft he'd perpetrated, and I took a couple of IDEA Control enforcement agents to meet with him while he was in the county jail. It was explained to him that his young eighteen-year-old son would soon finish his undergraduate studies; he was expected to graduate with honors at the top of his class, after which he'd come spend a year in Ronald's company, and he was not to dump the boy. He was expected to be himself at all times.

Could he "punish" him? Yes, I told him, but if you do him any permanent damage, we will not be as nice the next time we come for you. If you agree to this, then these charges will disappear. If you renege on the deal, then not only will these come back, but other more serious crimes that you've committed will be brought up. You will go to prison and be housed in general population, after all of your fellow convicts have been convinced that you are a child molester. What? No, we don't care that it's not true. Neither will they. Is that a yes? Then sign these papers, agree to allow us to use the recording of our little meeting, and it's done. Go home. Your son will arrive tomorrow morning. Be there.

At the end of the year with his father, Devin Craine was changed. His confidence in his father's winning personality had been exposed to him as a childhood misconception. Whenever he thought over his past in retrospect, he could now see that Ronald Craine had abused him emotionally and mentally while manipulating his opinions and feelings, all for his own entertainment. Craine cried as he talked to me about this, and I actually felt a bit of sympathy for the kid. I also saw the wisdom in Angeline's strategy and began to understand what she'd hoped to accomplish with it. She was deconstructing a potential murderer by readjusting the deviances in his personality while he was still malleable. Everything she did was geared toward that end. She'd even ordered me to call the young man by his first name after he returned. I was never again to refer to or address him as "Craine" as had been my custom. She told me, correctly, that such a way of addressing the young man was my means of keeping him at a distance, and what he needed was the exact opposite. I followed the Doctor's orders and it worked. After one of our talks, Devin Craine tearfully asked if I'd please take him to visit his mother.

I did him the favor of staying outside during the first part of his visit, but after a while, he insisted that I come in to meet her. Emelda Craine was tall for a woman, about five ten, and as gangly as a stork. She hadn't been an unattractive lady in her youth, but living a long time with regret and grief had not treated her very well. She tearfully thanked me over and over again for bringing her boy back, as did Devin. I wanted to credit Angeline, but she'd said that wasn't a good idea yet. After a little while, for me, all the bawling and tears made being in the house feel like being held captive at a sobfest, so I left him there to reconnect with his mother. Meanwhile, Angeline had met with Devin's uncles from the Aberjon and Wilson sides of the family. All in all, there were about nine men, and every one of them were his great-uncles, brothers of either his grandmother or his grandfather, who had fallen in love and married when they were both at relatively young ages. Both of his grandparents had also been the youngest siblings of their respective family units and very much loved. Besides his mother, he was the only surviving child or grandchild for both families. They were divided over the matter of race, but still were going to leave him almost everything they owned, anyway. Now, though, they'd been informed that their great-nephew was playing a vital role in a classified government agency.

She further suggested to them how, although it was clear that they didn't like each other, maybe they could all get together with him now, as he'd just discovered what kind of man his father was, and it affected him deeply. He was heartbroken, Angeline told them. He needed every family member he had left to get through this, and they needed to get along for his sake. Since his father was, all along, the only person in the whole drama who was universally hated by both families, all of them were equally touched by her plea and his efforts to reconnect with his mother, who was a beloved product of both of their families. They also assumed Devin to be engaged in the fight against Al-Qaeda in some top secret capacity, an idea met with approval from all of them. Regardless of their differences of opinion, they were, each and every one, old-school Southerners who prided themselves on their patriotism. They agreed on the basis of "being family," as well as love of God and country, to assist Devin in any way possible.

All of Angeline's strategy worked. Craine's grandfather and grandmother had been murdered as a racist hate crime, and the perpetrators never met proper justice. Each family had blamed the other for years. But the truth was revealed when they all got together and talked. Devin's uncles eventually realized how much alike they all were and formed genuine friendships with one another. Those friendships will last for the rest of their lives because once they can get past their race issues, Southerners are fiercely loyal to their friends, regardless of what skin they may be wrapped in. While the reunion was awkward at first, eventually, it became a real, meaningful thing, and this Devin Craine now has an extended family that loves him and cares about his welfare. It's everything that his former two counterparts wished for and neither received nor earned. Thanks to my dear Angeline, the Devin Craine of your reality will never find within himself any reason to want to kill the entire human race, Detective Caldwell.

Finally, Angeline allowed me to mention her role in the matter. She also recommended that he be permitted to see the record of our strong-arming his father into keeping him around for a year. She spoke to Devin herself after that. Angeline explained that she'd put up with his bad attitude and chose to work hard to help him reconnect with both of his parents because of her affection for me. She explained that I cared about him and she cared about me, that we wanted Devin to understand that love is not always fake, so he would comprehend the fact that his mother really did love both Devin and his father, Ronald. Angeline explained to the young man how, all along, love for him was the reason why Emelda had, over the years, put up with Ronald Craine's abuse and tried so hard to care for her son, not because she wanted to destroy his ability, but because he was her child and she loved him. The message got through. This Devin has grown into a different man because of those past events, Detective.

He has been humbled by cognizance of his own capability for mistakes in the way he treated Emelda. Craine is also a deep thinker, and gradually, the humility he'd learned began to show; his behavior toward his coworkers slowly started to change, and some of them have even found reason to like him. He was becoming the human being that the other two could have been. When the time was right, though, I called him into my office, gave him a speech about the excellence he showed in his willingness to face his former mistakes and the way he had chosen to apologize to his mother and worked to set things right, that these actions earned him a measure of my respect, that I thought so much better of him and the man he was becoming. Devin Craine left my office with tears in his eyes and a newly found pride in his own ability to do the right and honorable thing. After that conversation, I immediately attached him to then Lieutenant Robin Lacy's command. It was the best thing for the new Devin.

You want to know why? Well, here's why: changing a long-held view of another person isn't easy for anyone, including me. I found myself really liking the kid, but didn't want to get too much closer with him and one day succumb to the temptation to shoot him between his eyes or anything either. It seems that on some deeper level of consciousness, I will always see him as the mass murderer that the first one was and the second one almost became. In my eyes, the least amount of deviation in his behavior would have seemed to pose a threat to humanity, and I would have acted decisively against such a thing. For his own life's sake, he needed to be moved into a position that would not require him to spend a great deal of his time in my presence. Before moving him, though, I had him report to the infirmary for a routine checkup. That's when Kruger's people implanted our passive wafer-thin tracers in him. These were very much improved from the old will killer chip technology they'd grown out of. We call them "thumbnails," and with one tracer, we can locate any person anywhere all around the globe. Suffice it to say that if Craine gets into any mischief, we can get to him in minutes.

Power Reawakening

As for Nigel, even though he was officially considered no longer able to open the doorway into the nil zone, he too, would have a thumbnail tracer. If ever his ability manifested itself again, the brass reasoned, we should be able to locate him wherever he may be. Life went on, time passed, Nigel grew up.

When he became nineteen, Nigel chose, against the expressed wishes of his father, to join the marines. Of course he would. He performed as well as I had; again, not surprising, since we are genetically the same. My memories also may have been instrumental in his choice. Unlike myself, though, he chose not to go to the Naval Academy, preferring, instead, to go in as an enlisted man. I wondered if that was Lucius Carver's influence cutting through the fog of years gone by. As it was, Nigel was very good at his chosen occupation. He became a sergeant at twenty, and at twenty-one, he applied for and was accepted into Marine Raider training. But during his first mission after completion of his training, he started moving and fighting with the heightened ability of one of my MISTmen. After reviewing the reports, SECNAV demanded that I explain how that could happen, so once again, Nigel was poked and prodded. Analysis of his DNA proved beyond speculation what I'd already surmised some six or seven years earlier: that the MIST training I'd gone through had altered Nigel's metabolism. When we used DNA protein interactions in utilizing my childhood memories to fill the gaps in his, the MIST changes had begun. Nigel could now do the things we MISTmen do without the initiating DNA stimulation that the rest of us had to go through. The only reason that he'd survived that metamorphosis was our shared identity. Physically, at least, we are the same person. I wanted him to undergo MIST training, and SECNAV agreed, but it had to be done secretly in an undisclosed location. The brass didn't want any of his fellow Raiders to know about the MIST abilities, as it may have incited some to jealousy. I remember thinking that at least he was valuable to the DOD again, though it was for a different cause.

You see, Detective, your government has no way to implement that type of training, since for some reason, the men and women of this earth cannot live through the DNA alterations involved. It seems to be some sort of cosmic trade-off, because the inhabitants of this world also possess more natural intelligence when it's developed than the population of the other two similar realities, with only a few exceptions. Nigel was of a different world than either of ours, though, and not only is his intelligence on a par with the residents here, but he also had the physical capability to undergo our training, just needed the discipline. If he succeeded, then the Joint Chiefs felt that this United States would have its first and only homegrown MIST-trained supersoldier. For the same reason that I'd not allowed anyone to train their doubles on N-Prime, and as much as I may have wished to handle it myself, I assigned my new executive officer, Major Archimus Marcelon, to oversee his training instead. Marcelon loved Nigel as much as any of Crossover Team Alpha did, and he'd be fair, but also tough, since he knew that the young man needed such guidance to survive the ordeal. As expected, the boy passed through his training with flying colors. Since all MISTmen were under my command in IDEA Control, it was explained to him that he too would have to be attached to my command. This seemed to be the very thing he'd asked me not to do, attaching him to my own command thus. He chose to go forward with this assignment, anyway.

Although he was formally under my authority, SECNAV still occasionally deployed him with other units at times, depending on the nature of their mission needs, so to speak. Ostensibly, the DOD still viewed Nigel as the only homegrown MISTman, regardless of his origination elsewhere, so he was occasionally deployed without the rest in classified battles, black ops, and secret wars. He was better than I had ever been, hand to hand or armed and was without a doubt the best they had. Still, his existence and true identity needed to remain classified; consequently, he and his exploits have become an unconfirmed rumor and a legend among the men with whom he has fought. He has been decorated but, at this point in his life, doesn't remember any of those things about himself. Even those memories had to be taken away from him. An event that occurred after a particularly stressful operation led to that necessity. His squad had been involved in a dangerous joint Russian-American seek-and-destroy mission that took them to Cape Idokopas near the Black sea. They were hunting a terrorist cell whose actions were threatening the newly forged peace between the two superpowers, and in the course of the action, one of the younger men that he'd taken under his tutelage was killed. When they returned home, Nigel was on the way to see me when he came across Devin Craine, who was also headed to my office. As soon as they made eye contact, Nigel froze, a look of confusion momentarily crossing his face. Had I been in that hallway at the moment, I would have tried to get one of them out of there immediately, but I was in a meeting with Major Robin Lacy and Lucius Carver, going over training stats. All of a sudden, we heard Nigel's voice, booming like angry thunder. *"You!"* And a terrible racket followed.

I could hear Devin being slammed against the walls and Nigel shouting, *"You killed my MOTHER! You MURDERED her!"* Major Lacy, Master Sergeant Carver and I charged into the hallway, where Devin was yelling for help while trying to do his best to fight my boy off, but his efforts were as successful as a rabbit's would be against a lion. Nigel had grabbed him by his shirt to slam him around the hallway; then he began to choke Craine, holding the poor unfortunate kid with one hand around his throat, suspended about a foot above the floor, while deploying his Ka-Bar with the other. His eyes had started to glow with what looked like blue electricity as his anger increased. He slammed his victim against the walls a couple of more times, but by then, MPs were flooding the hallway. Master Sergeant Carver sprang forward and grabbed his arm, holding his knife back, while Robin Lacy grabbed his other one, trying his best to pry Nigel's fingers from Craine's throat; but Nigel was too strong for him. Finally, I yelled in command tone, ***"Stand down, Marine!*** This man is *not that* Craine!" Nigel dropped his victim, muttered something unintelligible, and stood to attention. I ordered Carver to escort him into my office, called the MPs off, made sure Craine was okay, and sent him to the medical bay along with Major Robin Lacy.

When I went back into the office to see about my boy, Lucius was sitting on the guest's couch, next to Nigel, his arm around the boy's shoulders, looking for all the world like a distraught father. Nigel was holding his head in confusion again, muttering, "He killed her, he killed her . . ." When I approached, Lucius quietly stood at attention, his eyes focused respectfully over my head. "At ease, Master Gunnery Sergeant Carver," I told him. He looked as if he wanted permission to speak freely, so I allowed him that. He deserved to say what was on his mind. We'd been through too much together.

He looked me in the eye then began. "Sir, I owe you an apology. I assumed that you were letting them do this to him because you're a coldhearted power-seeking bastard. But I see now what it's cost you to stay here while they fubar'd your boy's head. I know that if you hadn't been here to hold them back, what was left of his life would have been much worse by the time they were done, and I am ashamed to have ever distrusted you, General. Furthermore, I'd hate to imagine what they would have done to Nige, how far they would've taken it, had you not been here to hold them back. I am now and always will be at your command, General Renoir, sir. What are you orders for me?"

I took a deep breath and answered, "Master Sergeant Lucius Carver, I have stood as a barrier between Nigel and a raging flood of potentially dangerous, demeaning, and degrading procedures that would have stripped my boy of everything that made him who he was. When it seemed that he'd lost the ability to crossover, they preferred him as nothing more than a mindless DNA bank. There were some who wanted him confined to a military sickbay in some undisclosed location and sedated while they were working on their crossover tech. He was to have his DNA harvested as if this child were nothing more than a cornfield while his mind decayed. My determination to protect him and their fear of our MIST ability has been the only thing that has stayed that devilish plot. At the beginning of our disagreement, there were several attempts on my life and at least one on Angeline's, but all of these met with failure. When he was sixteen, I acted against certain individuals within their political structure, and as a result, there will never be another attempt against Angeline or me for as long as we are in this reality. But that will not protect Nigel should I fall. So I must stand as a wall until he can protect himself."

"Master Sergeant Lucius Carver, my orders for you are the exact same as the orders that you received when Nigel was a child. You are to look out for my boy while I do my sworn duty to him and our country. Ours—not theirs. You are to assist Angel and me as we walk him through his life for as long as you are able or until he discharges you from the necessity. You are to be as loyal to him as you have always been so far. I trust that this will not be at all difficult for you, considering the fact that you love this youngster as much as I do. You will be my main reinforcement on this front."

"Yes *sir*," Lucius replied as he saluted me, holding that position for a moment, then stood at parade rest. I appreciated his show of deep respect, but was just emotionally tired.

"Sit down, Lucius," I told him. He sat. Nigel, meanwhile, was still muttering the same thing, so I sat down beside him and gently said, "Son, your mother is not dead. She's safe at home, and she loves you." He looked at me, his eyes cleared up, and for a moment, he looked like a sleeper who doesn't know why he's been awakened. When he caught sight of Carver, he smiled, they both stood, then he hugged the big man like a kid who's just seen his favorite older brother again after several years, and I guess that's exactly what he was. As he hugged Nigel, Master Sergeant Carver had tears in his eyes.

Nigel didn't remember why he was so angry with Craine, or why he thought the man had killed his mother, or even that he had attacked anyone, and had no cognizance of the fact that he could have been dishonorably discharged or at least discharged due to "other designated physical and mental conditions" (referred to as an ODPMC discharge) because of something that he'd done. In the end, though, it was written off as a momentary case of battle fatigue. The boy never lost a man in combat before; so their handpicked so-called "analysts" pinpointed that as the problem and recommended his having a regular discussion of the matter with his Commanding Officer. That should resolve the issue, they reported. I was his commanding officer. No problem.

Had he been any other marine, there would have been no end to the trouble that his actions against Dr. Devin Craine had gotten for him. But when it was explained as a residual effect of his past crossover ability, the whole thing was dismissed. Top secret is top secret, and the brass desired no more investigation into the matter. After his debriefing, Nigel went to his barracks, left his rifle as well as his pistol, and disappeared. Resultantly, the CO of his Raider squad that had fought alongside the Russian military assumed that Nigel had gone AWOL and vigorously sought to court-martial him. Anything like that had to go through IDEA Control, though, and that brought me into the picture. Although the martial action he'd been involved in wasn't under my command, I met with the angry Captain to go over the matter, and that meeting went on long enough to expose the real problem.

It was professional jealousy. He coveted Nigel's MIST ability, had an idea that it may have been the end result of some top secret experimental treatment sponsored by the military, and wanted in on it, he said. When it was explained that the treatment would without a doubt prove deadly to him, he refused to believe that. When I also made it very clear that he himself was far too valuable an officer to risk in an attempt to MIST train, the man assumed there was an issue with his race and I wanted to deny him something he deserved. Unsatisfied with my explanation, he appealed to the CMC and got the same answer. Unsatisfied with that, he chose to schedule a meeting with a reporter, thinking of exposing IDEA Control. However, SECNAV made a deal with him before then. He would allow the Captain to undergo the training only if he agreed to sign a waiver of responsibility. Done. Time to begin. The man died in the first stages of the training, just as every other person from this reality had.

Normally, when Nigel returned after a crossover, he'd reappear right where he left or somewhere nearby, but this time, he returned out in the front yard of his father's home in Gentilly. His fatigues were bloody, and his Ka-Bar was still in his hand. It had recently been used, and he was wounded, coughing, struggling to breathe. He still thought himself surrounded by enemies and was attempting to defend with his blade. His father and brother were on the front porch when he reappeared, though, and they saw him step out of nowhere. His father, Raimond Narcisse Renoir, reported that Nigel's eyes seemed unfocused; also, he immediately crouched into a knife-fighting stance as soon as he reappeared and began slashing at unseen assailants, shouting to someone named Angeline, that she should run and run *now*. Additionally, Master Gunnery Sergeant Renoir told us that his son's offensive attacks were faster than anyone's eyes could keep up with. The whole spectacle was something they'd never seen before. Suddenly, Nigel's eyes focused on the location he was in; and once he recognized it, the young man stood down from his imaginary knife fight and passed out.

The entire family was there when it happened, and that stirred them up as if they were ants whose anthill had been kicked by some little boy. They hadn't seen Nigel in a couple of years, given that he hadn't shown up at their family dinners occasioned by the Master Gunnery Sergeant. They didn't know that their father had disinvited the young man, so it seemed to his siblings that he'd allowed his service in the Marine Corps to come between them. And now that they were all becoming young adults with busier lives, they missed him more, just as they missed one another more. All of these factors led to a confrontation that could have had disastrous effects. As soon as we'd picked up his tracer's signature, our people were already on the way, but before his family could get Nigel into the house, MPs and corpsmen arrived on the scene, under orders to escort the young Sergeant Renoir back to base so that IDEA Control could figure out how he'd opened the gateway again. They had administered morphine and were loading him into a military ambulance when his younger brother tried to board with him, refusing to be put off the bus. A struggle ensued, and the entirety of the Renoir siblings as well as a few of his cousins who were present got involved, turning the affair into a fistfight.

The neighbors were calling the police when, in the course of the action, one of the rookie MPs shot DeVries, after which Nigel, whom they'd considered knocked out by the painkillers, surged up, caught the man in his throat with his Ka-Bar, and grabbed his brother, disappearing both of them into *otherspace*. That display of his ability stunned the fighting parties into inactivity for a moment, ending the battle. Twenty minutes later, when he returned, DeVries Renoir was no longer wounded and was sleeping. Nigel was also healed. He passed out, anyway. After that, they were far gentler toward his sister Joanna when she decided to go along to the hospital with the boys. With their sister accompanying, Nigel and DeVries were subsequently airlifted to the Bethesda Naval Hospital, where both men were examined closely and certified healthy.

I arrived on the scene and, in private, explained to Joanna that DeVries would be released and the two of them flown home, but Nigel would have to stay since he had been accused of going AWOL and that was being investigated. She was assured that the matter was going to be settled in his favor since command knew that he was innocent, it's just that he'd been involved in a high-security mission, and no, I would not explain how he managed to appear out of thin air since that was also classified information. The family assumed he'd been testing some new military technology, and that idea was encouraged. Nigel was twenty-three, but our resemblance was beginning to show so much that Joanna asked me if I were one of their relatives. I assured her that I was and we'd talk that over later, but other things needed to be handled at the moment. She accepted that and agreed to make time for a future discussion. My older sister always was observant and practical that way.

IDEA Control did a thorough investigation and surmised that Nigel must have been assaulted with an energy weapon of some sort. The hole in his camos was perfectly round and had burned entirely through the garment; furthermore, its location indicated a solid hit through Nigel's left lung. His family, the corpsmen, and the military police had also reported seeing the hole in him but no blood issuing from it. His body, however, didn't even bear a scar. Even those he'd earned during his time with the Fight Club were no longer on him. DeVries Renoir was also thoroughly checked, and he too was in perfect condition. Even the cold he'd had was gone. He had no scars either. The Bethesda staff were racking their brains trying to figure out how that could be. I knew, though, that the healing light rays in the *between* zone must have been what did it. Their existence was one of the bits of information that hadn't been included in our debriefing back when we first arrived. In the following days, IDEA Control was informed that Interdimensional Asset One (ID-1), Nigel Boyd Renoir, was now of even more interest to the DOD and would remain Stateside until further orders came through.

There was more than one reason for such renewed interest, though; it wasn't just the resurfacing of his ability. The fact was that they wanted to get their hands on one of those energy weapons for reverse engineering, and they also wanted to find a way to expose wounded troops to whatever had healed the Renoir Brothers while they'd been within the in-between realm. So they ordered Nigel reactivated as a dimension crosser. His memory loss was progressive, though, and IDEA Control was now expected to stop it. We let them know that it simply couldn't be done without the possibility of inflicting some type of permanent brain damage, but all they heard was the word "possibility" as in not definitely. Since Nigel was once again classified as an asset, however, the matter of his personal safety was once again worth considering, so the question of whether or not to revive his memory of the world-walking power went to upper command for SECNAV, the CMC, and the secretary of defense to hash out.

It seemed that a compromise was eventually reached though, because soon enough, I received orders from The Commander in Chief and the Senate Armed Services Committee (SASC). I was to take a small detachment and go home. To return to ground zero of the original Craine-Muldowney attack, as a test of our new *otherspace* opening technology that was based on Nigel's DNA. They felt that there would be a lower likelihood of any inherent danger or armed conflict in that place; also, they wanted some samples of any human organic material that we may have been able to attain so that the lab could take a look at *that* DNA. They were close to having a cure for Craine's virus, they told us. That fact, in addition to the unforeseen revival of Nigel's crossover ability had the Joint Chiefs convinced this was without a doubt the right time to put all of our new toys to use. With their otherspace-crossing tech being as developed as it was, Nigel wouldn't necessarily have to be the one who opened the way in and out of there. We should be able to get there, attain our samples, and return with no problem; Sergeant Renoir only needed to ride along as an emergency escape device. SECNAV even gave a friendly pat on my back and assured me that now, we could set the lab further along the path to curing Craine's disease.

However, my sources within the lab reported something different. The DOD was, in truth, thinking of using the Devin Craine they had to duplicate and improve the original virus. They wanted a weapon of mass destruction, and since this reality had no access to key portions of his research, they were hoping he would reverse engineer it from any tissue samples that the expedition may have been able to attain for them. Because of our known immunity, almost all of the original Crossover Team Alpha were to go, Master Sergeant Lucius Carver and Kruger being exceptions, but Dr. Leonard would be included. I put my political weight behind forcing them to allow Devin Craine to go along too, just in case. Of course, my "just in case" was different than theirs, but who knew? Only Crossover Team Alpha.

Concerning Craine, Lucius, Kruger, and I expected Devin to become enraged over the incident between Nigel and himself, so right after it ended, we formulated a contingency plan to deal with such an eventuality. When the confrontation ended, he'd been whisked away to the med bay and we hadn't had an opportunity to talk since. I didn't hear from Craine for a couple of weeks after either, until one day when he came into my office and quietly asked if we could talk. Of course, I told him, as I placed my hand on one of my Berettas, which was holstered and hung under the desk in such a way that anyone sitting across from me couldn't see it. "Sir," he quietly began, "that Marine sergeant, he was ID-1, wasn't he?"

I assured him that was so. Nigel's identity had previously been kept from most of the lab people, especially Devin, so up until that moment of altercation between them, he hadn't known who ID-1 was. He shuddered then, as his mind went back to those moments when he was subject to

Nigel's attack. "His eyes," Devin continued, "they were glowing like electricity or something. I thought he'd kill me and could barely speak, but when you and Master Sergeant Carver came, his grip loosened. All I could say was, 'Tell my wife that I love her.' Then you ordered him to stand down, he dropped me, and I heard him say, 'What wife? You have . . .'and that was that. But I also heard you say I was not *that* Craine, so over the past two weeks, I've been doing some research to find out what you meant."

"And?" I patiently prodded while thumbing the safety on my Beretta to the "off" position.

Devin Craine raised his head to look at me, and I swear to you, Detective, that I have never seen such misery in any kid's eyes as in his that day. He went on. "Most of what I found was redacted, but I've seen enough to ask you, was it *me?* Was *I* the person who killed your world? Was it me who tried to kill your wife in the N-Prime reality? Please . . . I need to know. No one else will tell me the truth. If that's what I was in two other realities, how do I know that I won't become someone worse here?" The youngster almost choked as he continued further. "I-I couldn't sleep because I don't know that I won't become like them, and Doreen, she (sob), she said that I should come and talk to you about it, but I was afraid . . . I mean, how could you *not* hate me? How could you and Ms. Angeline *stand it* to look at me when you were treating me so well? (More sobs.) You've done so much for me."

So here it was. It was time. Devin Craine, in any of his incarnations, has always been a brilliant person, and this one was even more so. Sooner or later, he'd have found out what happened in those other places and would have put it together. After coming to an understanding of that possibility, Crossover Team Alpha created contingency plans for any villainous response he may have formulated, but no contingency was in place for this response—a young man, worried about who he could become and asking the only mentor whom he completely trusted for guidance and advice. Me. Another unbelievable turn in the road of our lives. As I've said, Angeline is a healer, Detective Caldwell, and the steps she'd taken to heal this kid had met with overwhelmingly successful results. I took my hand off my pistol and, in as kindly a fashion as I could, simply assured him: "Devin, it wasn't you who did those things any more than it was I who attacked you. Those persons were just individuals who wore your form, whom you could have become had things been a little different in your life and your world. But neither of them were you, and you will never be either of them." I then invited Devin Craine to come by my house that night, so that he, Angel, and I could talk it over. And yes, he could bring his young wife, Doreen, along. When I went home, Angel and I talked about it, but she didn't seem too surprised to find out that Devin had put things together, nor did she appear surprised at his reaction. In fact, she gave me the impression that she expected this.

So we had the Craines over, and Angel explained to them that we saw the good in Devin from the first day we met him (What do you mean "we"? I wondered mentally), and that was why we cared so much for him. In his case, unlike the last two Craines, that inner goodness had been given a chance and some room to grow stronger, and that was also why he wasn't in the same low sink as his two predecessors, she said. He had many people who esteemed him highly, a sweet young lady who'd loved him enough to agree to marry him, friends who respected him for the way he treated them and so on. We also found out that Devin had put together who the young Nigel was, and that had, as his wife said, "blown us away." So the night went on. Angel was only too eager to hear any news of Nigel, but was also deeply concerned with what was happening to his mind. She and I would have to have a long talk after they left, I knew. I wasn't too eager for it, so I let them all talk on and on into the wee hours. That night, Detective, was the first time that I began to see Devin as a different person than the other two Craines; and for him, that is definitely a good thing.

Devin Craine has now become my most reliable ally within IDEA Control's research and development laboratories. He has been assured that he will not become what his other two versions had been and has taken that assurance to heart. He has also espoused a different view of Nigel. Now that he knows the lad to be a younger version of myself, one who has had his mind manipulated and subjected to the whims of an uncaring government, he has become protective of the boy. As protective as any older brother would be. That also was a part of Angel's strategy with this Craine; she wanted him to feel as if I'd been the only real father he'd known because when he'd put together Nigel's true identity, as she'd known he would, then he'd have enough love for us to move him to find every way he could to repay the kindness of a beloved parent. I understood, then, how she'd done all that she could, not only to prevent the mass murder that Devin Craine could perpetrate on the human race, but also, on a more personal note, to help me protect our Nigel, the young man whom she'd come to view as the only son we'd ever have, since the genetic alterations that make us MISTmen also makes us unable to cause pregnancies. My Angeline also feels much better because she says that this is the *real* Devin Craine, the person he was meant to become. She also knows now that for "Petit Nigel Deaux," Crossover Team Alpha has a plan in place to ensure his well-being, a preparation that has existed since before we arrived here, and now, the Craines are on board. So yes, Devin was willing to join that expedition to what was left of our homeworld, and his life was no longer at risk from either Nigel or me.

Our force was additionally beefed up by the addition of Major Lacy with sixteen more troops. Why? Well, one can only surmise, Detective. Since it's not likely that they were meant as an anti-mutiny contingency, it was more likely that they were included as fodder for bringing the virus back here in case we couldn't get any other infected tissue. The mission planners either didn't know that anyone who passed through the nil zone was immediately rendered immune to Craine's virus, or they were counting on our miniscule DNA differences to render a different result. I was surprised that they'd send Major Robin Lacy into such risk, but from our subsequent conversations, I gathered that the Major hadn't made the connection and had worked hard to be a part of this. He honestly didn't know how contagious that virus had become. Although the information had been included in every report we'd made regarding Craine and Muldowney's Virus, that fact had been redacted from his copies of those same reports. I made a few advance preparations of my own, just in case, and we were ready.

What we found when we finally made it home again was soul wrenching. The battles we fought during our short time in our own world were grueling and costly. As far as the Department of Defense was concerned, the mission yielded little usable information and twelve deaths, one of them being Sergeant Thomas Bench, who had been with us through all that Crossover Team Alpha endured. We burned his remains and left them there. That was his home, as much as ours. He too has been just another one of Muldowney and the first Craine's victims. As expected, Major Lacy and his remaining troops were immediately quarantined upon our return then hopefully poked and prodded for a month after, only to be found uninfected. That had to be a disappointment, I guess.

Truthfully, Nigel is the only reason why anyone who went along on that expedition survived at all. No, I cannot elaborate on the details because what's there, in that place, as well as all that my boy did, is classified to the highest degree, Detective, but some of it you need to know. I can tell you that all of our brand-new equipment failed. We stepped into our old home, and a nightmare beyond anything any Hollywood producer could dream up was all we found therein. In addition, we were cut off from any retreat to safety. If Nigel hadn't done what he did on that excursion, all of us would have died in that graveyard of a world. My advance preparations had bought some time, but not as much as was needed. When it all fell apart, our company found itself in a no-win situation, expecting death. None of us would have returned but for Nigel. He could have fled and saved himself, in obedience to my orders, but that wasn't his choice. He brought us home, and only God knows how he did it.

He paid a price for that heroism, though. Once we stepped out of *otherspace*, it became visually obvious how much he was suffering inside. His own memories must have been clashing with mine and conflicting with everything else inside his head, causing him to come close to a psychotic break. He stood in the staging area looking around again and again, as if he'd left someone behind, a wild look of near panic in his eyes, hands held on both sides of his head, fell to his knee, then his knees. As he did, he kept saying, "Goodbye, Angeline," as if that mantra was all that helped him hold his grip on reality. He began to yell that he needed to go get her, that he couldn't lose her, and probably would have gone back there, but Kruger tranquilized him before his mental agitation escalated to that point. When they saw our individual camera recordings and read all of our reports, The President, SECNAV, and The CMC were so impressed with his actions that he was awarded the Congressional Medal of Honor for that day's deeds. It's sad that he doesn't even know it.

Meanwhile, what with their viewing of the record of his achievements and the return of his dimension-crossing ability, all the brass in the upper echelons of the Pentagon were thrilled beyond belief. They thought they had the first ever super-marine, so IDEA Control was ordered to restore Nigel's memories and afterward prepare him for additional action in the crossover field. But it seemed that no matter how hard Kruger worked, the memories only disappeared further. What a shame, I said, when they told me. But Kruger, Leonard, the rest of Crossover Team Alpha, and I had all we could take of seeing what was being done to Nigel. He was only twenty-three years of age, and IDEA Control had made him into a basket case. It was time for it to end.

INTERLUDE IV

A MOMENT AND
MOMENTS IN TIME

The dream wouldn't stop. Every time he closed his eyes recently, it would ascend out of the shadowy realm of his subconscious to torture him. Like everybody else, he had bad dreams at times. Never the same ones, though, and he could always awaken to a new day that kept him too busy to remember visions of the night before. But he could never seem to escape this one, and it was decidedly not one of his favorites. Lately, it had, in bits and pieces, begun occurring with more frequency, invading his mind even during his waking moments. If he daydreamed, it was there. Anytime he took a moment out of his busy days and nights to stop and think, it was there again, rising from the depths of his mind like some shark ascending toward its prey from the bottom of a cold black sea.

The events of that particular nightmare episode always started the same way. He and a party of fighters would emerge from some place where only he felt perfectly safe. They, for their part, hated that place. The Old Man, who was also the Commander of the group, would order them to start setting up a base camp, and the work began. The dream always blurred ahead then, and he'd hear one of the big-brain lab guys who accompanied the task force telling the old man that the city where they used to live was now totally submerged. The Old Man asked about his family home, and the top lab doc only answered with one phrase: "Gone, sir." The Commander's face looked ashen, and the Dreamer felt like a ton of lead had been dropped into his heart. That's why he concluded that The Old Man must have been his father, judging by the way they both felt the same sadness over the loss of their residence. The Old Man looked at him, noticed his grief, and said, "We had some good times there, didn't we, son?" The Dreamer answered, "Yes" and knew that he was right. This man must have been his father.

The dream skipped ahead again, and terrors would come. Where they originated was never specified in the setting. They just seemed to suddenly appear on the scene. There were huge rats the size of large dogs, with extralong razor-sharp tails, oversized knife-beaked birds that attacked like death from the skies, and the whole company of men were now having to fight off the horrors or become prey. During a short hiatus in the action, they tried to fire up the transports with their new versions of The Apparatus attached because that equipment was expected to convey the whole group back to the secure reality they called home. However, they'd soon discover how the circuits had all burned out during the transition, so, now, even though the transports could still perform their primary function of getting the men around within this reality, the zone-crossing devices had been rendered useless as vehicles of escape, effectively stranding them.

The Dreamer himself could have used one of the transports to flee through the zone, but the entire company would not have been able to escape that way since he thought he could only take one vehicle at a time. He'd be able to make it into this side and out of the other, perhaps even save some of the fighters, but he knew how that would work. The Old Man would have him go, taking along the lab geeks and the wounded, while he himself would stay and fight. He'd say he was sick of leaving good men behind and would choose to stay behind with them. But the Dreamer wouldn't leave his only remaining family member nor the rest of the men there to die.

Father even tried ordering him to retreat into the safe place, but he wouldn't. Even when some in the party fell, the Dreamer still refused to go, though his dad, as the Troop Commander, began to threaten him with court-martial. The two research techs would then step forward, oddly in sync, and mention that the unit probably needed the Dreamer to stay more than they needed him to go in case something else that they explained with big-word lab-nerd gibberish occurred and their explanation would be the only reason The Old Man would relent.

The group survived that fray then moved their base camp to a safer location in the foyer of one of the long-abandoned buildings, set up perimeter fencing to keep the rats out, and netted the broken roof to stop the birds. But none of them could possibly have expected the horror of the roaches that came in at night and ate human flesh. They hadn't encountered them before because the birds went into a feeding frenzy whenever the insects were available, and somehow the little creatures' hive mind had developed the precaution of staying hidden during the daylight and avoiding open spaces at night. With a sound like the basso echo of an organ in an abandoned church, he would hear his father ordering the troops to deploy flamethrowers as the roaches began to charge toward the big brains in their hiding place. But somehow, something had gone wrong with that equipment also. The company mech was working as fast as he could to fix that, since it was the one problem he could fix on this mission.

Yet another man was lost before the company could utilize flamethrowers, and they were able to use those only because that warrior sacrificed himself in a conflagration that held the insects' advance for a moment or two. His loss was particularly painful to the Dreamer since this one was one of the persons he'd known the longest, as well as one of their bravest. His remains would be burned no matter how long it took, for Father felt that this man deserved that honor, at least. "Small payment for all that he's given," Dad would say, and that phrase kept echoing throughout the dream as if it were a ball that some precocious little boy was bouncing off hallway walls.

The nightmare continued, and they lost one of the new men, his death (and it was a horrifying one) coming as he was saving one of the two lab guys from an explosion of flame whose origin the Dreamer couldn't pinpoint. Nevertheless, that tragedy bought more time for the party to use the flame-throwing weapons that saved their lives, although the rest of the equipment and stores so necessary for their survival throughout this mission were destroyed. Now they'd have to forage for as long as they were here in order to stay alive.

The Dreamer wanted to take everyone and go, but many of the less-experienced troops had lost their special uniforms—the only thing that would preserve their minds on the journey home, and that was an issue. He also discerned that The Old Man would not leave without these ones, and the Dreamer felt the same way. So he too would stay and fight. Because he used to hold an important post here, however, The Old Man also happened to know where they could find other special uniforms, and they fought their way to that place, losing two more in doing it.

Fortunately for the party, the location they sought was protected from the rats and the birds, a fact that gave them peace for a short time, but eventually, the roaches began to find their way in. The Old Man then put into play a weapon that he'd held in waiting for just the right moment to deploy. He'd insisted his troops acquire a little something extra wherever they could fit it into their packs: borax cleaner and quicklime, which he combined with a dry powder that he'd brought along.

It was a top secret chemical that supposedly would disintegrate organic material on contact. Borax would activate it much faster, almost instantly, in fact, and quicklime would increase its toxicity and scope. Of course, The Old Man explained, it was never meant to be used as a weapon or anything like that. *"Riiight."* the Dreamer remembered saying. He and his father would laugh then. Same laugh, same tone. They could both be very scary people, he guessed. As expected, after a disastrous first attempt, the roaches wouldn't cross over that mixture again, and for a while, the survivors had a measure of protection. Now, too, the couple of lab rats who had accompanied this quest could take a few moments and try to postulate a theory explaining what had happened here. No matter, the Commander told them, after hearing their thoughts. The party had to leave, starting with the lab guys because they would need those men's observations back home, and only the Dreamer could get them out.

So he ordered the Dreamer to take the doctors home and stay there, but only the first part of that order was obeyed. He took the two big brains to safety, yet nothing could stop him from returning for the rest. He went back to that dead world with the intent of making sure that all the survivors would make it home alive. Nevertheless, during his exertions, the Dreamer began having problems himself. Memories that he did not know he had started to haunt his thinking. He kept hearing HER in his mind, telling him to come home again to her. Telling him how much she loved him, and that particular memory began interfering with his ability. The dream reality suddenly jumped, and he was there, in her world again, fighting off the brigands in gray who had attacked the two of them.

The action got heavier; the Dreamer began to overpower his attackers, so the assailants used an energy weapon, searing through his chest, but he refused to go down. He bounced in and out of the zone until he'd taken them all with his Ka-Bar then turned to her and kissed her with all the passion in his heart while reassuring her that he was okay and would have to escape in order to come back for her. He began having a hard time breathing, but he ordered her to RUN, yelling the order again when she hesitated, tears forming in her eyes. Others were coming, he finally explained, and he couldn't both defend her and evade capture. She told him that she'd always love him, and he uttered two words that he never seemed to be free of when it came to her. When she did finally turn and run, it took all he had to stop himself from running with her, to take her back to wherever he'd come from. That was only a memory, but it froze his actions, leaving him unable to move because of his confusion. *"Where am I? Is this now or yesterday?"* he kept wondering.

She wasn't there anymore, but the fight, the sounds of battle, the guns were, and the Dreamer was once again back in that hell world with The Old Man and his men. He heard the sound of M4 CQBR gunfire, the scream of someone falling and being dragged away by the enemy, and knew then that the huge rats had breached their perimeter because the roaches had learned how to herd them into the chemical barrier until a portion of it had been depleted. Everyone was fighting for their lives while he stood as if a victim of catatonia. They were trying to defend him now, and more would be dying in attempting that. Unless he did something. Something drastic, fast, immediate. In an act of desperation, he reached into the safe place and pulled destruction out of there, a bad mood seeded in pent-up anger that manifested itself as blue electricity when it crossed from there into this world. He cast that upon the rats as well as the roaches that were driving them. What resulted were thousands of hostile targets burned into disintegration and simply gone, turned to ash. Their destruction caused a considerable hiatus in the fighting during which the human force got a bit of rest, temporarily. For that moment, however, when everything stopped and the enemy faltered, his company just stared at him, none moving. The Old Man was asking how he did it, but other memory visions were still battering at the doors of his mind, and the Dreamer could not answer without falling into another mnemonic trance. He had to act and act now, or no one would make it out.

So he let go of the faint trace of that woman he'd loved so much. She became like a soap bubble, and he had to let the memory of her perfumed kisses float away and burst. Then he could act. The Dreamer brought as many men as he could carry through, snatching them, one or two at a time, as fast as he could to safety then returning to the battle that had somehow resumed. Each time he returned, there were less and less fighters to keep the rats away from him, but the Dreamer kept going back. Finally, only he and The Old Man were left, fighting with the new laser blades that the quest had been issued; and the rats, sensing the approach of the roaches, were beginning to run from the only terror that was worse than they were, giving the two of them the seconds needed to cross into the safe place. The Dreamer finally got The Old Man out of harm's way, but they were both badly wounded, and it was too hard for him to open the door leading out of their refuge and onward home. He couldn't do it in that condition.

He therefore found the only medical help that existed in that area, using it to save himself and his father. But the process broke something in the Dreamer's mind, and he kept seeing HER, hearing her screaming for him. He thought he'd left her in that hell of a world and kept trying to get back to her. Suddenly, a hurricane of images and memories began attacking his thinking processes. He heard, as if coming from an abandoned well, other people yelling, other gun battles, an airplane falling, a car racing toward his mother in some stray memory; and there were more and more sirens. Through all the cacophony, however, he could also hear The Old Man's voice telling him that she, the woman the Dreamer had always loved, was safe, that she had neither been hurt nor abandoned;

and finally, he fastened his sanity to the sound of that voice and listened. After surfacing out of his mental whirlpool, He could finally open the door to their home again.

As they were arriving, however, the walls of his mind buckled; and he saw HER once more, in danger, in laughter, in happiness, in trouble. He saw her smiling at him and crying over him. He kissed her and watched her disappear. Over and over again, he kept having to say the same two words that he always seemed to have to say to her, as if speaking a spell that would bring them together again. But it wasn't working, and that loss was killing him moment by moment, bit by bit. He held his head because it seemed to be the only way he could hold on to HER and was about to jump back into that hell world to get her out, when darkness took him and he fell asleep.

Then it would all just go away. The Dreamer would wake up in the here and now. No danger, no special abilities, no guns. He didn't even know how to use the weapons of the dream nightmare. He was just an average person living an average life again. Still, he knew that something was missing. It was HER. She was what was absent, and that thought caused more pain than he could bear. Then he would again, just as before, always conclude that it made no sense to love a dream woman who wasn't real from a fantasy world that never existed. He'd sit for a while, clearing his head, trying to get his emotions under control, because of all the dreams that he could have, this one twisted his emotions and exacerbated his sense of loss more than any other. If only he knew what it was that he'd lost, he thought. After a moment or two of probing that thought as if it were an open wound, he shrugged his shoulders, went to the restroom, splashed cold water on his face, then got ready and went to work.

Saving Sergeant Renoir

I arranged another secret meeting with Master Sergeant Carver, Kruger, and Dr. Leonard. This time, Devin Craine was included in our plans, although it took quite a bit of explaining to convince Kruger and Leonard not to shoot the man on sight. We had to bring my Angeline in both to save Craine's life (again) and to help us implement our next strategy. Still, all agreed—that last time needed to be *the* last time Nigel would ever be used as a weapon or in any military capacity. We, with the exception of Angeline and the new Devin Craine, started this, and we would stop it. This nation has plenty of advanced weaponry and materials, with more to come, all because of our misplaced man-child. It was time for him to have his own life. We all regretted the fact that he'd lost his Angeline, and since that world was on to us now, watching and waiting for his return, it wasn't likely that he'd ever find her again. There seemed to be nothing that our team could do about that, though.

I took him to my wife since she needed to fabricate a medical report that would somehow disqualify the boy from serving due to some physical limitation. At the time, it seemed that this was the only way to free him of the slavery that I and my team had unwittingly delivered him into. Because it was possible that she wouldn't see him ever again, Angeline also wanted to spend some time with Nigel, to listen to him as he told her what his life was like. She loved him as much as any mother could and deserved to see him one last time before she disqualified him from ever serving anymore, which also meant that she might not ever see him anymore, either. So I took Nigel home to meet her—again.

She hadn't seen him since he was ten or eleven, as we'd deliberately left her out of what we were doing because I'd wanted my Angel to be

---

able to sleep at night. So of course, she was thrilled when I brought the boy in; she perked up more than I'd ever seen and kept talking, going on and on about how much he looked like me at that age, when I had to stop her and explain that he would probably not remember her at all. She looked at me, and her eyes said that she knew what we had done. I felt as if I'd betrayed her too; but when I tried to explain that none of us could have stopped the administration's activities because my reach just hadn't extended that deeply into the political fabric of this world at the time and, if I'd walked away, they only would have placed someone else, someone who couldn't possibly care about him as much, if at all, in charge of Nigel, she just *understood*.

She *knew* that I wanted someone who loved the boy to be in his life, and there was no one else of our Crossover Family whom I would have forced to stay beside him and watch, even *help* them ransack his mind. That I had to observe while my boy could have been made into a vegetable, only staying to be sure that he wasn't discarded like an old broken toy when they finished with him and that he would not be used as a thoughtless DNA bank for their *gadgets*. Angeline understood, as no one else was able to, what those years had taken out of me. I am not a man given to tears, Detective Caldwell, but they came that day, and I am so happy that she was the only one there to see it. Nigel has lost so much in losing his Angeline.

When he saw her, he stood and said, "Hello, ma'am." But the look on his face said that he was struggling again. He apologized for staring and told her that she made him think of his mother, but they looked nothing alike, and he couldn't figure out why she reminded him so much of Mom. While he spoke, tears began to roll down his face, but he didn't seem to realize that. She was kind and asked about his breathing, but when she returned to me, she was crying. Angeline certified his "bronchial disorder" and strongly recommended that he be given a medical discharge. Before she left to go to the hospital and her other patients, she turned around, looked at me, and asked, "I'm never going to see him again, am I?" I only wanted to look at my feet, but owed it to her to look her in her eye and tell her, "It's not likely." She looked down for a moment then raised her eyes to me again. There were many, many tears in them. "He was our only child, Nige," she said and turned to go back to work. I took Nigel and his certification away. The DOD also wanted a military doctor's opinion, though, so I sent Nigel to Lieutenant General Archimus Marcelon, our man's double in this world, a Medal of Honor recipient who commanded the Naval Hospital Corps School and, on more than one occasion, had worked with Angeline.

We'd occasionally enjoyed a dinner with his wife and him at our home or theirs, although we'd never mentioned his double or anything else about who we were or where we'd originated. But it was time to tell The General what we needed and why, so we also decided to tell him as much of the truth as he needed to know. He is a moral man who, once he understood all that had gone on, had no compunction against helping Nigel. The only thing he asked in return was a chance to meet and speak with his younger look-alike. He signed on, provided an additional certification of our boy's "bronchial disorder," and we took the certification to SECNAV. There was no more discussion after that. Nigel was given a secret honorable discharge and rotated into civilian living. Still, he was to be under constant surveillance for the rest of his life, and IDEA Control would be in charge of that detail.

That completed, we went to one more secret facility. Kruger and Leonard were already on hand, ready to work on his brain. It took months and lots of secret visits from naval psych doctors with consciences, but when they were done, he was as close to a whole person as we could make him. We made him a waiter because Craine and Muldowney both hated waiters, not even bothering to look twice at them, and we didn't even want to risk the possibility that some other Craine and Muldowney team from some other reality may find him. He had also been given childhood as well as adult memories to take along. Small payment for all that he'd been forced to give. We thought him totally unable to walk into otherspace ever again and were pretty sure that would make him next to valueless for IDEA Control's use.

Later on, Nigel moved here, to Florida, the year after his sister Joanna died in an auto accident caused by a drunken motorist and his brother DeVries got killed in a gun battle with a rival drug dealer. When he told me his plans, I knew what he didn't, that his choice of location was no coincidence; he had to be looking for *her* when he came here. Another Angeline. Not his, but the one from here, who'd lost her Nigel before they'd even had the chance to meet. Somehow, he just *knew* where the likelihood of his finding her would be highest. That is one of the mysteries about Nigel that can never be explained, the way his senses work to put together so much information that he seems to pull out of nowhere and arrange it all in concert, forming an accurate conclusion from that. According to

Kruger and Leonard's probability equation, however, it wasn't likely that he would find her before she got married. And if that were the case, then his heartache would only increase. We searched and found that it was, indeed, the case. I wanted to tell him this before he left, but if she were mentioned, it seemed possible that such a reference could break the conditioning that held his mind together. After he'd settled in to his destination, I had one of my men's wives rear-end him then appeared on the scene myself to direct him to the place where Dana worked, insisting that he be "checked out."

Major Lacy, on his end of things, had been suggesting to his daughter that Nigel might meet his approval, speaking as if he knew the kid from before, which he did, sort of, so she knew of him before he even walked in. It was also possible that her past memories were touching her psyche and accelerating their relationship. The whole operation was instigated for two reasons: our superiors had ordered IDEA Control to try to get these two together because Craine's DNA research gave their coupling the highest probability of producing children with the same abilities, and Major Robin Lacy actually did approve of Nigel dating his little girl. I went along because the brass had no idea that MISTmen cannot have children, and it seemed that Dana may have been able to ease the pain Nigel lived with. We hoped that some of that old attraction still remained. It did. They moved in together, but no children came. Eventually they broke up, but you already know all this, Detective Caldwell. Crossover Team Alpha has done all that we could to create a normal life for my boy, but it seems that normalcy is something that will never exist for long in Nigel's life, no matter where he lives it.

What concerns us here, at the moment, is that Nigel has begun making crossings into the nil zone again. So now, IDEA Control has been tasked with reacquiring Asset ID-1. There were also hopes of attaining Dana Lacy, who was never fitted with any tracer. If she got married, engaged, or anything of that nature, any children produced were to be monitored constantly by IDEA Control. At this point, it seems that something triggered Nigel's memories, and I need to know what that was. We know that he and the Angeline of this world met, but she was married to someone else as predicted. His tracer went off the grid a few times after that, but he did return, no worse for wear. Therefore, it follows that he did not go back into his own home world or he may not have returned at all, as they have been watching for him for years now. Lately, however, his tracer has winked out more, but it has returned faster, so he's going *somewhere* and he never stays long. Less than a second in some instances. What we need to know is where, why, and how.

On one of these excursions, Nigel somehow attained enough funding to pay all the outstanding debt that kept him and Ms. Dana Lacy together, pay for the home they shared, and turn that over to Dana. Upon learning of that, SECNAV and JSAC expressed a pretense hope that he hasn't used his latent MIST ability to commit any crimes in neighboring realities, but I know that he wouldn't. He is another version of myself, after all. IDEA Control managed to keep the IRS away from him by stepping in and explaining that this funding is related to an ongoing national security operation and that Nigel is one of our operatives for whom we supplied the money from classified sources. We also know that Dana regained her power of following him, but we don't know why her abilities seem to have become more like his. Another query that we are pursuing.

***

"I can answer some of those questions," Roan said. "But in return, I want to know why we found Dana's blood in her apartment and how her door got kicked off. Who was responsible, if not Nigel? And you still haven't been very clear about what you want from me." General Renoir looked at Roan as if he was measuring him. He sat down in the chair again, inviting Roan to take his former place across from him. Roan did. Leaning forward again, the general said, "Okay, I'll share what is appropriate and relative to the situation at hand, but we *are* extremely limited on time, maybe even more than we thought."

Looking the General in the eye, Roan leaned forward. He said, "You've been way too long winded for me to buy into that. Now tell me, please, General, *what happened* in Dana Lacy's house."

His host smiled. "Okay, you've made me laugh." (That's *what you call "laughing"?* Roan thought.) General Renoir continued. "As I've told you, Detective, we have found a way to open the door to otherspace. The problem is that all of our equipment needs a small amount of Nigel's DNA to act as a power source for opening the pathway, as well as for holding it open and guiding our men through. There are still a few things that need to be worked out with the system, but we recently had an unexpected chance to test it out, and it performed decently."

"That was when Dana followed Nigel through not too long ago, wasn't it?" Roan queried then added, "The thingamajig burned out when she returned, and two of your guys went to retrieve it. One got into a fight with Nigel."

General Renoir's gaze sharpened. "I see, now, that I should have found a way to record your conversations with him."

Roan was surprised. "It seems to me that you would have, General. You seem to be too thorough to have overlooked that," he said.

Again, the General smiled. "I did bug the place. Somehow, Nigel found every one of my eyes and ears then removed them. Lucius helped him with that, but we understand why. At least *our* people understand, that is. Whenever you walked into Sand Ridge, I was blind. And deaf. We tried to get a man into your house in order to copy whatever recordings you had, but again Nigel prevented that."

Roan's eyes widened. "How did—" he started.

The General looked down again and raised his eyes. Roan thought he saw a look of quiet desperation in them as General Renoir began. "Somehow he intervened. Our first man said that Nigel just *appeared* in front of him and knocked him cold. Our second man said the same thing happened to him, but Nigel sent a message back to me with this one. He pinned a note on the man. I was not to, in any way, overt or covert, try to put my hands on you, or to quote him, 'There will be hell for The Colonel to pay.' Even then, I wanted to take up the challenge, but the better strategy was to capture you myself and try to explain matters in such a way that you'd be willing to join our efforts."

Roan scoffed. "So you did 'take up the challenge,' as you said, huh, General? Guess you couldn't resist a fight, even against yourself."

General Renoir looked down for a moment, and Roan saw a slight smile on his face as he raised his head and told him, "Detective Caldwell, I'm not built to avoid any fights, most especially one against a younger version of myself."

THE HEART OF THE MATTER

Roan looked at the General for a moment. The man he'd considered a worthless criminal attempting to escape justice had chosen to protect Roan's own house. He was surprised at himself, that his judgment seemed to be so far off the mark. But then, the detective hadn't had all the information then that he had now. It was more surprising to him, though, that General Renoir seemed so disappointed in what Nigel had become, so he had to ask, "You seem entirely unsatisfied with the man he has become. Why does that bother you so, sir? Didn't you expect that sooner or later, he would adopt methods similar to your own? You trained him, didn't you? He is a version of you, isn't he? Besides, from where I sit, it doesn't look like you paid much attention to his warning."

"What worries me, Caldwell," General Renoir began, ignoring Roan's questions as he walked over to the bar for more scotch, "is the fact that Nigel was angry enough to threaten *me* personally. The only time I have ever seen him so heated with angst against me was when he breached *otherspace* at the age of fifteen. If his full memory has returned, as it momentarily did back then, he is in even more danger than he knows. All that would stand between himself and life as a vegetable or death in another realm is me." The General stopped talking for a moment then resumed.

"And yes, Detective Caldwell, I did expect him to eventually adopt my methods, but my methods come with a price. I have lost my most beloved son and am not sure how the other, less beloved one views me. I have seen grief in my wife's eyes as she looks at his medals and awards that we have kept and at what she thinks is her secret collection of pictures of the little Nigel. We all love to say things like 'If I had it to do all over again,' but that chance actually came my way, and it seems that things have turned out no better for all of my efforts to help. In the end, the constraints of my previous life choices and the world around me were immutable factors that made inalienable differences in all of my other choices."

"You know, that family relationship thing you and your wife have going with him seems all kinds of creepy to me, there, General," Roan began then continued. "I mean, think about it. You and your wife view a kid who's a younger version of you as your son, and he has the hots for a woman who is in reality the same woman he views as his mother. There's some seriously narcissistic and Oedipal crap going on here."

For a moment, the General just looked at Roan the way a high school principal regards a particularly substandard student and explained, "You must remember, Detective Caldwell, that although Nigel may be superhuman, the keyword in that composite is 'human.' Few humans ever choose to view their most cherished memories and assumptions as falsehoods. Somewhere, underneath all the layers of his mind, Nigel sees me as his father and my Angeline as his mother. That thought is precious to him, and even if anyone told him to his face and showed him proof that he and I are the same person, that my Angeline and his are the same, he would never choose to comprehend it. Anyway, getting back to another important point, Detective. What happened in Dana Lacy's house? To be honest, I can't say for certain. It appears that she was assaulted by party or parties unknown. Considering what has gone on around here recently, it may have been the man wearing the form of her father who ordered the attack on her. Nigel preserved her life and spirited her away to some reality that our forces cannot access."

Roan was again shocked. "How?" he asked.

The General looked at Roan as if he were that high school freshman who never listened. "Don't you remember that I told you how Major Lacy disappeared after testing the new crossover technology without permission or backup? They believed him to be lost, but when he returned after a week or so, no one questioned his story about wandering in the nil zone until he could find his own way out. He'd been replaced, and that's how it came about that Dana got hurt.

"They only knew of Nigel back in N-Prime, but while he was here, the false Major Robin Lacy accessed all the information we had concerning both ID-1 and ID-2 and was most likely to have been trying to kidnap Ms. Lacy. It seems that she'd fought them and, in doing of it, wound up bleeding. May have been cut by knife, grazed by a bullet, or punched in her face. Nigel joined the fight and left one of the assailants living, tied and bound. Lucius assured him that everything would be okay then called us and told where the captive could be retrieved. A little close scrutiny revealed that although they wore uniforms of the corps, the men were not marines or any other military. They were regular street thugs who were paid to do what they did. Even then, Major Lacy was not suspected. His double is the perfect intruder. After his first examination and interrogation, the petty crook that we had in custody hung himself. Oddly, all of our surveillance in the brig went on the blitz right about the time our lowlife did himself in. Major Lacy's double would have gotten away with his subterfuge had not Craine caught him removing a strange piece of technology from our main computer and called for the MPs, who subdued the Major. That was when the CMC called for my return.

"I was almost retired, you see. Losing Nigel forever as a member of our family was harder on me than I'd realized at the time and I was not the Officer in command of IDEA Control anymore. More and more of my time was being spent with Angeline, and I thought it was over. But then this happened. Ten minutes after I was back on board, I was able to confirm the fact that the Major Lacy we had in the brig was an intruder by checking his tracer output. There was none. Our man has disappeared now, and I had to take the helm again. That's why officers are not to go off alone into dangerous territory with no backup."

Roan cursed. "Why didn't you let me or anyone in the law enforcement community in on it right then, General?" he demanded. "We've spent all of this time thinking that Nigel was the perpetrator of a crime when we could have been helping him prevent another, or at the very least, we could have caught a real murderer by now."

Peering at Roan, the general said, "There was no need to involve you or any other police operatives. After all, what could you have done? We had our man, and the gunsel that Nigel left for us confessed easily. What murderer did we stop you from catching? Nigel's never been a cold-blooded killer."

Roan stood up. "Don't you *know* what's happened to Angeline Arlander? She's *dead*, and her husband may have been behind it. Your boy Nigel gave me this guy on a silver platter, and I was so worried about seeking justice for Dana Lacy first until George Arlander and his little boyfriend may have gotten away with murder! I didn't trust him, but if we'd had a little clarification about who and what Nigel is, things could have been handled a lot better!"

For just a moment, the General seemed shocked out of his mind, eyes lit with anger. "Angeline Arlander has been *killed*? Why? How do you know this for certain?"

"Because I *saw it*, General!" Roan answered. "Nigel popped into the room out of nowhere right after it happened, filmed the whole event with some palm cameras in that stealth suit your two mad scientists made for him, then sneaked the video into my house. I *saw* the girl murdered!"

General Renoir's face registered surprise. "What do you mean when you say he '*popped* into the room out of nowhere'?"

Roan was dazed for a moment. "Well, uh, I mean, he *popped* into the room out of nowhere," he answered.

"No, Detective Caldwell," General Renoir answered, slowly shaking his head as if he were trying to talk some sense into an unrepentant drunk. "Nigel has never been able to walk into *otherspace* or out of it from the interior of any building. He's only been able to enter other realities out of doors. Believe me, we *tried* to go from the inside of structures, but the boy couldn't do it, and his efforts were honest, as he had no reason to hide anything from me back then. There is also no way he could have gotten the cloaking outfit because it is being kept in a secure vault. Even if Kruger wanted to hand it over, he couldn't have because the vault is locked and can only be accessed by my . . ." General Renoir fell silent as some realization dawned over his thoughts.

"Right," Roan said. "Can only be accessed by your finger or palm prints, or maybe your own retinal scan, huh, General? When was the last time you talked to your buddy Kruger, anyway?"

The General replied. "Point made, Detective. But even if Nigel has somehow gotten his hands on the refraction suit, he still should not be able to use it in entering and exiting buildings from the shadow zone. It does nothing to accent his abilities even though it can be made active by his DNA signature. I know this because mine activated it when we tried it out, and it didn't accent any of my physical abilities."

"But you're not Nigel, General." Now Roan was the one sounding like a polite teacher who was at the end of his patience.

"Correct, Detective," General Renoir agreed, "but the suit still is what it is and what it is not. I can, however, think of another possible explanation for this new development in Nigel's abilities. They have grown as he has grown. I'm reminded of a time when I tried to lift my father's dumbbells and couldn't because they were far too heavy. I found those dumbbells after I'd grown up and realized that they were only thirty-five pounds. Lifting them was no problem then." So saying, General Renoir went to a phone on the desk and made a call. Roan heard him use Kruger's name several times, conjoining it with various expletives. Picking up his untouched scotch, he returned and told Roan, "Yes, Kruger just confirmed that he'd seen Nigel not too long ago. The boy just popped in from nowhere, he told me. He also confirmed that the two of them had a conversation, and he let Nigel in on the secret of the cloaking suit. He said that Nigel's memories are returning, but he cannot, as of yet, remember everything."

"Did you ask why he never contacted you about this?" Roan asked.

"Yes, I did," General Renoir answered. "He said that it was because he wasn't sure of what Nigel could or would do while he was present. After he left, Kruger did try to contact me, but I've been . . . incommunicado, you might say." He put his glass of booze on the table and stood eye to eye with Roan. "Do you know why they were after Ms. Lacy instead of Nigel, Detective? Because neither she nor Nigel are aware of the fact that her father is likely in captivity or dead back in Nigel's home world. Family members are normally the first persons who can tell when one of their own has been replaced by a double, and the false Major wanted to make sure that his cover wasn't blown. Also, Craine's research has suggested that the crossover gene may be carried on the mother's DNA more than the father's. Our Major Lacy was aware of this, and we believe he may have been forced to give up that information to his captors over there."

"So you still haven't told me what you want from me, General Renoir," Roan said. "I can't find Dana if you can't, and I have a couple of murder suspects to apprehend. My friends are waiting for me to get back. George Arlander's a murderer, and Angeline Arlander's blood is crying out from the grave. That's my main concern now. I'll handle the scumbags that threaten individual lives, and you handle the ones that threaten the life of the whole world."

A murderous anger flashed in General Renoir's eyes again, and Roan knew that the man wasn't angry about anything he'd said. Something else was irritating the man. *He's seriously pissed about what happened to her*, Roan realized. *He'd probably dump all this and go after George Arlander himself if he could. Not that I couldn't use his help. With all the toys and manpower he commands, I'd have both Arlander and Wesley Whatever-the-hell-his-last-name-is locked away forever, if they got that lucky.* The momentary anger in the General's eyes receded as he regained control of his temper.

"Detective, Nigel trusts you, and that is no small thing for him, believe me. He has contacted Kruger, not me, so I know that he doubts my intentions regarding himself, even if he does not remember why. We have reason to believe that Major Lacy may still be living, and even if he isn't, his daughter is still in danger. Since they've found a way through the zone from N-Prime, it is possible that they may be able to locate whatever reality Nigel has hidden Dana in. Kruger told me just now that if the boy's memory is returning, it will do so 'in spades.' He will have total recall, as well as eidetic memory. There will be nothing that he can forget, though he should be able to file recollections away for later retrieval, like a computer or something. It was part of what Kruger called a 'healing package' that he and Dr. Leonard built into their memory-suppression process. They felt they owed it to my boy to put him on the road toward gaining that ability. We need to open a dialogue with Nigel, and he will not allow this unless someone he trusts approaches him with the proposal. That would be you. We are also asking you, politely, to allow us access to your recorded interviews with him. Will you do this for us?"

Now it was Roan's turn to consider. *He's right. Nigel opened up to me, not him. I guess the guy does trust me. This is a big problem. That man never should have been in this world at all, and but for General Starched Shirt here, this might have been avoided. But then, it might not have been. Might have been worse, because the younger, badder Nigel would then be on the other side of this negative zone, or whatever it is, leading their troops into our world and swearing that he was in the right because he was serving his country. Hmpf. A flea and a fly were trapped in a flue. "Let us flee," said the fly. "Let us fly," said the flea, and together, they flew through a flaw in the flue. Emphasis on "together."*

"Okay, General," he replied. "I'll come on board. Though to be honest, I don't know what I can do besides telling him to give you a chance. In return, I'd like a little of your secret-squirrel-type help in confirming the evidence against my two suspects. What we got from Nigel's recording really is a smoking gun, but even an inept defense attorney could get it all thrown out in trial."

The General exhaled. "Thank you, Detective. Your assistance is appreciated. I will see to it that Mr. Arlander's confession is heard. If he had any accomplices in this murder, they too will be given to you along with all necessary evidence. What happens after the judicial system has convicted them, well, that we'll have to see. From now on, you'll be Special Field Agent Roan Caldwell, and I will see to it that you are paid hazardous duty pay. Will that be okay for you?"

"Fine with me," Roan answered, "but there is another stipulation I'd like to make. My makeshift team will come along with me at the same rate of pay. I've needed their eyes and ears on this, and they've been a lot of help. I have no doubt that you can arrange that with any local police department."

"Very well, then," the General said, walking over to the door. He opened it and gestured. Team Leader Sergeant Little's huge bulk filled the doorway as he walked in. He and General Renoir spoke in hushed tones for a few moments, Sergeant Little casting an occasional glance in Roan's direction. The General turned toward Roan after dismissing his man Little. He appeared slightly concerned as he told the detective, "Meredith and Billy Compton are with Nigel right now. That is your 'team,' isn't it? Yes? Makes sense. They were members of the other Roan Caldwell's team in NCIS. Well, they are at a house that belongs to Mrs. Arlander in a place called Beach City. Do you have any idea why they'd be there, Detective Caldwell?"

"No, General, I don't. I can say, though, that if they went there, they must have been looking for some evidence related to Mrs. Arlander's murder," Roan told him. In his mind, however, he was thinking, *Oh God, I hope the kids are all right. What were they doing, going there like that? Must have been following a lead. Wait, none of us knew how dangerous Nigel the Younger could be, but they're still alive, so maybe he didn't want to hurt them.*

Once again speaking as if he could read Roan's thoughts, the General said, "Well, I don't know what they were looking for, but Nigel was what they found. Certain others believe that he may be holding them as hostages, though that has never been his style. I, however, believe that he must be trying to recruit them, as I would have, with the intent of using their status as Law Enforcement Officers to help him pin this Arlander fellow."

General Renoir was ready to leave when Roan interrupted with, "By the way, General Renoir, did you consider the possibility that some of the things you've told me during our little fireside chat here may cause your cloaked-in-mystery superiors to question your loyalty to their system? I mean, they don't know about the medical blues in this . . . zone of yours, and there were, by your own admission, other things that you didn't tell them. If our conversation was bugged, you'll have to deal with that before you can be of any help to me, won't you?"

The General stared at Roan for a moment, as if he were weighing the man on some inner scale of trustworthiness. He seemed to come to a decision and replied, "You may have noticed, Detective Caldwell, that during our time together, there were moments when you felt a slight pressure behind your ears. I could tell by the way you occasionally rubbed that area with your fingertip. You're feeling it right now. Well, those were moments when the feed was being altered. What was heard outside of Crossover Team Alpha's surveillance was different from what my own devices have recorded and transmitted."

Roan's eyes widened. "You mean, you're working against the government now?" he asked.

"No, Detective," the general replied. "As I've told you, we found that our intentions toward Nigel, as well as our intentions with regard to the Craine-Muldowney Virus, were different from your government's intent. We have worked within the parameters of our oath to your government, but there are key points of difference that couldn't be reconciled.

"When Nigel was thirteen," General Renoir continued his explanation, "Crossover Team Alpha discovered a reality within which a version of Angeline has found and refined a cure to Craine and Muldowney's dreadful creation. She was an older Angeline whose husband died to attain the knowledge of this treatment, and because of her having spread that knowledge worldwide, she was considered by most as the savior of humanity on that planet. Others considered her an enemy of their gods. She'd risked her life to spread that cure as far and wide as she could. When we returned here, I floated the possibility of such a thing as a curative treatment to my superiors, and they clearly explained that should any type of thing be found, they would, for security reasons, need to lock it away and limit exclusive access to certain high-ranking members of the President's Security Council only. Even Crossover Team Alpha would've been denied the right to use it."

The General's voice took on an aspect of the quiet deadliness that Roan had come to understand as a sign of his anger. The man's hands tightened into fists as he talked. "Our conversation spoke volumes regarding their intent. When she chose to share the process with us, I'd promised that version of my Angeline that I would not permit her husband to have died in vain by allowing the cure to become classified property of a government bent on preservation of its wealthiest citizens first and foremost. I would surrender to death before choosing to break *any* promise to *any* Angeline Renoir."

General Renoir stepped back, took a deep breath to compose himself, and went on. "Thus, we of Crossover Team Alpha have concluded that while we will try to do all we can to benefit this America, it is simply not the country to which we originally obligated ourselves. Our purpose remains unchanged. We must continue with completion of Mission CureSearch, which means that we must now find a way to deploy the cure we have found into our home world, regardless of the risk to ourselves."

The room fell silent, and Roan could hear that the thunderstorm that had been raging outside was spent, its remaining rains fading into the distance like some troupe of wanderers who had lost their way. *What an adequate analogy*, he thought. *They lost their way, and without Nigel, they won't be able to find the trail back home.* As he regarded the man before him, who was standing ramrod straight like some road sign that had miraculously survived a hurricane, Roan achieved a sudden understanding within. He could *see*. He understood the man's hope, as well as how this General had done all he could to build a wall between what he himself was and what his younger version was threatened with becoming.

General Renoir had assisted in developing the crossover technology out of esperance: hope. Hope that the young Nigel could go back to a life of normalcy with the woman he loved because his ability would no longer be needed to save his own home world. But that hope was shattered by the nature of life in this system of things and the politics of power. Torn between obligations to two worlds that were completely different, yet totally alike with a third one in between, he was doing all that he could to care for what had become the only remainder of his people. At the same time, though, he was also hoping to complete a mission that didn't seem to matter anymore. And then there was his obligation toward Nigel the Younger. All of it had become too immense in weight for any man to carry alone.

"Okay, General," he started.

General Renoir turned toward him, looking as if he was preparing for another round of verbal sparring. "Okay? Okay what, Detective?" he asked.

Roan answered, "Okay, as in I'll help you because to do so would both help Nigel and remove a couple of murderers out of society. I'd feel better if you'd allow me the opportunity to talk to you and your wife together, though, and if possible, see all these medals and honors you say he has earned."

Again, the General looked as if he were weighing Roan. To introduce the detective to his wife would indicate an even higher level of trust in this man, he knew. He also knew Roan Caldwell to be worthy of such trust. "I agree to your terms," he said. "That will be arranged. Afterward, it's time to put you into play, Roan Caldwell. Sergeant Little will fly you back home. I have some things yet to do here, but we will give you whatever you need. Go out there and bring my boy back, Detective. Please. Sergeant Little will also lend a hand in filling whatever immediate needs you may request, within reason. If any other assistance is required as you go along, he will supply it."

The General turned and walked briskly out the door, as Sergeant Little saluted. Looking around, Roan noticed that General Renoir's glass of scotch was still untouched.

PRELUDE II

———

ADVERSARY UNSEEN

The young man sat alone in the room, waiting. What for, he didn't know. What he did know, in hindsight, was that they must have been searching for him for quite some time, and it had to have been an ongoing deep-cover operation; otherwise, one or more of his people on the street would undoubtedly have found a way to warn him. Dependency always bred dependability that way. Even his quick-minded cousins whom he'd been using as lieutenants had not been able to pick up on what the Enemy was up to; and this morning, after he got home from handling that business down in Mexico, agents had been right there in his residence, waiting for him. In the ensuing fight, two of theirs had gone down, never to rise again, and of course, his beautiful new studio apartment had been utterly trashed.

In the end, the home invaders won, taking him as a prisoner. There were too many of them there, waiting, and they used some sort of incapacitating technology that he hadn't yet bribed someone to get into his hands. Afterward, they'd somehow gotten him out, right past his own people, with none noticing. So, he surmised, the enemy must also have that hologram tech that he'd been hearing about, but contrary to what his spies had reported, it was online and activated. Faster than he'd expected. The sharp-eyed man made a mental note to self: "Get the moles to bring me up to speed on the bad guys' latest techno toys—if I get out of this alive." He couldn't understand why they hadn't just killed him already or at least given him a bone-crushing beating in repayment for the two they'd lost.

Without a doubt, he'd been a target of theirs for a long time now, especially after that peccadillo with the casinos dotting the Mississippi Gulf Coast right next door. Maybe that's what this is about, the young man thought. Whatever. He had no regrets for what happened there. How did a state that was the poorest in the Union only get as a far as being the second poorest in the Union after several billons-of bucks-a-year businesses like the casinos had taken over the entire coastline? There would never be a straight answer to that one. Didn't matter, anyway. They deserved what he'd done to them.

Not unexpectedly, a silent door in the opposite wall appeared, and a uniformed man walked in. The ribbons and medals he wore told the captive that the man was a colonel. A very brave and valiant colonel. What service branch, the prisoner couldn't tell—yet. "Who wears slate-gray uniforms?" he wondered aloud while trying to resist a mental panic. If the military had gotten involved, it meant that the Enemy finally had the entire government in their pockets, after all. The Colonel, for his part, only regarded him with a frosty smile. "We've been looking for a chance to spend some quality time with you for a while now," he began without preamble.

"Nice to meet you too," the detainee replied, with exaggerated politeness. "With whom do I have the honor of chatting today?"

The Gray Colonel just gave him that frigid smile again. He seated himself across from his prisoner and placed a holographic file chip on the table between them. It projected sheets of data into the air above it, and the Colonel began to silently read whatever was recorded on them.

The captive knew an intimidation tactic when he saw one, so rather than taking the bait and beginning to talk or ask questions, he just sat silently, a slight irreverent smile on his face, watching his captor read. He would have leaned back, put his hands behind his head, and relaxed, but the chair was a restraint chair, and he could only sit bolt upright, with his arms on the armrests. After a silence, his colonel spoke. "You're a very good hand-to-hand combatant. Just what we needed," he said, with no inflection at all in his voice. It was definitely not the tack the prisoner had expected. He laughed out loud. "Well, sir," he said, mockingly (extra emphasis on "sir"), "if you'll just deactivate the restraint field on this torture chair, I'd be happy to demonstrate just how good a hand-to-hand combatant I am."

"That's not one of our torture chairs," the military officer replied in a matter-of-fact way, seemingly still distracted by his reading. "Those are kept in a different location." The younger man stopped smiling.

Something went click in his thinking just then, and the prisoner said, "The fact that you have such humane *devices, yet I'm not strapped into one screaming my lungs out, tells me that you want me to do something for you, don't you, now? And whatever the dirty deed might be, you want to keep it secret."*

The Gray Colonel raised his head from his reading, and in his eyes, the captive could see that he'd struck a nerve of truth. Covering his own surprise with a steely stare, the colonel answered, "Everyone has blind spots. Did you know that? Of course you do. You always have. But you've tried to cover all or any of yours, haven't you?" The Gray Colonel paused for a moment, no doubt with the intent of causing his captive more discomfort. It worked, but the prisoner wasn't about to allow his anxiety to show. "Do you know what your problem is, though?" he resumed. "I don't think so. Well, I'll tell you. You imagine yourself as emotionally invulnerable, believing you have no soft spots that could be exploited, but you don't see that you really have two serious vulnerabilities. The first is your inability to discern your most serious weakness. Now, of course, you have no idea what weakness we could possibly have found in you, so I'll tell you, free of charge.

"You're known as a man who loves nothing, who attaches himself to no one. But that's only because this is a facade that you have created in order to protect what you really do love." The colonel projected a tri-dee photo of HER into the air between himself and the bound man, then went on. "We got your first mole . . . you know which one—the woman you convinced to compromise her father's security and surveillance system. She was destined to spend the rest of her existence in solitary confinement somewhere in a hole underneath Leavenworth for that little act of treason. We made sure you knew this, counting on your attachment to her as a means to capture and deal with you. Yet you seemed to do nothing. Not a big surprise, we thought. You have always used people with various moral—debilities to do your illegal drudgery, and then you've satisfied their inexhaustibly abysmal cravings as rewards for their work in your behalf. Yet if one of your agents is captured, all and any ties to yourself are cut, and that poor unfortunate idiot is on his or her own. So, of course, you'd abandon her. Or so it would seem."

The prisoner's eyes widened at what he was sure would follow. What had they done to her? He tried to lean forward, but the chair's restraining field held him tightly. All he could move was his head and neck. His lips twitched as if he wanted to speak, but was instead, holding his words in as well as his obvious anger.

Seemingly self-satisfied, The Gray Colonel shut his file chip off by pressing its side stud, then replaced it in whichever one of his uniform pockets it had been drawn out of. Folding his hands upon the tabletop, he continued. "Yes, as you have already surmised, we now know how well you have been caring for her. We don't know how you managed to suborn penitentiary robotics programming, but you did. I even went to Fort Leavenworth to see for myself and can honestly say that I have never seen a detainee there who has lived as well, with all the amenities of home, as she is living with. You have definitely cared for her. Even *her cell's sentry robotics' programming has been altered, and they have become her personal handmaidens and body guards."*

His prisoner interrupted with, "Hey, Colonel, did you ever get to see that movie, Inglorious Basterds*? No? Yes? Well, I just gotta say, you really remind me of the bad guy in that movie. You know, all talk, talk, talk. Why don't you just get to the point, man?"*

The Colonel didn't reply to his captive's badgering. Instead, he just gave the man another of his frigid smiles and calmly went on. "We were truly amazed that the prison's oversight systems had also somehow been distorted to make it appear that she was suffering the same as all the other guests with which she is sharing federal custody, but the puzzle of how you managed that only added to our understanding of the fact that you must have a deep personal resourcefulness which we could put to better uses. What we have wondered, though, is why, with this obvious ability to override top secret federal programming, you didn't just convince the prison to simply set her free."

The prisoner answered, "You said 'is living with,' not 'was living with,' so, then, you didn't take her comforts away?"

"No," the colonel replied, smiling coldly at his captive's obvious refusal to answer his tangential inquiry, "and we won't. But we will also not release her. Yet."

The prisoner's eyes stared with intensity at his captor for a long moment, then he laughed. "Aha! So you do *want something from me, and it is a big, bad, government secret. I think that's great, Colonel. The barter system at work. So why don't you cut the juice to this dentist's chair and let's get down to some horse trading."*

The Gray Colonel's cold smile returned. "No, again," he answered. "You still don't understand. Let's go back to that business about blind spots. Well, you see, it seems we have found another one of yours. Your problem is that you love. Though you hide it well, you still do love. Here you are, a confirmed criminal and would-be homegrown antigovernmental terrorist, yet you have such deep concern and love within. For a man in your chosen field, that's very dangerous. A critical liability, even. Your feeling for her is obvious, but what you don't see is how much you also love that tribe of cousins that you have been using as officers in your personal army. You love them, you love their families, you love their pets and their houses and their lives. But you can't show it, for if you did, some of the less trustworthy ones might turn on you. Or perhaps the ones you love more would be used as levers against you. You know this. Again, you always have."

The Colonel leaned forward, peering at his prisoner. He then began to explain. "Well, we're going to use them exactly that way. As levers. Starting with your least favorites, we will take away everything that matters to them, and though they may not be tortured to death, at least not immediately, we will break their minds and emotions into pieces, painfully and slowly, bit by bit. We will dismember their lives, their families, their happiness, right under your nose while you are watching, and you won't be able to stop it unless you do what we need you to do. Thoroughly, efficiently, and to the very best of your formidable ability." The detainee's face hardened as his captor continued. "We are well aware of your fiascos and forays aimed at changing the system. We haven't interfered because for the most part, your actions have not been harmful to the interests of national security. Also, what you had your people do to ISIS and Al-Qaeda's representatives—don't look so surprised, of course, we know about that—seemed to demonstrate where your true loyalties lie. You may not have a lot of love for your country's government, but you won't be a traitor either. Not yet, anyway."

Leaning back as if he were the cat who'd just eaten a very satisfying canary, the colonel in gray summed up his case: "Well, now we need you. We need your special abilities to deal with a possible threat that may be coming out of that phantom zone you disappear into and out of and we are not going to trade, barter, or negotiate for your cooperation. This threat may only be to our own soil at the moment, but the whole world could suffer from its long-range effects. So you're going to help save the world, son, whether you want to or not. Now, if you'll be a good villain and cooperate with us, then, when this is over, I just might see to it that you get her back. Hell, I may even let you be the 'hero' of the affair. After all, given the choice of exposing your organization or ours, yours is the one we'd choose for the media frenzy."

Colonel Gray Coat gestured, the restraining field went away, and the younger man stood and began to rub his wrists as if he'd been tied up. Tilting his head, he cast an appraising look at the colonel. A predatory smile began to form at the corners of his mouth. "Kind of risky, letting me loose like that, don't you think?" he asked.

The Colonel stood up and stared at the prisoner for a moment. "No," he answered. "It isn't risky at all, son." Then he blinked and vanished. The prisoner laughed. "A hologram, eh, Colonel? Guess you didn't want risk getting your highly decorated neck broken after all, now, did you?"

The silent door opened again, and a robotic drifted in, carrying a steel attaché case. Its smoothly metallic voice began. "Within this case, sir, you will find a uniform designed to help you better endure the physical anomalies that we suspect comprise whatever space is within the zone. As a side effect, it will also enhance your speed and strength, but if used outside of that area without proper authorization, its programming will kill you instantly." Its midsection opened, and a stack of official-looking documents floated out. "This is your waiver of rights document, acceptance of risk documents, medical and pay grade documentation, as well as a last will and testament, should you choose to use it."

The new Agent laughed. "Pay grade?" he sneered. "Since when did people who were compelled into government service get a pay grade?"

"It's the law, sir," the robotic replied, sounding as close to condescending as an automation could. The captive just smiled and stared at the machine for a moment or two. Suddenly and without warning, the young man's leg moved faster than a human eye could have followed, and the robotic's head flew off, leaving its remains to fall to the floor, emitting sparks and oil. The prisoner visibly relaxed then, mentally preparing himself for the inevitable flood of federal agents that he expected would no doubt swarm into the holding cell. Any minute now, *he thought.* I have to see how much they need me, and if they do come in, there's a little something I've been waiting to try.

But the door never opened. No one charged in to deal the captive any punishment for his blatant disrespect and destruction of government property. Five minutes later, Colonel Hologram suddenly appeared again. He looked with approval at the damaged machine. "I never did like the idea of using those things, but honestly, I've never seen one taken apart that fast with that much efficiency," he said. Turning to the younger man, he said, "You're definitely the man we want on this. But that's not normally like you, losing control and attacking a simple automation that way. You must be more shaken up than we thought. Nevertheless, you will still begin and complete your mission, or as I told you, others in your personal world will suffer." He looked once more at the smoking robotic, then said to the younger man, "You can be a scary person sometimes, son."

Looking at the cameras located at the junction of the ceiling and walls, the young man said, "When he wakes up, tell him to never again call me 'son.' He's not my father." After which, he stuck his finger into the holographic projection, right between its eyes. The projection immediately shorted out, with plenty of electrical discharge, and somewhere within the facility, the real Gray Colonel went into a seizure and passed out, having suffered a very nasty tazing to his forehead. The younger man quietly said, "I am a very scary person. All the time." He then opened the attaché case and began reading the suit's instructions in preparation for his first mission.

FRIENDS IN ABSENTIA

After the the dinner he'd had at his own home, General Nigel Boyd Renoir left Roan Caldwell there with Amadeus Kruger, Derron Leonard and his wife, and boarded a helicopter that was waiting on top of the building where he'd originally briefed the Detective. United States Air Force Major Martin Braggs was inside, finishing up with the flight plan from Patrick Air Force Base to Melbourne International Airport in Melbourne, Florida. He smiled the way he usually did as soon as he caught sight of his Commanding Officer striding toward him. Most of his coworkers didn't know that whenever things were sane enough for humor, the great and fear-inspiring General Nigel B. Renoir exhibited the best sense of humor of any commanding officer Martin Braggs had ever served with. He'd always make some observation, usually imparted with the utmost seriousness that would cause the officers to erupt in laughter during their staff meetings. Thinking of such moments always made Braggs feel good about serving under his General.

Major Braggs held hope that the crushing weight of command over such an open-ended mission would never kill the General's ability to laugh, and right now, the man was more relaxed than Marty had seen him in a long time. Good. *The Old Man's meeting with that bullheaded Detective Dude must've turned out well*, Marty thought. Maybe that guy's cooperation really *was* "the key to Nigel's future and our victory," as General Renoir had so aptly put it.

"Well, sir," Marty ventured as he took off, "is he on board with us now?" The General stared out of the window for a moment or so then answered, "It would appear so, Major. I believe that he'll be able to contact 'Petit Deaux' before I would. If this Detective Caldwell is the same as the others, his integrity of character will get through to our boy. If it works, we will soon be in a position to turn things around at home. Might even be closer to finding a safer way to deploy the cure." The pilot nodded. He knew that for now, that would be the only answer he'd get.

In a room within a Marriott Residence Inn located near the Melbourne International Airport in Melbourne Beach, Florida, Major Archimus Marcelon, Captain Walter Ralph Arthur McGrath, and Captain Logan Eller were "applying Mike-up," as the MISTmen referred to the procedure. It was a very painful process, part of the complex training they'd undergone so many years before. The men sat cross-legged on the floor, concentrating, marshalling their willpower for what they had to do. As they sat in silence, their facial features began to change: a widening of the space between the eyes, a jawline lengthened, a little forehead widening in some cases. The whole exercise would, when completed, cause the facial features of each man to change. Their looks would become just different enough to defeat detection through facial recognition security protocols. Each man could recall with utmost clarity the gravel-like voice of Colonel Jason Darting. "When you have completed this exercise, you will either be dead, or you will be Mike the nobody! Mike Plain Face!" Colonel Darting could go on with so many different "Average Mike" names and allegories that eventually the MISTmen began to refer to the whole process as "putting on Mike-up" or "Miking-up." It was rumored among them that the Mike-up process could even be used to change skin pigmentation or eye color, but no one they knew of had ever tried to take it so far. Not many of them could say what level of commitment such a choice would require; fewer wanted to find out. The changes were excruciatingly agonizing to make and maintain, only holding in place for as long as the individual's will could overcome the pain.

The men were all officers attached to Crossover Team Alpha, and they were about to walk through the Melbourne International Airport. When their faces were captured by airport security cameras, none of them needed to be identifiable. Equipped with keycards and passwords where needed, they would not be apprehended as they passed through the airport to a private hangar owned by Craine & Wilson Logistics. But then, being apprehended wasn't what they were worried about. They just didn't want to be recognized. When they arrived at their destination, they were met by Major Marty Braggs, who was waiting beside a Gulfstream G650ER, code-named *Little Bird*. The plane had been coated with their Refraction

Polymer shortly after the Preservation Hall Society purchased it from a failing real estate company at a tremendous discount of twenty million in cash instead of the sixty-three million that it was actually worth. That was one advantage of the housing market crash of 2008 in the world where Nigel the younger had been born. Overpriced, unnecessary toys formerly owned by real estate sharks could be bought at cut-rate pricing.

Once inside, the MIST officers let their biometric alterations fade away, took a moment to subjugate the pain, and then put on their OTTO gear. They were going to their base of operations for Mission CureSearch, a clandestine airfield located on private property in the place they called R-1, N-1 or N-Prime, Nigel's world. Before it left its hangar, *Little Bird*'s Refraction device was activated. Major Martin Braggs already had access to the flight plans of every aircraft between Melbourne, Florida, and Franklinton, Louisiana, so there was little or no danger of collisions on the ground or in the air. The plane taxied down its designated runway and took off with no unfortunate incident. No small feat, considering the fact that the aircraft was invisible to the outside world. In fact, there was no detection device in this world that could have pinpointed their location or presence.

Once over the Gulf of Mexico, Major Braggs reduced speed, activated the autopilot, and donned his own OTTO gear. He knew that the rest of *Little Bird*'s passengers had already done so by now if they wanted to survive the next few seconds with their minds intact. That done, he then opened up a panel located to the right of his pilot's seat. The panel would only respond to the palm prints of three persons: General Nigel B. Renoir, Brigadier General Benjamin Gary, or Major Martin Braggs. After determining the identity of the palm print, other nanosensors within would determine whether the person's hand was still attached to its body, whether or not the person was under duress, and whether or not the individual heart's harmonics and DNA frequency matched those recorded for each different personage with the clearance to open it. If the panel were forced open, the entire plane would disintegrate in an acidic fireball. Contained within the small compartment behind the panel was a small four-inch-by-four-inch copper box with the same safeguards, and within that, set upon its velvet liner, was an even smaller two-inch-by two-inch silver box with an attached USB. Inside of this silver box, suspended in a hyperconductive gel, was one baby tooth from a wide-eyed little boy who had once called Major Martin Braggs "Captain America."

For just a moment, Martin Braggs's eyes held tears as he regarded the box with its precious cargo. He hadn't personally seen Nigel in quite a few years, though all of Crossover Team Alpha's members had kept close track of what was happening in the boy's life. They all grieved with Nigel when his "Fight Club" members had been murdered, had approved of how he, as the Fight Club's Commander, had plotted his revenge on the killers, then cheered General Renoir's solution to that problem. Oh yes, they had gone to see his fights too, for none of them wanted to lose their connection with their beloved "Baby Marine." He wasn't just the son of The General, he was the son of Crossover Team Alpha; and when his MIST abilities manifested themselves, that just confirmed everything they'd held dear about the boy. He was one of theirs.

His reverie ended, and Major Braggs took the little silver box out of its compartment, then plugged its USB into a port on his control panel. Immediately, the plane's windows went black, a new feature for which Braggs was exceedingly grateful to Kruger and Associates. No one inside wanted to see the vista outside, least of all Martin Braggs. He still remembered the unfortunate events that befell him on his last two "firsts" through the nil zone: On his first flight through with a full crew, being knocked senseless by a treble clef, of all things. Later, when he had his first opportunity to walk through that hell, his stomach had revolted as soon as it was over. Not the most dignified behavior for the only Air Force Officer attached to an Elite Marine Squad.

Little Bird's engines began to whine as they did battle with the forces it passed through, and "the roller coaster ride," as Crossover Team Alpha called the passage, began. The plane heaved, seemingly in all directions at once, with excessive speed in all cases. The torture went on for three seconds, those three seconds that always went by like three hours, and it was over. The windows cleared up, the flight stabilized, and Roy-Bob Joseph's voice came over the radio. "Hey, Major! Major sir! Y'all all right in there?"

Braggs smiled at the man's lack of formality. "Yes, Sergeant," he answered. "Is the strip clear?"

"Shore as shootin', sir," Sergeant Roy Robert Joseph replied. "The Gen'rl's got thet conferince room all warm 'n' toasty fer ye fellers."

"Well, Roy-Bob," Major Braggs replied, "that's great, especially since we've got General Renoir with us this time."

380

The voice on the other end fell into an astonished silence. When it resumed, the relaxed tenor of the previous conversation had disappeared. "I'll notify Brigadier General Gary, sir. Will General Renoir require any special arrangements?"

"He says to tell General Gary that he wants to meet with him privately first," Braggs answered.

"Yes, *sir*," Sergeant Joseph answered with Marine precision.

He's worried that we have some sort of bad news. Major Braggs thought. *Wish I could tell him not to worry, but I have no idea why the General came with us this time either.* Braggs was pretty sure they'd all find out soon enough.

***

Brigadier General Benjamin Gary wasn't dead. He never had been. Not long after Crossover Team Alpha's arrival in R-3 and their first meeting with the President of the United States there, Crossover Team Alpha's Executive Officer appeared to have had a heart problem that could have led to his end in that world. All along, though, General Renoir had already chosen to order then-Colonel Benjamin Gary to return, take command of the Walking Dead Raiders and exercise oversight of the administration of all the Preservation Hall Society's assets in N-1, Nigel's world. Those assets were too deeply embedded there for any effective liquidation, and in that reality, Crossover Team Alpha had unrestricted access to every single bit of the internet. Nothing therein was unattainable for them.

The bugs and spyware that Kruger and Leonard originally created had now become an integral part of the World Wide Web there. Such a strategically strong position should never be yielded, and it wouldn't be. It also needed to be kept secure and uncompromised. Doing so required the presence of a capable commanding officer in that location, one whose loyalties were unquestionable, and Colonel Benjamin Gary of the MIST was the man for it. After Crossover Team Alpha's arrival in R-3, as Roan's world was referred to, the customary search for the team's doubles had gone forward, as usual. In this place, as in the several others they'd visited, they found that most of their doubles invariably had pursued the same or similar life courses as they themselves had. Over the course of their careers, some of those people had met with the same or better level of success as their own, others not so much.

The man who was Ben Gary's second was one of the latter. He was within a few months of the same age and had risen to the rank of captain when the accident that destroyed his family occurred. For this Captain Ben Gary, however, there was no relief to be found in an assignment to some other dimension. He had to live with his loss, and that affected him badly. His performance faltered more and more, so that eventually, his career stalled at the rank of captain. General Renoir and Colonel Gary immediately realized how this man could become part of their team; he was the same person as the Benjamin Gary of Crossover Team Alpha, with two very important differences: there was no Maureen Sampson or Crossover Team Alpha in his life. The commanding officers of Crossover Team Alpha felt that if those two things could be added, General Renoir could reasonably attain another man as valuable to him as the Executive Officer he already had, thus enabling the "original" Benjamin Gary to return to their N-1 headquarters. So he and the Colonel Gary of his world immediately set about concocting a plan, one that would allow the General to have access to one of his most trusted advisers as well as having that same man return to administer the assets Crossover Team Alpha had left behind.

Meanwhile, the Captain Gary of this reality had gone about his duties, day by day, with a growing listlessness. His was a monotonous existence that remained unaltered until a certain woman stepped into his drab world, bringing sunlight and vivid color to his life. She seemed to be everything that the man could have ever wanted in a partner, but eventually, the woman began to pressure him to do things that violated his position and oath. Captain Gary was in charge of requisitions, and his newfound love was, in reality, planted by a racist terror group. That organization wanted access to military hardware and had wrongly assumed that Captain Gary would share their views, considering the way his career had, in their eyes, been hindered by too much emphasis on diversification among Marine officers. Of course, their assessment of the man's character was wrong. They didn't expect him to go to NCIS with the situation, and even less did they expect to be infiltrated by one of that agency's operatives. Still, that was what happened.

When the dust settled and everything was over, Capt. Benjamin Othell Gary was promoted to Major and given an assignment that paralleled the very same one he'd had before. A listless and marginally effective posting. Truthfully, the man was expected to resign his commission soon. He continued to live a life of loneliness in his off-base apartment, dying little by little with every passing month, until the fateful day that he was contacted by a newly structured Black Ops unit known only as IDEA Control. He met and spoke at length with a General Renoir, who apparently came to different conclusions than every other superior officer who previously assessed him. Immediately after that interview with the general, Major Benjamin O. Gary was reassigned to IDEA Control and appointed to head up the agency's requisitions and supply division. He was also assigned a civilian assistant, one Maureen Sampson, whose charm and personality he found irresistible. Without a doubt, they became a couple, and to the Major, it always seemed that General Renoir knew this would happen. Actually, it was more likely, Major Gary frequently thought, that the general and his wife, Dr. Angeline Renoir, together comprised the driving force behind Ms. Sampson's being assigned to his office. Ultimately, it really wasn't important to him *whose* idea it had been to make the assignment—he was just happy to have her in his life.

Resultantly, the quality of his work improved as his whole disposition toward everything changed for the better. He was promoted, eventually, to Lieutenant Colonel, and with that came more assignments that required him to wear the uniform less. He frequently met with congressional members, business leaders, and the like, sometimes in undercover roles, other times in an official capacity. The Lieutenant Colonel was a "spook," as he still thought of such a role, and he was good at it. More than anything else, he had his General's respect, seemingly from before the moment they'd officially met. The man seemed to know, more than he himself had, what the lieutenant colonel was capable of, and Gary appreciated that. When he learned who Nigel was to the General, Lieutenant Colonel Benjamin O. Gary resolved to do all he could to help keep the young man safe. It was the choice to honor that resolve that ultimately cost him his life.

The end began when he was approached by a representative from one of the country's more clandestine and dangerous espionage agencies with a proposition: if he would assist them in attaining control over Nigel's comatose body, "strings would be pulled" in his behalf, and he'd become the commanding officer of IDEA Control. Such a command would, of necessity, come with access to all of that agency's resources, as well as any wealth resulting from its missions. No, the agent told him, Nigel wasn't comatose at the moment, but things may change soon.

When he finished his pitch, Lieutenant Colonel Benjamin O. Gary simply shot him in the face with his .45, then notified General Renoir.

Once again, his strength of character had been wrongly assessed. Within the next week, the agent officially became just another operative listed as KIA during a classified mission. The mastermind behind the plot, the handler who'd sent the defunct agent with his proposition, was soon exposed to IDEA Control; but Lieutenant Colonel Gary decided, against General Renoir's tacit recommendation, to do nothing that might harm the man. He saw it as just another case of a loyal officer being given an appalling mission along with untrustworthy intelligence and trying to do his best. He honestly thought that General Renoir's superiors would handle the problem more effectively. Before the higher powers could even get involved though, the cabal behind the scheme saw to that its man was moved to a different clandestine assignment. One month later, the newly-promoted Colonel Benjamin O. Gary and his wife, Maureen Sampson-Gary, were killed in an airplane accident that shouldn't have happened.

As he sat in the meeting room of the Franklinton home, the General's residence and Crossover Team Alpha's headquarters in Franklinton, Louisiana, General Nigel Boyd Renoir thought back to his last conversation with the other Benjamin Gary. It had been friendly and cordial, as all of their interactions were. No matter what world or incarnation, that man was always a good one and a loyal friend. The one here, whom he'd known longer, had been a member of the first class of MIST-trained Marines back home, along with him. They'd been friends from the day they met, back in Annapolis. Renoir was the first to answer the call for MIST training, Benjamin Gary following right behind him. Renoir knew that they would always be friends no matter what world they were in.

Using Nigel's baby teeth as beacons, Crossover Team Alpha could return here whenever the need arose now. General Renoir had decided that piece of information was one that did not have to be confided to the government of R-3 or Roan Caldwell in their recent conversation. It always amazed Crossover Team Alpha how such a small bit Nigel's of organic material could do so much, from setting up permanently open passageways between dimensions to establishing a firm link for telecommunications between the worlds. But the telecom link could only be used in certain windows of time, and each session had to be limited to two hours or less. Thus, General Renoir and Brigadier General Gary had been able to keep in touch over the years and synchronize their operations.

When Nigel crossed into his home world at the age of thirteen, Benjamin Gary and Maureen Sampson had been contacted immediately and sent to Broussard Park to meet him and ascertain the extent of public exposure as well as what, if anything, would be needed to contain it. They hadn't expected Federal Agent Roan Caldwell and his team to be on the scene before them, but that was what happened. They'd seen the rookie agent charge Nigel and Angeline with a drawn gun, and upon recognizing the glow that signaled imminent destruction within the young man's eyes, Brigadier General Gary shoved Maureen Sampson to the ground and covered her with his body, fully expecting to die there. They didn't see how that disaster was averted, but Gary knew that the young Angeline must have done something to stop Nigel from calling the conflagration from *otherspace* out upon them all. When Detective Caldwell and team approached to make sure that he and Maureen were not harmed, they pretended to be shaken up by the agent's charge in their direction with gun in hand. Okay, citizen, we apologize; the agent mistook you for someone else, yada, yada . . . Even as he saw that the two teens had somehow gotten away, he also recognized the pattern of speech in the federal agents' apologies; they were trying to find out how much he and Maureen had seen, whether they knew anything about Nigel. That told General Gary that they'd been expecting the boy.

Although pretending otherwise, he'd heard what the other agents had been yelling to their boss about: an energy spike that seemed to precede Nigel's arrival. The thought of MPIS being able to predict the boy's arrival chilled Benjamin Gary's blood. He, for his part, needed to avoid being detained for any reason, since General Renoir needed to know about this as soon as possible. So Maureen and Benjamin played dumb. "Oh, Agent Caldwell sir, we were *so* frightened . . ." so on and so forth. Anyone could see that their story was accepted as the truth, but he also knew that someone in Roan's office would run a background check on the two of them anyway, just in case. Hopefully, his "identity" would hold up: just a middle-aged moderately successful small business owner, out for a nice walk with his wife, in the wrong place at the worst possible time. The backstopping did hold up. The random businessman and his wife were dismissed as unimportant and consequently forgotten by Roan Caldwell and team.

When Brigadier General Benjamin Gary walked into the meeting room, his commanding officer, General Renoir, was standing at the window, watching the sunset. "It's been a while, Ben," he said without looking around. Gary smiled. *So it wasn't some worlds-shaking catastrophe*

385

that brought the old man here. Must be something else. He stood to attention and saluted. General Renoir turned and regarded his second in command. Benjamin Gary was about five ten, brunette hair, marine regulation cut, going gray at the temples. He had a friendly smile that usually made people feel welcome and comfortable in his presence, without the chiseled features and prominent cheekbones of a Martin Braggs. His face was lean, but seemed to be structured with more circles than angles. The man had steel blue eyes that gave the only hint of how deadly he could be, if necessary. He looked, for all intents and purposes, like an average guy from the suburbs who kept himself in decent shape, not a failure, not a celebrity. He'd chosen dress blues for this meeting with his General, saluted, and stood to attention as a gesture of respect. The gesture was appreciated.

General Renoir said, "Thanks, Ben, but you and I don't need to stand on ceremony. We've been through too much together, man. At ease. Sit. Let's talk a few things over." They seated themselves in two of the chairs that surrounded the conference table. At just the right time, Charles Lubkin, ex-navy steward turned "galley supervisor" for Crossover Teams Alpha and the Walking Dead Raiders came in with a pot of The Old Man's favorite chicory coffee and commenced service. He'd also remembered to include several of the authentic Danishes that the General favored. "Hello, Chuck," General Renoir said with a smile in his eyes. "How are your sons doing?"

"Excellent, General sir. I'll never thank you enough for what you folks did. They woulda spent the rest of their lives being held prisoner over there if it weren't for you." He too, stood to attention and saluted.

"At ease, Chuck. I appreciate the snack."

"Yes, sir," Lubkin replied before he exited the room. The brass needed to talk.

A slight pressure behind their ears told the two men that the anti-surveillance systems had initiated. General Renoir began. "The Angeline of that place has been murdered by her husband, Ben."

Gary's eyes widened. "Does Little Nige know?"

"Yes," General Renoir answered, "and his reaction is not at all what we'd have expected. He hasn't gone insane or charged off to destroy the man. He actually tried to enlist someone to help him bring the husband to justice. Someone we know well." Benjamin looked up from the cream he was about to add to his coffee. "Caldwell?"

"Yes, that man seems to be inescapable for us," Renoir observed then went on. "I've talked to that version of him on the other side earlier today.

He has agreed to help us open a dialogue with Nigel, in return for our assistance in getting these murderers to jail. Yes. There were two of them. It seems that the former husband, one George Arlander, has an . . . alternate choice of lifestyles. He apparently liked to mix AC and DC, so to speak. But all of this is just side drama.

"We have at least two other concerns of a higher priority," he explained. "Evidence indicates that Nigel's memories are returning faster than we'd expected. So is his ability. This event may have caused some override in his mental conditioning, thus forcing the ability to find other pathways within his mind through which to manifest itself. He can move in and out of the nil zone within structures now. As a second, though equally serious matter of concern, Major Robin Lacy has almost definitely been captured by MPIS over here. On the surface, it looks as if he may have decided to try making the walk over alone without authorization or backup."

Ben Gary cursed. "What the f—"

"Now, Ben," the general cautioned, "remember your station. We must be men who keep themselves under iron-like self-control at all times." General Renoir felt that the only place an officer should use coarse language was on the battlefield or when addressing the enlisted men. *Oh well*, Gary thought *All great generals have their quirks.*

Brigadier General Benjamin Gary stood up and walked over to the window, taking a moment to rein in his anger over Robin Lacy's seemingly rash actions and gather his thoughts. After a brief pause, he asked, "Why? What was he trying to accomplish, Nige?"

"I can't say for certain," General Renoir started, "but the story I told their SECNAV was all about how it may have been that Major Lacy had some reason to suspect imminent danger coming toward his daughter, Dana. They were also told how it's possible that he just thought he'd go in as an infiltrator, which was going to be his next assignment, anyway."

Benjamin Gary rubbed his chin with his hand then asked, "Nige, I know how you prefer to trust your officers' loyalties. What do you think, though, of the possibility that the same people who tried to turn my doppelganger have managed to turn Robin Lacy somehow?"

"No, Ben. That wasn't the case," came the reply. Now General Renoir stood up. He walked across the room to stand next to his friend. For a moment, the only sound in the room was Miles Davis's *'Round About Midnight.*

After enjoying the music for a minute, General Renoir exhaled. "Ben," he began, "the possibility exists that Major Robin Lacy *had* to cross over to avoid being captured or killed by his own double. They've found a way to cross or, at the very least, enter the void. The DOD on that side concluded that our Robin Lacy instigated the crossover, but I didn't record the entirety of my interrogation of their Robin Lacy. Under duress, the man told a different story. Somehow, their experimentation has added a reverse effect. If the entrants' duplicate is anywhere near the spot where one of theirs enters the zone, that duplicate will be drawn into this reality, like water flowing down a drain. There seems to be some law of substitution fault within their crossover tech that forces this. Anyone crossing from here to there must have the space they occupied on this side of the nil zone filled. "

Benjamin Gary felt his blood chill, then blaze as he considered the implications. He and General Nigel B. Renoir stood for a few moments more. "So now I see why you came here yourself. Nige, neither this world nor that one is ready for the repercussions of reality hopping. They don't know what they're calling in on themselves. The Graise will find them if they keep it up."

"Yes, Ben," General Renoir said, "they will. And if such were to occur, it could mean the end of their world. We saw the wasteland they made of ours. With our level of technical advancement, ours was one of the only civilizations that could have stood against them had not those two . . . *subhuman sadists* so effectively weakened humanity when they murdered ninety percent of the human race with their plague. That doomed us as much as the short destructive world war that followed did." Benjamin Gary stood with his head down. Paying homage to the honored dead, for just that moment. Then he raised his head and began to tell General Renoir how things had been progressing on his side. "Well, Nige, we at least haven't been compromised. As soon as Kruger, Leonard, and associates learned about the energy spikes, they were able to force the N-1 system to classify the ones around here as 'naturally occurring phenomenon.' Any traces that IDEA Threat Agency picks up here will be considered ordinary. We can also instigate identical, random spikes."

General Renoir nodded his approval. "So then Lucius Carver has been able to continue his visits with his wife?"

Gary smiled. "Yes, Nige, he has. I lost a bet on that, I know. Guess I owe you a C-note. We've got Little Kruger on board too. He's every bit as sharp as the one from our world. Actually, Nige . . ." The Brigadier General paused for a moment then added, "Maureen and I have kind of taken the kid in. Over the past couple of years, he's become like our son. His mother did wind up being taken away by their DHS, as we expected, and the boy was about to be put into foster care. No one here knew his potential. Glad we listened to our Kruger."

Gary seemed to be trying to get around to some personal request, his commander thought. General Renoir nodded sagely then said, "Ben, I'd like Maureen and you to take steps toward legally adopting the boy, please. I'll cut orders authorizing that for you. I know what it means for one of us to have an opportunity to become a father." Ben Gary regarded his general with a "thank you" in his eyes. He had to turn his head so that the old man wouldn't see any sign of the moisture therein. He breathed a sigh of relief and spoke again.

"We've recruited Leonard's parents to work for us too. Their current economic situation in this world would have guaranteed that little Leonard would never have grown up to use his gifts, otherwise. They were stuck in government-funded housing in the toughest and poorest part of Chicago. The father is way brighter than anyone knew, so I've installed him as head of a computer security company franchising agency. Additionally, we've found out who it was that accompanied Agent Caldwell when little Nige came over eight years ago. It was his Angeline. She was also the person he was with when they lasered him three or four years ago."

For the first time in a long time, Ben Gary had the satisfaction of seeing General Renoir truly shocked into speechlessness. "Wh—what? Is she . . . is she working with *them?* Against *Nigel?*"

Brigadier General Gary laughed. "No, Nige, she's not working with them. Actually, Roan Caldwell told us, sort of. He's kept her as a secret asset so that her life remains intact, safe from the MPIS interrogators, but he keeps a heavily encrypted log locked up tightly where he thinks they'd never find it. We found it, though, and added nano-safeguards to it after downloading a copy and bugging the thing. He doesn't even know. You see, sir, she instinctively knows when and where Nigel will be before his arrival on this side and after he exits *hellspace.* As far as we've seen, she doesn't know anything about us, so Roan was the only person she felt like she could trust. That's why she contacted him."

The General smiled. "Okay, Ben. You got me shook up there for a moment. But that is good news. Seems we may be able to help him get together with his wife, after all."

"There's more," Benjamin Gary interjected. General Renoir waited expectantly. "We've discovered that he took her into *Otherspace* unprotected back when they were thirteen years old, and she suffered no damage whatsoever. We also have yet to find out why Caldwell wasn't on hand the last time your boy visited. If he had been there, that fight may have been avoided. If he wasn't, then either he's been replaced since politics in this world are so partisan and cutthroat—he and Angeline aren't talking as much as we thought, possibly—or Nigel's breach was too fast and unexpected even for her to predict." Then he added, "By the way, the kid took down about eight to ten of their best. That boy of yours is nothing to play with."

General Renoir could hardly believe his own ears. "This Angeline can move through *otherspace*?"

Of course he's not surprised at what Nige Junior could do, Gary thought. *The Old Man knows what* he *could have done if he'd been born with his kid's ability.* "We're not sure if that's what it is," Brigadier General Gary answered. "Based on what we read in Caldwell's journal, it seems more likely that she can't. Although she can accompany Little Nige through there with no problem, she's never instigated a breach. Going by the way they feel about each other, she probably would have gone looking for him if it were possible for her."

"She would have," General Renoir assured him. General Gary took a deep breath. "Sir, you also need to know that we have found out that Nigel's brother DeVries is still alive and it seems that he, on the other hand, *can* move through *otherspace*."

General Renoir's gaze hardened. "Report," he said in that quiet, deadly tone that would have made anyone else want to run. Benjamin Gary, however, knew his friend. General Renoir was running a mental threat assessment and did not at all like what it was telling him.

"Last month, we measured energy spikes correlating to Nigel's. They were occurring, disappearing, and then reoccurring inside and around the casinos located on the Mississippi Gulf Coast. The traffic within their Law Enforcement Ethernet went up immediately as these spikes were happening. They were weaker, but still strong enough to get their attention." General Gary didn't realize that he'd stood to attention when he began his report, but General Renoir did. *He's worried. If this isn't Nigel, we may have another powerful enemy to contend with*, he thought, as Gary continued his report. "We narrowed in on the conversations and found that a person or persons unknown reportedly 'stepped out of nowhere' and robbed them blind. He kept disappearing and reappearing in the vaults, taking more of their money every time. When the guards shot at the person, he supposedly threw fire that consumed them. No evidence of heat damage or any other damage was found at the scene. Only the ashes of the dead."

"Why do you think it was DeVries and not Nigel?" the general asked.

"Lieutenant Carver assigned one of his MISTies to infiltrate the crime scene," Brigadier General Gary replied. "We searched for trace amounts of Renoir DNA and found a little bit. One of their bullets must've grazed him. We removed every bit of trace then checked the DNA wave frequency, sir. It matched Nigel's, but only to a certain percentage. The frequency indicated, with ninety-eight percent accuracy, a close relative, one to two years younger and male, most likely a brother. Also, the modus didn't match Nigel's way of doing things. We managed to find, within the police reports, a description of the suspect in the victims' debriefing of what they witnessed during the action."

Gary was smiling, now, which caught General Renoir's attention even more. His eyes hardened as he asked, "What, Ben? What else would you like to tell me about this?"

Benjamin Gary almost laughed when he replied, "Little Nige doesn't wear costumes to work. This guy did. He was dressed as some kind of Zorro with a *V for Vendetta* mask on."

General Renoir smiled. *No*, he thought, *Nigel wouldn't wear a costume, but if I know DeVries at all, he certainly would. And that particular look would definitely be his choice. He was always way flashier than me at times.* DeVries. Devvie. He really missed his younger brother, gone so many years ago. The General raised his eyes and said, "At ease, Ben. If it is DeVries, then, once again, I can assure you that we have nothing to worry about. Actually, he'll probably wind up working alongside Nigel, with us. We just have to get the two of them together."

"Well, sir," Benjamin Gary began, "I ordered Lieutenant C. C. Pendle to make contact and work with him loosely. He's been able to teach Mr. DeVries Renoir a lot about strategy and espionage. He's also been supplying him with some of our toys to use in the good fight."

General Renoir's eyes widened a bit. "Ben, that was kind of risky. But then, I imagine you'd already answered the question of whether or not he can go in and out of that place without being detected and traced by the Graise before making contact. Also, I honestly believe that if this DeVries met either his brother or me, he'd be easily recruited to our cause, but none of us could be sure. They didn't grow up together, though, and the Renoir family was dismantled early on in this world. These are things that cannot be ignored."

Benjamin Gary nodded agreement. "That is true, sir. But when I reviewed Lieutenant Pendle's reports, I realized that given the amount of time he's been bouncing in and out of *hellspace*, neither his existence nor his location have been determined by the enemy, or they'd have breached this reality by now. Young Mr. DeVries Renoir, for his part, has grown into the man your brother was back home. He can be trusted. He has your father's sense of honor just as you do. I'd also concluded that it was a risk, but it was one we really needed to take. He was already building an organization up on his own, and the PHS doesn't need to have any rivals here. Also, he's a good man, sir, with a real Robin Hood thing going on and would have done what he's doing with or without our help, but having him on our team is worth the risk."

General Renoir thought for a moment. He'd always trusted Benjamin Gary's judgment before, and this time would have to be no different. It was the only way he could effectively command two forces in two different realities and succeed. C. C. Pendle's selection as the person who would contact Nigel's brother was also a good choice. C. C. Pendle was a comedian and looked like it. His full name was Charleton Carlton Pendle, Charleton Carlton because his father thought that was a pretty funny name, and wearing such would likely cause his boy to have to grow up tough. The man was right. C. C Pendle was of average height, about five feet nine or so. The man was very dark skinned, well cut, and muscled in a way that made him look skinny whenever he was among the rest of the Walking Dead Raiders. He could be the funniest person in any room, but could also become the deadliest at any moment. The General also knew his own brother. DeVries would respond to humor when he wouldn't respond to anything else. Like most families with several children and little money, humor was one of the qualities that helped the Renoir family cope with the hard times. Yes, his second in command had chosen the right man for first contact with Devvie. Even though their family had not remained together past Hurricane Katrina, General Nigel Renoir was willing to bet that their tendency toward humor remained, and Benjamin had taken him up on that bet, so to speak. General Benjamin Gary had once again proven his worth.

"So where is he now, Ben?" he asked.

It was Brigadier General Gary's turn to take a deep breath before answering. "It looks like they may have captured him. If they have, that could answer the question of how they figured out a way to cross the zone. The internal MPIS communications we fished out of their communications tell us that they may also be using a hostage to coerce him into being their monkey boy slash hit man."

General Renoir nodded in agreement. He knew what it would take for DeVries to agree to work for any government agency against his will. "So now, Ben, we have hostages to set free. Robin Lacy as well as the woman whose life they are threatening in order to keep the string on DeVries. We will also need to snatch him out of their clutches, so that makes three rescues that need to be implemented. Most likely, the woman has remained unharmed. They'd never have gotten Devvie's cooperation, otherwise."

What *woman?* Benjamin Gary wanted to ask. Then he thought, *Of course he's figured it out. He knows what it would take to bend his own little brother.*

The General continued. "If I know my brother, they're using someone he's close to in order to twist his arm. That person is most likely to be one of our sisters or some other woman he values. We set her free, we get Dev on our side. The other person, our priority, is Major Robin Lacy. Have you gotten anything out of their net about where they're keeping him?"

"Yes, sir, we have," Benjamin Gary began. He waved his hand, and a projection manifested itself in the air in front of him. It looked like a five-walled prison citadel, built along the same plan as the Pentagon in Washington. "This is MPIS Detention Center A-21. It's located in Tule Valley, Utah, a perfectly dismal desert location with one paved road going through it, one prominent spring and lots of wild horses. They have the entry of the prison pentagon pointed due north. Weird thing with these guys; They love pointing things north."

General Renoir shook his head. "Well, Ben," he said, "that looks like a seriously hostile environment. And I suppose they're keeping the major stashed in some bunker deep, deep underground, surrounded by well-armed, ham-fisted guards."

Benjamin Gary chuckled. "That would have made sense, Nige, but they lost the funding wars the year they laid out the final plan and began construction for this monstrosity. So MPIS never got the money they needed to go underground to a great extent. There's only two sublevels, and they keep their torture chairs in the lowest. Actually, their justice department managed to have the use of torture without their explicit approval declared illegal. That means that the torture chambers and chairs are officially nonexistent."

"Oh yeah," General Renoir said, "those. I hate those types of things. Still, torture did work well for us with Muldowney of R-3, so I guess it has its merits."

"Yeah," Benjamin Gary agreed. "The one from here passed away crying like a baby and begging to be spared. Master Guns Carver and I were there to witness it. We wanted to make sure he died. Did you know that before he was executed, MPIS had tortured him for information about Savanne Road? You did? Oh well, moving on then. They'll likely have Major Lacy in the southern section of the sublevel. Without a doubt they're torturing him, but we have no idea what he may have given up by now. We've determined that this is also the location where they're holding DeVries Renoir. He's not in the sublevel though. They aren't torturing him, so they must want something from him. That's why we concluded that they want to use him as some type of agent."

"Well, Brigadier General Gary, I guess we'll just have to go get them out of there then, won't we?" General Renoir asked rhetorically. After speaking thus, he stood quietly for a few moments that stretched on. Any other person may have thought that the man had gone catatonic, but Brigadier General Gary knew better. His commander was going through innumerable mental visualizations from which he would draw his strategy. Some of the MIST trainees had the ability to mentally visualize thousands of probabilities per second, and these were the candidates selected to be commanding officers within the MIST Corps. Their training was always far more intense, with a greater potential for a painful death. But those who survived were the absolute best of the Marine Corps, which, in Benjamin Gary's opinion, was the absolute best of all armed forces, anyway. General Renoir was one of the first to exhibit what came to be known as visualization ability, and he was, to his men, the best there ever was. As he regarded his commander standing at the window, his dark-brown unlined face in a sleeplike repose, eyes closed, Gary genuinely regretted the fact that their civilization, which produced such men, had died.

The General had to be close to sixty years old now; and although he was still chiseled like a young man, still deadly as a sea snake, looking nowhere older than forty-five or fifty, the man was mortal and would die someday. The MIST training meant that his retirement age would be later than any other military branch officer's was, but the Corps would lose the last of the Visualization Commanders when that happened. Remotely, Brigadier General Gary wondered if the general's doppelganger son could be put through visualization training. Something he needed to talk over with the man later on. A "V-Officer" was not such a worthless thing, to be lost with no replacement. Meanwhile, the general's silence continued while jazz music from the likes of Wynton Marsalis and Miles Davis, along with Thelonious Monk and Charlie Parker played on in the background. General Renoir didn't *need* such music playing in order to do strategy visuals, he just loved having it when he did. Something else his executive officer wanted to keep tabs on. His general must never become dependent on outside stimuli in order to initiate the visualization process.

Renoir's eyes snapped open, and Gary knew what had to be coming next. "Okay, Ben, I have a plan," the general told him.

Not at all surprised, Gary simply asked, "Do you want to call an officer's briefing, or is this one for my ears only?"

"Call an officers' briefing, Ben. We'll need all hands on deck for this," General Renoir replied.

DEATH OF A TORTURER

In a far different location, Major Robin Lacy sat restrained in a chair that for all the world resembled a dentist's chair to his eyes. He couldn't see any bonds, but he couldn't move either, and it *felt* like he was tied up. Soon the little man with the funny glasses would return, and the questions would begin again. There was no pain involved, as of yet, but the questions were always hard to ignore. Major Lacy was glad that he'd taken the precaution of installing one of the improved will killer chips into his medulla oblongata. *What's a will killer chip?* he asked himself. *What was I thinking, putting it in my head that way?*

A sudden memory of a day when he was walking with the General came to mind. He could still recall The Old Man's speech: "Remember, advance preparation is an important key to military victory, especially in the shadows out of which we operate. The unknown can, by virtue of its very existence, come upon us unexpectedly, yet we can prepare for it all the same."

He could be wordy that way, General . . . Now why can't I remember his name? Major asked himself. *It's the will killer chip again, Rob. You're becoming as senile as General—What is his name, man? Come on, you've got to know it . . . Well, anyway, how do I get that thing out of my head?* He tried to think of the answer to that pummeling inquiry, but it wouldn't come. *Who improved this thing so much, anyway?* He tried to tell himself the name of the genius. It was . . .

All he could come up with was DC. *Why had he even come here to begin with? What was he after?* He'd wanted security for his baby girl, that's all. Wanted to be sure that she'd be safe. *Safe from whom? Does The Division know about us here?* Since he had no idea who or what "The Division" was, he could honestly tell them. "No. Don't know who they are." That was all he could tell them, though, nothing else. He could feel the frustration emanating from the little man with the funny glasses, but he had nothing he could give the man to help out with that.

The Little Man with the Funny Glasses who was seated beside the captive stood and stretched. Leaving his position bedside the I-Chair, he spoke to a uniformed colonel on the other side of the one-way digitally enhanced transparent steel glass. "Sir," he began after a proper salute.

The Gray Colonel came from behind the glass and gazed around the room for a moment, his sharp eyes missing nothing. Turning his attention to the Little Man with the Funny Glasses, he asked, "Well, Dawson, what have we gotten out of him?"

Looking down and shifting his feet, Dawson answered, "Sir, he installed something called a 'will killer' in his medulla oblongata before he was dragged over here through our equipment. We believe that it may be an organic assassination protocol and have taken measures to ensure that no service person whose name could possibly be shortened to any form of "Will" be allowed to participate in the investigation. Whatever this protocol is, it also interferes with the passive memory divulgence."

Exhaling in exasperation, the uniformed colonel asked, "How can you be sure that it's an assassination protocol? None of *our* assassins have ever made it to the other side or returned safely after they've penetrated the barrier. Somehow, their protocols invite death or catatonia when they're in there. Besides, he keeps saying 'will killer *chip*.' In my mind, that would imply something different."

"Sir," the little man began, "assassination protocols are the only technology that we have been able to organically weave into the human brain. Any other implant has to have *some* silicate trace elements. They are not as advanced as we are—the intrusion of five years ago taught us that. If we can't weave silicates into organic tissue, there's no way the guys on the other side could, given their comparative lack of technological development."

Gesturing toward Major Lacy with his chin, the Gray Colonel said, "He's not the same man from the intrusion. He looks older and is fair skinned. I've seen the footage. Did you ask him about that?"

"Yes, sir, I did," Dawson replied. "He once again got lost in a mental redundancy when we put that question to him. It's the doing of his assassination protocol, getting in the way like that."

The uniformed man stared at the little man for a while, making him squirm. "Well, keep working on him," he said. "Captain Robin Lacy was a friend of mine, and I'd hate to be unable to go rescue him if they have him. Dismissed." He strode out of the room, and the Torturer breathed a sigh of relief. He would not fail the Secrecy Commander again. That was never a healthy thing for a technician to do, even one as high in rank as he was. Dawson didn't want to use any of the torture chairs on this subject yet, but his objective was getting to be too hard to accomplish without it.

Additionally, he didn't necessarily want to burn this man's brain up with the chair, since any knowledge of that wonderful assassination protocol that he *must* have implanted would go, too. His options seemed to be disappearing, though. Maybe if he could just extract more information from that "Big Bernie" pervert, but the guy didn't seem to have any more info to give either. Still, the thought of putting that fellow through a few more rounds with the torture chair did warm Dawson up a bit. *Why not?* he thought. After all, good ol' Bernie could be fun. The little man just loved watching the way "Big Bernie" squirmed when the torment was applied.

"Well, Major, that's all for the moment," he said to the sweating semiconscious form of Major Robin Lacy "I'm going to work on an acquaintance of yours, and then I'll be right back for you." He just couldn't stop himself from chuckling and pinching his subject's cheek as he said that. *No matter*, he thought. *People who do what I do are supposed to enjoy it. I'm a rare breed. I have saved the lives of millions by removing the things that threaten them, even when those things walk on two feet, looking like humans . . .* And off the diminutive Master Torturer went, to spend more time with the hapless Bernie.

He was headed for Torture Room 13, sublevel B, East Wing, when he realized that the ground was shaking. There seemed to be a rumbling sound or something coming from outside, as if one of those sudden thunderstorms of this wasteland had again fallen upon the complex like an avalanche. That always happened out here in this godforsaken desert. He mentally dismissed it and moved on toward his goal, but another realization hit him. The ground was shaking.

Since when does the ground shake in a thunderstorm? he wondered. The shaking got worse as the thunder got even louder. *Something was headed toward the facility*, Dawson realized. Twisted though he was, Dawson was still quick-minded enough to comprehend what was causing the effects he felt. He also had the ear of a musician, so before anyone else in DCA-21, he knew, just by that sound, what had to be going on outside. *The wild horses are stampeding again!* he thought. Sometimes when he found himself alone at home, watching the gory horror movies he so loved, Dawson would think of what a shame it was that he'd never chosen a musical career. He could have passed away an old and wealthy man. In this, his thoughts were correct. He could have. His auditory sense was that good. As it was, though, the Little Man with the Funny Glasses would be neither old nor wealthy when he met his demise.

Dawson loved horses. He couldn't ride, and all horses seemed to hate him, but that never changed the way *he* felt. They were strong, powerful, and above all, *tall*. The wild ones had no one to answer to, no lesser creatures questioning their power to roam anywhere they wanted. Those untamed desert horses were everything he wished he could be, but never had been and never would become. He loved to watch the feral animals stampede. For him, it was the second most exciting part of this posting, out here in the middle of nowhere as it was. He had to go see them! In his enthusiasm, the former goal of inflicting unnecessary torture on Bernie was completely forgotten. Dawson ran for the stairs; he was claustrophobic and hated elevators. His choice of exits spared his life for a few moments longer. No sooner had he entered the stairwell than the wall he'd just passed collapsed into dust. Had anyone been standing there, they might have thought they'd seen some sort of movement, a tickling of the peripheral vision, perhaps, as eight barely perceptible forms entered DCA-21, sublevel B, east wing.

Meanwhile, strengthened by the adrenaline rush of excitement, Dawson was able to run all the way from the sublevels to the roof. He didn't want to miss the horses for anything, and judging by the sound, he'd already surmised that this had to have been the biggest stampede yet. He slammed open the door to the roof, startling one of the guards, who, upon recognizing him, sneered in disgust and lowered his weapon. *They all hate anyone from the Capital Punishment Corps anyway*, he thought. *Especially the torturers.* For the life of him, though, the Little Man with the Funny Glasses couldn't figure out why the regulars felt that way. In the end, he just chalked it up to professional jealousy. Everyone didn't have what it took to do *his* job and be good at it. Another attestation to the rarity of his breed, he figured.

None of them mattered, anyway. He'd only come up here to see the horses. Judging by the sound, this stampede had to be historic! His heart soared as he ran to the parapet that bordered the roof. When he could finally see the animals, Dawson could have cried for joy. They were *beautiful!* So very *beautiful!* He could see them, even through that huge dust cloud that they were stirring up. And oh, what a dust cloud! It looked like a great mother of a dust storm was roiling toward the facility, but he could still see the mighty horses in all of their diversity. Palominos, dapples, pintos, roans, blacks, grays, whites—every color of horseflesh was represented in all of its power. *There had to be thousands of them out there!* Dawson thought.

It didn't occur to him, at the time, to question why so many horses would be stampeding in a circle surrounding the facility. That was definitely not normal behavior for them. He was just too carried away in his joy at the sight before him to think of that immediately. It all seemed normal until he heard something that only a person with the auditory sensitivity of a natural musician could have discerned. It was a whistle. Not a whistle made in a toy factory or anything; this was a whistle emanating from human lips. Dawson instinctively knew the difference. Suddenly, his great joy drained like water fleeing a demolished and broken dam. *Someone was out there, in the middle of the stampede!* And whoever it was seemed to be *causing* it!

Now he felt only fear. What type of people could do this? Who out there in the big bad world could instigate a stampede like this and control it? He had no doubt that it was being controlled; for a fact, the human whistle he'd heard had come from *within* the megaherd out there. For that matter, he wondered, what kind of person could survive within such a maelstrom of wild horses, anyway? He peered closer. Something other than horses seemed to be moving within that equine pandemonium. He just couldn't fasten his eyes on it. The soldier who was on guard duty had a pair of binoculars trained on the spectacle, and Dawson could tell by the look on the man's face that he too was trying to fasten his eyesight onto something out there.

Suddenly, what appeared to be flashes of light began to strafe the roof of the prison, and the guards went down. For a moment, Dawson could only stare in disbelief. He hadn't heard any sound! No metallic whine, no report of any pistol or rifle. Just soundless tracer rounds from some invisible point in a silent sky! No sound of jet engines or helicopter rotors could be heard, and nothing that might pinpoint the origin of the incoming rounds could be seen in the night sky. Like most people who enjoyed hurting others, Dawson lived with a constant fear of his own death. Above all, he did not want to die in pain and discomfort, as had so many whom he himself had brought to such an end. That fear lent unbelievable speed to his legs as he fled the roof, running as fast as he could for the exit to the stairwell. Perhaps he would be safe within the lower levels, he hoped. After all, that was his turf, down in the torture rooms. He knew that labyrinth as no one else did. He also knew where his personal weapons were cached.

He never even considered the possibility that when he reached the lowest level, he'd need to proceed with caution. He was just so used to his small Kingdom of Pain being inviolable by official decree. The idea that anyone would trespass into his domain never even touched his thoughts. Who would dare? Didn't *everyone* fear the torturer and his enigmatic province in the lowest levels of hell? Oh yes, Dawson thought as he fled. Fear. Fear was power. If everyone feared the thought of being turned over to Correctus Johannes Dawson and his arts, then wasn't he the most powerful among them all? If he could just make it to his hell, where he was the only power, then no one could win against him.

Without a moment's hesitation, he slammed open the door to sublevel B, East Wing, and was immediately knocked unconscious by a blow dealt with his own Desert Eagle .50 caliber handgun, a personal favorite from his private weapons locker.

***

He was trying to climb a glass mountain. It was glass, all right; of that, Correctus Dawson was absolutely sure. Every time he got a little altitude, he'd slide back down. That's when he figured it out. He had to be trying to climb a glass mountain. Just like that fairy tale he'd read back when . . . *You drove him too far back*, his mind said. *Bring him forward a little more . . .* And the Little Man with the Funny Glasses was finally home at last, here in his Kingdom of Pain, where he had plenty of powerless subjects like Bernie to play with.

And how did that happen? How did you get Bernie?

"They brought him here to me after the *Liston* incident failed," Dawson told the glass mountain.

Why?

"Because the President said it was Bernie's fault that the mission had been exposed since it was his blog that outed the MPIS Secrecy Command's strategy."

We know about that, the glass mountain told him. Then it reminded itself, *He needs to tell it his way*. Dawson was in awe of the glass mountain's ability to speak to itself in that fashion, and he tried to think about it, but that line of reasoning burned his thoughts and made him stop. *Keep talking*, it told him, not in an unkindly manner.

Had "Big Bernie" not put out indisputable proof that the *Liston*, one of the navy's newest submarines, had really been the source of that nuke that went awry, he wouldn't have been here. But he'd done it to himself, hadn't he? If things had gone according to plan, that missile would have struck California (the President *hated* that State), and America would have blamed the North Koreans. Then with the nation finally united behind him, the President could have declared martial law and suspended the 2020 elections under the pretense of having to root out spies, enemy infiltrators whose activities had compromised the highest levels of Congress. He'd say he was protecting national security. That was the plan, anyway. But that pervert Bernie had put all that information out with his sickening blog, hadn't he? And now that great man, the billionaire president, and his whole cabinet, would be facing all kinds of legal trouble, and the plan would never succeed. Bernie the Betrayer had caused the country's political divisions to become even worse!

Dawson felt a surge of anger at betrayers, all of them. He wanted his beloved comrade, the glass mountain, to know more. "Why, the president's chief strategist had even suggested Bernie may have used some sort of Trojan horse malware to interfere with the nuke's guidance system, and that was the reason it veered north at the last minute and fell into the Beaufort Sea. The damn thing didn't even have the decency to explode and then the navy found it. Wouldn't be long before they—"

Stop! the glass mountain bellowed. *Your thoughts are meandering.*

Dawson felt guilt and hurt at the idea of his friend being angry. At that moment, he'd have done anything to restore their loving relationship. "I'm sorry. Please let me continue telling you whatever you want to know." He was ready to beg, beseech, implore, or supplicate, whatever it took for his sparkling companion to remain by his side.

It's okay, go on, the mountain said, and Dawson felt euphoric at the approval it radiated. He'd gladly tell the glass mountain a little more, if only it would keep on approving of him.

"Well, when Bernie's blog was traced and IDEA Control finally caught up with him, that overweight scum, Bernie, intimated that his inside information may have somehow come from the Interlopers. Since the president had decided that they were to be considered fake, and IDEA

Control contradicted the commander in chief by saying otherwise, the president began to fight for the man's removal from his lifetime appointment as head of the IDEA Threat Agency (ITA). His administration was a little worried that these holdovers from the previous president's administration, if they were allowed to remain in their positions, might have exposed too many secrets, anyway. That's why they attempted to dismantle the intelligence agencies."

Hmm, I see. So Director Caldwell is in trouble then, Correctus? the glass mountain asked. *Go ahead little fellow, tell me more.*

For a moment, Dawson's ability to communicate failed. He was always shorter than every other "normal" man he'd met, and whenever anyone drew attention to that fact, it angered him immensely. Surely his newfound friend wouldn't torment him by calling him a "little fellow," would he?

What's the matter, Correctus? the mountain asked, and the deep concern that radiated from it warmed the torturer to the depths of his soul. Who in his life had ever cared so much? *No one else has ever cared for you so much, Dawson. Just me. I used that as a term of endearment.* Yes. What did he expect? Isn't that what his friend called all of his little mountains? *Of course! Little fellows, indeed! But they were still mountains and larger than anything else in the world.*

At that moment, Dawson decided he'd tell his loving, kindhearted glass mountain everything. "I never believed a word the president said, Mounty, I only went along so I could keep torturing!" Correctus blurted out. There it was. His confession. That one statement categorized him as an enemy of the administration. "Please forgive me, my beloved friend," he pleaded.

Ahhh, but that only demonstrated how much more clever you are than the others.

"Yes, yes . . . that's the way it is, isn't it?" Dawson tearfully agreed. At that moment, he'd have done anything in the world to keep his friend's approval.

So that's all right, Correctus. You're forgiven, Mounty answered. The absolute relief Dawson felt once again lifted him up to new heights of jubilation. *Now, let's continue. Is Director Caldwell in any current danger?*

"Oh no, Mounty, he's always been too well connected for that. But the president had him dragged before Congress again and again, it's just that, well, there's nothing he can be accused of . . . He's too honest!" Dawson explained in desperation.

Indeed, his only friend in this entire cold, cold world answered. *Tell me more about why you were torturing Bernie, then. Why did the president have him brought to you? Tell me the rest of it.*

At that, the Torturer happily continued. "On top of ruining the *Liston* plan, that evil, godless perversion of a man posted a statement about how he'd once worked for the Interlopers. The whole world dismissed it as fraudulent, but the Secrecy Department of MPIS snatched him, anyway. They were commissioned to hunt down and capture anyone that the President and his Chief Strategist labeled as an enemy of the state. That way, they had a legal reason to snatch him without telling IDEA Control about it beforehand. With that done, that overweight, soulless *pig* was brought here to be tortured into confessing something that confirmed the White House's suspicions. He's been here ever since."

Dawson lowered his voice to a gleeful whisper and confessed, "I even brought his mother here and made him watch while she was subjected to all kinds of pain, but she died, and he became more resistant. I had to torture him even more after that." Dawson had an uncontrollable shudder of pleasure at that memory.

The glass mountain then asked, *What has he told you?*

It radiated such loving kindness that Dawson just wished he could hug it. Why, he'd joyfully tell this huge edifice anything it wanted to know! "The Interlopers are aliens who call themselves the division," he began. Lowering his voice to an informative whisper, he continued. "And they look like . . . like . . ."

Like what, Correctus? his beloved Mounty kindly cajoled.

"Like . . . BLACKS!" he told his friend. There, he'd said it. Without a doubt, good ol' Mounty would understand how Dawson felt about *that*.

What is the administration planning to do about it? Mounty asked.

"They wanted to purge all of them out of America," Dawson told his companion with glee. But his joy subsided as he went on. "That didn't happen though, because of the trouble it would have caused, so the Administration asked MPIS to do all it could without bringing ITA in. We were supposed to circumvent them, but that director of theirs found out and even now, there's more congressional hearings and the whole thing is tied up, and . . ."

His mind seemed to want to change channels, but he HAD to make his loving, caring friend understand, so he resisted the urge and proceeded with, "Why, the Chief of Staff had already drafted out a plan that—"

You're mentally wandering again, Mounty reminded him, with such great kindness until Correctus Dawson felt he could just die of happiness! *Continue answering my questions, please, Correctus Dawson.*

Yes! Yes, he would continue for Mounty and only for Mounty.

Good. Good man, Mounty expressed his approval of Dawson yet again. He'd said that Correctus Dawson was GOOD man! His joy was becoming so entirely complete that his eyes began to shed tears of emotion, and he was losing control of his bladder.

Dial it back some, Mounty told him. *We don't want to lose the torturer yet. He doesn't get to die enraptured to such an extent.* Dawson thanked Mounty for caring so very much about him. *Of course. Now tell me about Major Robin Lacy.*

"Oh. Him. Well, we captured him right after the inversion experiment. We were trying to use the ambient energy spikes as gateways to catch that big black alien who had the knife. Our major went into the lab after hours, where he activated the machinery and stepped into the void."

Why? Why did he do that? Was he ordered to?

"No, not at all. We think that he was trying to do what he could to put us at the top of the Federal Funding Commission's list for next year."

So it was a mistake? Was that Mounty asking? *Yes, of course it's me. No one else ever asks you anything*, Mounty reminded him.

Dawson felt tears of gratitude flowing down his cheeks. Of course. Mounty was the only person in the world who cared what the little man with the funny glasses thought. *Tell me more about—*

"Yes, I will, just please promise me that you won't hate me for being what I am. I don't mean to—"

That's enough of that talk now, Mounty kindly corrected. *Let's get back to the subject. How did the other Major Lacy get here?*

"We don't know. The aliens must have intended to send that double, but it seemed like our machines dragged him over before he was ready, but Secrecy Command was too clever for them. He was disoriented from the journey, and they trapped him like an animal. We analyzed his uniform, the spacesuit/jumpsuit thing he had on when he arrived."

What did you learn?

"Not too much. It self-destructed before the CSI team got very far. So the Secrecy Commander brought the false Robin Lacy down here to me. I was to expose his true subhuman nature and make him confess."

Confess what?

"All about the aliens' plan, what The Division Group is, how he got here, what happened to our Robin Lacy, any sort of intelligence."

How did your interrogation go? Did you attain any usable information?

Dawson felt a surge of regret and fear at his failure, but he had to answer, anyway. "No. He has an assassination protocol that keeps blocking me. I wanted to induce pain, but that . . ."

Assassination protocol? Explain.

"He calls it a 'will killer.' It stops him from divulging under passive interrogation. The Secrecy Commander wanted me to use aggressive pain, but I didn't want to destroy that assassination protocol. If I could sell it on the black market, why, there's an arms dealer who'll make me very rich, and—"

You're meandering again, Dawson. Let's go back to the subject of Bernie Syminski. The only concrete information you got was something about a group called 'The Division?' Come on, now, it's okay, you can tell me everything. Correctus Dawson felt a rapturous joy at the thought of being able to tell Mounty everything he knew. After all, there were so *many* secrets burdening his soul, now, weren't there?

"Mounty, did you know that I like horror movies?" he blurted.

Yes, Dawson I knew that. I know everything about you, now, don't I? We're friends, right? Dawson began to cry. He could hold it in no longer. Yes, Mounty was the only and most loving friend he'd ever have. He truly wanted to talk with his much-loved Mounty about any and everything. "Would you come by and watch some movies with me, Mounty? Please?"

Pathetic. Who told you that the Interlopers were aliens?

"When the President and his cabinet reviewed Bernie's early confessions, he declared that the Interlopers were aliens. Black ones. His chief strategist said all he needed was a good reason, and that declaration would make his plan acceptable to Congress and the general population. They felt that the idea of an alien world controlled by Blacks who had had advanced science and were competent enough to invade this one and escape, well, now that would generate a great deal of fear for the rest of us, the *real* Americans. Can you just imagine what ideas our Blacks might have gotten from that?" Correctus Dawson shuddered, but the warmth and empathy radiating from Mounty calmed his fear.

We exposed their subterfuge to the media, sir, Mounty once again said to itself. *That purge plan was debunked before it ever got anywhere.* The glass mountain seemed to radiate some sort of disapproval, and overwhelmed by grief, Dawson began to suffer heart palpitations. "Mounty, did . . . did I do something wrong? Are you angry with me?" he rasped.

If Mounty disapproved of him, the Little Man with the Funny Glasses would simply prefer to die before living any longer with that knowledge. *Pull him back. Convince him that he is still very important. We have time. The rest of them will be asleep for a long while, and all outside communications to and from the facility are proceeding normally.* Once again, Dawson's elation rose. He was important to Mounty! They would have *time* together! His life could be no fuller.

For the next few hours, the torturer told his friend Mounty everything he could. Everything he knew concerning the steps that had been taken to deal with the return of the Interlopers. He even identified every person scheduled for torture within MPIS Detention Center A-21. He didn't at all try to resist the urge to tell Mounty what wonderful plans he had for inflicting more pain upon the prison's inmates, how he loved to turn the intercoms within the torture wing on highest volume just so he could hear his subjects' screams. Surely, his glassine friend would understand and approve of him no matter what! Lastly, he told what the suit that had been given to the Casino Robber would do to that man over time, and that was when his relationship with his dear glass mountain changed.

For a moment, it felt like Mounty had distanced itself from him, and for fear of losing his beloved friend, Dawson offered a little more information. "We tried sending men into the void. Did you know that? Mounty? Please talk to me again. Mounty?" He once again felt the entire attention of his dear, dear glass mountain upon him, and that made him want to bare his soul out of sheer happiness.

Tell me about it. How did that go?

"Thank you for coming back, Mounty. I can't live without you."

Yes, of course. Now what about the others you sent in? How did those excursions go?

"We put preprogrammed assassination chips into their brains, but it seemed to invite death to every man we sent. Most of them didn't make it back, and the ones who did came out in a catatonic state. They died a week later."

Why did you send them in?

"Because we wanted them to find and kill that big Black Alien with the knife. He was the most dangerous one. Imagine what ideas people might have gotten from him."

Have you tried sending anyone in without these assassination protocols?

"No. The Commander in Chief and his Chief of Staff wanted only one type of person sent in. He specified assassins." *So then this assassination program is still in its infancy?* "Yes, it is," Dawson replied. *You've been very helpful, Correctus.* Mounty radiated so much approval in his direction, so much approval of *him* that Dawson's happiness began to swell to a level he could barely contain. He had become so giddy that he wanted to hug himself for glee when Mounty once again began to speak to him.

Correctus Dawson, you are the lowest form of life. Listening to you has been sickening. You've shown that you are truly the most despicable, debased example of a human that can be. Furthermore, you are a disappointment to me, personally. Therefore, I am depriving you of my company and my friendship. Now loneliness and silence will come crawling out of dark shadows for you, to steal your life with no more mercy than you have given others. Dial his conscience and sadness torment up to its highest.

After hearing that, Dawson's innermost feelings seemed to emit an audible *crack!* like some frozen rock, then began to cascade, circling from elation to misery and back, again and again. Then it was simply gone. All of it. No more Mounty the Glass Mountain. No more loving kindness or friendship. He was once again just the Lonely Little Man with the Funny Glasses. He was *so* heartbroken, *so* emotionally tired. It seemed to Correctus Dawson that he'd fallen under some silent avalanche of uncaring glass boulders that were splintering into thousands of shards of slashing grief, his heart had ripped apart, and he himself been left desolate and dry as the Utah desert beyond the prison's walls.

He sobbed and groaned as inconsolable sorrow ripped his soul into bleeding shreds of heartache and anguish. Something precious had been ruthlessly torn away from him, and now, his life was bleeding out in emotional pain as a wound would have leaked blood. When he opened his eyes, he was alone. Again. If he could have, Dawson would've leaned forward and held his head in his hands when he began to cry, bawling with the emotional abandon of a man who had found everything he ever wanted then lost it. A dormant part of his emotive capacity had been activated, taken to an unexpected high and broken. It had become the most painful thing he'd ever experienced.

Soaked in grief as he was, it took a few more moments before he noticed the darkness. The whole section was dark. Totally dark. It wasn't the darkness that stirred a flicker of fear to life within him, though. It was the silence. Being an unempathetic man, Dawson had never cared to learn anything about PTSD, so of course, he couldn't recognize the symptoms within himself. He was suffering from PTSD after his abrupt separation from his imagined friend Mounty. He'd also stopped paying attention to any of his conscience's feeble objections to torturing others, but now that human quality of his had been artificially magnified, over-empowered and that's why the silence was terrifying him so. MPIS Detention Center A-21 was normally bustling with activity, but not now. The only sound was that of the climate control units as they blew out cooled air and adjusted the temperature. There was a light coming from somewhere down the hallway outside, but no light anywhere in the immediate area, except for the torture chair's control panel. Yes, he was sitting in one of his own torture chairs, and the room was this one: torture room 13, his favorite, where he'd visited horrors and pains beyond imagining on so many enemies of the state.

Something seemed to move within the silence, and suddenly, he could see them all, his "victories." Some had blood streaming from their eyes, others had the drooping faces of stroke victims. Yes, his work could induce strokes, but he'd felt that it was only right. They had proven themselves inferior by their disobedience, and he punished them for it. They all confessed to their crimes in the end. But hadn't Correctus Dawson been disobedient too? Hadn't he sold secrets to arms dealers for money? Shouldn't *he* be tortured with the same ruthlessness? They started laughing at him for that thought, all of them, but their laughter had no sound, which only compounded the silence. Dawson felt the hair on his neck and arms rise. He sat upright, and suddenly, with a robotic whirr, the torture chair activated itself, increasing his immobilization. He realized then that he'd only been lightly immobilized all along, but still stuck here for his ghosts to torture with their skeletal hands.

His fear had become a palpable thing in the room now. He was sweating, but the water coming out of his pores was ice cold. It burned his sun-sensitive skin. The silence seemed to become louder, as if silence could possibly do so. Then he heard it. A sound. Like something was dragging itself toward the room.

There was a step, and then a drag. He could hear it, coming down that hallway, headed for his location. Drag. Step. Silence. He started to shiver and hoped that whatever was coming would not be able to see him in this darkness. His victims laughed their soundless laughs again, and it burned his chest, that lack of sound. Again, he heard the *thing* approaching the

---

409

room within which he was being held. Whatever it was, it was moving with the surety of pain and death. Step. Drag. Drag. Step.

Now he could hear it breathing, as if that were hard to do in this atmosphere. He tried to ask himself if the aliens were out there, but the thought drove his fear higher, so his mind abandoned it. His breathing became faster as his heart started pounding, but he couldn't get any air.

Drag. Step. Step. Drag. The thing's breathing became even heavier, and now Dawson could smell the creature that was approaching. It exuded every foul odor that could come from a living body. Sweat, feces, urine, infection. Dawson felt himself wetting his pants, but could do nothing about it. The thing was coming closer and closer. Drag. Step. Step. Drag. He could see its silhouette in the doorway now, and it was *big*.

It stood there for a moment breathing ragged breaths, exhaling a foul stench of bleeding mouth and broken teeth, a huge stinking shadow of malevolence. Dawson wanted to plead, to beg for his life. *Please! Please! Don't hurt me! P-please!* But he couldn't speak. The silent victims of his work had begun choking him, gibbering their soundless evil merriment, and it felt as if wet towels were being put over his face, to induce dry drowning. All of it escalated his fear.

Still, that *thing* just stood in its doorway for a moment, heartlessly watching Dawson's favorite device torture its chief operator; then it dragged itself closer. Step. Drag Step. Drag, now it was nearer.

He could smell its stench. Then it laughed too. Its face came closer to Dawson. "Y-you are no longer in control here," the shadow rasped as its foul breath seemed to wrap itself around Correctus's head like a blinding, stifling hood, forcing itself into his nose, his mouth, his *lungs*; and the little man with the funny glasses felt his bowels loosen.

It laughed again with a sound like wet blood being forced through a sponge. Suddenly, every light in the room came on, and Correctus Dawson found himself face-to-face with all that was left of Big Bernie, his favorite victim. The torture chair had changed him. His face and eye drooped on the left, and bloody saliva was drooling slowly from that corner of his mouth. His teeth were broken from their grinding together during his torture, and the man's tongue was still swollen from being bitten. His shirtless torso was covered with various blemishes from internal wounds, and some of them had ruptured, allowing blood and pus to ooze out. His left foot dragged along behind as he moved. All of it the handiwork of Correctus Dawson, King Torturer in his own little Kingdom of Pain.

Dawson would have sneered at this pathetic figure, but the memory of his fear was still too new.

"B-being tor-tortured isn't fun is it, y-you w-worm? I w-watched you tor-torture m-my mother to d-death," Bernie rasped. He shuffled over to the control panel, had to stop to breathe, then continued. "I a-asked The Colonel to ki-kill me. But he had something better in mind." He pushed a stud, and the arm panel in the chair opened up. One of Dawson's Colt M1911 service pistols floated out, coming to a rest in his lap. He couldn't believe what he was seeing. Did this useless hunk of meat think that he, the Master Torturer of MPIS Detention Center A-21, would put it out of its misery so easily? Or was Bernie thinking of shooting him and trying to make it look like suicide?

Dawson couldn't talk, or he would have railed at the useless carcass standing in front of him. He could move his head now, and when he looked up, he saw Bernie's foul mouth laughing again. "Y-you like that, huh? Well, it gets b-b-better." With a great struggle, Bernie pulled something out of somewhere, and Dawson's terror returned. It was his own .50 caliber Desert Eagle, being held in Bernie's formerly strong hands as a man would hold a rifle, and it was pointed at him. "I-I c-c-can't pull the trigger, but they fixed it, so it shoots on-on its own." Bernie laughed again, and this time, blood spurted out of his mouth. "W-we're g-going t-t-to kill each other. Th-the Colonel had th-them make this bracket-tt. I can r-r-raise it noww."

The Desert Eagle raised, its deadly muzzle pointed toward Dawson. Bernie said, "R-r-release." The chair released Dawson, and several things happened at once. He grabbed the Colt M1911, aimed and fired, all in one smooth movement. Two shots center mass. Even as those rounds flew through the air, the sole .50 caliber Desert Eagle round that Bernie had fired also soared toward the little man with the funny glasses. The bullets flew within one millimeter of each other; Bernie was hit with two in his chest and died even as his body flew backward from the recoil of the weapon he'd just used, slamming him against the transparent steel mirror. The little man with the funny glasses, however, was hit with a hollow point .50 caliber fragmentation round fired from one of the most powerful handguns ever made, and his body practically disintegrated.

Correctus Dawson would never retire as a wealthy old man. A closed-casket, top secret funeral attended by none but the chaplain on duty would be the last thing he'd ever have.

Outside, in the desert, Crossover Team Alpha and the Walking Dead Raiders carried Major Robin Lacy of R-3 to *Middle Child*, the CH-53E Super Stallion, their rendezvous point. Brigadier General Benjamin Gary took one last look at the sleeping MPIS Detention Center A-21, silhouetted as it was against the Utah desert sands, thought about how much he'd love to come back here and acquire one of those beautiful wild horses, then boarded the transport. About ten yards away, General Renoir, Lieutenant C. C. Pendle, and Sargeant Roy-Bob Joseph the younger loaded the unconscious form of DeVries Renoir of N-Prime into the waiting *Little Bird*.

INTERLUDE V

Sea Breezes and Memories

He was remembering. At least that was what it sometimes seemed like. Here he was, back home, walking along the Pontchartrain lakefront, near the street where she lived. (Hey, he wondered to himself, wasn't that a Frank Sinatra song?) But then, he was mentally wandering again, wasn't he? "I came here to find her," the young man told himself. "But I don't like it here. This isn't a good memory. I need to start it differently." So he moved it. Not the memory; he moved the world, because he could do that, couldn't he? Move the world. Never mind. He just wanted to be in a location that he found peaceful so that he could think. Now he was walking along the beach at night. It was a Florida beach, all right; the sands were white, and the full moon above made them glow like a fond recollection of yesterday's happy life. He wanted—no, he needed *the peaceful summer breeze that always blessed these beaches at night. Because he wanted it, the breeze came. So did the sights, sounds, and smells of that beautiful location under the full moon. Okay. Now he could start.*

There was a block in his heart and mind that he wanted to overcome, get around, or break through. He knew something; *it's just that he wasn't sure what it was. "It's time," he told himself. Nothing happened, so he told himself that same thing once more. Again, nothing happened. He started to despair. Something was going on within his brain, and he needed to know what it was. If any other person had found themselves able to access different worlds and realities, to find and talk to alternate versions of themselves, there'd be no end to the confusion and press coverage, he thought. But these things he'd been able to do over the past few months seemed normal to him, somehow, as if he were born to it.*

"What about the dream?" he mouthed silently. His thinking replied with a question, "What dream?"

"You know which one," he said to himself. "The nightmare with the rats and roaches. Maybe I can start there." He hated that nightmare, but the fact that it had begun to haunt him even when he wasn't asleep frightened him more than could be said. The young man feared going insane. But too much was happening nowadays; he needed to know what and who he was no matter the cost. So he relaxed his mind and called upon his nightmare, summoning it from the depths of suppressed memory. He felt it raging closer and closer as it boiled angrily up from the well of denial that it had been tossed into. His pulse quickened. His breathing became rapid and shallow as fear stalked him, and . . .

"Stop," She said.

"Wha-what?" he asked in confusion. "Who?"

"It's me," She said, and he felt her taking his hand, holding it with her own. Her voice, oh god, her voice; the sound of it touched his heart like warm honey and cinnamon rum on a cold day, and he thought he would fade for grieving her loss—again.

"Baby . . .," She said with that lilt that only people from their city put into that term of endearment; then she continued. "Baby, you don't need to grieve for me, since I'm not gone. I'm here, really here." He thought he could feel his heart choking on the pain again, for he so wanted her to be real, so wanted her to be alive once more. He touched her hand; it felt real, so he gently put his hand on the side of her face, then his other hand on the other side. He held her beautiful face for a moment, and then, because no man could have resisted, he kissed her with all the passion that he'd never dared express while she walked this earth.

His tears flowed with hers, and he had to tell Her, to finally say it. "I failed you. I'm so sorry that I failed you. I should have been there to stop them, and now you're gone, and I'll never be able to—"

"No," She said. "Stop. I would never want you to do this to yourself."

"No," he answered. "You wouldn't. She wouldn't. But you can't be her. I saw her die! I held you . . . her in my arms, and . . ." She smiled. That smile, her stunning beauty—the man felt physical pain in his chest now.

"Please," She said. "Stop hurting yourself. I'm not dead."

He looked at her for a moment, the sight caressing his eyes with love and warmth. The breeze moved her hair, and he could smell the natural oils she'd always used in it. He touched that hair, so soft and attractive as it was. "Okay, so you're a figment of my imagination, then," he told her gently. "I still love you."

She looked down, then up again into his eyes. "I'm not dead," she repeated. "I'm here with you."

"You mean, like a part of you still lives on in my memory or something like that?" Emotionally, he wanted to fade into her, into the hope that this embodiment of his lost Beloved represented. But rational thought interceded, and he recognized what this really was. What his calling on the nightmare had really been. It was some type of self-abnegation. Punishment he'd inflicted on himself for what had become the most epic fail of his life. Sarcasm forced other words out of his mouth then. "I don't believe in ghosts, babe, and if you're saying you're some type of mysterious spirit, then you've come to torture the wrong guy 'cause I already got enough torture on my plate. So as much as I love her, I've gotta tell you to bug off."

She laughed, a sound he always cherished; turned to look at the ocean; and started speaking to him again. "Look, Honey, you said it yourself—it's time. Time for you to begin recovering your memories, and I'm supposed to help you get through it without going crazy. The process was programmed into you when they had to take them away. They knew the memory of that trip back would be too traumatic for you to forget easily, so a neurobiological subroutine was programmed into your mnemonic recovery. It was coded to activate if you ever deliberately forced that particular memory up. Your mind would also call up a person whom you loved and trusted without question. The guidelines of the programming would force you to summon your remembrance of someone whom you knew, without any doubt, was still a living, breathing person. A dead one just would not help the process. The grief would sidetrack the progression. So, baby, somewhere out there, I'm still alive and you know it." She turned to face him, pushed her hair away from her face where the wind had blown it, then smiled that smile again. He looked into her eyes and knew; yes, she was alive. And he missed her more than words could say.

"How do I start?" he asked. "I mean, how do I accept that what I saw with my own eyes didn't happen, that you're not . . . gone?"

Now She had that thoughtful look on her face, and he knew she'd come up with an answer. "Well, there are alternate versions of both of us, aren't there? If there's a you who exists without me, then the reverse has to be true, yes? There's a me who's struggling through her existence without you, right?"

"Yeah," he answered, "but she may not be mine, *you know? My girl."*

Seemingly annoyed, she took a deep breath and reminded him, "You keep saying 'mine,' 'my girl.' Well, think about it this way, Boyfriend, if I'm 'yours,' 'your girl,' and it's a mutual thing, then that means that you belong to me and

I own you just as much, doesn't it? You do remember that we got married, don't you? And I'm not talking about that kid wedding, I'm talking about the last time you came to see me. We were both adults then."

He looked astounded. "W-wait a minute, now, when did we do it? I don't remember that at all."

She sat back, looked at him, pursed her lips, and tilted her head. Her mannerism. She was thinking of a way to reach him, he knew. To him, it seemed that her facial expression said she was torn between slapping him or believing his words, but then she thought of something that resolved that particular inner conflict for her. "They removed that memory right along with the rest of them, didn't they?" She asked. "And they never even knew how much they took from you, did they?" She closed her eyes for a moment and sat holding her hands in front of her face, fingers intertwined, looking for all the world as if she were saying a silent prayer while a lone silver tear rolled down her cheek.

"Okay, boyfriend," she started, after a moment. "When was the last time you remember seeing me?"

His face became as hard as stone. "When you died. I held you in my arms and felt the world caving in. I didn't even get to be the one who ordered them to cremate you. It should have been my right. We loved each other. We should've been a family."

She sighed in exasperation. "This is going to be harder than it seemed," she said. "I don't think I ever got to see your stubborn side."

"Okay, listen to me, please, Honey," she gently urged as she reached for his hand again and held it with both of hers. "You came across to me and we went and got married. You were in your uniform and had just come from some dangerous mission or something like that. It was the first time since they took you away that you'd ever come to me with your mind clear. That's why I didn't call the government man who helped us before. We went to my cousin Roy, the judge—you know, the one who lived over in the Garden District. Only, it wasn't the Roy I knew. He was older, and you said that we were in a different reality. He performed the ceremony on the condition that later on, when we could, we'd have a public wedding with all the bells and whistles for Auntie Momma. So we belong to each other, and I'm the right one, just as much as you are. Now, quit overthinking it and let's get started with your memories, okay?"

He stared at her blankly, still, so she went on. "We went headed over to someplace where we could be alone, and we were walking in the park beside the river by Cafe Du Monde and the market, when those soldiers in the gray uniforms started chasing us. You made a crack about how they looked like Confederate

Nazis or something like that, then pulled out a scary-looking knife and told me to run away. Four of them cornered us, and you started killing them. Then another one came. He had a lasegun and shot you through the chest. I wouldn't leave, so you yelled at me because you wanted me to escape and go. You told me that you were okay when we both knew you weren't." She beat the sand that she'd sat down on with her pretty hand as she spoke.

From the opaque depths of yesterday, a memory coalesced in his mind; She was going to school to become a doctor. He didn't want her to injure her hands. They were meant for saving lives, and she couldn't risk losing that. He gently grabbed both of them and held them to his heart. "Don't hurt your hands, Angel. You'll be needing them," he said this as if he really believed she was real.

"There was a hole in your chest, Nige!" Her voice was almost strident with concern, fear, and anger at him for sending her away when they both had known how much, at that moment, he needed her more than ever before. Her tears flowed like a gentle rain. "You kissed me and told me that you couldn't both defend me and escape yourself, so I needed to run and get off of the scene. That's what I did. There were more of them coming for you and you wanted to be able to fight."

Now he was staring at the white glowing sands, and his mind began to make the connections that had been left open for it. Confusion began showing on his face. "That-that was part of the nightmare dream, only I didn't recall all of what you're telling me, just the horrendous part."

She seemed encouraged by that admission. "Maybe that's why your mind kept pulling it up, Nige. You wanted to remember more about what we were doing while we were together that time."

He raised an eyebrow then asked, "So did we ever . . . er, uhh, you know . . ." She smiled with that flirtatiousness that made his heart beat faster and said, with total innocence, "Did we ever what?" He felt his face reddening while she laughed again.

She slapped his arm and said, "That was such a typical man question! Of course we did, you big beautiful idiot of mine. We just got married, after all! We spent the night in our pretty phantom zone because I'd told you how they were able to track your movements whenever you came to see me, so you wanted to go somewhere safe. We only left there because I had to get back to Tulane."

"Okay," he answered then added, "but I still think you're imaginary, so I'll just call you 'Figment.' I can't call anyone else by her name."

She rolled her eyes, and even that gesture was almost too much for him to bear. It was exactly how the real one would have reacted to his stubbornness. "Whatever," she said. "So what's the first thing you remember?"

—————

"I was lost, trying to find my way home. My family had disappeared in some sort of flood, and there was a toy in my hand that I needed to hold on to. I went looking for my home because something horrible was happening to our family. I found our house, and then . . ."

"Then what?" she prodded him gently.

"Then things changed, and that never happened. It was just a bad dream that faded away. It all changed. That flood never happened, and I was growing up at home with my brothers and sisters. Momma left us, and I started my Fight Club."

"What happened to your club?" she asked.

"Well, you see, Fig, that's one of the problems. I can't recall with any precision what happened. It seems that I went to college for a few years, and when I got back home, things had just fallen apart for the club. But that doesn't seem to be exactly what happened either."

She held her hand up at that. "Wait a minute," she said. "You're moving ahead too fast. We need to back things up. Go back to the flood and that 'you found your house' thing."

He looked at her for a moment, laughed, then started again. "Okay, so I thought it was my house, but there was someone else living there. They were very kind, and I . . . I think they may have been my real mother and father." They sat together in silence for a moment. The ocean's waves pounded against the shore in their timeless dance. The breeze stirred her hair, and he realized that he didn't want to move onward with this right now. He shouldn't have been able to feel her presence so acutely, for there was no possible way she could have been here. She was gone. He'd held her in his arms as she went.

The sea always smelled good to him on nights like this. Whenever the moon was full, its reflection made the ocean waves look like a field of sparkling diamonds to him. It made him feel safe and comfortable. "This can't be real," he said. "Not the Atlantic, that's real, but my being here with you, baby. It can't be real." She looked hurt, but he knew it was only because that was what he'd have expected. Somewhere nearby, a late-night walker was playing Sade's "The Moon and the Sky," and those words, along with the melody, spoke to his feelings about the figment of his imagination that was sitting beside him. To keep her there would cause him to die of heartbreak, but he couldn't bear to let her go either. So he continued, "I remember taking my father home, to the place where I was being kept, but then I also remember a different father whose home I grew up in. I remember Luke being my teacher, and I remember the skinny science guy too.

"Then that fades away, and I remember Luke being one of The Colonel's men and how we met when I was about thirteen or so. I remember everything about growing up with Devvie, Joanna, Marv, and Lisa. Then that memory goes away and I'm growing up living with The Colonel and his wife, but can't remember ever meeting her. What am I supposed to believe, Fig?"

She looked out at the ocean for a moment then replied, "Maybe both sets of memories are real."

"How could that be?" he asked her.

"That's what you have to piece together," she answered.

"Then what are you here for?" he asked in exasperation.

She looked at him with those eyes of hers, and he thought his heart would melt. But once again, rational thought brought him back to his senses. "Honey, I'm here to remind you that there is someone you love and who loves you. What's more, you need to remember that I'm a real, living person who's looking or waiting for you as much as you're looking and waiting for me. I'm here to give you hope and hand you a reason to keep going. You're starting to fade emotionally, getting tired, and you'd never be able to bear the onslaught of your memories in that sort of degraded condition. The stress would break your heart."

"Kruger," he said, as if all of her words had fallen on empty air. "Kruger. That's the skinny science guy who put you in my mind. I just remembered his name."

"See?" she said, and there was her beautiful smile again. "You're starting to remember, and you're not angry about it."

He laughed. "Why would I be mad at him? I liked Kruger as soon as I met him. I think that was when I was about six or seven years old."

She pursed her lips for a moment, and he knew that she was thinking of something. "Actually, baby, I don't think he put me in your mind. I was already there. Like I told you, I just happened to be the one person whom you trust with no reservations, and you've always known that I'm still alive. All Kruger did was put in guidelines for your brain to follow when you started your mnemonic recovery process. Right now, you're in what they call 'visualization mode.' It's some ability that only a limited number of people with your training are able to have. You can remember knowing Kruger since you were little, and that means that the repair process is going forward."

He stared at her for a moment. "So you're saying that I'm the one controlling this?"

"Yes, dear, you are," she told him then added, "I'm just here to help you temper the emotional feedback that's going to come from some of the memories you'll recover. You could be very dangerous if you lost control."

He cleared his throat. "Well, I am pretty good with my hands. I know that I'm good enough to kill a man in a fight, so maybe I am dangerous." She looked down at the sand between her feet. A minute passed, then another. She looked up at him and said, "Not that kind of dangerous. You're capable of being a danger that's much worse. You can channel energy from our phantom zone and make it do some very deadly things. I guess you're like some type of conduit or something for that. Another thing that you'll have to remember, but since you're older now than the last time you did it and your mind is clearing up, maybe you'll figure out how to control that too. Guess we have to work up to that level."

"How long will this all take? Months? Years? Days?" he asked with an intensity of bitterness.

"I don't know," she shrugged as she replied. "I guess that depends on how bad you want it." Her smile became flirty, and he laughed.

"Yeah, now that really is a good motivator. You, saying something like that to me. Okay, I'll work on this a little bit more every day, just to see where it leads." She touched his face, and the warmth of her hand brought tears that he didn't notice to his eyes. "If you're really alive, I want to, just once, not have to say goodbye to you again," he told her.

"I know," she answered. "I want you to be able to come back to me as much as you do." Then she was gone, and he was once again alone, accompanied only by the full moon and the sea, with its waves and breezes.

NEW FRIENDSHIPS, NEW FOES

In the Beach City, Florida, of Reality 3, a powerful thunderstorm coming off the Atlantic Ocean assaulted the coast. Four miles offshore, a United States Coast Guard HH-65 Dolphin flew through the same thunderstorm. It stopped and hovered long enough to drop something into the Atlantic Ocean, then flew back to its base at Coast Guard Station Ponce De Leon inlet in New Smyrna Beach, Florida. The guardsmen aboard had been ordered not to address the lone diver who was their former payload. His identity and mission were both highly classified. The man's name was Logan Eller; at least that had been the name he'd been given at birth and subsequently identified by for the greater part of his life. Since he'd began working his current job, however, he'd used several different aliases and been identified as several different people.

This Logan Eller was a super assassin of the highest quality. Posthypnotic suggestions designed to render it impossible for him to give away vital information, even under extreme duress, had been interwoven within the fabric of his psyche. His fingers, arms, legs and feet were laced with titanium in order to make his blows more deadly during any hand-to-hand combat. All the joints within his legs and arms were reinforced with a high-tension polymer spring interwoven within the tendons, thus giving him the ability to move considerably faster, strike much harder, and jump both higher and farther than a normal man could. Logan Eller, along with his fellow "One Per Center's Assassins" (OPCAS), had also been treated with the world's only true "supersoldier" serum, a steroidal substance unknown to the rest of the planet's population. His durability, strength, and stamina could, at times, be more than twice that of any untreated person's.

This was the Logan Eller who'd been born and raised in R-3 (Reality 3) where Nigel Boyd Renoir the younger had been inserted into a family that closely resembled the one he would have grown into adulthood with had a Hurricane Katrina not changed his life forever. This Logan Eller was, of course, not a MISTman, nor did he have a very concise idea of who they were. All he knew for sure was that they were an elite military spec ops/black ops unit, and they were tough. That was okay with "Wolvie," as he had come to be known to his employers (a name taken from the fact that his own first name was the same as a certain popular comic book character).

If there was a team of tough military men that he'd been pit against, he knew that he would just have to be tougher. It didn't really matter how hard the unit was, anyway, for according to the intel he'd been given, he'd most likely be facing only one of them, if any. The people he worked for had access to an entire network of intelligence agencies, as well as every bit of data in the World Wide Web, and their information had always proven trustworthy before. Some considered them to be "the Illuminati" of urban legend, but in reality, they could be more closely identified as the one percent of humanity that owned and controlled ninety-nine percent of the world's wealth. Of that one percent, six families owned the majority of *their* wealth, and those were the men and women whom Logan Eller of R-3 worked for. That was about one percent of "the One Percent."

Where fortunes, resources, or holdings were concerned, few things happened on this earth without their hands or bank accounts being involved. For more than a few generations, they'd profited from and often controlled all the political ebb and flow that shaped human civilization on the planet, even the seemingly random events that could and had, on occasion, been an integral part of the foundation from which sprang many of the world's bloodiest wars.

He'd been told his target was one of a group of persons who had come into this place from a different one, asylum seekers, with new technologies that were of great benefit to the country they'd settled into. No doubt that was also the country of their origin, back in wherever they'd come from.

None of *that* made any difference to "Wolvie" either. He knew that the political lines and national boundaries drawn by the world's governments were irrelevant to his employers. They controlled all or most of those governments, anyway. Even the worst wars and conflicts between the political powers were only expressions of angst between or tools of change used by the consortium he'd sold himself to, the ultimate "One Percenters." Political boundaries only mattered to Logan because the type of resistance his targets may put up had to have been influenced by the environments they grew up in. Targets that grew up in third world countries, for example, were normally more cautious and harder to hunt than those who had been reared in developed lands. Living in close proximity to death made people cautious that way. Where his prey came from mattered to Logan only because of such facts.

The current assignment was to incapacitate or kill a certain one of the otherworldly visitors. Reportedly, that person held the key to accessing all the riches of whatever place he'd come from, and Eller's bosses wanted it. To attain such, they needed the person's DNA; and although they preferred to harvest it from his living body, they could also attain what they needed from the man's dead body, if necessary. In Logan Eller's thinking, that meant he could take the man back dead or alive. This was the type of deployment he preferred. Keeping his targets alive always slowed him down and, on more than one occasion, had almost cost him everything. If an OPCA were compromised or captured, they were expected to escape after destroying the payload that they'd attained. Punishment by their overlords for such failure was always severe. Should escape prove impossible in the case of capture, though, there was only one option left to an OPCA. Living on to a ripe old age wasn't it.

His STIDD DPD (diver propulsion device) touched bottom, indicating that the water was now shallow enough for his emergence and the time for musing was over. Back to business. He'd come out of the surf about a mile north of the house where his objective was, then lope to the location, recon, and extract the target. That was the plan, anyway.

***

Meanwhile not too far away, in a house that looked occupied but was really abandoned, a man was about to begin speaking, to tell his audience of things and incidents that in other circumstances would have seemed utterly unbelievable. But other events were in motion that would prevent that conversation from ever occurring the way Nigel Boyd Renoir the Younger intended.

"Before you start telling us your tale, I have some questions that you need to answer," Meredith told Nigel, after she and her husband had been shown to the breakfast nook of the house that was once Angeline Arlander's.

"Go ahead," Nigel answered, sipping the coffee that Lucius had brought over after brewing it.

"Where is Dana Lacy? Did you harm her?"

"No. Dana is in R-10. So now that you know that, I guess you'd like to know what R-10 is."

"Okay, so what is it?" asked Billy. Then he continued, "If you're really interested in doing something about Angeline's killer, you have got to stop seeing us as your enemies, Nigel."

The younger man stared at Billy for a moment, as if weighing an answer. "Tell me, please, what do you know about what's been happening so far?" he asked.

He wants to see if we're telling the truth, Billy thought. Looking straight into Nigel's eyes, he answered, "You claim to be able to cross into different realities. It seems that this ability came upon you unexpectedly. You told Roan that you have no control over the timing of when this will happen, but right now, it seems that you've somehow changed that. You claim to have gone to one of these different realities and met some double of yourself who is married to Angeline Arlander's double there. Supposedly, this person just *gave* you a huge sum of money and some information that implicated George Arlander in his wife's death. According to you, he also warned you about the four hurricanes that blew through here last summer. When the old man talked to Arlander later on, that guy gave the impression that something you told his wife stopped him from making a business trip up north because of Hurricane Ivan. He wasn't very happy with you over that either."

"Yes, that happened," Nigel answered reflectively. "And because he listened to her when she told him, his life was saved . . . unfortunately. But," he added with an evil smile, "at least he lost a lot of money."

Billy and his wife exchanged one of those "see, I told you so" looks that married couples often share, and Billy continued. "Roan said you suggested to Dana Lacy that the two of you go back to the reality where your double and hers lived, to see if your visits had done any damage there in that place, where you said she was your brother's girlfriend, instead of your live-in paramour roommate. Or whatever you had become to each other."

Meredith then added, "You also told Roan that she witnessed something happening here. Since we've seen the video that you recorded the day Angeline Arlander died, we assumed that her murder was what you were referring to."

The young man's eyes flashed as he answered, "So you did see the recording. That must mean that you *are* working with Doc. Does it also mean that you two supercops have decided not to try to kill me again?"

"Okay, that's a fair question," Billy replied. "But also in the name of fairness, you did pop out of nowhere and startle us. For all we knew, you were a psychotic murderer who may have eaten your victim since there's no trace of her anywhere." Nigel looked down for a moment then over at Lucius, as if trying to muster up courage or strength for what he had to say next. Lucius's eyes held a look of compassion as he nodded and said, "Go ahead, Nige. You know we'll take all the help we can get."

Nigel looked around, sighed, and said, "That all-too-noble idea of going back to see if we did any damage isn't going to happen. I thought it over, and it seemed to me that I was just trying to fabricate an excuse that would allow me to go back to see that Angeline in her role as my wife. Or at least as the wife of some other me. I didn't do it because of the damage it could have caused. To all of us. Whatever repercussions there may be from our visit there, they'll have to handle it by themselves. Besides, I'd love to be able to hear him trying to explain all that to her. Dana thought that was funny too." He laughed a little, and the sound of it gave Meredith a chill.

This bastard's one step away from being a murderer, if he isn't one already, she thought. "Get back on point, you son of a—" she began, but then, considering their situation, she chose not to complete that thought. Instead, she mentally stepped back, took a breath, and chose a different approach.

Trying to sound as reasonable as she could, she said, "By the way, we would also like an explanation of how that stealth suit thing you're wearing does what it does too."

"Staying on point, Detective Compton, remember?" Nigel answered.

Meredith looked as if she could've shot Nigel right then. Instead, she took a deep breath and put on a pleasant smile that didn't hide the anger in her eyes. *Don't irritate her*, Billy thought. Clearing his throat, he began again. "Okay, look. The two of you don't have to like each other, but it would be good if we could just get down to doing something about Ms. and Mrs. Arlander. One we know was murdered, and we have Nigel on video, seemingly uninvolved in that crime. Right now, that's important because it could clear up any suspicion about your role in that. But, Nigel, we really need proof that you haven't harmed Dana Lacy."

Meredith cut in. "What we don't understand, then, is why were they even *able* to kill his wife? Why couldn't you stop that from happening? We were able to put everything, all of this together because of the stuff in that box—the same box that you supposedly slipped into Roan's house right under our noses. So if you had all of that evidence in your possession and that sneak-about suit you're wearing, well then, couldn't you have stopped him?"

Silence fell like a velvet stone in the room, and Nigel held his head down, fingers to his eyes for a moment, then looked at his two reluctant house guests. His voice sounded like that of a man who had been beaten and stabbed when he answered, "I tried to, but something attacked me as I was passing through the *between* zone. Something that looked like a gray convoy of whatever, I can't describe it. The thing knocked me out of the zone and into some abandoned jungle world. I went back in and destroyed it with the finger waters. It was emanating meanness rays, and that meant it would become a danger, so it had to be handled that way." Meredith looked at Nigel as if he had just been demoted from dangerously insane to irreparably stupid. She had what her husband referred to as that "this suspect is a real idiot" expression on her face.

Concentrating as she was on Nigel, Meredith didn't notice what her husband noticed after that statement. Lucius Carver's eyes widened, ever so slightly, and the man sat a little straighter as if he'd just heard something that caused him alarm. He'd looked down then, as if considering some mutinous thought. When he noticed the young detective's sharpened stare upon him, though, he reasserted his self-composure and regained his amiable sidekick disposition. *He must be worrying that his boy really is having some sort of psychotic break*, Billy thought. *Maybe we can use that to shake his loyalty to this guy. File it away under "to be exploited later."*

His wife, meanwhile, continued on with Nigel. "What bugs me," she said, "is the fact that anyone who has that piece of equipment you're wearing could probably be in several places within a relatively short period of time. You could've been the ground man on that murder and still popped in up the bedroom, just after the evil little Wesley What's-his-face shoved her off the balcony. That would make you seem innocent, and even make it look like you showed up just to help."

A cold anger gleamed from Nigel's eyes at the mention of Wesley, and in an emotionless tone, he answered, "There's only one thing I want to help Wesley do, Detective. I want to expedite his journey to Hell. He should never have even *thought* of touching Angeline. Your theory of my complicity in that act is not even nearly accurate." Meredith continued with, "So what do you have to offer that proves otherwise, cowboy?"

Nigel bowed his head and rubbed his eyes again, and to the detectives, he seemed to ripple a little, as if he were seated behind heat waves. Both Billy and Meredith Compton looked as if they weren't sure of what their eyes were seeing, but Lucius stood up and, very gently, like a father speaking to a son, said, "Nigel? Can you stay with us? Come on, Nige. Stay with us."

Nigel raised his head and answered, "I'll be okay, Luke. I'm getting better at controlling it." Appearing greatly relieved, Lucius lowered his massive bulk back into his chair. Looking at Billy, he said, "It's not the suit that allows him to jump in and out. He can do that anyway, with or without it. Sometimes he gets overwhelmed, and when that happens, he could be lost, really easily. Everything—all of his past, all that he was, and everything that he is—it's all closing in on him right now."

Both of the Comptons had to remember to close their mouths. "Wha-what do you mean it's not the suit?" Billy demanded.

Right at that moment, before the Comptons could get any answer, Lucius cocked his head as if listening to some musical note that only he could hear, then interrupted, "Nige, we're about to have company." Nigel, Meredith, and Billy all turned to him and stared. "Subdermal communication device," Lucius told them with an innocent smile. "Detective Caldwell is headed this way. One of my men will be bringing him." Nigel nodded sagely, as if this was no more than he expected.

Then something else occurred to him. The Comptons began to notice an almost palpable rise in tension from him as he spoke. "Luke, is this one that I know? 'Cause if it isn't, we just might have some problems. Especially after what happened with Dana's father."

"Don't worry, Nige," Lucius answered. "This guy's one of ours. Actually, you've already met him, but you may not be able to recall it at the moment." Nigel nodded. Lucius cocked his head, once more listening to some communication that no one else could hear then spoke. "Nige . . ." He motioned with his head in the universal "we need to step aside and talk" gesture. "I think that you and I need to go meet them in the front room." Turning to the Comptons, he added, "Please wait here. Roan Caldwell will be in soon. Nige and I have other things to deal with for a few moments."

Nigel got up from his chair to follow. "Lucius, that man is a suspect in a missing persons case and may even be a murderer!" Meredith blurted. "You're a fool if you think that we'll let him out of our sight for one minute!"

Lucius's back straightened, and his demeanor changed. He was no longer an affable, easygoing sidekick, and there was real danger emanating from his person. Slowly, he turned his head to look at the detectives, and they were both silenced by what they saw in his eyes. Quietly, each word drawn out with real menace, he said, "You *will* wait here, Detectives Compton. This has become a matter of national security now. For more than just this one nation. Don't say another word until after you speak with Special Agent Caldwell."

Billy spoke up then. "N-Nigel? Pardon me, but I thought that you were in charge here." Nigel smiled and shrugged. "When Luke gets like that, he's in charge, man. You don't screw around with a pissed-off Marine Corps master gunnery sergeant, and right now, he's pretty pissed off."

"Why? And why is he calling Roan 'Special Agent Caldwell'?" Billy asked, which seemed to irritate Nigel. "Look, man, I don't know. But if he wants me to get in there with him, I'd better go. Following a battle-hardened master gun's orders is how dozens of marines stay alive."

"You never made it as a marine, though, did you?" Meredith seemed to be taunting, but Billy knew better. She was just trying to give him a reason to stay and tell more of his story. Nigel smiled. "You're wasting my time. And I have no idea how Doc became 'Special Agent Caldwell,'" he said then turned and walked out of the room.

After he left, Billy and Meredith exchanged one of those "What the?" glances that married couples eventually become good at. "'*Special Agent* Caldwell'?" Billy mouthed.

Meredith looked at him and shrugged. "I don't know, babe, but it doesn't seem that we're gonna learn anything by sitting in here like two bad little kids. Besides, since when does the suspect get to give orders to the cops?"

"Okay," Billy said. "We go in. But remember, he took all of our weapons while we were sleeping."

"Damn. He did, didn't he?" Meredith replied. "Did he take our phones too? Anyway, *could* we call for backup?"

"I checked," Billy replied. "They were pretty thorough. But a lot of these old alarm systems utilized a hard-wired phone line as backup in case the thing failed or something. The main panel had always been mounted in the master bedroom's closet. Maybe if we can go break into that, we'd at least be able to call out for backup if we can't get to Roan."

As if on cue, Roan Caldwell walked in. "Hey, kids. Miss me?" he asked.

Meredith, as usual, responded first. "While you were out getting promoted to *Special Agent* Caldwell, we've been held captive by this madman and his flunky." Roan looked down a moment and smiled. He went over, sat down at the nook's breakfast table, and gestured for his protégés to join him. They did. "Well, Merry, it seems that I'm not the only one who's been offered a promotion." He began. "You and Billy could now be special federal agents on loan from the department. I got them to increase your pay plus hazard. It's been doubled. You've also got credentials to go along with your wonderful new money. Here." He placed two badge and ID holders on the table, one for each of them.

As they started to reach, he held up his hand and began again. "But . . ." Both of the Comptons stopped in midreach.

"Of course, there's a 'but' involved," Billy said.

"Right, Bill, there's all kinds of 'buts,'" Roan replied, "and they all stink."

"What's the deal, Roan?" Meredith asked.

Roan took a deep breath, exhaled, and began speaking as if trying to explain why Mom and Dad lied about Santa Claus. "Well, kids, our work is going to be highly classified, temporary, and we'll be involved with a governmental agency that doesn't officially exist. I *have* to be in on the job because, well, let's just say I'm already committed, with a vested interest. If you're in, then you have to stay in until the business is finished, at which point you'll be released back to the department after you've sworn to nondisclosure at the risk of imprisonment, or potentially worse."

The Comptons were totally taken aback. They looked at each other, then at Roan. "What have we gotten into, Roan?" Merry asked. "Is this Nigel guy more dangerous than we thought? I mean, like, is he . . ." Uncharacteristically, she ran out of words.

Billy took over the questions then. "Roan, who is this guy? Is he some sort of deep-cover government agent or something like that? And really, who is Lucius? You wouldn't have believed the change we saw in him a few moments ago. What's going on here?"

Roan rubbed his temple. "Until you either accept or refuse the offer, I can tell you some things, but not everything," he replied. "Nigel is the guy

---

we'd be working for, only it's not *that* Nigel. It's an older, more politically powerful version of him. He can't do what this one is able to do—nobody that I know of can, but he's in charge of a governmental agency that doesn't want *this* fella exposed. They want us to find an alternative way to bring Arlander and Wesley Whatever-his-last-name-is to justice so that the pressure is off this guy and, by extension, his older double. They've put a ton of resources at our disposal."

Billy and Meredith stared. "So is he telling the truth about all of this world-hopping and reality-shifting stuff?" Meredith asked.

"Again, Merry, I shouldn't go too deeply into it if you and Bill want to stay out of the thing, but let's just say that is very likely."

"Do you have some sort of proof, Roan?" Billy Compton asked.

"I do have a collection of recordings that I can show you, I've verified the collection's authenticity, Billy, but all of it's going to go kaput in a little while. Some super high-tech self-destruct timer is incorporated into everything. I've also seen all the evidence I needed with my own eyes," his mentor replied. "I've met Angeline personally. At least *another* version of the woman we knew as Angeline Arlander. She's alive, is an older woman, around fifty-eight, maybe sixty or so, and has been married to the older Nigel for many years now. So she is not Angeline Arlander. She's Angeline Renoir. I've seen pictures and reviewed records. They raised our guy from his childhood until he became a preteen. That's the man he's been referring to as 'The Colonel' but he isn't aware of who The Colonel really is, not yet."

Meredith thought a moment then asked, "Is it a possibility that he and this . . . *other* guy, this older man, are running a game on you, Roan? I mean, if they are the 'same person,' or more likely, a couple of relatives, then why would the one not be just as villainous as the other? They could have both been in on the murder of Dana Lacy or something."

Roan smiled wearily at Meredith. "Now, Merry, didn't I teach you to go where the evidence pointed you? Believe me, this is real. I've seen substantiation. No matter what we originally believed, the facts don't fit our theories. I can't show you those facts if you don't agree to their terms. So, my little pretties, it's time for you to make a decision here. There's a lot more to tell, but you guys have to decide for certain whether you'd prefer to be in or out."

An hour later, when Nigel returned, all three of the law enforcement agents were still there, Meredith and Billy inspecting their new credentials. Without preamble, Nigel began to speak. "We're about to have company.

The nasty kind. I'm supposed to stay in here with you, presumably to guard you, but—" He stopped in midsentence, went over to the refrigerator, opening it as if he were about to search for a beer or something. Leaving its door open, he then continued as if his behavior under the circumstances were not at all unusual. "I went to get all of your weapons back because I know how unnecessary guarding you would be. Here."

He placed Meredith's and Billy's armaments on the breakfast table. "In fact, I'd like to set up an ambush in the living room. I'll wait in the center. I always liked sitting in that big comfy chair she put there, anyway. And you guys will—"

Meredith stepped forward and began to speak then. "Nigel, I . . .," she began, stopped, turned to look at Billy, who had a very contrite look on his face, and Roan, who, for some reason Nigel didn't understand, seemed unable to meet his eyes for long, obviously having come to a different conclusion regarding the man he'd formerly wanted to see imprisoned for life. Meredith began again. "I want to say that, well, I —we, know that we may have been wrong about you, and, uh, well, let's just get what we have to do done, okay? We'll work together on your girl's murder. Those pricks are gonna pay for what they did to her."

Nigel clearly couldn't believe what he was hearing, and he was even more surprised at the sight of a tear forming in Meredith's eye. "Uh, well . . . okay then . . .," he said, looking at the three of them with more than a small amount of suspicion. He evidently wanted to inquire concerning the sudden change of heart within Team Caldwell, but something else was on his mind at the moment. "Uhm, like I said, we're about to have a visitor. A Blade."

Roan, Billy, and Meredith all looked at each other with confused "what now?" faces. Nigel seemed to realize then that they had no idea what a "Blade" was, so he clarified it as simply as he could. "A Blade is what you'd refer to as a superbad news. Luke stationed me here in the living room. We're pretty sure that I'm being targeted, and things could get pretty sporty soon. He'll be on stalking detail, and hopefully he'll be able to nab the Blade before he or she can make it into this room. As far as we know, they don't expect you guys to be here, but that could be faulty intel. Even if no one knows of your presence, it's too late to safely get you off the scene. The Blade may have been watching the house a while now; they love doing their recon. These guys are pretty good, and they tend to go through anybody who gets between them and their targets. They normally don't kill bystanders, but if you're here, then you're not likely to be categorized as bystanders. Should we wind up in the middle of a shooting gallery, you'd be more helpful if you deployed in three corners of the room. Stay away from the windows and keep your weapons drawn and ready. If you have to shoot, move immediately to a different location. Keep some distance between yourselves no matter what happens. These Blades are quick, but their omnidirectional movement can be pretty limited in speed. They can't change direction very fast for anybody who doesn't get that."

As they hustled into the designated room, Billy whispered, "Roan, what's a 'Blade' again?"

"Don't know, Billy," Roan whispered back. "These guys have all kinds of acronyms that sound like names and designations. But if they're worried about this person, then we should be too."

"A Blade is a professional assassin slash grab 'n' go man or woman. They're usually biometrically enhanced, and they're pretty tough. Everybody get low so that he can't see you through the windows," Nigel was saying as he opened the curtains and pointed each one of them toward a different corner of the room. "Now, please be quiet while I put on my baitfish act. Just be ready in case that Blade makes it in. I'd rather not be killed or captured tonight." They moved to their respective posts as Nigel sat in the chair he'd been raving about, and yes, Roan noticed, it did look very comfortable.

Angeline Arlander probably convinced herself that she'd bought the king chair over there for George, Roan thought. *But as far as I can tell, the guy never even came here after signing the place over to his wife. So now that I know what I do, it's obvious who she really had in mind when she got that thing. Poor kid. He doesn't even know how much he's lost. And now some killer cyborg is coming for him. But if this youngster can do even half of what his double and that Kruger guy says he can, or even a little of that stuff I saw in the recordings, then I don't know if I should feel more sorry for him or the idiot who's coming to try to snatch him.*

After sitting in the chair, Nigel picked up a remote and turned the television on, then went and closed the fridge door, returning to his place thereafter. Immediately, Billy Compton's attention was drawn to the television-like device. It was a curved ultrahigh definition set, one that he'd seen in his beloved *Popular Science* magazines. *But that was still in prototype development! It shouldn't be here!* he thought. He was beginning to wander out of his post toward the set when Nigel gave him a stern look as he shook his head in a barely perceptible movement. That joggled Billy out of his reverie and reminded him of the life-threatening situation they were all in. He returned to his corner. But the picture he'd seen on the screen was almost *too* sharp, *too* high-def, so he surmised that possibly, the thing had a deeper function than just being a high-definition futuristic television.

His supposition was, in fact, correct. The set that Nigel had activated also functioned as a baffler that interfered with an enemy's ability to detect infrared heat. The refrigerator in the kitchen was the same type of baffler. Thus, any device that may have been used for that purpose would not be able to "see" hidden individuals, as long as they weren't in close proximity to one another and were not present in any great number. With the set activated as it was, OPCA Logan Eller's infrared eye enhancements would not be able to catch Team Caldwell's heat signatures. That was one of the only reasons they would survive the night.

***

Behind a sand dune that was covered with palmettos and scrubby water oaks, Logan Eller stood stock-still, hidden from view through any of the windows of the beach house before him. The home was occupied, seemingly by one person: his target. Tracing the man's movements through the house by watching the variances and alterations in the light that was shining through the windows was a simple exercise for any OPCA. He'd followed the movement of the target as he went from the front room to the kitchen, opened the refrigerator, then went and sat down to watch the television. Apparently, the mark was relaxed enough to forget to close the door of the refrigerator for a moment before he began viewing the program since he had to go back into the kitchen to do so. As there seemed to be no sign of any other person talking or interacting with the man, it was easy to surmise that he must have been the only one here alone. Or was he? Not likely, Logan Eller thought.

After all, if this person's DNA strands were as important to his government as the Blades' bosses thought, then it wouldn't seem sensible that he be allowed to carry on in life without some sort of continuous surveillance. No government would want any foreign power seizing such an asset. Precautions would be taken. Surveillance teams would most likely be deployed to watch over him. Any such squad would also have to set up shop close enough both to guard their masters' prize against abduction and to keep eyes on his location and doings without being seen. In that case, spec ops people could and should be involved. No doubt, he could handle such individuals, he thought, but caution was still needed. More than one assassin had died because of overconfidence. He'd be careful, then. Logan switched his ocular implants into the infrared band just as the target remembered to get up and go close the refrigerator door. He wanted to verify that the man was truly alone, and everything was as it seemed. It was also important to be sure of what, if any, type of resistance he may be facing, just in case there was more to it than what he saw before him.

As he panned the vista ahead of him in infrared thermal vision, it became obvious that his caution hadn't been in vain. The target was indeed alone within the house, but surveillance was set up outside. There were three two-man teams deployed within the palmettos and water oaks just opposite of the blade's current position. Those guys were doing a pretty good job of remaining invisible, so yes, they had to be specialized forces. The fact that there were only six persons on the scene meant that these were some of the best. They'd be pretty skillful, but the Blades were on a different level, and none of these others could possibly be as good. Since there was no way they'd have known he'd be here tonight, Logan could surmise that none of them were on the lookout for an OPCA. *All this strategy and planning while the man inside the house just goes on about life as if nothing unusual was happening around him. He didn't even think of closing the blinds or curtains of that window he's sitting in front of. This guy is just another obtuse civilian. Probably doesn't even know what's going on out here. Taking his safety for granted.* Logan thought, as he sat back behind his sand dune to consider an approach.

In situations such as the one he was facing tonight, where there existed a possibility of battling an enemy who may have been able to put up a good fight, Logan was hard-pressed to remember that he was the type of operative whose success depended on his nonexistence in the eyes of any agency of any government. He was a brawler and had always loved a rowdy fight. But that wouldn't work in this setting. He didn't need to come up on any law enforcement radar either. So any plan that involved charging headlong into the enemy would not be viable. The random killing of any government's agents was not something that Logan's masters encouraged either, let alone the random killing of six such agents. Fortunately, he'd long ago learned the value of patience. Patience, the time-tested ally of all assassins, would get his objectives accomplished in a much more acceptable manner. So he sat back to consider optional approaches to the problem. Okay then. He'd use a different strategy: take out the watchers quietly and move forward afterward. Unfortunately, there'd be no brawl, and as much as he loved a good melee, the tactic he'd conceived *was* a more effective way to get this done.

The rain has become less of a thunderstorm and more of a rainfall. They've been out in the weather for hours, so those men have to be uncomfortable, he thought. *Even though they've no doubt been trained to endure such discomfort, they haven't seen any immediate threat for a long time, which means they'll be less cautious, so they will have to move eventually.* For what Logan had in mind, that movement wouldn't have had to be too much. Just a little restless fidgeting on their end would allow him to put his strategy in motion. So he sat and waited. It didn't take long. A man on one team moved to scratch his ankle, and Logan's targeting sensors had that team marked. On the second team, one of the agent's heads moved. That team was now in the assassin's sights. The third team had a more disciplined demeanor, so Logan had to wait just a bit longer before one of its members moved his hand to shoo some flying pest away. At this point they too were in his sights.

Now! Go! Logan kicked his servos into high gear and began moving faster than even an Olympic sprinter could follow. With deadly speed, he ran toward the hidden teams. It would take a minimum of three seconds for them to react if they ever saw him coming, so he moved just a little faster. He only needed to get within ten feet of his secondary targets. The dunes that they were hiding behind were in a sweeping line from the side of the house facing west toward the north then flowed from there down to the sand of the actual beach, so OPCA "Wolvie" sped to within ten feet of them and ran past while silently releasing six "twizzlers" from his wrist braces. Each of these was a two-inch-long nonflash powder-propelled dart with weighted, narcotized tips. They were heat-seeking missiles, literally shaped like "twizzlers" with acutely pointed noses and frayed ends. The shape was designed to make them more ballistic so that with the rotation it caused they could fly longer distances, with more accuracy. "Twizzlers" would home in on any temperature approximating the natural 98.6 degrees of a human being. They were programmed to aim themselves at anything with that temperature, a pulse, and surrounding human flesh. They'd target the jugular, deliver a blood-cooling poison that would immediately put the victim to sleep, then decay into dust five to ten minutes later. No evidence, unless someone died. Even then, though, there'd still be no proof in the postmortem toxicology report.

Their silence in motion was yet another advantage to the use of such "twizzler" darts. The target would never know what was coming. As he moved, Logan's infrared implants confirmed six hits. One man fought against the effect a little longer, lurching upright just before the toxin knocked him back down, and it was over. Now he could crouch and cross the sand unobserved by his main target, who was still watching the television. "Wolvie" could have accessed the place several different ways: from going up the stairs to the pool deck and attacking head-on, crashing the sliding glass door after jumping from the sand to the deck, or he could slip quietly into a position just outside, disable the locks with his intrusion kit, and enter. He wouldn't necessarily want to accomplish the mission with too much noise, but if circumstances demanded it, he would.

Before doing anything, however, he wanted to do a little more surveillance. He'd allotted a certain amount of time for each step of each possible strategy. Whatever he needed to do as he moved in for the kill, he'd use only the minutes slotted for each action. So he slowed his approach to fit that plan. Eller still wanted to be sure that the primary target was alone within the house. That had become a priority because he thought he'd seen more than one person inside, but there was no sign of anyone else showing on his infrared. He'd checked the domicile's records on his STIDD's internet uplink while swimming through the water to get here and was well aware of the identity of the property's owner. She was the wife of a man who owned a security company, and their marriage was in trouble. In his mind, that suggested the possibility that she'd be here with his target and the perimeter alarms and cameras may have been active. *Cheaters are always a paranoid bunch*, Eller mused.

An active perimeter alarm would summon local law enforcement, and that was something to be avoided. Besides, if the woman was in there with him, she could also be used as leverage to gain his cooperation or at least to distract him from putting up his best resistance. Not that this one would be likely to be able to put up much of an effective resistance, anyway. He'd also read the military record of the person he was going after. The fellow had joined the USMC and been discharged before ever being deployed. He'd just barely made it through boot camp. As an ex-marine, a part of *this* Logan Eller wondered how such a man had even gotten as far as he did. Some stomach or lung weakness was what finally washed his target out of the Corps for good. He wouldn't be too much of a problem, this guy. So "Wolvie" would once again be patient and take a little extra time for surveillance. Tonight's mission was a hunt, not a seek and destroy. He needed to keep moving toward the house, but caution was advised. He didn't want to harm innocent bystanders, but if there were any bystanders in such an isolated location as this one, well, they couldn't be very innocent, now, could they? Okay. All soldiers, no civilians then. Time to move.

Meanwhile, Logan Eller had no idea that he himself had become the hunted. Master Sergeant Lucius Carver, wearing OTTO gear and totally indiscernible from Eller's point of view, had been following his movements since he'd arrived on the scene. He'd seen the Blade hiding behind his sand dune, surveilling the house that Nigel and the Comptons were in. The MISTmen knew of the Blades (as they called OPCAs), but the Blades, for their part, knew practically nothing of the MISTmen. Crossover Team Alpha and the Walking Dead Raiders referred to the OPCAs as "Blades" because that was the way the OPCAs referred to themselves, using a shortening of the phrase "Blood and Death"—they were men and women meant to be used as scalpels in touchier situations, broadswords in other circumstances, depending on the needs of their masters. As of yet, though, the two units had never met in battle. Lucius had a strategy in place to intervene in Nigel's behalf, but he'd also been ordered to capture the assassin alive, so he wanted to see what his adversary was capable of before engaging. Due to the embedding that Kruger and Leonard had within the fabric of this world's Ethernet, every order and directive of the Blades' activity was accessible to General Renoir's cadre if needed, but the two groups had never been at cross purposes before then.

Master Sergeant Carver was impressed with the Blade's speed, accuracy, and performance. In anticipation of the upcoming conflict, he'd deployed Rondo Little with infrared misdirection devices; this world had not progressed to the point of developing anything like the OTTO gear that the MISTmen had, so the Blades were not equipped with any ability that mimicked starlight scopes or night-vision goggles. When the OPCA project was "on the table" for development, none of its contributors had access to any technology that could include the integration of night-vision capability into the ocular enhancement equipment they did have. The idea behind their physical design was speed and mobility without the encumbrance of carrying extra equipment, and since the technology existed for infrared capability within eye implants, that was what had been used.

———

Additionally, the nanotech utilized by almost all of an OPCA's systems and weaponry had been developed by Crossover Team Alpha's Think Tank back when it existed, so naturally, the MIST could access any of those systems and cause the OPCAs to "see" whatever *they* wanted them to.

That was the reason why Logan Eller thought he'd neutralized three surveillance teams that he'd been tricked into seeing. In reality, none had ever been there at all. What Logan interpreted as three two-man teams had been, in reality, an elaborate infrared countermeasure system developed by Kruger and Leonard's tech company. They called them "coconuts," and of course, the devices were about the size and shape of small coconuts. Each mechanism was loaded with microscopic electronic circuits that could create holographic projections. When viewed through infrared spectrum, they created images resembling whatever the programmer intended. Thus Logan Eller *thought* he'd observed the actions and reactions of two-man "surveillance teams," when the reality was different. His "twizzlers" were now in Rondo Little's possession and would soon be in Kruger's hands for further study. This was one weapon that the MIST hadn't seen in use until tonight.

The Blade was crossing the sand now, and Lucius began to move to interpose himself between that man and his objective, which *had* to have been Nigel, Lucius thought, as he picked up his speed to intercept. By now, he could discern his enemy's tactic. He'd stopped running, took a moment to orient himself in order to think something else up, and now was headed stealthily toward the only part of the deck that was low enough for a man to climb. Access through the glass door and straight into the living room. Just as expected. The virtual intel teams had been emplaced where they were just to nudge him into taking the very route he chose. Lucius began to run toward the Blade's location and got there just as Logan climbed the deck and began heading for its glass door. He easily jumped from the sand to the deck and charged. The OPCA, for his part, was caught totally unaware, but his reactions were nothing less than superhuman. Lucius charged right into the man's ribcage, wrapping his arms around him as he did so. Any other man would have had several broken ribs at that point, but not this one.

As he was being driven down to the deck, he twisted, locked his hands together, and pummeled Carver between the shoulder blades. With the force of his minihydraulics and servos, as well as the titanium lacing in his bones, Logan was able to smash Carver's grip loose. His opponent hit the deck, momentarily startled that anyone could floor him so easily. He recovered extremely fast, but the few seconds it took gave Wolvie all the time he needed to implement his first plan of attack. Even as he moved toward the glass door, he reached into one of his war belt's pouches and hurled a handful of bb's at it. With the force of the throw, they, of course, shattered the glass just as he jumped through.

At that moment, he realized that his optics were stuck in infrared mode (there was no way he could have known that Kruger had hacked his ocular system moments before). He could "see" his target as the man rose from his chair and seemed to try at escaping through the kitchen door, but his infrared heat image was all that the blade could discern. He couldn't make out any other images, so he assumed that there were no other persons in the room. He didn't see the Comptons and Roan Caldwell calmly raising and aiming their weapons in his direction. At the same time, a very angry Master Sergeant Lucius Carver followed the Blade through the door he'd just shattered. Logan noticed this, peripherally, but had no time to spare on it. He chose to pursue Nigel instead.

As he ran toward the doorway into the kitchen, he heard gunshots and felt bullets hit him from three different directions. *They have men inside!* he thought in anger. *How did I not see them?* One of the rounds had grazed his right shoulder and continued along that side of his back, burning a bloody furrow into his muscle. The other hit the rear of his upper left thigh, and the last punctured his left shoulder from the front, then continued passing between his clavicle and lung. That stopped him long enough for him to try to look around for his new assailants, thus slowing his momentum. Lucius Carver charged in and hit the man with a ham-sized fist, the blow spinning Eller completely around, right into Rondo Little's equally large fist. As he fell, Logan whipped out his Glock .22 caliber and, without turning his head, fired a shot toward the sound of running feet that he heard coming from behind. He hit the ground, but sprung up almost immediately, snatching out the stiletto that he'd sheathed on his left arm, charging toward Rondo in an attempt to break past and get to Nigel. He was getting desperate now and wanted to finish this as soon as possible. This unexpected battle was risking his extraction, and that was unacceptable.

Additionally, even though the blood had already clotted in his bullet wounds, he was still feeling weakened. So desperation it was, he decided. As he charged forward, though, Lucius Carver kicked him in the small of the back, forcing him into Sergeant Rondo Little, who grabbed his right wrist and twisted it, his anger-activated adrenaline increasing his natural strength as MIST-enhanced power coursed through his muscles so that he nearly twisted his enemy's wrist off his arm, thus forcing Eller to let go of the knife. Eller went to one knee, but as he rose to continue the fight, Lucius Carver grabbed his shoulder, forcibly turned the man, and punched him in the left temple. The Blade crumpled to the floor. The whole series of events occurred at such a high rate of speed until it was over far faster than it would have been had these been normal men. Before he could apply restraints to the defeated enemy, however, Carver heard a strained sob from behind him. He turned around and saw Meredith Compton lying on the floor with a bullet wound to her chest, victim of the Blade's random shot. Her husband had dropped his pistol and was holding her face in his hands, begging her not to leave him this way.

"Please, babe, stay with me . . ." The woman's breathing was ragged, and her blood was starting to slow as it exited her stricken form. "Don't go, Merry, I . . . I love you, babe, hold on, please . . ." Roan was rushing over to help when Nigel stepped in from nowhere and stood looking at the wounded detective in consternation.

At this moment, with his heart shredding itself apart at the sight of his beloved wife dying, a deep empathy for what Nigel had to have gone through at the sight of Angeline Arlander's death took root in Billy Compton, though he was unaware of it at the time. Nigel, for his part, could only stare in shock, feeling an acute empathetic pang. It hadn't been that long ago since he'd been saying the same thing to Angeline, the woman he would always love no matter where she was, whose life had also been unjustly taken in this place. He knew that there was no power Bill Compton wouldn't have appealed to in order to save Meredith's life. This, Nigel understood. He also knew that he *ought* to do something, and what was more, he felt somehow as if he was the only one of the onlookers who *could* do *something*, but he just didn't know *what*. Roan turned toward him and said, "Nigel! Take her to the blue lights!"

For just a second, a look of confusion crossed the younger man's face, but it passed, replaced by one of determination. He pushed Billy aside and picked Meredith up then disappeared again. Five minutes later, he reappeared with a sleeping healthy Meredith Compton in his arms. Her clothing were still bloody, but the bullet wound had totally disappeared.

***

When Roan ordered him to "take her to the blue lights," Nigel *knew* what the man meant. Inside his mind, another memory had clicked into place, and no further explanation was needed. He knew how and where to find the help that was required. Nigel wouldn't let this happen. The Comptons were only here because he'd indirectly set events in motion to get them to come. No, he could not allow such bereavement for them. Billy would not lose Meredith today.

After returning, Nigel walked over and gently put Meredith in her husband's outstretched arms. Bill Compton's tears upon seeing Meredith alive and well expressed the relief both men felt inside. Nigel put his hand on Billy's shoulder and softly said, "She needs to sleep a little bit now, Detective Compton. Take her over to the couch and lay her on it. She'll be okay. You're not going to lose her." The two men stood facing each other for a moment more. Billy's eyes hardened, and he told Nigel, "I won't forget. Ever. We'll never come after you again."

Nigel looked into the man's eyes and approved of the steel he saw in them. "You're tougher than you look, Detective Compton. I like that. I will never hunt you either." A chill ran down Detective Compton's back at the thought that such a person would ever have hunted him to begin with.

Nevertheless, he knew who this man was now. More importantly, he knew what Nigel wasn't. Not a cold-blooded murderer. Not any of the possible types of disgusting persons he'd formerly surmised the man to be. He was a man who had lost the woman he loved, and nothing would save those who had unjustly ended her life. In his heart, Billy Compton resolved that he would at least do this for the one person who could possibly have saved Meredith from certain death; he would help him do whatever he needed to in order to deal with those murderers.

Turning to Roan, Nigel asked, "How did you know? I-I didn't even know until you said 'the blue lights.'"

"I've been talking to some people who know a lot more about you than you know about yourself," Roan answered. "You still have a lot of friends out there, Nigel. They've never forgotten you or the things you've done for them."

The younger man stared at the detective for a moment then replied, "But I still don't have Angeline. And now, knowing what I could have done then only makes the pain worse." Roan wanted to say more, but a commotion coming from the direction of the kitchen interrupted any further conversation. Rondo Little had pulled the ski mask off the blade

---

and found himself staring at the face of someone who, in another reality, was one of his fellow MISTmen. At that moment, OPCA Eller had also awakened and was once more attempting to get past the two of them in order to assail Nigel, who had turned around to face the trio.

"Let him go, Luke," Nigel said. His voice was quiet, with a hardness of metal and rage. At the sound of his simple command, the three men ceased their struggle and stared.

"He'll kill you if he can, Nige," Lucius answered.

"I have no doubt concerning his intent," Nigel replied. "I've got something for him, though. Let him go." For a moment, Lucius Carver, Rondo Little, and the man they were struggling with stopped and looked at Nigel. "Nige, he'll kill you if he can," Lucius repeated.

"If he *can*, Luke," Nigel answered. OPCA Carl Eller's eyes lit with angry anticipation, and a wolfish smile came unbidden to his lips. Could it be? This fool wanted to take him on one-on-one? Might he still be able to accomplish his mission? If these spec-ops guys would just let him go, he had no doubt that not only would he definitely kill his target, but afterward, they'd be next. "Nigel, are you sure?" Roan quietly asked, even as the Blade stopped his struggles, hoping, just hoping . . .

"Yes, Detective, I am absolutely sure," Nigel replied. Afterward, Roan Caldwell would always recall this being the moment he truly realized that Nigel and the older man he'd previously met had to be two versions of the same individual. No other person he knew had such an ability to sound so menacing while speaking so quietly. To Roan, it seemed that what followed was happening in slow motion although he knew, intellectually, that the truth was entirely opposite. Lucius and Rondo looked at each other, Lucius shrugged, and they let OPCA Eller go. The Blade moved like uncorked lightning as he charged toward Nigel, pulling a thin-bladed Fairbairn-Sykes fighting knife out of a pocket hidden within his fatigues. Drawing the knife while still in motion, he brought it up and around in a deadly arc that would have ended with Nigel's throat being sliced open from one side to the other. Roan remembered bringing his Sig up for a kill shot on Eller, but his body was moving way too slowly. He could see Bill Compton leaving the couch where Meredith was peacefully sleeping, drawing his gun as he moved. Again, too slowly. Out of the side of his eye, he could see both MISTmen just standing there, seemingly buzzing of anticipation. *Why aren't they doing something?* Roan thought in his slow-motion world as he tried to aim his weapon. To draw a bead on a killer. To save an innocent man's life.

Suddenly, Nigel just *disappeared*, leaving Eller's knife to slice through empty air. The momentum of his failed strike almost took OPCA Eller off his feet, but of course, he recovered with the grace of a master martial artist or a ballet lead. Before he could even turn his head, though, Nigel reappeared behind his assailant, his eyes gone entirely charcoal gray. In his hands, held high, he was clutching something that Roan could only process as an upside-down round-bottomed bucket made of moving smoke, also colored charcoal gray. He slammed this over his assailant's head, and OPCA Eller, the human blade, immediately fell into Nigel's arms like a lifeless dishrag. Then they both just *disappeared*, like a blink in the light. Lucius Carver and Rondo Little beamed with unabashed pride.

Variants and Malice

In the Tule Valley, Utah, desert of the younger Nigel Renoir's home world, a rift opened in the fabric of reality; and four Stryker 8 × 8 multirole armored troop carriers, both painted flat charcoal gray, quietly rolled out. They stopped and waited in total silence for two minutes or so as an array of antennae and microsatellite dishes seemed to sprout on the top of each vehicle, rotating and moving as if searching for a sign from heaven or the desert. The APCs held their position until all of their antennae and comm devices began pointing in the same direction: toward MPIS Detention Center A-21, the maximum-security prison facility that the MISTmen raided just a few weeks before, where Correctus Dawson had met his ignominious end. Then they began to move slowly toward that location, assessing the world around them as they moved.

An hour later, four more of them appeared out of another rift. These headed northeast toward Sevier Lake. The men inside the troop carriers were human, though it would have been hard for anyone in this world to tell. They were dressed in typical military battle gear, just as any observer would have expected. There was one noticeable difference in theirs, though. Each soldier had something that resembled a large square backpack strapped onto them. Within each of these was an umbilical that for all the world resembled a rat's tail, about three inches' diameter, tapering to a sharp, hollow tip with a hypodermic-type needle point of about one inch in diameter. When deployed, this would penetrate the body of its target and inject a substance that reduced all the victim's internal organs into a liquid that would be extracted and stored under compression in the square receptacle on their backs. Underneath their outer clothing, each man's entire body was encased in what resembled a thin, rubbery, artificial skin in flat nonreflective gray. Beneath that, each person's natural skin tone was completely and totally gray. If the observer could have gotten close enough, he may have noticed that the hair, eyes, and teeth were the only parts where there were differences in the lightness or darkness of the grayness.

Otherwise, they were all monochromic men, without any variation even in the shades or colors of their epidermis. They were called the Graise because that was the name they'd given themselves a long time ago. They were here for the same reason that they'd been to General Nigel B. Renoir's world: to take as many normal humans as they could into processing in order to liquefy them, then collect the DNA-rich amino fluid left of anyone processed that way. They needed to ensure the survival of what the human race had become in their world, and the only way to get completely compatible DNA was to take it from animals or other humans who had not been subjected to forced mutation as they themselves had. They would, additionally, take any and everything of value that could be plundered from this Earth. That was their intent. They expected to face a fight, of course, but overcoming any such resistance was vital to their continued existence as a race, so they'd become very good at it.

The Craine-Muldowney virus of their reality had been concocted many, many years ago in an entirely dissimilar way for similar reasons. In their world, there had been no Division, no MIST, OPCA, or any other type of forces that may have stood against the two mad geniuses who had twisted humanity so. There was no Nigel and no Angeline. Blacen Muldowney had been one of the most prominent citizens of their United States, and Devin Craine had been the CEO of a pharmaceutical company with a questionable reputation. Using Muldowney's nanoengineering genius and Craine's natural brilliance in the field of genetic epidemiology, along with the covert approval and aid of their American President and his cabinet, they'd created a synthesis of nanotechnology and virology, an artificial genetic variance with the characteristics of a mutable virus; invented an airborne delivery system; and afterward, set in motion a top secret mass infection. Within six months, though, their pathogen had mutated so far beyond its original parameters that they could no longer contain it. Two years from the moment it spiraled out of its masters' control, the entire human race was infected. Irrevocably. That somber news had been delivered by Lester Holt in a historical NBC News Special Report. The President, upon realizing that he could not possibly have won another term, had conspired with his surgeon general, Mr. Blacen Muldowney, and

Devin Craine Pharmaceuticals to create a superbug that would be a final solution to all the perceived ills that had galvanized his "alt-right" base and put him in office. The Craine-Muldowney nanovirus was designed to target Black Americans (no one in that reality called them "African Americans" since the Continental African Congress, an American ally, resented that term vehemently), Jews and Central Americans, in that order.

But just as unto all plots of evil and malice, this one had grown far beyond the constraints of its creators. It was a virus like no other, a combination of micromachinery and DNA targeting ability that could reprogram itself to overcome any threat to its existence. Like all other racists before, these men had never accepted or had forgotten the fact that the human race is one race and that African DNA was present, to some degree, in most of the people who walked the earth. So for the first time, an American president was arrested in the Oval Office and taken away to Fort Leavenworth to await trial. Devin Craine and Blacen Muldowney, however, were both dead by then. One had been shot by federal marshals "while attempting to escape," and the other had been torn to pieces by an angry mob. The police had arrived just a little too late, it seemed. Meanwhile, the infection had also escalated: it was attacking the telomeric ends of human DNA; and children, always the most susceptible, began to age at a faster pace than their parents, who, in turn, were suddenly aging at a greater pace than their parents. Individuals over eighty years old were of the only genotype that seemed unaffected. So grandparents were watching as their successors died of old age while they themselves continued aging at a normal rate.

The virus spread around earth like a wildfire burning through dried grassland, and sooner than expected, babies began being born with skin as gray as old ash. Whenever that skin was broken, their blood would instantly fuse with any organic surface it spilled upon then absorb it, killing the nanovirus, but unfortunately also killing its host if the absorption managed to infiltrate the body. Human civilization began to topple, and as usual, the nations were preparing to go to war over the matter. Three years of unrest went by as the human lifespan declined until a newly elected President of the United States, Roan Caldwell, commissioned Leonard and Kruger Biotech, a reliable, ethical corporation, to find a solution to the problem posed by the virus, giving them carte blanche to conscript any person or persons within the sphere of American influence whom they may have deemed necessary to accentuate their efforts.

———

Within its first year, the company invented what became known as the EXOS-LK1—a breakthrough with worldwide implications. It was a masterpiece of microengineering, a protective polymeric external skin (named simply ExoSkin) that could process and deliver a DNA balancing drug directly into the body of its wearer through the epidermis. All that was needed was untainted, compatible DNA rendered into a liquid form. This presented its own set of problems, though, for all of humanity under a certain age had been tarnished. Most of the untainted elderly, however, began to volunteer themselves (or were volunteered) for liquification, that they might once more protect and preserve the lives of their offspring. Thus, the wisdom of the world began to disappear. It was too much to give, but was given anyway. So Leonard and Kruger Biotech went back to the drawing board and applied further refinements to their ExoSkin. When they were done, the EXOS-LK2 was created, and compatibility of donor amino acids only had to be within 70 percent of human. It was not a perfect solution, but it was the only one available. Now, however, the animal kingdom was in danger of being eliminated for the survival of the kingdom of humankind. And the world was still at war.

Realizing the magnitude of what was at stake; the survival and future of humanity, the American president Caldwell led a coalition of nations into a Non-Aggression Pact designed to last as long as the Craine-Muldowney viral threat to their survival was extant. Thereafter, any state, principality, or dominion that resisted the Pax Caldwell was attacked and eliminated, their compatible citizens rendered into the fluidic DNA balancing substance that could be administered through the ExoSkin, which had been mass-produced for all peoples through the industrial systems of the coalition nations. Soon enough, every ruler or group of rulers on the planet got the point and joined the Worldwide Federation. Finally, peace between the powers that be reigned supreme, and the human lifespan of the newer generations increased from twenty years to thirty, for as long as the amino fluid lasted. More years and more generations passed, and in time, the Craine-Muldowney virus (CMV) once again began self-modification, unnoticed, until the day that humans found they could not touch one another without the protection of the ExoSkin because the telomeric mutation would force fusion of anything human with anything human upon contact, instantly killing all living tissue. But there was more: further bad news soon had to be released to the public—human egg and sperm cells, which normally carried 23 chromosomes each, now carried

13 natural chromosomes and 10 nonreproductive nanites. Additionally, all nonhuman surface phylum on earth were now infected with their own variant of CMV, so they could no longer be used as donors for the ExoSkin's DNA balancing amino liquid compound (ALC). Mankind seemed to be doomed.

At that crucial moment in human history, First Contact had finally come. A benevolent race known as the Tola Bren, encouraged by the worldwide peace, landed seven ships in the Bonneville Salt Flats of northern Utah, hoping to befriend the denizens of Earth. With no understanding of the state of humanity's thinking nor the depth of their desperation, they chose to broadcast their intentions and their species' goodwill, along with an arrival date, location, and time, a year before they actually landed on earth, so as not to appear threatening. When the Tola Bren finally arrived, they were met with great fanfare. The leaders of all the world's governments turned out to welcome their visitors. They were asked, however, to remain in the location where they'd first landed so that the peoples of Terra could become familiar with them through podcasts, broadcasts, social media, and all other means by which humanity communicated. Lacking their host's imaginative maliciousness as they did, the Tola Bren had no idea of the fatality of such a decision, so they agreed to the Terrans' terms and remained where they'd landed, welcoming visitors, allowing the curious humans to take blood samples and cheerfully expounding upon the nature of Tola Bren technology, as well as its applications.

They'd found a sort of negative zone, they explained, through which they could traverse the vast distances between the stars to move from one world to another as fast as their imaginations would allow. It was, however, described as a dangerous course, since any Tola who went in without a skyship would always, without exception, wind up catatonic; but eventually, they'd learned to deploy probes into the zone. These probes would find routes to other worlds, then mark those routes with binary coding that allowed the Tola Bren to stabilize the pathways into courses that could be set and followed while remaining within the safety of their ships, and yes, this world had been discovered many of their life cycles ago, but they'd patiently waited throughout all the long years since for the time when humanity would become true creatures of peace, as they themselves were.

Finally, the day came when the Tola would be allowed to go out among the people of earth, to see more of their friends' world. Eight school buses arrived, to be boarded by thirty-one Tola Bren each, with four of them remaining behind to look after their camp. What the Tola Bren did not know then, nor would ever learn, was that their blood, although yellow, not red as human blood once was, still proved to have DNA that was, at most, 50 percent compatible with human DNA. Additionally, their cloning technology, open to all inquiries as it was, had shown their hosts how to keep their own race alive. They couldn't clone a human, but they could clone the missing chromosomes. All they'd need were 13 (or less) natural chromosomes from a male and the same amount from a female to create children now. Moreover, the biological technology the Tola Bren shared from their databases enabled humanity to create a recombination of their precious amino liquid compound so that its potency increased exponentially. With their new EXOS-LK5s in circulation, the life-preserving solvent they'd invented could be spread farther and last longer. In time, they predicted, the human lifespan could be raised to at least sixty or seventy years with these advancements!

Thus, the eight school buses transported their occupants 11.95 miles, from the Bonneville Salt Flats to a facility located in West Wendover, Nevada. Its construction had been under way for more than two years now, and it was finally completed. This was Camp Esperance, the world's newest liquification facility, specially designed to adapt to DNA that may be alien to earth. The Tola Bren were liquefied, their DNA's incompatible chromosomes "scrubbed," and the rest added to the Terrans' worldwide ALC reserves. That done, the commandos who had been waiting at Bonneville Salt Flats were ordered to take one of the Tola Bren's ships and force the four remaining ones to show them how to fly it along the pathways between the worlds to their home world while the other six ships, filled with more spec-ops commandos, followed.

So it was that on November 27, 2030, as their world reckoned time, that the first of many Graise attack forces took to the zone between the worlds. From that moment on, they would destroy every race they encountered, scrubbing its DNA and using that for their own survival. Unfortunately, for them, however, any hope of moving to some brave new world would come to nothing, and they would remain trapped upon the planet of their origin. Why? Because despite the fact that every other race they encountered breathed the same oxygen-nitrogen mix of air that humans had, the Graise always found that the CMV disease they carried would not allow them to breathe the air of any other planet for more than a year or two, at the most. The DNA within the pollen of local flora would eventually cause conflict with the nanite portions of the Graise blood, and that would turn all of their vital fluids into one deadly toxin. That was just fine with them, for they had neither desire nor inclination to leave the earth for long anyway. As an emotional, irrepressible side effect of CMV, the anxiety of such a move would cause their systems to go into overdrive and speed up the work of their inherent infection. So they could never have safely colonized any other planet, anyhow. They were trapped on earth. That limitation did not stop them from "farming" on other planets. What that term meant for them was this: they would no longer destroy all non-intelligent life on the worlds that they conquered. A certain number of native non-intelligent life-forms would be allowed to remain under the "care" of several large garrisons of Graise that were to be assigned on a rotational basis. Those remainders would thrive and then be used as an emergency source of ALC during the years between discovery of new worlds to conquer. Additionally, the planets upon which the Graise had wrought extermination still had natural resources that could be used to stretch the diminishing ones of their own world, so these resources were harvested and put to use for the good of the overpopulated Planet Earth.

Eventually, the ALC they stripped from the Tola Bren and others would be used up; it was finite, after all, and they would have to find other donors. Unlike they'd hoped, their lifespans did not increase past the ripe old age of forty to forty-five, but every race they encountered allowed them to exist for a few hundred generations more, until they ran out of worlds they could locate and reach. It didn't seem possible, but it happened at length. What must be understood is this: the Graise could follow courses that other races had lain out, but they were never able to create their own. Since the original onset of CMV disease, not one iota of their technological research had been directed toward anything other than the survival of the human race. They just didn't live long enough to explore very many new technological paths. So everything they knew, all of their science, stemmed from what was passed down through their predecessors or stolen from others, whom they'd always rendered extinct. Ultimately, they ran out of worlds to plunder and, having no other recourse, prepared for the extinction of what was once the human race within fifty generations, as their limited science predicted.

On some other world, in a different reality, a boy had been born. His name was Roman Marques, and he had the exact same affinity for the buffer zone between the worlds as Nigel did. Roman, too, could cross between realities; and because the natural law of that power seemed to always land the reality walker somewhere near his doubles' location whenever he crossed, it wasn't long before he too encountered "himself." He and his double really got along well, so they began to work together to improve both of their worlds. Roman's double was a successful, powerful, and determined immigration lawyer and used his vocation and influence to preserve his youthful duplicate from conscription by the government, promising them that he and the youngster would find a way to enable the crossing for others. So together, they founded a scientific research group to work toward that goal. Meanwhile, the two Romans were instrumental in "cleaning up" the Central American regions of both their worlds, from Mexico to Panama, including the islands in between. As drug lords, cartels, and dictatorships led by erratic men started disappearing from those territories, they became, once again, a safe place for families to live and raise children. Furthermore, all tourism profits were shared between the landowners and the working class. People no longer had to abandon their homes and run in order to survive. That, in turn, solved the immigration issues that threatened the peace between the Central American countries and North and South American ones. The two Romans were declared heroes, and the younger one was designated a National Treasure of the United Association of American States on both worlds.

Soon enough, the governments of both worlds arranged a Free Trade Agreement, and Roman's DNA was used to create routes between the realities (he was, of course, well rewarded, thanks to his older double). Little did they know, then, how they had doomed at least one of their homes. Because movement between the worlds created effects like the wake of a ship moving through water, the Tola Bren's probes reported the probable existence of a newly discovered spacefaring race to their masters. The return transmission ordered the probes to move their pathways to terminate at the location of this new finding. The probes obeyed and repositioned, later announcing, with great joy, that not one, but two worlds had been found. When they identified the inhabitants' species for their masters, a long silence ensued. For the probes, it seemed that communication had been terminated without further instruction, so they sent a query. In answer, they were told to confirm with extreme clarity, so the probes moved closer than caution allowed in order to do as their masters wished. One of them landed on one of the worlds, the other doing the same on the second world. From their locations, they cast pathway calculations back to the point from which their orders originated.

The Graise, for their part, couldn't believe their good fortune. Here were two more worlds that could be ravished for their survival. Additionally, the residents' being human meant a *100 percent* baseline compatibility on DNA. That, in turn, meant survival for *thousands* of generations of Graise to come! Consequently, three of the Tola Bren ships were prepped, and commando teams boarded. Cheered on by all onlookers, the assault troops entered the buffer zone and were never heard from or seen again. Their superiors did what they could to find them, but all that could be located was the debris of their skyships. Because the entirety of their research had been geared toward exploiting the technological advances of others instead of inventing their own, it took thirty more years, almost four of their generations, for them to figure out what went wrong. The problem was the way they'd approached the destination. They'd operated under the assumption that the ships would be travelling to a *different* planet. What they discovered, though, was unexpected: instead of traveling through the space around the earth, they were trying to travel through the same space occupied *by* earth because the destination was a different alternative reality populating the same point in the Milky Way Galaxy that they themselves did. The implications were astounding! There were other alternate earths, where the CMV scourge had not occurred! Other versions of their own galaxy that the Graise could plunder, if only they could access them! But there was a problem in the realization: they needed to learn how to create pathways and plot new courses through the buffer zone in order to move between realities, and the knowledge of creating these pathways through *otherspace* had died with its originators, somewhere among the stars and the bones of all those whom the Graise had rendered into ALC.

So they went back. Back to the unpopulated worlds that stood as final monuments to the Tola Bren. Oh, the Graise never totally destroyed any world, they'd just use up everything that didn't kill them on each planet, although there was always vast amounts of destruction left behind. They searched among what they understood of the Tola's research for a few more years while the generation that had seen the loss of the Last Commandos died out and another generation arose. These made a different decision: why waste so much time looking for some vanished technological secrets when there was still so much existing stuff lying around abandoned? So they gave up on the search for the secret of creating new pathways through *otherspace* and chose, instead, to repurpose the probes left unused amid the ruins of the Tola Bren's home worlds. They took a number of these to their earth and tried their best to reverse-engineer them. As things turned out, their best was good enough. When the work was completed, the Graise had built the first totally new thing since they had been fully human. They made probes that could home in on anything traveling through the nil zone, whether that travel was from one point to another or between the realities. Oh, their probes weren't capable enough to create new pathways, but they could at least point expeditionary forces in the direction of any others who may have been moving through *otherspace*. The problem was that there had to be activity for them to detect and pinpoint before their leadings could be followed. Something or someone had to be already using a passageway between the worlds, for that was something their equipment could detect.

Now, whenever Roman Marques, Nigel Renoir, his brother DeVries, Dana Lacy, or any other person born with the ability to traverse within the buffer zone did so, there was no way for the Graise to track them because they created no disturbance; they *belonged* there. But when others did so, without using DNA from one of these people *within* their vessels, then the zone was disturbed—such movement left a wake of sorts. When the worlds of Roman and his elder incarnation built their pathways, they did it by posting their reality walker's DNA in two spots then stabilizing their own passageways by referencing those two points. That type of travel caused rippling aftereffects that the Graise probes could detect and pinpoint, so that was exactly what happened. They found new targets. During the interim from the deployment of their probes and the resultant findings, the Graise scientists (such as they were) theorized thus: they were going to be moving, not from one planet to another, but from place to place on the same world, so instead of skyships (almost all of theirs had been destroyed, anyway), maybe troop carriers should be used. It seemed agreeable to the One World Federation Council, so that was how they chose to travel. Twenty years later, two and a half of their generations after they'd become aware of the two Romans' worlds, they sent their invasion force to one of them.

Roman Marques was thirty-five when the attack that ended his home civilization began. He was in his double's world when the natural forces within the crossover zone made him aware of the danger his people were in. The Graise had chosen to follow the probe that had landed on his primary world, once their new models found that piece of technology again for them. They'd had experience with planetary invasions before and knew that a single planet is far too large for one army to subjugate, so they sent millions and millions of troops. They had them, of course, because the CMV disease had rendered any sort of intimacy too dangerous, so without the ExoSkin, they couldn't even touch each other (they'd lost the science that could have adapted these for intimacy many generations past). Resultantly, the loss of such fundamental and necessary human behavior, coupled with the brevity of their lives, caused them to live from birth to death with a festering sense of anger, frustration, and resentment. Thus, there was no shortage of volunteers who, from the onset of adolescence until old age prevented them, were willing to fight and die in the Armed Forces of The World Federation. Additionally, Roman's world was populated by humans, not aliens, and no creature alive could kill like humans could, so the Graise found their goals much, much harder to achieve in that place. The resultant fighting almost lasted for more years and generations than they could give, with Roman's contribution to the defense of his home making things even worse for the invaders.

In the end, the Graise used their remaining Tola Bren skyships to deploy radiation bombs around the entire world, and their opposition disintegrated. Their own ExoSkins could scrub the radiation, or most of it, anyway, so they took the planet and began collecting any surviving humans as well as surface animals whose bodies produced hemoglobin, all to be rendered into ALC. As for Roman, they believed their bombs must have killed him since he'd never appeared on the field of battle afterward. They didn't know he could survive and live within the buffer zone, for their probes could not detect him; he belonged there. Roman, on the other hand, had not discovered his ability at the tender age Nigel had, so there was much he didn't know. For him, the "blue lights" effect was unknown until it found him as he floated along, nearly lifeless, saturated with radiation. When he recovered, his anger moved him to extend himself farther than ever before. He used the energies of the zone to destroy every Graise soldier walking his world, and because he was still able to exert himself more, he forcibly pulled all 300,000 human survivors from his world into Roman the Elder's and sealed both against the Graise for all time. The exertion killed him though, as he knew it would, and he was laid to rest on Roman Marques the Elder's world with all the honor that such a man deserved.

General Nigel Boyd Renoir and Crossover Team Alpha knew most of this. Their home world had also been attacked and ravaged by the Graise. As unto all tragedies, there was a starting point and a reason for this state of affairs, a state that never should have come about. After General Renoir had been assigned to leave their home reality with Crossover Team Alpha, others who themselves were powerful men within his government began to question the wisdom of sending *that* type of man forth with the mission of saving the human race. They didn't question his *dedication*, nor his *capability* or *determination*, they said. No, it's just that there are people who are like *us* and people who *aren't*, they rationalized. The General had been honest and forthright in his reports regarding the financial status of the PHS, and such honesty led certain members of the "elite" within his America to ask, "Why are we entrusting so much of our wealth to one of *them?*" As with every version of any empire, there were those who the people *thought* to be ruling and then there were those who were the world's *real* rulers. General Nigel B. Renoir's America, the United Federation of American States, was no different. There were also other social issues that would never be resolved, as long as some humans felt the need to believe themselves superior to others. Whether they credited this misbelief to divine right or natural selection, it was still a fallacy that held their reasoning ability hostage to the lens of their myopic worldview.

The world war that exploded into being as Crossover Team Alpha left R-2 did indeed annihilate a large number of that planet's population, as well as some of its less powerful governments, but the Craine-Muldowney virus soon forced that conflagration to end. Even as humanity continued to die, those who felt that such a man as this Black *General* had no right to what they saw as *their* riches made their move. Using political influence and snakelike manipulation of congressional leaders, they managed to force the new president to impel the majority of their remaining MIST operatives to go out and locate General Nigel B. Renoir. They were to arrest him for Desertion with Intent to Remain Away Permanently and Treason. His men would be similarly charged if they chose to remain loyal to him. Any civilians who assisted the General would likewise be charged with Treason. The problem that they faced, however, was the same as they'd faced before. They didn't have Nigel the younger. Without him, there seemed to be no other way to penetrate the zone between the worlds. But they had been working on a way to do this without the boy for some time now, and when the scientists working on that project were questioned about their progress, they revealed their newest development: a crossover technology that could be implemented by anchoring a pathway of sorts at one location and then proceeding to another and anchoring there. The anchors were, of course, portions of the Young Nigel's blood samples.

Meanwhile, Craine and Muldowney's virus mutated again, and even MISTmen began to fall ill. Their government completely missed or ignored the gravity of such an ominous development. The MIST process took what was once normal humans in peak physical condition and basically made such ones superhuman. Their immune systems were included in the transformation. This meant that MISTmen could go anywhere in the world without any need for vaccinations against foreign pathogens. If, however, a virus could mutate to a level that would allow it to threaten such powerful metabolisms, its virulence had to have increased exponentially. So when men of that caliber began falling ill of CMV, their superiors should have seen it for what it was—not a series of random occurrences, but an indication of a supermutation within the Craine-Muldowney virus. All MIST-enhanced men should have been isolated with extreme prejudice until CMV had run its course among them. Instead, the commencement date for the mission to find and capture General Nigel B. Renoir and Crossover Team Alpha was accelerated, and MISTmen were sent to arrest an honest man. Meanwhile, with its destructive ability mutated to such new heights, the Craine-Muldowney virus caused the human race to speed toward extinction even faster.

Then most of the animals that walked the earth also began to die. Only insects, vegetation, birds, and marine life remained totally immune. At that point, the world's resources would have been better used if uninfected humans had been sent to implement colonization of the moon or Mars, for that version of Earth had the technology to do it. Sadly, despite having such accelerated scientific advances in R-2, human nature had not kept pace. Not only was the monetary cost considered too high, but the remaining national governments would not work together so soon after a world war. Thus, each nation pursued its own agenda. Meanwhile in the United Federation of American States, armored personnel carriers were prepared, filled with MIST-enhanced marines, then sent out into the *between zone* to hunt one of their greatest generals, never to return. They were dying of CMV even as they left; they just weren't aware of it at that time. Thus, the natural forces within *otherspace* did not render them immune to CMV—its endemic energies actually exacerbated the effects of the disease. Every

MISTman who entered died. Even their OTTO gear couldn't prevent that. But their intrusion into the barrier did even more damage for their world and their people. It created ripples that the Graise could track and locate.

Eventually, the Graise found the planet that originated those pathways along which the last ill-fated MIST quest had traveled; and although they had never encountered enhanced fighters of that sort, they still remembered the cost of attacking another world populated by humans. Having learned caution after losing so many in the invasion of Roman Marques's world, therefore, they'd changed their strategy into one that made more sense. No large force would be sent in a type of blitzkrieg attack, as had happened before. This time, several Calvary Scout Forces in armored personnel carriers would go to assess the strength of their target world first, for there were prices that even the Graise were hesitant to pay. What their scouts found in R-3 proved thrilling and encouraging for them. The human race inhabiting the newest target world was weakened to the point of being simple sheep for slaughter, and the Graise didn't care why. Their EXOS-LK5 could filter and scrub whatever was depleting the population on that earth, so they didn't need to learn any more about it, they felt. It was time to send the invasion force, the scout units reported, and it was done. The Graise came in vast numbers with the expectation of "wrapping this one up pretty quickly," so to speak. But as is so often the case when it comes to human factors, the quick victory that the Graise had expected faltered because of two—the unknown and the unexpected.

Since this earth's entire environment had changed in the years since the inception of CMV, the necessities of the world's new ecosystem had created a predatory planet. Species *needed* to consume each other to survive. Only humans would not kill and eat one another. Though the Graise scouts had liquefied any and every living thing they could find, they hadn't suffered many losses before they sent back their first reports. This was because they hadn't yet stumbled upon the hordes of roaches that would strip them of their flesh nor the razor-beaked swarms of birds that attempted to do the same. And none of them had gone into the water. So when the Graise sent their first expeditionary forces, even the insects, birds, and sea life sought to kill them, for tainted though the Graise DNA was, it could still nourish the need that had become a part of the lesser creatures' metabolism. For their part, human survivors living in R-2 had learned that consumption of certain types of poultry, seafood, and vegetation would retard the progression of Craine-Muldowney virus. Though they were still dying from that scourge, they'd learned to gouge a few more years of life from the Grim Reaper and, thus, were stronger in health than their enemies expected. Additionally, they had developed a determination not to allow any invaders to easily take what they had given so much for. There were also normally isolated pockets of humanity, such as island dwellers, deep jungle tribes, and mountain communities whose cultures kept them away from the rest of the world, and these peoples were uninfected with CMV. The Graise soon found that these native humans' will to survive made life so much harder to retain and death so much easier to come by for any invaders.

The island dwellers they'd encountered would always retreat to the sea in the face of the Graise advance, for no matter how far or how deeply this earth's natives submerged themselves under the sea or how long they floated upon it, by decree of the Whales, a species newly advanced to full intelligence, those predators living within the waters refused to touch them. This was not so for the intruders who pursued them. Any Graise spotted above the waters or upon them was at risk of being killed and eaten. With all these factors, the subjugation of Crossover Team Alpha's earth gradually became a war of attrition for the Graise. But for that type of warfare, they had the numbers to spare, since deliberate overpopulation and inherent anger within their strain of humanity drove them on as much as the need for their version of the human race to survive. The ALC that could be distilled from these life-forms was an absolute necessity because it had been more than a hundred years and a thousand of their generations since the attack on Roman Marques's world. The guerilla warfare waged against them would have to be endured then, inasmuch as extinction seemed the only other option. So they fought on, no matter the cost.

Despite their high rate of losses, the Graise felt they still had the advantage, for throughout all the fighting, they had encountered no organized human resistance. That changed when Crossover Team Alpha and General Nigel B. Renoir, along with a supplementary force commanded by Major Robin Lacy arrived in that world. It was also the first time the Graise had encountered Nigel B. Renoir the Younger and MIST-enhanced Marines. The battle that followed their first contact with Crossover Team Alpha had been devastating for the invaders. They had no idea what the MISTmen were capable of, but they learned over the course of that conflict. Fighters though they were, the Graise died by the score. All that was needed to cause their death was for their EXOS-LK5 to be ruptured, and that was what their enemies did. General Renoir's forces took a heavy toll even as the vast amounts of enemy they faced forced them to retreat to various defensive positions.

They'd also captured and questioned more than one of these invaders under torture, something the Graise could never stand up to. Thus, Crossover Team Alpha knew who the Graise were, what they were capable of, how they traveled between the worlds, and had even learned what factors would draw the gray ex-humans to any location. Eventually, the sheer numbers of their enemies, coupled with repeated attacks of mutated birds and roaches by the thousands, forced General Renoir's exploratory force to retreat back to R-3. But the MIST never forgot the Graise and never forgave them. The Graise, on the other hand, were more concerned with Nigel and his abilities. Those who survived against him had been thoroughly debriefed when they returned to their own world. Their historians had then searched the annals for reports and accounts of any other encounter with such a person. There, they located detailed narratives of survivors of the battles with Roman Marques. These were compared with the most recent soldiers' recollections of Nigel's exploits and brought to the attention of their Central World Government. Meetings were held, goals set, and a Directive had been sent to all Graise military officers: should this person be encountered again, he was to be captured alive at all costs. He was seen as a weapon, one that could change the type of warfare in that location into a slaughter that the Graise could not afford, instead of the long war of attrition that had been working for them so far.

That battle with Nigel and all that it had wrought was over ten years ago. Of the Graise soldiers who fought in that first encounter, many were now over the age of thirty-five, in retirement homes, or dead of old age; but they never forgot what they'd seen, and that directive never went away.

FROM INJUSTICE TO JUSTICE

Shot. She had been shot. *Is this what it feels like to be dead? I must be dead*, Meredith Compton asked no one in particular.

"No, dear, you're not hurt. Not anymore, anyway." She recognized the voice. Her beloved Billy. He meant so much to her now. Only once before had she felt that way about anyone. It was back when she and Del were together. She thought of the black-skinned, green-eyed twins, Delroy and Fitzroy, though it had been a long time since they'd hung out. Not since what happened to Delroy.

"He says you need to keep on talking to her, and keep her talking. She was hurt pretty badly, but she's coming around. She'll be mentioning events from her past a lot. Hope you can take it, Billy boy," said another voice, and Meredith felt a surge of joy.

"Daddy! Is that Daddy?" she asked brightly.

He laughed just like her dad used to. "Close enough, dear," was his reply.

"Quit teasing him, Daddy—he's nervous enough," she said to the two shadows that she could barely make out. Dad laughed and moved off.

"So Delroy, then," Shadow Billy said, and she thought he sounded so cute. Like when other guys eyeballed her. Many years ago, when Meredith was a teen, she'd found two really good friends in Delroy and Fitzroy Spikes. Their names were common enough in Jamaica, where they were born, but their father, Richard Spikes, was an American police officer and her father's partner. Consequently, they and their mother had come to America, to Fort Lauderdale, Florida, where Meredith's family lived. Because their fathers were cops, most of the other kids weren't too fond of the trio, so they always hung out with each other. By the time they'd become young adults, the Spikes' mother had a very successful Jamaican/Caribbean restaurant, and the family was doing very well. Meredith thought she and Delroy might wind up married because they'd been dating for a couple of years. But Delroy was flamboyant (in a *masculine* way, she reminded Billy). He loved to lease the latest sport cars and always dressed like some young CEO. They were driving from Florida to New Orleans for their first Mardi Gras when they were pulled over, and Del wound up dying of a gunshot wound, no matter that he was neither armed nor resisting.

"Oh," Billy said, and the shadows cleared up a bit more for Meredith. She was lying on the bed in the guest room of Angeline Arlander's place, she realized. Her clothing had been changed; she now was wearing some sort of long, silky African-print caftan. She heard muted voices coming from the direction of the living room and kitchen, one of them she recognized as Roan's. He was talking to someone who sounded like Nigel. Billy looked like he hadn't slept in days, she noticed.

"Hey, Billy boy," she said, and he smiled.

"Glad you're back," he told her, with tears in his eyes.

He's been crying! she thought. *Now, why would he be—* Suddenly, she remembered. The muzzle flashed, she heard the blast, and she, Meredith Compton, was falling, going numb from a . . . *gunshot* wound? How did the Blade guy do that? He'd hit a moving target—*her*—almost dead center without even *looking* while he was running the other way! And they, the two military guys engaging the shooter in hand-to-hand, were moving so fast that they looked like blurs. Meredith was falling, trying to call for Billy, but he couldn't hear her. She hadn't wanted to end that way. There were just too many things she'd hoped to do. She wanted to have a little guy and maybe name him Delroy. It was too soon to go, so she fought against death, but was losing, she could feel it. Billy was holding her, and her vision started fading out . . .

"Billy," she began, "what happened to me? Did that bastard *shoot* me?"

Her husband's face looked more serious than she'd ever seen as he answered, "Yes."

"Where did he hit me?" she asked suspiciously.

"It was a center mass wound," Billy answered with almost clinical detachment. "Maybe your heart, or at least very close to it."

Meredith seemed to have forgotten to close her mouth for a moment, as memories of Delroy's body, lifeless before he hit the ground, crowded in upon her thoughts. *He flew backward. Parts of him came out of his back when the bullet exited. Did I look like that?* She didn't know if she was thinking it or asking it. *Did it happen to me that way? Now she was crying and could feel Billy holding her again. He was saying something* . . . Eventually, Meredith regained her self-composure. Still sniffling, she asked, "Why am I alive, honey? Why am I still here while Del is dead?"

With no angst whatsoever, her husband simply answered her, "Because Del didn't have Nigel, babe." She looked at Billy as if he were speaking some foreign language or had suddenly grown horns then asked, "What did he do?" It was Billy Compton's turn for tears as he told her what transpired after she'd been hit, how that little battle had ended with Nigel saving her life and then taking his would-be captor as a prisoner.

She almost didn't want to ask, but as an Officer of the Law, Meredith had to know. "What did he do with that 'Blade' guy? Did he kill him?"

Billy shrugged. "Don't know if the guy's dead or alive by now, babe. He says that he took him to his mad scientist buddy, that 'Kruger' dude who was in the briefing material Roan showed us. What happened to him after that, I don't know, and honestly, I don't care. Nigel could have tortured him to death on the kitchen table right in front of me, and I still wouldn't have done a *thing* about it."

As he spoke, her husband became more agitated than she'd ever seen. Then he said, "Meredith, that *person* almost killed my *wife!* Whatever is happening to him is no more than he *deserved*!"

"Okay, Bill," she said. He was different now. Seeing his wife fall to a gunshot wound would have changed any man, she knew. Experience taught her that. "Is that him I hear out there talking to Roan? Yes? Well, I'd at least like to say thank you." He moved as if to help her get up, but to her surprise, Meredith found such assistance unnecessary. She felt fine, no, better than fine. *What did he do? I haven't been in this great a shape since I was a teenager.* Her knee injury was gone, and that constant nagging pain in her lower back simply didn't exist anymore. Meredith had to know. Her mind was too inquisitive to just *accept* things like this, so she had to go ask Nigel herself.

After returning to the Arlander home, without OPCA Eller, Nigel had gone to Angeline's closet and returned with the caftan. He'd handed it to Billy, saying, "I don't think it would be good for her to wake up in those bloody clothes, Detective Compton. Ange loved these African dress things, and your wife looks to be about the same size. Why don't you take her into the guest room so she'll be comfortable when she comes to?"

Billy had looked at Nigel with gratitude in his eyes then. "Thank you, Nigel. From now on, you can call me Bill or Billy. That's what my friends do," he'd told him.

"We're friends then, Detective?" Nigel asked. "You no longer consider me a murder suspect?"

Billy Compton looked at the caftan he was holding, then raising his eyes to meet Nigel's, answered, "I almost lost the woman I love today. We know, as cops, that it could happen to any of us at any time, but no man wants to see it happen to his wife. Meredith means everything to me." Grief seeped into his voice, but he continued. "I'm not as intuitive about people as she is, but I know a good person when I meet one. You're not a victimizer of innocents or a hardcore murderer. I say that not only because of what you did for Meredith, for me, but because anybody who could do the things you can, well, if you wanted to be a soulless murderer, who could stop you? If you had no morality, you'd have slept with George Arlander's wife and killed him if he tried to intervene, but that isn't what you've done. After he took her life, you still could have just murdered him and made all the evidence disappear, but instead, you tried to get help from the law the only way you felt would work." He looked at his sleeping wife. "Whatever you are, you're no cold-blooded murderer." He shifted a bit, like some shy kid who had spoken too much, looked at the caftan he was holding again, and repeated, "Thank you, Nigel. You can call me Bill or Billy from now on. You've earned that much and more of my respect." Then he went and gathered up his peacefully sleeping wife.

Turning to Roan, Nigel asked, "Can we talk in the living room, Doc? I guess you have some more questions to ask."

Roan yawned and stretched. "Sure, Nigel, but I've already had most of my issues about you resolved. It seems more like you should have your questions answered now." After grabbing two Beck's beers out of the refrigerator, they seated themselves in the living room. Nigel began by confessing, "I was the one who put that new bottle of bourbon in your living room, Doc. Pappy Van Winkle. The best." Roan looked astonished for a moment, but it passed.

"Yeah, I kind of suspected so," he replied.

Nigel had a question to ask now. "How did you know about the blue lights, I mean? How did you know that I would understand what you were telling me to do?" Roan held the cold beer against his forehead for a moment. The weather outside was heating up. *With that glass door broken, it'll be pretty wicked in here until the sea breeze pops up.* He hadn't realized that dawn had broken. *Early morning, and everyone here has been awake for more than twenty-four hours. Everyone except Meredith, that is.* He could hear Nigel asking again, "Doc? How did you know?"

God, Roan thought. *I'm so tired.* "Nigel," he asked, "are you tired?"

Nigel looked like someone had just asked him to explain four-dimensional space. "Whu—" he started and then Roan saw the realization wash over the younger man. He scratched his head then said, "You know, Doc, I'm not. Not at all."

"Right," Roan said, "and you've been awake just as long as anyone here. Me, I'm wiped out, and Billy there probably is too. He'll realize it for sure as soon as Meredith wakes up. By the way, how long will she be out?"

"Depends on the severity of the wound, Doc. That one was pretty bad. If I hadn't gotten her there in time . . ." Nigel stopped, his gaze seeming to turn inward as he finished the sentence, slowly as if recalling something from long ago. "If I hadn't gotten her to the blue lights in time, she'd have died. Then nothing more could have been done. It'd be good for her if he kept her talking when she wakes up, she'll want to talk about her past a little bit, so it might be easier to let . . ."

Looking up, as if unable to believe what he'd just said, he asked, "Why did you ask me that . . . You . . . you *knew?*"

"Yes," Roan assured him. "I knew how that question would make you think. You're not tired because you've had the same kind of specialized training and physical alterations as Lucius and that Rondo Little fellow. You can do what they do *and* what you do. You just can't remember all that. Yet. I'm going to check on Merry and Billy. Sounds like she's coming around." Roan stood slowly, the way a tired man does.

Before walking off, he turned around and said, "By the way, Nigel, you couldn't have saved Angeline Arlander. You didn't know how to. But you have given us enough to prosecute the men who took her life. Why did you give us this case when you're perfectly capable of closing it yourself? Think about that. I believe you feel that you'll be needed somewhere else, and you're going. Soon. There's the reason why."

Nigel didn't know how to reply to that. He had indeed been feeling pulled in *some* direction, he just wasn't sure which. But Roan was saying something more as he walked out of the living room. "Hey, do you mind if we search the other guest rooms? Nobody's to go into the master bedroom until after I look it over. There may be some sort of paper trail that can convict Angeline's murderers. Physical evidence is pretty much compromised, after all the action that's occurred around here in the past twenty-four. If there's anything found, we'll talk later."

Looking as if he couldn't believe it, Nigel answered, "Well, this isn't my house, Doc. It was Ange's, and I've only been using it as a hideout, so I mean . . ." Roan let the younger man run out of words then did him the favor of completing the thought he was trying to express. "So you're saying since it's not your place, you have no authority to allow us to go through the bedrooms? If that's what you think, then ask yourself, who did she really have in mind when she bought that chair you were sitting in out in the living room? Fits you pretty perfectly, yes? Right."

Leaving Nigel sitting in his chair with a confused look on his face, Roan went in to see how Merry was doing. *There, that'll keep his mind going the right way. That lanky Kruger fellow told me not to try forcing the kid's memories to return, but nobody said I couldn't give him something to think about that might help move things along*, he thought.

Nigel was still sitting there, deep in thought, when Meredith walked in. He stood up when he saw her, and for a long moment, a weighty silence filled the air between them as they faced. Meredith, not knowing what else to do with her hands, seemed to be wringing them, and tears began to form in her eyes. "How did you do it?" she blurted. "Save me, I mean? That shot should have . . ."

Nigel looked down to spare her the embarrassment of expectation, and the charged silence dragged on for a few seconds more. "It seems that I have access to some sort of healing rays inside the phantom zone," he almost mumbled. "I put you in the blue lights, and they fixed you."

"I . . .," she began then stopped as if to remember her words. "I-I don't know what needs to be said or how to say 'thank you' for something so *big*, Nigel. I . . ." Her words faded, and the tears that held her feelings in threatened to flow as her voice broke. She put her hand to her mouth like a barricade against any expressions then dropped it. "I almost lost *everything!* If you hadn't been here, I don't know . . ." The tears were flowing freely as she put her arms around Nigel and kissed him on his cheek. "I'm sorry for the way I dealt with you. I was ready to believe you were the lowest and treated you that way. Then you go and save my life as if none of that ever happened. It says a lot about who you really are. Thank you, Nigel." She hugged him very tightly; then while he looked for all the world like a kid who had just been embarrassed in front of his pals, Meredith let go and patted Nigel on the chest. "Thank you. From both of us," she said once more while gesturing toward her husband, who was standing in the doorway, smiling.

Nigel looked at the two of them and replied, "I know now that you weren't after me. You were here for Angeline's sake. For that, I thank you."

"We're going to get these guys, Nigel," Meredith told him as Billy nodded agreement in the background. Right then, Roan walked in and said, "Okay, your man Rondo tells me that he's already sent for some people to 'secure the scene, sir,' as he put it. Hey, what's with that guy, anyway? Has he got something against me?"

Nigel smiled as if at some private joke and replied, "No, he doesn't, Doc. Maybe you look like his dad or something. They weren't very close. Besides, he's not *my* man, he's The Colonel's man. I trust him, though. Have for a long time now."

Roan, looking as if he'd seen something no one else had, asked, "How do you know that, Nigel?"

Nigel's smile disappeared like a fog after sunrise. His face took on a confused look, and he answered, "I-I'm not sure how I know, Doc, I just do." Team Caldwell exchanged meaningful glances, and Roan said, "Actually, that's a pretty good sign, kid. That hell zone of yours must be doing something to help your memory."

Nigel stared at Roan as if he'd just seen a suspicious-looking tattoo on his forehead. "What do you know about my memory, Doc? I mean, how do you know?"

Roan didn't back down from the younger man's intensity. "It's something you've been struggling with for a long time," he began, with a teaching tone that Billy and Meredith Compton knew all too well. "That's the *what* I know. As to the *how* I know, well, *think*, Nigel. The Comptons arrived first without me, and First Sergeant Little out there, he was my transportation. Put all those facts together, and what do they tell you?"

Nigel's eyes lit up with anger. "Are you working for *The Colonel?* Did he snatch you off the street and somehow convince you to be another one of his *flunkies?*" he demanded, through gritted teeth.

Well, at least he doesn't look like he's about to burn me with that weird lightning or anything, Roan thought. *If he were that angry, I'd probably be french-fried Caldwell or worse by now.* Sighing as if he were some tired old father, he answered, "No, Nigel, I'm not working for The Colonel. I'm working for you."

That statement completely derailed Nigel's ascending anger. "Since when?" he asked. "I'd hoped you'd take her case, but I didn't pay or formally hire you, and you did come here with a brand-new federal job classification, so it all smells like my godfather's doing."

Roan was about to say something, when Meredith interrupted with, "Nigel, nobody here is like you. I know that you want answers, and you could probably go on for another twenty-four hours, but Bill and Roan are dead tired right now, and this place is just not the best venue. Can we go back to Roan's and take this up later? They aren't going to be any good to anyone if they try to work a case while dead. I can look over everything we've got while these two get some sleep. Bill can be pretty aggravating when he's tired."

Nigel looked at Meredith and smiled a little. He liked her much more now. Her personality seemed to be as similar to Roan's as a daughter to her father's. "Okay, Detective Compton. You guys go get some rest. I'll help Luke with some things he's doing and then we'll get together."

"By the way, Nige," Billy started, "where is Lucius?"

"He's tailing Arlander," Nigel replied. "We don't want him and little Wesley What's-his-name skipping town without our knowing where to find them. Ole Georgie's been doing some odd things lately. Looks to us like he's got some newly hatched evil murderer plan afoot."

"Nigel," Meredith cautioned, "don't do anything that might make you a suspect again, okay? Let *us* be the ones to put those turds where they belong, please. Besides, life in prison would be just the right hell for a coupla pansies." Like a big brother answering his bossy little sister, Nigel said, "Okay, Detective Compton."

"And call me Merry, will ya?" she told him. "We have *got* to be friends now."

"Okay, Merry," Nigel answered. "I can't swear not to harm those guys, but I will promise you that before we take any action, we'll contact you. Will that do?" Roan, Billy, and she all nodded at the same time. "Okay. Deal."

As they headed toward the door, Nigel's demeanor suddenly became more serious and he added, "By the way, Doc, the *facts* tell me that my godfather *has* gotten involved somehow, and I'd like to know what manipulations he's up to now."

"Yes, he is involved, but not the way you think, Nigel," was Roan's bleary-eyed reply. As the group walked past the marine police guards who had arrived surprisingly soon by Roan's estimation, he advised, "Maybe you ought to ask yourself why you get so worked up about him, anyway. Take some time to really concentrate on it. You might just uncover more of your identity if you do."

Nigel opened his mouth as if to speak, lost the words, then shut it. "Okay then. Maybe he is trying to help out," he conceded.

"You don't know the half of it," Roan mumbled as he and Billy got into the Comptons' car and Meredith took the wheel. As they drove off, Nigel stood silhouetted against a sky clearing itself of the few remaining wisps of thundercloud that had obscured the sun. *It's about time things started clearing up*, Roan thought. Sleep claimed him like some forgotten lover.

He remembered getting home and going to bed, then nothing more. By the time Roan Caldwell awakened, the day was almost spent. Merry was still up, studying something, and he could smell freshly brewed coffee. People follow set patterns within their own homes, and because he was no different in that respect, Roan went into the kitchen and began to prepare a brunch. Billy woke up a few minutes later. Smelling bacon and eggs, he came into the kitchen saying, "Oh my god! What did they hit us with? I've never been so *tired*!"

When he caught sight of Meredith, they both felt new tears. He went over to her, and the two of them held each other for a while. "Okay, lovebirds," Roan said. "Break it up. We've got work to do. You act like you almost lost each other forever or something." It was just the right thing to say. Both of the Comptons laughed a little. "Well, Merry," Roan began. "What are you thinking?"

Merry gestured toward the paperwork she was reading and answered, "There's nothing from Angeline Arlander's Beach City home that we could use to get anything else on Georgie and his little friend, let alone an arrest warrant or two. Since her death, that place has had more traffic than the I-4 at rush hour, so that's pretty much a compromised crime scene. There's just too much that we couldn't explain to a judge. We'll have to try another way. I was hoping to find something new in this stuff, but there just doesn't seem to be anything usable there either."

"What about his financials, guys?" Billy asked hopefully. "Maybe we should go at him from that angle. Could be something there." Roan, on the other hand, had stopped speaking and was leaning on the kitchen sink, staring out of the window. Merry and Billy had fallen silent and were simply waiting for whatever the man might say next. After a few more moments, he turned toward them and asked, "How did you know to go to Angeline Arlander's house? What's more, how did you find the one that belonged to *her*?"

For a moment, the younger detectives seemed confused. "Well. It was in the newspaper clippings, and—" Billy started. Meredith finished the sentence, "And since there were so many of the same variables here, we decided to see if that was the same too."

Roan nodded sagely. "As things turned out, you were correct, yes? It was the same house, same address."

"Yeah, that's the way it went, Roan," Billy cautiously replied.

"So what are you saying?" Roan walked over to the table and picked up some of the papers Meredith had been going over. "So what if that isn't the only thing that's the same? What if the George Arlander who lives here has an ex-wife who died or disappeared under suspicious circumstances?"

Billy and Meredith both blinked, looked at each other, then started going through the stacked papers and notes with renewed zeal. Roan went back to his kitchen. The day was moving on toward evening, so he knew they'd get very little done with such a late start. *Okay, tomorrow then*, he thought. *But we'd best get this wrapped up as soon as possible. If things are allowed to drag on as they have been, I don't even want to consider what Nigel may be tempted to do with George Arlander. But our little team is playing catchup. If Arlander murdered his first wife, the man has already gotten at least a five- to eight-year head start on us.* Roan estimated a minimum of four to five more days would elapse before his team even had one complete report on paper to use as a guide to the *starting line* of the whole ugly business. They needed eyewitness accounts, insurance documentation, bank statements, a coroner's report, if there had ever even been one. Angeline hadn't had one, so her predecessor may not have. All of this and more would be needed before any investigative boots could even hit the ground, and once the case progressed that far, he'd need more than just the three of them to chase down every possible lead. One whole workweek, just to get started. That was too much time. He'd need an army of investigators to wrap this up before Nigel did something dangerous.

So thinking, Roan went to his bedroom, reached under his bed, and found what looked like a carrying case for someone's laptop. It had been placed there by one of General Renoir's agents, right after Roan had consented to his own "special federal agent" posting, no doubt. He laid the case on his bed and opened it. The console within was much thinner than he'd expected, and of course, its phone was attached via USB cable. Much to his surprise, however, it was a cell phone, similar in style to any iPhone. As he touched the handset, he felt a slight tingle in his palm, and a nonobtrusive red light emanated from the ultrathin console, scanning his face. He'd been told not to close his eyes when this happened, so he didn't. Roan touched the home button, the phone lit up, and he saw only one contact on the home screen: Little Roy. It made him laugh. He touched that contact, put the phone to his ear, and after the first three rings, heard the polite voice of USMC MIST First Sergeant Rondo Little, IDEA Control. With no opening niceties, he said, "Acknowledged, Special Agent Caldwell. What can I do for you, sir?"

Two days. That was all it took for IDEA Control to compile every report, documentation, and firsthand account that Roan and his two juniors needed to begin their investigation. Team Caldwell had also learned by then that they too had been assigned an acronym. They were considered an extension of IDEA Control and thus referred to as the "Extension Team Caldwell." Or ETC. When she heard how their Mist-enhanced teammates called them "the Et Ceteras" or "the Extras," Meredith rolled her eyes and said, "Very funny, Roan." Roan himself suspected First Sergeant Little as the originator of this pejorative nickname. When it came down to it, though, it really didn't matter how they were referred to because all of their requests were treated as priority one. Once he'd explained what was needed to First Sergeant Little, the matter was handled with marine efficiency. The result was a pile of reports that had been printed and neatly stacked on the coffee table. He and his fellow agents hadn't even needed to leave Roan's bungalow to accrue more reports or corroboration. After the second day, First Sergeant Rondo Little called in just to check and see that everything "the Extras" needed had been attained. Roan thanked him, and the Extras settled down to review all the information acquired regarding the life and death of George Arlander's first wife, Irene.

As things turned out, the Mr. George Arlander of their reality had, indeed, been married to one Irene Arlander for at least eight years. She'd struggled with alcoholism during most of that time, it seemed. That, in turn, caused her husband to desire her company less and less each year. Resultantly, he buried himself in his work, just so he wouldn't have to deal with it, he later said. He'd hoped to start his own business installing home security systems in White Plains, New York, where they lived, but the problems and issues that came with Irene's alcoholism constantly interfered with the process. That sad affair had trudged along for about seven years.

Early in the eighth year of the marriage, however, Irene Arlander and her suspected lover, one Robert "Bobby" Landis, absconded to a secluded "spiritual retreat" within a rural community in upstate New York. Additionally, Mrs. Arlander owned a home about an hour's ride away from that place, the house being located at 2875 East Lake Road, right on Skaneateles Lake, in the charming village of Skaneateles, New York. The way he told it, George Arlander had driven out there three months after their separation, hoping to make things work and reunite with his wife. He'd heard that Irene had abandoned the drinking habit and Bobby Landis was no longer involved in her life. It seemed that the youthful Mr. Landis found a younger paramour while in spiritual retreat at the Sanctum of the Holy Blue Zen Eucharist Infantine, and that was why they were no longer a couple. Unfortunately, when George arrived at her home, he found his wife floating face down in Lake Skaneateles.

The ensuing investigation was inconclusive. Bobby Landis had no less than three women, ex-meth addicts all, who would alibi him. They claimed to have been involved with Mr. Landis in a "Holy Bacchanal of Zen" ceremony (the lead investigator noted this as a long-winded way of saying "orgy") several times during the week of Mrs. Arlander's death. Because of the great spirituality of the matter, they said at least one of them were obligated to be with him at all times during the week of the ritual, which just happened to include the day on which Irene Arlander had died. They could even describe "Little Bobby's" private tattoos. One month before the event, George Arlander, for his part, had gone to and remained in Panama City down in the Florida Panhandle, with the intent of assessing the area as a possible location to move his business to, hoping it would fare better there than in New York. He'd even supplied the number of his business contact, a Mr. Charles "Chuck" Reddick, in that area. His story checked out also.

The coroner's report, when it was completed, showed that Irene Arlander had been extremely drunk when she wandered out onto her boat dock and leaned against one of its railings, which broke, thus causing her fall into the icy waters of the lake, where she'd drowned. Despite all this, Lead Investigating Detective Stewart Bauman's notes also indicated his hesitancy at ruling out either Arlander or Landis as suspects. He'd gone to the scene and walked it himself. Something wasn't right, he felt, so he'd kept up the pressure on both of them. Eventually, though, George

Arlander's lawyer filed a complaint, prompting the DA to come down pretty hard on Detective Bauman. Although choosing not to consider the case closed, he'd left the two men alone. Accordingly, the DA's office ruled Irene Arlander's death an accidental drowning caused by overdrinking, and George Arlander got a huge insurance settlement. With this, he moved South to Central Florida and started his home security business. No one knew where Bobby Landis had gone.

Early in the morning on the third day after his call to First Sergeant Little, Roan walked out onto his back porch and watched the waves break on the shore for a moment. He wanted to formulate a plan that would allow his team to pin Arlene's death on her husband. In his mind, he agreed wholeheartedly with Detective Stewart Bauman's conclusion as much as Meredith and Billy's. That broken railing as a catalyst incident was all too familiar to Team Caldwell. That was why he knew, they all *knew*, that her death hadn't been any more accidental than Angeline Arlander's had been. They also knew that Nigel's recording of that evil act would not only be very hard to explain, but the application that allowed such a thing was also nonexistent, not even conceived of here. No one in their world had any idea of what "backpulse tech" (as Nigel called it) was, what it could do, who invented it, what principles it was based on, et cetera, et cetera, and so on. What they needed was a reason to reopen that Skaneateles investigation. They also needed a reason to make it a federal case. That way his team could be involved.

As he stood there, thinking, Nigel stepped out of nowhere onto the beach below. He wasn't wearing his OTTO gear, though. With jeans, leather jacket, motorcycle boots, and the stubbly beard, he looked more like a lone biker. "Hey, Doc!" he called out cheerfully, waving. "I figured it was best to show up out here than in your house. I wouldn't want Merry to shoot me again."

Roan forgot to be surprised at the manner of the young man's arrival since he was more shocked to hear that Meredith had once shot Nigel. "When did she shoot you? I hadn't heard anything about that," he replied. As he began to walk up the stairs, Nigel told him, "It was when they first arrived at Angeline's place. They got rattled when I sneaked up on 'em. By the way, you guys got any coffee here? Luke and I've been watching George Arlander creep around Daytona. It's Bike Week there."

"Well, uh, sure," Roan affirmed. "What brings you here anyway? Thought you were on stakeout."

By then, Nigel had reached the landing and was facing Roan. He looked down for a moment, and when he raised his eyes, there was anger in them. "You remember how I'd promised that before we took any action, we'd contact you? Well, it looks like it's time. Arlander's been making plans to leave the country. I think your visit spooked him, Doc. He's going to try for Morocco because they have no extradition treaty with the United States. His intent is to file for citizenship when he gets there, and Wesley's been conned into thinking they'll meet up at the airport in Orlando, but Arlander really intends to leave out of Titusville. I'm gonna catch him and burn him down before then."

Roan calmly took a sip of his coffee, but inside, he was extremely distressed. *It's always something, isn't it? Now, we've got to stop this man-child from committing murder, no doubt with Lucius's cheerful assistance and at the same time convince him that we have a better plan. What's next? Could this case get any more convoluted?* He noticed Nigel standing impatiently, waiting for him to say something. *Okay, here goes.*

"Thanks for letting me know, Nigel, but I'm not the one you made that promise to, is it? It was Meredith." Nigel blinked then said, "Yeah, right, um, so they're in there? Okay." So saying, he went inside. As soon as he was out of sight, Roan called Little Roy. After he'd told him what Nigel just said, First Sergeant Rondo Little replied, "We're aware of that, Special Agent Caldwell sir."

"So what are you going to do about this, Sergeant?" he asked then added, "We need Arlander alive, son."

"Master Gunnery Sergeant Carver has already begun to work on that, sir," came the stiff reply.

"I'd like to talk to him before he does anything that ruins our case then," Roan insisted.

"General Renoir hasn't authorized that, sir," First Sergeant Little replied. "Let me talk to General Renoir then, *Marine*, or am I not authorized to speak to *him* either?"

"You do have that authorization, sir," Rondo Little replied with military crispness. "Hold for just a moment, please."

I must've gotten on his nerves with that one, Roan thought.

Sooner than he expected, there was an almost inaudible click, and the General himself was on the line. "Yes, Detective Caldwell. What do you need me to do that Sergeant Little couldn't do?" Again, Roan was struck by how much his voice sounded like Nigel's. *Of course it does. They're the same person*, he reminded himself. "General, I need to talk to Lucius Carver. I think he's about to do something that'll ruin any chances we have at legally disposing of George Arlander."

There was a short pause, and the General answered, "Perhaps you should tell me what you have, and I'll see how we can all tend to this matter in the same way." After Roan's explanation of the evidence he had, and what he'd hoped to do next, General Renoir asked, "So you'd like to find a way to make the investigation a federal one so that your team can take it over, exhume the body of the former Mrs. Arlander after it's been buried for this long- six years, I believe, in order to see if she was poisoned, locate and capture this Bobby Landis, attain his cooperation, stop Mr. Arlander from legally leaving the country, and talk to Master Gunnery Sergeant Lucius Carver in an effort to get him to influence Nigel to stand down. Correct?"

Feeling a little foolish, Roan replied, "Well, it does sound like a lot, but that's about the size of it." The ensuing silence lasted long enough for Roan to think the General had hung up. Just as he started saying, "Hello? General Renoir? Are you still with m—" The General spoke again. "Very well, then, Detective Caldwell. We'll get these things done. First Sergeant Little will call you with the results. By the way, there's one more thing I'd like to discuss while I have you on the line."

Here it comes, Roan thought. *He's about to dress me down for going over his man Rondo's head.* The General continued. "Things would undoubtedly work out for the better if you and your team were to enfold Nigel within your investigation. Get him occupied and keep him busy. At the very least, such a course could ensure his continued cooperation with you. He may not show it, but the murder of Mrs. Arlander has angered him to an extreme degree. He needs to be involved in the process of capturing her killers. At the very least, such a course may stop him from taking upon himself the need to dispense justice."

"Uh, thanks, General, but I think we'll be okay with our current lineup."

"Very well then, Detective Caldwell," the general replied. "Thank you for informing me of your progress." The line went dead. *Not much for saying goodbye, I guess*, Roan thought. *Probably used to giving orders and having people shout "Sir, yes, sir!" whenever he says anything. Still he is my boss, so I'll see what I can do. "Enfold Nigel within your investigation." Who talks like that anyway? Hopefully, the kid in there never does.*

He dumped the last of his coffee out on the sand and went inside. As he entered his living room, he could hear the young people talking. Meredith was saying, "And that's where we lost the trail. This Bobby Landis guy just seems to have dropped off the map. Crawled back under his rock, or whatever these types do." She was in Roan's chair, Billy sat on its arm, and Nigel was in Laura's chair. All three were looking at a photo of Bobby Landis. *Well, I guess he's already been "enfolded within" the investigation*, Roan was thinking when Billy noticed his sour facial expression and elbowed Meredith, who looked for all the world as if her dad had caught her playing with his shaving kit. He cleared his throat and stood up.

"Um, Roan," he started, but as usual, Meredith finished up for him. "Nigel knows who Landis is. He's seen this leech in pictures at the Arlander's house. Not the one we were in, but the other one, where you interviewed Georgie and Wesley. He thinks that Bobby might have been another one of Mr. Arlander's little do-boys."

Nigel, on the other hand, was still looking at the picture. "Yeah," he added. "A few of us from the restaurant were at their house, having an after-work drink or two." He stopped for a moment as if about to summon a painful memory then continued. "Angie showed me this picture where her excuse for a husband was sitting at a campfire with *this* dude. She said his first wife had taken it on one of their camping trips to upstate New York. I said that the way they were cuddled up looked pretty gay to me. She would usually punch my arm and tell me to be polite whenever I said something like that, but this time, she didn't. She just shrugged and then showed me something else."

He was getting angrier as he spoke, Roan, Billy, and Meredith could tell. *"He needs to be involved in the process of capturing her killers,"* General Renoir had said that. *Well, I guess he would know, wouldn't he?* Roan thought. Putting his cup down and using his best de-escalation tone, he asked, "What else did she show you, Nigel?" It worked momentarily. Nigel calmed visibly and replied, "It was a scrapbook that he had. She and I were in his office library, and now that I think of it, this may have been the reason we were in there to begin with. She hardly ever took anyone in there. But she showed me the pics on his desk then went to his safe and opened it. She thought it was funny that he believed he could lock her out of the thing . . ."

Nigel's eyes were somewhere else, as if he were looking at some internal memory, so Roan calmly pushed a little more. "What was in the scrapbook, Nigel?"

"Young men. Some naked, some not. He always went up to Panama City for fishing trips, and all these pictures were taken on those trips. George and other guys, all having a few good times with one another."

Nigel's rage seemed to be under control, but he was still simmering underneath. Roan could see it in his eyes when he looked up again. "You know, Doc, I don't hate gay people—they're just as human as anybody else, but if this was George's life, why couldn't he just come out with it and go *live* his life? They both would have been happier. And I think she had some idea. She said that there were about to be drastic changes in their relationship. You know what? I *knew* it, man, I *knew* that they'd be divorced, but I wanted to be Mr. *Noble*, Mr. *Honorable*, so I didn't even try to hold her, kiss her, or anything, and that's all she wanted from me then!"

His voice seemed strained as he went on. "She *knew*, Doc. She *knew* that he wouldn't just let her go! That her *life* was at risk! That must have been what she was trying to tell me, and I was so *intent* on keeping it *clean* 'til I . . ." Flashes of orange were crossing his eyes like ripples crossing water, and a static charge seemed to be filling the air.

Suddenly, Meredith's hands were holding his. "Nigel," she said, with the forced calmness of an experienced cop. "Nige, *listen* to me. You wanted things to be *right* if you and Angeline had gotten together, man, that's all. You wanted your relationship unblemished so that there wouldn't be any doubts between you, right? There's nothing wrong with that, do you *hear* me?"

Apparently, Nigel did. He visibly calmed and said to Meredith. "You remind me of my older sister Joanna. She could—" Right then, his phone rang. "Hey, it's Luke," he said brightly. "Give me a moment." Then he went into the other room.

After his exit, everyone in the living room breathed a sigh of relief. "Merry, what were you *doing* just then?" Billy demanded. "He could have blown up or dragged you off into that whatever zone, or something!"

Merry answered, "I had to, Bill. I can't be afraid. If the fear takes over, then I'm worthless as a cop on the street. Scared cops kill innocent people. If I let fear control me now, I might as well become a house mouse." Her husband started to say something more, but the look of determination on his wife's face said it all. He shut up.

Right then, Nigel reentered the room. "Well, it looks like ol' George isn't going anywhere. He loves to speed whenever he drives on I-95, and this time, he got pulled over by Florida Highway Patrol. His Corvette looks exactly like one reported stolen this morning, so they searched it. The plate number didn't match, but they found something called Rohypnol III in his baggage. It's a controlled substance that comes in from the Carolinas or somewhere, which makes it federal. They call it 'the lady killer' because of some big case that went down a couple years ago. Luke says you ought to be getting a phone call soon."

As if on cue, Roan's encrypted phone rang. "Hello?" he answered.

"Acknowledged, Special Agent Roan Caldwell." First Sergeant Little once again. The sergeant reiterated some of what Nigel had just said and added more. Rohypnol III was a drug that had been developed in the former Soviet Union during the bad old days of the Cold War. It induced simulated drunkenness and exacerbated susceptibly to suggestion in anyone it was administered to, and its existence was, of course, a state secret. Any person caught with it was subject to federal prosecution.

Due to this drug, many a "drunken" NATO agent had been walked out of public places by "friends" concerned for their safety, usually turning up later on various television channels and news shows in order to denounce their NATO country of origin. After that, they'd normally disappear forever. Time went on, the Cold War ended, and certain chemists from the old bloc set up laboratories in Cuba, intending to concoct and distribute Rohypnol III (RHp3, or ripped-three), along with other drugs of that sort in America, the world's largest market for narcotics. One of their distributors happened to be the owner of a certain Captain Chuckie's Charter Fishing Company in Panama City, frequented by Mr. George Arlander, among others. Thus, the manner of her death could be a cause for a federal investigation team, such as Roan's, to order the exhumation of the former Mrs. Irene Arlander's body and have it transported to the nearest DEA laboratory, located in Syracuse, New York, for examination. New developments in toxicology testing could determine what type of (if any) drug had been administered before death and, if so, how long before. Should any traces of RHp3 be found in the victim, that would constitute reason for an investigation into possible terrorist activities, meaning that the Patriot Act could be invoked in order to refuse any suspect's right to legal counsel.

After explaining all this, First Sergeant Little asked, "Will your team be taking the investigation, Special Agent Caldwell? If so, the authorities in Skaneateles need to be informed. I have a contact number." Roan had no words. A chill went through his body when he thought of how fast this had been done and all that it took. He hadn't realized the scope of IDEA Control's influence, or maybe it was General Renoir's influence. If he could get this much done so quickly, what could he *not* do? A man with that kind of power could make Roan's whole team disappear without a trace. However, one calming thought did occur to him: *His wife loves his younger self as a mother does a lost son. He loves his Angeline and sees this Nigel as his son too. If young Nigel does something dumb, he could wind up impelled into service by the government again, and that could spell the end of his life as a free man. Possibly the end of General Renoir's family. So of course, any decent husband and father would move heaven and earth for his family. Maybe he really doesn't intend to make us disappear after this case is resolved. He may even be grateful.*

He almost didn't hear Sergeant Little asking, "Special Agent Caldwell? Are you still there, sir?"

Shaking his head as if to dispel an icy mist, Roan answered, "Yes, First Sergeant Little, I'm still here, and my team will be taking on this investigation."

"Very well, sir," the man replied with his usual efficiency. "There is one other thing. The General has stipulated that you use Nigel Renoir and Master Gunnery Sergeant Lucius Carver as additional investigators. They will locate and secure Mr. Landis while the Extras work with the Skaneateles authorities on the exhumation, investigation, and intelligence. Master Gunnery Sergeant Carver should be arriving at your location within the next five minutes. You will discuss the information you have with him and request his assistance. He will agree, and you will assign Nigel to accompany him. After their departure, a separate car will take you and your team to Orlando. There you will debrief Mr. Arlander, following which a private aircraft will take you to New York."

Roan felt a little aggravated at that and replied, "What if I feel that neither one of them needs to be involved? I may want to do this my own way—those two might kill Landis or something, and a dead witness is pretty useless to me."

"You may want to do that, sir," Sergeant Little replied. "But General Renoir also would like you to know that this is not optional. After you give Master Gunnery Sergeant Carver his assignment, you may handle all other matters relating to the investigation as you see fit, but you *will* follow these orders. Is that clear, Special Agent Caldwell, or would you like to speak to General Renoir about it?"

Well, I guess big Rondo Little is still pretty salty over our my going over his head after our last conversation, Roan speculated. "No, Sergeant Little, that won't be necessary," he told the man.

"Very well then, sir," Rondo replied, with less severity. "After we have disconnected, please go to your phone's security console. When the scanner beeps, touch the green button. This will acknowledge that you have received and understood your orders, following which a hard copy will be hand-delivered by Master Gunnery Sergeant Carver." *Click.* The line went dead.

Alrighty then, Roan thought as he took the phone to its security console. *Here I am, following orders . . .*

Satisfaction. That word described Roan Caldwell's feelings about George Arlander's predicament as he and his team boarded the *Little Bird* thirty-six hours later. He'd never forget the expression on the man's face when he and Meredith walked into the interview room where Arlander had been placed. That had gone about as well as expected, with Arlander first demanding his lawyer and then turning as pale as death when he realized that no such person would be coming. Additionally, he'd been implicated as a party involved with terrorists because of his connection to Charles Reddick's charter fishing business, a suspected front for a domestic terror cell, with connections to Al-Qaeda. The purchase of Rohypnol III ("ripped-three") hadn't even been expressly mentioned until Mr. Arlander offered that information in exchange for immunity from prosecution for his testimony against his former friends. The man actually seemed to think, according to him, that the orgies that he and his associates involved themselves in while on their "fishing trips" had been the worst thing Mr. Reddick was engaged in. Yes, he knew that it was an illegal drug that he'd purchased, but the only reason he did that was for "personal use," he claimed. He just had no idea *how* illegal that drug was. Oh, by the way, he *had* seen a few other things that Chuckie Reddick bought from his Latin friend who sometimes joined them, and maybe he could verify what he saw and who he'd seen, if the feds would guarantee immunity. Why, on one relatively recent occasion, he'd even seen something that could indicate a plan for use of ricin or sarin against certain governmental officials and/or their families, but his memory wasn't up to par, what with his being afraid of incarceration at some black site in Cuba and all.

In the end, George Arlander thought he'd been pretty clever, Roan thought. He actually did have information that Homeland Security needed to know. Additionally, there absolutely *had* been a plot to harm certain IRS employees' family members through an airborne deployment of sarin gas at two or more elementary schools in an act of domestic terrorism. Of course, that wasn't going to happen now. Reflecting upon this drew Roan to another realization: the General *knew. Yes, George thought he was pretty clever, all right, but he was out of his weight class when it came to General Renoir. He must have known what was afoot with Arlander's associates, and now, not only had that plot been foiled, but by George's own admission, he had Rohypnol III in his possession within the timeline of his first wife's death and his second wife's official disappearance.* The orders delivered by Lucius Carver had included a very specific directive; neither Angeline nor Irene Arlander should be the subject of the first interview. Instead, George Arlander would be interrogated about the purchase of the drug RHp3 with the intent of forcing him into exposing any other terror plots extant.

When "the Extras" arrived at Orlando International Airport for their flight to New York, they were met by an air force officer who looked for all the world like one of those guys Roan used to hate back in high school. The man was tall, handsome, well-tanned, and had a smile that most women caught their breath over. His blond hair had some gray within it, but that just seemed to make him more attractive. Roan and Billy both resented the guy, at first. Meredith, of course, didn't. He was picking up their bags when Roan understood that this must've been Marty Braggs.

"You're Major Martin Braggs?" he asked. The pilot flashed his all-too-handsome smile. "Yep," he answered. "That's me." He again smiled, this time while looking appreciatively at Meredith, who seemed amused at the attention, like a teacher whose kindergarten student had given her a Valentine card. Billy moved closer to his wife.

"So are you one of these Special Forces guys?" he asked. Marty snorted. With honest good humor, he answered, "Well, I may *look* like the Mighty Thor, but when it comes to heroics, I kinda perform more like SpongeBob." Billy and Meredith both broke out in laughter. *Sponge who?* thought Roan.

After they were settled into the plane, Martin Braggs turned to Roan and said, "Special Agent Caldwell, I was supposed to relay a message from the old man to you." Roan, visibly exasperated, breathed a huge sigh. "Okay, what does he want to order me to do now, Braggs?"

Marty Braggs laughed and said, "Yeah, I know, man. The General can be a little overly intense sometimes. Kinda reminds me of a fat old walrus goin' all possessive over some iceberg that nobody wants." A mental image of the ever-serious General Renoir's head on a fat old walrus's body, tusks and all, was just too funny, so Roan couldn't help but laugh.

"You've got to know the man to get that one," he said to the Comptons' confused looks. *Now I can see why Nigel likes this guy so much.* "Well, what is General Walrus's message, Marty?"

Martin Braggs smiled back. "He said to tell you that you're at the helm, now, sir. From this point on, the investigation is all yours." He slapped Roan's shoulder like some old drinking buddy. "Go out there and do what you do, man."

After that, he headed for the cockpit. As if something had just occurred to him, he added, "By the way, Luke and Little Nige wanted you to know that they've got some guy named Bobby Landis in custody. They'll be waiting for you when we get there."

A FORK IN THE ROAD

Once upon a time, Robert "Bobby" Landis had been a very handsome fellow. But that was a different time, and obviously, a very different Bobby Landis. That one had been a younger, more cocksure "Bobby L" who seemed to think that he had the world on a string and could do with it as he wished. The human wreckage sitting forlornly on the guest side of the desk in the interrogation room of the Village of Skaneateles Police Department was so far away from the person that had been in George Arlander's pictures and videos until Roan, on the other side of the observation glass, could easily have thought that maybe Master Guns Lucius Carver and Nigel the younger must've grabbed the wrong man.

He sat in the interviewee's chair of the interrogation room, slumped and beaten, with unkempt hair the color of old dishwater, missing and broken teeth that made his mouth resemble a ragged, worn-out saw blade. His eyes were shrunken and seemed a little glazed, as if he'd seen too many things that he hated remembering. On his feet were frequently-taped excuses for Nike tennis shoes, with a few dirty toes poking out here and there. Of course, his pants and shirt were in little better condition, and above all, the man *smelled* badly. The overall impression he gave was that of a person who had given up on everything a long time ago. *Well, I guess that's what homelessness does for you. Or maybe that's what taking part in the murder of someone who tried to help you does for you.* Roan was thinking. They had pretty much gotten the whole story of Irene Arlander's relationships, life, and emotional crises by this time, because, unbeknownst to most of the people in her life, the woman had kept a journal. In addition, DEA testing of her remains revealed that she had indeed been dosed with RHp3; overdosed, even. They knew that George Arlander had been the only person in her life who had access to that particular drug, but now, in order for George to be charged with anything in this case, the dots needed to be connected between him and the results of the chemical residue tests performed on his former wife's body.

Detective Stuart Bauman, who had joined in the investigation at Roan's invitation, thought that there was no way to connect George Arlander to the man they had in custody, or to Irene's death and that bringing Landis in would prove to be yet another dead end, but Team Caldwell had seen the recording of Angeline's murder. Detective Bauman, however, had not, as Roan felt that it was too soon to introduce their supplementary evidence for his review. Since The Extras knew how Wesley had been involved in that particular crime, they believed it entirely possible that Bobby Landis played a similar role in the previous one. At the moment, Landis was exhibiting extreme discomfort with being in the small interrogation room. The temperature had been turned up and no doubt, it was getting warm in there.

After a long enough wait, Meredith and Detective Bauman entered the room. Sounding very sunny and cheerful, Meredith said, "Oh my, it's so *hot* in here. Let me adjust the temp." She did so and seated herself in the chair on Landis's right. Bauman seated himself across the desk from him. She looked at her suspect and smiled. "How are you, tonight?" she asked. Without waiting for any reply, she continued as if chatting with an old friend. "You know what, Bobby? This village of Skaneateles, it's incredibly beautiful! My husband and I just *love* it here. In fact we were thinking of buying a place out by the lake, there." Bobby muttered something under his breath, to which Meredith cheerily responded, "I'm sorry Bobby, dear, I didn't quite catch that. So, anyway, we were looking at a house to buy and guess what? We found one! But it's been empty for eight years, and rumor has it that you know a whole lot about the place. We have an address here . . . let me see . . . oh, here it is . . . 2875 East Lake Road, right on Skaneateles Lake." Bobby's eyes widened and his raggedy mouth gaped. Suddenly her demeanor changed, and Meredith was dead serious. "What do you know about this house, Bobby? People say all sorts of things about it, you see. Why some of the neighbors remember seeing you, or at least the Bobby you used to be, out there. After eight years too! That's rare. You and George got pretty loud with the orgy-parties sometimes, and then, there *you* were again, hanging out with his wifey. Oh, Bobby boy, they just thought you were *so* scandalous!" Bobby Landis blanched like someone had thrown ice water on him.

"Why am I here?" Bobby asked, loud enough to be heard this time. Bauman then put a file down on the desk in front of him.

"Oh, we just want to show you some pictures, maybe get your viewpoint on some things," Meredith replied.

"Do you remember Irene Arlander?" asked Bauman.

Bobby blinked, then said "N-no, I mean, uh yes, I might have once, but I don't right now." Bauman glared and asked.

"So, is that a yes or a no? What are you saying, man?"

"I-I, well it's been a long time and . . ."

"So, you *don't* remember her?" Meredith asked nicely, then continued, "Because she would never have forgotten *you*. Did you know that she kept a journal, Bobby?" Bobby stared blankly. "Yeah, she did. The only reason that Detective Bauman here didn't find it sooner was because his investigation was mysteriously shut down," Meredith said. "Would you like to know what she wrote about you?" Bobby Landis opened his mouth, said nothing. "Okay, I'll read some of it to you." Meredith put the old journal on the desk and opened to a page she already had marked. "Here's what she thought of you, Bobby. 'I think that Bobby is a very kindhearted kid. It's just too bad that GA is using him so. We have spent these last few months getting to know one another.'"

"Were you lovers, Bobby? Is that what this was?" Bauman asked with a leer.

Landis flinched and stuttered, "N-no it wasn't like that. I-I wasn't sleeping with Reeney, we just . . ."

"'Reeney,' huh?" Bauman said, "So you were that close, huh?"

"N-no," Landis answered. "I don't want to talk any more. Can I go, now?"

"No, you may not." Meredith answered him icily. "I'm going to read some more for you. Here's another journal entry, dated a couple of days before she left that wacked out retreat the two of you were hiding out in. 'I really have come to trust Bobby more, but last night, I heard him talking to GA on the phone. They're supposed to run off together, or something. I'll never forgive GA, but Bobby has come to be like the little brother I lost. I love him that way, and I believe that he's being fooled just as much as I was. That man doesn't care about Bobby, me, or anyone else. I'll try to warn him. Maybe he'll listen, and run away from GA before he gets hurt too.' So did she warn you, Bobby?"

Landis was looking down now. "Come on, 'Bobby L,'" Bauman encouraged, sarcastically. "You took your only friend's man. I mean, god knows you didn't have any other friends then, and you sure as hell don't have any now. What were you planning?"

"I'll read another entry for you," Meredith said. "And you'll really want to pay attention to this one. 'Haven't heard from Bobby for a while, but last night he called. He wants to have dinner with me tomorrow! I said we ought to go out, but he told me that he loves my pot roast, and asked me to make it tomorrow. Can't wait to see my little brother again!' Know what's so special about this one entry, Bobby?" Meredith asked.

At the same time Detective Bauman opened his file and put three pictures on the desk in front of Landis. One was a picture of Irene Arlander in life, smiling. The second was a picture of her body as it had been found floating in Lake Skaneateles. The third was a picture of the desiccated remains recently exhumed. Landis turned ashen.

"Oh myyy . . .," Bauman taunted. "Look at that face. You look like you've just seen a ghost, 'Bobby L.' Something scare you? Or is that your guilty conscience? Isn't *this* what you did to her, how *you* repaid her for caring about a sorry, backstabbing jackass like 'Bobby L'?" he added with more sarcasm.

Meredith said, "So you *do* know what was so special about this entry, after all, right? It was written the day before she died. Or was killed. That happened the next day. What's more, we had her body exhumed. The DEA lab ran tests on it and want to guess what they found, 'little brother'?"

Bobby Landis leaned forward and shook his head. "No, no . . .," he mouthed. Aloud, he said, "It shouldn't have happened. We were supposed to be happy, and Irene, she . . ." he couldn't finish.

Sounding like a concerned father, Detective Bauman said, "Get it off your chest, son. What about Irene, Bobby? She what?"

"She was supposed to be all high on that rufie and then I could get her signature on the divorce paper!" Landis blurted. He sniffled. "I liked her. I mean, George told me that I was only supposed to—to . . ." Meredith looked at the observation glass, then turned back to Bobby.

"Let it out, dear," she told him consolingly. "You've been holding it in all this time, and look what that's done to you." Bobby Landis looked at her like a penitent begging for absolution.

487

"I was only supposed to get her to agree to give him an uncontested divorce before she wandered into the water—so when I got Skaneateles, Reeney and I went to the Sherwood Tavern, I put that stuff in her drink there, and George, he'd cut the railing at the house while we were out. But the rufie wasn't working, because by the time we got back, she was supposed to be pretty slammed, and she wasn't . . .," he sobbed and went on with his statement, "so when we got back to her house, and she asked me to get her a bottled water, I put more of that stuff in, but all of a sudden, it was like, it all hit her at one time, and George and me, we had to carry her to the railing and lean her against it, then it broke, and she fell . . ."

Meredith put her hand on his shoulder in the kindly fashion of an older sister. "Come on, Bobby, tell us what happened. You deserve a good night's sleep." She urged.

Head in hands, Bobby began to sob. "I did that. I did that to her. George told me that we'd go away together, but he just needed enough money to take care of us and . . ." Throughout the rest of the interview, Bobby Landis continued tearfully spilling facts about he and his former partner's orchestration of Mrs. Irene Arlander's murder.

With Bobby Landis's confession, Skaneateles Police got what information they needed to request an arrest warrant for George Arlander in connection with his first wife's death. He would eventually be tried by the Onondaga County Homicide Prosecutor for that misdeed. Because of the ongoing federal investigation into sale and distribution of RHp3, however, he would be tried by the United States Justice Department in federal court first. Additionally, due to his association with Charles Reddick, a known domestic terrorist with connections to a hostile power, the very man who had been his alibi witness in regards to the Irene Arlander matter, homeland security also wanted to detain him, and now, Mr. Arlander's situation had become a very dire one indeed. All of this, Roan explained to Lucius and Nigel as the three of them talked in the lobby of the same Sherwood Inn where Irene and Bobby had been on the night of her death. This was where IDEA Control had arranged for The Extras to stay while working the Arlander case. Roan liked the place, and of course, Billy and Merry had been quite impressed. This was way more than what they'd been used to in their former jobs. Lucius and Nigel, on the other hand, seemed a bit uncomfortable in these surroundings. At the moment, Nigel, who, for some reason, had taken to wearing sunglasses all of the time, had his head down and was massaging his temples.

"This Bobby Landis guy will plead guilty in front of a judge and he isn't trying to make a deal or anything, so Mr. George Arlander's chances of beating this charge are pretty slim. Even if he does, there's no way that the man will ever step out of a prison for the rest of his life." Roan was telling the young man, "What about Angeline, and what he did to her?" Nigel asked. "Then there's Wesley." He added, almost spitting out the man's name in disgust. "He was in on it too. Is there any way that my recording can be used to pin him?" Right then, Lucius spoke. "Nige," he began, "Rondo contacted Detective Caldwell earlier. Turns out that the out-of-state home security company that originally installed the alarm system at her house in Beach City referred the former owner to a telecom company whose specialty was installation of home monitoring systems." "Oookay . . .," Nigel answered in a "So what does that mean to me?" tone, so his mentor continued, "The former owner of the place used to publish adult magazines, which means that the *idea* of his placing hidden cameras in the bedroom wouldn't be unusual, for that type of guy. There's also an old work order which 'unexpectedly' turned up in the installer's records. It proves without a doubt that there were cameras there."

"What that means," Roan added to Lucius's explanation, "is this: if those cameras were running when it happened, and we can access that footage, along with Mr. Landis's confession, it could be enough to put Wesley what's-his-name behind bars forever," he said, hopefully. "I'll just have to see if I can get a search warrant for the property. This business that Arlander's involved in should be enough to make that happen."

"So you can't use my recording, you're not sure if you'll get a search warrant, and we all need to hope that some old cameras have caught Angie's killer in the act. Humph," Nigel answered. "Maybe I should have just burned 'em all down from the start, but I listened to Luke."

Master Gunnery Sergeant Lucius Carver seemed to think of something right then, so Roan looked at him expectantly. "What, Lucius?" he asked.

"Look, Detective Caldwell," Lucius started, and although he was clearly speaking to Roan, he was looking at Nigel as he went on, "you really need to contact First Sergeant Little as soon as you can about this camera situation. It's not as hopeless as my snotty-nosed Baby Marine here seems to think. In fact, I can say without a doubt what you'll be told when you do call." Now he focused on Nigel. "The hidden cameras have already been found by a property maintenance company that no one knew your girl hired before she—passed, so no search warrant will be needed.

The workers will testify that they found, not the cameras, but a recording that led them to the cameras. That recording will actually be the one you made, Nige, only it'll be doctored so that it fits the technology that was available when the cameras were installed. Regardless of that, this Wesley guy will still be identifiable. What he did will be obvious. That way, your recordings will be admissible in court, with no questions asked." Roan opened his mouth to say something, then shut it and took another drink from his shot glass of bourbon. Nigel stared at his friend for a moment, then said, "It's The Colonel, isn't it? He's the only one who could get all of that done." Lucius nodded. "Why, Luke? Why is he trying to help? I thought he'd forgotten me."

"He never would do anything like that, Nigel," Roan interjected. "You may have had some misunderstandings, but I can honestly tell you that he has never wanted to see you hurt. I was there when he learned what happened to your Angeline. Yes, that's right, I was talking to him. In fact, I'm the guy who told him about it. Anyway, he was just as hurt for you as any godfather or parent would've been. He was also pretty pissed off. He didn't want you to do anything that would endanger your future, so he's taken care of it his way, and he did it for *you*."

Nigel seemed pensive for a moment. "You know, I can't even say for sure why I've felt so much anger at him. Besides Angel, he's the only person who's really been there for me since Devvie went, and"—he suddenly stopped speaking, rubbed his eyes with his fingers and repeated—"Devvie, man, ol' Devvie . . ." For just an instant, the air around Nigel seemed to ripple, as if emitting heat waves.

"Nige . . .," Lucius said, cautiously. "How are you doing, man? You all right?"

"I'm dead tired, Luke," he answered. "I've been feeling some sort of pressure, like—anxiety or a—*tenseness*. It's like something's coming down the pipeline, and I *need* to be there to deal with it. I just don't know what's coming or where I need to *be*. Gives me a headache, man." Lucius nodded, never taking his eyes off of Nigel, then said, "Why don't you go get some rest man? It's zero dark thirty and we've been pushing it for five straight days between watching Arlander and looking for that Landis zombie. It was aggravating. This stuff may not be new to you anymore, but it's still taxing." "Yeah, yeah, okay, big man," Nigel replied, "you're right. I'll go hit the rack. But I'm gonna take one of these bottles of Crown with me, Luke. I need to get drunk."

"See you in the morning, Nige." Lucius said, then included, as Nigel headed off, "Hey—you did good with this, kid. Handled yourself well. Might make a Marine of you, yet." Nigel beamed. "Yeah, man, thanks. You better get outta sight before somebody here calls the cops on *you*, big man," he answered. "They can't hit what they can't see," Lucius replied, with his best Muhammad Ali imitation. Nigel laughed as he headed for the stairwell.

After he left, Roan turned to Lucius. "So what can we expect from here?"

"I don't know, Detective," Lucius replied. "You're the special agent, Lawman, so you tell me."

"No." Roan shook his head. "I'm not talking about the investigation. I'm talking Nigel. What's with never taking off the sunglasses these days? He looks like Stevie Wonder or somebody."

Lucius laughed a little before answering. "Something going on with his eyes. He's not losing his vision, or anything, but his eyes, well, let's just say that the Nigel's-about-to-put-you-in-the-hurt-locker light keeps flashing up in them. Seems he isn't making it happen, but he doesn't know what else is either. You've seen the heat lightning that seems to have followed us up from Florida, right? I think that's got something to do with it, cause his eye-lights always go live right before or after. Don't think he's noticed the connection yet, but I have." Roan was stunned. "Has that ever happened before?" he asked.

Lucius poured himself a double shot of Roan's bourbon, leaned back and said, "No. Can't say I've ever seen it, before, but it sure did motivate the homeless community in Syracuse to give us honest answers when we asked questions." He smiled at the look on Roan's face, raised his glass in a toast, and finished it off in one draught. Then he stood, stretched and said, "Guess I'd better hit the rack, too, Special Agent Caldwell. We've decided to drive to the airport in Syracuse tomorrow, instead of Nigel leading the way through the hell zone. He's worried about what might happen if we went through there again. Says he's being pulled in some other direction every time he goes in there."

Roan's eyes went wide. "Is *that* how you guys have been getting around?"

Lucius laughed again. "Yep. That's how we got up here from Florida, that's how we've been getting here and there. That's also how we got the zombie here from Syracuse so fast. Hit him with a slappy and walked right over after we found him."

Roan had to ask, "What about the gaps in Nigel's memory? I thought he'd be spotty for a while. I mean, I don't know if I'd trust a guy in that condition to walk me through some creepy *otherspace*, Lucius."

Lucius sat back down and explained, "My job is to take risks so that people like you don't have to, Caldwell. The General lined this procedure out. He calculated how Nigel's reaction to my presence would stabilize his ability. We go way back, so the kid doesn't want to see me hurt. That's why he insisted that we be attached to your unit, for now. He wanted me to push Nige a little, so that his memories would hurry up and come back." "Wow" was all Roan could say for a moment. "You were put in danger so Nigel could recover faster? That's—I mean, what if your General's calculations had been wrong, man?" Lucius looked like Roan had just insisted that the earth was flat. Then he said, "You don't know General Renoir. Goodnight, Caldwell." And headed up to his room to turn in for the night.

Roan had to think this through. *With whatever's going on with his eyes and memory, Nigel could be dangerous. People could die just because he got his signals crossed. Lucius trusts Nigel the elder, but I can't say I do. I think I'll ride along to the airport with them tomorrow, just to make sure that nobody gets hurt. Billy and Merry can come along later.* Thinking thus, he finished off his drink and took the bottle to his room. The following morning, as he tried to explain his reasoning to the Comptons, they just looked at him like he was insane. "Roan, if Nige does go haywire or something, how do you propose to *stop* him?" Meredith argued. "It is something you ought to consider," Billy added. "What do you think you'd do? Shoot him? And with Lucius guarding him too?" Roan looked a little embarrassed. "Well, I really didn't think it through, I guess," he said. "Still, I'll ride with them, anyway. If things go south on us, maybe I could help talk Nigel down or something. I'd like the two of you to ride in a different vehicle out to the airport in Syracuse. There's no need for everyone to put themselves in danger here. In fact," he continued, "I'm going to have to *order* you not to ride with us."

An hour later, Meredith, Billy, and Roan were riding with Master Sergeant Lucius Carver driving and Nigel, who was riding in the front passenger seat of the armored Ford Expedition that had become IDEA Control's transport vehicle. Its rearmost passenger seats had been stowed, and that part of the vehicle was absolutely filled—what looked like at least half a ton of baggage had been loaded in and covered with a blue tarp.

Master Sergeant Carver was wearing what Roan surmised to be the MIST camos that the general had told him about, and Nigel was wearing his now-familiar stealth suit. Because it was a Saturday, the ride was only a thirty-nine-minute trip, but all three of The Extras fell asleep along the way.

He was remembering. *Marjorie. Giselle. Laura. I'm sorry. I should have been faster. I should have been less arrogant.* It seemed that he was telling General Renoir something, but no, the General was saying something to him, only, Roan had heard it all before. *The next thing I remember was a feeling of wrongness—as if the laws of physics were in open rebellion.* He knew that he was asleep, but for some reason, it didn't feel like normal sleep. Words of conversations past kept coming into his mind and flitting away like frightened birds. He could hear Laura reciting their wedding vows, saying yes when he proposed. He heard Nigel speaking again, only this time it was the younger one. *Some odd feeling of being in a different where or when crept up my back and made the hairs on my neck sort of rise, you know.* Roan doubted what he was hearing, thinking the man in front of him must be insane, or pretending to be, when he heard him speak again. *Somehow, I knew that this was an Elsewhere. My body tingled all over and my bones felt as if they wanted to jump out of me for sheer excitement or confusion. Something was right, but everything was wrong.* Roan felt the vehicle hit a series of bumps in the road, and Lucius stood in front of him in his dream. *He wants to be gone before the end of the week and said that it's time to tell you everything. You're the only one he'll talk to.* The vehicle hit another bump, and dream Lucius was telling him something, with a shrug. *He has ways of doing things that no one can explain. Nige! Nige!* Dream Lucius was getting louder, and all of a sudden he seemed to sound every bit the marine master gunnery sergeant that he was "RENOIR, NIGEL B! YOU WILL WAKE UP! ANSWER THE MASTER GUNNERY SERGEANT—NOW!" The vehicle stopped hitting bumps and rolled to a smooth stop at the same time that Roan forced himself to awaken. He saw that Bill and Meredith had the exact same look of confusion on their faces as he must have, and that they, too, had just been jolted awake. In the front seat, he could see Lucius shaking a sleeping Nigel, who seemed unable to awaken. Somewhere along the way, the master gunnery sergeant had managed to pull the hood of his OTTO gear into place and looked for all the world like some camouflage-alien with glowing eyes. Roan opened his door and spilled out of the SUV, vomiting, while Billy and his wife did the same thing on the other side. Feeling a little woozy after forcibly evacuating his stomach, he noticed the dry heat around him, then the hard-packed ground the SUV had come to a stop on. *Actually, this ground looks like it used to be hard packed. Something came through here recently. The tracks say horses. A lot of horses . . .* He was thinking when he heard Billy asking, "Where are we, Roan?"

"I—I don't know." He answered as his mind seemed to snap back to reality, and his sight sharpened. Meredith was looking around warily, Sig Sauer in hand. Billy was coming over to help him up, the world was spinning, and Lucius could be heard in the background, "Master Gunnery Sergeant Lucius Carver, USMC487908765. We have arrived in N-1, R-1, and are not sure of our position . . ."

The Extras looked around them in disbelief as Lucius continued, "Contact with Crossover Team Alpha H&S actual, I say again, this is . . ."

"N-1 R-1? That's what he said they called Nigel's homeworld, isn't it Roan?" Billy was asking. "Baby Marine is down. EVAC needed, I say again . . ." Lucius was still speaking in the background.

Roan was standing, now, using the Ford Expedition they'd been riding in to hold himself up, when his eyes caught sight of a structure in the distance. It was a prison, obviously. What was more, he'd seen enough of them to know that this one must have been a Super-Max. "Lucius!" he called. "Is that a prison?"

Lucius came over. "Yeah, Caldwell, it's a prison," he answered. Then, raising his voice and sounding like a platoon leader addressing his troops, he announced, "We have now entered Nigel's homeworld, people, and we are 1.05 klicks to the south of MPIS Detention Center A-21, which you see before you. It is located in Tule Valley, Utah. It is also the scene of a relatively recent military action taken by The Walking Dead Raiders, our second squad of MIST in this world. Because of their humiliating defeat in said action, the staff of that big gray box in the distance has been armed and primed. We will, therefore, stay out of range and out of sight, as we await evac." The Extras looked at him in silence.

Meredith repeated, "*Nigel's* homeworld? Seriously?"

"Yes, Agent, that is correct," he answered, with military seriousness.

"How?" she asked, while everyone was getting back into the SUV. "How did Nigel do this? And what happened to him?"

Lucius's tone softened. "I don't know, Agent Compton," he said. "He was asleep, and somehow, he still opened up the passage. I was driving, but as soon as I saw what was happening, I let the wheel go and pulled my hood. You guys couldn't wake up, so that was probably his doing too.

You've never moved through the zone before, and you had no protective gear. That's why you dumped your bellies as soon as we hit shore."

"He also seems to have brought us out far enough away so as to be unnoticed by the prison staff." Billy added, "There's something like a little mountain or a tall hill to our left. Looks like we could pull behind the rock outcropping there."

"Out*standing* observation, Compton, Billy," Lucius said as he turned the vehicle around and headed for the outcropping Billy had seen. Once they'd gotten out of the prison's line of sight, he handed Billy a pair of field binoculars and put him on sentry duty. After that, he enlisted Meredith and Roan's help to remove several bags and weapons from the vehicle.

"Well, Master Gunnery Sergeant Carver, you do not believe in travelling light, do you?" Meredith asked as they were unloading.

"Nige's idea," Lucius answered. "He had a very *strong*—premonition." As if on cue, Nigel, still buckled into the passenger's seat, groaned. "He's trying to fight his way back to consciousness," Lucius told Meredith. They put the bags on the ground, and he started going through them, looking for something. Eventually, he found three earwigs in sanitary containers and a flat disc that was about two feet in diameter and one half of an inch thick. This he put down on the hardpan ground. He touched a small button in its middle and the world around them seemed to pop. Again Roan felt that familiar, miniscule pressure behind his ears. "It's a refraction field," Lucius told them, almost apologetically. "From the outside it looks like our location is just another part of the rocky hill behind us, and we can't be seen or heard, but we can see and hear what goes on out there. Here—take these earwigs and put them in. We'll be able to stay in contact, in case someone has to go outside the field, and with these, you'll be able to walk in and out through it. Otherwise you won't."

Master Gunnery Sergeant Carver then went to the pile of gear, grabbed a powerful-looking rifle, two pistols, two knives and lastly, a twenty-four-inch blade that looked like nothing more than a short glassine sword. Lucius was headed toward the SUV to get Nigel when Billy called out, "Hey, Lucius—are they going to be coming for us in cars? There's something that looks like a convoy headed this way, and it's coming from the south!" Lucius's demeanor changed instantly. He became a blur as he moved faster than their eyes could follow from the Expedition to Billy's sentry post, handed Billy his earwig, took the binoculars, and looked at the approaching vehicles. Whatever he saw made him let out a tirade of expletives and move even faster as he sped back to the SUV, where he unceremoniously snapped Nigel's seatbelt with his bare hands and threw the young man over his shoulder like a sack of potatoes. He moved from that position to Roan and Meredith's in an instant, moving like a freeze frame—far too fast for their sight to follow. He stopped right in front of them and put the sleeping man down.

Lucius cocked his head, then, as he had previously done when communicating through his subdermal commlink and said, "Master Gunnery Sergeant Lucius Carver USMC487908765 to Crossover Team Alpha H&S actual. We have visual contact with the Graise. Four APCs, estimate thirty-two-unit load, five klicks out. Request permission to engage. Yes, sir, General Gary. Baby Marine is secured with Team Caldwell, R-3 and they are 'unk' for this fight, sir. Wilco, sir." When he looked their way, they once again saw danger in his eyes just as they'd seen for just a moment back at Angeline Arlander's house. "Our backup is about six hours out," he said without preamble. Facing Roan, He began, "If I get KIA'd you *will* protect Nigel. *Do you understand*, Agent Caldwell?" Roan stammered, so Lucius repeated, louder and with more intensity, "DO—YOU—UNDERSTAND, AGENT CALDWELL?"

"Yes," Roan replied, "yes I do, Master Gunnery Sergeant Carver. Go do what you do."

Lucius nodded, then pulled his hood and disappeared. All they could see of him was a manlike shape that matched the background and seemed to be moving, the way a person's hand could be seen moving under a blanket, but no one could fasten their eyesight on it for long. Lucius reached the barrier and disappeared. Nigel groaned again. Billy and Meredith walked over after he'd gone, and asked Roan, "What was that? Who in the world are 'The Grays,' Roan?" "I can't say I know for sure, guys," he answered. "There are certain—branches of the military that wear gray uniforms here. From what I've been told, they're a pretty heinous bunch and they've been out to get sleeping beauty here for a while now. Could be those are the guys that he's gone to mix it up with."

"But this is America, right?" Billy asked.

"Yes, but you know that already," Meredith answered him.

"Right," Billy said, then added, "what I was thinking is, if this is America, and Lucius is going into combat against any branch of the United States Military, then doesn't that make him an Enemy Combatant representing a foreign power?"

Roan was about to answer when Nigel yelled "LET—ME—GO!" and sprang to his feet, a Ka-bar that he appeared to have pulled out of nowhere in his hand. He crouched into a knife fighter's stance with a wildness in his eyes, looking for some foe. It took a minute for him to come to himself enough to recognize who he was with and that there were no enemies surrounding him. "Doc?" he asked as he lowered his weapon, not seeming to notice that the Comptons had begun to reach for theirs. "Where are we?"

"Well, it seems that we have come to the reality where you were born," Roan answered calmly.

Nigel looked confused. "Wait. What d'ya mean 'the reality where I was born'? How did we get here, wherever here is?"

"Hey—uh, guys . . .," Billy, who had returned to his sentry post and was looking toward MPIS Detention Center A-21, started to say. "Guys, I think something's happening at that prison."

"What do you see, Billy?" Roan asked.

"Where are we? What prison?" Nigel demanded from behind Roan. "Why has Bill got the Sat-Glasses? Where's Luke?" "One thing at a time, Nigel," Roan replied. "Billy, what do you see?"

"They're coming this way. There's Hummers with machine guns on top, what looks like some sort of bearcat, and a troop transport truck, the kind with the open back and big wheels. It's loaded with soldiers, and they're all wearing slate gray uniforms." At hearing that, Nigel's face changed. "Gray uniforms?" he repeated. "You mean, like Confederate Gray?" "Well, yeah, almost," Billy confirmed. "But there's something different in the gray, like it's modernized." He crossed the space with the same type of speed that Lucius had, and was suddenly standing right next to Billy, startling the man.

"May I see the Sat-Glasses, please?" he asked politely. Billy handed over the binoculars. Nigel looked in the direction of the prison, and then in the direction that Lucius had been looking. "Hmmm," he murmured. "Two FMTVs, Three armed Humvees, A coupla Growlers. Yeah they're seriously looking for somebody or something nasty." He handed the glasses back to Billy and put his fingers under his chin as if considering some life conundrum. "Well, Luke did tell us that this place had recently lost a fight with some Walking Dead Raiders or whatever his guys call themselves here . . .," Billy started.

"Where's Luke?" Nigel asked again.

———

Roan went over to Nigel and said, "He gave us these earwigs and went out there," he responded as he head-gestured toward the refraction shield. "He told me that if he was KIA'd, then I should protect you. As a matter of fact, he *strongly* insisted on it."

Nigel nodded sagely. "I appreciate that. It won't be necessary anymore."

Roan sighed. "You somehow dragged us to this place and this location, and you just woke up from a half a day's unconsciousness. How are we supposed to believe that?" Meredith, who had been uncharacteristically quiet, answered for Nigel. "Whatever was going on with him, Roan, I think it's over." Nigel nodded agreement. "She's right, Doc. Now, I need to talk to Luke. One of you raise him on your 'wig,' please." Meredith did it for him. "He said that he's gone dark. Says you'd know what that means."

"Okay," Nigel replied, "guess I'll just go to him, then."

"You're different, Nige," Meredith said, with just a note of suspicion. "What changed?"

Nigel, who had begun sorting through their weapons dump, stopped, and for a moment, stared out into nowhere. "I think . . .," he started, paused, and continued, "that I've somehow become more—attuned, if you can understand what I mean, Merry. What needs to be done right now and how to do it is suddenly pretty clear to me. Somehow, while I was incommunicado, something happened. It's like I feel—tuned up. That's the only way to explain it." He picked up three weapons and gave one to each of them. "Neat guns!" Billy exclaimed. "What type are they?" "Special Operations Forces Combat assault Rifles. They're called SCAR-H STD, or MK-17s"—he stopped a moment, as if just now thinking of something forgotten—"do any of you have military experience?" Roan and Meredith did. Nigel had fetched an earwig for himself, and began to explain his intent. "Luke probably figured you were unqualified for fighting either the guys in Gray or the ones in that other group [yes—I did say "other group"]. That's why he left you here. I, however, do not share his view. I *know* what you can do. I remember now that Doc and Merry have military experience, and Billy there is highly proficient with weapons."

"How would you know that, Nigel?" Roan asked.

"Not sure," Nigel responded. "Since my tune-up, I can remember some things with perfect clarity. Other things are pretty fuzzy, but, like, I comprehend what each of these weapons can do, what their designations are, and on and on. Somewhere, I remember seeing a sort of statistic sheet on each one of you, but for the life of me, can't remember where or why I'd be looking at something like that . . ." He got quiet and stared at nothing for a moment, then shook his head. "Anyway, about my plan. Those guys coming from the prison are MPIS, and they're pretty unpleasant. By the way, Bill, what are they doing? They should have been here by now."

"They stopped to look at the ground," came the reply. "Looks like they're interested in how it got all churned up there. They may have seen our tracks too. They're taking photos and talking to someone over the radio."

"Okay, so here's what I want to do . . .," Nigel began.

Master Gunnery Sergeant Lucius Carver thought that maybe the Old Man's kid was going nuts. He'd just *appeared* and explained his strategy. He was more than used to Nigel's strange way of appearing out of nowhere, but it was the fact that this time, he'd come with a *strategy*, and delivered that game plan with the same self-assured confidence as The Old Man. Lucius ran The Baby Marine's idea past General Gary, who was his commanding officer in this reality, and in what he thought was a surprisingly quick decision, the general ordered him to proceed according to Nigel's directions. By the Master Guns' estimation, however, implementing this maneuver would result in a fight between this United States' Military and the Graise. *Perhaps that wouldn't be a bad thing,* he thought. *This world is fully populated, and having the same enemy wouldn't hurt international relations. The combined military forces of this planet, provided they can work together that much, amounts to about sixty million guns. They're way ahead in weapons development than the other worlds were too. We're ahead of them, but Lord knows the only reason we can't drive them off our homeworld is because we don't have the numbers. And the Graise did win only because Craine and Muldowney had killed off more than nine-tenths of the human race back home. The kid said that I'd know when to start shooting. Okay, here goes . . .* Lucius knew that the Graise had no way to tell that he was standing little more than 1.5 klicks northeast of their position, so he pulled the hood on his OTTO gear and stood up. Hefting the light machine gun Nigel had brought, he began to cautiously pick his way from his observation post in the rocks to the hardpan below. The ground was, of course, open desert, meaning he'd have to stay hooded in order to remain unseen by his target. The camo blanket that the weapon came with would keep it invisible to the Enemy, so that wasn't a worry. After a short run, Master Gunnery Sergeant Lucius Carver was in position one klick north of where the Graise had stopped. *Four APCs, and they're still waiting. They must be bringing in reinforcements. Either that, or they've got another force in a different location, and they're on comms . . .* Just as he was considering such thoughts, someone fired a Command-line-of-sight missile from the direction of the MPIS forces on the northern side of the Tule Valley toward the Graise vehicles that Lucius was watching. The missile was still flying when Nigel appeared in front of him with a FIM-92 Stinger and fired in the direction of the MPIS forces to the north, then disappeared. Of course, the Graise had noticed the death flying their way, and begun evasive attempts, but it was too late, and one of their vehicles exploded as the missile hit it. Master Guns Carver thought for sure that he had begun hearing gunfire from the direction of MPIS Detention Center A-21 when Nigel suddenly reappeared next to him with yet another light machine gun, then lay down next to his position and opened fire. Lucius did the same.

"Okay, Luke, Let's fly, man—*run!*" Nigel shouted.

They got up and ran toward the direction of the MPIS force. All of the ensuing confusion interfered with the Graise's ability to bringing their deadly antipersonnel weapons to bear on the two fleeing men and apparently, Nigel had counted on that. As they ran, he grabbed Lucius' sleeve and took the two of them into *otherspace*.

They came out behind the rock outcropping where Lucius had left The Extras, but Nigel kept running right toward the rock itself. They got closer, and passed through into their makeshift hideout that had been created with the "Peek-a-boo-plate," as they called the Portable Refractive Shielding Generator. Within it they found Roan, Billy, and Meredith, flushed with excitement and exertion.

"Wow. That was fun!" Billy was saying.

"We may have just started a war, Bill," Roan said correctively.

Meredith said, "Yeah. Sounds awful." But her eyes were also bright with excitement. "It was still fun," she added. Roan tried to hide a smile. Luke looked questioningly at his protégé.

"I had them do the same thing you did," Nigel explained. "But since I couldn't take them into the buffer zone, we just redeployed the Peek-a-boo-plate a little farther away, and they ran into cover before MPIS could recover enough to shoot at them." Luke kept looking at Nigel, like an older brother who was about to trounce his younger sibling, so Nigel continued, "I know—'*We do not attack the United States Military.*'" Nigel had obviously had that drilled into his mind, but he added, "We didn't kill any of them.

The missile hit the ground and blew, but it was far enough away so as not to harm any of their men. the Graise, now. Those guys, I *did* mean to harm."

"By the way," Billy began, "what do you mean when you say 'the grays'? Aren't those guys who we just shot at wearing gray?"

"Those fellas are not the problem," Lucius began, but Nigel finished with, "They're just an inconvenience. It's the guys coming from the southern end that are the real problem. They're called the Graise, spelled g-r-a-i-s-e. At least that's what they call themselves. They're here to liquefy every living human being that they can, for some reason."

"They destroyed the world that we originally came from," Lucius continued. "Or at least they completed the destruction that a coupla mad scientists had already begun."

"Yeah, we know parts of that story," Roan told them. "General Renoir told me about Muldowney and Craine."

Lucius looked quite shocked at that. "He must really trust you, man," he said. "Most people have to have a pretty high-level clearance for that."

Nigel, for his part, just looked mystified. "Muldowney and Craine? Who's that? a law firm or something?" he asked.

"Before your time," Lucius answered. "Let's just say they're the reason for a whole helluva lotta trouble. Let's see what's going on outside. Whaddya got there, Detective Compton?"

Billy, who, for some reason, seemed to have become the Master Gun's favorite person for sentry duty, answered with, "The prison force just thundered past our position, so I guess they've got the red eye with ill intent for those Graise." Gunfire could now be heard from outside.

"Where did you get that stinger from, Nige?" Master Guns Carver asked.

There was an uncommon silence from Nigel, prompting all of his companions to look expectantly in his direction. "Uhh, uhm, well, the uh . . ." Obviously embarrassed, Nigel, looking at his feet, faltered in his explanation.

"Nigel?" Lucius, sounding like an elder brother whose sibling had just gotten them both in trouble, pressed the young man for an answer. Nigel looked truly embarrassed as he continued, "The, uh, Barrier told me where to go, and so I went, and there I was inside of some sort of armory, and the Barrier told me to get the stinger, and what needed to be done with it . . ."

"What do you mean, 'the *Barrier told*' you where to go?" Master Gunnery Sergeant Lucius Carver demanded through grit teeth. "Why did we just start a planet-wide war? And how did you know about the Graise, but not Craine and Muldowney? How did we wind up here *anyway*?"

The Extras looked from one to the other, not knowing what to do in this situation. It was the first time that they'd seen Lucius apparently angry over anything Nigel had done. "Easy, Lucius . . .," Roan cautioned. "I'm sure Nigel has an explanation . . ."

"He'd better have something to say, or he'll find my size-twelve boot up his young . . ." Lucius started, but was interrupted by Nigel saying, "I've always trusted you with my life, Luke, so how is it so easy for you to stop trusting me?"

Master Gunnery Sergeant Lucius Carver stopped, sighed, shook his head, and said, "Look around you, Baby Marine. You've never done anything this *big* without telling me something, *anything*, first. What's going on, man?"

Finally regathering his composure, Nigel raised his head and met his friend's eyes. "The Barrier between the worlds is self-aware," he announced, continuing with, "he's trying to save himself, and the Graise are destroying his fabric, his *being*." Silence dropped like a millstone among the group.

"How do you know it's a *he*?" Meredith asked. Everyone looked at her. Her face reddened. "I was just wondering how he knows this Barrier thing's a *guy*, that's all."

Everyone just looked at her for a moment, until Master Sergeant Lucius Carver's baritone laughter broke the tension. "Okay, Detective. Good point, but, Nige, we *need* to *know* what's happening, man."

Nigel took a deep breath and began his explanation. "When we left this morning, I fell into the phantom zone and . . ."

"Phantom zone?" Billy asked, with just a tinge of excitement in his voice. "Like in the Superman comics?" Meredith rolled her eyes.

"Uhm, yes—I mean, no. Our phantom zone is just what she . . .," Nigel began, stopped as if confused by some half-recalled moment of time, then went on. "No. Never mind that. It's not like the Superman Kryptonian prison or anything. Look, just to make it quick here, these Graise have been doing *something* that has the Barrier pretty unhappy and it wants them stopped. It kind of brought us here because it knew they would be here."

"Wait a minute, Nigel," Roan was asking, "what do you mean, it told you? Does this—entity—*speak* to you?"

"Well, no," Nigel answered. "It's more like feelings or—impulses, something like that. I just know what it's saying, because I just . . . *understand* it, the way you understand a foreign language."

"So why did it bring us here? Nigel? Is it because you were born here?" Roan asked.

"I wasn't born here, Doc. I was born in New Orleans," Nigel replied. Lucius chuckled. Roan looked like a football coach who was about to yell at someone. Nigel continued his explanation, "As I understand it, Doc, this reality is one of the more scientifically advanced ones, and they could beat the Graise, which would set whatever damage they've been doing back long enough for the Barrier to fix itself."

"But they'd have to mobilize their entire world to do it," Lucius added as if he finally understood the message his protégé was attempting to convey.

"That's right, Luke!" Nigel said excitedly. "Actually, I've never *seen* or fought with these guys, but the Barrier kind of told me who they are . . ." Lucius looked away, and that caught Nigel's attention. "What, Luke? Do you know something that . . ." He did not complete his sentence, as a distant explosion from outside seemed to make their hideout shake.

Billy ran back to his post near the perimeter of their refraction shield and raised his satellite glasses. "Hey, I think that this fight is almost over," He announced. "The guys from outer space or wherever are winning. Wait a minute, what are they . . . oh, my *God!*" He dropped his binoculars and blanched.

"What is it, Bill?" Meredith demanded as she ran toward him "Babe, are you okay?"

"Yeah," Billy muttered. "The Graise they-they have rat tails—and I just saw them . . ."

For the second time that morning, Billy Compton found himself wanting to vomit. "They sucked the soldiers into themselves!" he told Meredith who had put her arms around him.

"Rat tails?" Nigel asked, "What rat tails? The dream. There were rats, and roaches and, and . . ."

Lucius ordered Billy, "Detective, you will move *away* from the sentry position. *Now*," his tone aggravated Meredith, who hadn't seen the change that was coming over Nigel.

503

"Hey, Master Guns, why don't you let up? My husband's not in the—" she started, but Roan was gesturing her to stop. She noticed then that he and Lucius both had their attention fixed on Nigel.

"Rat tails?" he said again. "That was in the dream. There were rats, big ones, and . . ." He looked up and she saw that his eyes had gone blue with electricity, or some energy like electricity. The color alternated between fiery reds and yellows, then back to electric blue. He was walking slowly, as if in a daze, toward the sentry post that Billy had been occupying. As he walked, hands open, fingers splayed widely, small lightning that duplicated the colors of his eyes moved beside him, as in some bizarre energy field centered on Nigel. "They *attacked* us, and I had to *leave* her!" His words ground through clenched teeth that were also bleeding dangerously colored light.

"Nigel . . .," Meredith said slowly, holding out her open palmed hand toward him, a peace gesture to calm an angry hurricane.

"Nige . . .," Billy said as he moved protectively in front of his wife who had done the same to him a moment ago. Together, the couple moved slowly away from the front of their refractive shield wall. "Nige," Billy repeated, "we're your friends . . ." Nigel stopped moving toward the exit long enough to turn his head toward them and repeat.

"They had *rat tails!* They *killed* our men! *I had to leave her, just to stop them from killing her!*" His voice had escalated, as had the energy that was pulsating throughout him and from him. Suddenly, with an almost primal roar, he surged out of the protection of their shielding, and the sky began to storm the colors of his anger. For the second time that day, Master Gunnery Sergeant Lucius Carver let out a stream of his favorite expletives. He donned his hood and dashed out into the Tule Valley Hardpan after Nigel.

A Tale of Two Brothers

DeVries Renoir woke slowly. Actually, he tried his best to make it *seem* like he awoke slowly. Truthfully, he'd tried to milk the knocked-out thing for as long as he could. That was because of the way they'd nabbed him. He'd been looking over that new suit, uniform, or whatever it was that The Gray Colonel had given him. The instruction book (yes, it came with an *instruction* book, as if its wearer was expected to be an idiot or something) described it as a Kevlar-Polymer Body Armor outfit. Supposedly, it was proof against pointed or edged weapons, as well as "high-impact projectile damage," such as would result from bullets.

"Well, that's just the way it goes, isn't it? I get a bulletproof suit, plus a government paycheck, and just when I'm about to try it out, somebody zaps me," he mumbled.

"I hear you, Devvie, so you might as well quit mumbling like you're the only one in here. You always did have a bad habit of doing that. Tells your enemies too much about what's going on inside your head," someone who sounded like Dad told him. He opened his eyes. "Besides, it wasn't a *free* bulletproof suit. It was doctored with an addictive that would have gradually rendered you totally dependent on MPIS. They were going to make you into their junkie," said the Dad-sounding guy.

DeVries assessed his current situation, now that they knew he was awake. He was lying on a hospital bed within what must have been the most luxurious clinic ever, and his hands were tied to its frame with some sort of electronic zip ties. There was a television mounted to the wall past his feet, and the evening news was on. A very comfortable-looking chair with a *Batman* comic book left face down in the seat was beside his bed, and to his right, an aquarium was set into the other wall. Near the door, in the darker part of his half-lit room, someone was sitting in a different chair. All DeVries could make out was a man's seated silhouette.

Creepy, he thought. "Why am I tied up?" he demanded. "Because not only do we know what you can do with your hands, we also know that you tend to shoot first and ask questions later and that doesn't need to happen until I talk to you about some things." The silhouette replied.

"*Man*, you sound like Dad," he repeated to whoever it was that was speaking to him. "Is that you, Pop?" he asked again. "They told us that you'd disappeared in the Kandahar province." The Dadly guy laughed again. The light over in the corner of the room was turned on by the silhouette that he'd addressed the query toward, and the man who was sitting beside the lamp stood up and spoke. "I'm not Dad," he said, "I'm your brother Nigel."

DeVries regarded the man with a stunned look. A moment passed, and he started laughing. The man looked like this was the last thing he'd expected. It was just too funny, what with that confused look on the guy's face and all. He seemed to be unsure whether he should laugh or be insulted. That made DeVries laugh even more. Between breaths he managed to say, "And you with the lights all off, and then . . ." Composing himself a bit more, he finally managed to say, "Man what a drama queen, dude! Kazam! Lights on! And then you're all serious, like, with the 'I'm your brother, Nigel.'" General Renoir almost laughed himself, when he heard it put that way.

"Okay, I might have been a little bit *too* dramatic with it, Devvie, but really . . ."

"But really," DeVries interrupted, "you *can't* be Nigel, because my brother is *dead!*" He was unaware that he was shouting as he continued, "He fell off the roof, into the water, and we *lost* him! So, don't—you—*dare*—try to use his memory to make me do whatever it is you want *now!*"

All of the laughter stopped. The general looked down, then up again into DeVries's anger. "Yes, of course. The anticipation of seeing my own brother again was so overwhelming until I failed to realize, I suppose. That would have been the last time you'd seen *your* brother. Look at me, DeVries. Who do I *look* like?"

"You look very, very much like my dad, but then, I've seen a lot of dirty tricks done with look-alikes, man. Even done some myself. So you could be anybody."

General Renoir returned to his chair, seated himself, and stared at the blue-lit fish tank that dominated the wall behind the desk for a moment. After a short pause, he began to speak. "I guess the loss of Nigel *would* have changed everything for our family, here," he started. "Momma was probably pretty devastated, because I, or rather he, was her favorite, before things went wherever they did in her mind, or so it stands to reason." DeVries had gotten quiet. "You have a birthmark on your back. Upper right shoulder. It's shaped like a lightning bolt," the general said.

"So? Anybody in the government would know that," DeVries answered.

"Yes, they might," the general replied. "But *anybody* wouldn't have known that Auntie Amynthe and Auntie Emmeline used to call you 'Little Black Lightnin',' until Auntie Marguerite said you really should've been called 'Little *Yellow* Lightnin'' because you were too *yella* to be *black* anybody. She never knew how much that hurt your feelings, but you told *me* about it."

DeVries remained quiet, so General Renoir continued, "I was seven, and you were six. You had fallen in love with Sarah Delacour from down the street, so you asked me if you should give her a kiss. We didn't know why that was important, but since we heard Momma and Joanna saying that the man on TV should give the girl a kiss, well, we figured that was the thing to do. So we snuck into Mom and Dad's room to steal one of her little chocolate Hershey's kisses, for we truly believed that'd get the job done."

"That was before The Storm. She caught me going through her dresser . . .," DeVries started to mumble.

General Renoir looked at him. "And when Marvin heard why we got a whuppin', he laughed at us and said we were just *too* stupid," he completed.

"Joanna punched him in his eye for that. Then she told me that you have to put your lips on the girl's lips for a kiss, and," DeVries began, "and you said that you would *never* do that because everyone knew that the Delacours ate snails!"

General Nigel Renoir completed the story and laughed, truly, this time. Tears were in his eyes. "When," he started, then stopped for a moment to get his emotions under control, "when we were teenagers, Li'l Lisa found Marvin's little black book of girl's numbers, so the two of you called his girlfriend Jeretta, and she pretended to be a girl named 'Corenna' who Marvin was two-timing with, and oh, god, did she do a job on that one!

She made sure she sounded like a girl-nerd. Even snort-laughed a lot!" The General was smiling again as he recalled that prank.

"It was his cell phone," DeVries muttered. "Li'l Lisa hacked it. Nigel was—gone by then."

"Yes, of course there would be differences," the General said, reflectively. "Very well, then." He stood up and started removing his shirt. "We all have lightning birthmarks. Marv's was on his upper left shoulder, mine is in the middle, right between my shoulders. Joanne and Lisa have half-circle shaped lightning marks. Joanne's is on her upper left shoulder and Lisa's is on her upper right. Lights up," he commanded the room. Its lighting grew brighter. He approached the bed, took off his undershirt, then turned so that DeVries could see his birthmark. It was very obviously a lightning bolt, located right in the middle of his back, between the shoulder blades.

Though he could not have explained with words how he knew, DeVries just *knew*. This *was* a Nigel, but not as he'd known Nigel, and maybe not even *the* Nigel he'd known. "How did you get so *old?*" he demanded.

"First things first," the General said as he donned his shirt. "Push the green button on the nurse call near you right hand, please," he told DeVries. When DeVries did, his bonds popped loose. "You know, I can be pretty dangerous, man . . .," he started to say.

"Not to me," General Renoir replied. "The only thing I'm concerned with is the fire that you throw out of that phantom zone . . ." He stood near the chair he'd been sitting in, continued speaking, "But would you really attack me, Devvie?" DeVries had stood, and began massaging his wrists.

"I don't know. Might just try," the younger man answered. "Tell ya what, kiddo," Old Nigel replied to that, "I don't throw fire or bounce in and out of the nil-zone like you do, but if you want to take a shot, I'll give you a free one, long as you stay on my level of things."

DeVries grinned like a wolf. "So 'fisticuffs' only then, huh?"

"Yes, that'll do nicely," Old Nigel said.

DeVries moved into a boxer's stance, knees bent, hands up, and shuffled toward his brother, who was standing as if nothing was going on while he started putting his shirt back on. "I almost feel bad about beating an old man down," he started to say, as Old Nigel finished buttoning up and started tucking in. "But, if you're stupid enough to give me a free shot, well . . ." He began to advance on his target. Without warning, Old Nigel moved faster than DeVries had ever seen any man go. Suddenly, he was behind his younger brother, delivering an open-footed kick to his trailing leg, which was the one most of any man's weight is on when using a classic boxing stance. DeVries' leg buckled, and he started to fall, but Old Nigel grabbed his shirt with his left hand before DeVries could go down, then lifted the man completely off of the ground with that one hand. Moving with the same amazing speed, he took his brother over to the bed and slammed his body down on it. The bed broke with a loud crack.

Devries wheezed to catch his breath and then slowly said, "Owww. Ouch. I [wheeze, wheeze] thought you said I'd get a free shot at you."

Old Nigel, back in his chair now, laughed. "What are you, stupid or something, kid brother? Daddy always said, 'If a man is dumb enough to give you a free shot, then learn him a lesson 'bout why ain't nuthin comin' free but death and trouble.' Besides, you were going to try to fake a jab, then come with that super-fast left uppercut. Got me a few times with that when we were growing up."

By then, DeVries had finally caught his breath. "How [cough] did you move that *fast?* You're not even breathin' hard and you're *old*, Nige."

"Well, let's just say that they changed some basic things about my metabolism. We have a lot to catch up on . . ."

Right then, the door opened, and Angeline came in. "Nige, What are you guys doing in here?" Looking at DeVries trying to sit upright on the broken bed, she said, "I knew you couldn't hang out with your little brother for long before you two broke *something.* Hopefully, it's none of his bones." She went over to the bed and looked at him for a few moments. Tears started forming in her eyes as she checked his pulse. "It's so good to see you again, Devvie," she told him as she checked his breathing with her stethoscope, felt his sides, and said, "Be more careful with that super-strength of yours, dear. I think you've bruised his ribs near the clavicle," she said to her husband.

"Well, serves him right for trying to beat up on an old man, my dear," General Renoir said.

"Mmm-hm . . .," Angeline replied as she checked DeVries' breathing again. "Well, he needs about two days' rest before he does anything strenuous. You just got him back from that awful prison yesterday, and it seems that he'd been beaten on and narcotized before that, I'd guess." Then Angeline patted her brother-in-law's back, kissed his cheek and said, "We both really love you, Devvie." To Nigel, she said, "Come down and eat when you're ready."

"Have you prepared a lunch, Angel?" the General asked hopefully.

"No," she replied as she headed toward the door. "You're going to. That's why I came to get you an hour early. The galley awaits."

After she left, DeVries sat with mouth open. "Who, I mean—was that your *wife?*"

"Absolutely," General Renoir replied. "I had one of my men bring her here before we got you out."

DeVries exclaimed, "Man, she's *seriously* good-lookin' for an older gal, but what happened to *you?* And how did she know who *I* was, when I've never even *met* her? Is it because of the metabolism changes that you mentioned?"

Old Nigel laughed. This was the best he'd felt since leaving his world. "Devvie, you're my brother, and at the same time, you're not. Let me tell you where we came from and how we wound up here . . ."

It took a long time, Angeline's help, and a lot of supplementary evidence to convince him, but in the end, DeVries recognized that General Nigel B. Renoir was at least a version of his brother. Two days later, they were sitting together on the general's front porch, casually drinking beer, when DeVries asked, "Hey, Nige, why didn't you just show me all of those pictures and birth certificates from the start?"

"Because it was more fun to trounce you," Old Nigel answered.

"So you're about Dad's age, and still a bad a—" Devvie repeated. "That's crazy but cool, man *and* you're the General in charge of all *this?*" He waved his arm to include everything he'd seen at Crossover Base One. "Man, you got lucky, Nige!" Old Nigel seemed to stare off into space for a moment.

"It doesn't feel that way, Devvie," he said. "How come you haven't asked me what happened to the DeVries in *my* reality?" DeVries got quiet.

"It was the way your wife reacted when she saw me, Nige. She cried. So I figured that the DeVries she knew must have died badly or something."

General Renoir let out a long sigh. "He was drafted during the Vietnam War. Devvie did way better in the army than anybody expected. He made sergeant by the time he was twenty-two. He died in battle at twenty-four when his platoon and another were ordered to take a certain hill that was important for strategic reasons. Intel got snafu'd, and they were sent up the wrong hill. None of them knew that the enemy had placed howitzers at the top. It was a slaughter. Their lieutenant fell, their first sergeant fell, and Devvie was the senior NCO left alive. As a direct result of his leadership under fire, they managed to take their wounded off of the field when they implemented an organized retreat. Almost all of the men in his unit, as well as those who had been in a couple of other units made it out, but a larger force of NVR regulars ambushed them right before they made it to their base. He stood them off while his men made it to safety. By the time air cav got there, he had fallen. At least they prevented the enemy from mutilating his body. He was posthumously awarded the Congressional Medal of Honor. We have it here, and I'll give it to you if you want. Guess it's yours, anyway."

The Renoir brothers were quiet for a moment. Then DeVries asked, "What about Marvin, Joanna, and Lisa in your world. What happened to them?"

Old Nigel became quiet for another moment under thoughts of regret. "They were all living down in Florida when the Last War broke out." He eventually began his reply. "Dad was living with Joanna and her husband. He was more than ninety-five years old, and bedridden. Marvin was an oceanographer, Joanna was a structural engineer, and L'il Lisa had become an aquatic civil engineer. They were seeking funding for an undersea city project, last I heard. We hadn't spoken for over ten years when I was sent off on this mission. I believe they blamed me for Devvie. They still thought that I could have used my rank to get him a safer posting. Believe me, I tried, but I was barely out of Annapolis, and he was an army draftee. Any efforts I could have put forth would have been in vain, anyway, because once he really began to like the army life, he called and told me in no uncertain terms how much he appreciated what I was trying to do, but he'd appreciate it more if I'd just stop." Old Nigel put his head down and rubbed his eyes. Then he went on. "You told me that you had finally found out where you wanted to be, Dev, and I left you there. Now, I wish I hadn't."

DeVries swallowed hard. "I-I don't know what to say to that, Nige," he said.

Old Nigel shook his head and reassured his brother. "It's all good, Dev. I know that you're not *that* DeVries, but it's still really good to see you alive again. Angel tells me that I was different after you—went, and I believe her. I'm just going to try to keep you alive this time."

"Wait a minute, now," his brother began, then continued, "I'm a grown man, Nige, maybe not as grown as you, old dude, but I'm nobody's child either. Besides I can do things that your real brother couldn't."

Old Nigel looked at DeVries for a moment, and said, "I know, Devvie, but I'd still rather see you alive than not. That's why I dispatched a team to go get your girl out of Leavenworth about four hours ago. They should be headed back soon."

DeVries's eyes lit up as he jumped to his feet, threw his beer, and called his brother several foul names, then added in a few threats for good measure. Nigel sat stoically, drinking his Becks Dark beer throughout his brother's tirade. "How do you even know who she *is?*" DeVries demanded.

Old Nigel responded with, "Her name is Dana Lacy. Her mother was what you people here call African American, from Mobile, Alabama. She graduated from Jackson State in Jackson, Mississippi. She was an air force officer when she and Robin Lacy, Dana's father, met. You met Dana during Mardi Gras shortly after her parents had been posted at Keesler Air Force Base in Biloxi, Mississippi." He stopped as if checking some report that only he could see, then went on, "Her mother was killed when her plane went down in the Persian Gulf. When Dana found out about her father's complicity in in an attempt to commit genocide against Blacks and Latins in these United States, she lost faith in the administration and joined your efforts to disrupt the current economic status quo. You and she have become emotionally close, and you value her highly. Still, you gave her an assignment of gathering information from her father's files, but she was apprehended in the act." Devries was calming down, so his brother continued, "You used some of our tech to deceive the surveillance systems in Leavenworth, but MPIS has some hotshot colonel who made a personal visit to check her status. Thus your subterfuge was discovered, but the Gray Colonel allowed her to retain her amenities in order to keep you in line."

DeVries slowly sat down. "*Your* tech. What do you mean *your* tech? How did you know all this? Was my buddy C. C. really working for *you?*"

Old Nigel said, "I'm your brother, but I'm far older than your Nigel, and have been doing this for longer than this version of you has been in existence, Devvie. Thus have I learned the value of research, patience, and planning," he continued with, "Yes, Lieutenant Pendle *is* one of my officers, but he is also your friend. He requested permission to assist you in your endeavors long before our people had confirmed your identity. Once they knew who you were, the question of whether you would sell, barter, or trade our secrets to unsavory interested parties no longer needed to be brought up. So he requested to be placed next to you as an advisor. I wasn't here at that time, but my executive officer approved Lieutenant Pendle's request." Old Nigel stared out into the distance for a minute, then told his brother. "The rescue mission has been a success. To all outside observation, however, it will appear that Ms. Lacy remains in custody. By the time any information to the contrary is uncovered, she will have disappeared. The rescue team will arrive here in two hours."

"Why weren't you here?" DeVries asked.

"What?" the General asked.

"Why weren't you here when your people found out about me? Where were you?" DeVries asked again.

"I was in another reality, with your 'real brother' as you so eloquently put it," Old Nigel answered.

DeVries blinked. "Is he okay?" he asked.

"That's what I'm trying to insure," General Renoir replied. "He met an Angeline who is his age over there, and they fell in love. She was married to another man, though, and Nigel refused to assail their marital bond. In truth, he was living with a different version of your Dana Lacy at the time. *Her* mother was third generation Irish. Their situation ended, and a little while afterward, that Angeline's husband, along with a cohort, murdered her."

DeVries whistled. "Was it because of Nige?" he asked.

"No." General Renoir assured him. "The man was living a double life. He was a homosexual, but was attempting to hide that fact, which no doubt deepened his frustration. In the end, however, he murdered her over money. She was about to divorce him, and it seemed that the courts would have awarded that Angeline a great deal of the man's assets and monetary gains. That was his motive for taking such a heinous course of action."

"Do you *have* to always talk like that, Nige?" DeVries asked.

Old Nigel was puzzled. "Talk like what?" he asked.

Imitating Old Nigel's voice, his brother mimicked, "Nigel refused to assail their marital bond . . . assets and monetary gains . . . taking such a heinous course . . . along with a cohort . . ."

"Yes," the general replied. "I do have to talk like that. Now, would you like to hear the rest of it or not?"

"Yeah, okay, go 'head," DeVries said as he returned to his chair.

"Your brother had begun to regain his memories by then, and—"

"You know, I'm still not sure how I feel about what you guys did to him, with that memory suppression and stuff," DeVries cut him off.

"As I've explained, Dev, he needed to be removed from danger, and that was the only way to do it without hurting him physically. They would have made him into a comatose DNA bank, just so as to continue using his living cells," the General told him. "Besides, the process was designed so that the memory loss would gradually decelerate to zero, then reverse its course at whatever pace Nigel chose to set."

"So the whole thing works kinda like a yo-yo or something, right?" DeVries asked.

"Yes, Devvie," he was told for what seemed to Old Nigel like the hundredth time. "Yes," General Renoir responded, again. "When everything inside of his mind is integrated, he will likely be able to remember all that he sees and hears, as well as everything that has gone before in his life."

"So what about this dude who killed his girl? What's going on with that? Have the cops nabbed him or anything?" DeVries wanted to know.

"No, Dev, they have not," Old Nigel replied. "But I was getting around to explaining how that has been handled."

"Oh, I interrupted you didn't I? I'm sorry, Old Nige. Finish telling me," DeVries answered.

Old Nigel sighed and continued his narration. "We were concerned that Nigel would go and destroy the man who committed that atrocious crime. What? Yes, Devvie, he can pull ruination out of *otherspace* just as you do. I thought I'd explained that to you already, during your briefing sessions, when I told you the entire story . . . what do you mean, you 'went to sleep'? Never mind. If Nigel had gone after George Arlander with his emotions in such disarray as they were, there may have been no end to the slaughter he may have wrought. He could easily have annihilated hundreds."

"I don't know, Old Nige," DeVries said to that. "I can take out maybe ten to fifteen before it's time to pop back into the shadow zone and recharge, but that's all. Only ten to fifteen, and maybe a car or a truck. So I don't see how my brother could do hundreds."

For a moment, General Renoir stared out at the compound and activity that made up Crossover Base One. "DeVries," he said. His younger brother heard the seriousness in the way he spoke and quietly waited. "I've seen him not only destroy enemies by the hundreds, but also their vehicles, helicopters, and everything else, all at one time." Turning his head to look intently at DeVries, the General said, "If you can be considered a weapon of destruction, your brother must be considered a weapon of *mass* destruction. I believe the difference in the level and type of your abilities must be a consequence of the differences in the manner in which you both first entered *otherspace,* as well as what age each of you were when you made that breach. How did you come into your power?"

"I first found my way into the shadow zone right after Dad was officially pronounced MIA in Kandahar. I wanted to find him, because there was no way that Dad would just be *missing.* He had to be dead or captured." Now it was DeVries's turn to become deadly serious. "I was nineteen, and kept staring at the city of Kandahar on a map. I looked at pictures in books, in magazines, online, on TV, and one day, I got so angry at the hopelessness of finding Dad that it felt like I was having a heart attack or something. I felt dizzy and stumbled, then fell. When I got up, I was in Kandahar City. I tried to find my way around, but couldn't speak the language and when I finally came across some American soldiers, there was just no way to explain how I got there, why I was in the area, or anything. At least no way of explaining that they would believe." Devries stopped speaking, went to the cooler for another beer, then resumed his narrative. "They 'detained' me. I was put in some military holding cell, or whatever they call it, and there I sat, all burnt up with anger. The heat in that place was burning me up, too. I wanted to get out before they took a mug shot or whatever, and I knew there was no hope for help. So I focused on wanting to get home, and all of a sudden, I *knew* how to do it. I stepped into the shadow zone over there, then stepped out of it and into our apartment, over here."

"What of the fiery destruction that you hurl upon your enemies?" Old Nigel asked. "How did you learn that? Was it instinctive?"

DeVries looked at him for a moment, and said, "Man, the way you talk, Nige. It's kinda cool and nerdy at the same time, I mean how did you—"

"Devvie," the General interrupted. "Focus. The fire. How do you do it?"

"Oh, yeah. That. It's not really *fire,* see? It's, well, it's like—like, really *intense* emotions and feelings that are kinda running wild or floating around inside the shadow zone, and when I need to have a weapon, I use it as one. Kinda similar to the way you squirt water out of a water gun, but with the effect of a flamethrower. Then the fire just fades away."

"Can you cross between realities?" his older brother asked.

"Nope. Never tried, don't know how to start," DeVries replied. "Well, I mean, I never knew anything like that was possible. I only started going through the zone a little while back, and the flame throwing kinda came to me by accident a few months ago." Devries suddenly looked as if a new thought occurred to him.

The air around him began to ripple as he stood up, faced the elder Nigel and said, "I hope you haven't got some idea of doing to me what you did to Nige. You need to know that if you try anything like that on *me*, I'll kill you right there and then, for him and me both."

"That isn't why I'm asking these things," General Renoir responded. "Although, from my perspective, your assertion seems to be quite fair, you should know that my forces wouldn't see it that way. Even if you were to succeed in any attempt to dispatch me at all, well, immediately after killing me, you'd find yourself engaged in pitched battle with all of my command, such as it is. I'd rather not see so many of them killed, nor you, as that would be the only possible outcome. Besides, your life isn't at risk in the same fashion as Nigel's was. He was but a boy when he came to us and at any moment, they could have held Angeline and I as hostages in order to force his cooperation. His youth would not have allowed him to bear the thought of sacrificing us for his freedom. I do not apologize for my course. What I allowed wasn't an easy thing for anyone to see being done to a younger version of themselves."

"I—uh, I hadn't thought of that," DeVries said, as the rippling effect stopped. "So what do you *want*, Old Nige?" he asked. "Why am I here waiting for your men to bring Dana? Listening to you tell me about my brother that I might never get to see again?"

The General sighed. "Because there is a larger threat coming to your Earth. They're called the Graise, and we, along with your brother, have fought them before. Also, Nigel's real girlfriend is here, in this reality. She's another version of my wife. They have been involved since he was about ten or eleven years old, maybe even longer. She can sense Nigel's arrivals before they happen. Either the Graise or MPIS would be happy to capture her. We can't allow it. She needs to be guarded by someone who can access *otherspace*. Additionally, if Nigel does wind up battling the Graise again, even with his abilities, he'll need help. You can be counted on to do either or both of those things with complete loyalty to your brother."

"But I don't know him, Nige, and he doesn't know me," DeVries objected.

"He knows you," Old Nigel responded. "He grew up with a DeVries from the time he was about twelve years old. He also has my memories of you. I gave him those, to replace what was stolen. You are his favorite. He'll remember you and the things the two of you have done together."

"Well, I don't know *him*, man," DeVries restated. Old Nigel looked his brother in the eye and answered with "Yes, you do." They regarded one another for a long moment, until DeVries looked away and replied, "Maybe so. Is there anything else I need to know, General?"

"Yes. There is," Old Nigel replied. "I have a report that the Graise have already sent at least one scout troop into the nil zone, but Nigel encountered and dispatched them while he was in there, despite not knowing who they were. Others may be coming. On another front, I have been in contact with an investigative team formed to bring those men who murdered the Angeline of the Earth Next Door to justice, and that matter is proceeding well. With his memories returning, I feel that you may meet your brother again soon. No one can successfully resist the power of the way things were meant to be. He will eventually come back here, even if he doesn't know why. You will encounter him then. Please try not to fight him. He's far more amplified than I am."

"That almost makes sense," DeVries said. "Him being more amped-up than you, I mean."

"That is true, though for different reasons than you might have in mind, Devvie. Additionally," General Renoir began, "we will release you with a conditional allowance. You work with us, and my forces will not act against our cousins whom you have organized into soldiers for your cause. By the way, what *is* your cause, anyway?"

DeVries looked a little abashed at that question. "Err . . . uhm, we—we don't . . . umm we don't exactly *have* a cause, or anything like that. It's just that there's all these people who don't have the means to take care of themselves, with almost no way they can survive, but all, and Nige, I mean *all* of the funding for low-income people has been eaten up by the corporations that control Washington, so uhm, yeah, I like to think we help those type of people out, sometimes—paying bills for them or buying them food, maybe a car, if a family needs one, and we keep the really bad criminals from goin' buck wild on the little people. We even managed to buy back one or two of the homes that people lost after Katrina."

"I see. You robbed the casinos on the Gulf Coast, but without taking *all* of the money, which kept the heat on your group to a minimum. Hence, you laundered those funds through a couple of fake businesses, from which you then implemented your 'Robin Hood' activities," General Renoir conceded.

"Yeah, man, that's pretty much the way it goes," his brother agreed.

"Then how do you explain to your beneficiaries the relatively luxurious manner in which you and your Kinfolk Crew live?" the General asked, then continued, "Eventually, they will see you as common thieves, not as benefactors. You'd be seen as being no different than those drug dealers whom you have strong-armed out." DeVries' mouth dropped.

"To continue," Old Nigel went on, "now that you have escaped their clutches, MPIS will be waiting for your resurfacing. We did what we could to make it seem that you died in the Utah desert. But, if you show up and continue your former activities in the haphazard way that you have doing, do not doubt that they will act on their threat against our relatives. It's time for you to take a different approach, Devvie."

"Well, what do we do, then, Nige?" DeVries asked.

General Renoir stood up, stretched and fetched himself another beer. He sat on the railing of the porch and allowed his mind to enter visualization mode. DeVries thought he had gone catatonic, at first, but he waited, which, for him, had never been an easy thing to do. He was starting to wave his hand in front of his brother's face when General Renoir finally spoke again. His hand shot out and grabbed his brother's. "Devvie," he said, "you're about to become the CEO and chairman of an entirely legal charity."

DeVries looked confused, "Huh? You mean like the Red Cross or something?"

Old Nigel replied, "Okay sure, if that's how you'd like to see it."

"How will it work?" DeVries asked.

"Well," General Renoir began, "when your brother first brought me across the nil zone to this reality, I was commissioned by my government to plant roots in this world, in case we ever need to utilize such a system. Thus I formed a charity entitled the Preservation Hall Society. Its stated purpose is the preservation of New Orleans's cultural roots, as well as its genealogical and literary history. We are going to create a branch that will be tasked with the prevention of the gentrification that has spread like wildfire within New Orleans since Katrina. It will be known as New Orleans Against Gentrification."

DeVries smiled. "Okay, NOLAG. Don't you mean New *Orleanians* Against Gentrification, though, Old Nige?"

518

"No," General Renoir replied. "If it's New *Orleanians*, that will imply that only specific people, or types of people are interested and involved. To the ears of political conservatives in this reality, such a thought could suggest some sort of dangerous group involving angry individuals. If the name is New *Orleans* Against Gentrification, that implies an effort emanating from the very bones and roots of the city *itself*. It would appeal to people who may not mind contributing to or being involved in a *moderate* fashion for the sake of their *city*, which they themselves are a part of."

DeVries smiled. "Good, very good," he said. Then he asked, "Will we *actually* be fighting gentrification, Nige?"

"Yes," General Renoir replied. "You will buy back those homes that were lost to families who had owned them for two generations or more, although three generations would be better. Your group will assist these families in finding employment and education, right through to postgraduate college and university levels. That way, the talent born within New Orleans will be more prone to remain in New Orleans. Your main goal will be assistance for New Orleanians who do not have financial means for such things. Their ethnicity and race *must not* be a factor in this, but their economic situations will have to be, as long as their families have lived in New Orleans and its surrounding parishes for three generations or more. Continue to do all you can to keep the criminal element at bay within these communities. How you do so will be at your discretion, as long as you remember that your charity *must* remain free from accusation, or its function will be impeded. You will need a staff of permanent employees, and they need to be able to make a very good living as such, because that will reduce the likelihood of corruption within the ranks, hence, our cousins, and possibly our brother and sisters here will remain involved. You will also make a very good living. Additionally, this could mean that you might become quite the public figure. With such positive notoriety, MPIS will be hard put to initiate another kidnapping attempt against you or your employees. Will that do, Devvie?"

"Hell, yeah, that'll do, but how will all of this be paid for, Old Nige?" Devries asked.

General Renoir responded, "The PHS has become a multinational organization, Devvie. We have made financial investments that have paid off significantly. We have invented and patented things that will never draw much attention, but will pay off. Things like advanced USB cabling, gaming apps, tempered steel-glass, for phones first, and later, for other applications. This has become a multibillion-dollar company that will be used to restore our homeworld when the time comes, but in the meantime, we invest. So we will be your financial backers. That will dovetail nicely with the stated purpose of the PHS."

DeVries' face lit up. "When do I start?"

This time, General Renoir smiled like the wolf. "There is one other price to be paid beforehand, however, and you will pay it," he said.

Suspicion returned to DeVries' voice, and his smile faded as he asked, "What do you want for this, General?"

"You will help your brother Nigel in battling against the Graise." General Renoir answered, "You will guard his interests as if they were your own. You have the ability to access *otherspace* and a limited amount of its potential, so you will not only help protect your world, but you will also protect your own flesh and blood, as well as the woman he loves. Do you consent to pay this price, DeVries Renoir?"

DeVries looked shocked. "You call that a *price*?" he asked. "I get to see my brother who we all gave up for dead, we have a chance to fight together, and for this, I get paid to be the top dog of this hot new charity? I think you're the one getting ripped off here, General Old Nige. The only thing I regret is not having that cool bulletproof battle suit . . ."

Old Nigel smiled. "Forget about that useless, limited, inadequate excuse for battle armor, Devvie. We've got a better outfit for you. How about you going into battle bulletproof, armed, and invisible? Will that do?"

Devries smiled. "Okay, so like I said, when do I start?" General Renoir nodded. "Very well, then," he said while looking at his watch, "Lieutenant Pendle will come and escort you to General Gary, with whom you will discuss the parameters of your needs for the mission. He, in turn, will authorize and implement your *reasonable* requests."

"What about you?" DeVries asked. "Are you going somewhere else?"

"Yes." General Renoir confirmed, then told him, "In the other reality, Nigel should be in New York State by now. He and his companions will most likely have their investigation completed by the time my wife and I arrive. I will have to be on hand to make sure the individuals involved with the other Angeline's murder pay the price according to the law."

He looked at his brother for a moment, then hugged him. "I hope to see you again, Devvie," he said. "You'll have dinner with Angeline and I tonight before we leave, I hope."

"You act like we'll never see each other again, Old Nige," DeVries said.

Old Nigel smiled. "That possibility exists," he said. "But, no matter what, you will, at least, see *your* brother Nigel again. He has some of my best people around him, but he needs *you*."

INTERLUDE VI

THE POWER OF THINGS
THAT WERE MEANT TO BE

Angeline Duplessis really hated coming out to Utah, but she had come anyway. Her mother and father had urged her without letup. "Probably trying to set me up with some other loser," she thought. That had become one of her mother's favorite pastimes, it seemed. She wanted to just tell her—oh god did she ever want to just tell Auntie-Momma, "I'm already married! I've been married for five years!" But, for some reason, the words just never came. Indeed, she and her Nigel had gotten married the last time he'd come over. Unlike all of his previous visits, he was coherent when he came to her that time. With his thinking ability unimpeded, he proposed, and she accepted. For her safety, though, they resolved to keep it to themselves. He'd come just for her, he told her, and this time, it was something he did willingly, not by accident. He was in the military, now, and some war he'd recently fought had made him more aware of his own mortality, so he wanted to marry her, for any one of his upcoming missions could be his last. If he had to go to his grave, he said, he'd rather go knowing that he'd married the only woman he'd ever love, in any world. So they went and got married. She'd thought of calling Agent Caldwell, but instead, decided that this was not a time for his involvement. This was a time for Nigel and her.

She trusted the Roan Caldwell that she'd met, for the man had proved that he was trustworthy in the way he'd treated her Nigel when he'd come over with his head all jumbled up from whatever evil things they used him for in that other place, where he was stuck. So, even though Agent Caldwell, and later, his wife Laura as well as their two daughters had become friends of hers, she still just couldn't bring herself to call him the last time Nigel had come. Laura, now, she did want to call, for that woman was a lot like Auntie-Momma. Angeline knew,

———

525

however, that if she were to call Laura, then Laura would be under obligation to tell Agent Caldwell, who would probably have to do something governmental or official, and that would have spelled the end of Nigel and Angeline's wedding plans. She thought back to the time he'd come over wearing earrings, dressed like some sort of motorcycle rebel, confused, rambling about losing his fighters, feeling lonely and looking for her. Something bad must've happened in his life on that other plane of reality, or whatever the place was, because she could feel his inner pain and sense of loss. His emotional agony was intense, and being unable to find solace anywhere, he'd come to her. Her, and no one else. It was normal for her now, being able to know that he was coming and when he'd arrive. That time, she'd headed out to the park, thinking and hoping that they'd meet there as usual, but before long, the place was swarming with soldiers in gray uniforms. Lots of them. They were making people leave. There had been a terrorist threat, they said. Not unusual, since Broussard Park had become a minor tourist attraction. She knew though. Their arrival on the scene so quickly could only have indicated that they'd found a way to predict his arrival. Angeline dropped her eyes and filed out of the park with everyone else. Agent Caldwell was there, too, with his team. She started to walk toward him, but his eyes told her not to.

She felt Nigel coming closer that day, and when he stepped out of the phantom zone, it looked to her like he was about to be mobbed by soldiers the way rock stars get mobbed, but she heard Agent Caldwell ordering them to stop. She couldn't see with her own eyes because of the crowd, but if she stretched her feelings she could see through his, in a way. One or two of them crept forward, apparently hoping to draw blood samples or capture him, but then one of the soldiers disobeyed agent Caldwell, attacked her Nigel, and pandemonium erupted. She saw him fight for the first time ever that nigh —it was a magnificent, graceful, and frightening thing to behold. He moved faster than the human eye could see, punching, kicking, clotheslining his attackers, but as often as they fell, they'd get up, since he was holding back, because he didn't want to hurt her but was afraid he might (as if she'd be in with that crowd). She felt his emotions escalating toward destruction, and even though she couldn't touch him in order to help him hold back from doing something awful to those innocent people, she tried her best to telegraph her presence, her love, and compassion to Nigel. She tried to project the word "RUN!" through her feelings and apparently, it worked. He broke loose from the melee and ran, then disappeared.

Nigel left the park filled with disorganized bedlam, military men and women who were groaning, holding their heads, arms, legs, and other injured parts of their bodies, and all the while Agent Caldwell was yelling at one of his people about calling an ambulance. After doing that, he began looking around for clues. Angeline crept close enough to get his attention, and when he looked up, gave the international "Shussh" sign, then motioned for him to follow. When they were out of sight, Agent Caldwell, of course, began to interrogate her about Nigel, but she informed him in no uncertain terms that she'd tell him nothing, but if he would help her, she'd get him in a position to talk to Nigel, only if he promised not to try to arrest the young man. He agreed, they got in his car and she took him to the spot where Nigel was going to be. Sure enough, he popped out of the zone right there. They pulled next to him, and Angeline called his name. Her presence was the only reason why Agent Caldwell wasn't attacked and wounded, or worse. Nigel got into the front seat, then Agent Caldwell and Angeline talked to him. For some reason that she didn't understand at first, though, Agent Caldwell kept telling Nigel not to look at Angeline. He told Nigel "You're probably bugged, and you do not want them to know about her! I'll protect her from them by keeping her identity a secret, but if you come back, I will have to let them take you into custody!" So he wouldn't turn to look at her, and for some reason that hurt her worse than seeing the state he was in. She could feel how much that hurt him too. He wanted to, at least see her, she knew. She felt him getting angry, his emotions escalating again, so she told him the truth that she'd held dear all this time. "Nigel," she intended to say that she loved him, but the words came out as if they had their own intent. "I know you love me." She felt his emotions settle as she said it. That had been the one right thing to say to him at that time, in that moment. "And I love you just as much," she'd continued. Then she felt his tears and longing. "I know," she answered those feelings too. "I feel the same way."

"Look at me, kid," Agent Caldwell had said, then, "I think I know who's sending you over here in this condition, and I've got something to say to him." He relayed his angry message, and they drove to a place where it was safe for her Nigel to walk away and disappear. After that, she and Agent Caldwell, along with his family, had become closer friends. Still, Angeline believed that if The Good Agent found out that Nigel and she had been married, he'd be angry because she hadn't told him that he'd arrived. But she didn't feel obligated to Agent Caldwell or his family as much as she did toward Nigel and herself. She had been at Tulane when she felt his approach, so Angeline had gone to a private location where no one would see him, and waited. This time, though, he proceeded with caution. He reached out of their phantom zone and pulled her in. As always, she was awed by the beauty of this place that was also a non-place. She also knew that they were totally safe from the gray-uniformed soldiers or any other threat as long as they stayed inside. He gave her a ring unlike any she'd ever seen, and

they stepped out of their phantom zone, into a courthouse. He told her that this wasn't the world that he'd been stuck on, nor was it the one where she lived. They went to the judge, a longer-lived version of her cousin Roy, and when they stepped into his chamber, there was an older, very dignified woman there, along with a big, dark-skinned man who had the brightest smile and looked like an old Marine. He was with his wife, who was African. They were to be witnesses of the marriage. The dignified woman had brought Marine Dress Blues and a bridal gown with her, and the clothes fit both of them perfectly. Angeline was surprised at how much she liked the dress. Apparently, the matriarchal woman had the same taste in wedding dresses as she. After they had both changed and returned to the judge's chambers, that woman stepped over to her, held both of her hands and said, "You're a younger version of me, and I promise that you'll never regret this. I never regretted marrying the older version of him." The judge cleared his throat, everyone assumed their places, and the wedding began. Afterward, the guests gave Angeline modest little gifts, and Nigel took her back into their phantom zone.

Later that night, she wanted to walk the riverside, Angeline remembered. They both knew he'd have to go back to that other place and stay for a little while longer, especially since he was now in their Marine Corps. Still, they needed to plan their future reunion. So they thought that maybe they could go to Woldenberg Park late at night, walk along the river and talk without drawing attention. But some of the soldiers in Gray stumbled across the pair, and attacked the newlyweds, not realizing how they'd signed their own death warrants. He fought them off, taking their lives so that they wouldn't identify her, and yelled at her to run, to leave him behind, because he couldn't live if she got hurt, captured, or killed. Angeline didn't want to leave her husband, especially after she saw a laser bolt hit his chest. More Gray soldiers were coming. Still, he refused to fall, telling her he could cure it in the phantom zone and then yelled at her to run. "I couldn't defend us both!" he said. "They don't know that I'm with you or that I love you," he added, "so, please, leave before they find out." So Angeline ran. She knew he'd survive. Even now, while she was sitting out here in this bone-dry Utah desert, she knew he was still alive. It really didn't matter what nice guy Auntie-Momma might summon up from her endless batch of interns, Angeline's answer would still be "No. Not interested." None of them could possibly be better for her than Nigel, anyway.

She looked around the Sunstone Knoll camp again, crowded as it was with different people, almost each and every one of them members of some tech team sent out to estimate the cost and impact of this project, and wondered why she'd even bothered to come out here with her parents. True, she did need a break from her studies, but not that badly. She should have stayed home in New Orleans. But when they told her that they were going out west to help put in a wind-farm power plant and fresh water supply for a natural salt mining operation the State was planning, she just had to see. That's what she told herself at first, anyway, but that didn't hold up as a good enough reason to be here, when Angeline thought about it. There was something else, but she couldn't put her finger on it, cognitively. Uncle Rene was a mechanical engineer and Auntie-Momma Severine was a hydrologist. Angeline guessed that maybe she herself had just come along in order to see the two of them working together. It made her think of him, of the day when she and Nigel could work together. That reasoning didn't hold up either, really. There was something deeper going on with her. She saw that pretentious intern, Roland Jefferson Ronald Bharker III, coming out of his camper to go along with her, and wondered was this some biological clock thing. She was approaching twenty-seven, after all, and maybe she wanted a regular family, or something. Auntie-Momma had decided to send the two of them with an assignment to a location called Sevier Lake Reservoir number one, about two miles along the road out there, US Route Fifty, or something like that. It was about five miles of actual travel southwest of the base camp. They were to gather soil samples for her, and gathering the prescribed amount would likely be an all-day task. She hated the thought that maybe Auntie-Momma was right. Maybe she did need to move on. Maybe Nigel wasn't ever going to be able to come back. He was an active duty marine in a world that she couldn't get to, after all. If she did have to move on, though, it wouldn't be with an overblown, spoiled, self-important man-baby like Roland Jefferson Ronald Bharker III. She didn't care how wealthy the guy's Daddy and Mommy were. Besides, every time he opened his mouth, this kid proved that he had no idea how misogynistic and racist he was, how far out of touch with the common people whom Angeline would be serving once she finished her studies. He'd never experienced the fear, loss, and insecurity that resulted from surviving a Katrina while losing his parents and his home, never had the humbling experience of having to endure through suffering that was out of his mommy and daddy's control, and it showed.

That thought brought her back to Nigel, again. They'd met at that godawful orphanage, and she'd felt the pain of every beating he'd endured, right from the start. She knew when he'd slip away to wherever it was he went to find happiness, she just didn't know, at that time, where it was he'd go. Later on, her family found her, she was adopted, and her life went one way, while Nigel's life went another. Then that day had come when she saw him in the park. He was so serious for a little kid, as always, and as always, he'd found her again. He told her, in the way of a ten-year-old, that he'd become a marine. She didn't believe him, but she liked him, anyway, even if he did tell tall tales. Later on, he'd just turned eleven when she felt him coming to her house, appearing in the back yard, stepping out of nowhere, and he was hurt. How it happened, Angeline didn't know. Fortunately, it was a Saturday, so Uncle Rene and Auntie-Momma Severine were sleeping late. Angeline had gone outside to find him there, holding his head, moaning. Had she been any other eleven-year-old girl, she may have run for help. Angeline wasn't just any eleven-year-old-girl though. She was who or whatever she was to Nigel, just as much as he was to her, and they were meant to be inseparable. She went down the stairs to him, and grabbed his hands. That was the first time she'd come to know exactly what and where his escape into his safety zone was. The knowledge passed from him to her through touch. That was also the first time their emotions truly synchronized. She felt his pain and confusion more intensely than ever before.

"Nigel!" she called "Nigel! Let me help you." His mind stopped racing for a moment, and he told her that he'd had to save his father and the other marines in the war, and doing so had hurt, but he didn't know why, or what exactly he'd done. It was something he got out of the la-land, and maybe it was too much, he managed to say. So she told him to do the only thing that made sense to her. She told him to go back in there and see if he could fix things. He didn't want to go alone though, so he asked her to come with him. She went. That was the first time she'd seen their phantom zone, and to her eyes, it was the most beautiful place she'd ever been. Inside the zone, she sat beside Nigel on a euphoric thought that presented itself, and they floated along for a while. He was feeling better already, he said. Then a tornado of some sort of happy emotions/word/events swirled down from above and went through her, into him. They put their arms around one another and floated along while Nigel's mind healed. After his clarity of thought returned, they stayed there for a while longer, just playing and being kids, then she asked him to take her home.

The events of that day provided her with a path to follow through life. That was why, fourteen years ago, now, she'd decided to become a doctor, and throughout the days, months, and years that passed after that, she'd never gone through an interval when Nigel wasn't present in her heart, as constant as her shadow. She remembered that horrible day in Broussard Park, when he was trying to marry her, but some maniac attacked the place and she ran home. The thought of that kiddie wedding made her laugh a little. Who but Nigel would come up with an idea like that, and who but Angeline Duplessis would go along with him? She thought of all the other times he'd come to see her, even that visit when he'd brought the other girl. That was an aggravating turn of events, but Nigel's life was in danger on that occasion, also, and if it hadn't been for Agent Caldwell, he might have wound up as an experiment in some lab. Angeline didn't much mind if it had happened to the girl, but when it came to Nigel, she was determined to protect him as much as she could, even if it meant sending him back to those people in that different world with that irritating—Dana. That was her name. She hated sending him back with her, but she also knew that Dana didn't have the same emotional connection with Nigel as she had. No threat there. What bothered her more was the way both Nigel and Dana's statements seemed to suggest that Nigel's father was the one doing whatever this was to his own son. If he couldn't trust his father, who could he trust? That left one person—her. He was alone, except for her. She wanted to go back with them, for his sake, but Agent Caldwell feared for her safety. So did Nigel, and his was the advice she decided to heed.

So she'd stayed, and she'd waited. There had been moments throughout the years when she could feel him longing for her. It wasn't an imaginary feeling, Angeline knew that. It was him. Every time she felt it, she'd known that Nigel was trying to find a way back, but couldn't. Her mind came back to the present. The GPS told her that this was the spot they were looking for. She stopped the company Hummer that Uncle Rene had insisted she ride in (alone, he'd emphasized—at least he wasn't trying to marry her off, for which Angeline was inexpressibly grateful) and got out to unload the equipment. Her pompous helper was getting off of his dirt bike, once again running his mouth about how she might have enjoyed the ride more if she'd rode on it with him. Angeline tuned him out. She considered his advances sexist, selfish, arrogant, and just all-around aggravating. She was preparing to dig out some of the mud with her spade when a strong uneasiness came over her at the same time that sounds like explosions and gunfire reached their ears. There were always gun guys out here, shooting for fun, so the sounds shouldn't have affected her this way, but . . . something was wrong, she knew it. Or maybe, something was right, she really couldn't tell which feeling was correct. Her emotions seemed to be fighting one another, roiling in confusion and straining to break loose.

Angeline realized that she was crying, and Ronald Jefferson whatever-his-name was asking her if she needed him to hold her, when suddenly, the sky exploded in color, as if heat lightning were attacking the blueness of its expanse. It was him. He was here, and his power had grown. Something was happening over in the hardpan valley where that prison was located, and whatever the conflict, it was focused on her husband. She wondered why she hadn't felt him coming, but also realized that she had. Somehow, as long as a month ago, when her parents asked if she wanted to accompany them, she'd known. She'd known that he would be here, and her presence would be urgently required. How that happened, she neither knew nor cared, at the moment. He was angry, and that anger was ascending. She felt him reaching for a zenith of expression in fire and destruction that he intended to draw from their phantom zone. He meant to utterly destroy something or someone, but somehow, she knew that channeling the level of power he was reaching for would drain his life. She wondered. Why? It occurred to her then that she was screaming her question into the air. "Nigel! Why are you so angry? Nigel!" The answer came on the wings of a hot wind emanating from that valley where he was. "I HAD TO LEAVE HER, JUST TO STOP THEM FROM KILLING HER!" "Oh, my god," Angeline whispered. "You think I'm dead! Oh Nigel, baby . . ." Right then Ronald-Roy-whoever grabbed her left arm. "Hey, sexy, let's get out of here before . . . urk!" Angeline landed an open-handed blow right under his overly-prominent Adam's apple, and he went down. Nigel was here. He needed her, and she needed him. She ran to her jeep, got in and sped off in the direction of the Maelstrom.

REUNIFICATION . . . INITIATING

Nigel ran and ran. He ran so fast until there were moments when running felt like flying. When he was a kid, he could remember how his mother sometimes said that he "Ran so *hard* that day . . . ." He'd always wondered, then what does that mean, to run *hard*? Different words would go through his mind as he grew up, words like *concentrated, strong, tough, arduous, demanding, heavily, seriously, vigorously,* but later in life, he'd realized that running hard, playing hard, loving and hating hard all meant the same thing; doing whatever he did with all that he had. So he guessed that meant he was running hard right now. The Barrier agreed; Nigel was bringing all of his heart into the fight that he was running toward. All of them were there—the ones who had killed Thomas Bench, one of Crossover Team Alpha's originals and someone who had always been kind to The Baby Marine, as well as the ones who had forced him to separate from the love of his soul, just to keep her heart beating for a while longer. They were all there, in the same place, and Nigel would have his due from them. He was moving so swiftly that at times, his feet left the ground for long minutes, and a rain of hell was storming along with him. There! He could see them better now, the Graise with their rat-like extensions that sucked everything a person was out of their bodies, leaving empty husks of skin and bone—they were fighting the soldiers in gray, who had assailed Nigel and his newly beloved wife with their energy laser-gun-things, the same weapons they were now using against the Rat-men, shooting as many of the Graise as they could, all the while, losing numbers in a futile, desperate fight.

Within the eye of his thoughts, he saw Angeline, when they were lost little children in an orphanage managed with cruelty, playing together. He remembered when his father told him that they needed to get back to their world, and he had to say "Goodbye, Angeline" for the first time. He watched like some outsider when she ran to him, overjoyed because her aunt and uncle had found her, they were coming to take her home. He'd had to say "Goodbye, Angeline" to her again, then, hadn't he? He saw her in the park, where his mother would take him to play, just because she knew Little Angeline lived nearby. He recalled every day that he got to play kid games with her, cowboys and girls, fireman and rescuee, Superman and Wonder Woman. He recalled the day the maniacs in the car drove through everyone just to attack his mother, and he had to say a swift "Goodbye, Angeline" to her as she fled for safety. Nigel jumped into the air, as high as he could go, and with his hands, he reached into the essence of the Barrier and grasped firm hold onto ropelike tendrils of anger, rage, and bitter desperation, to pull these into the physical world around him, where he intended to use them to flay to nothing the evils that plagued his life, as represented by the combatants below him on the floor of the Tule Valley Hardpan. He never would know that, as a matter of fact, he'd gone high enough to disappear from sight, but his mind wasn't on the physics of the act, anyway. What his mind was on was the time and times again that he'd had to say "Goodbye, Angeline." The day when he'd gone to see her with a Dana who was far younger than he remembered, and the time when he'd gone because he'd seen an older version of his beloved, aching with loss and bereft of her Nigel, but still brave and determined enough to formulate a cure for the man-made disease that was ravaging her world, which would have died without it, and even to *her* he'd had to say "Goodbye, Angeline." She was gone, and today, he would follow her if he had to, just to destroy all of *them*. Both the Rat-men and the soldiers in Gray would pay for his pain today, even if the effort destroyed Nigel.

He felt the tendrils of emotions within the Barrier becoming solid destruction in his grip, while he remembered the two of them, Angeline and himself, as adults, and how he'd chosen to forgo the comfort of her touch for both of their sakes. "Goodbye, Angeline" from that restaurant, from the coffee shop, from her house, where he felt, now, that he should have stayed. Nigel was descending now, at thirty-two feet per second per second, and still, time seemed to move across the screen of his memories at a snail's pace. He saw Lucius below, fighting against the Graise that had him surrounded, and that vista bifurcated, half screen-like, with the way *she* felt as he held her broken body in his arms and said his final "Goodbye, Angeline." All of it made his heart feel as if it was tearing so he taxed the Barrier for even more destruction. In the pain of his heart, he tried to reach deeper for more emotional magma, but it seemed that he'd hit some type of barricaded ceiling composed of her feelings for him. The upper limit that stopped his progression toward self-destruction kept telling Nigel that she lived still, loved him still, and it would not allow him to take any more energy from the buffer zone between worlds and realities that the Barrier was. Because upper limits could do that inside of *otherspace*, it also identified itself; it was Angeline's love for him, and would resist his immolation. *That's okay,* he told it without words. *I will use what I already have,* and he continued his fall toward those enemies on the surface. He would kill them all. Not Lucius though. That man had been his loyal friend, and he would not die today. *"HOOD UP, LUKE!"* Nigel cried out with the voice of a Titan as the earth seemed to inch closer. He pulled Luke into the Barrier and thrust him out into the safety of the shielded area where Caldwell and his team were. Then Nigel hit the ground, and the storm of hell that rode his wake as unto the wings of a falling eagle broke upon the remaining Graise.

***

USMC Master Gunnery Sergeant Lucius Carver ran as fast as he could after Nigel. He could see The Baby Marine ahead of him, running with strides that elongated with his speed. The sky, as if a coconspirator, had begun to drop lightning all around Nigel, and it seemed at moments, that those were giving him sort of an extra lift, like some overenthused concertgoers helping their favorite rock star to crowd surf. Lucius cursed. He would never catch the kid at this rate. They both could move faster than an eye could follow, but not as fast as ethereal lightning, electricity, or whatever that was. He contacted Crossover Base One as he ran and apprised them of the current situation. Backup was still three and a half hours out, but General Gary had been in contact with The Old Man, who was on the way, and use of *otherspace* passage was authorized. Good. That would cut the time to three seconds or less, and soon everything would be in place. Then they'd drop MIST on those Graise bastards for sure. He was gaining on Nigel now, so he increased the speed. Just as it seemed he'd catch the kid, Nigel jumped. He jumped and kept going up, up, higher, and higher. Lucius's eyes followed, even as his feet kept him moving in the direction of the pitched battle between the Graise and MPIS. He stopped after a few more yards, though, pulled his hood off and stared into the sky after his ward. As Nigel rose, the storming heat lightning that crowded the atmosphere seemed to suddenly center itself on him. He vanished into a pinpoint in the sky, and all of the lightnings and thunders followed him, leaving nothing but sunlight and wild blue yonder. Meanwhile, the entire spectacle went unnoticed by the combatants ahead.

Master Gunnery Sergeant Carver was still staring into the air when he became aware of the proximity of the Graise, running in his direction. *Shouldn't have pulled my hood off,* he thought. *Their eyesight isn't very good, so they must have locked on to my heat signature.* With his hood off, the camo suit he was wearing had reverted to its regular gray color, its refraction ceased, and to the Graise, he no doubt looked like one of the MPIS fighters. *Not that it would have made any difference. They'd attack me no matter who I am.* He heard a metallic *chic-chack* followed by a *whooo-ooosh,* a sure indication that one of them had deployed their rat-tail-like penetration and suction cable against him. It was coming in low, headed for his upper right thigh. If that thing penetrated his skin, all of his internal organs would have been rendered into liquid by whatever they injected into his body, then sucked out like sludge. *Not gonna happen, pal,* thought Lucius as he jumped six feet into the air, spun into a somersault and came down on the trunk of that cable right where it connected to its human carrier. While he was somersaulting, Lucius deployed his twenty-four-inch Laze-Blade. As he landed, he slammed his boot down, breaking the hose loose from its pack, spilling the pre-ALC mix it contained onto the desert floor, and thrust the Laze through the Graise soldier's armor, piercing the man through his throat. *Scratch one.* Then he heard the sound of many more boots running his way. His enhanced hearing told him that reinforcements had arrived for the enemy. Between their fight with MPIS and Nigel's earlier act of sabotage, this particular scout troop's numbers were cut from thirty-two to about fifteen, and that should have been all that Master Gunnery Sergeant Carver had to deal with, but more of them had come and the bad guys' numbers had to be up to sixty or so by now. Unless something drastic happened, this would indeed become USMC Master Gunnery Sergeant Lucius Carver's Last Stand, but he would without a *doubt* take along as many of the enemy as he could for his ride with The Blind Widowmaker.

Although the enemy was moving fast by any other standards, Master Gunnery Sergeant Lucius Carver's hyper-accelerated senses were faster. He removed the clip of his M4 CQBR and replaced it with another one that was loaded with Graise-specific BD rounds. *He wasn't even supposed to know that these existed, let alone what they were, but somehow, Nigel had not only known all about these BD's, he'd also known where we kept them, how many we had, and which ones were programmed for the Graise.* the Master Gunnery Sergeant thought as he switched clips faster than any eye could follow. *That memory deal must be starting to work in his favor now. He's beginning to remember everything the Old Man knows. It's about time.* He faced the oncoming enemy fighters and began firing. Slice the pie left, slice the pie right. The Graise fell far faster than they expected, for every single one of the thirty rounds in Lucius's clip took another one down. If a round missed, it would turn in midair just to find its target. After clearing the immediate area, Lucius dropped the weapon, letting it hang in its harness, since the barrel had gotten too hot. It would cool momentarily, but for the moment, he drew his Laze-Blade. This weapon's design was based on the traditional USMC Ka-bar, but its blade was twenty-four inches of metallic Palladium glass made with an internal microwiring that would coat it with a self-contained laser. It was exclusive to the MISTmen, and, given enough time, could cut through the side of a tank without damage to itself. They were called Laze-Blades or, of course, the Laze. Each one was tuned to the specific DNA wavelength of the man to whom it had been issued, thus insuring that no other person could ignite its laser. Master Gunnery Sergeant Carver looked around at the destruction he'd wrought. Graise corpses littered the ground around him, their blood fusing with the hardpan valley, then slowly turning to dust. He saw that at least thirty-five or forty more were standing, slowly advancing toward him, weapons drawn. By now, they knew that this man wasn't MPIS, and that they were once again facing the MIST. They'd only ever killed one of these type of men before, but in so doing, they'd learned that ALC rendered from such enhanced men as he was had an extra potency that made it able to extend farther—it was usually isolated and used for their wounded or reserved for the upper echelons of Graise society. Because of that, their officers would want his body left whole. That was why they were in no hurry to open up on him with their M4 Carbines.

Master Sergeant Lucius Carver raised his Laze and was saying "Okay, then, come and get . . ." when the heavens suddenly darkened and the air began to crackle. *"HOOD UP, LUKE!"* the sky thundered. All of the combatants stopped and looked up to see Nigel descending rapidly with eyes that blazed color into the atmosphere he was flying through. Each of his hands held whips of lightning that started at the same base, then separated into living, writhing flagellum of hues varying from warm-to-hot spectrums of luminescence, all of it resembling nothing so much as The Hydra of Greek mythology. His words became black minicones, deadly, pointed shards that ripped through the Graise closest to Lucius, tearing them from top to bottom. With only seconds to comply, Master Gunnery Sergeant Lucius Carver donned his OTTO hood, activating his camouflage. He felt himself being lifted, forced into *otherspace* then thrust out onto the ground in front of a startled Team Caldwell, four miles away, at the other end of the Tule Valley Hardpan, within the refraction field of the Peek-a-boo-plate. Before anyone could speak, they all heard an extremely loud explosion coming from the southern end of the valley, where the Graise were. They could feel the effect of that blast, though it could not have been defined only as a wave of heat or light. It was physical, but the sound was accompanied by an emotional after-effect that washed over them all, like a release of some long pent-up feeling. About twelve seconds afterward, they felt the ground below them heave like an ocean wave. Again, it was as much an emotional, intense body wave of relief caused by some impassioned catharsis as it was a physical ground-quake.

Moments later, Nigel appeared in front of the group. His stealth suit smoked, although none of it was burned. He looked extremely tired, "You okay, Luke?" he asked. "I burned 'em all to ashes, man . . ."

For a moment he wobbled unsteadily but managed to murmur "Oh, and your son is here, Master Guns" before he fell to the ground.

***

First Lieutenant Charlton Carlton Pendle was "on the stick" of Crossover Base One's CH53E Super Stallion, the *Middle Child*. His copilot was First Lieutenant Walter Ralph Arthur McGrath. The rest of *Middle Child's* passengers included Captain Lucius Carver Jr., in command of the current mission, Master Gunnery Sergeant Gabriel Puccini, Gunnery Sergeants Antoine Rochon the younger, Roy-Bob Joseph the younger, Staff Sergeant Len Li and two more sergeants, Morgan Reynald and Oscar Juarez. They were going to get The Baby Marine, Master Guns

Carver and whoever-the-hell-else the guys had dragged into this reality with Nigel's latest unexpected crossover. By General Gary's orders, they were originally restricted from entering *otherspace* and limited to flying through the atmosphere while in refraction. That meant a six-hour flight from Franklinton, Louisiana to the Tule Valley Hardpan in Utah. It was, of course, the second time in as many months that The Walking Dead Raiders had to make this journey. Charleton Carlton Pendle hadn't felt the least bit of regret over the damage they'd had to do in that place the first time. His civilian pal DeVries had been in danger then, as had some Major from the Earth Next Door. As for MPIS, well, they definitely hadn't given Lieutenant Pendle any reason to love them. That group had been directly responsible for the demise of his father and indirectly so for his mother and sister's deaths. Additionally, they had deliberately abandoned his unit to be killed or captured. Sure, it was true that such an outcome was clearly possible from the moment that mission to Russia had been greenlit, but what none of them had known, at the time, was that their deaths or capture had been the expressed intent. None of them could have known how completely they'd been betrayed. Had General Renoir and Crossover Team Alpha not been there, Lieutenant Pendle's unit would have been dead, or worse, prisoners in some secret Russian hellhole. Even with Crossover Team Alpha, however, they still might have all been lost, but for Little Nigel's mass rescue of both units, at great personal cost to himself. All sorts of pain due to MPIS treachery. Of that The Walking Dead Raiders were positive, for Captain Carver and his officers had quietly spearheaded their own after-action investigation, without General Renoir or General Gary's knowledge (or so they thought). Resultantly, they'd learned exactly how deeply the deception of MPIS had penetrated the American political system. Since then, that organization had even collaborated with a hostile power in order to put their own man in the White House, and succeeded. Whenever he reflected on the work he'd been doing with General Renoir's forces, he'd think of how stunned the average American would be if they'd known how close their country had come to having its government hijacked and remolded into a dictatorship.

He'd seen The PHS avert a nuclear strike on the state of California, and had been involved with collecting and publicizing evidence proving the existence of that plot. Lieutenant Pendle himself, along with every ranking officer of The Walking Dead Raiders, had witnessed, with their own eyes, verification that MPIS had become an enforcing arm for the president who attempted that devilish act. They were informed of all the details because that was the way General Renoir ran his outfit. He, along with General Gary, considered strategies, made decisions and then presented those as well as all pertinent information to his officers. All of his officers, senior and junior, would be made privy to facts and proofs that influenced their general's decisions. Renoir felt that their having such knowledge would insure the long-range success of their goals. They were not officially a part of any government in existence, which sometimes made things harder, and at other times, easier, but at least their actions were not implemented to further secret agendas perpetrated by shadowy politicians in darkened back rooms, either. After General Renoir and Nigel saved their troops from that disastrous scouting mission into Crossover Team Alpha's own homeworld from Earth Next Door, General Gary and The Walking Dead Raiders, following General Renoir's orders, had used all of the information gained from the ill-considered and dangerous excursion to make their own expeditions to that place (had the top brass on that other Earth heeded General Renoir's advice, none of the deaths in his unit may have even happened). The expeditions made by the general's forces from Crossover Base One, however, were not subject to adjustments and poor planning by some self-serving governmental agency, so none of their men died, despite their many skirmishes with the Graise in R-2. Thus, The Walking Dead Raiders had learned more about the Earth where Crossover Team Alpha had been born. They'd learned what their brothers-in-arms and fellow marines once had and lost. Every man in their MIST outfit had made the trip several times. That Earth had almost been at Star Trek level when it came to technological advances, and every marine of The Walking Dead felt that if their elder brothers' world had been given just a few more years, maybe that version of the human race could have somehow achieved all that science fiction promised. Still, nothing they'd accomplished over there had been enough to stop evil men from doing evil things with the knowledge they possessed. Humanity fell, and then the Graise had come.

Generals Renoir and Gary's strategy also required their forces to learn all they could about the Graise. These people, if they could still be called that, embodied all that humanity hoped never to become. If they lived to forty-five years, they were old and bedridden, the way a Centenarian, in Crossover Team Alpha's world, or a ninety-year-old here, in Pendle's world, might be. At fifteen, the Graise were full-grown men and women, having earned none of the wisdom that commonly came with growing to adulthood, and they were speeding toward the golden years of their thirties. Their survival as a race depended on stealing life from others, and they would never be able to simply touch one another again. Anger was the sustenance of their psyches from start to finish, because, on some deep, instinctive level, they all *knew* that their situation wasn't fair. All of General Renoir's men had learned how that version of the human race had come to *this* from documents and recordings they'd found in Graise vehicles and on their bodies, as well as interrogations of captured Graise prisoners. He remembered the outrage that showed on General Gary's face when he'd learned how, many thousands of their generations past, different variations of the same two evil men that caused the downfall of his homeworld were ultimately responsible for instigating the downfall of a previous version of the human race, as well as all the evils perpetrated by them since they had become the Graise. All of this due to other incarnations of Muldowney and Craine. It seemed that, in every reality, any fruits of their joint efforts were predestined and doomed to be irreparably wicked.

Lieutenant Pendle thought more about DeVries Renoir. He wondered how Little Nigel would react when he met his brother. Would the kid remember? C. C. Pendle and DeVries had hit it off very well. As a Marine officer, he'd found he could admire the younger Renoir kid's moxie. The boy had built an army and moved to take back as much as he could of what the twisted system had taken from his relatives and him. Dev had come into his power and used it to make relevant changes for real people. Pendle approved of that. Plus, the guy could be pretty funny, sometimes. It was good to finally be working with the kid on an official basis.

He laughed a little as he thought of DeVries Renoir. He almost didn't notice Cap Carver trying to get him on mikes. "Yes sir, Captain?" Pendle asked.

"We've been ordered to jump through the hell zone, Lieutenant Pendle," Captain Carver told him. "When we get to the other side of it, continue running cloaked."

"Captain Carver, may I ask what's going on, sir?" Lieutenant McGrath asked as he sounded the warning for total OTTO cover.

"We just got a spurt from Pop," Captain Carver answered. "It seems that he and Baby Marine have engaged the Graise. Just to make the crap deeper, the enemy has sent in double reinforcements."

"Understood," C. C. Pendle responded. "Hood up, we're about ready to do it, Captain Carver, sir."

"Captain Carver, What about our special package, sir?" Lieutenant McGrath asked.

"He went into the zone about three minutes ago, Lieutenant," Captain Carver replied, as he entered the cockpit. "Said he felt a pull from there that he had to go answer. Maybe he bailed." As they spoke, *Middle Child*, powered by another of Nigel's baby teeth, moved into the *nil zone*.

"Captain Carver, I know the package personally," Lieutenant Pendle said. "He is not a coward. If he left already, it's more than likely that he'd be trying to hog all of the killing for himself, sir."

Captain Lucius Carver Junior came into the cockpit and clapped Pendle's shoulder. "The man's courage was never in question, Lieutenant. He let the sergeants know that he was about to try something he'd never done before, then jumped out of the chopper. No 'chute. Wrapped himself in light. The kid's got showmanship, that's for sure. He's that 'with a flash and a bang' kinda guy. Can't see The Baby Marine ever putting on a light show like that."

As if on cue, everything around the *Middle Child* lit up with the brilliance of the sun. The vista outside resolved itself into a scene that their minds could grasp, unlike the normal state of affairs within the barrier. All of the light resolved itself and suddenly, it seemed that the *Middle Child* was flying toward the underside of a mushroom-shaped funnel cloud that was striped with alternating patterns of light and darkness. At the bottom of the spectacle like a drain at the foot of a funnel cloud, was Nigel, set in a classic flyer's pose, one leg straight, the other bent at the knee, his arms outstretched above in a Y. Lightnings of varying warm-to-hot colors were flashing from his eyes, and all of the light/darkness of *otherspace* seemed to be getting pulled toward him. He came up from below, hung in place momentarily, then dropped, as if falling through some hole that had opened right underneath.

As he went, all of the spectacle that the occupants of *Middle Child* were seeing went with him. Pendle couldn't resist speaking. "Umm, what was that you were saying, Captain Carver, sir?" Captain Lucius Carver Jr. slapped Pendle's flight helmet and laughed. Right then, the chopper's systems all went haywire – the aircraft was being dragged along in Nigel's wake, and had begun to bank too hard. It was ripped out of *otherspace* with a tremendous jolt, and for the next few minutes, Both Lieutenants C. C. Pendle and Walter R. A. McGrath were intensely fighting to keep their bird aloft. Meanwhile, in the valley below them, the Graise had called for reinforcements the moment their encounter with MPIS began, and Master Gunnery Sergeant Lucius Carver's initial attack with BD rounds ended just as eight more heavily-armed Graise APCs arrived, their occupants spilling out with murderous intent. There were at least sixty-four soldiers on the ground surrounding the master gunnery sergeant when Nigel hit the earth, and his impact immediately disintegrated all of the enemies near his touchdown location. The whips of lighting in his hands he used to destroy the rest of the soldiers and their equipment as they exited the armored personnel carriers, then attacked every one of those transports, burning everything into ash. Still, with at least one tendril of his weaponry, he reached up and steadied *Middle Child,* subconsciously recognizing that vessel as a friendly. The two USMC First Lieutenants seemed to breathe a sigh of relief as one person. They and every other warrior within once again owed their survival to Nigel Renoir the Younger. They'd say "thank you" later. For now, though, the area was about to get crowded. MPIS air and surface attack craft were issuing from DCA-21, crossing the four miles between that location at the north end of The Tule Valley Hardpan to the Graise's entry location at the southern end of the valley, all moving at top speed. Simultaneously, more Graise vehicles had begun pouring from their entry point, and this time, they were bringing in aircraft. This fight was about to escalate. As much as the MISTmen may have wanted to join in the fray, Captain Carver had his orders. Since they were still in Refraction and undetectable, the mission could be completed. They were to retrieve Master Gunnery Sergeant Lucius Carver, Sergeant Nigel Renoir, and whatever guest stars had made the crossing with them. So *Middle Child* flew northward.

REUNIFICATION . . . PROGRESSING

"*She's here,*" The Barrier said. It didn't actually *say* those words, as much as it *intimated* that fact to Nigel through its emotional bond with him.

"*Who's* here?" the young man wanted to know.

"*He's going to help her,*" it added, as if he should have known who it was referring to.

"Who?" Nigel asked again.

"*Them. They love you.*"

"Well, that's nice to know," he answered. "But it would also be nice to know who the *hell* you're talking about!"

"*Them,*" the Barrier replied.

"Oh, my god, we're just not getting anywhere, are we?" he said to the Barrier.

"We're not getting anywhere, are we?" someone else echoed, as Nigel floated along in near-tranquility. *Sounds like Merry.* Nigel thought "Who are you talking to, Nige?" Big Luke asked. Nigel opened his eyes. He was within the refraction disc field, with his friends.

Nigel sat up. He was a little light-headed, but he felt less tired. "Master Guns . . ." He was happy to see that Master Gunnery Sergeant Lucius Carver had survived. "What time is it? What's going on outside?" Nigel asked.

"Our backup is here. They're hovering while they look for a safe LZ. It's hittin' the fan between the Graise and MPIS out there," Lucius answered. "And it's only about thirteen-thirty."

"Seems like it should be later," Nigel replied.

"Who were you talking to a minute ago?" Meredith asked. "We were worried that you'd gone unconscious again."

"I was talking?" Nigel asked. The Extras looked at him with that "we know you're faking" look that friends sometime have.

"You need to tell the whole story, Nige," Master Gunnery Sergeant Carver said. "Need-to-know basis doesn't apply here right now. They're not civilians anymore." Nigel and his mentor regarded one another for a moment. Then he sighed. "Okay, then. I was talking to the Barrier again. Or, rather it was talking to me, only it wasn't *talking* the way we do. It was more like, emotionally projecting whatever it was trying to say. It told me that '*She's* here,' then it said that 'he' was going to help her, but it couldn't seem to be capable of any more specifics. Then it told me that '*they*' love me. I kept asking who it was talking about, but the Barrier seemed to think I just ought to have known. Very aggravating."

Everyone else exchanged looks. Nigel noticed that. "Ooookay . . .," he started, "it seems like everybody here knows more than I do, after all." Lucius and Roan exchanged a meaningful glance.

"Don't you think it's time for him to know, Master Gunnery Sergeant Carver?" Roan asked. Lucius opened his mouth to speak, but Billy spoke up.

"Your Angeline is alive and lives here, in this reality," he said.

Nigel stared at him until Billy's face reddened. "What are you talking about, Detective Compton?" he asked with frighteningly quiet seriousness.

Meredith stepped forward and took Nigel's hands in her own. "We all know how much you loved Angeline Arlander, Nigel. So don't feel as if we're saying she didn't matter. We've just learned that another version of her lives here, in this place, and the two of you know one another already. What's more, she's been in love with you all this time." When Nigel didn't answer, she let go of his hands.

He stood up and said, "Well, when are we out of here, Luke?" As if the previous discussion never happened.

The others looked at each other for a moment. Lucius shrugged. "As I said, Nige, Captain Carver is looking for an opportunity and an acceptable landing zone. We're safe for the moment, and he doesn't want to dodge ordinance in order to set down."

"Are we safe, Lucius?" Roan asked him. It seems that a couple of bombs, rockets, or whatever have hit our little shelter here already."

"I think I heard a few stray shots hit it too," Billy added.

"I wouldn't worry about that," Lucius replied. "It would take a lot bigger to breach this peek-a-boo field."

"Wait a minute," Meredith interjected. "We just dropped a bombshell on Nigel here, and then we're going to move on to another subject just like *that*? Don't you think we should at least spend some of our precious time talking about how he *feels?*"

Lucius scoffed, politely (something none of the others had ever seen done so well until then) and the rest of them got quiet. Nigel seemed uncomfortable with the sudden attention to his feelings, but he replied anyway, "I think that I've been suspecting something like that. I keep having these—moments, when I kinda get into this, I don't know—fugue, and I remember, or have waking dreams, something like that. The last time it happened, I saw her, or, rather, a—manifestation of her, if that makes any sense, and it really wasn't her. But she said that when my memories started returning, I'd call on a recollection of someone who I completely trusted to help, but that it also had to be a person whom I knew to be alive. She said that I was in something she called 'visualization mode,' and that her presence was part of a neurobiological subroutine. I just assumed it was some figment of my imagination."

When Nigel mentioned the "visualization mode," Roan noticed a slight change in Master Gunnery Sergeant Lucius Carver's demeanor. *It's almost like he's excited about something,* he thought. *I'm not sure I even want to know, but I'll ask him later, anyway. Privately. If this is something monumental, well, good. If not, I don't want to have my people blindsided.*

He turned his attention back to Nigel who was still speaking. "She told me that *they* had to take my memories away, and that's what worried me. I want to know *who* had to take my memories away and why."

At that moment, Lucius tilted his head to the side as if listening to something only he could hear, which was exactly what he was doing. "Okay, people," he raised his voice, sounding once again what every marine master gunnery sergeant under fire sounded like. "We are going on a hike. Captain Carver has landed our transport on the other side of this hill. Four more marines and one officer will be arriving very soon. We will escort you for about one klick. Sergeant Nigel Renoir and I will be in OTTO gear, you will not be. You will, therefore, stay within the protection box we create for you along with him. You will also bring your weapons. This will ensure that we safely attain the transport. Is that understood?" The Extras understood.

"What about the SUV and all of this stuff that you and Nigel brought?" Billy asked.

"We leave that here," Master Gunnery Sergeant Lucius Carver responded.

"Aren't you worried that someone else might find it?" Meredith asked.

"If any unauthorized penetration of the refraction field occurs," Nigel responded, "the peek-a-boo plate and everything within its sphere will self-destruct. Everything. So don't forget to bring your baby pictures." Lucius laughed at that. Billy and his wife looked confused. "Inside joke." The Master Guns answered to their confusion.

"I think they mean that you should make sure to get everything you need out of the SUV," Roan said. Meredith went over and got her bag out of the Expedition. Lucius took Nigel aside and told him "Nige, The last these men heard, you were a marine. So, don't forget to salute the lieutenant."

At that moment, five men seemed to appear out of nowhere. They were First Lieutenant Walter R. A. McGrath, Master Gunnery Sergeant Gabriel Puccini, Staff Sergeant Len Li, Sergeants Morgan Reynald and Oscar Juarez. Master Gunnery Sergeant Lucius Carver and Nigel both stood to attention and saluted the lieutenant as he stepped forward. He smiled and spoke with an obvious New Englander's accent, "Master Gunnery Sergeant Carver, is your party ready to depart?"

"Yes, sir," Lucius responded. The Lieutenant's gaze lingered on Nigel for a moment.

"You've grown pretty big now, Baby Marine. Or should I refer to you as Sergeant Renoir?"

"Whatever designation the lieutenant prefers, sir," Nigel responded, sounding for all the world like an imitation of Lucius.

Lieutenant McGrath smiled. "At ease. That was some fine work that you men did on the Graise out there," he said.

"Thank you sir," Lucius responded to the lieutenant's smile and the other marines' beaming pride. *They love this kid, their "Baby Marine,"* Roan thought. *Even the officers are proud of him.* Lieutenant McGrath came over to Roan and extended his hand.

"USMC First Lieutenant Walter McGrath, sir. Pleasure to meet you and your team, Agent Caldwell. It's time to get you out of here. Once we get outside, our troops will box you in, but please, move forward only when we tell you to, stop when we tell you, and stay within our perimeter."

Roan looked him in the eye and responded with, "Understood, Lieutenant McGrath."

Just as everyone was ready to start moving out, Nigel's eyes lit up with a chartreuse color. It was bright and blinding, then it went away, leaving Nigel looking as if he needed to hurry to some other location. "What is it, Marine?" Lieutenant McGrath demanded.

"I have to *go*, sir—she'll be captured or killed if I don't get there! The Graise—*they're about to attack her!*"

"Permission granted, Sergeant Renoir," Lieutenant McGrath replied. "Complete the mission and meet us at Crossover Base One. *Go!*" Nigel disappeared.

***

A few minutes earlier, as the *Middle Child* flew toward the location of Master Gunnery Sergeant Lucius Carver's locator beacon, the battle between the Graise and MPIS started heating up on the floor of the valley beneath. Tracer rounds were flying from one group toward the other, and they were still about two miles apart. There were also low flying helicopters coming in from the Graise's portal entry. After ascertaining the safety status of the group he was here to extract, Captain Carver ordered his pilots to climb to a safe altitude and put the *Middle Child* on autopilot while he looked over a holographic map of the land below, searching for a safe LZ. If it could be avoided, he didn't want to risk exposing his marines to either of the battling parties down there while they were in the middle of a firefight. As their aircraft automatically maintained altitude and hover, Lieutenant McGrath asked for his assessment of the fight they were watching.

"Well, Lieutenant," said Captain Lucius Carver Jr., "as I see it, MPIS's reinforcements are coming from DCA-21, and the Graise's troops are likely coming straight from their homeworld. MPIS is gonna start strong, but eventually, they'll lose this engagement," he predicted.

"Why's that, sir?" Lieutenant McGrath asked.

Captain Carver gestured toward the prison. "They've fortified this position since the last time we were here. That facility is now at almost one hundred percent occupancy, and most of the occupants are battle-tested MPIS fighters. Their people are all stationed nearby, in the prison and on its grounds, so they have reinforcements on site, but that's still a finite number of guns," he began to explain.

Then he turned to McGrath and asked, "Can *you* tell me why their defeat in this battle is inevitable, and what that implies, Lieutenant McGrath?"

McGrath thought for a moment and answered, "The Graise's people are coming from farther away, but there's probably thousands, no, *billions* of them lined up back at the ranch, all waiting to jump on the next transports out. They've been planning this for quite a while now, so they're all ready to go. Meanwhile, these poor MPIS screws had no idea that the Graise existed or that they would attack today, so they're not combat-ready. Additionally, because they don't want to risk coming in last for congressional funding, they will refuse to request assistance from any other branch of their military for as long as possible. They have the upper hand at the moment, but the Graise will just never stop coming."

"What do those facts tell you, then, Walt?" Captain Carver asked. McGrath and Pendle looked at each other for a moment as a realization washed over them.

McGrath answered Captain Carver with "The Graise will undoubtedly win this engagement and take over Detention Center A-21. At that point, they will have captured the equipment that MPIS used to create their reality crossing portals at the same time that they will have attained a defensible command post from which to launch further operations against this Earth."

A silence fell upon the troops in the *Middle Child*. Most of them were of this reality, and all of them had seen what the Graise were doing in Crossover Team Alpha's world, so they were determined not to allow such a thing here. "Master Gunnery Sergeant Puccini!" Captain Carver called out. Puccini stood to attention.

"Yes, sir!" he saluted. Captain Carver answered, "Please inform our fellow marines of the reasons why this Earth will not fall to the Graise."

"Because we will not *allow* them to take DCA-21, we will not *allow* them to establish a command post, and we will not *allow* them to win, *sir!*" Puccini responded.

"Excellent, Marine. At ease." Looking around the chopper, he continued, "When we get our people on board, we attack the Graise and drop refraction shielded SMART-mines on the ground in front of that portal, since this is the only one that they've opened up at this time. We'll slow down their advancing forces long enough for the MPIS reinforcements to arrive. I've been in contact with General Renoir, the mission is greenlit, and he sent backup. *Little Bird* is fully armed and flying a holding pattern above us with Crossover Team Alpha and the rest of our unit, while she awaits my go. Our Brain-Boys back at base have sent a satellite-recorded, time-lapsed account of this little brouhaha to IDEA Control, and he is already causing a stir in Washington. Hill AFB will likely be sending air support soon, whether MPIS wants it or not. We *will not allow* the Graise to get a foothold on our world, Marines." Master Gunnery Sergeant Puccini stood to attention, saluted, and every other man did the same.

As one, they said, "OO-RAH!" Captain Carver returned their salute, then turned and entered the cockpit with Lieutenants Pendle and McGrath following. The *Middle Child* moved to land behind the hill where their passengers were located.

They landed in the designated zone and the rescue party set out for their destination. Gunnery Sergeant Rochon, for his part, donned his OTTO gear and slipped quietly out to post as overwatch security. He would make sure that no unexpected visitors from either side of the conflict came toward the *Middle Child* unseen or unchallenged, if necessary. At the same time, he'd gather as much intel as he could regarding the events unfolding out in the hardpan. While Lieutenant McGrath and his party set out to pick up their objective, Rochon made his way toward the sounds of combat from the other side of the hill. He was a USMC Scout Sniper, so he also needed to scout. He gradually made it to a vantage point from which he could see most of the field of battle. As Captain Carver and the other officers had surmised, the fight was turning toward the Graise. Their sheer numbers were overwhelming MPIS. Graise helicopters were strafing them from above, and infantry just would not stop pouring in through that portal. Two or three AH-64E Apache Guardian Attack helicopters had taken off from DCA-21and were making their way across the valley to engage the Graise's versions of the same unit. They were doomed, Rochon knew. The Graise had an advantage in numbers. They also had something else—an EMP cannon that would eliminate electrical signals within a human body, rendering its victims immobile. It was designed to stop enemy troops without doing physical damage. That way the Graise could easily siphon their enemies' vital fluids off, with less risk to their troops. The disadvantage of that pulse cannon, however, was its size. It could only be mounted in a vehicle as large as a helicopter or larger. Still, General Renoir had been looking for an opportunity to capture one. He felt that it could save lives. Well, the MIST might be able to get one today.

It only took about two and a half hours for the rescue party to return. Remaining unseen in this terrain was easy for them, but not for Roan, Billy, and Meredith, therefore, the whole group had to move slowly, so as not to draw attention. Their MIST escort, however, was invisible to most eyes. At least to most untrained eyes. Rochon reported their approach to Captain Carver and settled down to wait. The antiaircraft turrets mounted on the walls of DCA-21 began to cough out their deadly ordnance, and he knew that the Graise's choppers had finally made it across the four miles separating their entry portal from the prison's walls. That, in turn, meant that possibly, all or most of the MPIS personnel would have been eliminated. Their secondary mission was even more urgent now. Mentally, he urged Lieutenant McGrath and his people to hurry up. Eventually the small group entered the *Middle Child*, and overwatch for this mission concluded, he followed. Like the rest of his brothers-in-arms, he, too, was disappointed that their Baby Marine wasn't with the party, but all of them understood Lieutenant McGrath's decision to let Nigel go do whatever the Barrier was urging him to. His was a different case. No matter how much the kid wanted to try, he would never be a "normal" marine (not that any of the MISTmen could be called such a thing anyway). Nigel was a beloved part of their MIST family, but he was still an outsider. No one else could do what he did. Antoine Rochon knew what that felt like. He was a USMC scout sniper, the only one attached to then-Lieutenant Lucius Carver Jr.'s Raider unit and a loner, as many sniper experts tended to be. Until that night when they'd been abandoned to the enemy and General Renoir's unit was there to save them, that is. He was as shocked as anyone else to meet an older version of himself from a different earth, and it was rather off-putting, at first. Until he realized that the other wasn't just a copy or a replica. It *was* him. Same childhood, same family, same home, everything. They had the same secrets, the same tendencies, and now they had one another. It made life easier. So he could understand why DeVries's presence with their unit would be important to Nigel. His brother would be the only other person who could truly understand what it was like to have an affinity with the hell zone they sometimes traveled through. So thinking, Antione Rochon made his way back to the *Middle Child*.

***

Angeline Duplessis-Renoir rode her Hummer toward the disturbance in the sky, pushing the huge vehicle as hard as she could. Her inner feelings told her that Nigel must have gotten her message, because at the last moment, he'd stopped pulling energy from the phantom zone, and that saved his life. She was relieved, but her heart also told her that the need for urgency hadn't abated. She *needed* to get to him, not only to save his life, but also because he was hers, and she missed him. So she rode on through the dry heat toward that valley where the prison was. For her, there was no uncertainty concerning his whereabouts. He was up ahead, in that valley. She remembered the name of the place, now—they called it the Tule Valley Hardpan. She'd be there soon. Angeline had no idea of how grave the situation was in the location she was headed toward. If she had gotten that far, she would have driven right into a pitched battle, behind the Graise's lines. Fortunately, she never made it to the Tule Valley Hardpan during that battle. As she sped along, she heard the gunfire and explosions continuing, which made her feel more desperation. *Uncle Rene said that they sometimes have war games out here,* she thought. *That's why those sounds are there. Maybe Nigel's involved. He was in the Marines the last time we . . .* She couldn't complete that thought. But she did notice the sound of diesel engines that seemed to be emanating from some point up ahead. *Right. So now there's some sort of construction work going on up there too,* she was thinking.

The average American never believes that their homeland could become a battleground, because no such thing has happened since the Civil War era, and though Angeline was anything but average, she still shared that view. So, to her ears, the sounds she heard coming from the road ahead must've meant some sort of heavy equipment was in use. *Great* she'd been thinking. *All I need is some road construction crew getting in the way.* Well, nothing was going to stop her, Angeline decided. She'd find Nigel and, this time, she wouldn't leave him, no matter *what.* They were married, now, and he wasn't going to get away with saving her life at the cost of their losing one another again. The construction vehicles were closer now. She had travelled little more than four miles down the road, and was right at the location of a landmark known as the Hummingbird Natural Arch when Angeline Duplessis-Renoir came face to face with the Graise. The machinery she'd been hearing wasn't construction equipment at all, she realized. Right in front of her were four Graise APCs, arranged in such a way as to block the entire road. As soon as the soldiers inside realized that a possible all-terrain vehicle was headed their way, they'd stopped and arranged their transports so as to do just what they were doing—form a roadblock by parking front bumper to rear bumper from one side of US 50 to the other. The land was too flat to stop any all-terrain vehicle from simply going around their checkpoint, so they'd set ambush points as part of their preparation, just in case the approaching Hummer was a military vehicle. No version of Angeline was familiar with military tactics at this age, so she had no idea that she should do anything but stop. She didn't know the difference between marine or army transport vehicles, friend or foe. To her eyes they were just big army trucks of some sort.

In addition to stopping Angeline, the Graise had detained a crew of young motorcyclists who were headed for the Tule Valley Hardpan in order to race their bikes. There had initially been four bikers and an RV with four more of their friends riding along behind. When they'd seen that these were not US Army vehicles, the young men had fought to escape. Now there were only two left. Scattered along the ground were six humps of leftover skin and bones. Angeline may not have known what military vehicles were ahead of her, but she did know what she was seeing in the side of that road. So when she did stop her vehicle, she didn't get out. Instead she reached into the back seat for the Mossberg 500 Tactical 8-Shot pump-action energy bolt shotgun that Uncle Rene had insisted she bring along. He'd said that there could be coyotes, wolves or mountain lions out in this desert, and he'd prefer she go armed. At the time, she'd thought that he was probably thinking of two-legged predators more than anything else. Just as she got the shotgun, the prisoners that the Graise were about to liquefy seized upon the moment's distraction and attacked their guard. What ensued would always seem to Angeline to be the event that made her believe in evil.

The two men overwhelmed the Graise they'd attacked and knocked him to the ground. Then one of them got ahold of the man's firearm and turned it on the others. At the same time, the second man had gotten ahold of his guard's knife and was stabbing him viciously in his throat. Angeline would always remember wondering why the knife attacker was so angry and how come the victim's blood looked—*gray?* That's when she saw the Graise deploy their liquification cables. One struck the Mad Knifer right between his shoulders, the other struck the would-be Rifleman's belly before he could pull the trigger, and both men seemed to crumple from the inside, like dried-out autumn leaves in a child's hands. Everything she was seeing resolved itself into a stark scenario. She could see the Graise cables pumping fluid from the men's bodies and into the tanks they carried like obligatory steel backpacks. She was in dread, but Angeline still retained enough self-control to back away from the Graise at high speed and do a power turnaround with the intent of heading the other way. The whole maneuver was executed with the seamlessness that could only have been achieved by a first-timer. But she never got to the part where she sped off in the direction she'd come. The Graise soldiers lying in ambush shot out her tires. She retained enough presence of mind to use the brakes to prevent anything worse from happening to the vehicle and to allow her time to get her shotgun ready in preparation for a fight. All of a sudden, one of their cables punctured the driver's side door and withdrew, tearing it off and taking it along. Angeline pointed her shotgun and fired it as best she could. The recoil knocked her toward the passenger side of the Hummer at almost the same time that another Graise cable tore it off. Meanwhile, her "beginner's luck" continuing, the blast from the Mossberg tore her primary attacker's head to shreds, spilling gray blood and brains everywhere. Still another soldier was rushing over to take that one's place and drag her out of the shelter of the Hummer, though, while the one who had snatched off the passenger side door was freeing her cable from its wreckage. Angeline knew that this was her end then. She would never survive these things, whatever they were. *Nigel, I love you. You were all I ever wanted*, she thought.

Suddenly all of the soldiers near her were decapitated with different rays of yellow light. The door to the phantom zone opened, and he somersaulted into the scene outside. As he completed that move, daggers of blue and bright green light flew from him and speared more of the gray attackers. He actually took a moment to do a hero pose and laugh before he flew into action again, making a rope out of the sound of his own laughter and whipping it around and around, tearing more of their attackers in halves. He was wearing a different uniform now. It was something like a flight suit and either everything they'd shot at him had either missed, or his suit was bulletproof. Even the cables the gray-blooded soldiers shot at him before he'd either speared or sliced them hadn't had any effect. For just a moment, the bad guys stopped their attack. Probably to figure out what had just happened and how to proceed.

"N-Nigel?" Angeline asked. She wasn't sure. There was something about him that wasn't the same.

"Well, not exactly," her rescuer said as he turned toward her and pulled his hood back. "I'm Nigel's better-looking brother, DeVries. Since you're my sister-in-law, I guess I'll let you call me Devvie."

Her jaw dropped. "There's two of you? I only ever knew Nigel. You're shorter than he is, you know." DeVries' smile faded as Angeline continued, "He never told me about . . ."

"That's because he doesn't know," DeVries told her. "They fried his brains and he doesn't remember anything. We should—" at that moment, the Graise APCs began shooting rapid-fire machine gun rounds. DeVries was hit, but not before he threw a stubbornness shield bubble from out of the Barrier to surround Angeline. The bubble surrounding his sister-in-law held fast as he rolled along the ground. Eventually, he stopped himself. The rounds began to bend around him as he drew on the Barrier's abstract energies for Acts of Evasiveness that would deflect their trajectories. "YOU'RE PISSIN' ME OFF!" He yelled and his words became force arrows that hit the APCs but still did not stop their attack. He was trying to make his way back to Angeline in order to affect an escape for the two of them. As he moved, he threw daggers of sickly, yellow-green hatred at the Graise soldiers who had begun trying to make their way toward Angeline. DeVries hadn't had the military training that his brother had, though, so he didn't notice that one of the APC vehicles had broken off from the engagement and started a flanking movement. The Graise were determined to capture him, if they could, since they thought him to be Nigel. Meanwhile the remaining troops and APCs had begun to let loose with everything they had against DeVries and Angeline within her shield. Nevertheless, he was shielding himself while trying to mount an offensive at the same time, and it was going slowly. He somehow understood that Angeline's shield wasn't a concern, for it would hold out forever, if it had to, since the Barrier was intent on protecting her as much as DeVries was. Outside of it, the battle continued. Devries's outrage at the impasse was building, and he felt he needed to reach for something more, but—*what?* He wondered.

Suddenly, he recognized that something powerful and angry was coming, but had no idea what, or where it was coming from, when he saw that Angeline had felt it too. She was looking up and saying something. Even some of the Graise had started staring at the sky above. So DeVries looked up also. What he saw almost made him drop his stubbornness shield. The sky above looked like a pot of gumbo in a rolling boil. There was every sort of red color moving and twirling, wheeling, and pirouetting, along with chartreuse–colored lightnings tinged with yellows and blues. All of the lightnings charged toward one point and then seemed to turn earthward the way migrating birds and beasts all turn at once. Within the cacophony of colors, he could see someone, a man—and intuitively he perceived that this could only be Nigel, falling upon his enemies in the power of his anger. Everything seemed to move in slow motion as DeVries called to mind the Older Nigel's words, *"If you can be considered a weapon of destruction, your brother must be considered a weapon of mass destruction.* "Oh, mon Dieu . . .," DeVries muttered, "he is *so* gonna bring some serious pain to these guys . . ." And as Nigel hit the ground, his lightnings and fires came crashing down along with him.

There was the same physical-emotional upheaval as before, but DeVries and Angeline felt it more acutely than The Extras had, for they, too had special connections with the Barrier and all of its abstracts. A cloud of dust rose from the desert floor, obscuring everything for a few moments. It combined with the barrier energies that Nigel had unleashed, then rolled outward, and DeVries saw his brother, on one knee, his fists on the ground, cracks emanating from where he'd just landed so violently *Now, that's an entrance!* he thought. The dust cloud rolled away in the direction of the Graise soldiers who'd survived, carrying all its annihilation and obliteration along, expending it all against them, reducing every single one to ash. The APCs and their occupants, however, had suffered the most immediate damage. Two of them were crushed as flat as a plastic container on the interstate would be crushed, and a third was balled into a metal ball—again, crushed the same way an empty water bottle would have been. Nigel stood, slowly, his eyes blazing a chartreuse color that swiftly faded. When his vision cleared, DeVries could see that his brother's eyes had focused on him. First they registered disbelief, then joy.

"Devvie?" he asked.

"Yeahh . . .," his brother replied slowly.

"DEVVIE!" Nigel yelled, then ran over and swept him up in a bear hug. "I thought—I thought, I mean, we'd *lost* you, man! Oh, man, Oh, man . . ."

Then he turned his head and caught sight of Angeline. His mouth dropped, and his eyes began to tear. "Ange. My angel . . .," he said, as he started toward her.

"I'm not dead," she told him through her own tears. She was walking toward him, reaching for him, when the Graise dart hit. Nigel's eyes suddenly clouded, and he fell to his knees, mumbling "Get her to safety, Devv . . ." then pitched over sideways to the ground.

"NIGEL!" Angeline screamed. At the same time his brother sprang into motion. DeVries charged toward Angeline, grabbed her, and disappeared into the zone. He came out of it in General Renoir's house.

Angeline was still screaming "TAKE ME BACK! HE NEEDS ME!" When Angeline the elder, along with Lucius Carver Senior's wife, came running. "What *happened*?" she demanded.

"They got *Nigel!* Those gray *connards* got *Nigel!*" DeVries shouted. "She tried to go with him, but I *promised* to protect *her*, so I brought her here!"

Angeline the younger was becoming hysterical, now. "LET ME GO!" she screamed. "He's my *husband*, and *I'm not going to lose him again!* Not going to . . .," she murmured, even as she fell asleep from the sedative slappy that Angeline the elder had applied to her neck.

***

After everyone was aboard, *Middle Child* lifted off and contacted *Little Bird*. Major Braggs relayed their battle orders. They were to take out the Graise Helicopters while in refraction. An easy enough mission, since the *Middle Child* was armed with BD rounds as well as Graise Hunter missiles that would target the all-pervasive nanites saturating the gray ex-humans and everything they produced. If a missile somehow missed the helicopter, it would hone in on anything else with that signature composition. Things got complicated with the additional objective though. Captain Carver was expected to find a way to deactivate one of the Graise attack choppers, capture its pulse gun, mount it in Middle Child, and fire a burst at the Graise's entry rift. That was how the portal that had been opened in the Tule Valley Hardpan would be closed. (The enemy would without a doubt open another one, since they now knew how to find this reality, but, considering the Graise's limited technical ability, the tactic would at least buy a little more time for the different governments of this world to decide on an approach in confronting the upcoming invasion.) Meanwhile the *Little Bird* would target the battlefield with smart-drones that were preloaded with an incendiary version of General Renoir's Boron Quicklime. This was the same chemical that he'd used in the Exploratory

Mission to R-2, but some changes had been made in the composition of this batch. The science acquired from Blacen Muldowney of R-3's Nano-tech research had been combined with Kruger and Leonard's work, producing the current version of Renoir's Quicklime; a chemical compound infused with predator nanites that would that would target the titanium and internal programming the Graise nanites were composed of. These were delivered within an advanced, self-igniting thermite. Thus, it would burn through the enemy's armor, their equipment and their bodies in the same way regular thermite would. Any of the tiny predator nanites that did not land on Graise targets would still be destroyed by its own ignition. It was a nasty weapon, but a necessary one.

Meanwhile, the MISTmen used what was known among them as Repulsion Parachuting to get to the Hardpan floor from the *Little Bird*. Every human body produces an electrical field- it's not a very strong field, but in the world that Crossover Team Alpha came from, the Think Tank of days gone by had learned how to program military camos with a polarity reversal feature. What this would do for their soldiers was this; their personal polarity as expressed by their individual magnetic field would be reversed in relation to the polarity of the earth's magnetic field in whatever location they might be in when they needed to jump from an aircraft onto a battlefield. Opposite polarities repel one another, so the repelling force between the soldier and the earth they were jumping onto would force that person's fall to decelerate. That was Repulsion Parachuting. Put simply, every military force in General Renoir's America could jump to ground in refraction without traditional parachutes and land safely. That was what the marines in Little Bird had done, so now, when the aircraft deployed the anti-Graise drones, Crossover Team Alpha and any of The Walking Dead Raiders who had been on that aircraft would be on the ground, having jumped without being seen by either MPIS or the Graise that they were fighting. They were going to mine the ground in front of the Graise's entry portal as "plan B," but if the marines on the *Middle Child* could force one of those Graise choppers down, they were prepared to swarm it and capture one of their pulse cannons as "plan A." So they waited for a signal from Captain Carver before taking any action. Only if the MPIS forces were close to being destroyed would they act before Major Braggs released his deadly cargo.

***

Colonel Roderick (Rod) Lichsten was in unfathomable trouble. The recent failures and losses within his department had undoubtedly put his career in jeopardy. Because of the covert nature of his work, it was also quite possible that his life and Janice's, as well as their two little boys' lives, would also be imperiled. He was known in MPIS as "The Gray Colonel" and had been appointed Secrecy Commander over the most covert arm of that branch of the military. He was responsible for DCA-21 and all its inmates, as well as several assassinations carried out by his own hand. He was also in command of multiple top-secret operations involving information-gathering against various persons and elements considered threats within the other branches of the United States Military. From his perspective, it seemed that all the recent misfortune befalling his command had to have been orchestrated from behind the scenes by some party or parties unknown. He had been deeply involved with the Commander-in-Chief's plot to undermine ITA and its Idea Control Director Roan Caldwell, so he wondered about that man's possible involvement in the series of unfortunate events that kept befalling his people and his command. Were these incidents all a part of some sort of revenge plot launched against him? Was this Roan Caldwell less of an honest man than he seemed? Nobody in the shadowy world of MPIS could possibly have been *that* upright, so it was hard for the colonel to believe that anyone else could have been. Colonel Lichsten had spoken to Correctus Dawson on the day of the torturer's unfortunate demise at the hands of an escaped prisoner, and still felt aggravation over Dawson's lack in achieving any progress. Regardless of the man's occasional ineptitude, he was the best there was at what he did, so The Gray Colonel had held out hope that some excellent insights may have been coming from the Little Man with the Funny Glasses, but that hope was gone.

He resented the fact that the Tiny Torturer (as he had been derisively referred to within MPIS) died before mining any significant information in relation to Major's disappearance and replacement by that intruder. Dawson had been sloppy and incompetent in the way he'd handled that assignment, and now, not only was the impostor gone, but that Casino Robber with the amazing ability (or technology) to mimic the Broussard Park kid's abilities had disappeared also. The Gray Colonel felt that the two events were somehow related. Not that there was anyone still around who could be questioned about it. He could only surmise that the prisoner who killed Dawson must've had outside help (nobody who was in that man's physical condition should even have been able to *lift* a .50 caliber Desert Eagle, let alone fire one.) and because he had vanished, Mr. Casino Robber seemed to be the only logical suspect. He, The Gray Colonel, had every intention of despoiling and slowly, painfully pulling apart every person that man had ever loved, starting with Major Robin Lacy's traitorous daughter, but now, he was neck deep in the toughest fight of his entire valorous military career. He had not been on the field at the start, for his staff officers insisted that he, as the ranking officer, should command the soldiers from the comm room, while remaining in contact with MPIS headquarters, so he had. But things were beginning to go badly out there, and the reports that made their way back to him seemed chock full of unbelievable, incredible tales. Colonel Lichsten was a man of many bad traits, but cowardice wasn't one of them. He also was fanatically concerned with the well-being of his soldiers. He felt that right now the men needed to see him out on the field. The battle outside had been going well at first, but now it seemed that just as the sun began to set, all hope of MPIS winning this battle had begun to go down with it. Colonel Rod Lichsten thought back on his world history classes during his time at the university. Julius Caesar was always one of his favorites. He'd worn a red cape so that when his troops were in pitched battle, they could see him fighting alongside them and take heart. It worked for that great man, so Colonel Lichsten had adopted the same practice. He donned his own red cape, and along with his staff officers and his aide, mounted his armed Humvee, then headed out to the battlefield.

What he saw when he got there turned his face ashen. His soldiers were fighting, but the enemy just never stopped coming. They also had three AH-64 Apache Helicopters in the fray. These were floating along like wasps, then they'd dip the nose, and several MPIS soldiers would drop everything and fall to the ground like puppets whose strings had been cut. After that, the enemy soldiers would walk over, extend something that looked like a rat's tail out of their backs and the stricken MPIS soldiers would seem to have everything that they were sucked out of their bodies. That was by far the worst thing The Gray Colonel had ever seen done on a battlefield, and it crystallized his hatred of this enemy. If these were the Interlopers, and this was what they had planned for his world, he was determined to do everything in his power to bring hell and blood against them. If he survived. For now, though, he had to turn this fight around so that his men would take heart. He ordered his aide to head for the thickest part of the melee, then chose to man the energy gun mounted on his transport himself. His soldiers needed to see him fighting along with them. As they headed into the battle, Colonel Lichsten truly proved his worth. His forces had begun to lose heart, but the sight of him, blasting the enemy into oblivion, red cape flaring with the wind, strengthened their resolve. He shot at the helicopters, even managed to graze one, but it didn't slow the thing down much. He was looking at it when an RPG round exploded in front of his vehicle and darkness took him.

He woke up, and his Humvee was tilted at a terrible angle, everything on its front right side destroyed. Colonel Lichsten, bleeding from a wound to the right side of his forehead, stumbled out of the vehicle and checked his personal laser pistols. The enemy soldiers were almost upon him, and he wasn't going down the way in the same way those poor unfortunates who got their insides sucked out had. He couldn't see very clearly, but it seemed that even more of the enemy troops had arrived and their numbers were doubled, at the least. *Too many. There's just too many,* he thought as he lifted his pistols. "General Custer's last stand . . ." He chuckled through grit teeth. Suddenly, tracer rounds by the hundreds began to fly from some unseen source above and behind him. Every one of the rounds hit one of the enemy troops, even if that round had to curve and dip like some sort of heat-seeking missile. He could hear them whizz the way that flying bullets do as they flew past him, but he never heard gunfire, never saw any muzzle flashes from anywhere. Those rounds just seemed to come from thin air. When it ended, the immediate area was clear of enemy troops, but there were still too many of the them swarming the battlefield and Colonel Lichsten's command was still falling apart before the never-ending onslaught of gray-blooded attackers. *Where are they coming from?* he wondered. Through the blood partially obscuring his eyesight, he could see that they had flanked him, and he was about to be surrounded. This was it, then. No matter what new MPIS stealth tech might pop up to save their skins, he and his unit were going to die here. He'd honestly thought that he'd win. He had the reinforcements and the firepower, but none of it made any difference now. DCA-21 was going to be overrun and captured. He intended to get to the flare kit and fire off the blue one. That would signal an orderly retreat to his location for all surviving troops, so that maybe his forces could have withdrawn to the prison and made a stand there. He never managed it. Suddenly the entire sky lit up and the hundreds of enemy fighters covering the land caught fire. Colonel

Lichsten knew thermite when he saw it, but he had no idea how this was happening. He was standing there, shocked, when a man *appeared* right in front of him. At the same time, four others appeared, and The Gray Colonel was boxed in. "Colonel Lichsten," one of them began, "I'm going to need your laser pistols." Another of the men stepped forward and relieved him of those, then handed them to the one who was obviously in command. Immediately, the commander pointed them at the floundering helicopter that Lichsten had wounded. The aircraft went down, while at that moment, *something* destroyed the other two Apaches and more men *appeared*. These charged the downed Apache with inhuman speed and boarded. He heard the abrupt report of gunfire and everything inside the helicopter got quiet.

"What are they doing in there, soldier?" he asked in his best command tone. No one answered. He was about to approach the one in charge when one of the others stepped in front of him and blocked his way.

"Sit down, Colonel Lichsten," the first man answered casually. "I outrank you."

The Gray Colonel was shocked. What was a *general* doing out here in this mess? As if he could read thoughts, the general said, "I'm here to coordinate and execute a mission that will give you and your world more time."

"What do you mean?" the Gray Colonel demanded. The general held up a finger to quiet him, then stepped away. Colonel Lichsten tried to see what he was doing, but a very large younger man stepped forward to within an inch and blocked Lichsten's view.

After a moment, the general returned. "We're the ones you've been referring to as the Interlopers. For years now, we've been battling the Enemy that you're currently mixing it up with," he said, then continued, "they call themselves the Graise, and they devastate civilizations to preserve their own with that liquid they make out of people. There are billions of them on the way here, so your world will need to do whatever they have to in order to survive the coming assault." As he spoke, another unbelievable thing happened. Rod Lichsten never saw where it came from, but suddenly, he was aware of something *big* sitting on the ground behind him. A CH53E Super Stallion had materialized there. He tried to turn around, but the four men who were holding him only allowed him one brief look. Then the general spoke again. "Colonel Lichsten, we're about to end the current problem you're having, but it won't be done for free. You've seen what is facing the entire human race on this planet. We consider you a despicable, slithering person, but you're tenacious enough to push for worldwide unification with no regard for your own safety or career. You're also an extremely fine officer and a dedicated champion of humanity who's about to be sacked and executed. Believe me, we know this is your superiors' intent because we've got a copy of the order. We've already taken measures to protect your family, and that wasn't done for free either. Just another reason why we've selected you for this mission. In return for our assistance here, you will do all you can to unify this world against the Graise, even if doing so requires you to act against your former agency and its bosses. You will, from this point on, work with ITA. We'll try to put in a good word with IDEA Control for you."

"So," Colonel Lichsten began, bitterness dripping from his tone, "Caldwell is working with you, isn't he? I knew he was *too* honest."

General Gary laughed. "No, Colonel, he is not. Even if we approached him, he would refuse. That's why we choose to work with you. You're dishonest, but in all the right ways for us. You won't let this world fall any more than he would." The general started to walk away, but he turned as if he'd just remembered something else. Rod Lichsten could see the anger in the man's eyes as he said; "Oh, and the next time you are in the presence of a superior officer, *you will salute.* Knock him out. He doesn't get a slappy so he can to go to sleep the easy way. Have a good rest, Colonel." The very large younger man stepped forward, stood in front of him, smiled, then punched him. Stars flared behind his eyes, and darkness took Colonel Lichsten.

***

DeVries didn't even know why he had just *acted* on that New Nigel's command to get his girl Angeline to safety. He hadn't even made any snappy, smart-aleck remark or anything, he just *obeyed* the guy. As he watched the older Angeline tending to her younger counterpart, he realized that at some point, he'd been convinced. That other guy *was* his brother, and he *did* know DeVries, although the knowledge wasn't shared between the two of them, meaning DeVries didn't just suddenly *recognize* the guy who was his brother as *the* Nigel his family had lost, but all along, he had known that one belonged here. He was the *right* one, if such could be said of someone with multiple copies. He shook his head, as if to dispel the thought of multiple copies of any person. At any rate, he was getting tired of sitting around here waiting for Old Nigel to show up from the command center, or wherever. A couple of military guys had come in after word got out of his brother's capture by the Gauze, or Graise, whoever they were. They'd told him that "General Renoir has ordered you to await his arrival." But he wasn't one of the general's military monkey-boys, and thus under no obligation to obey like one. So, he wasn't going to wait. He was going to go get Nigel. He hadn't attained the same affinity for communicating with the Barrier as his brother had, but he could receive communication in the form of feelings relayed to him from within it. He knew how to find his brother, so why was he waiting for this Old Nigel-General guy to tell him what to do? He decided to go and go now. Just as he stood up to leave, Old Nigel walked in. "DeVries, I . . ." And DeVries was gone.

He was flying and floating, walking and gliding. Emotions in solid constitution, actions, reactions, words that took form, thoughts that had feelings. Colors that made stars, stars bounding, rebounding, musical notes with their own intelligence levels, feelings who spoke with no words, empathetic tornadoes that were able to communicate thoughts and feeling from one person to another, random personality quirks from random people long gone and still to come. All these things and more made up the substance of the Barrier. It was an abstract environment with physical effects, and it defied all human description. The Barrier had been at risk ever since the advent of the Graise, and it needed to preserve itself for the sake of multiple worlds it cradled and protected. Because the threat originated within humanity, it needed humans who could abide its environment. No normal human could survive within it, though, and that was why something different had to be done. The Graise's violent elimination of so many species and decimation of their worlds had begun to affect the balance of life that kept the Barrier stable, and the Barrier was what kept all the worlds and their many versions from colliding. If it fell apart, such an event would lead to extinction along all lines of life, and that ran counter to the Barrier's reason for existence. The Graise were human, and though there were other species populating the thousands of worlds and versions of those worlds, they simply didn't have the imagination and drive that humans had. So it seeded minute portions of itself into the human worlds that abounded within it. All these infusions didn't graft into the DNA they'd been aimed at. Some of them did, but the effect wasn't what the Barrier was trying for. Then Roman Marques was born, and he was everything the Barrier needed. The problem remaining, however, was the Barrier's inability to communicate with its agent. It had no way to call Roman into itself, or to converse with him on the outside. Thus, Roman Marques discovered his own ability at a later age, which meant that he wasn't as effective a reality walker as he could have been. Later, the Graise found his world and committed another crime against the peacefulness holding the Barrier's substance together. They crossed from one reality to the next, bringing total war and extinction to a world of humanity for the first time since they had become what they currently were. The chaos reverberated within the Barrier, racking it with waves and waves of pain. It almost weakened its hold on its purpose.

It wouldn't give up though. It was only a matter of time before the Graise would discover other realities, or at least other ways to travel farther into the outer space of their own, since they were always searching for new worlds to exploit and destroy. So it began its own search. It couldn't "see" humans as clearly as if it were one, but it could *feel* for a precise combination of DNA that could accept its gift. In this way, it came upon the Renoir family of one reality and the Lacy family of another. It still couldn't communicate as well as it hoped (yes, the Barrier *hoped*) but it found it could do a much better job of seeding within this DNA pool, and resultantly, could pull at least one of the new agents toward itself whenever that one was in a certain emotional state of despair and/or desire. That was how Little Nigel had found his way into it so many years ago. The Barrier developed an affection toward this human child, for he was unlike the Graise, and unexpectedly, the small human loved the Barrier in return. Little Nigel fled into its demesne whenever he was in emotional turmoil, or just needed to escape his post-Katrina situation. The Barrier provided him solace, and from him it learned how to communicate with its agent, but that wasn't anything that would be available for its use yet, as the child it coddled could not have withstood such communication for a long time to come. Eventually, Nigel found his way to the elder Nigel's world, and the Barrier became aware of the bond between Nigel and his Angeline. It also recognized its own handiwork in that bond, no doubt the residual effects of its past attempts at seeding itself. There was a Nigel and an Angeline born within every Human reality since that attempt, and each coupling had been beneficial to the world upon which it had occurred, *when* it had occurred. Thus, it infused some of itself into the younger Angeline's DNA through Nigel's touch, as protection for her way back when the younger

Nigel had first brought her into its realm. Later, when DeVries broached its boundaries, it came as close as it could to euphoria at its own success. There were *two* reality walkers from the Renoir family, and one potential from the Lacy family! Now, though, Nigel was in danger and DeVries was trying to find and save him. The Barrier, for its part, was determined to preserve both. They were crucial to its survival and should not be lost. Since it couldn't communicate with DeVries as effectively as it could with his brother, it was determined not to let the Graise leave its realm until the younger brother had found the older. That was the reason why the Graise's path constantly seemed baffled on this particular trip back to their home. Additionally, the Barrier used its internal currents to push DeVries toward the Graise vessel carrying the unconscious Nigel. He would catch up with it long before it reached its exit point.

Lieutenant Cadmium Breen considered himself the luckiest of the unit. Today he'd earned his promotion to a Captain in the United Planetary Armed Forces of Altered Humanity, and he was only sixteen years old. That meant that he could become the youngest soldier (since the Arch-Commander) ever to attain such rank. *His* platoon was the one that finally captured the Monster of Mayhem mass murderer feared by generations of Graise soldiers. All it had taken was one sleeping toxin dart at the right moment, and the Giant fell. Right now, the Towering Figure of Terror was snoring away on the floor of their APC. Lieutenant Breen kicked the man just to be sure that he was asleep. The guy just grunted and went back to his snoring. It wasn't fair. This killer had outlived even the best soldiers of the generation that he'd first encountered, and here he was, snoring. Some of the toughest they had, dead of old age while this monster went on with his life. Lieutenant Breen kicked his captive again. His temper was getting the best of him, he knew. But he couldn't help himself. This piece of garbage probably had some mommy and daddy. The Graise didn't. Their zygotes were produced in laboratories and inserted into a woman's fallopian tubes with surgical machines that would not fuse with the surrogate's body.

Almost every Graise pregnancy ended with a cesarean section and the death of the mother. Didn't matter. They had neither fathers nor mothers, couldn't touch one another and Lieutenant Breen would be an old man before this guy even started showing any age. Gods, they all *deserved* to be liquified into ALC! And why the *hell* wasn't this platoon home yet?

"Hey, Dorsen!" he shouted at his driver. "What's going on up there? We should have been home by now!"

"Don't know, LT," Dorsen replied "The route keeps shifting and we have to compensate." Right then there was a loud thump on the outside of their APC and the thing rocked like a boat.

"What the . . ." Lieutenant Breen was starting to say when the side of the vehicle was punctured by something that looked like a chrome-colored laser ray. From its point of penetration, it began moving in a circle, cutting through the plating the way a can opener cut through a can. The Graise began firing their weapons with one accord, but the inside of an armored personnel carrier has never been an ideal location for discharging high-powered weapons, so that activity didn't go too well before the soldiers stopped. Right after that, the side of the vehicle was ripped away, its passengers exposed to the full effect of *otherspace*. Catatonia overcame every one of them within seconds. DeVries didn't have to do a thing after that, except to pull his brother out of the drifting wreck.

As they sped along on some hyperactive exclamations of children long past, He tried to revive his brother. "Nigel! Wake up, man! C'mon, Nige, snap out of it!" DeVries had gone deeper into the Barrier than he had ever been in order to find his brother, and he wasn't sure if he'd be able to find his way out. "I don't want to slap you, here, man . . .," he was saying this when a thought-tornado-storm hit them. It only lasted for a few minutes of relativity, but it had profound effects on the brothers. It *shared* between them. It opened Nigel's memories, his own as well as those that had been contributed by the older version of himself. These were shared with DeVries's memories of both Nigel's absence and his family members who grew up alongside of his younger brother, so that they understood each other now, in this moment. DeVries learned who his brother was, and at the same time Nigel learned what this version of DeVries's life had been. They recovered from its effect with a different view of one another. Additionally, they both understood the Barrier's desperation over the activities of the Graise. When they recuperated, they were floating upside down in relation to one another, but face to face.

"Thanks for saving her, Devvie," Nigel said. "I don't think I could have stood it if I lost her too."

"You really are *our* Nigel," DeVries replied. "We thought you were gone."

"I kept your Batman safe," Nigel told him. "Don't know where it went though. Seems like I left it somewhere on the trail behind me."

"That creepy Old You probably has it, Nige," DeVries answered. "He likes Batman too."

"Of course he does," Nigel said "He is still *me*, after all. But I thought he was my dad too."

"Yeah, well, don't start talking like he does, Nige. That You uses way too many words."

"Hey, man, you always thought my vocabulary ability was cool, Devvie!" Nigel replied. "Different me. That DeVries is dead, ain't he?" his brother asked.

"Yes, but I'm not going to let that happen to you. Dev." DeVries scoffed. "Don't need protection, man. I got it." Nigel laughed at that. "Right. Mr. 'got it.' So how do we get out of here, then?"

"All right, all right . . .," his brother said. "So you know this stuff better than I do. Okay. What's our next move, Mr. Titan?"

"We're going to secure both Angeline and your Dana Lacy, then we have a fight that we need to get into."

"With who, Nige?" DeVries asked, then went on, "If you're mad at that creepy old general, you need to remember that guy is *you*, and whatever he did was just what *you* would have done. Besides, I think you're pretty cool as an old dude."

"Nah, Devvie, I'm not mad at him." Nigel reassured him. "I was referring to the Graise. That's who we get first."

***

There was so much that Angeline Renoir wanted to say to Angeline Duplessis-Renoir. She wanted to tell her what her life with her own Nigel had been like, what to expect, what to do. She wanted to tell her younger self about the younger Nigel, how cute he'd been as a little boy, and how it felt to have a near-double of her husband live as her son. So many words that needed saying, stories that she felt should be told. First, though, she needed to awaken her patient and prevent the girl from panicking over her Nigel's capture, then explain that Angeline Renoir and Angeline Duplessis-Renoir were the same person in different lives, at different ages. She remembered her husband telling her that the younger Nigel had done this twice already, with two other versions of himself. How that worked out, she didn't know, but she had to try. So she allowed the younger Angeline to awaken from the "slappy sleep" on her own. When the younger woman awoke, she'd want to know where she was and who the people around her were. Angeline would just answer her double's questions and let it go wherever it would.

Right then, Angeline Duplessis-Renoir awoke. "Where am I?"

"You're safe," her double replied. "I know that you're worried about Nigel, but please, rest assured, he'll be fine. Can you go into that whatever-it-is-zone to get him?"

Her younger self dropped her eyes. "No, I can't," she answered.

"So what do you plan to do to help?" her elder asked.

"I'll call Agent Caldwell and see if he can find out anything."

Angeline Renoir laughed, politely. "My husband can do more than Agent Caldwell ever could. He can go into that zone and find him," she said.

The younger Angeline sat up. "Can we try that? Who is your husband?" Angeline Renoir smiled.

"You already know him," she said. "He's an older version of Nigel, just like I'm a different version of you." *There. I've told her. I hope she can handle it*, she thought.

Angeline Duplessis-Renoir's eyes lit up. "That makes sense," she said. It was surprising enough to render Angeline Renoir speechless. "What do you mean, dear?" she asked, after a moment.

"When Nigel and I got married, we went through our phantom zone to a place that he said wasn't his home or mine, and an older lady brought wedding outfits for us to wear," Angeline Duplessis-Renoir answered. "She brought a wedding gown for me, and Marine Dress Blues for Nigel. Everything fit like it was made for us. She said some things about having enjoyed her life with him, and how I was a younger version of her . . ." Angeline Renoir held her hand to her face as if trying to summon up an idea. "We have a lot to talk about," she told her younger version.

***

Roan Caldwell had never seen anything like the ending of the Battle of The Tule Valley Hardpan. He wondered how in the world could so much destruction be wrought, so many shots be fired, and so many explosions could go off without *someone* in a position of power noticing all of this and acting. From the moment he and his party boarded the Middle Child, he'd seen the Graise and their activities for the first time with his own eyes.

He'd seen MPIS soldiers die and the MISTmen attack. They truly did perform at a superhuman level. At this moment, he would have loved to talk to General Stuffed-Shirt Nigel about everything, including his questions regarding the unconscious soldier they'd dumped into the chopper with his head hooded. "Valuable asset," smiled the dark-haired middle-aged man whom he'd intuitively recognized as General Benjamin Gary. "I'd like to talk to General Renoir, if I can, General Gary," he said. "I guess I shouldn't be surprised that the great Roan Caldwell recognized me right off." He looked around and added, "Don't worry, you'll definitely be talking to the general, but I think he's also going to arrange a little meet-n-greet between you and yourself first. At least the 'yourself' that lives here." Roan couldn't believe that he was serious.

"Why?" Roan asked.

"Because this Earth needs his help," General Gary told him, and continued, "if we were to approach him, he would only see us was a threat, and wouldn't believe a word we said. Regardless of how you yourself view us and our activities, you, at least, know what's at stake. Nobody can convince a person as well as a person can convince themselves. That's why we got you out after completing our mission here. You needed to see it all because now, you're going to convince your counterpart who lives here to work with us."

REUNIFICATION: COMPLETE

Nigel hovered along, thinking. Somehow he needed to come up with a way to stop these Graise from destroying the Barrier that had come to mean so much to him. It had done more than anything or anyone else to preserve his life. He knew that General Renoir had also done what he could, and even now, he wasn't feeling any real intense anger over the actions that version of himself had taken in trying to prevent his younger duplicate from becoming a mindless DNA bank, for that was surely what would have become of him, had General Renoir not been there. Still, the Barrier held a special position in relation to Nigel Renoir the Younger. This place (person or thing? he wondered) had been his first refuge after Katrina. He never wanted to leave the Barrier during his childhood years, but at that point in his life, his young body could only tolerate its widely varied abstract/solid/tangible-intangible environments for a small amount of time, so it would gently expel him. Every time he returned, though, he'd become more and more acclimated to being there, and eventually, he could even pass through it to other places. Later still, he'd become aware of ways he could use the forces that swirled and moved within these environs. He heard a squeak, or rather, a sound that translated as a squeak, then turned to see DeVries idly kicking a beginning suspicion of some lover's infidelity that had casually floated near him. *He's bored,* thought Nigel. *Funny how, no matter what reality I find him in, DeVries is still DeVries.*

"Hey, Devvie, what's eating you?"

"Nuthin,'" his brother answered.

"So then why do you have aggravation lines around your head and why are you kicking that minor jealousy around like that?"

"Is that what this ugly little thing is? A jealousy?" DeVries asked, as he kicked it again. "Maybe we can throw it at the Gauze, Graise, whoever they are. Make 'em so jealous that they'll just kill each other." Nigel somersault walked over to his brother. "You know who they are. They're already angry because of their short life spans and inability to touch one another. If we used that jealousy on them, it could have a reverse effect, and make them even more pissed off at us. Such a shared, communal feeling would increase their morale, and thereby increase their ferocity in a fight."

"Nige, you're starting to sound just like Old Geezer You. That's not good, *mon frère*. Stop before it becomes permanent." Nigel laughed.

"Okay, man, whatever. Hey, you got any ideas about putting them off our Earth?"

DeVries grinned. "Yeah. How 'bout we kill 'em all? With what we can do, it shouldn't be too hard." Nigel turned his head.

"*What*, Nige?" DeVries asked defensively. "You know we could get it done. Probably in one day or so."

"Dev, do you have any idea how *many* of them are coming?" Nigel asked.

"A lot," his brother replied, "but Old You told me that you're a weapon of mass destruction. So, let's go and mass destroy."

"Is that what he said, really?" Nigel asked.

"Yeah, Nige, that's what he said. And before you go all reflective thinking on me, let's get out of here. I got your girl to safety, but I gotta make sure that Dana's safe too."

"Didn't the General tell you that his men had already done that?" Nigel asked, then continued, "Because if he said so, believe me, he did it."

"Nige, that was over a month ago, and we've been staying in that military cultist compound that Old Nige put together ever since they got her out. He's building a charity for me to work through, but in the meantime, we're supposed to stay on base so that the guys in the gray uniforms can't get to us," DeVries said. "All this crap that's hittin the fan just started, though, and I think I oughta make sure she's good."

Realization materialized above, washed over Nigel and then swished away into the depths of the Barrier. "DeVries, Renoir, you're not entirely comfortable in here, are you?" he asked in disbelief.

"No, man!" his brother yelled. "I never stayed in here this long before! It's kinda creepy!"

"Well, we can't just go out there and start making war on billions of people, even if they are Graise, Dev. I'm not talking about any high-fallutin' fake morality against the act of fighting a people whose sole aim is to terminate our world or anything, it's just that the exertion would kill *us*," he told his brother, then added, "we need a strategy, man. If we just go out there, start hitting them hard and what-not, we'll eventually burn ourselves out and they'd still be coming."

DeVries floated/jumped up on an unfinished explanation that happened to be hanging around. He thought for a moment, then asked, "Well that Old Nige is an Army General, right?"

"He's a *Marine*, and don't get 'em mixed up again, Devvie," Nigel replied, and this time he was being defensive.

"Hey, don't get pissed off about it, man!" Devries answered. "My point is, well, I mean he's all old, experienced and everything, right? And he's a *general*, which means he should be the Nigel who has all kinds of strategic ideas, so maybe that's the guy we ought to be talking to about plans to get rid of these gray *connards*."

Nigel smiled. "That's a bad word! If ma-Mair Olivet was here, she'd smack you or wash your mouth out with soap, or something!"

DeVries looked like he'd been unexpectedly hit with a cold-water balloon. "Well, I'd run. She'd never catch me," he said. The Renoir brothers laughed, and the nature of their merriment lit up the happy musical notes that kept wandering near them.

"Okay, DeVries," Nigel said, "let's go ask the General. I was supposed to meet them at Crossover Team Alpha H&S anyway."

"What the hell is 'Crossover Team Alpha H&S,' Nige?" DeVries asked as they left the Barrier.

***

Roan Graham Caldwell, ITA director, code named IDEA Control, sat at his desk, once again looking over all the photographs and satellite footage that had mysteriously appeared in his e-mail two days ago. He was looking at a full-on, pitched battle out in the Tule Valley Hardpan in Utah. He'd tried to verify what was going on out there, but MPIS wasn't talking. He'd almost decided to let the whole thing go when Quentin had come in with a report of multiple extreme increases in the levels of ambient electromagnetic static suddenly occurring in the area of the Tule Valley Hardpan as of that morning. *That could only mean that the boy from the Broussard Park Incident has to be involved*, IDEA Control thought. Even then, Roan wasn't sure of his conclusion, because that kid had never made this big a dent in the atmospheric whatever. This looked like more like an invasion force than a single, lone traveler. But then, that boy would have been a full-grown man by now, so he could be spearheading an invasion. This was why ITA had been created, to prepare the nation for such a possibility. Lately, however, the new administration had really done all it could to neutralize this agency. Caldwell knew that they'd been working with MPIS to undermine his authority and power, but it hadn't worked so far. He was increasingly thankful that the original ITA charter had not allowed for his removal by executive order and allotted an adequate amount of operating funds annually. Thus, his agency had no need to involve itself in the yearly Congressional funding wars. The president who formed ITA had seen to that. He felt that any outsiders who attacked Earth would likely be able to replace key individuals within the government if they wanted to. The incident in Broussard Park, as well as The Savanne Road Affair, convinced the congress back then, and the ITA charter was approved as it stood. Since the new administration, though, Roan had been in battle after battle on Capitol Hill, while more and more frequently, MPIS had denied his agency's access to their overwatch equipment and other resources. He'd known that they ran a Super-Max out in Utah but had never been able to get any more concrete facts about it. Until now. Its floor plans, activity list, duty rosters and prisoner manifests, along with complete records of everything going on within had been included in the e-mail communique that he'd received.

Back when the new administration first declared political war on ITA, he would loved to have put down his badge and moved on with life, as Laura urged, but the Interlopers haunted him, and he just couldn't walk away. If they came back in force, with what he'd seen when it came to their ability to war, he knew his Earth wouldn't stand a chance against them. Then there was the matter of young Angeline Duplessis and her beau. He hadn't seen the young man since way back when, and as far as he knew, neither had Ms. Duplessis. Angeline. She'd become friends with Laura and the girls after the last time that the Broussard Park kid (his name was Nigel, Roan remembered) had come over and left, so in a way, he always had the young woman under surveillance. If things stood that way, he felt that he'd know when Nigel was on the way back. Then this happened. When he received the information that he was currently perusing, Roan had immediately taken it to the President, who had refused to see him. Since it was as important as it was, though, Roan had then gone to other governmental agencies and their directors, trying as best he could to gain the president's ear. If nothing happened, he'd have to take this to the press, but the thought of doing so angered Roan. This big battle in Utah pointed to a serious, credible threat and it wasn't going to get any better. Fortunately, the threat seemed to have been contained and limited to the Tule Valley Hardpan in Utah, but his country needed to be prepared. Once again, he asked himself if this could be the Interlopers, returning with Nigel as their top soldier. He thought of something then. Reaching for his phone, he called Laura. After a ring or two, she answered. "Hi, honey. What's going on?" she answered with her warm fireplace on a wintry day tone. "Hey, dear, there's something I'd like you to do for me, please." "What is it, Roan baby?" Laura asked. *She knows something's wrong. Her tone changed*, he thought. "Would you give Angeline a call and see if her guy's been making any appearances, please? Let her know that I may need to talk to her. I don't want to scare her, or I'd call her myself." After a moment's hesitation, during which he knew that his wife had decided not to ask any more questions, she replied, "Okay, dear, I'll call her, but I don't think that she'll be able to meet with you for a few days." A strange feeling came over Roan as he asked, "Why not?" "Because she's gone to Utah with her parents," Laura replied.

Bill Thomas Compton was the same height as his counterpart but was also a few years older and a few pounds heavier, with moustache, goatee, and a scar bifurcating his left eyebrow that continued around behind the eye. He came into the ITA office where his wife, Meredith was issuing orders to the Probies. It seemed that everyone was running around like ants whose ant bed had been kicked open. *Something serious is happening,* he thought. *Roan pulled me off a stake-out on a high-value target and people are running around like it's the end of the world. Meredith's stressed too.*

"What's happening Agent Compton?" he asked his wife. She just gestured toward their TAC with her head. "In there," she replied. They went over to the retinal scanner, got scanned, and entered. Inside, they found Troy Quentin sitting in one of the audience chairs. As soon as he saw them, he stood and put his finger to his lips. A very angry IDEA Control was almost yelling at the Secretary of Defense, "What do you *mean*, you can't access those satellite feeds? *Don't you know that our people are getting killed out there!* You have the ambient static information *right there on your desk,* man! *Read it!*"

Meredith whispered in her husband's ear, "Those guys from Savanne Road are back, and it looks like this time, they've come with an invasion force." Bill felt his heart and spine turn to ice.

Meanwhile, the Secretary of Defense seemed to have had enough of being yelled at. "Look, Director," he started yelling back, "I have checked the report! There's nothing I can do without a direct executive order! I can't override the president! He's given MPIS complete authority over this!" Calming himself, the secretary of defense continued, "And they're *not* talking, Roan. They don't *want* our help there. It's going to take more than your belief in an ongoing alien invasion to get the president's attention."

"What will it take, Mr. Secretary?" Roan asked.

"Completely plausible, credible and undeniable proof given to someone other than the president," the secretary replied, then added, "and don't ever *scold* me again, Director. You need every ally you've got in Washington." With that, he disappeared, and the screen cut off.

Roan turned toward Bill and Meredith. "Where's Quentin?"

"Right here, Director," Quentin responded.

"Okay, so we're all here, then?" Roan asked. His team nodded almost simultaneously. "We have a problem," Roan started to say. "It seems that the Interlopers have finally decided to make their move against us and . . ." Suddenly, the lights flickered, all of the technicians' heads fell down on their desks, and the screen lit up. Roan and his people turned to see a message repeating itself there.

ROAN CALDWELL, THIS INVASION IS NOT OUR DOING. THE FORCES THAT ARE ATTACKING YOUR EARTH ARE ALSO OUR ENEMIES. WE OFFER YOU OUR ASSISTANCE. WE WILL MEET WITH YOU AND YOUR TEAM ONLY AT THE

SAVANNE ROAD LOCATION. TOMORROW MORNING 0900
HOURS. YOU WILL NOT BE HARMED.

Roan, Bill, and Meredith stood with their mouths agape. Then Bill
turned to his boss. "It has to be them," he said.

Roan nodded. "It *is* them."

"Do you think it's a trap, Roan?" Meredith asked.

"Anybody that can do what they can wouldn't need to set a trap," he
told her. "If they're willing to offer their help, we'll take it."

Troy Quentin looked at them. "Who was that?" he asked.

***

After witnessing The Battle in The Tule Valley Hardpan, Roan and
his team, The Extras, had been ushered into a large house within what
had to have been the command post for Crossover Base One. They were
seated in a living room with the high ceilings and accompanying fans that
kept so many houses in the deep South cool during the humid summers.
A tall dark-skinned man, Charles Lubkin, who identified himself as once
having been a navy steward, had seen them to their rooms last night (or
early this morning) when they'd arrived with the crew of *Middle Child*.
Later, when they awakened, they'd missed breakfast, but Mr. Lubkin had
promptly ordered his chef to see to their needs. The general would be in
later to talk with Agent Caldwell, he explained. Meanwhile, they were
guests, and per General Renoir's orders, were to be treated to the finest
hospitality. That was earlier. Now they sat here, waiting. He was supposed
to be along any minute now. *Apparently, there's a lot going on at the moment.*
Roan observed. Men in military gear were running to and fro, vehicles
were being moved into formation, and to Roan and Meredith it looked for
all the world as if they'd stepped onto a Marine base that was at Threatcon
Charlie or Delta. *All this manpower and advanced armament, unattached to
any government. These people have built a small army within the borders of the
United States. They could be the most dangerous threat in existence here, once
this business with the Graise is over.* Roan thought as he watched from the
porch of the house where he and his team were staying. *But they have got
some godawful good coffee.* As he considered the scene before him, the men
guarding the house stood to attention just as a Humvee with a four-star
tag on the front pulled up.

One of the sentries hustled to open the door and General Nigel B. Renoir stepped out. He was accompanied by General Benjamin O. Gary, Lucius Carver, who wore the insignia of a newly minted sergeant-major, and First Sergeant Rondo Little. General Renoir greeted Roan and gestured toward the living room he'd just exited. "Are the Comptons inside, Agent Caldwell?" he asked. Roan nodded an affirmative. As they all walked in together, Roan managed to mutter "Congratulations on the promotion, Sergeant-Major" to Lucius, who smiled back. As the company followed General Renoir to the conference room, Meredith also noticed the man's new insignia. "Congratulations, Lucius," she said with a smile. Any further attention or communication ended as General Renoir began to speak. "Please be seated." Normally, all of his officers would have been there and seated before the commanding officer arrived, but The Extras, although well-disciplined in their own way, weren't military. General Renoir and General Gary seated themselves at the table, while Sergeant-Major Carver and First Sergeant Little stood at ease close to the walls behind them. General Renoir nodded to Sergeant-Major Carver, and as he crossed the room to activate the antisurveillance system, First Sergeant Little dimmed the lights.

For the next thirty minutes, everyone in the room watched as the Graise's history, origins, and intent was explained through video clips of the events that had taken place in R-2, the home reality of the MISTmen. After it ended, and the lighting was restored, General Gary stood and began without preamble.

"What you saw yesterday was the beginning of a very long fight for the inhabitants of this reality. We believe that the Graise will not stop coming unless total annihilation stops them. That's because annihilation is what the Graise are facing in their own world. Unless the man-made disease that makes them into what they are is eliminated from their DNA, this is how they survive. As far as we've learned, the fluid they produce with the liquified remains of their kill is what permits them to live to the ripe old age of between thirty-nine to forty-five. Any Graise who survived yesterday's encounter will be too old to fight in another five or six years. A thirty-year-old Graise is equivalent to a sixty-five-year-old, in your reality."

Roan and his team looked at one another in disbelief. They knew better than to start asking questions right now, so General Gary continued. "They began as humans, but a man-made viral outbreak changed them hundreds, maybe thousands of years ago. Right now, they reproduce, as far as we know, only by artificial insemination, and every birth causes the death of the Graise woman who carries a child. They cannot touch one another without their bodies fusing together, which causes them a painful death. So they spend their lives in frustration. Although our intel suggests that the earth of their origin may be altered enough so that they might not use these there, we do know that for everywhere else they may go, their biological exoskeletons are the only deterrent that prevents them from fusing with the world around them and instantly dying. They originally swept through the stars in their own reality, destroying and rendering every life form that they encountered into ALC—that's what they call the end product of living beings that they dissolve. Again, that was hundreds, maybe thousands of years ago. Since then, they have started using some of those worlds in their own reality as farm worlds resourced with non-intelligent creatures that they can capture at will. Still, they are constantly on the search for new sources of stock for their liquefication procedure."

He stopped as Charles Lubkin entered with one of the house staff to refresh their drinks. When that distraction ended, General Gary resumed with, "When the Graise locate a new target world, they take the time to increase their numbers all around their own Earth, which has a united government. As far as we know, going into battle for new sources of ALC is like a sacred religious duty for them. Every single Graise is born to fight this war. They can't *wait* to die for the cause, and by the time they attack their target, they come by the billions. They've found this Earth now, so there will be billions more coming. What you saw yesterday, well that's not even the tip of the spear. Questions?"

Roan started. "How do you know all this?" he asked.

"We've been mixing it up with these people for five or six years now," General Gary told him. Then he continued, "Thanks to Little Nige, we developed a means to get back to our own reality, where these guys have almost overrun the place. By the time we got home, they'd been there long enough to dig in and fortify their positions. We've been battling them over there ever since. They're born to do battle, but they are not in any way the best there is at it. Their immaturity often interferes with good fighting sense. We've taken their compounds and retrieved books, recordings, and other personal items. Our men have also captured and interrogated plenty of prisoners, including some of their officers. Through all of the information gathered, we've come to understand more about them."

"You also have some psychological profiling equation, or something like that, don't you?" Roan asked.

General Gary answered with, "Yes, we do. But please keep your questions relevant to the presentation we're currently engaged in, Caldwell. We don't have a lot of time to spare on unrelated explanations."

Billy raised his hand. General Gary looked at him and said, "Detective Compton? You're raising your hand?"

"Um, yes, are these Graise considered human?" Billy asked. General Gary blinked at the thought, a rare thing for him. "Yes, they are. But they aren't human like you and me. They've been altered by a viral infection that's attached itself to their genes. The Nazis were more human."

"How do you know that they're still going to be coming?" Meredith asked, adding, "Your super-soldiers pretty much succeeded in shooting that EMP weapon at their portal, so that door is closed now, right?"

"Correct," General Gary affirmed. "But imagine someone shooting grappling hooks at a certain target in the dark. If one of those hooks catches, then the shooter has a pretty good idea about where to aim for his next shot. The more hits he gets, the more he will get. That's the way it is for the Graise. They've located this reality, so they'll be trying for it again real soon."

"So how long do we have?" Billy asked (he didn't raise his hand this time).

"We can't say for sure," General Gary told him, "but it normally takes about forty-eight to seventy- two hours for them to open a second entry point again after the first incursion."

"You said that the viral disease they have is man-made," Meredith said. "Who did this to them? Because if it was some outside force, that person or group may be more of a threat than the beasties they created." The room got quiet for just a moment.

Then General Renoir spoke, "The Graise's current condition is the end result of a viral disease created by their versions of Blacen Muldowney and Devin Craine, many hundreds or thousands of years ago, on their homeworld." Then he added, "And please don't refer to our troops as *soldiers*, Meredith Compton. They're Marines."

"Okay, so what would you like us to do, then, General?" Roan asked. "Why are the three of us here, listening to this well-arranged presentation, instead of being carted back to our own reality?"

General Gary looked to General Renoir, who said, "I'll take over from here, Ben. Thank you." Gary sat, Renoir stood, clasped his hands behind his back and began. "You've all been briefed regarding the crossover attempts MPIS has been involved in, but you were not informed of the fact that those very actions were what allowed the Graise to locate their reality. I chose not to include the information in your briefing because it was not relevant to you at the time. Since then, Sergeant-Major Carver has given us a full report regarding the manner of your arrival here, as well as Nigel's assertion that the *otherspace* zone is alive, intelligent, self-aware and able to communicate with him. I considered sending you back to your own place ASAP, but the events following your arrival have given me pause. Nigel instigated a confrontation between MPIS and the Graise, but if he hadn't, the prison within the Tule Valley Hardpan would have fallen to the Graise by now, and they would have a heavily fortified base from which to begin operations here. He told Sergeant-Major Carver that this course was advised and assisted by the *otherspace* entity.

"Changing our focus, the competition between the governmental agencies of this America has caused deep-seated resentments among them. Those resentments inhibit communications, and every agency is incredibly territorial. They don't work together often or well. That facility in Tule Valley is under jurisdiction of MPIS, the agency most hated by all of the others. However, they have the backing of the current administration. If they were in danger of elimination, no other agency would care to help, but this administration would pull funding from wherever it could for MPIS. They have a—symbiotic relationship, of sorts. Enter the Roan Caldwell of this reality. We have learned that our past interactions with his team and him wound up being a catalyst that has propelled him into the directorship of an agency that has immutable legal authority to force all these others to work under his. He cannot, however, exercise such far-reaching authority without solid, incontestable proof that there is a real and immediate threat from beyond his earth. This is where you come in."

"You want us to convince him, right, General?" Roan asked.

"Yes, that is what needs to happen. I neither believe in evolution nor coincidence. Based on these factors, along with Nigel's own assertions regarding it, we now think this may be the reason why the *otherspace* entity dragged you here along with him. This version of Roan Caldwell would not trust anything we tell him, so he has to hear the facts presented from someone whom he will consider a credible source," General Renoir replied. "Do you have any reasonable objection to making contact with him and explaining what you've seen?" Roan, Billy, and Meredith exchanged glances.

"How would you like us to do it?" Roan asked.

"We have arranged a meeting with his team and him tomorrow afternoon. We'll transport you there at 0600," General Renoir responded.

"That's fine with us," Roan answered for his team, "but there's just one more thing we'd like to ask about, General."

General Renoir's eyebrow raised. "What would you like to know?" he asked.

"Where's Nigel? Taking him along would help convince my counterpart. Is he back from wherever he disappeared to yet?" Roan queried. An uncomfortable silence fell among the marines in the meeting room. *Oh, no . . .*, Roan thought.

After a moment, General Renoir said, "Nigel saved his Angeline, but in so doing, he has been captured by the Graise."

The Extras stared in disbelief. Roan's face showed his astonishment. "How did . . .," Billy began. Meredith's hand was covering her mouth as if she were afraid of what she might have said.

"So what are you doing about getting him *back?*" Billy demanded. He was angered at the thought of Nigel being abandoned, and it was showing in his vocal tone. "It seems to me that the focus here should be on saving Nigel's *life* more than talking to some big shot version of Roan with trust issues!" The men in the room shifted uneasily. They did not like to hear anyone addressing General Renoir with such disrespect.

"Billy"—Billy was about to keep on going, but Roan cut him off— "Billy, *stop.*" He stopped. "You don't talk to a Marine General like that." Roan advised him as a father would. "Especially not in front of his marines. General Renoir won't abandon Nigel. They're probably working on a way to find him right now."

Billy Compton's face reddened. "I apologize, General Renoir," he began, then added, "Nigel saved my wife from dying, and I'd do anything I could to help him." Everyone else relaxed. Down to a man, they'd felt the same frustration.

General Renoir nodded. "Your aggravation is understandable, Detective Compton. You're no coward, but you've never been military either. We don't hold the same expectations of you as we do of our own. [*That had to be one of the most politely delivered insults I've ever heard,* Roan thought] Nigel, however, is neither alone nor abandoned. Our side also has an additional asset deployed. He will succeed in bringing our boy back, or die trying."

After the meeting ended, Roan and General Renoir once again found themselves talking. The general wanted Roan to know everything he could about his counterpart. He briefed Roan on the man's family, their friendship with Angeline Duplessis-Renoir, the versions of Bill and Meredith Compton he worked with, and so forth.

As their conversation continued, Roan eventually had to ask. "Who's this asset you sent for Nigel?"

General Renoir smiled, a rare thing for him, Roan thought, then told him. "It's his brother DeVries. He has the same ability that Nigel has, but to a more limited degree." There was, however, something Roan wanted to know.

"Then why aren't you using the two of them as weapons against the Graise? They're the biggest guns you have."

The general stood up. After a minute, he began to explain, "These young men will undoubtedly join our efforts to contain the Graise, but they'll have to do so on their own terms. While we are confident of the decision they'd make, we cannot depend on the help of such natural forces as the Renoir Brothers in our war with the enemy. Normal humans cannot command hurricanes or tornadoes. To try doing that is to invite disaster. So we have to train to defeat the Graise on our own. Any contributions that Nigel or DeVries Renoir choose to make toward that end will be cheerfully accepted, but not depended upon."

***

Roan Graham Caldwell, William (Bill) and Meredith Compton, along with Troy Quentin, rode along Little Bayou Black Road on a Louisiana morning. A fog marking the cold-to-hot weather change from a cold Winter to a warmer Spring, was obscuring most of the surrounding vista. *The last time we came up this road, I was driving my Ford Crown Vic from the auto pool,* Roan thought as he watched the scenery go by. *Now I'm in an armored Chevy Suburban with Billy driving and our vitals being monitored from my agency's headquarters in Washington. Satellite surveillance follows our every move, and we have covert escort and assist teams shadowing. My, my, how things have changed in fourteen years.*

"Why are we pulling over, Bill?" Roan asked. "Did you see something?"

"Umm, boss, that's the problem," Bill Compton replied. "I'm not the one pulling over. This thing is doing it by itself." Without warning, every one of them received a text message. *Your escort has been rerouted to Morgan City and your satellites retasked. You'll leave your vehicle in the bank's parking lot. It's Sunday, so the lot will be empty. We will provide transportation from that rendezvous point.* Regardless of Bill Compton's efforts at reassuming control of the vehicle, it pulled itself over and parked at the South Louisiana Bank branch that was nearby.

"What now, Boss?" Bill asked. *He calls me "Boss" when he's nervous.* Roan thought.

"We wait, Bill," Roan ordered. "As I said, if these people wanted to spring a trap, there's nothing we could do to stop them. Everyone keep your hands away from your weapons." As if on cue, a black Ford Expedition just *appeared* one parking spot over with two armed Marines in short-sleeved dress blues standing at ease, awaiting Roan and his people. "Okay, here we go," he said. They got out of their Suburban and into the Expedition to begin a long, silent ride to the house at the end of an unnamed road that ran perpendicular to Savanne Road.

Their arrival this time was much different than before. This time, they were welcomed by Charles Lubkin and his household staff, who ushered them into a dining room where there were breakfast pastries and excellent coffee, Roan thought. They ate a little and then the same two marines who drove them to the house came to lead them into a meeting room where three people sat at a conference table, obviously awaiting their arrival with nervousness. When the doors opened, one of them stood, and the other two did the same. *What would it be like to meet yourself?* Roan had always wondered, since the first time he'd encountered the Interlopers. He wasn't sure, but the impression he'd gotten from the words that general had said never left him. *Another Earth. Another America, some other me and another you.* Well, here it was. He, Bill and Meredith were meeting themselves, and it was so strange that it seemed almost like some out-of-body experience. Of course, there was the first impression, each person looking at what they considered a "duplicate me" with resistance to what the eye beheld, then came the criticism at their own foibles and weaknesses exaggerated in their own eyes, and finally, acceptance. Roan Grayson Caldwell was only younger than Roan Graham Caldwell by two years, but Billy and Meredith Compton of The Extras were younger than their counterparts by seven years, thus leaving them closer to Troy Quentin's age. Regardless the age difference, both Roans were older than both sets of Comptons. They all stood looking at one another in disbelief for long enough to make it uncomfortable. Then Billy Compton said, "Meredith, babe, you are gonna be so *hot* when we get older!" She looked at him like she couldn't *believe* he'd say that about another woman, then realized he *wasn't* talking about any other woman . . .

That broke the tension enough for the two groups to begin speaking. The only person with no double present was Troy Quentin. "Wow! Are these guys clones?" he asked. "Can the Interlopers *clone* people?"

"No, we're not clones," Billy Compton began to say, "that technology doesn't exist in our reality. Does it exist here?"

"No, it doesn't," Meredith replied. Looking at Bill, she said, "Honey, you were so *skinny*—I'd forgotten . . ."

"Well, he's not exactly skinny, Merry, he's just younger . . ." Bill was talking to Meredith, at the same time that Meredith of The Extras was saying to Billy, "He's not *fat* or anything, Billy, I was just saying that if you pushed the weights a little more, then maybe . . ." The two Roan Caldwells, on the other hand, were just staring at one another as if they needed to talk, but couldn't, at the moment, like two islands of silence in a sea of conversations. "Was your mother . . ." "Did you guys ever go to . . ." "How many . . ." "Why did you grow the . . ." "Do you have a scar on . . ." "Did your dad . . ." What did you call . . ." "Do you remember having . . ." Suddenly both Roan Caldwells let out a loud whistle, then each one looked as surprised as the other. The room quieted down.

"We need to sit down and talk," said Roan Graham to Roan Grayson, and by extension to the both sets of federal agents in the room. "I don't imagine we could do it without being overheard?" he asked his counterpart. Both of the marines at the door tilted their heads as if listening to a sound only they could hear, then promptly left the room. At that moment, The Extras felt a familiar slight pressure behind their ears. The ITA team did, also, but they didn't know what it was.

Roan Grayson then addressed his elder version. "They've just given us total privacy. What would you like to know?"

After two hours, the door to the conference room opened, and General Renoir walked in. All discussion stopped as the general walked to the head of the table.

"Good morning, Director Caldwell," he started. "It has been a long time since we first met here. Many unfortunate incidents lie between now and then."

"What is your relationship to the boy from the Broussard Park Incident?" Roan Graham Caldwell demanded.

"Your counterpart didn't tell you?" General Renoir asked.

"No," IDEA Control answered. "He's convinced me that he is who he says he is, that the attack in Tule Valley is real, and you're willing to help us convince the rest of the country. But he feels that the Broussard Park kid is a subject I should discuss with *you*."

General Renoir looked as if he were considering an unexpected development for a moment, then he said, "Very well then, Director. After we conclude our primary business here, I will meet privately with you."

Roan Graham Caldwell looked relieved. He continued speaking, "He's also told that he personally has seen these . . . Graise? That's what you call them, right?"

"Yes, that's right," Renoir confirmed. "As you and your team are about to. Right now." General Renoir tilted his head and said, "Bring the prisoner in, First Sergeant Little." The door opened again, and First Sergeant Rondo Little brought in a bound Graise soldier with the hood of his EXOS-LK5 (military-issue) EXOskin pulled back so that the gray on gray features of his face were exposed. Master Gunnery Sergeant Puccini followed the duo. Every civilian in the room expressed surprise in a different way at the sight before them. Roan Graham Caldwell, however, stood up. "I don't believe it!" he exclaimed. "*Rondolaine!* You're *alive*? How? They told me that . . ." The First Sergeant looked at General Renoir, who nodded and said, "Sergeant Rondo Little, you are off duty for the next thirty minutes. In fact, we will adjourn for that amount of time. Master Gunnery Sergeant Puccini will take charge of the prisoner." First Sergeant Little handed the Graise over to Puccini, who took control of the POW and walked him out.

Right after that, Rondo Little exclaimed, "*Unc!* Uncle *Roan!*" He ran over and grabbed the smaller man in a bear hug.

Several conversations began among the people at the conference table as Charles Lubkin and three of his staff came in with food and drink. Roan Graham Caldwell smiled and laughed as he talked with his huge nephew, which seemed to shock both teams, but Roan Grayson Caldwell was shocked the most. "*Unc?* Uncle Roan? He's his *uncle?* What the . . .," he muttered.

Meredith and Billy Compton wandered over, "And here you thought he hated you," she said. Rondo Little, in the background, surrounded by Roan Graham Caldwell's ITA team, was talking more than The Extras had ever heard.

"They planned to abandon us, and we were going to be killed or captured. General Renoir and the kid saved our bacon, Unc. Our whole unit was as good as dead." The elder Roan even had tears in his eyes as he listened. "And these *Graise*, they're serious trouble. I've seen what they're doing on the General's world. If we don't beat 'em back, the whole Earth is in danger."

During the break, General Renoir sat quietly observing from the chair at the head of the table. Roan Grayson Caldwell meandered over and began a quiet conversation with the general.

"I've always felt that you're that guy who leaves as little up to chance as possible, General." Gesturing toward his counterpart, he asked, "How much of today's activity was timed specifically for this reaction?"

General Renoir almost smiled. "Pretty much all of it," he confirmed. "First Sergeant Little is related to your counterpart through a sister that you never had. When she and her husband were killed in an auto accident, young Rondolaine was sent to live with the father's family, who turned out to be quite a villainous brood of amoral people. He was constantly in trouble with the law until the day that police officer Roan Caldwell, his uncle, took him into a gym and uttered a challenge. If he beat Rondo, the young man would join the military. If not, then the young man would be free to run the streets as he saw fit. You can see how that went. His uncle saved his life, and I counted on their bond to make today's events more palatable to Director Caldwell."

"Aren't you worried about First Sergeant Little running off to see his uncle and cousins?" Roan asked.

"Not really," General Renoir said. "First Sergeant Little is a Marine NCO and a man of honor. Additionally, if MPIS were to learn that he still breathes, his uncle, his cousins and he would be marked for death immediately. That would necessitate a firefight between my forces and theirs. None of us want that right now." He turned to look at Roan. "I'll admit to having been surprised at the fact that you told your counterpart to talk to *me* about Nigel, instead of relating your own observations. I appreciate your discretion. I'm not ashamed of our shared identity, but the knowledge of it could have severely biased your counterpart's opinion before our meeting."

"Well, General, are you going to tell him what your kid can do?" Roan inquired. "The youngster can protect himself, now, can't he?"

"I'll consider it," General Renoir replied. "But I have come to realize, Agent Caldwell, that the young man Nigel is not a *duplicate* of me, he *is* me. I am quite positive that should this threat of invasion continue, then this whole world will soon be aware of who Nigel and his brother are." He let that sink in for a minute, then added, "And, Roan, I think you would do well to remember that this man is also not a *copy* of you, he *is* you. It will help as you deal with one another."

Roan head-gestured toward Rondo Little. "I thought that the kid there hated me. So I'm his uncle, huh?" Again, General Renoir almost smiled. "That's one of the situations where your differences have more bearing than your similarities, Agent Caldwell. He resented being unable to tell you, but he obeyed his orders."

He gently tapped on his water glass. The ringing drew all attention to him. He stood and started speaking, "First Sergeant Little, you remain off duty for another twenty minutes. You may be seated with Director Caldwell, if you like, or you may spend that time elsewhere."

"Request permission to remain, sir," Rondo stated.

"Permission granted. First Sergeant Little, you will remain posted beside the Director until otherwise ordered. Now we will continue." He stood, clasped his hands behind his back, and began, "Director Caldwell, we have two mutual problems. The Graise and your Earth's unpreparedness. We are going to help you."

"If this isn't your Earth, why are they a problem for you?" IDEA Control asked.

"It seems to us that you could just jump into your spaceships or whatever and leave," Bill Compton added, continued, "so why are you concerned with helping us? What difference does it make to you?"

"Are you people in a war with these 'Graise' too?" his wife asked. "I mean, you've been here all this time but never come out and identified yourselves or anything. What are you doing here? Did these guys clean your clock back home and chase you off or something?"

"Our Earth is currently battling this very same enemy," General Renoir confirmed, "but no one 'cleaned our clock,' as you put it, Agent Compton."

"What happened, then? Why is all of this, the meeting with our doubles, and your guys showing off this captured—whatever it is, why is it happening? What do you want?" Roan Graham Caldwell asked.

"Now we finally come to the crux of the matter," General Renoir said. "Our world fell long before these people arrived. Two of the most nefarious human beings ever born there caused the fall of humanity by instigating a mass infection with a super-virus they created."

"So that's what you meant by . . .," IDEA Control started.

"Correct, Director. That is the event I referred to the last time we met here," General Renoir affirmed. He gestured, and First Sergeant Little went over to press a button on the wall behind him. At that, a holographic projection appeared above the conference table. "The Devin Craine-Blacen Muldowney super-virus that attacked human DNA. We called it CMV. When they deployed it, their actions proved to be the catalyst leading our Earth into its Third World War. Just as that conflagration begin, my command was sent to find a cure somewhere among the vast amounts of parallel earths that exist. Our mission was a success, but when we returned, things had changed for the worst, and this enemy was already entrenched in our Earth." As General Renoir continued his narrative, images correlating his account appeared and faded. "From what we have learned since, the Graise arrived right after World War Three ended. More than ninety percent of humanity was gone by then, and there was little, if any, defense against them." He stopped for a moment as if to gather himself, resumed, "We have gone home and engaged them in battle several times, then returned and sheltered in this reality while we prepare for further encounters, but a planet is huge, and that war will continue for quite some time. We do not need to have our fallback position here overrun by these ex-humans who have wreaked so much havoc upon our own people. If they meet with sufficient resistance right now, their ill intent toward your world will never be realized. We need your various nations to join together in fighting the Graise, because as I've mentioned, they will be coming by the billions. We will throw in our assistance, but yours is the only agency we will work with, Director Caldwell."

"Will you be sharing your advanced technology with us for this?" Bill Compton asked. "No, because you won't need it," Renoir replied. "You have almost sixty million men and women bearing arms on Earth in this reality, not mentioning your equipment and various types of weapons. Your military forces have the capacity to defeat the Graise here, whether your different governments cooperate with one another or not."

"Then what do you intend to do to help them?" Roan Grayson asked.

"We will destroy the Graise portals. This must be done after these doorways have been used at least once. Your forces will meet them in the field, and while the invaders are being dealt with, we will cut off their escape and shut the entry point used to gain access to this Earth. We will also share every bit of information we have gathered about them with you in credible format. You will announce their threat to your world, as well as the fact that the Interlopers have secretly been working with you for the past two years, supplying intelligence on your current foes. Additionally, we will transfer all captive Graise to your custody. This will solidify your power and influence over the agencies that you must conscript, as you have been given a charter to do."

"So will you subject *your* organization to us?" Roan asked. "I mean, people in power are going to want to have a say in whatever you're doing here."

"No, Director, we will not, for precisely the reason you've just mentioned. Your current administration is unrepentantly, incorrigibly corrupt, your congress is too divided to pursue any logical moral course regarding your President's obvious criminality, and the welfare of your citizens are ground into axle grease by corporate giants. As political interests destroy your America, the rest of the world descends into chaos. Your earth is less than a centimeter away from total self-immolation because of your current mismanagement. We will assist you because the Graise are a universal threat, but we will not put ourselves under your authority. We have to attend to our own Earth first." This condemnation was delivered unemotionally and authoritatively.

"Now, wait a minute," Director Caldwell began, "you people have not at all been working with ITA. We haven't even spoken to one another in fourteen years, but, as I see it, we'd be lucky if they don't arrest *us* for collusion with a hostile power."

"That won't happen, Director," General Renoir replied. "We have proof of the depth of that corruption I spoke of, including a secret plan to subject one of your fifty-two states to a nuclear attack. This plot was concocted by your current President, along with his then Chief of Staff, and activated by MPIS. We prevented it. Your current administration has engaged in countless other underhanded, illegal acts and every one of them have eroded your government's hold on its nation. We will give you all that we have collected regarding these matters, as well as one other asset."

The door opened again, and Colonel Rod Lichsten, wearing two black eyes and MPIS Dress Grays with no rank insignia, came in, escorted by Major Archimus Marcelon, Lieutenants C. C. Pendle and Walter R. A. McGrath, all wearing marine officer's dress blues. All four saluted General Renoir and stood at attention. Roan, Bill, Meredith, and Troy each sat up or leaned forward. "At ease," General Renoir said. The military officers complied. "Do you know this MPIS officer, Director Caldwell?" he asked. "Yes," IDEA Control said. "That's The Gray Colonel. He's been a thorn in our side for a long time."

After that, the Gray Colonel was hustled out of the room and immediately put into a slappy sleep. "Well, the Gray Colonel belongs to you now. He will cooperate with and assist your agency. We know he will do so wholeheartedly and without duplicity because the administration, through MPIS, has his family and him scheduled for termination. My people snatched his family from the jaws of death not too long ago, for his former commander had ordered the execution of his family performed first. We have proof of this also. As things have turned out, cooperation with your agency is his only hope," General Renoir said. "We will relay the coordinates of his wife and sons' location to you after you have returned to your office with the Colonel. You will decide his fate as well as theirs."

"Why?" Roan Graham asked.

"If you mean why did we hide his beloved family even from him, it was because we couldn't be sure that he wasn't complicit in their attempted murder. We've seen MPIS officers sacrifice family members in order to prove loyalty to their commanding officers," General Renoir replied stoically.

Sighing in exasperation. Idea Control asked again, "Why are you giving *us* all of *this?*"

After a moment's pause, General Renoir said, "Because we have found Roan Caldwell to be an honorable man in every reality. Your character and the overall character of the teams you have created has been one of reliability and honesty. We also have a deep appreciation for the kind way in which you have dealt with young Angeline Duplessis. Our young Nigel would be lost without her."

"I didn't know she was one of yours," Director Caldwell replied.

591

"She isn't. She's one of yours, as is Nigel," General Renoir said. The ITA team exchanged startled glances. Their host continued, "Still we have raised him, and he means a great deal to us, as does Ms. Duplessis."

General Renoir took a moment to let that sink in, then continued, "All of this has been done so that you may know we mean you no ill will. Without a doubt, the Graise will return within forty-eight to seventy-two hours or so, and they will come by the thousands, then millions, and finally, they will come by the billions. You need to prepare your nation and your world, if possible. Director Caldwell and Agent Roan Caldwell, we need to have a private conversation right after this, but you need to get the ball rolling as soon as possible, Director. As for the ITA team and The Extras, spend as much time as you wish in chatting with your duplicates, if you like. You will find The Gray Colonel confined within your vehicle when you get back to it. Will the two Caldwells accompany me, please?" General Renoir left the conference room, with Roan Graham and Roan Grayson Caldwell, First Sergeant Rondo Little following. With that, the first Inter-Reality Conference since the days of Roman Marques ended.

***

Nigel and DeVries stepped out of the Barrier and into the front yard of General Renoir's home right next to Crossover Base One. "Why didn't we just step out into the house?" Devries asked.

"Because I've gotten shot by surprising people that way. It hurts," his brother answered. "If the General and I are the same person, then I can promise you that his wife is armed."

"But she's your wife too, right, Nige?"

"No, she's more like my mom," Nigel said.

"So if she's like your mom, and the young her *is* your wife, that's kinda creepy, don't you think?" DeVries asked.

Nigel looked annoyed. "Nah, Dev, it's nothin' like that. One's more like a mother to me, and the other isn't, that's all."

"Riiight," DeVries said. Nigel punched his shoulder—hard. They would have started wrestling, but a feeling washed over Nigel, and he knew *she* was coming out to meet him. Her.

She came out the front door and ran into his arms. "I'm not dead," she repeated.

"No, you're not," he told her through the smell of her perfume, the smell of her hair and his tears. Angeline. The woman whose loss moved him to cross realities when his power should have been gone. Angeline. The one whose memory moved him to do all that he'd done. She'd held on to her hope for him when he hadn't even remembered who she was. Angeline had been a constant that Nigel always reached for, and with his memory restored fully, he now knew why. It was the power of things that were meant to be. She was why he would not get lost within the Barrier's immense vastness, no matter how many times or how far he'd ventured into it. Angeline. The anchor that moored him to his own reality as much as the best of humanity. Nigel once held a dying version of this woman in his arms and thought that his world would shut down with her death. As much as he grieved over that Angeline, she was ultimately, just a projection of the one that was real for him. He determined right then that he would never say "Goodbye, Angeline" again. He would hold onto this woman through hell or high water, for he'd seen what losing her had taken away from his life. He held her for as long as he could, finally the embrace ended.

"I'm not *that* much shorter than he is . . ." DeVries cut in from somewhere off to the side.

***

It would take some time, they all knew. There was so much that needed to be accomplished, but everything had to start here, with Nigel the Younger and General Renoir. Neither man would have been complete without Angeline, so she had to be involved. Nigel and DeVries Renoir had returned just as General Renoir's contingent were leaving Crossover Base One in order to meet with the Roan Caldwell who was the Director of ITA, code named IDEA Control. That meeting was too important to put aside, so General Benjamin O. Gary and Sergeant-Major Lucius Carver were chosen to go and collect the Renoir brothers. They met at General Renoir's house. Nigel was, as always, pleased to see the Sergeant-Major. He hadn't seen General Benjamin Gary in many years, and the last he'd heard, the man had died in a plane crash.

When he saw the general again, Nigel's eyes teared as he shook the man's hand. "I'd salute, General, but it appears that I'm no longer enlisted," he'd said.

"No, Nigel, you're not. But you'll always be a Marine, and you're still one of Crossover Team Alpha's." General Gary smiled.

Unexpectedly, Nigel grabbed the older man in a bear hug and lifted him. "I'm glad that you and Maureen didn't die!" he exclaimed. Of course, General Gary was somewhat embarrassed. Sergeant-Major Carver seemed about to burst from holding in laughter at General Gary's discomfiture. This was their Baby Marine all right. He was back, once again knowing who he was. More importantly he knew who they were. General Gary would likely have "read the riot act" to anyone else who did that, but this was "Little Nige" and that was the only thing that made it okay. He did want to talk to the younger man about his visualization ability though. There was every possibility that the DNA copy of General Renoir's memories to "Little Nige" may have resulted in duplicating more than just childhood recollections that Nigel once needed. That conversation would happen later, but at the moment, another Graise attack would be coming, and preparations needed to be made.

The Graise wouldn't stop, everyone knew that. They *had* to invade other worlds in order to insure the survival of their version of the human race. While neither Nigel nor his brother were currently military, their contributions could be the foundation for any defense, so they had to be included in the strategic planning sessions. Thus, they were also given a very generous line of credit as assets. No one was worried about Nigel, but the brass felt that DeVries needed to be made comfortable for a while in order to cement his allegiance to their needs. DeVries was both like and unlike his older brother, so even though he agreed to commit himself to assisting in their efforts, he still needed to get away from it all before the war started, or he couldn't bring his best self to the fight. So he, Dana Andria Lacy, Nigel and Angeline Renoir had all gone to the beach—in Grace Bay—Providenciales, Turks and Caicos. General Gary shook his head in appreciation when Sergeant-Major Carver told him that. *Oh to be young, in love and able to walk through interdimensional portals,* he'd thought. *Well, if anybody in creation deserves a break on the beach, Little Nige does. These Graise are going to be bringing a hellstorm with 'em when they come back. Maybe I'll have him take Maureen and baby Kruger somewhere safe 'til this is over.* He turned to look at the view from the window behind his desk. *How long do we have before they come back?* he wondered. *Nige has got to get that Director Caldwell to come into the fold and work with us—soon. If he doesn't we just go with plan "B," I guess.* For the MISTmen, it was simple.

—

They would not take "no" as an answer from Director Caldwell. If he chose not to accept their assistance in publicizing the threat posed by the Graise, then Crossover Team Alpha would proceed without the ITA. As an information-gathering society, the PHS was still very active. Where information could be gathered, it could also be disseminated. This world would not be caught unawares, if any of them could help it.

The day passed, another one dawned, and no Graise attacks were recorded. This worried Crossover Base Alpha. The Graise were a very scheduled culture—a necessity caused by the brevity of their lives, so they never missed a window once they began an attack on a target. That fanatical adherence to schedule, along with their relative immaturity, had worked in favor of the MISTmen during many of their excursions into R-2, General Nigel Renoir's home reality. General Renoir had returned home from his meeting a day and a half ago and still no word of any attack anywhere. His wife had told him how the young Nigel and his Angeline had done pretty much the same thing that he and Angeline Renoir had. They'd gotten married privately and planned a public wedding for her adoptive mother's sake. General Renoir was not at all surprised at the location where the young couple had gone; it was a location that he and General Gary often took their wives to whenever they needed to get away from the base and its duties, but, he wondered, *Did the boy have to go so far away just to get to the same place?* He was in his office preparing for a return to R-3 with that reality's Roan Caldwell and his team, The Extras, who were going to be permanently assigned to IDEA Control of R-3, when his phone rang. He pushed the "speaker" function and a holographic projection of Roan Graham Caldwell, along with his team members appeared. General Renoir could tell by the way they were assembled that he'd been called from their TAC.

"What can I do for you, Director Caldwell?"

"We've got a spot on the NBC news tonight," he began without preamble. "They'll show some of the footage from Tule Valley, but they're not willing to present it as a leading story."

"I see," General Renoir replied. "Are they at least going to present it as a *serious* story?"

"Not sure," IDEA Control answered. "They didn't seem to take it seriously at all. They tried to cross check with a few other sources in Washington, but, of course, they couldn't get any confirmation." "How can we help, Director Caldwell?" The miniature director and his team looked at one another uncomfortably.

"Director?" General Renoir prodded. The Director of ITA cleared his throat.

"Well," he began, hesitated, "we were thinking, if you'd have your kid make a public announcement, maybe show them something that they'll believe . . ." General Renoir raised an eyebrow. "Well, ordinarily, I'd leave that choice up to Nigel after explaining the necessity, but as it is, he isn't here now."

"Do you think you could talk to him, wherever he is, General?" Director Caldwell asked. "See, that's just the thing, Caldwell. He isn't *here* now. He and his brother took their young ladies to a very nice beach, but not to its location on this plane of reality," General Renoir answered with the barest hint of annoyance.

The ITA team seemed disappointed, and they were, but after a moment's thought. Roan asked "General, is he with Angeline Duplessis?"

"Yes," General Renoir replied. Roan Graham Caldwell breathed a sigh of relief. "Well, that's one worry off of my mind. Her mother and father have been calling my office and my wife. They're worried to death about her. Seems she went missing about the time of that mini-war in the Tule Valley. They're refusing to evacuate until they find her."

"Who's ordering evacuations?" General Renoir asked.

"It's MPIS," Roan answered. "We believe that they're trying to hide all evidence of the Event."

"I can give Angeline Duplessis's family a call, if you'd like, Director," General Renoir suggested. Roan looked thoughtful. "It might work better if a Marine Officer contacted them, assuring them of her safety. I'm sure you can come up with a logical reason for her absence, General. They may just listen to you," He said in acceptance of General Renoir's suggestion. "Would you like me to text their number?"

"No, Director, I already have it."

Roan looked confused for a moment.

"How did you . . . oh, never mind. I forget. They're your in-laws too, somehow. General, this whole another you another me thing can really get confusing sometimes."

"Yes, I agree, Director," General Renoir agreed, then cut the call short, automatically activating Kruger and Leonard's failsafe and once again baffling the director's attempt to trace his location.

Twenty minutes later, he was talking to Rene and Severine Duplessis via Skype. The image they saw was altered just enough to make him unrecognizable to them if ever they met in person. He politely informed them of the fact that yes, there had, indeed, been an emergency that arose in relation to war games conducted in the region of the Tule Valley Hardpan, and thankfully, young Angeline happened to be on hand when it occurred. Her medical training had come in quite handy, and the USMC would see to it that she got credit toward her degree for her contribution.

Where was she now? Well, yes, Mr. and Mrs. Duplessis, that's the thing. You see, she met a fine young Marine Sergeant from a very wealthy family while she was working with the Corps here, and, well, you know how young people are—it seems that when the young man cashed in on his accumulated leave, and, well, they went to the beach in Grace Bay, Turks and Caicos, with his brother and some other young adults. Yes, yes, the sergeant is a marine of excellent performance and reputation, the kind of guy we'd call a 'squared-off marine,' and he has never been known to gallivant with various women or anything like that. As far as we know, it appears that the two of them met long ago when they were children in New Orleans, but what with the hurricane and all . . .

"Yes, Mr. and Mrs. Duplessis, I'll have his CO contact him and tell Ms. Angeline—that's the name, correct? Angeline Duplessis? Yes, we'll have them call you later today or tomorrow. The young marine? His name is Sergeant Nigel Renoir, and we'll have him speak to the two of you, also. No, no, he's not facing any disciplinary action, but, well, we'll just have to have a good ole heartfelt USMC conversation with him, won't we? Yes, yes, we can wait until after you speak to him for that, Mrs. Duplessis, yes. Thank you for your understanding, we'll handle the matter right away. What? What do you mean, rumbling? The ground is rumbling there? It's just occasional, you say? No, we're not doing any underground testing, but perhaps some other division of the military . . . yes, thank you Mr. and Mrs. Duplessis. Look for a call from your daughter soon."

After the call ended, General Renoir took a moment to consider what Mrs. Severine Duplessis said about rumbling underground. He was a mechanical engineer, she was a hydrologist. These were not dim-witted people. They would know if the region they'd been searching for a week or more was prone to unexplained seismic activity. If that ground-rumbling was just something to be expected, they wouldn't have found it an odd enough occurrence to ask him about underground testing, which they would know had to be classified, if such were in the process. No, Mr. and Mrs. Duplessis had asked about the source of that mysterious rumbling because they *knew* it didn't belong. General Renoir made a call to Kruger and asked him to retask their satellite (Yes, Crossover Base One had a satellite deployed. More than one, really.) that was watching the Tule Talley Hardpan. General Renoir wanted to have its underground imaging system activated and concentrated not only on the Valley, but on the surrounding hills and rock formations. While he waited for the results, he went to his home. There was something that he and his beloved Angeline needed to do for Nigel and *his* beloved Angeline.

Rene and Severine Duplessis were ecstatic. Mrs. Duplessis finally heard from her daughter via Skype. They'd met her young Marine too. Severine was pleased to no end with her first impression of the man. He was respectful, handsome, and very much in love with Angeline. She was surprised that her girl had kept him a secret, but Angeline explained that he was active duty and frequently deployed. Because his was a special operations unit, many of those deployments had to be kept secret, so Angeline had kept her engagement to Nigel quiet. Yes they had set a date, but could they get back to her with it later, please? She just wanted to enjoy his company for now, since he may be deployed at any time. Mr. Duplessis was hesitant, as all fathers are when it comes to their daughters, but the young Marine had treated him with respect too. He and this Nigel fellow would have a talk soon, no doubt. The Duplessis couple would sleep well tonight. With that done, General Renoir could concentrate on the results of his scan. What he saw made him raise that right eyebrow again.

Immediately afterward, he contacted General Gary. "What's going on, Nige?" he asked as soon as their contact was secured.

"Ben, it appears that the Graise have a gifted commander," General Renoir told him.

That gave General Gary pause. "What do you mean, sir?" he asked.

"We know that their culture has deteriorated to the point where it doesn't produce any great people," General Renoir began, continuing with, "this is why their tactics rarely, if ever, change. Yet they have adopted a drastic change in tactics over in the Tule Valley. They're trying to blast tunnels and use them as an entry point to launch their next attack from." General Benjamin O. Gary knew that there was no need to ask, "How do you know?" or "Are you sure?" as many people would have. General Nigel B. Renoir was one of the last of a select group, known as "V-Officers" and quite possibly, the last one their civilization would ever produce. There was no need to ask anything more than "What do we need to do now?" So that's what General Gary asked.

"Stop them," General Renoir responded. That was the only reply he needed.

To End It

As soon as Nigel, Angeline, DeVries, and Dana arrived in front of General Renoir's home, they were met by a contingent of their favorite people. General Renoir, General Gary, Lieutenant C. C. Pendle, Sergeant-Major Lucius Carver, and First Sergeant Rondo Little were all there. Immediately, Nigel and DeVries were whisked away to the command center while Angeline Duplessis-Renoir and Dana Andria Lacy went in to discuss matters with Angeline Renoir.

***

The Tule Valley Hardpan at night was a beautiful place, Nigel thought. He'd always loved looking at the indigo sky. It made him think of escapes aboard seafaring ships and warm nights under faraway skies. Not tonight. The stars twinkled and glittered with the same cold, beautiful fire that they always had and always would. Tonight, he was here to do whatever it took to protect the Barrier, as it had protected him. He didn't hate the Graise as his older version did. But then, they hadn't overrun *his* world after it had been weakened by a nuclear war, either. He did know, however, the merciless nature of his enemy. They destroyed worlds that they had no right to set foot on, and that was bad enough, but in addition to that, their wanton cross-reality warfare on other Earths was causing the substance of the Barrier to unravel. If that continued, then the worlds would come into destructive contact with one another. The scale of death and destruction following such an event would be too grand for his mind to process. *That sounded so cliché,* Nigel thought.

—

600

"Hey, Nige, you're doing that reflective thinker thing again." Devries cut into his reverie.

"How did you know?" he asked his brother.

"I know who you are now, thanks to that mind-storm-tornado in the *Hellspace*."

"Yeah, that was a moment, huh, Dev? You ready to do this? The troops await us." The two of them were standing near the small hill where Nigel, Lucius, and The Extras had sheltered on their first day here. Now they were waiting for . . .

The ground rumbled and instantly, the Renoir brothers sprang into action. Nigel disappeared into the Barrier, seized tendrils that emanated the thunderous effect of a political upheaval in one of the many worlds, and these he thrust out to his brother, along with calming and mellowing effects of Grandmothers throughout time, so that DeVries could handle the vast amount of power that was coming toward him. Devries absorbed it all, directed it into two opposite points, and thrust it into the rock he was standing on. It penetrated all the way down into a chamber that was formed by a tunnel that the Graise had blasted out. They'd began in an underground ALC facility located in the Tule Valley Hardpan of their own reality. Their newest Arch-Commander had come up with this novel idea, based on a premise that tunnels would protect them from observation by the satellites of their target world. World Military Command originally ignored her battle plan and chose to send in a couple of Calvary Scout units. They both disappeared, so they sent two more. One of the second unit's APCs made it home and reported a battle, how the Monster of Mayhem from Trouble World was there, along with the super-soldiers that normally accompanied him. So the Graise sent an invasion force, and it never returned. Additionally, the new portal had been forced shut.

After that, Graise's World Military Command listened to Arch-Commander Dana Lacy's battle plan, hoping that her new strategy would get them into the world they'd just discovered. Their first foray had been beaten back. Such a thing never happened before. Now they were creating an access tunnel that would start in their own reality and end in the New Find's reality, so, moving the reality crossing equipment into the basement of the ALC facility, they blasted a tunnel into the bedrock there, in their own reality. Their intent was to begin a crossover into the new Earth while still underground as the tunnel lengthened. Once there, they would begin to tunnel toward the facility that housed the New Find's crossover equipment. If they could make it to that structure, they could seize the machines it contained and use it as a forward base for their invasion forces. They'd blast here and take the debris to their world for disposal. Once they captured the structure in the other Earth's Tule Valley Hardpan, why, millions and later, *billions* of Graise soldiers would arrive, subjugate that Earth, and every human living on the New Find would be liquified, as they deserved to be. That was the Graise's plan. What they didn't plan on was having to deal not only with the Monster of Mayhem, but also with his brother.

Devries and his brother formed their spike into two intersecting tunnels that would hit the Graise's subterranean passageway at ninety-degree angles. Nigel took one side, and DeVries pushed another aspect of his passageway into an intersection of the same type from the other side. With that done, Nigel anchored the entire route through the Barrier. Now the forces attached to Crossover Base Alpha could flank the Graise invaders and attack from both sides while they were still inside their tunnel. They themselves would launch their assault from within the demesne of the Barrier. Nigel would lead one wing through *otherspace* and DeVries would lead the other wing. General Renoir had about twenty-four MISTmen under his command. One general, one major, three captains and two lieutenants, seven officers, all totaled, and fifteen noncommissioned officers. During the years since they'd found themselves stranded on R-1, General Renoir and General Gary had implemented a long-range plan to build their forces in preparation for the day that they'd go home to cast the Graise from their world. They had many more men and women in their Crossover Corps now, all vetted as thoroughly as they could by the best means they had. Every member of their forces had been recruited from their own homeworld and put through basic training in Nigel's world. There were also many more MISTmen now, as this was the one of the reasons for their many excursions into their own home reality. Another reason was the cure for CMV that had been developed by an older Angeline in another reality. Her husband, USMC Colonel Nigel Renoir, had given his life in delivering that cure, and she was willing to share it with every country or world that needed it. Every person, family group, and community they'd been able to preserve in General Renoir's World had needed it. Many of the people they'd saved there, such as Charles Lubkin and his family, as well as every other member of their support staff, chose to join General Renoir's forces in gratitude or anger over the Graise. This was where they'd found their reinforcements. Now General Renoir and his forces were about to engage their enemy once more, to deny their entry into Nigel's world, and expose the threat of the Graise to all its people. They entered the Barrier following Nigel, and at a certain point in their forward progress, their forces split, half following DeVries.

***

Arch Commander Dana Lacy was far from the person who had once lived with Nigel, or the woman who now loved DeVries. She was Graise, and as such, hated the unfairness of being such. As unto all her people past, that hatred was transferred from the injustice she could not control to all other non-Graise life forms. She intended to conquer as many of them as she could in her short lifespan, so that future generations of her race could live, and maybe one day they could live to what should have been a normal human age. At twenty-five years, she was almost past middle age and into the realm of being a senior citizen. Because of her gender, she'd spent most of her time trying to prove her value as a military officer. Even though the Graise's world lived under a united government, there were always separatists who wanted to go back to the old ways, so, there were countless domestic mini-wars and police actions needed. Dana Lacy of the Graise had distinguished herself in battle by the time she was sixteen, and a Major. Their government tried to keep her from off-world excursions, but there were also pockets of survivors among the various farm worlds they dominated, and at times, these created disturbances that required intervention by an expeditionary force, usually one commanded by Dana Lacy. Eventually, she became The Arch-Commander of all United World Federation Military Forces and this was her moment in history. The tunnel was large enough now. They couldn't take any tanks through it, but infantry and light vehicles could pass through it. Forward Company E-22 would go through first, then the Arch-Commander would send the Death's Head Battalion through. Their intent was to exit on the other side and storm the fortress after Forward Company E-22 blasted through its walls.

Nigel and General Renoir waited in a location that was within the Barrier, but close enough to its exit so that they could see without being seen. General Renoir found it to be the strangest sensation he'd ever experienced. He was standing *within* the rock wall of the Graise tunnel, like a ghost or something. With him were Sergeant-Major Lucius Carver and Major Archimus Marcelon, in command of the 140 marines that were in this Battery, called "Battery A." Although he couldn't see through the wall on the other side of the tunnel he knew that DeVries and General Benjamin Gary was there, with Sergeant-Major Puccini and Logan Eller, who had received a field promotion to Major, also commanding a battery of 140 marines ("Battery B," of course). Somehow, Nigel would know when they were in position, and they would step out of *otherspace* and into the tunnel, deploy their refraction camos, and wait. Eventually, Nigel gave the signal and the troops moved out of the cover of the Barrier and into the brightly-lit tunnel. On the opposite side, the others did the same. The end of the tunnel started glowing as the Graise activated their crossover tech, and all of General Renoir's marines deployed refraction, as did General Gary's. The portal opened, and they came through, about 160 Graise Soldiers. Some of them went to the end of their passageway and begin to set charges on what was the outside wall of an underground storeroom within DCA-21. Before they could finish, General Gary's grenadiers, armed with upgraded M320s, launched their nonconcussive energy flechette grenades into Graise Company E-22, with destructive results. They were caught completely off guard, and Battery B used the advantage gained with the element of a surprise attack to complete their victory. The firefight didn't last long, since Crossover Team Alpha was using Graise-specific BD rounds. Of the few Graise that survived, most refused to surrender and fought to the death, but Crossover Corps Alpha chose not to kill them all. They wanted to keep some alive.

***

Arch-Commander Dana Emily Lacy stood on a walkway that lead to the office facilities of the huge underground ALC factory. She was there to review the Death's Head Battalion, commanded by Lieutenant-Colonel Ross Johnson. The portal was opening again, and they were ready, anxious and eager. The success of their mission would gain the first foothold in a new Earth for the Graise. At the moment though, there was a commotion going on down there, with officers and noncoms raising their voices. Because their attention wandered when a group had started playing the latest hip-hop song on the PA system, the soldiers were being commanded to re-form ranks before marching into the portal. Their NCOs and officers were livid, of course. How *dare* these kids embarrass them in front of The Arch-Commander! Although they didn't know it, she wasn't at all angry or otherwise nonplussed. The Arch-Commander knew that the average Graise soldier was still a ten or eleven-year-old person in a full-grown adult body. Yes, they did think like the adults of old most of the time, but they were still what they were, and there would always be moments when their long-lost, nonexistent childhood would assert itself. All that mattered was their ability to follow orders in battle and that they retain a healthy hatred of all non-Graise life.

As the ranks finally formed for review, she thought her peripheral vision caught movement. She wasn't sure, so she ignored it. Still, something about it nagged at her thinking. Feeling a slight pressure behind her ears didn't help things either. She was just suddenly *uncomfortable*. Then it happened again. The arch-commander turned toward her Prime General, Sub-Commander Fadl Al-Basan, to see if he'd noticed anything, but at that moment, she heard the unmistakable sound of a bullet flying in her direction, and his head exploded before she could speak. Suddenly, true pandemonium broke out as the crossover equipment, both engines, exploded at the same time that Lieutenant-Colonel Ross Johnson's head was burst apart by another sniper's bullet.

"Sniper! Find cover!" she cried out in anger, and the call was taken up by the officers and noncoms on the floor below and up here where her command staff was assembled. That's when she remembered the intel that had been nagging at her thoughts—the super-soldiers from the Trouble World! That invisibility they were known to have, that way of moving so that you could just barely see it except in peripheral vision—they were *here*! *Here*, on the Graise's homeworld!

Dana Lacy hadn't become arch-commander due to inability to act, so she cried out, "Take cover and deploy smoke!" *That would baffle the sniper for a little while, at least, long enough for someone to spot him or her,* she thought. Her command was never heard by the soldiers under review though. Confusion had broken out on the floor below. Her Sergeant-Major was hit within seconds after her senior officers had been and the Death's Head Battalion was being cut down by what appeared to be tiny heat-seeker missiles flying from the walls of the floor below. The snipers (she felt that it had to be at least two of them), were also singling out the officers and noncoms, who were being eliminated with superhuman speed and efficiency. Dana had taken cover behind a wall just inside of the facility manager's office. Every now and then, she'd peep around the door or through that small window that she was hiding under. Then she heard automatic weapons fire and knew that the soldiers had started shooting randomly, trying to hit something, anything. She heard screams of agony as her forces occasionally shot each other and knew that some had actually deployed their ALC cables hitting their own.

She had to do something. So Arch-Commander Dana Lacy stood up from her concealment, walked boldly to the railing overlooking the floor and called out, "Why are you hiding like cowards? Come out and *fight like real soldiers!*" All the mayhem below stopped, and men appeared—a company-sized force, along the walls of the floor. They wore camos that were only a shade less gray than her troops' utility gear, and every one of them drew two-foot-long miniswords that lit up. Most of the Death's Head Battalion was gone, but there were still enough to fight. Her people were filled with anger and resentment over their fallen comrades, ready to die, and motivated entirely by unreasoning hatred of these *regular* humans. Even her hatred was breaking the restraints of her self-control. *"Kill them all!"* she ordered through clenched teeth, and the fighting began.

She couldn't take her eyes off of the spectacle below. Her people were shooting, deploying cables, and using their knives to the best of their ability, but they were still being slaughtered. Their foes could move unlike anything she'd ever seen, and the tenor of the fighting told her that they hated her people just as much as the Graise hated them. She knew by then that no help was coming, for she'd called several times, and no one answered. They were alone with these people. Dana aimed her sidearm toward the floor below, hoping to take out at least *some* of the warriors that were killing her people, but one of the snipers shot her weapon. It hurt, but the bullet didn't penetrate her hand either. At that, Dana's thinking cleared up, and she realized, *They want to capture me alive!* She was determined not to allow this, so she pulled her service blade, which was promptly shot out of her hand, again, without penetrating her suit or her hand. *Of course. If the ground soldiers were enhanced somehow, their snipers would also be,* the arch-commander thought. She was charging forward, now, thinking of casting herself into the bloodletting below. If she survived the fall, and her EXOS-LK5 didn't tear open, she'd force her own death at the hands of the super-soldiers before she'd let them capture her! Unexpectedly, one of them appeared in front of her and knocked her down with a body-block. She tried a foot-swipe to take the man off of his feet, but he was too fast. He jumped, bending his knees, and she missed. She used the momentum to spin around, hoping to land a hammer blow to the back of his knees, since he'd likely be a little off-balanced when he landed from his own jump. The blow connected, but the enemy flipped backward and landed on one leg. The other one he used to land a full-force kick to her face, and the lights went out for Arch-Commander Dana Lacy.

She awoke to the sound of quiet. *We lost*, her mind said. *You failed.* She was blindfolded, and didn't know if any of her people had survived the encounter with the super-soldiers from the Trouble World, but she did know she *had* to get a message out, somehow. Central command needed to know that this enemy had found their way to the Graise homeworld. *I didn't know their capabilities. Never was deployed there. But this company is stuck here, now, since they've blown the crossover machinery. If I could just get word out, there'll be nowhere they can hide on this earth.* She wasn't reaching for any excuses, but honestly, she knew that if she'd had at least one deployment to these people's homeworld, if she'd seen them in action at least once, her forces could have put up a better fight today. Arch-Commander Lacy was correct in that, but the moment was over, and she was a captive now. She was sitting in a chair within the factory manager's office, unable to move, but she didn't see any bonds anywhere on her. They had taken off one of her gloves and her hand was exposed. At this point, she felt that she was just waiting for the worst death one of her people could experience. Death by fusion. A small plate, one foot in diameter was under the chair, though, and the low humming it emitted indicated that the plate was possibly the cause of her paralysis.

The door opened, and she could tell by the smell of the air that she was still on her own Earth. *Maybe, if I could just . . .* "Please don't," someone said. "I don't know why they blindfolded you. It wasn't really necessary." The blindfold was removed, and she found herself looking at a tall man with a doctor's demeanor. He too was a colored human. Very fair-skinned, with blond hair going gray. She hated him and his little round glasses instantly. A medical alarm beeped, and the tall man leaned closer to look at her eyes. "Hard to see through those special facepieces you wear," he said. "But I think that your hatred response kicked in. It's an intrinsic particular to your people's specific CMV infection." He smiled at her, and she hated the whiteness of his teeth. "They call me Kruger," he told her, as if she should care.

"I'm gonna kill you and liquefy what's left," she answered.

"I'm sure you would," he replied.

The door opened again, and three military men walked in. They were of different colors, too, so her hatred spiked again, causing the annoying beep to sound itself. One of them spoke, "Are you the officer that came up with the idea of tunneling?"

"Lacy, Dana Emily. Arch-Commander, Serial number 238756909. United World Federation Armed Forces," she replied while fastening her gaze at a random spot just above his head.

The man, a huge dark-skinned fellow, looked at her and smiled without malice. "So you *are* the officer that came up with the idea of tunneling, then?"

"Lacy, Dana Emily. Arch-Commander, Serial number 238756909. United World Federation Armed Forces," she repeated while fastening her gaze at a random spot just above his head, again.

The man turned to look at one of the others, his superior officer, who said, "Thank you, Sergeant-Major. I'll take it from here. She's not a threat at the moment."

One of the other men moved a chair to face her, and the speaker sat down in it. "I'm General Nigel B. Renoir, United Federation of States Marine Corps." The arch-commander started to reiterate her former statement, but the general held his hand up. She waited. "I already know who you are, Dana. I have no questions for you. We are taking you with us. If things go well, you'll be thankful that we did."

At that moment, another man stepped out of nowhere. He looked exactly like this general, so Dana surmised him to be the man's son. Her hatred increased. The medical machine beeped again. "I got everything we needed, sir. We'll know when and where their attacks are coming," he said. "We can leave whenever you're ready."

He turned to look at her and smiled. "Dana, you make a pretty good-looking older woman, for a Graise. Do you collect coffee mugs, still?" Her eyes widened.

"Kruger," the general said. The tall man approached and reached out for her hand, causing her fear to spike. The annoying beep sounded continually this time. Due to her strong-willed self-control, her lips never moved, but her mind was screaming *Stop! Let me die in a fight! Not like this! Not like* . . . and blackness took her. "Now, the Graise will go back to being entirely predictable," General Renoir said.

***

Two days later, ITA director Roan Caldwell received a call from General Renoir. "The Graise will open four portals. They want to move on Washington and Moscow, but they don't want the exposure of crossing over into a large city. They've selected two smaller towns in each country, both near to these capitols."

"Where?" Roan asked.

"In America, it will be Bailey's Crossroads, to the southeast, and Glenn Dale, to the northeast. In Russia, they'll arrive in Dimitrov, to the north and Klimovsk, to the south," General Renoir said.

"Well, you guys also told me to expect an attack within seventy-two hours of the Tule Valley Incident, but that never happened."

"Yes, Director, it did," he responded. "You just never knew it was happening."

Roan felt a chill as General Renoir continued, "We have intervened in that scenario, but your forces will have to handle what's coming next. Your whole world is about to become a battlefield, Director. I suggest you start applying your powers surreptitiously at this point. Make some calls to that agent you've turned in Russia. He needs to be a hero. Then go to the Tule Valley and apply the upgraded military version of Ground Penetrating Radar that MPIS has stored there. You have the authority to walk in and do so. Without a doubt, The Gray Colonel will be of assistance in this."

"What am I looking for?" Roan asked.

"You'll find a tunnel underneath the southwestern wall that is large enough to accommodate the light infantry whose bodies are lying askew there, and ground vehicles, which are also in the tunnel, having been destroyed. There will also be some Graise soldiers who are immobilized. They're disarmed, unconscious, and their ALC cables have been detached. They'll die there if another day passes. Notify the press. We have several reporters already awaiting your call."

"How long before . . ."

"The Graise will attack in three days, Director," General Renoir said, ending the call.

***

Things moved faster after that. The evening news broadcasts confirmed what was already being discussed on social media. The director of the Interception of and Defense against Encroachment of Alien Threats

Agency (which many Americans did not even know existed) had found positive proof of an invasion attempt right in the Tule Valley. Furthermore, the agency publicized satellite images of a pitched battle in the Tule Valley Hardpan between these invaders and MPIS, which went viral. The director of ITA, Roan Caldwell, held a press conference to inform America and the world of the fact that he and his agency had, in line with their original charter, been using the Interlopers as an intelligence gathering force. They were refugees who fled a world overrun by the very same aliens who now threatened earth. No, they were no threat to humans, and no, they would never be available for an interview, as they preferred not to be a circus sideshow. The only thing he would confirm regarding the Interlopers was that they were humans, also, and they had, indeed come from a different world. Yes, he had attempted to inform the Administration, but was ignored. The reason he was going public now was because these same forces that had been found decimated in the Tule Valley Tunnel were going to invade again. When? Three days from now, and here's where. The silence that ensued as Roan Caldwell read the names of the towns targeted by the Graise also went viral. For the next two days, rumors, accusations and unrest filled the airwaves and social media. The Administration was threatening to arrest the ITA team and dismantle that agency for perpetrating such an elaborate hoax. The Russians were accusing America of attempting to sow unrest within their peaceful realm. But the world waited.

Three days after Roan Caldwell's announcement, at precisely noon, four portals opened up. In America, they were located in Bailey's Crossroads, to the southeast of Washington DC, and Glenn Dale to the northeast. In Russia, portals opened up in Dimitrov, to the north of Moscow, and Klimovsk, to the south. At the beginning, one division of Graise charged forth through each portal. In all four locations, the ferocity of their attack drove back the underpowered defenses that had been placed there just to satisfy public outcry. The defenders rallied, but by the time that happened, two more divisions per portal had set foot on their planet. Eventually, in both Russia and America, the native forces bottled the Graise up so that those portals became useless for them, and closed. Within seventy-two hours, four new portals opened up, two in China and two more in Africa. Four divisions of Graise fighters per portal ushered through, and the Graise War continued. Eventually, human wars ceased. They had to. The Graise portals that opened up in Syria and Venezuela proved that. In both locations, almost a whole nation of people had been subsumed by the invaders, and due to the constant fighting previously raging in the Middle Eastern region, almost none of the surrounding nations were strong enough to cast them back. A full year after their first attack, they did what Isis had done before them, and captured territory in Syria, covering vast swathes of land from which they could safely sally forth to battle their neighbors. They could also move troops and equipment into that area, so now the fight for survival of the human race on R-1 intensified.

***

Roan Graham Caldwell sat in his office in Dubai, reviewing reports of the fighting around the world. Humanity was winning everywhere except in Central America and Syria. He had a meeting with The Joint Chiefs of Earth Defense in an hour and he wanted to be sure that he had all his facts lined up. General Renoir sat across from him, with a cognac in hand. True to his word, his forces had thrown in to help Roan's Earth when the general deemed it appropriate. That was why humanity had persevered here, because of victories won due to Crossover Base Alpha's interventions. They would win, Roan was sure of it. It's just that there seemed to be no end to the Graise armies. Just as the General predicted, they had begun to come by the millions, and would likely start coming by the billions soon enough. Nigel and DeVries had been involved in the fighting, too, and they were becoming folk heroes and urban legends. They were tired of the war, though, and from within the Barrier itself an idea of how to end the fighting had come to Nigel. That was why General Renoir had come today, to show Roan what Nigel and DeVries had cooked up.

After looking the plan over, he asked, "General, I understand that when the guys draw on the Barrier's energies, they pay a physical price, right?"

"Yes, that's true," General Renoir confirmed.

"Well, then, if they try something like this, on this scale, couldn't it kill them?" Roan asked.

General Renoir stood and walked over to the window, stared at the ocean for a moment, and responded, "They were going to do it anyway, you know. Would have tried it by now, but we let them in on a project we have going. If it succeeds, the problem of the Graise may be ended forever. We need time though. Nigel, however, isn't entirely willing to wait, and where he leads, DeVries follows. That's why he wants to apply his solution to this Earth instead of the Graise home, so that our project can proceed."

The room fell silent. He turned to Roan then and said, "Yes, it would kill him, if he were to try it alone, but he has his brother and his wife. They anchor him when he's in there, and it increases his chances of survival."

Roan looked down. "Okay, General, I'll put it in front of the Joint Chiefs and see what they say." "This will end the fighting, Director. After that, it'll be up to your nations to live with one another. We'll be going back home to deal with the Graise there."

"Is there any way we can we help?" Roan asked.

"Possibly," General Renoir replied. "But in order to be of assistance, your world will have to stay united after this is over, and none of us know if you can do that."

"True," Roan agreed. "Only time will tell."

***

In the location known to the MISTmen as R- 3, George Arlander sat in his cell, being miserable. He was entering the fourteenth month of a forty-to-life sentence, all because of that sorry-a "Bobby L." Irene had, in George's mind, gotten what she deserved, no less. He'd taken her life and dismissed her as if she'd never had any value at all. Then there were the federal charges, as well as the upcoming trial in Florida for that useless broad, Angeline. *Thanks, Wesley,* he thought. *You had to open your big mouth about everything, didn't you? Wonder what deal you made. You sissy-bottomed fag. I never liked you anyway.* He'd tried to pin that one on that waiter that she had the hots for, but somehow it had gone sideways and here George was. He was becoming angrier now, and thought of punching his cellmate when the guy got back. That wouldn't be a good idea, though, because his cell mate was also his Owner in this place. "Larry Liverface" was a huge, smelly, abusive member of a racist motorcycle gang, and he'd laid claim to George Arlander as soon as he'd arrived here. He was supposed to have Larry's laundry done today, or he'd get another beating and be loaned out again. He'd thought of murdering the man, but George Arlander was too much of a coward for that. He'd meet with his lawyer and complain again, but that probably wouldn't help. His lawyer, the person who had assured him that knowledge of his "alternate lifestyle" would be kept confidential, that not even the guards would know. Well that assurance hadn't held much water, had it? He intended to move some money around, put a few words out, and have Larry Liverface, Wesley Chumley Keller, and Bobby Landis killed. George had the money to do it too. A lot of his assets were still safe, he'd made sure of it. As he was thinking, *something* happened, and that waiter walked into his cell, carrying what looked like a dead body over his shoulder. He was wearing something that looked like a military flight suit. *Kind of hot,* George thought, *but he isn't my type . . .* He wanted to slap himself for that lapse, but, instead, crowded his thoughts with anger. "What are you doing here, you nig . . ." Nigel punched him in the mouth before he finished. George fell to his knees, holding his mouth. His teeth felt loose. Why, he would . . . and he was knocked out by a blow to his jaw.

Georgie Porgie, Puddin' and Pie, Kissed the girls and made them cry, When the boys came out to play, Georgie Porgie ran away.

Someone was singing, and he hated that stupid poem. *Mom. I hated you for singing that poem to all the girls. . .* George Arlander woke up, finding himself all tied up, lying in hot sand and covered in—*bacon grease?* "Wha . . .," he tried to talk, but his jaw was swollen.

"Hey, Georgie, relax," Nigel said from somewhere. "Listen." He could hear— was that—*Wesley?* whimpering, crying, begging. He looked up at a sun that burned his eyes. "Desert?" he croaked.

"Nah," Nigel answered nonchalantly, "you're right in the middle of what was once the hottest city in Texas. Austin. I love the music here. Well, not here, exactly. In a place very much very, very much like it."

George croaked.

Wesley whimpered. "Oh!" Nigel said "I almost forgot. Back to your . . . situation. Let me help you up, there." George felt himself being pulled up by his collar. As soon as he was upright, he could see what was left of Wesley. The man was still alive, but he probably wished he weren't. He was suspended by a plastic—looking ropelike material that cradled his body with what looked like three skeletal fingers on each side, and one that went between his legs. This was attached to a bent light pole that stopped working a long time ago. There were ruins of a city in the background, and he was hung in a standing position with his hands at his sides, as was George. Only his toes would have touched the ground, when he had them. He didn't have them anymore. All that was left of his lower legs were bone. Pieces of his torn flesh hung and dripped from his thighs, and a few giant roaches were joyfully feeding on those. There was blood around his mouth, and his head was lolling to the side. George's stomach revolted, and he vomited. Nigel looked down at it a moment. "Well, that's helpful," he said.

"It's definitely going to shorten this ordeal for you,"

George croaked again. "You . . . monster . . ."

Nigel looked at him. "You know, it's funny. I've been called that over and over again by enemies that are less human than you, but believe it or not, their way of killing innocent people, well it's more humane than you two guys' way. At least they don't kill people's hopes or break their hearts in the process" He walked around George.

"Angeline didn't deserve that, you know. We *did* want one another pretty badly, I'll tell you that. Still, can you guess what she refused to do?"

George Arlander croaked again.

Nigel continued, "She never would cheat on you, piece of dirt that you are. What's so pathetic, George, was that I never really pressured her to either. I thought I was being *honorable*." He scoffed.

"Well, here's the part where I tell you how you die."

Waving his arms to encompass their surroundings, "This," Nigel began, "was once a thriving, vibrant world. They were about to go out into space, even. But, George, you *know* how evil men can be. You are, after all, Mr. Evil Murderer of Wives yourself. You've done it twice, right? No answer? Well, anyway, the evil guys created a super-virus that not only killed hundreds of thousands, it also caused a nuclear war, after which a *more* evil alien race came along and attempted to subjugate whatever humans survived. They wanted to suck the humans' insides out through a tube."

George croaked again

"Yeah, I know— *Yuckk*, Right?" Nigel said as if he were speaking to his best friend from middle school. "Well, don't worry, Georgie Porgie. Some valiant and honorable humans have survived and are battling bravely for the future of humanity in this world. Not that *you'd* know anything about valiance, honor or bravery, huh?"

"It wasn't my fau..." George began, but his captor glared him into silence, then continued his narrative

"Now, that battle is still going on, but don't worry, George, none of the combatants will ever come here. Not only is the weather too hot, but it's hot with radiation too." He looked up at the sun. "Gonna be dark, soon, so I'd better hurry this up, huh?" he continued, then, "well, you know how they always say that rats and roaches could survive a nuclear war, and the end of the world? Can you believe that turned out to be true? Underneath this sand, though, lives a certain slug that survived too. These slugs love to do what—you guessed it, they love to eat *flesh*. They climb on the target, secrete some acid-like substance to liquefy their food, then ingest it through their skin." He leaned closer. "Here's where things get sporty, George. The roaches that you see there nibbling on little Wesley, well, they consider the slugs a delicacy.

"It's true. They go *crazy* when they know these things are around. They swarm, and they eat whatever they swarm over, little roachie bite by little roachie bite. Now what I'm going to do, George, is lower you 'til your toes touch the sand. Then I'll cut your tongue out and throw it down, so that all the hungry bugs will visit you tonight. At first, they send a scout expedition, which is why your boy Wesley there has only lost the lower part of his legs. The next night, they come in force, and eat the target to the bone. So this is definitely Wesley's last night. Maybe yours too, since your vomit may make them realize they don't need to find out how you taste. Oh, don't worry about me. My suit here has repulsion tech, so my feet never really touch the ground. They don't know I'm here."

If Nigel had laughed maniacally, his own upcoming death would have been easier on George Arlander, somehow, but there was no laughter in Nigel's eyes or demeanor. "You know, George, if you'd killed her out of jealousy, because you thought she and I were doing the 'friends with benefits' thing, maybe that would have merited an easier death for you. But that wasn't it, was it? You killed her that way because you *thought* she was going to take your precious *stuff!* Well, Georgie, your money was gone the day before I took you."

He leaned forward, pressed a stud on his gauntlet, and some type of electrical current flew from his suit and hit George's jaw, deadening the nerves and forcing his mouth to hang open. Nigel held an extremely sharp knife in his hand, now, and with the other hand, reached into George Arlander's mouth to hold the man's tongue as he cut it out. George wanted to scream, but his jaws were not functioning. He couldn't *feel* the knife cutting his tongue, either.

Meanwhile, Nigel continued speaking as if this were all normal. "All of your ill-gotten gains, every single bit, have been given to her family, legally, along with your written confession of your multiple misdeeds. No one at the prison will miss you, either. See that body I left, that was another

---

version of you that had done worse things, believe it or not. He got a shiv to the liver and checked out. That shiv will be found in your cell, and Larry Liverface will get a longer sentence, maybe even the death sentence. So at least you can gain a little peace from that thought, huh?" He dropped George's tongue, and it flopped to the sand.

Nigel went on, "So this is goodbye, George. Enjoy the Wesley show tonight. The little critters love to come out after dark." He turned and started walking away. He stopped, turned around to face George Arlander, gestured toward his own mouth and said, "You're gonna feel that in the morning. If you survive the night, that is. You're gonna feel a lot of things in the morning." He stepped forward and disappeared.

***

Special Federal Agent Roan Caldwell sat in his chair in his beachside home, a snifter of the good ole Pappy Van Winkle that Bill and Meredith Compton had bought for him sitting on the side table. He never asked them how they knew what day his wedding anniversary fell on, but he was grateful for the fact that they never forgot. Every year, they'd gotten him something on that date, but then they'd leave him alone, knowing as only close friends would, that Roan preferred it that way. Tonight, he was looking at pictures of his lost family, something he'd just started doing again. *I could never have brought myself to do this before*, he thought. The pain was too acute. Things had changed since— Nigel. Roan often wondered how that lost man-child whom he'd first considered a dangerous suspect was doing now. At least the youngster had found his Angeline. At least Roan also knew that another version of Laura and the girls were still happily living with another version of himself. That was what really had changed the way he felt on this day.

Roan was looking at Laura and his wedding picture, now, and for the first time in years, he could smile about it. Nigel's words from the day they first met came back to his mind *"It's about a woman too. I mean, after all, isn't that what almost every man's story is about?"* "Well Laura," he said to her memory. "I guess the kid was right about that part of it." He still felt that both incarnations of the Nigel that he'd met were men who were a little too— amoral in the way they approached certain matters of Law and Justice, but, then who was *he* to say? Wasn't he the guy who shot The Tenement Slasher on public TV? If he had a "do- over," he'd do it again, too, wouldn't he? "Guess I would." he said to the picture of Laura, Marjorie and Giselle that he was now looking at.

Seemingly from nowhere, he heard Nigel the younger asking, "Hey, Doc, can I come in?" "Sure." Roan replied. "Why not? I was just thinking about you— sort of." Suddenly, Nigel stepped into his living room out of nowhere. "Whoa!" Roan exclaimed. "I didn't expect you to just *pop* in like that! You could just use the front door, you know." Nigel looked at his feet, then met his friend's eyes. "I wasn't at the front door, Doc." He quietly said. Roan stared at him for a minute. "You were in that Barrier thing, place or whatever it is? You were watching and talking to me from there?"

"Yes, I was, but that's not something I do just for fun. I just wanted to talk to you. It's important" Nigel said.

"How important? Is it a life or death thing? I mean, you guys are still in the middle of fighting a war over there, aren't you? Or has that whole thing been resolved already?"

"Yes, that's true, we are still in a pretty big fight, but that could go on and on for quite a few years, unless something drastic enough to put an end to it happens."

Roan's eyes narrowed. "And you've got something in mind, right, Nigel? I thought so. How does it involve me?" Nigel looked at his feet again and up at Roan. "It doesn't." he said. "I'm here because I don't think I ever said 'Thank you' for your efforts in bringing those two guys to justice for what they did to her." He reached into the backpack he'd brought with him and withdrew a very expensive-looking bottle. "This," he said as he held the bottle up so that the light reflected through the amber liquid within, "...is a bottle of one of the most expensive cognacs in the world, *Henri IV Dudognon Heritage Cognac Grande Champagne*. The bottle is dipped in 24 K Yellow Gold & Sterling Platinum and decorated with 6,500 certified brilliant cut diamonds. It's worth about two million dollars." Roan whistled. "Yeah, what you did meant that much to me." Nigel said as he handed the bottle over. "I hope it's good." Roan said. He and his visitor laughed. "Yeah. There is that." Nigel said. The laughter stopped, and Roan stared at Nigel for a few heartbeats. "Nigel, what's going on? Why the sudden visit and the far too expensive gift?" Nigel turned his head and stared at the wall. "Let me try this again, son." Roan started. "How's the war going?" Nigel looked toward his friend again. "They come through their portals, the World Military Force beats them back, and we close their portals. Devries and I destroy them and their equipment by the thousands, but they still keep coming."

"How's your Angeline doing?" Roan asked. "Is she okay?"

"Yes. She and the other two Angelines are working on a cure for the Graise's condition." Nigel said.

"Really? That's a pretty big undertaking. How do they hope to get it done?"

"Well, we have the older Angeline, and she's the person who found a cure for the CM virus in her reality, we have the Angeline who was my mom helping her and we also have two Krugers and Dr. Leonard working on the problem. You'd like the way the eldest Angie thinks of it, Doc. She said that they have to look at it as a crime scene and work backwards from there." Roan laughed a little. "I see that you have one of those big glassy knife-swords like Lucius's now. I noticed it in your bag there." Nigel smiled. "Yeah, I do. The Colonel—I mean, The General, he had it issued to me. Devvie was green with envy, but his DNA couldn't light one up, anyway…"

"Nigel, I appreciate your visit, but something's bugging you. Tell me what it is, son." Roan interrupted. Nigel looked him in the eye and said, "This thing I'm going to do to stop the Graise War on my world could kill me, Doc, and there's someone I want you to meet before I try it. Give me a minute." He stood up, stepped into nowhere and returned with—

Laura! Oh my god, it's her! *I should have guessed!* Roan thought as he stood up and tried to breathe. His heart was thumping, his head was spinning, and suddenly the air in the room seemed too thin. He tried to talk, but could only say "I—I…" Her dark skin and the beautiful white teeth of her smile was overwhelming him. He tried to stand, felt himself falling, but she rushed forward into his arms, holding him up with her love and affection. "*Roan!*" She exclaimed "Oh, my god *Roan,* it's *you!* We never thought we'd see you again!" Roan was mute, unable to utter a word, so Nigel began his explanation. "Doc—" he said, "Doc, you need them.

You need your family, or the pain of living without them will break you, now that you've seen the things you have." Roan just held Laura as tightly as he could without crushing her, and it seemed that all he could do was squeak "How? Why?"

Nigel looked for all the world as if he wanted to cry as he explained himself. "I found her in the older Angeline's world. Her husband, Roan Caldwell, worked with the FBI for years, trying to expose widespread corruption in the police department of one of their largest cities, and eventually, they succeeded. He won, but about a year ago, he was murdered, his body dissolved in hydrofluoric acid. A couple of FBI agents who worked with him, Bill and Meredith Compton, exposed everything and took the perpetrators to justice. They'll hang for what they've done, but I got involved and talked to Mrs. Caldwell and her two daughters, Giselle, who's thirteen and Marjorie, who's ten. They just want you back, and they're willing to move here if you'll have them. Both sets of Meredith and Bill Comptons— the people you know in this world and the ones of that reality were in on it. The ones from over there also send their best regards. They know who you are because I've brought them over for a few surveillance runs— I can do that now— bring one or two people over without them wearing any OTTO gear. Anyway you were their teacher there, too, so they have promised to clear everything up on that end. That's *if* you want Mrs. Caldwell and the girls to stay here with you. We talked to her Giselle, and Marjorie before we tried this and they know to expect differences in the you of this world, but they want their Roan back, and well, you're their best option. Just tell me what *you* want, and I'll do it for you." Roan saw tears form in Nigel's eyes as he was speaking. "You— you *know* what I want!" He answered as he held Laura, not wanting to let go. "Please," he continued through his tears, "please, bring me my little girls, Nigel."